The Black Isle

The Black Isle

Sandi Tan

GRAND CENTRAL
PUBLISHING

NEW YORK   BOSTON

Grand Central Publishing
Hachette Book Group
237 Park Avenue
New York, NY 10017

www.HachetteBookGroup.com

Printed in the United States of America

RRD-C

First Edition: August 2012

10 9 8 7 6 5 4 3 2 1

Grand Central Publishing is a division of Hachette Book Group, Inc.

The Grand Central Publishing name and logo is a trademark of Hachette Book Group, Inc.

The Hachette Speakers Bureau provides a wide range of authors for speaking events. To find out more, go to www.hachettespeakersbureau.com or call (866) 376-6591.

The publisher is not responsible for websites (or their content) that are not owned by the publisher.

Library of Congress Cataloging-in-Publication Data
Tan, Sandi.
  The black isle / Sandi Tan.—1st ed.
    p. cm.
  ISBN 978-0-446-56392-5
  I. Title.
  PS3620.A6836B57 2012
  813'.6—dc23

2011028120

For all my ghosts,
including you

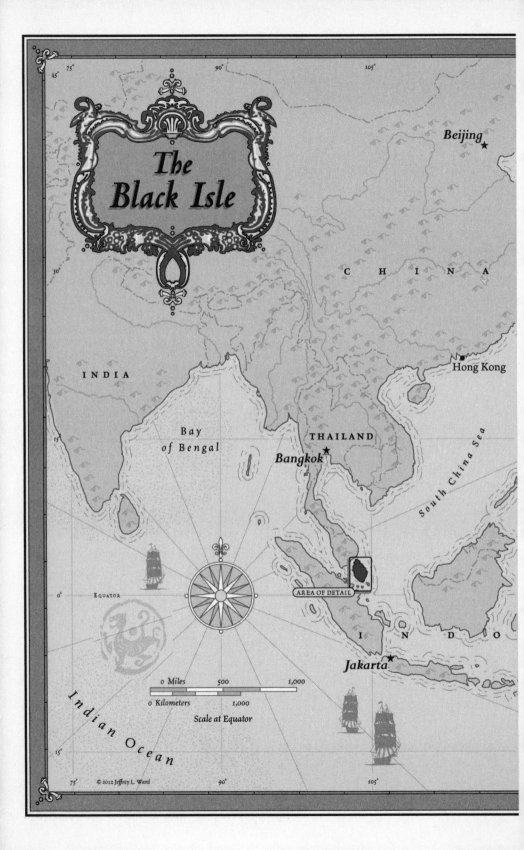

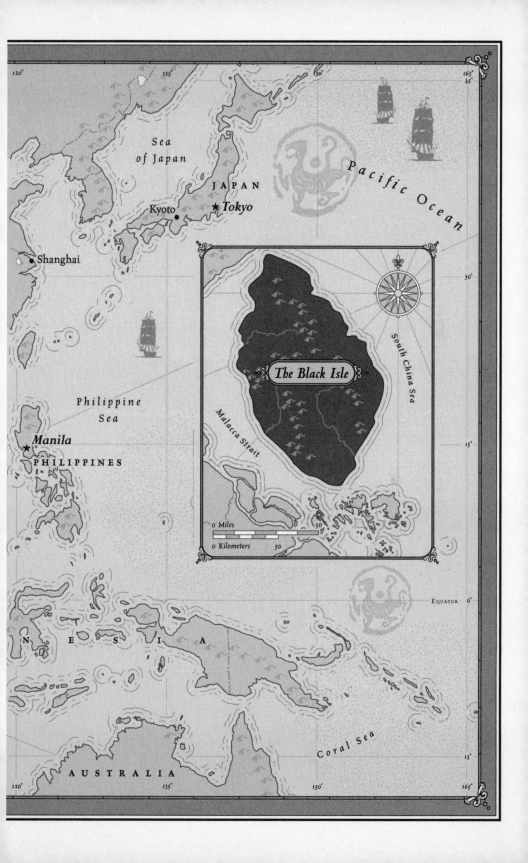

Take care, night is approaching... Wash your hands, go on your way, to your home, to bed.

COMTE DE LAUTRÉAMONT
Maldoror

—PART ONE—

The Haunted

Anyone who has lived as long as I have, and who has done the things I have, knows there will come a reckoning. Mine announced its arrival quietly—in a library, no less.

Every Saturday, like a faithful grave-tender, I would go to visit a certain book at the Archive of Wartime Affairs. The book was part of my private curriculum—my research, if you will—not that I ever had to worry about secrecy. This being 2010, the Archive, perched atop a crumbling billiards parlor, is little known and even less loved.

This morning, however, my book is gone. It's not in its usual hiding place, the dankest corner in War Crimes, wedged behind an encyclopedia on genocide that never sees any traffic. Reaching into the empty space, I feel the panic of a mother who arrives at the schoolyard only to find her child missing.

But my breath returns: Two librarians are pulling books from the shelves. Anything that is jaundiced with age or crippled of binding—no matter if it's the *Communist Manifesto* or an introduction to hara-kiri—if it looks old, out it goes.

You may ask, Aren't archives supposed to be forever? Well, forever's a meaningless concept in Asia. Here, only the present is eternal.

I head over to the wheeled cart by the exit where they've quarantined the discards and begin sifting through volume after dusty volume. Miraculously, I spot the red jacket of the book in question, *my* book, its unwieldy title embossed in faded gilt down its spine: *After the Ghost: Good Shepherds in the Post-Colonial World* by the Flemish couple Lucas Van Kets and Marijke Jodogne, long out of print and impossible to obtain. I clutch the volume to my chest.

The younger librarian, a fashionable girl with raccoon eye makeup, clops by in her fur-lined boots. She stares at me, smiling. Loony old coot, she must think, haunting this pathetic place all the time.

Yes, it *is* strange that I should feel such intense attachment to a book that nobody else cares about. When it first came out in 1974, I wanted nothing to do with it. The work purported to be a survey of the so-called Third World following the eviction of the British, French, and Dutch, quick sketches in which the colonial masters came off badly, yet not so horrendously that anyone reading it in the West would feel too queasy. The final chapter included a brief interview with me, flabby with misquotations, alongside an unflattering snapshot of myself picking up bones at a cemetery. It was egregiously miscaptioned, "Native girl practicing witchcraft."

When the authors perished in a boating accident a few years later, I began to forgive them their errors. For all its blunders, *After the Ghost* was the closest thing I would ever have to a record of my achievements, my failures, my life's work.

I flip open the old hardcover and sniff its musty, reassuring scent. Then I race my dust-covered fingers to the closing section on the Black Isle.

But…what's this?

My pages are missing, stolen—all of them—ripped out along the margins. And the photograph…

Black marker scrawls, a crazed spiderweb of them. *Somebody's given me the face of the devil.*

Immediately I lose all bearings. My fingers grow limp and the book plummets to the ground. My head throbs. Things flash black, white, black, white, black, white.

I must have made a desperate sound because Raccoon returns, wearing a nettled frown. I point to the book, now lying on its spine, the amputated pages exposed for all the world to see.

"Who would do a thing like this?" I suck in my rage. "Why…?"

Shrugging like the impatient youth that she is, she plucks the book from the floor and plops it back onto the cart. "It's falling apart, anyway."

"Yes," I say, "I suppose it is." I give my book one last squeeze and leave.

On the way home, I pick up a few essentials at the mini-mart. When I emerge through its sliding doors, the air is sweet with the scent of blistering chestnuts. Above the squat gray buildings, the sky is perfectly clear—cloudless, nearly two-dimensional in its monotony—just as it was the day I moved here exactly twenty years ago to pursue my private studies.

Happy anniversary.

Cutting through the blue expanse are two dark specks, on opposite ends of the horizon, advancing in straight lines. Both are speeding toward some invisible meeting point. I stand mesmerized. Is this love or is this death? One of them will surely swerve. Surely.

They crash head-on with a muffled smack and plunge to the ground as one. A few feet from me, the shocking, liquid thud arrives almost before their bodies hit the pavement, a mess of black feathers with twin beaks: Crows.

This is not good. Not good at all.

In all my years in this city, I've never seen anything quite like this. Crows colliding. It's hard not to think the missing pages have something to do with it, that they've untied some secret knot within the world.

My head's on fire once more. I have to get home and lie down. My doctor says I . . . Damn what the doctor says. I take to the shortcut, as fast as my feet can manage. The alley's never been a problem—it's well lit and I know every chipped cobblestone and blind corner like the back of my hand.

But out of nowhere, brisk footsteps come running behind me. Before I can turn, something rams into my arm, sending my bags into the air. I look up and see a teenage girl jogging, headphones as swollen as donuts. She hasn't even noticed.

I gather up my fallen things, the groceries of the insignificant old woman I've let myself become: loaf of bread, tub of margarine, ten bars of dark chocolate, two bags of prunes, and a carton of eggs—broken. These I abandon to the rats.

"Are you okay?" someone yells from an open window. At least that's what I think she's saying.

"I'm all right," I lie. "I'm all right."

Slam, lock, bolt, chain. Home at last.

I strip off my clothes and run the hot water till the bathroom mirror is fogged. This is the only way I can bear to look at myself these days.

These dried mangoes hanging from my chest? They used to be breasts.

My legs? Sexless, hobbling candlesticks. As for the gray skin flapping from my arms, it would be generous to call them bat wings. Then again, I can't complain. I shouldn't even be alive, technically speaking.

I soak in the bath, replaying the day's uncanny sights. Were they omens? Or am I turning into a nervous old ninny?

The second I step out of the bath, the telephone rings. A rare occurrence, now that circumstances have robbed me of every friend and acquaintance. So I let it ring. And ring. And ring.

After the tenth ring, my answering machine clicks on. I hear the voice of a woman with an unplaceable accent: South African? Dutch? Or perhaps she taught herself English watching *The Sound of Music*. She says she's a professor, surname Maddin, Christian name Mary, then adds, a bit too casually, "I'm an admirer."

I shudder.

"You don't need me to tell you that you were a legend in some circles. And when you disappeared...well, that only added to your mystique." The voice pauses. "I've wanted to chat with you for quite a while. But of course I've had to track you down, which wasn't easy, and then find the nerve to call, which was in many ways even more difficult."

There is something in her approach that makes me uneasy. Too ingratiating. And the timing of the call...I pick up the receiver and tell her to go to hell.

"My, is this really you?" She sounds amused.

"How did you get my number?"

"That's confidential, I'm afraid."

Wrong answer. "I'm going to hang up now."

"Would it be better if I just showed up at your door?"

"Don't you threaten me!"

She sighs, as if I'm the one who's making trouble. "All I'm asking is that you talk to me. It concerns your life."

"My life?"

"Just hear me out, please. I'm writing a book about superstition in twentieth-century Asia, or rather, the impact modernization has had on indigenous belief systems in that part of the world."

"Biting off more than you can chew."

"No doubt." She chuckles vacantly to humor me. "But here's the thing.

When I was starting my research, I occasionally came across mentions of you. Good things and bad, depending on who was doing the writing, but mostly unkind."

Is she baiting me? "All right, just to be clear, I don't give interviews. Be sure to relay that to your fellow historians."

"Actually, *madame*, most of them think you're already dead."

To my astonishment, that wounds me. "Well, maybe I am."

"But I never once believed that, not for a second. People like you live forever." A pregnant pause. "And so I tracked you down."

"How?" I keep an unlisted number and mind my own business. I'd deliberately dropped off the map years ago. Centuries, it feels like.

"Your very presence is defined by your absence."

"Enough with the riddles."

"I've been doing research on three continents, at all the best libraries. You began appearing in several pretty arcane articles between 1972 and 1999, usually as a footnote, always described as a 'shadowy, behind-the-scenes figure.' That got me intrigued—of course I had to know more. Over the next year, I managed to locate a handful of sources pertaining to you, but believe it or not, each time I went to one, all I'd find was a black hole. Literally. Library after library, book after book, line after line. On all three continents. Whenever I turned to any page that mentioned your name, the passage would be completely crossed out—with black ink. And if the section was long, entire pages would be torn out. And I'm talking about rare historical records kept in libraries with the highest levels of clearance." She takes a breath. "Somebody—and this person or persons must really be obsessed—has been cutting you out of history."

I swallow. "Cutting me out of history?"

"Everywhere. Even online. As far as the Internet is concerned, you don't exist." She lowers her voice. "Every place I looked over the past year, you'd disappeared. So I deduced, if you were actually dead, why would anyone bother with this erasure?"

I have long accepted that no trace of me exists in the official histories of Asia—that's been my life's great bargain. But am I really now disappearing from unofficial accounts as well?

"Look, we really should talk. Face-to-face. And we must hurry. The night is closing in."

A warning, is it? "Who are you? Who sent you?"

"The real question is, who are *you*?"

"Tell me how you found me, Miss Maddin."

"Not over the phone . . . You of all people should understand." Her voice grows silkier, more conspiratorial. "Please. Let me in. I know I'm the only one who can—"

I hang up.

And instantly regret it. She's the only one who can *what*? I wait for the phone to ring again. If she's as persistent as she says, surely she'll try again. I wait. And wait. And wait.

I sit by the phone the rest of the evening, keeping Schumann's "Scenes from Childhood" low on the turntable so I won't somehow miss her call. It never comes; only a dead knot tightening in my gut.

First the mutilated book, then colliding crows, now this. All in the same day.

Signs. If my life has taught me anything, it is not to disregard signs. And there's something weird about her use of the phrase *the night is closing in*. What academic speaks like that? This is no professor.

If my brother were here, he'd tell me this feeling of doom was merely indigestion, paranoia resulting from cognac on an empty stomach, followed by half a bar of chocolate. My doctor would scold me for eating the wrong things, saying I'd only hasten my coronary tsunami. But they would both be wrong. Naïve and wrong. Something black and toxic is moving closer and closer to me. I can almost smell its sour edges, feel its burning miasma reaching for my throat, my heart, my soul. It's death, then, my brother might say. Well, perhaps. But I've stared death in the eye for years, and never once had I felt the kind of nausea now churning through me. No, this is something more destructive than death. I sense evil. A devouring mouth of ill will that isn't about to let me off with a quick and happy end.

I've made many enemies over the years, among both the living and the dead, so reprisals should come as no surprise. Yet they do. Anger, jealousy, regret—I am no freer of these emotions than anyone else, but for the first time in perhaps twenty years, I feel fear. Fear has finally returned to claim me, a woman nearing ninety, a shadow of her former self who, if that strange woman is to be believed, is vanishing even from history itself.

I have worried for decades about this moment—this reckoning—and the time, it seems, is about to come.

The doorbell goes off at 2:37 in the morning. Is it her?

I swipe the cleaver from the side of my bed and hobble to the door. But through the peephole, nobody. At least, no one I can see.

As I back away from the door, the neighbors' dogs begin baying with a morbid fearfulness that chills me to the marrow. I can't tell which is worse—the basso woofs of the hound next door or the Pomeranians at the end of the hall squealing like children being strangled in their beds.

I turn off every lamp and light the red candle—a memento from long ago, untouched for years. Whenever it burned fast, I knew something was wrong. It's racing tonight. The flame chases the wick down to nothingness in five minutes flat. Normally this is the work of four hours. I sprinkle bone ash across the doorway, another rite from another time, and utter a chant I inherited many moons ago from a former friend now long gone.

Finally, I sit in my rocking chair, knife perched across the knee.

Sometime in the night, my eyes close. When they open again, there is a flurry in the air. The distinctive cold, prickly draught I know only too well.

Sure enough, in the dark, my eyes make out an uninvited guest. His hair is white, his shirt and pants headstone gray.

The sight of him, after all these years, in this city, makes me tremble. This is the man I owed everything to. But why here? Why now? I cannot think of what to say, except, "What do you want?"

As he'd done countless times before, he fixes his sunken, rheumy eyes on me. His lips flex to reveal a mouth with small, jagged teeth. Still human, but only barely.

"You're one of us now," he hisses, his voice thin, dry, snakelike.

I recognize the presumption of his claim. This is no invitation to join a club.

Before I can curse him, he vanishes, taking with him half the heat in the room and all the air in my lungs. My struggle to breathe only proves he's wrong. I'm not one of them. I'm still alive.

Nine a.m., I grab the phone before the first ring ends. "Yes?"

The professor jumps in immediately, as if our conversation hadn't been interrupted. "I want your story. I *need* it."

Goose bumps scurry across my arms.

"In exchange, I'll give you what you've been searching for."

My heart almost stops. "I'm not searching for anything."

"You're hunting," she says. "That's what you do."

"Miss Maddin." I pause to steady myself. "Why are you so interested in my story?"

She thinks for a few seconds. "I've always had this need, you know, to dig beneath the surface of things. To uncover and protect the truth, I suppose, in places people never think to look. And to right wrongs."

To right wrongs? Would she do that for me? "Where are you?" I ask.

"Ah," she says, with the care of one who knows too well the world's dangers. "Not far."

Darkness is closing in. "You better hurry."

The professor says she'll give me what I've been searching for. Could she? I mean, how could she even know? Unless . . . And the ghost . . .

I take a tranquilizer and potter around—Nutella sandwich, undies in the wash, warm milk and prunes, my heart all the while going *pit-pat-pit-pat*. I try to revive myself with a nap. No luck. Before long, it is night again.

I pull open the bedroom curtains and gaze out. Lights dot the surrounding high-rises. Children, perhaps, talking to strangers on their computers. Confessing their sins. That the young keep vigil while their parents sleep—there's poetry there, I suppose, although night is never really night here, not in the romantic sense anyway. The sky is an orange luminescence, the by-product of six thousand tower blocks and the metropolis that spreads itself yonder, the glimmering grids of one endless electric paddy field.

Darkness has long been extinguished in this part of the world. Some call it a compromise, others a blessing. There are millions of us, living in exactly the same apartments, under our shared tangerine sky. For years, I felt that this anonymity was the best fortress I could ask for.

But anonymity is not the same as annihilation. One is about the present, the other is about the past, and the two should never be confused.

You're one of us now.

No! I'm still alive.

It is inevitable that my past should return. I'm an old-fashioned woman with an Old Testament faith in symmetry. What goes up must come down. Every action has an equal and opposite reaction. Life for life, eye for eye, tooth for tooth.

The Professor and the Ghost. One telling me I'm disappearing, the other saying I'm already on the other side. Two faces of the same terrible coin.

The Professor . . . is it possible she could be my salvation? Will telling her my story save me from becoming one of *them*?

I must do it. It's my best hope.

I root in the petticoat drawer for the voice recorder—a present to myself after watching a dreary Canadian film about Alzheimer's that nevertheless made me quake—and slot in fresh batteries and tape. I trust the permanence of tape. They let words live on long after the air has died. My story shall survive. To prepare, I give my throat an antiseptic gargle: to ward off the rot of mendacity.

In the mirror, my blue teeth smile back at me.

Permit me to cast the first stones.

All my life, people have tried to erase me, in big ways and small, publicly and privately, thoughtlessly and with supreme, awe-inspiring malevolence. All my life.

But I refuse to let them win. They will not wipe me out.

I will not become a ghost.

— 1 —

A Child's Hands

THEY CALLED ME LING. Names don't come much more forgettable than that. And my story didn't begin on the day of my birth, August 3, 1922. I was just a wailing blob that day, and thus no different from all other blobs in history that were pulled screaming from their mothers' loins and then subjected to the universal rigmarole of walking and talking, eating and sleeping. I was told that I mastered those skills more quickly than most, so eager was I to win my parents' affection as well as some invisible contest against time that only I knew about. But again, this precocity was far from a defining character trait. I was a young child. And babies are in general uninteresting people.

My real story began in the summer of 1929, on my seventh birthday. Or, more correctly, *our* birthday. I was older than my brother, Li, by four or five minutes, a race I won, I always believed, by being closer to the gate and not by the heartless bullying of my weaker twin as the midwife insisted. (Chinese midwives! Always rooting against girls!) I was undeniably a stronger baby than Li—I cried louder, kicked harder, weighed more—but I plead my case that in the womb, there was no pushing and shoving or malicious piggery. Of course, when Li emerged emaciated, his wail barely a whimper—and a boy, no less!—everyone listened to the midwife. They all blamed me.

As soon as we were born, my parents tried to counter the injustice. What happened in Mother's belly was out of their purview, but so long as Li and I lived in their house, under their care, they would make it up to him. They always gave him whatever he wanted; he always got the first pick. From the moment the midwife washed the blood off her hands and wobbled down the stairs, it no longer mattered that I was the eldest. The roles were cast: Li was the hero. I was the sidekick.

By the time of our seventh birthday, Li had grown into a vigorous boy, a natural leader, taller than me by two inches. He led and I followed. He became my protector and benefactor. If he was offered a cream puff, he would ask for two so he could give me one. Soon I no longer had to fight or choose or pine. I got used to coming in second and began to prefer being his shadow—there was never any pressure to be original or brave. One should never underestimate the joy of being underestimated.

In looks, Li was nothing special, just your generic little prewar, middle-class Chinese boy in flannel shirts and corduroy shorts, always smiling, always smelling faintly of chalk. I had my hair in two pigtails and wore pinafores made of flannel and corduroy, surplus fabric from the construction of Li's shirts and shorts. Neither of us had any distinctive features or battle scars; no stranger passing us on the street would stop to cry out in glee or in horror. We might as well have been invisible, as far as the wider world was concerned, two children drowned in an endless sea of black hair and narrow eyes. But to me, Li was the handsomest boy in all of China.

His things filled our house: model cars, dancing bears, books about planes and warships, many ordered from America. "What will I get for my birthday?" he'd ask, months before the actual day. "Anything," was Mother's invariable answer. "Anything your heart desires."

This never became an issue until the day of our seventh birthday. I always took whatever they gave me, be it pencil case, scarf, or slippers, so I was never a problem. And until then, Li's taste was conventional—our parents held boats, planes, and trains on reserve at the toy shop until he made up his mind—but for our seventh, he kept his request secret until the big day. I saw him go over to Mother and whisper in her ear.

"No," Mother said definitively, and stormed up the stairs.

There were two ways of looking at Shanghai in those days. It was either the Pearl of the Orient or the Devil's Den. There was no in-between; you belonged to one camp or the other. Our mother evidently belonged to the latter. She had been raised in a cloistered Suzhou compound by spinster maids who taught her to fear and loathe the outside world. Her fear was so great that it rendered the binding of her feet unnecessary—there was no risk she'd run off anywhere.

Shanghai only heightened her nervousness. None of the hedonistic thrills of big-city living for her. She was happiest in her dark little rooms, where she could pore over opulent catalogs, oversee the help, and fret in peace. Indeed, her unnatural pallor that came from staying indoors was considered quite fashionable. But there was a price to her agoraphobia. The feral love affair Li and I had with sunlight and nature caused her great anguish. It only proved to her that she had been inadequate in her job. What provident mother had children who needed to leave her house to seek fun?

That's why she felt profoundly wounded when Li, for his seventh birthday, whispered these simple words: "Take us to the park." She doubtless felt he was attacking her weakness with a son's malice. Her "no" resounded through the house, the louder for being the only time he'd been denied.

Our home on Rue Bourgeat was everything that a good middle-class town house should look like, at least on the outside. It was in the French Concession, which telegraphed that we belonged in the happy bourgeois world of cosmopolitan Shanghai, and it had the requisite white walls, which proved that we could afford to hire painters to undo the darkening effects of the region's inclemency. We even had a waist-high wrought-iron gate in the Kensington Gardens style, an ornamental barrier between our front step and the toothless kumquat and lychee vendors who traversed the dusty pavement. We cherished our borders. To the outside world, we were solidly, stolidly middle class. Within our walls, however, we were less complacent, a young family fraying at the edges as our financial situation grew grimmer and grimmer by the week.

In spite of our straitened circumstances, my parents retained domestics— two amahs, Sister Kwan and Sister Choon; a cook; and a part-time errand boy. I should also include the rickshaw coolie duo who served us exclusively on weekdays. Nothing would have gotten done if we hadn't had help, for Mother wouldn't leave the house and Father, a dreamy idealist, had so little interest in the physical world that he could barely remember the name of our street, let alone the location of the butcher's or the spice shop.

As a practical concession, we leased out the servants' quarters, and this little room was piled from floor to ceiling with low-quality women's sandals (and their persistent tang of cheap tannin), overstock from Mr. Wang's footwear emporium on nearby Avenue Joffre. Their space thus usurped, our servants slept anywhere they could come nighttime, on lumpy blankets by the dying embers of the kitchen brazier or crouched under the crook of the stairs, knees tucked beneath their chins to fend off the plague. Mother assured me that to the people of the lower classes, this was still rather luxurious. Most of Shanghai, she said, lived in rat-infested shantytowns on the banks of the muck-filled Suzhou Creek or were packed like sardines inside crowded junks where only the luckiest got to lie on straw mats.

We slept on the second floor. My parents had their own room, large enough to accommodate, aside from their featherbed, a brass chamber pot and a folding screen hand-painted with a hundred cranes in midflight. I know it was meant to be a picture of serenity, but it always filled me with panic to gaze at the screen—the cranes looked as if they were fleeing some sort of catastrophe, perhaps an earthquake or a prodigiously good shot. The elder two children, Li and myself, shared a small, nondescript room adjacent to our parents', and our infant sisters, Xiaowen and Bao-Bao—strangely enough, also twins—slept in the hallway on a cot that had once belonged to a consumptive great-aunt. Nobody wanted to say that she died in that rickety thing, but the stains on the mattress seemed to me brutal evidence.

Hanging on the wall above the twins' cot was an oil portrait of our parents on their wedding day, as wide as a broadsheet and nestled in a gilded frame. They were outfitted in the latest Western styles—he in a suit with a cravat, strangely dashing in his quiet way, and she in white lace, looking waxier than usual, as if she had been carved out of a huge candle and then dredged through powders and rouge. Her mind seemed to be elsewhere and her lips were crooked with a kind of half smile. An unhelpful aunt must have told her this was the proper way to pose. This image of Mother I found disturbing. Her eyes followed me whenever I crossed the hall, accusing eyes that seemed to know even before I did that I would someday disappoint.

Unlike her mother, who'd been a celebrated Suzhou beauty in a city famed for its beauties, Mother's charms weren't self-evident. There was a bit of the tadpole about her—bulging eyes, weak chin—and to disguise the fact, she spent hours arranging and rearranging her hair and face before every lunch or cocktail invitation. Much to the puzzlement of new friends and the exasperation of old ones, she nearly always decided at the very last minute that she couldn't leave the house and would forgo the meetings. Friendships suffered, and so did her confidence.

Over the years, her fear and poor self-image had worked so well in tandem, each reinforcing the other's sinister hold, that they completely crippled her social life. She turned her attentions by sad default to the running of the household, becoming a quarrelsome matron who rose at six and dressed for nonexistent balls, all for the purpose of ordering the help around. From the way she screamed at the amahs and steamed around the house, I sensed that her quirks frustrated her deeply. Her great concern was that our neighbors would never think of her as anything but well put together and of us as anything but angelic and that they'd never suspect the awful truth that we were, alas, a struggling little ragtag troupe headed by a pseudo-intellectual whose station in life as a schoolteacher meant that we'd never in a thousand years be rich.

Father plodded through his role as paterfamilias. I remember him as having a perpetually pursed mouth, his thin lips pressed firmly together lest the fried fish roiling in his gut came leaping out. The idea of family made him queasy in general, the reality of it even more so. He'd wring his hands like a woman whenever the twins started bawling; then he'd either go out for a long walk or put on a record—opera in German usually, a language he didn't understand and therefore felt unburdened by. Looking back, I don't think poor Father was ever prepared for the size of our household—not just the aggrieved, high-maintenance wife but also additional headaches in the form of four children and a rotating roster of resentful servants. This was a storklike gent who preferred to be left alone and might have been best suited to the life of a medieval scholar-prince, emerging from his pavilion once in a blue moon to stretch his skinny legs, stroke his beard, and sip Huangshan Mao Feng tea harvested by an obedient band of snow monkeys. Yes, in a different universe, Father would have been sitting atop a craggy mountain memorizing obsolete tracts on thousand-year-old scrolls instead of mopping up vomit or worrying about grocery bills.

It may surprise you, then, to hear that my parents were considered very much a modern couple. They had married out of choice, back when the rest of the continent still abided by matches devised by Machiavellian fathers and meddlesome aunts—two goats if you'll take her off my hands, and all that. They must have once thought they were in love. Sadly, untutored as they were in the demands of romantic commitment, they'd each picked for themselves their worst possible match. Father ran cold, Mother ran hot, but their yin and their yang were grossly misaligned. Marital calamity has been built on far less.

That our parents made an odd couple was obvious even to us. Idiosyncratic, yes; inattentive, to be sure. Yet their odd union produced me, my twin, and the other twins. The baby girls Xiaowen and Bao-Bao made up for our parents' character flaws twice over. Fuzzy of forehead and forearm, the pink-cheeked pair sang and romped around every day, satin ribbons fluttering in their hair. They were my mascots, my greatest allies in the house, and their presence made me infinitely happy. I convinced myself that they were the magical Peach Children of old folklore, with supple fruit flesh that made them seven and a half times more adorable than their human counterparts as well as impervious to all mortal danger, so long as they stayed together.

We all hold on to what we can, I suppose. In those days, I clung to the idea of the twins' innocence and purity, and they clung to my legs as I prepared for school every morning, chanting in duet, "*Jie jie*, don't go! *Jie jie*, don't leave us!" They wanted to keep me at home with them, where they could shield me from danger with their downy little arms. I always left for school with a heaviness in my heart. They weren't just blindly echoing Mother's words about the dangers of the world. In their way, the twins were reminding me so I wouldn't grow too bold and forget: I wasn't the hero of my own story. Not yet.

Li went upstairs to find Mother. I followed. We whimpered and moaned shamelessly and found glee in it. Why did we persist in antagonizing her? Mother asked. Maybe in the autumn, she said, but not now. It's summer. Who knows what deadly germs are lurking in the air? And, anyway, couldn't we find our fun indoors?

So find our fun indoors we did, at least for a while. We were sufficiently unattended. Father was teaching school; Mother was shouting at the amahs upstairs. The cook was having her siesta, dozing upright in her rattan chair, and the errand boy, as usual, was nowhere to be found. Each potential deterrent thus accounted for, we crept into Father's study—a room no bigger than a broom closet and even more cramped—and went to his precious goldfish. The pair were named Wu Song and Wu Dalang, after two brothers in Father's favorite classic novel *Water Margin*. Li dropped ten garlic cloves into the water, which the goldfish pounced on with their greedy, sucking mouths. Then, with nervous titters, we waited.

As expected, the first bubbles emerged from Wu Song's tail, his plumbing being quicker. These were followed by more robust ones that took both goldfish by surprise. Air shot out their rear ends, sending them forth like rockets. Luminous projectiles! Both fish banged their stunned faces into the glass. The bigger the emission, the stronger the collision. *Phoot! Thump! Phoooot! Thuuummp!* Li had fed them garlic many times before, yet they fell for the trick without fail, over and over. After a few minutes, the flatulence wore off, and Wu Song and Wu Dalang resumed their mindless circuits. It was as if nothing had ever happened. Li grew restless again.

Mother was in the midst of writing a letter, but we were merciless in our demands. Exhausted by Li's doleful pantomime of gazing out the window and my extravagant sighs, she finally relented.

She called in Sister Kwan. "Take them straight to the park and only the park. At no time should you ever let go of their hands. And keep them out of the sun!"

As Sister Kwan nodded, I saw the tears well up in her beady Cantonese eyes. She was so easily intimidated, the poor girl. I wanted to tell her that Mother was all bark and no bite but felt it wasn't my place; it seemed disloyal to side with the help. The other amah, Sister Choon, older and grimmer, was to remain home and watch the twins. I still remember the scowl on her face as she locked the front door behind us.

As we walked, I asked Li, "But why the park?"

"I wanted to test Mother."

"Why?"

"To see if she really loves me."

"Does she?"

He gave me a look I couldn't decipher.

Like many green spaces in Frenchtown, the *Paradis des Enfants* was immaculately manicured and easy on the eye. The only difference was that everything in it was scaled for tots, and to a perverse degree: All the shrubs were within crawlers' reach, all the flowers short enough for the tiniest petal-sniffing *enfant*. The Parisian-style gas lamps came up only to Sister Kwan's chin, and the benches similarly favored the wee. Nothing loomed too tall, not even the trees—those that grew higher than six feet had their heads lopped off. The whole place was safe, sedate, a mini Versailles ready to receive the woozy tumbles of wobbly footed babes.

The two brief times we'd been taken to the *Paradis*, we always eyed the European youngsters of our district skipping along in their starched sailor suits, licking ices and lollipops while amahs of all ages skittered after them, pleading with them in pidgin to *no runnee*. Today was no exception. The pampered little devils were out in force, terrorizing pigeons with high-pitched roars and tucking sweet wrappers into the mulberry bush.

I observed Li watching them. In the center of the park stood a circular rose garden enclosed behind a formidable fence that barred "All Chinese and Dogs." Even though Sister Kwan had explained that this was for *our* safety—"Those red roses are fed on the blood of Chinese children!"—Li's jealousy was evident. He stalked and stared. I felt envy for the foreigners, too, but mine was different. Many of the children were roaming unsupervised, and it made me realize that never in my seven years of life had I walked, let alone run, in any public place without some zealous grownup holding on to my hand until it was slick with sweat, as if I would suddenly disappear the instant they let go. This, I felt, rather than size and complexion, was the crucial divider between the Chinese and the Europeans: Their hands were always free.

While the privileged thronged in and out of the rose garden, we stayed on the commons. We made our own fun. Sister Kwan was given to dizzy spells, and we had a fairly good idea of how to trigger one. Li and I ran rings around her like twin engines fastened to her wrists. Very soon, our human carousel had to sit down. She staggered to a spot under a shady Japanese maple and, much to our delight, fell unconscious with a gasp. Li and I were now alone, with a million options open to us. Should we peer into the mulberry bush and count the sweet wrappers? Should we stick leaves in Sister Kwan's hair? What should a boy freshly seven and his agreeable accomplice do?

Somebody else answered our question. A Chinese man, tanned and slim in the Southern way. He was very old, possibly the oldest person I'd ever seen, with a thousand wrinkles, a long white beard, and a black wool cape—this, at the height of summer. He had a cinnabar walking cane that he didn't seem to need because he walked well—too well, I thought, for a man his age. On his cane were intricate carvings of hundreds of couples, all intertwined in some communal embrace that stretched from its foot right up to its handle, all in the throes of some sort of wretched ecstasy. I couldn't take my eyes off the thing.

A polished gold watch attached to a chain fell from the old man's waistcoat when he bowed to shake our grimy hands. Li lit up as soon as he saw it.

"Greetings, my little friends," the man said. He had a marvelous accent, speaking what I thought was very mandarin Mandarin, untainted by the singsong cadences of the Shanghai dialect. "I was wondering if I could ask you for a favor."

Without waiting for an answer, he began walking. I tapped Li on the arm and we looked back at Sister Kwan—still unconscious under the tree. We now followed our new leader, who walked at an unnaturally keen pace. We had to take three or four steps for every one of his. When he led us beyond the places we knew, past the rose garden and past even the hedge maze where only forbidden lovers went, I grabbed Li's hand.

All of a sudden, the man stopped in his tracks. He turned and looked directly at me. "Do not be afraid." It was an order, not friendly reassurance. "How will you ever discover new things if you're always fearful? Fear is our greatest enemy."

Li shook my hand off and glowered at me. "He's right, you know." Turning seven seemed to have given him the illusion of awesome power. Normally I would have kicked him in the shins to remind him I was still his older sister, but we were in unfamiliar waters. We were following a strange man. And this strange man was leading us deeper and deeper into the unknown. I now hoped that Sister Kwan would wake up and come charging after us.

We came to a small, dark, windowless hut, perhaps a gardener's shed, on the far edge of the park. I could tell from the height of its door that, unlike everything else in the *Paradis des Enfants*, this hut was sized for grownups, and quite unapologetically so. A huge, old-fashioned padlock secured the rusty handle, and I was grateful that the old man showed no interest in disturbing it. Then my heart sank. Behind the hut was a stone wall about ten feet high. If anything went wrong, there'd be no escape.

The dank, fecal odor of fertilizer hung in the air, much like the sewer, only denser and more beastly. I scanned the area. Nobody else was around.

The laughter of children sounded as tinny as mosquitoes, and incredibly far away. My stomach tightened and again I reached for Li's hand.

"We should go back," I whispered, hoping the old man wouldn't hear.

But of course he heard me. Sighing, he shook his head, then addressed Li and Li alone: "Young man, you seem like a leader. Don't let the girl fill your mind with fear. I need you to be brave and strong. You must not disappoint me."

It was then that we heard the baby's cries. They were coming distinctly from the dark hollow between the hut and the wall, a space of uncommon darkness. The man lifted a finger—wait here—and went toward the source. We stood still, exchanging anxious glances.

After a while, the man called, "Young man..."

Instantly, Li went.

I had no choice but to follow. As much as I dreaded seeing the baby, being left all by myself seemed even more frightening. Out of the sun and into the shadows, the temperature dropped.

Our eyes took a moment to adapt to the lack of light. At our feet was a shallow rain gutter, lined with velvety black moss. It felt like we were suddenly in a cave. The baby's wails increased in pitch and intensity, as if it could sense our approach and wanted us to hurry.

The hairs on my arms stood up and my pulse quickened. In the drain lay a quivering gray puddle. I saw its watery blue eyes and froze.

It was a kitten, not much bigger than a ball of yarn. Its fur was frayed, exposing snatches of baldness, and its hind legs were bent in such a way that I could tell they had been broken in several places.

"The handiwork of neighborhood thugs," the man said, sighing again. "Boys from the countryside with nothing better to do." For a moment I felt his grief. He said that the kitten belonged to him and that its name was Xiao Huangdi, or *Little Emperor*. "My heart aches to see it in such obscene agony. I want nothing more than to end its suffering. To bring it the peace it deserves. It's only right. But you see, young man"—he turned to Li— "this is a job for a child's hands."

Like a soldier reporting to his general, Li pulled away from me and took three steps toward the trench. In that moment, I felt the lifelong connection between us, our bond of blood that I'd always taken for granted, not merely slip away but *snap*. A clammy uncertainty was left in its wake. For the first time in my life, I felt completely, horribly alone. The nausea came at me in waves and was suffocating, endless. I choked back the urge to throw up.

Calmly—too calmly—Li got on his haunches and examined the kitten. Just as casually, he placed his hands on the creature's head, caressed its tiny ears, and then lifted it by the loose flap of skin on the back of its neck. The pitiful thing sensed peril and swiped at the air, swaying like a ragged pendulum. It mewed for its life; it was begging, desperate. How could Li not see this? How could he not hear this? Instead he gave the old man a quiet smile, as if posing for one last photograph with his beloved pet.

"Please, sir, tell me what to do," Li said. His eagerness to please sickened me even more. His voice was as sweet as treacle.

The kitten looked toward me. Tears fell from its eyes. If someone had told me then that it had a human soul, I would have believed him absolutely. These were not the eyes of a dumb animal but the pleading eyes of a sentient, intelligent creature tragically aware of what was happening and yet unable to stop it. It was an accident of size, of species, that the kitten could not fight back. But the feelings were no different. I would see those eyes time and time again during the course of my career. The eyes of someone dying alone and terrified.

"Brother, don't!" I yelled. Li did not respond. He'd either grown deaf or I had become irrelevant. "Don't hurt it! Please!"

The old man continued watching Li. In a flat, unemotional voice, he said, "Break its neck. Quick but firm."

My brother nodded, matching his solemnity.

The kitten fought at the nothingness as Li's fingers closed around its neck. My brother, murdering an innocent being with the same soft hands I'd held just minutes before. A child's hands.

I couldn't allow it. I lunged forth with all my might, aiming to snatch the kitten from him but instead I found myself hurtling onto the grass yards away. The old man. I never saw his arm move.

The kitten's mewing grew muffled, but its terror was undiluted. I picked myself up and screamed one long piercing scream to cover up the horror. Even so, I heard its tiny neck snap with a crisp click. An unnerving hush followed. When I peered at Li, the lump of gray fur had gone slack in his hands. He let the lifeless bundle fall to the ground.

The old man nodded at him with avuncular approval and pulled from his pocket a small disk wrapped in shimmering gold foil. I knew at a glance that it was butterscotch candy, the kind we'd ogled in shop windows but were told was too expensive to be wasted on children like us.

"Young man, I want to thank you for your time. And your courage." The man handed the reward to Li, who accepted it gratefully. He then turned to me with a supercilious smile. "Nothing for you."

Usually Li would have protested on my behalf, but this time he didn't.

Lowering himself to the drain with great agility, the man scooped up the dead kitten in the palm of his hand. In one seamless motion, he folded up its legs and tucked the carcass into his pants pocket like a used handkerchief. With the same soiled hand, he patted Li on the head, his fingers slithering through the forest of my brother's hair before finding a comfortable hold and kneading his scalp. Li closed his eyes and tilted his head back. When he opened his eyes, his features went slack, as if he'd been blessed. I will never forget that look, that taint.

The man waved at the distance and smiled. "You are now free to go."

Li turned to me. There was a new coldness to his face that I didn't like. I found myself wishing we hadn't disobeyed Mother, that we hadn't caused Sister Kwan to faint. But for the first time in my life, I couldn't share those feelings with him.

"Don't you dare say a word." He made me swear as we ran, him clutching the butterscotch disk like a prized talisman. "And don't expect me to share this with you."

He needn't have worried. I wanted none of it. I did, however, want my brother back.

Running to the commons, I had to keep slowing down to wait for Li. The violence seemed to have sapped his vigor, for he paused every so often to catch his breath. Gray rings appeared around his eyes, the kind I often saw in hungry beggar children. And his scent, too, turned strange. No longer did he smell of chalk, of cleanliness; he now smelled slightly off, like rice vinegar. Could the same thing be happening to me? Could turning seven mean having less energy and a new odor? But no, I was running at my usual pace and smelled like my usual self. These changes seemed to be occurring only in Li.

When we returned to where we'd left Sister Kwan, she was hoarse from shrieking our names, her eyes rimmed red with worry. Her bun had come undone, leaving streaks of black hair plastered to her tear-stained cheeks. For the first time, I realized how pretty she actually was. In a different, perhaps better world, she would have been a rich man's plaything. When she saw us, she clutched us to her chest and I felt the shivers coursing through her. Her shaking masked mine.

Sister Kwan never told Mother about her fainting spell or our little detour. Most crucial of all, I kept my oath—I never breathed a word to anyone about the old man or the kitten. Or the sweet. To everyone apart from Li and me, and maybe the invisible guardians of the cosmos, that encounter never happened at all.

Why do I mention the guardians of the cosmos? Well, because that night, following the day my twin and I became two separate people, was also the night I saw my first ghost.

— 2 —

A Child's Feet

WHEN LI AND I RETURNED from the *Paradis* that afternoon, Mother and Father were in the middle of something. Neither noticed the scuffs on my arms, the stains on my dress, or Li's uncharacteristic exhaustion. At first I was relieved to be home. Then came cold, hard bewilderment as I heard the exchange of foreign place names—names with the forlorn musicality of Hindi, Khmer, Malay. They rang of great distance, of sweat and rot and jungle. I could tell my parents weren't discussing holiday plans. What they were discussing I had no idea.

Li collapsed onto the living room settee. I offered to bring him a glass of milk.

"Scram," he mumbled, turning away. "Just get me Sister Choon."

Left alone with my thoughts later that night, I wondered if I should have been more forceful at the park. I could have stood my ground, played the big sister. I could have stopped Li from following the old man, from putting his hands—his soft, warm hands—on that helpless kitten. I could have offered to take the poor thing home instead of standing there dumbstruck, no better than a pathetic crybaby. But no, I *was* a pathetic crybaby, shattered by the sudden realization that my twin wasn't as bound to me as I'd come to believe. We'd only seemed tethered because something was perpetually holding us together—whether it was Sister Kwan's iron grip or the prison walls of our mother's house. Or the narrow bed we shared, where the only way we could both fit was to lie back-to-back.

Li, his back pressing against mine, slept as soundly as a baby, the day's disturbing adventure apparently already forgotten. He had on his new blue satin pajamas, a birthday surprise from Mother, the arms and legs overlong so as to last through another year of growth. In the moonlight, he shone like an iridescent eel at the bottom of the ocean. The butterscotch disk peered out from within his tightened fist, an otherworldly compass leading him to new places without me, no doubt.

Still in my old pajamas—no new ones for me—I continued to toss and turn. The air was dead. I could hardly breathe.

Summer nights in our house were hell on earth. Mother, fearing contagion, ordered all windows shut after dusk, trapping in the heat of the day and turning the whole place into a tomb. On July and August nights, the air heaved with moisture and the walls gave off centuries of human must—the smell, I used to think, of a dying man's last breath (though this was before I learned what *that* actually smelled like).

Naturally, when the muggy air in our bedroom turned dry and chilly instead of hotter and stickier as I tossed and turned, I knew something wasn't right.

"Li?" I tugged at his sleeve, my teeth chattering. No answer.

I reached for the blanket and when my fingers grazed my bare thigh, I jumped: icicles! My fingers were stone cold. Had a window blown open? No, everything was still, the same as it was. But my heart had begun to pound, and I felt a deep, throbbing ache behind my eyes. The nausea I felt earlier in the park returned, pursued by a tingling of the tongue. The hairs on my arms rose to attention. Something was about to strike—a meteor, perhaps, or a typhoon. Something monumental.

In the dark, I plotted the quickest route to my parents' room. Don't trip on the cot in the hallway. Abandon Li, if necessary.

My breath emerged from my nostrils in pale wisps as thick as incense smoke. Thicker, when I exhaled through my mouth. Could I be on fire? Or was this the pneumonia or influenza that crept in through windows and carried off so many children in their sleep? Those terms had been thrown at me so frequently that they rang like place names in my mind. Was I already dying?

Then I saw her.

She was old. Thin as a beggar woman. White hair pulled back into a tight bun.

Her white tunic and black slacks instantly told me she was—or had been—an amah. Silently, she took three paces forward and stopped at the foot of my bed. I realized when I tried to sit up that I was paralyzed. It wasn't fear. Emotion didn't enter into it at all. A kind of supernatural glue was holding me to the bed. I couldn't move a muscle or even blink.

I'd heard many stories from Sister Kwan, and in them, ghosts were usually vengeful harlots or poorly tended goats, alternately screeching for blood and bleating for sympathy. This one was neither wraith nor beast. Her skin was ochre. Her eyes lacked the sparkle of life that is noticeable only when it's missing. But she looked at me with such a beneficent gaze, dead eyes notwithstanding, that had I been a religious little girl, I might have taken her for some sort of nun. She didn't fit the description of a ghost. For starters, she didn't frighten me at all.

Aside from her jaundiced complexion and the pant legs that vanished into thin air, she looked to be solid, three-dimensional. Real. Not floating. No unruly hair or black holes for eyes. She could have easily passed for one of the amahs we had working for us, or one of their friends. But a part of me just *knew*, and I was flooded with a mute, abstract sadness. She conveyed absence, silence, loss—like the primordial emptiness that entered my mind every night before I drifted off to sleep. Had my tear ducts worked, I would have wept.

I could tell she had lived a long life, but it hadn't been enough.

I wanted desperately to question her, but my mouth could form no words. What did she want? Did she have friends over there? Was she lonely?

It was possible that she registered my questions, but her expression remained unchanged. She looked at me and only me; Li did not exist. She reached out slowly with both hands for my feet—bony, immobile things poking out of the wool blanket I'd long outgrown. I was happy to offer her solace, if that was what she sought. I held my breath, certain I would soon feel the coldness of her claws. I watched as her gnarled fingers wrapped themselves around my toes, one set in each hand. To my surprise, I felt absolutely nothing. But could *she* feel me? It was hard to tell. I studied her features and committed them to memory: black mole just under her left eye, unusually high cheekbones, the pronounced overbite I'd often noticed in the servant class—essentially a kind face. Regulation amah uniform, white jade bangle around her right wrist, no earrings. I told myself to report these specifics to Sister Kwan in the morning.

Out of the blue, she made a noise, a soft gurgle in the back of her throat, like someone about to gag. Or speak. She tried again, but all she could manage was a single guttural word:

"One..."

And just like that, she vanished.

I could now wriggle my toes and part my lips. I hissed, just to make sure my voice had returned. The air lost its sepulchral bite and my skin was again coated with sticky summer perspiration. The melancholy was lifted from me. I kicked off the covers and leapt to the floor, peering under the bed. But no, there wasn't an old woman lying there with her joints folded across her chest like a giant bat.

I flew back to bed. I couldn't wait to announce my achievement to Sister Kwan—I saw a ghost and wasn't scared!—and watch her mouth fall open in wonder. "You brave soul," I could almost hear her say. Did Li see her? No, it was me, only me. I was first. I was special.

My brother, meanwhile, continued to doze unfettered. I thought about shaking him awake and telling him about my encounter, but I knew he'd only fly into a rage and call me a liar.

Should I keep the sighting a secret? Reporting it might make my parents fear for my sanity; they'd always considered themselves too modern for ghosts. But Sister Kwan...she would understand.

A new, loving warmth wound its way around my torso, as if the bed were caressing me back to sleep with damp, heated hands, coaxing me away from the sharp snap of wakefulness. I snuggled into its embrace and closed my eyes. Every part of me relaxed. The warmth spread farther. Seconds later, I felt a hard kick to the shin—Li. He'd jolted awake and was crying out, furious:

"Damn you, Ling! You peed on my new pajamas!"

Around the year 250 BC, the Taoist philosopher Han Fei put forth a malignant theory that unfortunately became a founding principle of Chinese art. Since everybody knew what dogs and horses looked like, he said, they were the most difficult subjects to paint, whereas demons and goblins, being invisible, were child's play. In other words, realism was high art because it involved control and discipline, whereas abstraction was the refuge of charlatans. Ever since that time, the imaginative arts suffered. Works of imagination would never again be as prized in Chinese culture as mundane still lifes of birds and chrysanthemums or groves of soporific bamboo. And this attitude infected the rest of Chinese thinking: Originality would never be as revered as rote learning and the manufacture of flawless reproductions. Copying became our métier.

Having seen my first ghost, I knew I had to produce as accurate an account of the encounter as I could so nobody could accuse me of a flight of fancy. Details would serve as proof that the dead amah I saw was as real as a living one. I waited for the right moment to confide in Sister Kwan. Not Li. He had been my secret sharer once, but no longer. After breakfast, we were separated into our respective routines, our respective routes to our respective schools.

Every morning at seven, Mother placed our fates into the hands of our servants. Quite literally. With our hands tightly clasped in theirs, Sister Choon took Li by rickshaw to the boys' school at one end of Frenchtown and Sister Kwan took me to the girls' school at the other. Both amahs waited by the gates until lessons ended at noon, at which time they escorted us home, again by rickshaw, again with our hands tightly enclosed in theirs. At no point in the journey would the amahs let go of us to scratch an itch or even to hold on for dear life when the rickshaw puller swerved to avoid a flattened dog.

It was hard in those days to find a moment without either of the amahs hovering over us, nattering acridly in Cantonese and pulling our ears for the smallest infractions—hawk-nosed Sister Choon especially, but even my favorite Sister Kwan was not immune to ill temper. We were small and had no concept of privacy, so we rarely begrudged their interference and abuse. Chinese children, I suppose, never took scolding very seriously unless it was a person of authority who was doing the scolding, in which case we cowered and cringed and cried. (We Chinese children were preternaturally aware of status.) Yet because we spent most of our time with these grown women who, due to their lack of education, retained a childlike credulity, they often became our confidantes.

Sometimes on the trips to and from school, when I had Sister Kwan all to myself, I would ask her for stories of the strange—the weirder the better. She considered herself an expert in the field. All the amahs did, coming as they did from superstitious families in the South who worshipped their ancestors at dilapidated shrines and said prayers to rice grains. From Sister

Kwan I'd learned that a cat could turn a dead man into a vampire by leaping over his corpse, that the beautiful maidens men met on byways at night usually turned out to be ghosts, and that wayward monks could sometimes subsist for decades inside the bellies of large carp.

I loved her stories. They told of an ancient China steeped in magic, color, and fine breeding, far removed from the fetid, gray, unsmiling world that was our Shanghai. Her stories helped to leaven the unpleasant encounters that were such a frequent component of city life. Whenever we passed the distended corpse of a beggar on the street, she'd mumble a Taoist blessing and assure me that the person must have been cruel to his parents to deserve such a fate; whenever our rickshaw man took us past one of those wretched funeral shops that considered baby coffins appropriate for its windows, she'd tell me American children used them for storing their dolls.

"There was an old amah in our room last night," I told Sister Kwan.

Her eyes widened in anticipation of a juicy story, so I proceeded to describe the encounter in detail. We were in the rickshaw, away from Mother's disapproving ears and punishing hands.

"The mole..." Her expression was uneasy. "You're sure it was under her left eye and not her right eye?"

"Positive."

"And her hair was completely white?"

"Yes. As snow."

"The jade bangle was white, not green?"

"White as her hair."

"Oh dear, oh dear." Sister Kwan muttered a quick oath. *Amitabha. Amitabha. Amitabha.*

"What's wrong?"

"You've just described Sister Yeung."

"Sister Yeung?"

"You don't remember her, do you? She used to take care of you when you were a baby." Sister Kwan released my hand and clutched at her temple. "I wonder what she wants, coming back." She looked at me. "Did she say anything? Did she frighten you?"

"She touched my toes."

"She did?" Her eyes widened again. "What else?"

I shrugged. "She tried to say something but vanished before she could say it. Anyway, I wasn't scared. I don't think she meant any harm."

"Oh dear." *Amitabha. Amitabha. Amitabha.*

"What's wrong?" I pinched her arm. "Tell me!"

"The first thing that's wrong is that Sister Yeung died when you were two years old. She threw herself into the Huangpu River. The other thing that's wrong, my child, is that faced with her ghost you felt no fear."

I didn't tell anybody else about the ghost amah. Sister Kwan did. Even after I made her swear repeatedly that she wouldn't. Her betrayal sent prickles of rage up and down my spine. These Cantonese farm girls were no better than the water snakes that slithered through their paddy fields!

That evening, the amahs gathered in the kitchen with the cook and started boiling noxious mountain herbs and ground-up mutton bone. The entire house reeked of wet soil and rot, like a cemetery after the rains. Sticks of incense smoldered at the kitchen shrine. I begged the amahs to stop—the ghost meant me no harm! No harm at all! I tugged at Sister Kwan's sleeve but she went on as if I weren't there.

"Why are you doing this?" I moaned. "Was Sister Yeung a bad person? Tell me! I want to know. Come on, tell me about Sister Yeung!"

The twins were wailing, constipated, and carrying their potties, still attached to their bottoms, like musical chairs around the sitting room. Li chased them, though not in earnest. From her restless pacing upstairs, I could tell that Mother was in a foul mood. It would only be a matter of time before she found out what was going on downstairs. Father remained, as usual, oblivious. He sat in his study on his straight-backed, cushionless chair, nose stuck in a book of Tang dynasty poetry, fingers dancing to some private meter.

Mother clopped down the stairs in high heels. "What's that infernal stench?" Her wrath was inevitable. "Sister Choon, what do you think you're doing? Why aren't you watching the babies? Ah Ying, where's our dinner?"

The servants said nothing. It was the first time I'd seen them openly defy Mother. Sister Choon unwrapped twigs, dried fungus, and unknowable black berries from paper parcels and handed them to Ah Ying, the cook, who pounded these things into smaller and smaller fragments with a stone pestle, then scraped the paste into the earthenware pot. Sister Kwan watched the bubbling cauldron, murmuring to herself, rubbing the bright orange rosaries in her hand.

"Ah Ying, I am speaking to you!" Mother stormed into the kitchen. "I paid good money for that duck and I expect to feed my family with it. Now clear out that pot and start cooking dinner. As for your incense, Sister Kwan, how many times have I told you I won't have those things burning in my house?" She swiveled around and caught me hiding under the altar of the kitchen god. Her eyebrows twitched. "What are *you* doing here? Don't tell me you're part of this coven."

"Let her be, madam." It was Ah Ying who spoke, the usually wordless cook who always did as she was told and kept her eyes on the stove.

"What is this? Mutiny?" Mother grabbed my wrist and twisted it. I groaned.

"Madam," Sister Choon said calmly. "Perhaps we should have explained our actions. We're cleansing the house with a protection spell. You see, Sister Yeung returned last night. We don't know what she wants, but we don't want her causing any mischief."

"Sister Yeung? What are you talking about? That woman died five years ago."

"That's precisely what we're talking about. Her ghost was seen in this house last night. She must want something. You recall she didn't exactly have a happy death."

"Who's responsible for these rumors?"

I held my breath and tried to make myself as inconspicuous as possible. Too late.

Sister Kwan turned to me. As her outstretched finger formed an accusation, I felt a burning hatred for her—her hypocrisy, her cowardice, her class. She averted her eyes.

Mother gave a harsh laugh. "And you grown women are foolish enough to believe the words of this little fantasist?" She went straight for the boiling pot and grabbed it with her bare hands. For a second I feared she would fling it at me, but instead she dumped its throbbing contents down the drain. The servants jerked back from the putrid steam.

"Enough is enough. Ah Ying, start cooking the duck. Sister Choon, please make the twins stop crying. And you," she said to Sister Kwan, "give this girl a bath. A well-scrubbed child doesn't make up stories." Sister Kwan was slow to take her cue and Mother lost her patience. "Oh, forget it. I'll bathe her myself. Just go and open some windows. I can't bear this smell. You're driving me insane, the lot of you."

As she washed me, Mother made no mention of any ghost. To her, the whole thing had been a figment of my fevered imagination. I didn't dare bring it up either. She cleaned me in grim silence, a maid scrubbing a stained spittoon, her thoughts so distant that she forgot I was made of flesh. I hated it when she bathed me. She was always unnecessarily hard, digging her nails into my scalp and rubbing the rough cloth across my back until I gripped the sides of the tub. But I never cried out or whined; I never wanted to give her any satisfaction from hurting me.

At one point, Li came to the doorway and stood watching us with meaningful silence, like someone who hadn't been let in on a secret but wanted us to know he knew it anyway. He'd been strangely quiet since the park. Mother shooed him away with a light kiss.

As I dried myself, my skin still raw, she grabbed both my shoulders and forced me to look into her unaffectionate eyes.

"Sister Yeung was an unstable woman. Whatever happened, happened a long time ago. It's all in the past. I don't want you listening to any more of the amahs' rubbish. They're cheap, ignorant country girls, full of silly ideas. You are a city girl. You're educated and come from a good home. If you believe their stories, then you're no better than they are and I might as well give you away to the orphanage. Let me know if you want that, and I'll tell the rickshaw man to take you there."

After toweling dry my hair and putting me in pajamas, she sent me back downstairs with a hard smack on the bottom.

I scampered back to the kitchen area, where the servants were wordlessly and grimly preparing dinner. On tiptoes, I crept up slowly behind Sister Kwan, who was at the chopping board slicing ginger. I got as close as I could and then roared with all my might. She jumped and dropped the knife. "Aiyah!" Her left thumb began to bleed. I glowered at her as I made my cocky exit to the back door.

"You wicked child! You demon!"

In the back of the house, by our small garden patch, I found Cricket, our errand boy, tending to the lilies with complete disinterest. A chunky, sullen kid of about fifteen, he was supposedly Ah Ying's adopted son, which meant he could have been anything from her nephew to a child beggar she'd taken in from the slums. Everybody called him Cricket because he spent all his spare time catching spiders and moths, yet for some inexplicable reason refused to touch crickets. He was my last hope; he'd been around the servants long enough that he might have overheard gossip about Sister Yeung. I rarely spoke to him because his position in the house was so ambiguous—he was young enough to be my brother, yet he was one of the servants. At the same time, he never displayed the deference to us the other servants did, so I never knew how to gauge him. Mother, on the other hand, made it plain she couldn't stand his insolent face. To cut through the awkwardness, I bribed him with a box of matches printed with a picture of a half-naked girl. He fingered it awhile, then pocketed it.

He pulled out a newsboy's cap from his pocket and put it on to hide the pink birthmark on his forehead. Sister Kwan had once joked it was shaped like a penis.

"They said she was always unhappy," Cricket grunted in his thick Shanghainese patois. He unscrewed a glass jar and released a hairy black tarantula. Possibly to scare me, he let the creature run up and down his bare arm, where the thick flesh was mottled with bites and bruises, old and new.

"What else did they say?"

"She had a younger brother in Canton who swindled her out of her money. Blew it all on gambling"—he smirked—"and girls."

"But why did she kill herself? It's just money."

"She was an old woman. It was her life savings. She'd set aside the money to build herself a house to retire in. They said she'd even found the perfect spot in her ancestral village. Next to a lake, supposedly, with lily pads so big you could sit on them. This was her dream. So you see, it wasn't only about money. It's about the trust lost between brother and sister."

I imagined Li's betrayal in the park amplified by ten, a hundred. And I remembered the hollow, empty feeling Sister Yeung had brought to my gut. I internalized her grief in an instant.

"You're too well-off to know disappointment." Cricket unleashed another spider onto his arm. He watched for my reaction. "People like you will never have empathy."

"What do you think her ghost wants?"

34

"Sorry, Your Highness, I've told you what I know. I don't believe in ghosts. I only believe in things my eyes can see and my hands can touch."

"But I saw her myself, I swear."

"The Song dynasty scholar Zhu Xi once said, 'If you believe it, you will see it. If you don't, you won't.'" He brought both spiders so close to my face that I was staring into their multiple eyes. "Me, I don't like scholars. I think they're all sissies. So I say the opposite. I believe in spiders because I can see them. Want to touch?"

Over dinner that night, Mother's revulsion for Father reached another of its increasingly frequent peaks. I think I was the only one in the house who ever registered her looks of nausea. In each grimace, she conveyed exactly what she thought of him—that he was worthless, unmanly—and betrayed her enormous self-pity, her sense that, deceived by his love poems and genteel manners, she'd married a pauper when she could have had a prince.

She sprang from the dinner table before her tears fell, and shot up the stairs.

"Bad stomach, Mother?" Father asked without looking up from his food. A door slammed.

Father turned to Li and me and shrugged. "Must be something she ate."

We polished off the braised ginger duck, though it was awful; the amahs' herbs had left a nasty aftertaste in the pot. I felt sure I could detect Sister Kwan's blood in it.

After dinner, I went to play with the twins. They pretended to be baby pandas, fighting for choice bamboo—me—but I had other things on my mind. As soon as Father stepped outside for a cigarette and Li was taken upstairs for his bath, I abandoned the twins and rushed into the study.

I climbed into Father's chair and sat at his rosewood desk, surveying his things. Framed photographs of the entire family lined the far edge. They were taken the year before in a studio in the American Settlement. We all appeared unnaturally stiff, posing against painted backdrops of trellises, sunsets, and Greek columns. There was one of Li and me flanking a cardboard cocker spaniel that even at the time I thought looked ridiculously fake. Father did his work surrounded by these pictures of us yet never paid us any attention when we were in the same room with him. A strange irony. But in these pictures, we were perfect: backs straight, hair groomed, clothes starched, smiles locked into place like a model army. It was probably how he preferred us—flat, silent, pocket-sized.

Pulling open the drawers, I located what I'd come for. Father's Four Treasures. Not his four children, of course, but his calligraphy tools: a brush with purple rabbit's fur, an ink stick made from compressed pine soot, an inkstone carved out of river rock, and finally, a ream of pure white writing paper. In one of his more affectionate moments, he'd told me that with these four portable Treasures, it would never matter where he was or how little money he had because he could always dream up a better world for himself in letters. It would take years before I stopped thinking that those were the ravings of a deluded old fool.

With only the two goldfish watching, I worked Father's implements the way I'd seen him do it: grinding the ink stick on the stone with a few drops of water to produce liquid ink, then dipping the brush tip lightly in the black puddle. On a fresh sheet of paper, I wrote in huge letters:

> *I know who you are.*
> *I can see you.*
> *I want to help.*

I fanned the note dry, folded it up carefully, and ran upstairs with it tucked in my pajama pants. Should Sister Yeung appear again that night, I would be ready. If she could see my toes, she would certainly see my message.

That night, as soon as Li's breathing grew steady and regular, and—more tellingly—his fist loosened around his butterscotch talisman, I placed the note flat over my feet, words in full view. I tried to stay alert and wait for the ghost, but to my great frustration fell asleep.

Sometime during the moonless night, I woke. The air had again become very chilly; Sister Yeung must surely be close. My hunch was confirmed by the dark silhouette in the far side of the room, a humanoid form moving slowly closer to me. I wriggled my fingers and toes to make sure I hadn't been turned into a statue again. I was free—Sister Yeung had decided to have mercy on me. As she approached even closer, I saw her white tunic and black slacks.

"Sister Yeung," I whispered. "I understand you. I want to help you."

A thin arm reached down and lifted my note. I held my breath. With a rude crunch, her hands balled up my offer.

"Hey!" I whispered violently, trying to keep my voice down.

The amah took another step closer—Sister Kwan. Betrayed again! She came to my side and I expected a slap, but instead she pressed a small mirrored amulet into my hand.

"You mustn't encourage her, child. Protect yourself with this."

I didn't want her stupid charm. I threw it on the floor. She picked it up and placed it back in my hand.

"Don't let her touch you again. Keep this to repel her. It's for your own good."

"No!" This time I hurled it across the room. Sister Kwan clucked her tongue and after a fruitless search for the thing in the dark, gave up. Before leaving, she said to me, "Sister Yeung could be very dangerous. Prior to drowning herself, there was an incident..." Here she paused dramatically.

"What incident?" I hissed.

"She tried to take you with her."

"She tried to kidnap me?"

"Worse."

I understood her meaning perfectly. But was Sister Kwan just trying to scare me?

After she left, the room was once again silent. The chill returned. I could feel my legs begin to stiffen. Oh, why had I tossed away that amulet? It hadn't even occurred to me that Sister Yeung could have meant any harm until Sister Kwan put the idea in my head. I watched as my breath again cooled into white spirals. My entire body was paralyzed, but this time my head remained unaffected—I could move my lips and my eyes. A small improvement. I could sense Sister Yeung's approach.

In a matter of seconds, she became whole. She came toward me exactly as she had the previous night—there was not the slightest variation. This time, however, I was free to scream for help. Yet, as before, I felt no desire to do so. The fear Sister Kwan had tried to instill in me was needless, even hateful. There was something very sad yet strangely calming about Sister Yeung's ghost as she gazed at me with those passive, unblinking eyes.

"Sister Yeung," I said quietly. "I know you. I want to help you."

Again, Sister Yeung reached with both hands for my feet, her movement and expression an exact facsimile of the night before. When she squeezed my toes, I again felt nothing. But this time, I paid closer attention. Her fingertips were shriveled and as tiny as a child's, smaller even than mine. I had heard about poor children hired by silk factories to fish out silkworm cocoons from boiling tubs with their bare hands—the job left them with stunted fingers. Sister Yeung had those fingers. Looking at her face creased with time's unstoppable passing, I had a flash of recognition: She would never be young again. I began to weep.

"Sister Yeung, can you hear me?"

"One day...," she started to say. "One day..."

Her body seemed to melt away, and once again, I was alone in the dark.

The next day, in the rickshaw to school, I refused to let Sister Kwan touch me. Her thumb was wrapped in a much bigger bandage than needed, exaggerating the injury sustained at the chopping board. Each time she tried to grab my hand, I let out a piercing scream. Finally, the rickshaw man told her to leave me be because I was attracting too many stares. He didn't want the police or, worse, the Republican Army after us.

"Did you keep the amulet I gave you?" Sister Kwan tried to make conversation, casting herself again as the concerned guardian.

I ignored her.

"It was blessed at my temple by a very powerful priest. He has ended droughts."

I stared out at the row of street carts next to the crowded tram stop, all of them hawking breakfast crullers and hot soybean milk to commuters in a hurry. The grease smelled delicious. I wished we could stop.

"She always liked you, you know. Sister Yeung. You were her favorite. That's why we were all so shocked about what she tried to do to you."

Lies. All lies.

"I suppose she was afraid to go alone," she continued. "She was probably lonely."

"Everybody's lonely," I snapped back.

That night I was ready with a new note for Sister Yeung.

> *You are a good person.*
> *I want to be your friend.*

Even if she couldn't hear me, she still might be able to see the note.

Hoping for a new outcome this time, I threw myself onto the floor as soon as I felt the onset of the cold, leaving the note where my feet would have been. I wanted to see if Sister Yeung would behave any differently.

She came, moving forward exactly as she'd done before. When she stretched out her silkworm-factory fingers, I thought she would pick up the note; instead her hands passed right through the paper, as if it were liquid. She squeezed the spot where my toes would have been and didn't seem to register the note. She appeared to be operating in a completely different plane, not seeing things that were there and seeing things that were not. It felt as if I were watching a film loop—her actions were completely identical to the previous nights. I had to break her routine.

"Sister Yeung!" I whispered. She didn't turn but instead continued to gaze at the dent on the bed where I would have lain. "I'm here, Sister Yeung. Over here!"

As if in response to my words, she started to speak, without turning her face:

"One day...one day these little feet will grow big..." Her voice quickly began to wither into echoes, as if coming from deep down a well. "And they will carry you far, far away from all of us."

"Sister Yeung!" I tried again from the floor. No reaction. "Please!"

The moment she vanished, I was flushed with grief and shame. How did she know? How could she have known?

Sister Yeung had unmasked me, voiced my most personal, most private secret—a fantasy I'd never shared with anyone. Yes, I had thought frequently of escape. Yes, I had dreamt about fleeing my family. *I wanted my hands to be free.*

I wept quietly at the foot of the bed for a while before crawling back in. Li stirred but miraculously did not wake. The butterscotch medallion sat in his palm like some magical tram fare. When dawn broke, my pillow was soaked with tears. Sister Yeung never returned. She must have found what she had come for.

Soon I, too, got what I was longing for.

That Mother and Father were moody was nothing new. Had we been any richer, or any poorer, they might have given in to the silken promises of the opium den; that they did not, I remain eternally grateful. But where once the two of them sank into what the amahs termed the Sulks, each moping around in a private gloom of their own, they now openly banged heads—an unthinkable move for Father, who had spent his entire life dodging conflict.

"Things will work themselves out. You'll see!" Father would say.

"That's all you ever do. Defer, delay, deny!" This was Mother's usual retort.

Whenever these clashes grew too intense, a quaint old propriety kicked in; they clamped down and reconvened in their bedroom with boiling tumblers of tea. There, with the door closed, they lobbed accusations at each other until the acrimony wore them both down and a blackened silence took over.

Our fate was sealed by two other events happening in quick succession. First, Father lost his job. His spineless principal, under pressure from a growing cadre of antibourgeois parents, decided that the teaching of poetry to twelve-year-olds was a waste of resources. Then the stock exchange crashed in New York, which meant that our stock exchange, too, was crushed in the ensuing depression.

Things had not worked out according to Father's lazy faith in goodness happening to the good. By default, Mother, that well of negativity, won.

We were called in to a family caucus.

Father, decided our matriarch, was to redeem himself in the Nanyang—the South Seas—a band of tropical islands that were seemingly immune to the ups and downs on Wall Street because its assets were material. Real, as opposed to the intangible, theoretical realm of stocks and bonds. The world would never stop needing tin, rubber, palm oil, tobacco. Mother's reasoning was that even if Father had to take on humiliating work in the plantations, at least we knew nobody there who could gossip.

He was to remit money home to us at the end of every month. And if the situation looked steady in the longer term, he could send for us, as many of our compatriots had done with their families. A few had even been known to thrive in the heat and dust.

Father mulled this over and emerged with a counterproposal: "I will take Li with me. No boy should be without his father."

Rather than argue, Mother conceded instantly—here Li probably got his answer about whether Mother loved him—but under one condition: "Ling. Take Ling, too."

"Twins should never be separated," she said. "They're two halves, yin and yang. They can never be a whole person unless they remain together."

Imagine Mother, chief debunker of ghost stories and myths, coming up with a theory like that!

Inwardly I was scared but thrilled; outwardly I pulled long faces. Li, too, bemoaned his impending exile. But for the first time since our day in *Paradis*, I saw some of the old spring in his step. I caught him whispering to himself, half excited, half fearful: "I'm going to be an Overseas Chinese."

Overseas Chinese. As in "Mr. So-and-So is an Overseas Chinese, which accounts for his poor taste in suits" or "Mrs. So-and-So is an Overseas Chinese, so you can't expect her to know how to fry eels." I'd been raised to think of the Overseas Chinese as a separate race, an underclass of lost souls deprived of basic things—sometimes an eye, sometimes an ear, but mostly proper manners and the ability to speak Mandarin like they meant it. They were the banished tribe, the wanderers, the deserters, the outcasts. Different, set apart, marked for life.

I had to put away my biases. For I, too, was about to become one of them.

The night before we set sail, there was a mournful air about the house, a feeling of missed opportunity too late to be salvaged. We played gramophone records by Shanghainese divas warbling about lost love in a minor key while the amahs stuffed clothes into two crowded trunks reeking of mothballs.

Mother sat on the couch with Li lying across her lap, both completely lax, almost comatose, both sets of hooded eyes staring into the distance while she massaged his little hands. Nobody spoke. The twins must have intuited our impending separation because they chased me around the downstairs, clinging to my sides like barnacles. Each time I pulled free, I got no more than three steps before having to surrender again. I lay flat on my back on the rug with both of them sinking their warm, heavy heads into my armpits, feigning sleep. I didn't want to look at them. I couldn't bear it. I let their heads fall to the floor and then crept away, only to have them catch me once more.

Through the door, I could see Father slumped at his desk, drunk on plum wine. The family photographs stared back at him. He picked up the frames in turn and whispered the name of each child as he encountered their image. I didn't have the heart to tell him that he'd mistaken Xiaowen for Bao-Bao. He didn't touch the one of Mother seated alone; perhaps he had forgotten how much wheedling and how many vials of tranquilizers it had taken him to get her out of the house and into the studio. Or perhaps he did remember but was now suddenly sentimental about it. I wriggled out of the twins' embrace and went to him.

"Why don't we take these pictures with us?" I said.

"We can't." He rubbed his thumbs over the one group portrait, all of us standing, somewhat stunned, before a painted sunset. "These are the only pictures your mother has of us. It would be like robbing her of her memory."

But by not taking them, I wanted to say, we would be robbed of ours.

Then I realized. Better to forget.

I HEAR HER VOICE IN MY HEAD as I make myself a pot of pu-erh tea. I hear *his*, too, of course—but his I've been hosting in my conscience for years, as constant as the beating of my own heart.

I want your story, she said. *I need it.*

The dense black leaves unfurl with the help of a spoon, but, like memories, they are old and stubborn. After a few quick stabs, they turn the water into ink. Medicinal ink that tastes of rot and regret.

But where is my inquisitor? I'm impatient. If I tell her my story, I will not have lived in vain, my deeds vanished without a trace.

There's another reason I want her here—and quick. Unlike the fearless child I was, I am now afraid to be alone. I'm shaking. My remembering has forced open a whole city of graves. In speaking their names, I've surrounded myself with ghosts. Mother, Father, Li, Sister Kwan . . . I see them as clear as day. And this has only been the beginning, the innocent days of childhood.

Please let my savior arrive before I reach the darker depths.

These memories, once unleashed, can be held back no more. I gulp my tea.

Hurry, Professor!

— 3 —

The Doldrums

THERE WERE AWKWARD GOOD-BYES at the dock with Sister Kwan and our rickshaw man, the latter whose calloused hands I shook for the first and last time. They were standing in for Mother—the woman could not transcend her phobia, not even for our departure. Blotting out my sorrow at this maternal absence, I gawked at the leviathan that would soon remove me from the unhappy pit that was old China.

The boat was enormous. Li elbowed me for calling it a boat. "It's a *ship*," he barked. He'd even heard a smartly dressed gent refer to it as a floating island. I conceded the point—this was no mere boat. The vessel had a trio of towering smokestacks in brick red and black, each larger than our entire house. All three leaned back ever so gracefully like ladies having their hair done. There were seven stories of living space, under which were storage vaults and boiler rooms, deep in its bowels.

As passengers embarked, a group of painters with harnesses around their waists were being hoisted up along its side, having just stenciled on the ship's new name, the SS *Prosperity*. Father explained that the vessel used to sail the transatlantic route exclusively, but the Depression had forced it to pick up business in the South China Sea. Its real name was being kept a secret. But what of names? Europe's loss was our gain.

I shuddered with glee as we stepped aboard and saw the long, lifeboat-lined boulevards on either sides of the sun deck. I could already picture Li and myself racing up and down them. Sister Kwan wasn't here to rein us in with her iron claws; Mother wasn't here to mutter. And since Father never willingly touched us, our hands were now completely free! Just to find our living quarters, Father had to study the map and lead us through labyrinthine stairways, elevator lobbies, mahogany-paneled landings lined with chrome handrails, and, most strikingly, a high-ceilinged dining room with peacock wallpaper and crisp white linens. Floating island? This was a floating city!

Then I saw our room. The three of us entered a dark little vacuum not much larger than Father's study. Eight feet by eight feet, if that. Against the near wall were two narrow bunk beds, the kind even coolies might complain about. Father said he'd take the lower one; Li and I were to share the one above. Seeing our dismay, he began to pace the room. The wallpaper was a sickly green, with an interlocking vine motif. Most depressing of all, there was only a single porthole that we were all to share—a miserable disk of sooty, unwashed glass through which we were to get our sightseeing done, presumably while seated at the one careworn chair perched in its shadow. Six days and six nights we had to spend in this cell. I tried not to think it was a portent of things to come, the plummeting tenor of our new life amidst the natives and grass huts of the Nanyang.

"Is there a mistake?" Li finally said.

Father shook his head. "This is what we paid for. Third class on this ship is equivalent to first class on the kind of ship people normally take on this voyage. So we should think of ourselves as being in first. We should feel fortunate."

"What about first class on *this* ship?" Li grew impatient. "Can't we go there?"

"Only third class is open. The rest of the ship is closed."

"Mother wouldn't approve."

"Your mother isn't here, is she?" Li kept quiet. Father continued, stating what I would come to think of as his life philosophy: "Boundaries are made for good reason. They set different people apart, and this is how we keep the peace."

The horn sounded its low signal. As the SS *Prosperity* pulled out of the harbor, I thought about all the beauty spots of China I'd never get to see now that I was about to become an Overseas Chinese. The Ming emperor tombs outside Beijing. The poet Du Fu's thatched cottage in Chengdu. The scholars' rock gardens of Suzhou. These places would soon sound as foreign and fictional to me as the Jade Rabbit's home on the moon.

Except for the panda-filled forests of Sichuan Province, I felt absolutely no connection with any of China's supposed cultural treasures. Beyond family, my concept of "our people" didn't stretch very far. I'd felt beggar children—brown, with beaky Uighur features—hurling rocks at my rickshaw. I'd experienced the rank betrayal of a Cantonese servant girl like Sister Kwan. These weren't "my people." In most cases, we didn't even speak the same language. The all-purpose lumping together of everyone who happened to be born on the same enormous landmass was willful madness.

The first night on board the SS *Prosperity*, after a dinner of smoked ham sandwiches that Ah Ying had packed for us in waxed paper, Father sent us to bed. He said the waves were making him dizzy and he had no energy to watch us. We had no choice in the matter, as we all shared the same little cabin. Li took the side of the bunk nearest the wall while I got the outside, the result of much haggling—we were both afraid of falling off the edge—and as at home, we slept back-to-back. Li had his nose pressed against the wallpaper, so tight was our space.

My fortune was free, I consoled myself, my path uncluttered. The stars blinked their affirmation through the murky porthole, instigating the wild patter of my innocent heart. Before long, exhausted with anticipation and lulled by the waves, we all fell asleep.

To my surprise, Father had brought with him English language instruction books. The very next morning, he began giving Li lessons in the third-class cafeteria; I was not included—apparently I wasn't important or clever enough. Father was no expert himself. Embarrassed to be seen struggling through the language alone, Li was clearly his alibi. Unsurprisingly, father and son became, through their shared new lingo, a colony of their own. Li gave me the cold shoulder, knowing that in the power dynamic of our new family unit, he'd better choose wisely.

"We have no choice," I overheard Father say as they stumbled along, learning the alien alphabet. "Where we're going, we'll need to know English."

"Where's that?" Li asked.

"The Black Isle."

The Black Isle! Until he uttered those words, I hadn't even known where we were headed and somehow never found the inclination to ask.

The Black Isle, where they spoke English! I pictured hairy Englishmen wearing sarongs and living in grass huts. Horrified, I covered my ears. I didn't want to know any more.

I walked off my rage. But the farther I wandered from Li, Father, and the rest of the passengers, the more closed doors and deserted hallways I encountered. Unlit hallways in the windowless depths of an ocean liner are unfriendly indeed. Father had not exaggerated—most of the ship was empty. Paying customers were relegated to the drabbest portion of the ship while pretty stairways and exquisite promenades gathered oceanic dust. I ran down promising corridors lined with doors numbered in gold only to find each and every one of them locked. I kept expecting to run into someone who'd scold me for being where I shouldn't be and spin me toward whence I came, but no such person ever materialized, not even a crew member on an unauthorized smoke break. All I heard was the low hum of the ship's tireless engines chugging along and the wooden floorboards creaking beneath my feet. These sounds became my constant companions.

I hoped to find the peacock dining room Father had walked us through, but every door I tried refused to budge. Was that area now closed, too? Were all the nice parts of the ship locked away? The third-class cafeteria was a teeming lunchroom, the air dense with tobacco smoke and recycled grease, the windows frosted with the dew of communal sighing. Diners stood in line for food served in trays, just like at school, except most of the passengers were grownups, many with children in tow who were older than me. What a humiliating arrangement. What a far cry from the peacock room.

Finally, deep inside the belly of the ship, a couple of floors below the observation deck, a pair of heavy steel doors gave way. There were words in English above the door frame, in what I would come to know and love as Art Deco script. I couldn't read them, but I detected a smell I recalled from a class excursion to a swimming club. Chlorine. A funny place for this smell. Curiosity got the better of me and I pushed through the steel double doors. Sure enough, a pool.

It was cold in the room, probably because every surface in it was tiled. The walls were ivory, pierced with horizontal striations of turquoise, and the pool itself was done in mosaics on the aquatic theme of blue. Ribbed chrome sconces flickered, and the stripes they cast on the water gave it an atmosphere of high drama, like a stage set anticipating the entrance of gloomy players. Lounge chairs lined the pool, all empty, their long, gray silhouettes peopling the room with silent spectators.

"Hello?" I called. My voice echoed loudly through the cavernous chamber. I heard water splashing. Someone was swimming laps, freestyle. A young girl in a red swimsuit with a matching red cap, about my age. Odd that I hadn't noticed her first thing. She barely lifted her head. I had to think twice about disturbing her—she seemed so intense. I watched her swim a couple of more laps and when she didn't pause to breathe, I called out again, louder. "Hello?"

"Hello," a voice answered behind me. I jumped. It was a man in a Western-style suit. His face was in the shadows but his Shanghai accent was unmistakable. I wondered how long he'd been standing behind me.

"So this part of the boat is open?" In my nervousness, I'd slipped and called the ship a boat again. Thankfully, the man didn't mock me.

He stepped into the light, revealing thick brows and dark European features. "It's open," he said in perfect Shanghainese. "To you and me, everything's open."

His words confused me, so I changed the subject. "Are you that girl's father?"

He smiled. "Do I look that old to you? No, that's Rachel," he said, as if it explained everything. "Come, let's not disturb her. She's very...serious."

He guided me to the other end of the hall, where there was another set of doors, identical to the ones I'd entered. I watched the swimming girl while we walked toward these doors, hoping she'd finally lift her head and let me see her face.

"Oh, don't stare," the man said in a friendly voice. "Rachel can be awfully shy."

In his gentlemanly fashion, he allowed me to enter first, unlike Father, who always rudely pushed ahead. I found the smell of his cologne delightful. His hair was so long that its curly ends brushed his collar. Had Mother seen him, she'd have sent him straight to the barber. To me he was the very picture of masculine grace. Here was a complete stranger who was kind, gracious, well spoken, who took enough of an interest in me to show me around, while my own father cowered like a scared sheep in his third-class ghetto, incurious, unquestioning, passively believing the lie that the rest of the ship was closed. I decided then that I would never share my findings with Father or Li.

The doors led directly to the peacock salon. It was as if the man had read my mind.

I gasped and raced in, the flimsy soles of my shoes immediately buffered by luscious, endless carpeting. Nobody was here, not a soul. A hundred tables were set—starched white napkins atop expensive china, no fewer than three wineglasses per diner. Strains of watery music emerged from the next room. My flesh tingled. Somebody was practicing the harp. The gas-lit chandeliers flared on together at this moment—puff!—and the mahogany pillars glistened with fresh polish. A huge banquet was certainly in the cards for some lucky passengers tonight.

"How do you know where everything is?" I asked. "We've only been at sea one day."

"I've made this passage many times and know how dull it is if you confine yourself to one area. My wife lives on the Black Isle."

"And you live in Shanghai?"

"Mostly."

"Don't you miss your wife?"

He smiled ruefully. "I never stop missing her. Even when she's standing right before me." He walked to one of the large windows on the sides of the hall.

It was nearly evening. Stars were rehearsing their twinkles, and a blushing band of peach light lingered at the end of the horizon, fading slowly down the waterline.

"Look at the water," said the man.

As the sky dimmed, the black ocean came alive. Fairy lights, maybe thousands of them, bobbed up and down with the waves, each flashing pink, blue, and silver at different intervals. They formed a dense garland around the ship, their colors unsynchronized, yet harmonious, even hypnotic—pink, blue, silver, blue, pink, pink—like a soft electric glove easing the ship through the dark water.

"Jellyfish. They light the paths of ships at night so the ships don't collide with whales or the sunken galleons on the ocean floor. These jellyfish are the seeing-eye dogs of the marine world. They're possibly the cleverest creatures on earth. People underestimate them because they don't make any noise, but they have their own way of speaking. Whenever they flash like this, you know things are going to be all right. I wanted you to see them so you'd know that things are going to be all right."

I nodded vaguely.

"It's late now. You better run along back to your family."

Needles of panic. "But I don't know how to get back."

The man pointed to an elegant mahogany door with an inlaid anchor done in red cherry. I ran to it and placed my hand on the brass handle; then I looked back, sorry to have to abandon my handsome newfound friend.

"See you tomorrow?" the man asked. My mood lifted. "Shall we meet again at the swimming pool?"

I beamed. "What time?"

"The same time, after lunch. I could give you English lessons."

My heart leapt. "You know English?"

"And Hebrew and French and Russian. Not by choice. History forces some of us to learn a little of everything." He waved good-bye. "*Au revoir, mademoiselle.* 'Til we meet again." He turned back to view the water.

I bit my lip, then asked, "What's your name?"

"Odell." He smiled, charmed that I would ask.

"See you tomorrow, Mr. Odell."

As I ran toward our inelegant cafeteria, guided by the cloying scent of pork trotters being drowned in fat, I thought it odd that the man never asked me my name.

After the peacock room, everything felt even more inferior. The cafeteria floor was covered in cheap third-class linoleum to catch the spills from clumsy third-class hands. The silverware was third class, lightweight and malleable; when our aluminum forks scraped the bottoms of our aluminum trays, they made the harsh squawks of dying parrots. Everybody huddled over their food like ragamuffins guarding their rations. There were teachers, clerks, and shopkeepers among us, yet they were all behaving so disgracefully, as if third class was a state of mind and not simply a ticket price.

Li nibbled at his undercooked yam, prodded the congealed fat around the overboiled pork, and told Father he felt sick. His complexion was green, as if his blood vessels had been eclipsed by those foul wallpaper vines.

The following morning, I skipped lunch and smuggled my unsupervised self back to the swimming pool. The girl, Rachel, was already doing her laps. Odell sat in a lounge chair, as if he'd been expecting me for some time. As promised, he walked me through the ship—the ballroom, the hairdressing studio, the squash court and gymnasium, and the wood-paneled galley where first-class dinners were prepared, with its army of gas rings and railcars of humming iceboxes. He told me the names of everything in English. Parquet, pommel horse, aperitif—how grand those words felt on my tongue!

In the depopulated shopping arcade, elaborate cut glass panels unfolded across two facing walls like parallel comic strips. The tableaux were vivid with monsters and men whose near nakedness made me blush.

"They're Greek," explained my guide. "The weather's very warm there."

He went on to narrate the two tales inscribed in those panels. In one, a young hero named Perseus went on a quest to slay Medusa, a deadly Gorgon with snakes for hair who turned men to stone at a glance. Aided by special gifts—sword, shield, and flying sandals—Perseus emerged triumphant, Medusa's head wriggling in his hand. In the other panel, another hero, Theseus, faced off against the Minotaur in its labyrinth. Also aided by a gift—a ball of string—Theseus survived and laid rest his beast.

The pictures were luridly exotic—Medusa's head dripped blood—but I was struck by a glaring imperfection. "Isn't it cheating," I asked, "if the heroes had outside help?"

Odell laughed. "Have you tried slaying a Gorgon? You need all the assistance you can get." He pursed his lips. "Actually, you remind me of another Greek character, a stubborn young girl who never wanted any help. Pandora."

"Was she a hero, too?"

"To some." Odell twitched his brows dramatically. "To others she's a *villain*."

He followed this with the story of Pandora and the infernal box she opened, a parable whose old-fashioned moralizing provoked my deepest yawns.

"Tired, are you, Pandora?"

He flicked a switch and a series of sconces fired up along the walls, hissing and flickering uncertainly. I realized that until then, we'd been standing in near darkness. We were in the first-class lobby, surrounded by clusters of empty settees and ashtrays set on kingly pedestals. Nobody was manning the welcome desk and we passed right through. At the mouth of a corridor lined with numbered rooms, Odell paused.

"Feel free to use any room here you like. You'll find they're much more comfortable than the ones in steerage."

I ambled down the hallway and chose a room at random. Room 88. It felt like a lucky number. As Odell promised, it was unlocked. The room was easily four times the size of our pathetic cabin. A double bed, big windows, frilly drapes—everything done in genteel pink and cream. I looked back to thank Odell but he was gone.

I hadn't thought I was tired but no sooner had I collapsed into bed than I submitted to slumber. When I woke, the sky was dark. My stomach rumbled. Dinnertime.

The peacock salon was not empty. I stopped at the doorway, wondering if I'd be caught in this forbidden zone. A long-legged blonde in a shimmering gown danced a somber tango by herself in the silence, by the stage where no musician had yet been installed. But she was fully absorbed and seemed not to mind my presence.

I sauntered in, trying to decide which of the hundred tables I should sit at.

"Pandora." Odell was sitting by a trompe l'oeil window at a table for two. The Mediterranean countryside, bursting with butterflies and olive trees, spread out along his arm. "You look lovely tonight." I blushed and walked nimbly over to join him. He tilted his head at the dancer. "Don't worry about her."

He pushed his steaming bowl of meat and rice, apparently untouched, toward me and handed me his fork with a flourish. I promptly forgot all my manners and started into the food. The rice was fluffy, the sauce tangy, the cubes of beef so pinkly tender they practically melted on my tongue. Even with my childish palate, trained on Ah Ying's salt-lashed casseroles, I knew what I was tasting would be hard to surpass.

"Beef Stroganoff," he said. "The chef's specialty. He cooked for the Russian imperial family during the old days. I can tell you like it."

He watched my unladylike gorging with his sad eyes, and I grew self-conscious.

"I shouldn't be stealing your food." I pushed the plate back toward him, but the meal was already half gone.

"Nonsense. There's plenty more where this came from. It's a pleasure to watch you eat. One of these days you should join my wife and me at the Metropole for tea. We're there the last Sunday of every month, without fail. The Metropole's famous for its high tea. You remind me a great deal of my wife, actually. Pei-Pei. That's her name."

My cheeks prickled again. "Your wife's Chinese?"

"Very much so."

"Do you have children?"

He shook his head, regretfully.

"Why not?"

"It's difficult when I live in one place and my wife lives in another."

"Why don't you stay with her on the Black Isle?"

"There's no place on the Black Isle for someone like me. You'll see what I mean. It's not like Shanghai over there. It's a jungle. People are less open-minded."

"Then why doesn't your wife live with you in Shanghai?"

"Do you always ask this many questions, Pandora?"

"Stop calling me Pandora." I put down my fork.

"Have you noticed something unusual, Pandora?" He smiled, pointing to his lips.

I covered my mouth: we'd conducted our entire conversation in English.

In the company of my good teacher, I had absorbed this new knowledge like a thirsty sponge. But here's the truth. This was due less to talent than to *empathy*, and it would be much later before I'd come to understand—or rather, accept—the difference.

Both Li and Father were seasick again, taking turns at the bucket out in the corridor. Between the two of them, the door creaked open and clanked shut all through the night. I was tempted to tell them about the rooms in first class, but I held my mouth shut.

When I woke in the morning, Father and Li were gone. I instantly regretted my secrecy.

"They're in the Isolation Ward," said an old widow who shared a cabin with her middle-aged daughter. "It's at the tail end of the ship, down several very dark, very steep flights of stairs. My girl's there, too. Best you wait here and keep me company. Come, come." She handed me one of her knitting needles, which I was to hold still while she tied endless loops around the other. I flung it down and fled.

The Isolation Ward? I had to find Odell.

A crew member intercepted me on the promenade. A stocky Chinese sailor so tanned he looked almost Indian.

"I have to meet my friend at the swimming pool," I told him.

"Rubbish, the swimming pool is closed."

"No, it's not. That girl Rachel swims there every day."

The sailor's lip quivered. "Rachel? You saw Rachel?"

The sailor didn't wait for me to answer. He grabbed the collar of my blouse and dragged me through a set of doors marked CREW ONLY and then down a long corridor rattling with noisy generators. The ship seemed to pitch more dramatically in that tight space. At the end of the way was a frosted glass door with the word ENGINEER painted in gold. It opened even before the sailor could knock. A lank, sinewy European in a crumpled, unbuttoned shirt stood on the threshold, his white hair in a mess.

"What is it now?"

"This one says she saw the girl. In the pool."

The European's pale blue eyes widened for a split second; then he nodded, almost subliminally, as if deciding on the terms of some internal pact. He unfurled his wrinkly hand in the direction of my face and I flinched, but all he did was flatten his palm against my forehead in a grandfatherly way. "No fever."

He placed his thumbs below each of my eyes and gently pulled down my lower lids. "Normal."

Squatting down until our gazes were level, he addressed me in halting Mandarin: "Where your people?"

"In the I-Ward, Mr. Rosen," said the sailor.

"In that case, they'll be back in their cabin shortly. The I-Ward is overcrowded. Too many first-time travelers. The Chinese can be very imaginative when it comes to ailments." He shook his head, dispersing white hair across his balding pate. "This one's probably no different. Take her back to her room to wait and make sure she doesn't wander off again."

The sailor pulled me gently out of the engineer's office.

I resisted. I knew I had to register my outrage before it was too late. But where I found the courage for my outburst, I do not know:

"How come Rachel can go there but not me?" I shouted.

The engineer responded in a voice heavy with regret. "Rachel does whatever she pleases. And I'd appreciate it if you didn't tell the others about my daughter."

With that, he shut his door. I heard a record squeal on—minor-key piano music full of clashing chords. But I had questions. Rachel was his *daughter*? He looked so old.

The sailor's hand gripped mine as he walked me back, so I wouldn't "wander off" as the engineer had so insultingly put it. Reaching third class, he slavishly repeated his overlord's demand: "Don't go around spreading rumors about the girl, you hear? Just stay in your room and be good."

"Why?"

"Because we cannot afford chaos on board."

"Why?"

"Are you playing games with me or do you really have no horse sense? Couldn't you tell that Rachel isn't like us?"

"Because she's a European?"

The sailor sank down to his haunches and looked into my eyes. "No. Because she drowned in that pool ten years ago."

So Rachel was a ghost! My flesh tingled with this secret, special knowledge. So Sister Yeung wasn't the only one. Like that dead amah, Rachel hadn't scared me or harmed me, and I remained untouched, unchanged. The only unhappy consequence of my sighting was that it had rendered the sailor and me into two very different animals, with nothing more in common. My maritime guardian sat on the lone chair in our cabin, staring out the porthole, halfheartedly whistling "It's a Long Way to Tipperary" and playing with a loose thread on his shirt. I sensed he was now afraid of me, as if seeing ghosts instantly gave me some strange power. I couldn't wait to hear what Odell might make of the news, since he, too, had clearly seen the little swimmer.

Finally the door clicked open and the sailor popped up from his perch. Father lurched back, startled to see a strange man in the cabin; I watched his guard go up. I was relieved to see Li, but he was still green-faced. He darted to the bunk, pushing me aside.

The sailor was only too happy to leave. He shot me a look of caution—*Don't tell*—then slipped out the door.

Father waited till he was gone before uttering a word. "I didn't want to wake you this morning. I took Li to the sick bay. The doctor says he has anemia." Father's face creased up. "Not enough nutrition. And there's nothing they can do about it until we get to shore."

"They have beef Stroganoff," I offered, "in first class."

"Will you stop?" Father was suddenly livid, his rage incommensurate with my words. His eyes flared. "I've no patience for your lies!"

"But I ate there!"

The back of Father's hand came crashing across my face.

Father, who'd never scolded or struck any of us. Only four days in, and this journey was already changing us. My gentle father was turning into a brute, my athletic brother into a weakling, and I was left to fend for myself in this upside-down world.

I was the island, not this treacherous ship. I was the one floating by my lonesome in the vast ocean. My face burned from the slap, and again from my tears.

"Your brother is sick and here you are gleefully making up stories." Father sat on the rickety chair and gazed out the porthole, just as the sailor had done. Was I so repellent that neither of them could bear to look at me? After a while, he glanced at me, surprised I was still standing where he'd left me. "All right. All right. Stop crying, will you?" He beckoned me over and pulled out a fraying handkerchief. When he daubed my cheeks with it, I smelled orange peel and naphthalene, the comforting scents of our old Shanghai. "Aiyah, I only have one handkerchief. Look how you've ruined it."

I sucked back my tears, but this only produced jagged, hiccuplike sobs. Father clucked his tongue. "What am I to do with you?" We both turned to Li, who seemed to be asleep but not restfully so. Greenish veins were winding down his temples like tendrils. His lips were tinged blue. "What am I to do?"

I felt his despair. We should have stayed in China; we could have found a less drastic solution.

Suddenly and roughly, he grabbed my wrist. Another first. I relaxed, expecting an apologetic caress or at least an avuncular handshake. Instead, he snatched a paring knife from the nightstand and brought its tip perilously close to my open and vulnerable palm.

"Father...," I pleaded. Hadn't he hurt me enough?

"Don't make this any harder for me. We have to do this for the greater good."

He plunged the sharp blade into the fleshy ball of my palm and I shrieked in pain. Clamping me between his knees, he held me still—the man possessed more animal strength than I'd ever given him credit for. The blood streamed down my arm in two crimson ribbons, making his grip slippery, but this only tightened his resolve. He rose from the chair, and it fell back against the wall with a crack. Clutching my hand, he dragged me toward the lower bunk.

He placed my bleeding hand over Li's mouth, pressing my cut against it until his lips pulled apart. I felt Li's teeth rubbing against my wound but his eyes remained shut. Was he really asleep or just pretending? Seeing my blood smeared across his mouth like lipstick, I felt ill.

"Drink," Father whispered to his beloved son, tears forming in his eyes, too crystalline and proud to fall.

Li drank.

Although I couldn't know it then, the balance of power between my twin and myself—a delicate, unspoken understanding natural only to those who've shared a womb—had begun to shift. I was now Li's benefactor; it was my blood that kept him alive.

Maybe because he sensed this unsettling change, Father watched me hawkishly. We went as a pair to the cafeteria for our meals, ferrying food back to Li, who stayed in the room to rest. To improve my circulation, we took solemn, repetitive hikes together on the sports deck, circling the smoke stacks until I memorized every crack and ding in the paint. Each time he caught me looking at a stairway or door, he chastised me with a painful squeeze of my arm or with a harrumph if others happened to be watching. Back in the cabin, I received a hard smack for every liberty-seeking glance. Escape proved futile.

Yet it wasn't exactly escape that I craved. I was thinking about Odell.

I had so many questions for him: Was he like me? Could he always see the dead? Was he ever frightened? Would I be? Part of me prayed that he would come back to third class and rescue me, but an even greater part dreaded him seeing me like this, kept under lock and key by an unworthy guardian.

Every morning, under Father's supervision, I fed Li his cafeteria break-fast and lunch. Every night, again under Father's watch, Li fed on me, reopening the gash on my palm by first peeling off the scab with his teeth, then sucking on the clot until life flowed afresh from my veins to his and we became one continuous artery.

When Li felt better one evening after his "dinner," Father was able to take him outside for some fresh air. Once they were safely gone, I saw my chance and stepped into the dusk.

The ship had entered an equatorial zone of dead calm in the South China Sea, an area that was known as the Doldrums because nothing there ever stirred. The air stayed warm and sticky day and night without varia-tion. It was notorious for driving sailors mad with restlessness. But not just sailors. I felt the suffocating humidity burrowing deep into my pores like a pox that was impossible to scratch off.

Running breathlessly along the twilit promenade, I was instantly drenched. Sweat trickled down my chest and legs like tickly snakes. Every door to first class was now locked. My boundary crossing must have pro-voked these measures. I cursed the engineer. Why so much fuss over one little ghost girl? Why the fear?

Halfway down the walkway, I climbed up a ladder to the next deck, panting from the extra weight the Doldrums seemed to have piled onto me. Up there, my path lit by the most halfhearted moonlight imaginable, I faced a grim mechanical wasteland—spigots, the elbows of unfriendly pipes, the yawning mouths of massive ventilators.

Suddenly the floor shook with a low, vibrating blast, and my ears, bones, everything shattered. The call of Satan's own trumpeter. I fell to the ground, plugging my ears. Eventually the noise ceased. Nerves still ringing, knees still soft, I ventured forth.

I looked out at the water. It was alit. Not with jellyfish this time but with undulating flecks of gold. Reflections! Adjusting my eyes, I glimpsed on the horizon a swath of land. Its modest hillocks were packed with the silhouettes of curious giraffes, their long necks bending to one side. Electric lights were ablaze on some kind of dock.

It had been days since I had seen anything but water, and even this unpromising atoll romanced me. It loomed closer and closer with each passing second. The giraffes turned out not to be animals after all but tropical palms, their trunks yielding to a nonexistent breeze. Firefly dots of light flickered in the blackness beyond, like a hundred children waving mirrors from dark windows.

"They'll forget you," said a child's voice. It echoed strangely, as if it had come from yards away or from some forlorn corner of my mind. "They always forget you."

But no more than five feet behind me, amidst the knots and necks of pipes, stood a girl in a red swimsuit. Rachel, of course. Again, I felt no fear. Water flowed from her nostrils and mouth and cascaded down her waxen, silvery skin. Her eyes were bloodshot and her cheeks, possibly once rosy, were sallow. Here was a sweet girl made plain by chlorine and death, nothing at all like the carefree little Europeans I'd seen in Shanghai. She sighed with an old person's sobriety and turned to leave.

"Wait!" I cried. "Who's going to forget me?"

The look on her face sent a spear of ice through me: She had the eyes of the kitten in the park, soon after its fear had stilled, the eyes of one who had seen enough to not place any faith in human beings. Somehow I had already failed her.

From deep within its belly, the ship released another plangent, metallic wail. I felt subterranean brakes groaning into place and was thrown against a standing pipe. When I picked myself up, Rachel was gone. All that remained was a puddle where she had stood and the unmistakable scent of the swimming pool.

Cold panic tore through me. *They'll forget you.* I dashed toward our cabin.

How long had I been gone? Hours? Third class was deserted. Nobody was in the cafeteria, not even the old codgers who usually sat around playing checkers and smoking Red Lion cigarettes. The reek of tobacco breath still hung in the air, telling me they couldn't have strayed far—but where to? Down the entire third-class corridor, cabin doors had been left gaping, indecent, and through each I peered uneasily into unmade bunks, evidence of hasty departures. My legs wobbled as I approached ours.

Our room was empty; all our things were gone. Father and Li had abandoned me.

I caught a glimpse of myself in the mirror: I was in pajamas, and embarrassing ones at that—pink flannel imprinted with bouncing rabbits, the left shoulder seam splitting, the underarms salty with perspiration. I had no idea where Father intended for us to lodge, no address, no names of distant relatives who might be standing on the pier in their grass skirts.

My legs were betraying me also. They now threatened to buckle. With a final surge of energy, I climbed to the top bunk and curled up against the hideous green wall, hoping the vines would emerge from it to fold me in, enmesh me in leaves and lichen until everything, everything, was over. But I couldn't keep my eyes closed; tears were pushing their way out.

Footsteps down the corridor. I jerked up. "Father?"

A face appeared in the doorway—not Father. It was the tanned sailor. "There you are!" He sighed. "Come, hurry." He came directly to the bunk and seized me, flopping me over his shoulder as if I were a pig to market.

Over the shaky gangway from ship to land, I glimpsed a strip of dark water, teeming with what looked like luminous, fluctuating tulips. Baby jellyfish, still uncertain, still unformed.

Incense, the pious kind Mother despised, laced the air on land. But as soon as we entered the covered terminus, a dilapidated pavilion with wrought-iron pillars, all I smelled was rank body odor. Although electric ceiling fans buzzed far above our heads, it felt as though we'd entered an enormous oven. A teeming oven in which each person had distilled his or her entire life into a single trunk and consequently guarded it with unnatural and often undue hostility.

"Welcome home," the sailor whispered in my ear as he set my jellied feet down on solid ground in the middle of thousands of people I'd never met. "Your father and brother are waiting for you under the big clock."

He nudged me in the right direction. I couldn't see them, but the pale yellow clock face loomed like a moon above the flurry of sticky elbows and sweat-mottled backs. The moon clock had but one arm. What a terrible place this was that even the port terminal clock would be missing an arm! Presently I realized my mistake: The minute hand was tucked behind its brother.

It was midnight.

— 4 —

Dirty Island

THE BLACK ISLE was the largest in a chain of some thirty or forty islands scattered along the equator, the smallest of which sprouted no more than a fishing shack and a cluster of palms. East to west it spanned fifty miles, north to south a hundred fifty.

Far from being the center of things, however, the Island—as it was called by the locals—sat like a dull guest in the northwestern corner of the Archipelago, itself an unpromising clutch of crumbs with only the pull of the earth holding it in place. This arrangement seemed entirely provisional, and you got the sense from looking at the map that even the Isle might someday wear thin gravity's welcome and simply float away.

Yet the Black Isle's place was as solid as Gibraltar. The British East India Company had owned and operated the Island since the early 1800s, running it as a city-state, much like Florence or Venice at their peak, albeit with Anglo-Saxon stoicism instead of Latinate bravura.

It was the shiny opal in the empire's Far Eastern crown—Britain's only territory with a deep natural harbor *and* the right climate for the cultivation of such planter favorites as rubber, tobacco, and nutmeg. And being equidistant between India and China, the Island made an ideal stop for British ships ferrying opium. But as to the portentous timbre of its name, the mighty colonizers could not be blamed. It was a literal translation of the native Malay *Pulau Hitam* (Island Black), perhaps a bitter wink at its shadowy history as a pirate's lair before the coming of the European.

It was this dark aspect that we saw on the night of our arrival at the tail end of 1929, dreaming of a better life.

The entryway into the Isle was flanked by a series of greeters, starting with poker-faced Chinese guards who divided up the thronging new arrivals. Those Chinese men who spoke fluent English and wore spectacles were pulled from the queue and directed to a separate, less busy area.

"Special treatment!" Father sputtered. He pulled out his comb to neaten his oily, unwashed hair, but then struck me with it instead. "Why did you run off without telling me? If I didn't have to go looking for you, I would have cleaned up!"

Years later, I realized that *our* queue had been the lucky one. Because they looked educated, those well-groomed men were interrogated about that scourge of Eurasia, Bolshevism, and were given cavity probes for tell-tale proclivities. Those who gave the slightest cause for suspicion were promptly thrown back on the boat.

At a second checkpoint stood a corpulent British inspector whose sole duty it was to shake hands with us newcomers. This was no friendly gesture, however; he was on the lookout for smooth hands. Smooth hands, too, raised red flags. Father, with his fey, scholarly mien, fell into this category, but fortunately for him, his bedraggled tagalongs (me in torn pajamas, Li of the green face) allowed him to pass through unmolested.

We slept on hardwood benches in the terminal building until morning. At daybreak, packed and smelling like sardines, we were carted off in rickety buses and dropped off en masse at the main depot in the center of the city.

The city began on the Island's southern tip, and from this Victorian crucible civilization boomed. What I saw that first dawn was a typical frontier town, much like what I would later see in pictures of Bombay, Sydney, Johannesburg: a clique of European wedding cakes standing close together, frowning valiantly through the heat and dust at the endless circuit of zigzagging trolleybuses. Everything was overwhelming—the noise from horns, engines, cursing in a dozen languages; the smell of coal smoke, frying oil, sewer rot; and even the people, who were all sizes and shades. Most terrifying of all were the rogue taxicabs that flew over curbs, sluicing in front of man, beast, and automobile, honking all the way. The moment we stepped into the street, one of these wild jalopies, puffing putrid black smoke, came within a foot of ramming us down; at the last second, it swerved away, its Klaxon horn battering our eardrums. I held on to Father and Li, jumping, squealing, and weeping at every honk. Finally, Father flagged down the most sedate one of them to whisk us away.

I gaped out the window. Along the edge of the road, unruly with meandering snack carts and billboards selling Vicks cough mixture and Flying Horse bicycle tires, moved a grave procession of twenty or thirty men. They wore thick black robes and marched two by two, their hooded heads piously bent, their pace in keeping with some shared bereavement. As we slowly glided past them, I saw that under each of their overhanging cowls was a solemn, unyielding darkness.

"Why so quiet all of a sudden?" Father asked me, not unkindly.

"Those men," I whispered, pointing.

He looked. "What men?"

I shuddered and let the subject drop. Unlike the ghosts I'd met before, these men unnerved me; they were too remote. Worse, there was now nobody I could tell, not even Sister Kwan, who, for all her shortcomings, at least believed me. Would these visions never end? I curled up into a ball and shut my treacherous eyes.

A different kind of dread fell upon me when we reached Chinatown and the knot of lanes known as Bullock Cart Water, so called because a station for working beasts used to stand there. I knew Shanghai was gone forever when the cab pulled up to our narrow four-story row house: Jet-black mildew covered its walls, pink patches of brick exposed like bare skin. We had come all this way, endured the long voyage, for this? What's more, we had to lug our own cases—no servants ran out to help us. No Sister Kwan, no Sister Choon, not even chubby, grouchy Cricket.

Li fought back his tears as we lugged our possessions up steep, dark, creaking stairs to the third floor. It was a small but real comfort that I wasn't alone in my dismay. I kept waiting for him to say something to Father, but he never did.

When we came to door 31A, its red paint flaking off where vandals had scratched a huge and ominous X, Father pulled me aside.

"Your brother's not feeling well," he said softly, slipping me a few coins. "Go downstairs and buy some *baos*. They will cheer him up."

I knew pork buns were Li's favorite, but where was I to find them? This wasn't Shanghai. Did people even eat *baos* here? Nevertheless, I did as I was told. The longer I could delay facing the squalor of our apartment, the better. I ran all the way downstairs, taking care to avoid the festering mound of feces I'd spotted on the second-floor landing. A rat hissed at me from some unseen hole.

The shop on the ground floor of our row house was named House of Great Hope. It didn't sell *baos*; what it had in its tall glass cabinets were male-potency elixirs made from deer antlers and cobra hearts. The side-walk in front of the building had been commandeered by a wordless duo: a barber who cut hair in the open and a coffee man who used an old sock as his strainer. No *baos*. I ran down the street reading the signs—Long Last Incense, Great Eastern Fortune-Teller, Gold Star Herbalist. At the end of the pavement clustered five women with no faces. I rubbed my eyes, but it did no good; each still had a creamy blur in place of features. Though they looked Chinese in their white pajamas, their frenzied chatter was no dialect I'd ever heard. It was closer to shushing, the admonishments of stern librarians.

I turned back before any of them could spot me. But no sooner did I move away than something raced up behind me and tapped my shoulder. I shrieked.

It was not a ghost, just a man who seemed like one—a scrawny, white-haired Indian sadhu with gray-black skin and a pale smear of volcanic ash between his eyes. He was barefoot and wore no more than a muslin loin-cloth. Each time he waved his arms, he unleashed the reek of rotting meat.

I clutched the coins tightly but he didn't want money. No, he fixed his magnetic, bloodshot eyes on me and shook his dirt-encrusted fist at the cosmos.

"*Very dirty*, this island...This island, *very dirty*."

Having uttered this strange greeting, he nodded at me and ambled away at a leisurely pace, taking his fleas with him.

We shared apartment 31A with two other newcomer families, the Can-tonese Wongs and the Hakka Koos—both half families, torn down the middle like ours. Each clan made do with a room of two bunk beds and a wardrobe. Ours had me nostalgic for the ship. There was just one window and it overlooked an alley favored by whistling, lip-smacking pimps. Luck-ily, there wasn't any room here left for ghosts.

The common area was just wide enough for a table and a single bench, so the families ate in turn, which was just as well. The drab monotony of our dinners—rice, salt fish, pickled vegetables—was a constant source of shame. With these dismal dinners gurgling in our bellies, Li and I spent every dusk hiding from the black-skinned Tamil who went shirtless from door to door, chanting: *"Karang guni...Karang guni..."* We had talked ourselves into believing he was a jailer coming for naughty boys and girls. It was only after speaking to the Koos that we discovered our foolishness: *karang guni* meant "discards," not "children." He was only the dustman.

In that tight space, a tense, unspoken rivalry grew between the three fathers for jobs, schools, food. There were always unhappy looks whenever a child from one family was caught playing with one from another. After a while I realized why. We had entered a kind of limbo, a transitional period in which we were meant to form no ties, exchange no secrets; it was the loathsome interregnum we were never to speak of again once we settled into our *real* lives as respectable Islanders with our own private apartments. Already we never spoke of our passage on the ship. The collective amnesia Father, Li, and I feigned just had to keep on expanding.

And so our first weeks passed.

Mosquitoes sucked at our blood, geckoes shat in our food, and we fell asleep—even in the stony heart of Chinatown, with no sea view and nary a sprig of green—to the howls of wild dogs and the arias of ten thousand insects. Still, we dreamed.

Li and I were sent to free day schools run by missionaries—Oldham Boys for him, St. Anne's for me—but contrary to literary cliché, we were not put to work weaving rugs, nor were we set upon with paddles and canes by mad, grinning nuns. We paid in prayer, yes, but lucky for us, the good brothers and sisters wanted first and foremost to turn the children of the Black Isle into learned little people—catechism came only after Chaucer, mass only after math.

St. Anne's was a two-story Victorian box on Emerald Hill, just beyond the business district. Its founding donor was one Ignatius Wee, the rare philanthropist of Chinese descent who did not demand the place be named after him nor that a pair of snaggletoothed *foo* dogs flank the entryway. The only visible marker of Mr. Wee's generosity was a plain brass plaque outside the staff room with the simple legend IGNATIUS WEE, PATRON. The somber gray building could have passed for a tourist landmark had it not been for its notorious former life as an asylum, a memory the nuns had done nothing to rub out.

On my first day there, I learned a new word, which, I suppose, boded well for my education.

"Guano," announced Sister Enid Nesbit, the apple-cheeked and uncommonly kind headmistress, anticipating what must have been the question most asked of her. "That's not frosting or candle wax. It's just guano."

We were standing outside in the midday sun. She was pointing at the school's roof, from which weird gray spears hung from the eaves like stalactites, blackening with each successive monsoon.

"Guano?" I asked meekly, every bit the new girl whose father was so underinformed as to enroll her in the middle of term.

"Guano is feces, or more specifically, bat feces." Sister Nesbit beamed, almost house-proud. "There are pigeon droppings mixed in there, too, of course, but it is still mainly bats. We've loads of bats. You could almost say we're quite—"

"Batty?"

She laughed. "Could be...though I was actually going to say we're quite well fortified for a convent school, because guano makes for excellent gunpowder."

Sister Nesbit, I would later learn, was the product of a Calcutta birth and fifty-odd years spent shuffling between the port towns of the empire, a history that helped explain her ability to turn every mishap or disgrace into an opportunity for learning.

In truth, I had not paid much heed to the discolored walls. Instead my eyes were transfixed by what I saw through the windows: waxen European women, clearly not students or teachers, staring out of the classrooms like dress shop dummies. They did have faces, or at least partially—gray-rimmed eyes and smudged noses, no mouths—and they were naked, their bare breasts varying in shape and sag.

There were *so many* of them. My school was a gallery of dead women.

Sister Nesbit was oblivious, but my arms were covered in gooseflesh. I was ashamed for these women, yet also terrified, and tried to conceal my nerves with excessive smiling.

"I can tell you're going to do very well here," Sister Nesbit said, all maternal encouragement as she led me inside the building whose darkness her bright attitude had scant prepared me for.

What saved me was the nuns' generosity of spirit, which forced me to put on a brave front, day after day. Was I terrified of the mouthless, naked specters that crisscrossed the classrooms? Of course I was. Did I dread morning assembly at Shaw Hall, with the long-haired schoolgirl dangling from the ceiling fan, shaking out her final spasms inches from Sister Nesbit's wimple? I felt sick every time. I even grew numb whenever the nuns spoke of "the Holy Ghost" in prayer.

The most dreadful room in the building was also the one impossible to avoid: the toilet. Windowless, pungent in the extreme, and lit by a lone bare bulb, it had five mossy stalls, each fitted with an oval hollow in the tiled floor that always became clogged by noon. A low bank of sinks lined one wall, their mirrors cracked and smeared with dark, unwashable stains that looked suspiciously like old blood. One didn't need a special gift to know that unspeakable things had happened here. The first time I stepped into the gloomy room, I saw four naked European women lying on the grimy white tiles, their bluish, milky rib cages marred by cuts and bruises, their eyes staring at me. The stalls were worse—each had its own phantom guardian crouching behind the door. Every time I entered, I thought of the sadhu's words—*very dirty*.

I yearned to tell Sister Nesbit that her school was swarming with horrors. Yet how could I crush the nuns' illusions with my righteous testimony? Ghosts would have proved false the efficacy of prayer, a practice they were working so hard to instill in their two hundred impressionable young wards; ghosts would have attacked the core of the missionaries' idealism, that the dark Isle was worth illuminating. This was assuming, of course, that the sisters took my warnings seriously at all. Surely I could close my eyes and hold my tongue long enough to absorb a few years of verbs, adverbs, and long division, skills that would help me transcend the narrow rooms of Father's world?

The alternative was clear: hard child labor, Bullock Cart Water forever. Damnation.

I don't know what Li's scholastic life was like in those days, but it couldn't have been much grander. I watched him grow into a quiet boy plagued with bouts of exhaustion, chained to a thrice-weekly regimen of boiled pig's blood to curb his anemia. On his good days, he played sports with his mates—soccer, rugby, rounders, badminton—and this meant that we grew into very different people. I devoured books, whereas he read nothing at all. We increasingly had nothing to talk about. We continued to sleep back to sticky back like a two-headed beast: he with the gold toffee disk tucked into his hand and me making tense, tight fists. I suppose we each, in our own way, were praying for a better future.

Everywhere in our neighborhood, however, steps were constantly being taken to protect the past, which, to most, meant the dead. The zealous staged street operas in Teochew and Cantonese to distract their ghost relatives from mischief, burned "hell money" to support their netherworldly spending, and placed six-inch blocks in entryways to prevent the unwelcome ones from supposedly gliding in—not that any of these measures made a bit of difference, as I often felt like telling them.

"Don't you stare at me," Father barked at me one afternoon when I returned to find him nailing a small, hexagonal mirror above our room door. "I bought this from the Taoist temple down the road. Better safe than sorry, don't you think?"

To my dismay, our father had become superstitious. Once so modern, he now absorbed the old-fashioned panic around him. He grew gray and gaunt, losing most of his hair and a quarter of his body weight. To hide his sunken chest, he developed a pronounced hunch: A bone that looked like a baby's elbow jutted out of his upper back, just below the neck. The old stork was turning into a camel. His fearfulness meant that I had to act bravely at home, as I did at school, to spare him additional worry. Naturally, I never mentioned the eyeless old man who had begun appearing every night at the foot of his bed.

Through the early 1930s, even during the Japanese invasion of Manchuria and the sneak attacks culminating in the occupation of Shanghai, Mother stayed in touch. At first I would rip open her letters the moment they arrived, savoring any news of the twins, but I soon found that to read Mother's letters was to be driven mad with frustration. The little ones were very well, she always wrote without variation, and she was very well, too. No mention was ever made of the checkpoints that were reportedly making daily life so impossible or of the nighttime gun battles between the Republican army and the Japanese military that we heard so much about on the wireless. I learned more about occupied Shanghai from the mass boycott of Japanese brothels in Chinatown than from anything Mother cared to share.

She always signed off, "Yours sincerely, Mother." No love, no kisses, just cordial sincerity, as if she'd been forced to pen these missives at gunpoint when what she really wanted to do was go out and dance on the beach. I had a theory that she was being held captive by the Japanese, but when I shared this with Father, he laughed so hard—and so acridly—that I thought the throbbing vein on his forehead would burst.

Not that Father, I suspect, ever painted her the full picture from our side. He wrote home every other month and sent along whatever money he could save, but steady work kept eluding him; not one of his clerking positions had lasted longer than two months. Most of the Chinese bosses were from Guangdong Province or Fujian, few of whom spoke English and none of whom had the patience to penetrate Father's Shanghainese-fattened Mandarin. The lingua franca of the street was in fact Malay. Even the European *towkays* (bosses, in the Island vernacular) had to pick up a few words of it to make themselves understood to the help.

Father resisted learning. But it wasn't all his fault; bad luck kept his spirits down. The Depression had left this part of the world tattered and raw. Walking to and from St. Anne's, I saw rickshaw coolies squatting in the shade, some without fares for days. Beside them were construction workers (many of them Chinese women), wharf laborers, beggars, all stooping together in what at first appeared to be silent solidarity but, at a second glance, was clearly bewilderment so deep as to have rendered every single one of them speechless. Only their children had the enterprise to beg, filling the district with their ubiquitous cry: "No mother, no father, no supper, no soda!"

After school, I often sat on a stone bench in the traffic island dividing Spring Street, the main artery of Chinatown. This island was tiny: just a small, raised slab with barely enough room for the bench, a hibiscus bush, and the pedestal where Mr. Singh, the Sikh policeman, stood directing traffic with oversized canvas sleeves fastened to his arms like wings. It was here, watching the throngs in cars, trams, buses, and on foot, that I received my practical education.

The Chinese, who made up a little more than half of the populace, came in a wide variety, from slave to millionaire. The ones known as Peranakans, whose families had been in the Nanyang for generations and proudly spoke no Chinese at all, fared the best. The rich ones swanned into Chinatown in big cars, trailed by uniformed servants, eager to distinguish themselves from the newcomers. The indigenous Malays mostly worked as drivers and laborers or led self-sustaining lives as fishermen; though most were poor, their lives were still in general not as dire as those of the South Indian Untouchables who took the worst jobs: hauling stone and removing night soil. The *karang guni* men were of this caste. Then there were Parsee, Arab, and Jewish shop merchants. These fluid types weathered the hard times better than most because they maintained family everywhere and did business with everyone. I found them admirable, if always a little sly.

Looking down on us all were the Europeans, who rarely stepped into Chinatown except on ghoulish excursions to see the death houses of Sago Lane, where old amahs rented bunks and waited to die. From the gin-soaked specimens I saw, I concluded that the Island's Europeans were of a much coarser grade than those of Shanghai. Perhaps this was because they felt they owned the place rather than tenanted it, as in China.

But the heartening thing about the Black Isle was that, aside from the colonials, everybody mixed. Even in Chinatown, you would find a Taoist temple devoted to the goddess of mercy, a Hindu temple with stone buffalos stacked in a gaudy pyramid, an Anglican church with services in three languages, *and* a boxy run-of-the-mill mosque, all on the same street. Around the corner, there might be a synagogue, a *kramat*—the tomb of an Islamic holy man—and an Armenian church standing cheek by jowl.

I told myself that ghosts were just another facet of its lush, equatorial diversity—the dead walking among the living, everybody sharing the same air, the same soil. This die-and-let-live attitude was part of the Island's social contract. As much as some of them frightened me, I had to learn to get used to them.

From my perch on the Spring Street traffic island, I witnessed the stirring of this cosmopolitan mélange. It was sitting here that I felt myself becoming an Islander and not just any old immigrant, any old Overseas Chinese who continued to dream of the Middle Kingdom. My day felt incomplete if I didn't greet passersby in at least four languages—*vellikum* to the Tamil road sweeper, *cho sun* to the Cantonese butcher, *selamat* to the Malay watchman, *shalom* to the Jewish money changer. To the random lost soul, I trained myself to look away and solemnly nod, which was a language unto itself.

The ghosts of the aged *Samsui* women troubled me the most. Shipped away from their villages in Canton to haul stone on the Isle, these un-married women, with their uniform of red head cloth and blue pajamas, seemed like nuns forever betrothed to the dust. I always felt butterflies in their presence even though, thank goodness, none of them addressed me. The sickly feeling would fade a few minutes after they did, and I would once again be reabsorbed into Spring Street's bustling human swirl.

On my braver days, which typically meant after I'd been puffed up with praise or high marks from school, I would force myself to walk home via the dreaded death houses of Sago Lane, where the loneliest amahs and coolies went to die. On these confident afternoons, I felt the same nauseat-ing emptiness I associated with Sister Yeung's first visit, yet I saw no ghosts. Rather it was on my bluer days, when things had gone less well at school, that I would see them. The barred windows of the death houses would be crowded with the faces of the migrant dead, staring out like passengers on a motionless train. Was rubbish-strewn Sago Lane the view they'd chosen for all eternity or did they not have a choice? I had nobody to ask.

And on my worst days, when I felt particularly put upon, there was even more. I could *hear* them—a soft, murmuring stew of regional dialects, like a sonic compass to rural China. I could never make out the individual voices, but the emotions transcended them all the same: desolation, nostal-gia, regret. In a word, homesickness. Their pain was so powerful I tried to imagine my way into it.

Feel, I told myself. Think of the twins growing bigger without me, think of all the smells that had made our old house home—orange peel, soy milk, jasmine water, mothballs. I slowed down my breathing, tried to parse the world from the exiles' perspective. Yes, I was an Islander, but I understood their loss.

Gradually, my good days and my bad days made no difference. They were always there, and I always saw them.

Because this was the tropics, Spring Street had other exotic visitors as well. One day, as I was sitting on the island, the afternoon traffic inexplicably began dividing into two streams. From his already high vantage point, Mr. Singh the traffic controller stood on tiptoes and brought a sun-shielding hand to his brow. He widened his eyes and began waving his canvas wings, looking as if he were trying to fly away.

"Tiger!" he gasped. "Tiger!" But the more he flapped those wings, the more he attracted attention to himself.

Before we could even think of fleeing, a bushy-jowled beast materialized between the parted rows of cars and buses, his orange fur luminous against the blacks and grays.

"Stop waving your arms, Uncle!" I shouted at my frantic companion. "He'll think you're calling him!"

The tiger sauntered down the center of Spring Street, its eyes aimed at our island.

The bustling street went silent as the king of the jungle made his approach, the pads of his mighty paws sounding *thup . . . thup . . . thup* on the scorching concrete. Although I knew I should have been scared, there was something very soothing about his ease. I was riveted by his magnificent slouch, the black stripes on his face that looked at once lazy and so artfully inked, and the effortless intensity of his yellow-green eyes—eyes that locked onto me as if I were the only person who mattered in the world. I don't remember what Mr. Singh was doing when I reached out, hoping to stroke the great cat's whiskery cheeks, but I will never forget the luxuriant purr the creature gave me, nor the tilt of his snout as his pink tongue leapt out and snapped at the air.

As I took a step closer to him, the black hood of a Ford Model T rattled into view and slammed into my feline friend with a loud crack, sending him flopping to the ground ten feet away.

"Take that, you bugger!" came a cry from the driver's seat.

I feared the beast had been killed, but he was back on his paws in seconds. Shaking his majestic head, almost sighing, he padded toward his aggressor, the car now backing away, and stared down the driver, a quivering Englishman. No roar, no claws, just a look of deep disapproval. Then my tiger turned, shot me a parting glance, and bounded in orange flight back to the forest.

Flush with adrenaline, I could feel my attachment to the old country evaporating. Even if I'd fought it—and I really didn't—Shanghai never stood a chance.

During my fifth year at St. Anne's, in 1934, I was made class prefect.

Sister Nesbit anointed me at assembly, while the hanging girl of Shaw Hall writhed and twitched just above our heads.

"For your leadership qualities and good marks." Sister Nesbit smiled as she affixed the blue rectangular pin on my pinafore. "For being cheerful and brave."

Cheerful and brave? It hadn't occurred to me that this was how the world now saw me, so immaculate had my act become. Cheerful and brave—I liked that. Finally, somebody had grasped that I was special. For the privilege of junior sainthood, I was to continue what I did so well: exhibiting model conduct and being an exemplar of Positive Thinking. In other words, be a shining light in the dim, dark corridors of our frightening institution. I smiled until my cheeks ached.

Following my coronation, I became a heroine to the meek at the primary school. I showed them how to tie their shoelaces and how to protest when the drinks seller short-changed them. "Pharisees!" I taught them to shout.

My afternoons were spent proselytizing on behalf of the school library, for which I was paid with an extra borrower's card. I was friendless anyhow and regarded the work as character-building time well spent. Not only did reading distract me from the school's more disturbing ghosts, but also books were perfect shields against the condescension of the wealthy Peranakan girls, mercantile blood flowing thick in their boorish veins, who flocked together at recess and went out of their way to tell me, "You know, you speak quite good English for someone from Chinatown." They never invited me to their parties, so I held my own with *Huckleberry Finn, Robinson Crusoe,* and *Little Women,* and in these fictional stars found true and fast friends.

One morning, Sister Nesbit interrupted one of my bookish communions to place me in charge of a new girl, a tiny person with a runny nose. She looked all of seven, though Sister Nesbit said she was my age, twelve, and a refugee from St. Hilda's, whose rural setting had ill suited her.

The girl reached for my hand. It was like being touched by the paw of a dead rabbit, that was how small and cold her hand was.

"My name is Dora Conceição," she peeped in a toddler's voice. "I have a heart murmur."

As soon as our headmistress left us, I snatched my hand away—I was too old for such sentimentality. Nevertheless, a well-intentioned comradeship was formed. Her isolation reminded me of my earlier self.

"Sister Nesbit told me you have no friends," she said. "I was like you at St. Hilda's. It was lonely for me there. Don't you ever get lonely?"

"No." I smiled. "I've got books."

Dora Conceição was of Portuguese, Chinese, Indian, and Malay stock, "with a touch of Dutch," she said proudly, which explained her wavy hair and milk-tea complexion—a custom, made-on-the-Black-Isle blend. But her genes had not imbued her with the sixth-generation native's careless ease. She followed me everywhere like a lost puppy, her dolefulness contaminating my every joy. You see, I had worked so hard to evict my fear, to betray no trace of my weakness, and Dora Conceição was afraid of everything, especially things she could not see.

Her fearfulness might have been bearable in another, less "dirty" environment, but because our schoolhouse was so full of dark corners, locked rooms, and endless staircases, her whimpers tested my charity, over and over.

"I feel queasy," she would complain as she ascended the stairs, clinging to the banister that in my eyes was slick with blood.

"Do you think someone died here?" she would ask me in the musty music room, exactly three feet from the ghost of a naked old crone standing in the corner, rocking herself back and forth.

"There's nothing here," I would say. "It's just dusty, that's all." Or: "Maybe it's those beans you ate." Oh, the false denials I had to make. Eventually, she'd believe me. She had to.

No such luck. A few weeks into being saddled with this inconvenient ward, I noticed that she'd begun to neglect basic hygiene. Every day now, stains appeared on the skirt of her blue pinafore—yellowish blotches that dried and slowly browned.

"You smell!" I told her at lunch one afternoon after a frustrating art class in which every apple I tried to paint turned out looking rotted.

To her credit, Dora did not burst into tears. She simply sat there on the canteen bench, her legs too pathetically short to touch the ground.

"It's just that I am so frightened," she said quietly.

"What's there to be frightened of?" I shot her a bright grin. "Are you mad?" After the failure of denial, I felt shame was the key. The girl would be shamed into bravery.

"The rooms, the darkness, the entire school. Something's not right." She clasped the crucifix on her necklace and her eyes reddened. "I can feel it in my heart."

"I thought you said your heart was defective."

"My heart is very sensitive. I can feel things other people can't. At St. Hilda's, when I was in certain corridors, my heart would beat so fast. One time, I felt a cold hand brushing my hair."

"This is not St. Hilda's. We're in the city, surrounded by thousands of people. You have to rise above that kind of superstitious nonsense." I knew I sounded like Mother, but I had no choice. I was class prefect; I had to keep up some semblance of order. "What's the matter with you?"

Her tears gushed now. I looked around to make sure no one was watching—a prefect who made the new girl cry was not likely to remain prefect for long. A few busybodies glanced over, but most of the girls in the canteen were busy eating their noodles and chicken wings and chatting. Nobody cared about Dora Conceição.

"I don't like the toilet here," she mumbled. The truth behind her smells was being unveiled. "There are things there...I just know. My heart can feel them."

"Stop that. You are twelve years old—or so you say. Yet you're so terrified of our school's toilet that you'd rather wet yourself." I clucked my tongue. "Gracious!"

"But there are—"

"All right, let's go." I pulled her to her feet. There was no other option. I had to perform the charade myself—take her to the haunted toilet and show her there was absolutely nothing to fear.

At the toilet, no other girls were present—no living ones, at any rate. Dora Conceição clutched at the door frame for dear life while I pulled at her blue pinafore. I had intended to coax her but my irritation resulted in this forceful tug-of-war.

"Come on, you cowardly custard! There's nothing here!"

"I can't," she whined. "Oh, my heart..."

"Stop it!"

One of the naked women on the floor decided to writhe her way toward the entrance. I repositioned my foot so she wouldn't brush against my ankle. Not that I would have felt anything.

"Why did you do that?" moaned my smelly protégée.

"Do what?"

"You moved your leg. Why did you do that?"

"I didn't do anything. You're being crazy again!"

Garnering my ruffian strength, I ripped her from the doorway and dragged her to the nearest stall. That little twig could really kick; my shins would be black and blue.

"Don't! Please, don't!"

I did it anyway. I pushed her into the back of the putrid cubicle and held the door shut from the outside. As she begged and yanked at the door, the lonely bare bulb began to sizzle and strobe, sending eerie flickers across the room. Thankfully, its buzzing helped to camouflage her yowls.

"Don't come out until you're done. Have some respect for yourself!"

I held the door until I felt her resistance fade. The poor thing had finally recovered her good sense. I washed my hands, stepped over the blue-gray bodies wriggling sluggardly on the floor, and went off to history class, proud that I'd accomplished a task worthy of my prefect's badge.

After the final bell rang, the sisters were atwitter in the staff room. I felt their anxiety all the way from the library, at the opposite end of the building, and I couldn't concentrate—on reading, on writing, on anything. As the emissary between the teachers and the flock, I knew it was my duty to investigate. I raced down the unlit corridor, flicking on the lights as I came through, straining to hear the words echoing through the building. *Scandal . . . reputation . . . Literacy Council . . .*

The nuns were gathered in the darkness, six senior teachers sitting around Mother Hen Nesbit's desk, six junior teachers standing behind them. Lit by an oil lamp at Sister Nesbit's side, the group resembled a cabal posing for Rembrandt's brush. I clicked on the overhead light, and all eyes turned to me, squinting.

"This doesn't concern you," said Sister O'Hara, the old giraffe who taught reading. "Do go away. This is not the time."

I looked for support. "Sister Nesbit?"

With an ominous sigh, my protector emerged from behind her gargantuan table. She walked up to me and placed a somber hand on my shoulder.

"Did you not hear Sister O'Hara? This isn't the time, child."

"But I'm a prefect! I'm not like the other girls."

With quick fingers, Sister Nesbit unpinned the badge from my uniform. "Now you *are*." There was a new hardness to her face that made her seem very English.

I was struck dumb by this unexpected robbery. Tears welled up in my eyes but I vowed to stand my ground. Sister Nesbit returned to her seat.

"The parents have been informed," one of the young sisters reported, sniffing. "They've been told to collect her body from the mortuary."

"Whose body?" I cried. "Who are you talking about?"

Not Dora Conceição, please. Not her.

Sister Nesbit's chair screeched as she leapt to her feet. "That's quite enough from you!" Her eyes were now red. "If you must know, a girl died in our school today—the new girl, Dora Conceição. Does her name ring a bell? I had *specifically* asked you to look after her, and you did not. She died because you *failed* to look after her..."

The world went pitch-black.

When I came to, I was in the sick bay. Sister Nesbit was at my side, kneading her rosary. She tenderly made the sign of the cross.

"I apologize for my harsh words earlier. It really wasn't your fault at all, and I was wrong to suggest it was. It's just that her passing came as such a terrible, terrible shock to us. I do hope you'll forgive me."

"How...What happened to her?"

"Dora had a weak heart...and it suddenly gave out. In the toilet, of all places. It's probably more my fault than anyone else's. *I* knew she was frail. But even I could never have imagined...I mean, the toilet!" She shook her head. "Sister Fernandez found her lying on the floor in one of the stalls. Curled up like a sleeping babe, Sister said, her thumb in her mouth. The poor, poor lamb. May her soul forever rest in peace."

I wanted the whole world to fade away again. But consciousness refused to leave me, and I was sent home to Bullock Cart Water with tram fare and smelling salts, doubly bereft—robbed of my prefect's badge *and* my self-respect. I knew I was to be blamed, of course. I'd been blind and arrogant.

At home, neither Father nor Li noticed the new empty spot on my chest, and it dawned on me that neither had ever registered my appointment in the first place.

The next few days at school were filled with prayers for Dora Conceição. The Union Flag was even lowered to half-mast. Girls who had never paused to give her the time of day sobbed into their handkerchiefs, as if they'd lost their favorite cousin, and Sister Nesbit announced she would install more lights in the toilet. Still, in the corridors, the dead went grimly on and on.

She had joined the mournful chorus in the toilet, of course. I saw her in that damned cubicle every time, staring back at me with lifeless saucer eyes, her modesty setting her apart from the others. She wore her stained blue pinafore.

Being a good convent girl, I found something to be thankful for even in the midst of this tragedy. It was the fact that Dora, like her otherworldly colleagues, no longer possessed a mouth. My crime would go unreported.

Forgive me, Dora Conceição, for my sin of pride.

A few days later, Father returned home all smiles.

"I found a job. A real job." He handed out parcels of hot, fluffy pork *baos*. One bite and I knew they were the good, meaty kind, not the usual ones stuffed with sauce and gristle. This meant Father was confident in his self-deceit. "I signed a contract. We will leave for up-country next week."

Li threw me a skeptical look, then turned back to Father. "Up-country? But isn't that all jungle?"

Father laughed and pushed another bun into his boy's hand. "I'm going to manage a rubber plantation. It'll be good to be away from the crowds, don't you think? Fresh air, quiet. You want to grow tall and strong, don't you?"

Li looked to me, hoping I'd say something.

"What about school?" I asked, though I was actually relieved at the prospect of escape. Ever since Dora's death, all I saw at St. Anne's were ghosts; the living had become mere shadows.

Father snorted. "You can read and write, can't you? That already puts you ahead of three-quarters of this population. Besides, it will do you good to get away from those nuns before they start suckling you on the blood of their saints. I don't want you growing strange whiskers." He smiled, pleased at his own formulation.

In the end, we had no say. At twelve, Li and I were still dependent on Father—we were his property. We began to pack up our things. It was a testament to our poverty that this task did not even take a whole afternoon.

A week later, our window was shaken by a loud rattling. I looked out and saw one of those rogue taxis I'd once been terrified of, a seven-seat carriage soldered over a Ford T chassis. They were known as *mosquito buses* because of their buzzing engines and unorthodox flight paths. We hadn't ridden in one since the day of our first arrival. Going places was done by rickshaw or on foot—everything else was deemed an extravagance. The driver was a skeletal Malay, his hand already perched over the horn, acting out the stereotype that his people lived to honk.

Father was in good spirits and unusually garrulous. "I've hired Ahmad and his bus for the whole day." He clearly relished the idea of hiring a *bus*. I admit I was charmed. "On the way up, we'll be passing through the city. I want you to set it to memory because in a few years, we'll be back here to conquer it. I promise you!"

Although he probably didn't understand Shanghainese, the Malay driver smirked—a silly man's hubris sounds the same in any language—and stomped on the gas.

With Bullock Cart Water vanishing behind us, my mood lifted. So long, bad dream! Farewell to old chains!

Without warning, we zooted past the liveried doormen of the legendary Balmoral Hotel. Our driver jumped the curb to bypass a Rolls-Royce, nearly running over the foot of a rotund Scot. The man cursed us in a pungent brogue. We—especially Father—cackled. Ahmad replied with shrieking Klaxon honks. *Ah-ooh-gah! Ah-ooh-gah!* Out the back of the cab, we assessed the legendary Balmoral as its ostentatious bulk shrank to the size of a postage stamp.

Li gripped a handrail and arched his neck for a better look. As if voicing my thoughts, he whispered, "Not so grand after all."

Our driver disregarded the stop hand signal from the Sikh traffic policeman at the junction of four busy roads, and our near-collision with a crowded trolleybus was celebrated with yet another tooting of the horn. *Ah-ooh-gah!* We hung on tight to every fraying hand strap, giggling nervously. D'Almeida Place, where the wealth of the Isle was made, flew by our eyes. Goliath bunkers in imported stone flanked by Corinthian pillars, impossibly tall eight-story office buildings fused to one another, all christened with names familiar from adverts for rubber tires and fox furs: Jervois, Sohst, Guthries, Fraser, Dunlop, Firestone... *Ah-ooh-gah!* Lying between the biggest buildings were vacant lots, waiting to be assigned future lives as hotels and brokerages.

At the mouth of the Black River, which snaked its way through D'Almeida Place, stood a cast-iron statue on a stone pedestal. Not of a founding father but a Bengal clipper, its sails fully unfurled, a potent symbol of the British East India Company to which the Isle owed its existence. The water was packed with bumboats, each painted with large, sad eyes. We could hardly see the brackish river but we could certainly smell its fetor, perhaps even greater proof of its existence. Tanned Chinese and Indian men, bare from the waist up, were heaving rattan baskets full of vegetables from the boats to the warehouses lining the banks. Plump Chinese overseers watched from the shade, shouting.

"Look at them," Father told us. "Which would you rather be? The man giving orders or the man taking orders?"

"I'll never take orders from anyone," said Li.

Father chuckled. "Then you'll like it up-country. Up there, we'll be the boss."

Li sat back, a smile sneaking across his face.

I was eager to give Father the benefit of the doubt—his new buoyancy was a nice change—but could we ever really be the boss on this island?

Looming over the river was lush, fern-covered Forbidden Hill, so called because pirates had made their nest there for hundreds of years. Though I couldn't have known it then, the Hill would one day ruin my life. A dozen or so figures dotted its steep sides, climbing up and down like pale spiders, undeterred by the terrain: ghosts. All of them. As long as they were on the Isle, no living soul could truly be boss.

"Uncle"—our driver pointed—"they say that hill *very dirty*."

"Dirty?" Father scoffed. He had clearly never heard the expression. "Then they better ask somebody to wash it clean, right? Come now, Ahmad, take us to where the rich towkays stay!" He turned to Li and me. "We might as well see where we'll be living someday."

Our carriage sped out of the city and into the unchecked splendor of Tanglewood. This was the plushest of the colonial estates, the last gasp of civilization before the jungle began. Winding, shaded lanes with Scottish names—Inverness, Glencoe, Dalkeith—were lined with the large "black-and-white" bungalows I'd read about at school, each a fiefdom unto itself. I saw the much-praised black timber frames, the zebra-striped verandah shades, and the blazing white walls. The effect was watered-down Tudor, yet, like so many things on the Isle, attractive in its own mixed-up way.

"Europeans stay here?" Father asked our driver.

"Peranakan Chinese also," came the sneering reply. "They think they are *orang puteh*. U-rope-pien."

We galumphed over a python, stretched twenty feet across the road, already turned *paillard* by a dozen earlier cars. Everywhere we looked, moss coated walls, tree roots buckled footpaths. And the mad profusion of plants! It looked as if vines would lasso the whole enclave into oblivion if its gardeners so much as took an afternoon off. Missing from the picture, however, were the owners of these homes. Those, Father said, hid indoors with tumblers of gin until the moon showed its face.

A fugitive strain of German opera blew into the cab, along with a breeze. *"Tannhäuser."* Father smiled, puffing up with recognition. However, I knew that it was in fact *Das Rheingold* because Sister Nesbit had been playing Wagner at assembly. Father leaned forward. "You know opera, Ahmad?"

His tone made me cringe. Ahmad flared his nostrils and floored it until we were well out of the gramophone's range. He slowed the car when we neared a mansion on a knoll, set back from the road. Its black timber highlights had been painted over in white and its sides extended into wings. In front, a porte cochere pushed out, club-style, and a black Bentley sat parked in its circular driveway like a well-fed dog. Neither gardeners nor ghosts sullied the perfect setting.

"This one Wee house," said Ahmad. "You know, Ignatius Wee, that rich baba?"

"Of course," said Father, so brusquely that I could tell he had no idea.

But I knew Ignatius Wee. Or rather I knew his name and, as prefect, had polished with Darkie toothpaste the brass plaque bearing it. So this was the way our grand patron lived, more European than the Europeans, on manicured, ghost-free grounds. The gap between his castle and our guano-encrusted asylum was vast indeed. Did he have any idea how dirty his school was? Would he even care?

"His father, Old Man Wee, make money in rubber," Ahmad went on. "But Ignatius Wee only know how to spend money—give to schooling, to church, his own kind only. Never give to poor people. These rich babas, they got no use!"

"Rubber...," Father cooed to himself, hearing only what he wanted to hear. "I say, I say." He was mapping out his own rubber-derived destiny, buying imaginary manses next to these first-class men. If them, why not him? He roused me with a slap on the cheek, uttering, "Rubber!"—a word he made sound fatty with promise. Ever the good sport, I obliged him with a tiny nod.

Li's eyes were devouring the Wee house. I could tell from his furrowed, sweat-soaked brow that he was entertaining some private resolution to become very rich. Like father, like son. I wanted our villa on the green, too, of course. But could Father get us there? As the family pragmatist, I had to think, Were we setting ourselves up for heartache?

North of Tanglewood, the suburbs came to an abrupt end. The roads turned into narrow dirt lanes pocked with the stink of animal ordure. Flies buzzed into our car. Through overgrown bushes, we glimpsed the haphazard sowings of family farmers too dispirited to care; roosters, all feather and bone, staggered from plot to plot in slow motion. As we drove by this seemingly never-ending patchwork of indifferent soil and corrugated tin shanties, I fought my dismay: This was exactly what I feared our future would look like.

"Eh! *Eh*! Why you bring us here?" Father growled to Ahmad as a gaggle of emaciated geese trudged across our path.

"You want scenic tour, right?" our driver replied provocatively. "I show you where Malay people stay."

"No need." Father shook his head. "No need to frighten my children."

The coward blamed us, when we were *all* afraid.

Storm clouds charged together, crowding the sky and bathing us in an artificial night. The air simmered against my skin. No one in the taxi said a word, as if any sound launched into the atmosphere would send rain crashing down upon us.

A ten-car traffic jam slowed us on the dirt road into the jungle—there was a police roadblock, out here in the middle of nowhere. Ahmad offered to circumvent it by cutting through marshland, but thankfully Father said no. We soon saw the cause of the holdup: swamp clearance. But not just any routine swamp clearance—this was Jervois swamp, the largest of the mangrove wetlands that the government had been trying to drain for years. The city was constantly running out of living space. A year before, this had been jungle; next year, maybe a school.

A Sikh policeman in a yellow slicker walked from vehicle to vehicle, leaning his turban into each driver's window. His pants were knee-high with reddish mud. Finally he reached us. "Prepare to wait, ah." Enormous trucks rumbled ahead.

"What's happening?" Father shouted impatiently.

"Swamp clearance, Uncle."

"Yah, I know swamp clearance, but how come we wait so long?"

The policeman considered for a moment. "A dead body is down there— female." He peered into the car, and seeing Li and me, lowered his voice to a whisper. "With two small choo-ren. She drown them first; then she drown herself."

"*Aiyah . . .*" Father clucked his tongue. "What a waste."

"Yah, boss. So young some more."

I shivered. Fifteen minutes later, the roadblock was removed and our line of vehicles clattered slowly through like a funeral procession. Even our driver had grown subdued.

Roots and fresh mud mixed uneasily in the brush. Three long, un-marked vans were parked on the side of the road, shielding the traffic from the investigation underfoot. But of course we all peered between their bumpers and saw three bodies covered in tarpaulin—one large, two small. The small ones were both the same size. I had a sudden vision of Mother and the twins: This could have been them, driven to harsh measures by despair. If it was bad being tethered to Father, I didn't dare imagine what life must have been like with Mother. That woman seemed capable of any-thing. I remembered her tantrums, her threats, the sharpness of her claws against my flesh.

I scanned the scene for ghostly signs of the woman and her children, ex-pecting to find her watching the inspectors from the vine-entangled bank or perhaps reliving over and over the moments before her regrettable act. I wanted to see if she was indeed remorseful, if she at least looked sorry for what she'd done to her helpless babes. But . . . nothing.

Evidently I assumed wrong. In the years to come, I would learn that death, like life, will always find ways to surprise you.

— 5 —

Blood Hill

ALL WE SAW WAS GREEN—a hegemony of green.

Green enshrouded everything. As Ahmad drove us north of the city, toward the plantation, the trees, shrubs, stumps, took on unexpected shapes—the Eiffel Tower, fornicating dragons—random acts of nature that were like deliberate provocations from some puckish topiarist. In the undergrowth, hidden from all eyes, loomed a shadow economy of snakes, lizards, spiders, scorpions. I heard their hisses. I knew that if the car slowed down even a little, they would swarm out and engulf us.

"By the way, Uncle," Ahmad said once he had dropped us off and collected his fare. "My name is *not* Ahmad! Why you Chinamen like to call us all Ahmad? We got names. My name is Ishak bin Shamsuddin."

He sped off, leaving us in front of a bungalow that sweated mildew and slime—the caretaker's house. Our new home. I couldn't picture what it originally looked like, for it came swathed in never-ending waves of climbing plants. Knee-high grasses beat a path to the front door, cracks in the walls hemorrhaged three different types of fern, and the windowpanes were opaque with moss. On the roof, a clan of gray monkeys romped possessively, staring down at us with pink, sarcastic faces.

"Ooo-oo-oo-oo-Ooo!" they cried.

This was our auspicious welcome. I almost wept.

On the front lawn, a rusty flagpole flew a rain-mottled Union Jack at half-mast, the unwitting result of both gravity and lackadaisical knotting. Father told us that the previous caretaker—English, a drinker—had taken home leave three months earlier, but for reasons unknown never came back. He shrugged. "His loss is our gain."

Pulling out his pocket knife, Li cut away some surprisingly tenacious pitcher plants. Half-digested beetles fell out of these bright green cups, and his hands became covered in sticky, bitter-smelling sap. It looked poisonous.

"Careful," I said, handing him my handkerchief.

"Nonsense!" Father pushed my hand away. "We're going to tame this jungle. We're going to be masters here."

He kicked the front door open.

Inside, it was almost black. The bungalow had the thick, earthy reek of exotic plant matter new to our urbanized noses. We turned on the lights and explored. It could have been worse: There were three bedrooms, so we would each have our own room, not to mention a sitting room, a study, a kitchen, and a full, hot-water bathroom. If only the smells of algae and animal waste hadn't filled every corner.

The kitchen greeted us with presents left behind by some considerate soul: *Malay for Mems*, a phrasebook made ratty by desperate thumbing; a half-drunk bottle of Beefeater gin swimming with dead ants; and a farm implement similar to a pitchfork, with its middle tine sawn off. I would have found the latter intriguing even without the attached handwritten note: *During cases of amok, place affected man's neck between the tines and pin him down. Best of luck!*

Before we left the city, we'd been warned repeatedly about amok, a now-common term that had its origins in the Malay world. During amok, rural men, supposedly inflamed by the fullness of the moon or the pull of the sea, fell into temporary fits of lunacy that saw them murdering their own families and neighbors. The phenomenon was said to be rife up-country. But we could see no evidence of it around us—except this ridiculous fork. Surely men who went amok would have broken into the caretaker's house or at least tried to tear through its vines.

Father spread open a map of Melmoth Estate's 498 acres. Our plantation was divided into two distinct and equal lobes; east and west halves grew narrow at the center, where our house sat, and rounded out at the fringes like the two lobes of an enormous heart. The workers' dormitories ran along the northern periphery of the west lobe.

On paper, the wilderness only began beyond the plantation. But, of course, these boundaries were a legal fiction—we'd already seen the jungle pushing toward our door.

Even a cursory glance outside showed us that no work had been done in months. Tall lalang grass covered the lobes; the rubber trees were overflowing with sap. Father's duty, it dawned on me, was really foremanship at caretaker's pay. He was to whip the plantation back into working shape.

"War in Europe is looming," he told us, his optimism undimmed, even as Li and I exchanged skeptical glances. "Nobody can fight a war without rubber. They need boots, tires, raincoats. We're going to be rich!"

We spent that first night accosted by strange noises, their origins unseen. Monkey calls mimicked infants in peril; tree branches randomly crackled and collapsed. I had the ability to see more than most, and still the jungle baffled me with its invisible noisemakers. Toots, hoots, hollers, and screams came in orchestral variations—falsetto, basso, cheery, mournful, staccato, on and on. I assigned each note to a different creature, only to discover later on that I'd got the whole thing upside down. The growls were not tigers but bullfrogs; the croaking was not frogs but jet-black horned macaws.

The next day, Father woke us before dawn. "Get up! Time for work!"

Pruning shears in our hands, we marched through the lobes. The east lobe was overgrown and swarming with mosquitoes. Father looked around anxiously. "Where are my workers?"

As if in reply, the sound of distant laughter came from the west lobe. We followed it until we came to a clearing—and a tropical tableau: swarthy men kicking a ball around while their womenfolk lolled in the grass, gossiping and feasting on papayas, rambutans, and chikoos. Dozens of small children traipsed around in the nude.

Father's face grew red. He tore into the makeshift arena, huffing and puffing with rage. The rattan ball flew at him and lashed his buttocks, making him yelp. The crowd cheered at this stroke of genius. Even angrier now, he shook his shears at the bare-chested footballer nearest him.

"I your boss now," he shouted in pidgin Malay to all those gathered. "Listen to me! I want you to cut-cut!" He pointed at the shears, then at the creepers choking the rubber trees. "Cut those things! Make pretty-pretty!"

The workers tittered, then resumed their game.

Catching his breath, Father turned to Li and me. "We have to give them some face. They'll come around in a few days." We returned to the house to wait for this magical transformation.

Evidently, these rustics—half of them illiterate Tamils and the other half illiterate Malays—had never encountered urban Chinese before. They looked upon us as freakish interlopers, aliens who were neither white sahibs nor dusky communalists like themselves. We had disrupted their sense of the natural order. It took them days to grasp that we'd begun to occupy the caretaker's house, not that it got them working.

A week later, still no change in the lobes. The grasses continued to grow unabated, and the vines ran riot. We trekked out to the soccer field once more. This time, Father brought along a machete-like parang, the jungle man's tool of choice. It looked so unwieldy in his puny hand, I felt sure he would accidentally slash one of us.

He waved the rusty sword at the indolent group. "If you like, use this! Look! I'm not playing! You want to eat, yes? You want your children to eat, yes?"

They jeered. The rattan ball flew toward him once more; this time he dodged it.

"Monkey! Monkey!" a small boy yelled. Everybody laughed.

"Look! I'm not playing!"

He stalked over to the boy who had caught the ball and grabbed it from him. Then with the mania of a furious child, he clopped it to bits with his parang.

The crowd thought it was hilarious.

Time and again, Father's attempts to rouse the workers failed. Three weeks on, he had all but given up. He locked himself in the study—*to think*, he told us. But he was resolutely *not* thinking. His days were spent communing with his Four Treasures, writing out Tang Dynasty poems from memory in ink and brush. Escaping.

Imaginary clouds and mountains became his refuge, while the plantation teetered on the brink of chaos. The owners sent telegrams from the city, and these sat unopened on the dining table, spoiling our appetite every night—not that we had much to eat because there was no money.

There's nothing quite like lawlessness and poverty to make a person yearn for order. I became nostalgic for St. Anne's—even the triple inconveniences of early rising, uniform ironing, and homework. I missed the city with its full palette of colors, not just this monochromatic green. I even missed the hairy, desiccated chicken wings sold at the tuck shop. Did I sacrifice my schooling for this? I longed to be pushed, prodded, fed, *tamed*, whereas I knew that out in the country, it was left to me to do my own taming.

Unlike Li, who'd cast away his uniform to a Chinatown urchin like a seasoned philanthropist, I clung to mine and all it represented: discipline, routine, civilization. On the bungalow's front step each morning, I stood at attention. Dressed in the white blouse and blue pinafore of St. Anne's, I raised the flag while singing my school song:

> *Glad that I live am I*
> *That the sky is blue*
> *Glad for the country lanes*
> *And the fall of dew . . .*

Li mocked me mercilessly. But order was my vote of dissent against the messy uncertainty of our lives. Li's rebellion was more prosaic. He gave Father hell in the form of door-slamming and chair-throwing disagreeability. We were twelve and full of energy, with nowhere to direct it.

Finally, one morning, starved for food and drunk on inertia, Li decided we had to save ourselves. We began tearing open the stack of telegrams. The latest threatened Father with dismissal—and a legal suit for false representation—if the plantation failed to ship rubber within the month. I secretly wished this would happen, but Li held firm.

"I'll play soccer with the men. To win them over." His voice was weighted with grave determination. "I don't care. We *have* to succeed. We have to. I'm *not* going back a failure. I told everyone we were going to be rich."

So this was why. His pride was at stake. "But how will we make them obey us?"

"These people are like children. None of them can read or write. They believe idiotic things. They're easily bored. Remember this, and you'll be able to boss them."

Miraculously, my brother was right. He took charge of the west lobe, and I took the east. Workers in both listened. They probably found us amusing: Two twelve-year-olds barking orders from bicycles and never taking no for an answer. For me, it was like being a prefect all over again.

When they humored us, we humored them. The women of the east lobe insisted on playing with my hair. I gave them free rein with coconut oil, pins, and curlers, ending each session looking like a Tahitian princess, sprouting bouquets from my ears. Li won the respect of the men on the soccer field and promised to teach them rounders—but only after they met the quota.

As the days wore on, the men and women reestablished the routines that had once given their lives meaning. They trimmed the grasses; they cut the vines; they collected the tree sap. Work was like a language they'd momentarily forgotten but regained once gently prodded.

Or maybe that's the happier interpretation of events. Looking back now, I can imagine they feared us, for there is nothing so capricious as a child with power. The plantation became functional again, if not yet thriving. And while I viewed my lobe as a burden, Li was a natural towkay. He carried the amok fork with him on his rounds, resembling a little devil with his trident.

Money began trickling in. It now seemed possible to dream of moving back to the city—and bringing over Mother and the twins.

Our hope had been that once things were in order, Father would resume his place in the field. But he kept on demurring, saying he was not ready, that he needed still more time. In a matter of weeks, the provisional had become permanent: Li and I ran the plantation by ourselves.

We developed a rigorous routine. Every morning after my flag raising, I changed out of my school uniform and into my work clothes while Li waited for me. We bicycled together before splintering off to our respective lobes as we came to what we called Blood Hill, a gentle rise half a mile from the house, barren but for a cluster of banana trees. When we first arrived, the trees were on the verge of death but Li nursed them back to health—it was his little pet project. They rewarded his efforts with robust, voluminous swatches of bloodred bananas. Ever suggestible, he believed that the red fruit kept his anemia at bay and ate them religiously. Not that his superstition was altogether wrong—bananas have been shown to be highly nutritious.

Until noon each day, Li and I surveyed our matrix of rubber trees, neatly planted by what had to be German cartographers. Every trunk was marked with big white arrows pointing down, down, down toward the ground, each V an open wound dripping with sap. Sarong-clad females twice and three times our age collected the milky lifeblood from these notches. This was rubber tapping; the sap was latex—rubber in its rawest form. Our job was to make sure nobody spilled a drop of this precious liquor as they sashayed back to base with five-gallon tins perched atop their heads. And that they didn't sashay too slowly.

I called the girls our Javanese Milkmaids, though they were neither Javanese nor milkmaids; that's how starved I was for poetry in that most unpoetic of workplaces. In the afternoon, when the equatorial sun blazed at its most pitiless, Li and I convened indoors at the processing hut, which we called our factory, to watch over the male workers as they turned the "milk" solid with acid and pressed it into sheets that could be taken to the city in a lorry that came through once a week. I had no funny nickname for these men, however, so afraid was I that they'd come to the house with parangs in the dead of night.

Father took the money we earned, but none of it trickled down to us. We were fed and given shelter, but that was the limit of his largesse. He said no to the new shoes Li asked for and the books I desperately wanted.

"We're his dogs," Li grumbled to me many times. "And what do we get fed at the end of the day? Scraps."

"Maybe he's saving up for Mother and the twins."

"Maybe."

Three years passed. Three years during which our bodies went through bewildering changes. First I outgrew Li. Then he caught up and sprouted half a head taller. His voice broke. I started menstruating—an event that terrified me more than any ghost sighting. It was only from the kind women in my lobe that I learned I wouldn't die from it. I developed curves, breasts, all of which made the St. Anne's uniform harder and harder to squeeze into. And we both became captive to our many, ever-shifting moods.

After a childhood in the city where we seemed to live in two separate worlds, our shared sense of persecution reunited us in the jungle. To further estrange ourselves from Father, we began speaking to each other in English. Li even joined me at flag raising, singing his school anthem alongside mine:

In days of yore from Western shores
Oldham dauntless hero came
And planted a beacon of Truth and Light
In this Island of the Main . . .

I reveled in the fact that I was no longer the family black sheep. If anyone was the odd one out now, it was Father. He clashed with Li at every opportunity. Watching my brother explode was like watching a storm crackle or a wild horse break free, and it was especially exhilarating when the furor came without warning or provocation. Li would enact wickedly accurate impressions of Father fending off sunlight like a spineless vampire or take mocking stabs at his halting, unidiomatic English. Father called him *unfilial*—that most overused of Confucian damnations—and made feeble threats of expulsion that were met only with derisive laughter. "Who would run this plantation for you, then?" Li would sneer. "Your Four Treasures?"

One evening, the inevitable occurred.

Li came to the dinner table nursing scrapes from a bicycle accident.

"If only Mother could see what was happening to us," he said, glowering at our mousy paterfamilias, who was stuffing his mouth with the rice our labor had earned. It had been months since either of us raised the subject of Mother to him. Her letters had dried up, and with the Japs rampaging all across China, neither of us dared to speculate out loud about the missing half of our clan, even though I was sure we were all haunted by those thoughts.

The veins on Father's forehead quivered. "Your mother is no longer relevant to us. She stopped being relevant the day we left Shanghai."

"What do you mean?" Li was livid. "How dare you write her off just because *you* failed to send money back to her?"

"Your mother banished us."

"She banished *you*. You took us along because you were afraid of being alone."

Father pursed his lips and thought for a few seconds, giving himself over to moral superiority. "Before we left, your mother and I had a divorce."

A divorce? Was he being metaphorical? A pair of gray monkeys shrieked outside the window, but nobody moved.

"You're lying," Li finally said.

"What about her letters?" I asked. "If she really banished us, why did she bother to write us those letters?"

"*I* made her write them." Father pounded a fist against his chest. "It was *me*! *I* begged her to write those letters, for the two of you. She may no longer be my wife but she's still your mother. And you both read them, so you know. It was like wringing blood from a stone. Wasn't it clear she had no interest in either of you?"

Li backed away from the table, his lips curled in a mixture of disgust and disbelief. "Go to hell!" he spat in English. "And I hope you burn!"

He raced outside, leaving the door wide open behind him—an invitation perhaps for me to follow. He was running toward Blood Hill.

My thoughts flew not to Mother, whose kisses had always felt insincere, but to the twins, the little baby girls I'd not thought about since our arrival at Melmoth except as abstract, sentimentalized symbols of purity. They'd become cooing ambassadors from a vanished way of life, forever frozen in midsong. But Xiaowen and Bao-Bao were not even babies anymore. They were now nine, older than I was when we left.

In that instant, I was hit with the guilt of abandoning them that fateful morning, sneaking out of the house like a common thief while they slept. Had I no heart? I was their beloved *jie jie*! Seven was never that innocent an age—I had to have known that losing them was the price of my freedom. Yes, yes, I did know, yet I'd still chosen flight.

I took off after Li, but two steps beyond the house, I felt a hand reach up my throat from within. I fell to my knees and vomited on the footpath until I was drained.

An hour later, from the living room window, I watched two monkeys dancing in my grotesque puddle. Then the rains came and washed everything away.

Our plantation wasn't much haunted.

There were a few wayward spirits, of course—every place has them, no matter how "clean"—but far fewer than one would imagine from a cursory inspection of the surroundings, what with rapacious jungle and the macabre shrines the natives maintained. I learned that how a place looks has little to do with how much supernatural activity it actually hosts.

My guess was that the people who worked here never had much chance to be alone. The tappers slept in overcrowded barracks, segregated by sex. We had a hundred workers living in three such hives, each about the size of the caretaker's bungalow, and many of the workers even had their families with them. They slept in cycles. The first shift rose at four and by five were already out and about, collecting and transporting sap; the second shift rose at noon to make fresh cuts in the bark or to press sap into sheets in the factory. When not working, the workers sang, ate, bathed, and worshipped together—living for them was very much communal.

Ghosts, in contrast, are mostly solitary. As a woman of some experience, I have a theory as to why this is so: Those emotions powerful enough to transcend death tend to be ones experienced *alone*. Only when alone do we truly open ourselves to fear, lust, hatred, regret, and desolation in their most tenacious forms.

Having little privacy, and therefore little opportunity for such deeply personal emotions to fester, the workers were not a haunted people. This was not to say that they were slaphappy simpletons, easily appeased with white rice and a clean bunk, just that there was no time for introspection.

In plainer words: Li and I worked our men and women to the bone.

We could tell the Malays on the plantation were not like the Islamized Malays we had known in the city. They adhered more closely to the beliefs of their ancestors than to the teachings of Mohammed, although orthodoxy did inform their practice of circumcision—and polygamy. Instead of mosques, they built makeshift shrines to gods whose names we didn't know and knew we'd never be told. On these woebegone altars we saw unusual items of devotion, including the umbilical cords of babies left to rot on black stone cubes.

"Malays are aimless by nature," Father always said, "so we might as well let them worship something. As long as it doesn't interfere with their work..."

Where our Tamil workers were like Tamils elsewhere on the Black Isle—highly adaptive and highly motivated—our Malays were ruled by superstition. Their chief grievance was Blood Hill, which they took great pains to avoid, often walking an extra half mile so as not to even see it. They had their own name for the mound: Tomb of the Dead Girls. The older workers believed no crop would grow on it because unwanted baby girls had been buried alive there generations before. Others said it housed the corpses of unfaithful wives.

I looked for signs of haunting on Blood Hill but never saw anything, not that I would have shared my findings with anyone. As for the blood bananas that grew on the hill, Rani, my most trusted Tamil girl, told me why the Malays feared them. Rural Malays believed that banana groves harbored the vengeful she-demons they called *pontianak*.

"They are women who die giving baby," she said. "That's why they like to kill pregnant girl. They jealous!" During full moon, the pontianak emerged from the space between two adjacent banana trees and went in search of prey—that is, very pregnant women. They drove their long claws into the mothers' bellies and drank the fetal blood, although during desperate times, they were known to eat even men. If a woman died in labor, the Malays took extreme measures to prevent her from becoming a pontianak. They stuffed glass beads into her mouth, placed an egg under each of her arms, and stuck needles into her palms so the corpse could not open her mouth to shriek, spread her arms as wings, or flex her hands in flight. "But the number one way to stop pontianak," Rani said firmly, "is do not grow banana tree."

I told this to Li repeatedly, and he took offense each time. Blood Hill was his monument. If the Malays could just see what marvelous fruit the trees produced, he insisted, they would stop fearing. "Then they can plant bananas all over the place!"

It was this willful arrogance that led Li to take a heavy, freshly plucked phalanx of blood bananas as a gift to Mina, one of his Javanese Milkmaids, on the day she was to give birth. I tried to talk him out of it and felt a shiver of déjà vu at his stubbornness: He'd been like this at the park in Shanghai. Ever since Father mentioned the divorce, this callous streak in him, subdued for years, had been reemerging. Perhaps proving to himself that he wasn't a weakling like his father, he was constantly priming himself for a brawl.

I was cleaning a catfish for dinner when Li stormed into our house with the bananas intact and threw the lot onto the foyer rug.

"Mina's father had the gall to tell me to leave! And all those women— his *wives*— standing around him—not one stopped him! He's got a strange hold over them. I've heard he fancies himself some kind of magician or witch doctor. But if he really knows magic"—he smirked—"why's he working on a plantation?"

"He probably doesn't work. He probably makes his children do the work instead." I retrieved the bananas before their red juice could stain the carpet. "Anyway, I've told you how much the Malays loathe bananas."

"But I want them to know they're *wrong*! What makes these bananas special is that they thrive where nothing else will grow. I want them to stop being such primitives."

I laughed dryly. "It's not our place to change anyone."

"Isn't it?" He snatched the bananas from me and cradled them to the kitchen. "Aren't we here to manage this bloody place? Aren't we here to civilize them?"

"*Us*? Civilize them?" I laughed again. "We're as trapped as they are!"

"You saw this place when we first got here. We've saved it."

He had a point, but the argument led nowhere. We'd cut back the vines so our house was now filled with light. But were *we* any more enlightened? "I hope Mina wasn't too upset."

"I wouldn't know. I let them all go. The whole goddamn harem."

Father, who had been quietly listening to our conversation, rushed in from the study. His glasses slid down his nose. "What do you mean, 'let them go'?"

"I told them to pack their things. I told them all to go to hell."

"How many of them?" Father asked, his voice tremulous.

"How should I know? Ten, twelve."

"Even the girl?" I asked.

"Even that bloody ingrate, Mina!"

"But, Li, she's about to have a baby! You know she can't go anywhere!"

"That's her own problem, isn't it! Besides, I think there's something unnatural going on there. She's got no husband, you know?"

Father looked sick. Not because he bore the workers any affection but because he dreaded losing their labor. He scurried to the locked drawer in the study where he kept our cash and coaxed out a bundle of ten Island dollar bills, each the equivalent of a worker's weekly pay. I was thankful that for once, he was doing the smart thing. I knew how unforgiving our quota was; we couldn't afford to lose any workers. Father stuffed the money into his pocket and went to put on his shoes.

"Where do you think you're going?" Li leapt to the front door, his eyes electric. "Why are you trying to undermine me? They're *my* workers—they listen to *me*!"

When he and Father stood face-to-face, I suddenly grasped that Li at fifteen was now taller than our old man—taller, stronger, and fiercer. Father now appeared limp and wizened; there was no way he would dare fight his son. With lowered eyes, he walked silently to the kitchen and disappeared out the back door.

Li ran after him, shouting, "You make me do your dirty work and then you undermine me! Undermining me when *you're* the goddamned cheat and the goddamned coward!" He turned to me. "He can go all he likes. They're *our* workers. They won't even know who the hell he is. They'll just laugh at him."

It was true. Father had no clue which tapper was pregnant, let alone which hive she lived in. He held no sway. I had to go after him.

"Ling!" Li snatched my arm as I started for the door. "Don't you dare! Are you trying to make me look bad? Why must you always be the hero?"

Our eyes met. His anger turned to pleading in a flicker, but my stare let him know that I wasn't giving in. Out of nowhere, I was knocked backward, the base of my cranium slamming against the door. From the horror in Li's eyes, I knew that he had struck me, even before the burn settled on the left side of my face.

"I'm sorry . . ." He reached for my cheek but I smacked his hand away.

"You're a bloody idiot, you know?"

I raced out the door and leapt onto my bicycle. I didn't let myself slow down until I passed Blood Hill and was sure that Li wasn't shadowing me. Then I pedaled hard all the way north to the hives.

Through the open doorway of hive 2, I could see my father surrounded by a crowd of workers and their scruffy children—all of them female except for an athletic, white-haired Malay who conducted himself like some sort of a village elder. Mina's father, clearly. His hands rested on the waist of his batik sarong in righteous indignation.

As I dismounted my bicycle, my father sank to his knees and lowered his torso, bit by bit, until his forehead kissed the ground.

The kowtow. I'd never seen it performed before and instantly understood why—the nakedness of the subjugation was excruciating. I burned with shame and fury. Why this mortifying gesture when money should have sufficed? How would he ever gain the respect of our workers again? How would *I*? Father, the defeatist! If there's anything I despise in a man it's this kind of weakness.

I was about to flee when Mina's father cleared his throat. He pointed one languid finger in my direction. One corner of his mouth rose to form a lewd, lopsided smile. He muttered something that made Father pull himself off the ground. Sweeping the dust off his hands and knees, Father stole a furtive glance at me.

The old man's lips moved again: "Your daughter—pretty girl."

He beckoned to me in a way that made my hair stand on end: fondling the air as if squeezing an invisible peach. I pretended I hadn't seen him and leapt onto my bicycle. As I sped away, I heard him ululate like a hyena, each laughing cluck rising in pitch and derangement.

Evidently we would not lose those workers, after all. But forgetting that insidious old pervert was another matter. I cringed at the memory of Father's kowtow.

Hurrying home, I noticed something I must have passed hundreds of times but never fully registered: a black wooden shrine hidden along the outer edge of my lobe. Its presence surprised me because I had ordered all shrines moved to the recreational area. As I neared, I realized that my first impression was wrong. This was not a shrine but a hut with a large, rusted padlock on the single door. No windows or any other opening. The woodworking was superior. It had none of the splinters so common in up-country huts. It was free of lichen and moss, again odd in this supremely humid landscape. The whole structure seemed designed to vanish into the night, yet I felt a tug of the familiar.

My mind was too preoccupied with the day's disturbances to give it further attention. Later, I told myself, later. Sunlight was fading rapidly, as it does at the equator. I rushed back to the house.

That night, my left cheek wore a purplish bruise where Li had punched me. I said nothing to Li or to Father. Did he even notice my face? Around midnight, in my bedroom, I heard a distant roar from the plantation hives, followed by a fit of joyous drumming. Mina the Milkmaid's child was born.

Soon an admired relative would "open" the newborn's mouth by dipping a gold ring in honey and placing it in the baby's mouth until he or she began sucking it. The idea was that the child would magically absorb some of the traits of the ring bearer. For the baby's sake, I hoped this sponsor wasn't Mina's father. I now understood why Li had found him so infuriating. The man had the air of a deposed king plotting his way back to power. The lewd gesture he gave me betrayed a chilling lack of restraint.

The drumming didn't die down for hours. I was finally drifting off to sleep when my door creaked open. Someone was entering my room. Instinctively I reached for the knife by my bed, but it was just Li, in his pajama bottoms. Through the scrim of my mosquito net, I saw tears glinting in his eyes.

I stayed under the covers because, like him, I slept topless.

"I'm sorry." He walked over and lifted up an opening in the net. "I promise I'll never hurt you again." The ferocity of the day was no more. This was a chastened boy.

I let him touch my cheek so he'd know that, although he had hurt me, the injury wasn't serious or permanent. I didn't hold a grudge—my anger had already been shunted toward Mina's vile father.

"I can't sleep," Li said. I knew what he meant. I, too, often had trouble sleeping because I'd grown accustomed to the warm lump next to me.

He climbed into my bed, the way he'd done a thousand times when we were children in Shanghai, on the boat, in Bullock Cart Water. It was the most familiar thing in the world. I turned to my side, but Li, instead of turning his back to me, faced my spine and wrapped his arms around my bare waist. He sank his face into the back of my neck; I felt his every breath. It was a surprising comfort. I closed my eyes.

We lay like this for a while before he spoke again. "You're my best friend in the world." I knew he meant it.

"You're mine." And I meant it. We really had no one else.

"We're bound, aren't we?"

"Yes. We're bound."

"Forever?"

"Forever."

He gave the nape of my neck a little kiss. "Your skin's so soft." When I showed no objection, he grew braver and gave it a longer kiss. And then a longer one still, until his mouth ranged up and down my neck and onto my shoulder. My flesh tingled and I let out an involuntary whimper—which we both took to mean approval. He moved his hands up toward my breasts and I felt the first prickles of shyness.

"I'm not going to hurt you," he whispered in my ear. "I promise."

I relaxed and let him explore. It was erotic, yes, of course, yet also spiritual—I was being embraced by my other half, my missing half. When he touched me, I felt complete. He draped one leg over my thigh and pressed himself against the small of my back so I would know his desire was urgent. When he reached down the waist of my pajamas, I found myself sliding up to meet his fingers, inviting them to venture further. Without discussion, we removed our pants. I swooned when I saw the full extent of his love for me, but that feeling soon washed into many others, equally pleasing, equally intense. Our movements felt dreamlike, as if we were both really asleep.

In bed together, we were freed from the soul-deadening quotas of the plantation world. None of the daytime rules applied, yet our connection was made stronger precisely because we spent our lives under those constraints. Instinctively, we did whatever felt good, wonderful, ecstatic. Rubbing, pinching, licking, the tickling of a sensitive spot with a kiss of air—everything but the act itself, which both of us, even in our hallucinatory state, knew was a bigger step than we were prepared to take.

Eventually I rolled over and met my brother head-on. He looked handsomer than ever—the handsomest boy I'd ever seen—and my heart was filled with joy that I was the one he'd chosen to love. That I was the one he'd chosen to explore and conquer.

We remained in each other's arms until sunrise. But instead of feeling sapped from the lack of sleep, I felt nourished. Love nourished me.

At the flag raising, we resumed our usual, chaste positions and sang our anthems, for Father's benefit. But the ceremony now felt like a hollow, childish pantomime, much more of a sham than it had always been. I also noticed, for the first time, how ridiculously small my uniform looked on me. Even after letting out the hem completely, the pinafore still stopped short of my knees, and the area around my chest was a very tight fit. After securing the flag, I shot Li a secret smile and hoped Father wasn't watching from the window. He wasn't. Li returned my smile and when I went back to my room to change, he followed me. Without bashfulness, I removed my clothes in front of him, and without bashfulness, we entwined again, kissing as if the ten minutes we had before the workday began were the last ten minutes we would ever have.

The following three nights, Li continued his visits, and each night, we danced closer and closer to the precipice from which we knew there would be no return.

"I don't think I can hold back any longer," he gasped between kisses.

He raised himself over me and we knew the precariousness of our situation.

"No, don't move." He pinned my arms down. With a look of torment, he began nuzzling my neck until he could formulate his thoughts. "We can't go on like this. You're driving me mad. I feel like I'm about to burst."

"Then burst."

"But I want to be inside you . . . Don't you want me inside you?"

"Yes, I do, but . . ."

"But what?"

"It doesn't feel right . . ." I meant morally. Physically I knew it would feel divine.

"You moan when I touch you." He brought his lips to my breast and let his tongue run across my nipple. I whimpered. "We are meant to be together, you and I. We're two halves. You know this." He licked his way down my chest to my abdomen, which he teased with small pecks before plunging his mouth between my thighs. I moaned loudly this time and feared that Father would hear us. But Li kissed me until I was brought to delirium. He only stopped when he knew from my tremors and the arch of my body that I was completely his. "I love you. I promise I won't hurt you."

He launched himself back up and was again atop me. This time, he pried my thighs apart with his knees. The coarseness of his movement stunned me.

"No!"

Everything from here on unfolded with disorienting speed, like falling back to earth after an opium dream. I tried to push him off me, but he was too strong. I tried to slap him, but his face was buried in my neck. I kicked at his legs to no effect. Finally, as a last resort, I forced my hands between us and gouged my nails into the part of him that only minutes before I had kissed.

Li hissed like a wounded beast and leapt from the bed, almost tearing down the mosquito net in his retreat. "You tricked me!" He raised his hand to strike me but held back, remembering his promise. He glared at me in silence for a minute, seething, then grabbed his pajamas from the floor and stumbled away. His door slammed.

I lay in bed, sobbing. Had I done the right thing? His body had felt so *natural* against mine, and I could not deny my desire for him. I wanted to experience the act; I was ready for it. My body was more than ready. But I knew that my first lover shouldn't also be my... Then again, we weren't like other brothers and sisters. We were two halves, incomplete on our own and whole only when together.

I woke the next morning sapped. Unnourished. Unloved.

For the first time in three years, I couldn't summon up the energy for flag raising and decided then and there that I would abolish the practice. When I went to fetch my bicycle, I realized that Li had already gone on without me.

I did not see him again until dinnertime, picking at the vegetable curry he normally devoured, his face clouded over with bruised pride and self-hatred. Father didn't seem to notice anything different—insolence was insolence to him—but I registered all the minute changes. I slid my foot to Li's under the table. He didn't pull away, nor did he respond.

That night, I brooded. Had we brought ourselves to the point of no return? Had I really tricked him, as he'd put it, led him on? Thinking back, I realized it often had been my hands that did the exploring, my moans that egged him on. But still, we'd begun in unison, hadn't we?

Exhausted by worry, I finally drifted off.

Sometime later, I felt a weight on the bed behind me. How long had it been there? Also present was the dense, coppery odor of wet soil.

"Li?"

No answer. Still half asleep, I tried to turn and face him, but was pushed facedown on the bed with an unfamiliar roughness.

"Stop it, Li!" I thrust my foot back, but there was nothing where I should have felt his legs. I could not turn my head either. This couldn't be my brother, could it? Someone was applying pressure to the nape of my neck, and my arms were pinned down. I reached out for my knife but my fingers grasped at nothing. I was paralyzed.

A pair of hands tore down my trousers. I tried to scream but another hand, a very cold hand smelling of fresh mud, clamped itself over my mouth. My assailant remained invisible, yet his moves were anything but amorphous. When my pants tangled around my ankles, he impatiently ripped them apart. Freed of them, he splayed my legs wide and forced my face into the pillow so deeply I could barely breathe. It was a measure of my childish delusion that even in this position, I believed I would some-how be able to fend him off—with my rage, with my wits, with the sheer force of my will. I was, after all, different. Special.

I felt his full weight on me and tried to buck.

But my body was crushed. I was being buried alive. My lungs ached from the lack of air; it burned just to inhale. I told myself to surrender. There would be less pain if I surrendered. This was the end.

My ignoble end.

Then, all of a sudden, gasping madly like a near-drowned girl, I realized that the devil—and his nauseating smell of moss and earth—had bolted. He had left me stripped bare, shaking, in tears—but intact.

In taking me to the edge of doom and setting me free, he was taunting me with his strength and his mercy, as if to say, *I don't need your permission. I can claim you whenever I want.*

A trickle of red ran down my left thigh. My monthly visitor had come a few days early.

At breakfast, Li shot me a warm, conspiratorial smile. I left the table with-out a bite.

"What's the matter with you?" Father asked, with his usual abrasiveness. "By the way, I have something to tell you two."

I didn't wait to hear it.

Li tore after me and stopped me by the bicycles. My reaction to the sight of him, the smell of him, was physical. I was shaking. I couldn't look him in the eye.

He reached for my arm but I pulled away before he could taint me. "Let's forget the whole thing and be friends again."

"Friends?" I was ashamed that my voice sounded so thin.

"It's just as hard for me." There was something uneasy in his manner. Guilt? Shame? "But we're stuck here together. So we should at least try to get along."

"You promised you wouldn't hurt me."

"I did—and I haven't."

Liar.

"Because of what you did to me—"

"What *I* did to you?"

"—we can never be friends."

"Wait!"

I didn't wait. "Stay away from me."

Riding off, I wandered aimlessly around Blood Hill, anything to delay facing my workers. I had to keep moving until the shaking stopped. The night's bleeding, too, had left me pale and exhausted. My authority was integral to my work—it was all I had. I refused to let them mock me the way they had mocked Father. Already the bruise on my cheek from the other day had caused some of my girls to titter. I pretended I hadn't noticed, but of course I had—and it stung.

Circling Blood Hill for the third time, I saw a truant Milkmaid sitting at the top of the mound, deep in thought and singing to herself. Brazenly so, it seemed to me. Already the disobedience had begun. Choking back my tears, I threw the bicycle aside and marched up the hill.

As I neared, she vanished. A ghost! The first I'd seen on Blood Hill.

I reached the heart of my lobe at least a half hour late, still trembling. My Milkmaids were in order—everything was the same. Nobody stared, nobody laughed. I peered over my shoulder to make sure no one was whispering behind my back. Nobody was. The girls barely even registered my presence. Not only did they not joke around, they were doing their work with far greater diligence than usual. In fact, the Milkmaids were working so well that the only explanation I could come up with was that some punctual, efficient doppelganger of mine had already been there, walking my rounds ahead of me. Making me, in other words, a shadow of myself.

The whole morning had an uncanny feel, as if I'd entered a world in which I didn't exist or was already dead. My flesh prickled at the slightest breeze. A black moth landed on my cheek and refused to leave. My eyes kept picking out the peculiar: A leaf became an insect; a cloud formed two perfect lobes. The grasses hissed. Mysteries lurked.

And then an image leapt to my mind: the wooden hut, standing where it shouldn't be. *That* was the most peculiar detail of all. Even in my unhappy state, my intuition told me that whatever was in it might explain everything, that perhaps it was calling out to me. I cycled back to where I had seen it, along the easternmost edge of my lobe.

Sure enough, it was there—thank heavens for that—and every bit as out of place as it had been. Yet it felt so elemental, so familiar. Slanted roof, black walls, one door, enormous rusting padlock.

And an elbow. A human elbow jutting out from behind the hut.

I moved in and heard the telltale sounds of disobedience. Murmurs, soft laughter. The rustling of feet on damp grass. I dismounted my bicycle and crept closer, the better to surprise my wayward Milkmaids. I set my sternest glare as I reached the corner and peered over the edge:

I saw Li—and I saw *me*.

Or some incarnation of me in my St. Anne's uniform, shoulder-length black hair just like mine, pressed against the hut, her face nuzzling Li's neck. They were enveloped in each other, Li and my other self. The uniform's skirt was hiked up in Li's hand—my double wore no undergarments!—and one of her bare, tanned legs was locked across his pale buttocks. Li's pants were at his ankles. He plunged into her and she moaned. Instinctively, I covered my mouth. He thrust again. She grunted, lewd and uninhibited. And as she turned her head in ecstasy, I recognized my doppelganger.

It was Zana, one of the Malay Milkmaids from my lobe. Her hair was usually pinned in a knot over her head. She must have been at least twenty. I'd never liked her, and now I knew I'd been right.

I watched them longer than I should have. Then I quietly pushed my bicycle away from the hut and, embracing the pain, pedaled to a patch of long grass in the shade. There I dived off the bike and crouched amid the leaves, waiting for the pounding in my head to subside. Black moths landed on my skin, and I did nothing to dissuade them. More and more came, and then an enormous brown and white moth landed, its triangular wings marbled like batik kites. They were small comforts. To exorcise Zana, I thought of every word I knew beginning with *z* that wasn't her name: *zeal, zenith, zoology, zero . . .*

I knelt there, my arms covered with insects. Not just moths now, but flies, spiders, beetles, each little stinger staking their claim on my flesh.

Let me say this clearly now: It wasn't so much the sight of Li and that girl that had disturbed me; it was the smell they produced together. Their vile perfume was like an oceanic burp that had crept inland and clung to the air. Prawn carcasses and musk.

I crushed a horned beetle in my fist and watched its gritty black nectar pool across my palm. A single leg twitched once, twice, and then no more. I pressed this bitter paste against my nose and sniffed deep for anything, anything that could help me erase the lingering scent of my twin with my twin.

— 6 —

The Jungle

I WANDERED THE DARKENING PLANTATION, flinging myself against the ground.

My arms, knees, and shins were bruised and sore. But I wanted them bruised and sore. I clutched at the tall lalang, pulling my hands along each blade until my palms were crossed with cuts. I wanted these cuts; I cherished these cuts.

I came to a mossy pond and strode waist-deep through the sludge, emerging with black leeches clinging to my legs. I watched them grow fat with my blood before I tore them off. They left holes on my calves like weeping stigmata.

I was bleeding for my shame, I told myself. How could I not have known that proximity was a great deceiver, that it was loneliness that had driven me into my brother's arms? This was convenience, not love. All I'd gained was a phantom comfort, as cold and bloodless as any ghost.

I stripped off my sodden clothes and buried them under a rock. I walked steadily and did not slow until I was well past the boundary of our lobes and into the untamed jungle. The grasses tickled my chin; the wet air quivered with living chatter. Mosquitoes the size of wasps came to me and suckled, painting my flesh in dots and welts. But I did not scratch; I did not flee. Instead I pushed deeper into the rainforest. The mosquitoes quit; the itching ceased. I went deeper still. The pythons and cobras slithered away as I neared. I glimpsed the hooves of animals, both slow and fleet. Tapirs, mouse deer, tigers. They all ran from me.

I no longer felt any fear. I no longer felt any pain. I no longer felt anything. I was now a thing of the jungle, indistinguishable from its roar, its bite, its venom, its ancient, untouched darkness.

I bled into it, leaving a trail of red in the grass.

Around me, the scent of fern, soil, and orchids made the most sublime perfume. There was shade where I sought shade and quiet where I sought quiet. In this primeval cave, nobody could find me; nobody could hurt me. And I no longer had Li to care about.

Two days and two nights I spent in this wilderness, sleeping and fasting, crawling on all fours. Through it all, I was at peace.

On the third morning, a cool breeze woke me and I received an epiphany. What had attacked me that night in my room was neither man nor ghost, but something in between. Who'd have such power? And be apt to abuse it? Mina's father. The way he'd leered at me at the hives—it could only be him.

I was now ready to reenter the world and mete out my revenge.

I crawled back toward my lobe on all fours, the jungle still very much alive within me. I found the rock where I had buried my clothes but didn't touch them. They belonged to the old me.

As I neared the eastern edge of my lobe, who should I see sashaying along in my St. Anne's uniform but Zana. Instead of collecting sap, the trollop had strayed off the common path and was idling by herself, humming a Sumatran love song. In her arms, she cradled an empty milk tin, as if nursing a child. Tramp!

I stood up in the bushes and hissed. She glanced around but didn't see me. I hissed again, more viciously. When her eyes finally found me, naked, my flesh covered in mud and sores, she froze. Her milk tin fell to the ground with a hollow thunk. Glee coursed through me. I leapt out of the grass and pranced in her direction. She stood there shaking, but frozen. With each step I took, her fear trebled.

Mere inches from her face, I bared my teeth and snarled. My breath must have been terrifying. She shuddered but was too overcome to flee. Staring into her eyes, I whipped out both hands and smeared mud across her quivering face.

I let her stumble away, sobbing like a child, then shrieked with pleasure at the top of my greedy lungs.

There was a strange black car in the driveway. Could Father have sent someone looking for me? As far as I knew, nobody had come. From the outside, the house appeared placid, no better or worse than I remembered it. I slid in through the back door and slipped into the bathroom.

I examined my naked self in the mirror—the angry cuts, welts, and bruises. It looked as if I'd been pelted by a mob. Though mosquito bites dotted my arms and legs, the spider bites were worse. They left itchy scarlet buboes across my back and under my breasts. My pubic hair was caked with mud. When I tried to unpeel a clump of dirt from it, a bright orange beetle scuttled out and buzzed into flight. Lower down, some of the leech marks on my legs had closed into scabs, while others were leaking yellow pus streaked with blood.

I hardly recognized myself. My hair was long, tangled, greasy. My tongue was a sickly green. Yet I looked invigorated; there was a new determination to my jawline, a new brightness and depth to my eyes.

First, I had to let my body heal. After that, revenge.

I took a satisfying soak in the bath, after which I dressed myself in long sleeves and pants to cover up my sores. I combed my hair, finding a new, left-side parting that most flattered my looks. I wished I had rouge for my lips but I didn't, so I bit them to bring out some color.

There were voices in the sitting room. From the hallway, I saw that Father was entertaining somebody—a pudgy European, sweating through his linen suit. I knew Father was trying to impress him because he had brought out the good china and put Wagner on the gramophone. The stranger, however, did not impress me. He remained seated like a pasha when I made my entrance.

"Ah, Ling, there you are," Father addressed me in English, artificially gregarious. Although he smiled, I could feel his eyes chastising me for my disappearance. "You were out, so I could not tell you. Master Robby is our visitor. He arrive last night."

Master Robby? This was no master. The man looked well over thirty. No youngster had crow's-feet like his or that bulbous cauliflower nose.

"My name is Robin Melmoth, but really, do call me Robby." Melmoth was the name of our plantation. Did he own it? If so, why was he pretending to be much younger, like some affable schoolboy?

"Are you hurt?" he asked.

I was startled by the question. He pointed to the cuffs of my trousers, where a few bleeding sores were visible.

"I see you like to play rough." His eyes swept over my body, studying my contours, passing a multitude of lascivious judgments behind his fake-innocent grin.

I stared back at him, passing judgments of my own.

Father cleared his throat. "She usually not so quiet." He muttered to me in Shanghainese: "Speak up, girl. His father owns our estate. Do you want him to think they've hired a dumb mute?"

"Where's Li?" I asked Father in English.

He replied in English: "Your brother is outside, of course. Working in the plantation. He work very hard."

It was sad how hard Father was trying to dazzle this blob. Sadder still, he had no choice. His family paid ours.

"Your father's told me quite a bit about you and your brother."

I stopped breathing.

"Master Robby last time stay in this house, when he small."

"That's right. I spent my earliest days in this very house. Your room was mine. We've slept in the same bed, I daresay." The man threw me a wink. "Those were the good old days. Carefree living. There was another family up the road, you know, the MacDougals. But they got homesick for Tongue or whatever ghastly Scottish hamlet it was, and Father bought their land from them for a pittance. That's why the estate looks like it's made of two halves. The irony, of course, was that having bought the MacDougals's land, we became the only people here—I mean, apart from the natives— and my parents couldn't bear the isolation. We returned to the city when I was nine. Mummy missed the shops; Father missed the bars. But I never minded it here, honestly, not a bit. Now's a different story, of course—one minute outside and the mozzies are all upon me. Swarms of them. They really can smell an outsider's blood."

"Master Robby is going to Oxford University to study next week," Father interjected again proudly, as if such prestige would somehow rub off on us. This only made "Master Robby" blush and look at his ruddy hands. Was he embarrassed at being the oldest undergraduate ever admitted?

"Indeed, going 'home' at last," he said.

I felt his quotation marks; one didn't need to be Sherlock Holmes to know he wasn't painting us the full picture.

"Father suggested I come here for a final visit, one of the few good ideas he's had in a decade. And I thought, why not? Things change so quickly on the Isle. The next time I'm here, all this could well be shops, hotels." He smiled. "The three of you run a tight ship, I must say."

The *three* of us? I almost gagged. Father had done nothing in years.

"I told Master Robby he can take his old room back. You share with Li."

Father had a genius for demanding exactly what I didn't want to give. I knew he was punishing me—both for my disappearance and for having witnessed him abase himself with Mina's father.

"I'll sleep on the settee," I offered.

"No, you share with your brother. No discussion."

Robin Melmoth looked ready to say something. But the deceitful creature in him pursed his lips and sipped his tea, pinky aloft.

Just then, Li bounded through the door, red from the sun and drinking thirstily from his canteen. He grimaced at the sight of Master Robby. Evidently they'd already met. Yet what surprised me was the look on his face when he saw me. He seemed shocked. Shocked and—after the split second of relief vanished—dismayed.

He disappeared out the door without a word.

Our strange visitor had not arrived empty-handed. When everyone gathered for dinner, he brought in a crate of groceries from his car, as if a critique of my modest chicken stew. I had, however, a strong suspicion that these items were meant solely for his consumption and not intended as gifts: Beefeater gin, tawny port, brandied fruitcake, ten tins of treacle, and a pot of Marmite. I was unfamiliar with all of these things—except for the gin—but carried them dutifully to the kitchen.

It is astonishing how one new person can alter the mood of a household. Father relaxed and played the gentleman host: He saw Melmoth's arrival as a release valve for all the tension that had been collecting between us three. Li remained morose: He saw Melmoth as a spy sent by the rubber bosses. I saw Melmoth as a harbinger of something dreadful, even though he himself seemed fat and harmless. I sensed deceit, and the danger that deception wrought. What was his game?

We would just have to wait and see.

After dinner, I found the St. Anne's uniform returned to my wardrobe, freshly washed and still warm from the iron. Perhaps the fright I'd given

Zana had chastened her. More likely, Li had ordered her to do the washing once their fun was over—a servant was still a servant, after all. Li mentioned nothing of it, and I didn't question him.

We exchanged only a few words.

"That Robby guy," I said. "He gives me the willies."

"Same here. He keeps eyeing you, you know, like you're something to eat."

"Well, he *is* a pig."

Bedtime was fraught, as I feared. Sleeping on the floor of Li's room was out of the question. There were too many insects and vermin. I erected a wall of pillows between us on his bed and I afforded him no intimacy—not that he asked for any, now that he had his pliant Milkmaid.

His old toffee disk was on the bedside table next to me, its gold wrapper slightly tarnished. I was amazed he still had it. Such faith—but in what?

Li waited until it was completely dark before he said anything. His words had the pious, formal tone of a much-rehearsed speech.

"When you disappeared, at first I felt terrible. Like I'd chased you away."

"Then why didn't you come looking for me?"

"I did." I heard him swallow. "Now, don't hate me for saying this, but after a while...after a while, I felt freed. I almost wished you wouldn't come back."

I did hate him for it. Yet I understood. During my time in the jungle, I, too, had felt liberated—of him, of Father, of all responsibilities, and, above all, of guilt.

"Say something, please," Li said. "Are you cross with me?"

"To be honest, I wish I hadn't come back either."

My statement hung in the air like a disease. I couldn't tell if he was wounded by it or was preparing to return with a more cutting barb.

"You look...different," he finally said.

I pulled the blanket over my welts.

"You're prettier. But I don't feel..." He searched for the right words. "I mean, I feel...I don't know...it's like *fear*."

The next morning, I wanted to be left alone, to lie in bed nursing my sores. But of course that was impossible. There were tappers to be overseen, quotas to be filled.

Since Li had confessed his wish for my absence, I decided I would make him feel my presence doubly, triply, spitefully, by surpassing the day's quota and making up for the losses that occurred while I was gone. I would work my girls close to death.

I cycled to my lobe and was greeted by an unfamiliar hush. A good third of my Milkmaids were not there. Those who did show up stood clustered together, exchanging anxious whispers until I shouted at them to resume work. One of them, a gray-haired Tamil who should have known better, ran away wailing as soon as she saw me.

"Come back here, you old bag!" I shouted in a tone that struck me as unnecessarily fierce. My voice sounded much more forceful than it had just days ago.

None of my threats could detain her. The girls stared at me as if I were a barbaric enforcer. Soon after, two Milkmaids tripped and lost entire tins of milk to the grass.

"What's wrong with all of you?" I snapped. Nobody said a word, bound by some sorority of silence. The crickets roared. "If nothing's wrong, do your bloody work!"

I pulled aside Rani, the Tamil girl I trusted. Her eagerness to practice English usually made her a good conduit for gossip, but today even she seemed haunted.

"What's happening?"

"Nothing, miss." She stared at the ground.

I gripped her thin black wrist to get her full attention. I asked her again.

This time, she relented. "Zana say she see pontianak yesterday, miss, coming from jungle."

So that's what it was. My little prank had caused a mass hysteria.

"But the pontianak didn't harm Zana, did she?" I asked.

Rani shook her head reluctantly, as if there was more she wanted me to force out of her. I twisted her wrist till she yelped.

"So?"

"Miss, you know that girl who have the baby?"

"Mina, you mean?"

Rani nodded fearfully. "She die last night."

I groaned. Her father would surely be looking for someone to blame.

"She have many, many pain, miss. So much blood come out. Now everyone scared she become pontianak."

"What about her baby?"

"Baby die also."

"But I heard the drums. I thought the baby was fine."

"They say Mina father make baby die. Then pontianak cannot eat baby."

"*They say, they say.* What about what *you* think, Rani? Where's the baby's father?"

"Miss..." She glanced around nervously. "Mina father is *bomoh.* He use magic to do bad thing. Miss...Mina father and baby father is same-same."

Her words echoed my worst fears. I felt myself sinking in a wave of nausea.

Tears pooled in Rani's eyes. Remembering Dora Conceição, I released her wrist.

"Miss, please don't say I say this...please..." She backed away, ready to run.

"Will there be a funeral?" I pressed.

"Her father don' wan' bury her. He make her wear dress red in color. You know what red dress mean, miss?"

Vengeance. The old man wanted Mina to come back and wreak havoc.

"Tonight is full moon. That's why everyone so scared."

I told my Milkmaids to take the rest of the day off. We couldn't afford the stoppage but I had no choice. I had to confer with Li about what to do next.

When I cycled to his lobe, I saw that even more of his Milkmaids were missing. Li himself was nowhere to be found. Was he off with that hussy again?

I rushed to the milk factory—deserted. A tap dripped water into a rusty basin. Vats of sap sat idle, skin hardening across their surface. The men had fled, leaving their rattan soccer ball on the foreman's stool.

I pedaled home. Perhaps Li would be there. Naturally, Father wouldn't be. This was Friday, the day he made his weekly pilgrimage to Ulu Pandan, the nearest village ten miles away, via hired taxi. He made the trip ostensibly to stock up on groceries but somehow always found an excuse to stay past midnight.

Only Robin Melmoth was in the house. He was sprawled on the settee, still in his nightshirt, sipping a glass of some brownish spirit and flipping through *Malay for Mems* with a nostalgic twinkle.

"Air the clothes—*jemur pakaian*. Air the mattress—*jemur tilam*. This is dirty—*ini kotur*."

He reeked like a saloon; the soles of his feet were jet black.

"Well, hello, young mistress," he said when he finally noticed me, his face red from drink and from the crush of seat cushions against his cheek. "You know, your room smells of frangipani. Funny smell."

"Have you seen my brother?"

"Always looking for him, aren't you? It's not natural, you know. But I suppose life can get lonely here in the country." His eyes stayed on me as he sipped his drink. "As a matter of fact, your brother was just here. And then he wasn't. Funny chap."

"One of the tappers, this girl . . . she died last night."

"Memento mori." He turned back to the booklet, as if he hadn't registered my words. "Polish the golf clubs—*gosok kilat kayu-main golf*. Rub hard—*gosok kuat*." He grabbed my wrist. "Sit down, will you? You're giving me a frightful headache."

"What should we do?" I shook his paw off. It disgusted me to have to seek a buffoon's advice, but he'd once lived here. There was a chance he'd know.

"What should we do?" he repeated. "That's the eternal question. To be . . . or not to be."

I now saw that he was hopelessly drunk; the reading had been a charade.

"Come, sit. Let's ponder this a moment, shall we, funny girl?"

A half-empty bottle of port was stuffed in a crease between two cushions, and I reached for it. With no warning at all, he lunged at me.

I leapt back and his mouth struck my shoulder, leaving a slimy trail of spittle on my blouse. He looked confused, even hurt.

"That was most uncalled for!" he said, nursing his reddened chin.

"You're not going to Oxford, are you?"

My words worked like a splash of cold water. He cackled mockingly. "Lookee here! Clever Chink girl like you, wasting away in the jungle. Why aren't you in the city, with all the other clever Chinks? Full marks to you! I'm not going anywhere." He challenged me with narrowed eyes. "My dear papa gave me up to the army, said it would do me good. I disagreed. I suppose this makes me a deserter, a coward. But tell me, why should I sit in a trench and freeze my toes off for the bloody king?

He's got no loyalty to me. I'm just one of the bastard children of the empire, no better than a blackie bent over tea leaves in Assam, no better than *you*."

He reached for the port, but I slapped the glass out of his hand.

"A girl's dead, you monster!" I screamed.

"Yes, yes, I heard you the first time..." He worked his face into a serious expression. "Here's what I propose..." His eyes rolled back in their sockets and he collapsed into the cushions, snoring.

I closed and latched all the windows and waited for Li's return. He never came.

I sat in the muggy house with the sleeping whale, more than willing to offer him up to the natives in exchange for my brother.

Hours into my vigil, the smell of brush fire began to permeate the house. Opening the front door a crack, I saw orange flames rising on Blood Hill, framed by the purple sunset. The banana trees twisted like women being burned alive.

Bloody idiots! I freed the bottle of port from under Robin's arm, shook the liquor out, and shattered it on the front step by holding its neck. Clutching this saber-toothed bouquet, I bicycled through the rapidly diminishing twilight.

Amidst thick plumes of smoke, a person appeared on Blood Hill, fanning the flames with two large fronds.

"Stop that!" I ran up the steepest side, brandishing my weapon.

"It's me! It's just me!" The figure was Li, trying hopelessly, foolishly, to blow out the fire. "My trees..." He was crying, crumbling. "Mina's father made them burn down all my trees! But my trees didn't do anything! My trees are innocent!"

I couldn't remember the last time I saw Li cry. My poor brother, blinded by his devotion. His fanning only made the flames leap higher.

"Go home," I said. "Guard our house in case they try to burn it down."

"That Robby chap's there! Let *him* guard it."

"Him?" I was too exhausted to explain. "I'm going to look for Mina's father. Go home, please! Just go, and wait for me there!"

He studied me, the pious solemnity of last night returning to his face. "All right."

We raced down the hill together, night wrapping tight around us. At the base, he embraced me swiftly:

"Kill him," he whispered.

Over Li's shoulder, I saw columns of shadowy figures marching through the plantation grids. Their pace was strangely placid, as if this parade had been ordained by some bullying high priest: Mina's father. There wasn't enough light for me to tell if they were living or dead, but I had my suspicions. Ghosts did not take strolls in packs.

"Bring your bicycle inside," I told Li. "And hide Robin's car key. Don't give them anything."

I watched to make sure Li left Blood Hill before I started pedaling north.

Rain clouds were clustering, like tighter and tighter gray fists. I passed more of our workers, most carrying cloth bundles. They averted their eyes and I didn't slow down to question them. Where did they hope to go in the dark? The nearest village was ten miles away, the nearest main road two or three miles beyond that, and in between were pythons, kraits, and cobras that could rise up taller than any man.

After what seemed like forever, I reached the dormitories, the hives. All three barracks appeared to be vacant—their doors left gaping wide. Every lamp had been extinguished, even those hanging outdoors. The whole area was silent. No crickets chirped—even they knew better than to linger here.

I stared at the open doors, each an invitation into a black hole. I stepped through the middle doorway—Mina's hive.

"I am looking for Mina's father!" My voice echoed in the abyss.

I waved the shard flower. Its jagged teeth caught the moonglow and threw dots of light into the darkness. I needed more light. I found a box of matches by the door and lit up a battered old kerosene lamp.

The dormitories had no sitting rooms, only a small common area with one long table and bare benches. Attached to one end of this dining area was an outdoor kitchen consisting of three brick braziers and a tap over an open drain. The place smelled of coffee and toddy, the twin engines of the plantation worker: one to rev him up, the other to bring him down. At the other end, the common area filtered into a corridor that led to two long sleeping rooms: one for men, the other for women and children.

The men's room reeked of the armpits and crotches of the poor laborers now trudging through the jungle. Hard, narrow bunks were stacked three high, as on a battleship sailing off to war. There were eighteen bunks in all.

The women's room threw off a stench far worse. A few feet from its closed door, I felt like gagging. Even holding my breath, I could taste the sour bitterness of rotting meat. The last thing I'd smelled this foul was a four-legged carcass lying by the Ulu Pandan river, so hollowed out by maggots that I couldn't tell if it'd been cow, mule, or horse.

The door opened into a dark chamber, its windows covered with canvas panels nailed into the sash. Small candles burned on the floor in one long line, their red wax oozing to form pools that looked like caked blood. I propped open the door with a brick and entered. More filthy, endless bunks and the crosshatches of their shadows.

Immediately, my skin began to itch. Flies. They buzzed and grazed my arms, my face, by the score. I brushed them away but they kept returning.

Reaching the farthest mast of beds, I knew I had come to Mina's body. The coppery, putrid odor of old blood emanated from her—a ghastly note distinct from the rot. I held the lamp over her. Her face and upper torso were covered with a bloodstained blanket. Below her long red smock extended a pair of gray, calloused feet, their toes permanently curled down and crawling with maggots.

Her stillness unnerved me. I'd never seen a dead person who wasn't in motion. I realized with a shudder that I had never really seen a corpse.

"Mina, are you here?" I enunciated clearly, over the rumbles of thunder. "Mina, I want to help you."

I spun around. The candles burned steadily. Nothing moved in the shadows.

But she had to be here. If I were her, I would return. I would want to bare my rage, voice my outrage against my father, against the world that allowed him to use me.

"Mina? Mina . . ." Each time I spoke her name through the empty hive, I felt her isolation, her fury.

Here I was, just a young girl myself, my body covered in sores, standing all alone in an abandoned plantation. Why had I been left to defend it? Where was my worthless father, my cowardly brother? I wanted to hurl my glass weapon into the darkness and flee into the night, along with all my workers.

Truly, I wanted nothing more than to go far away, back to the city.

But the instant I ran out of the hive, the storm smacked down on me. The heavens had unlatched their floodgates, and rain was descending in denser and denser sheets. There'd be better days for running away. Pelted by the deluge, I dropped to my knees, suddenly and vividly aware of my own mortality.

In the end I would die alone, just as Mina was all alone.

Thunder shook the ground beneath me. This was no time for self-pity. I pulled myself up and sprinted toward home. All around me, the rain clacked against the ground like a million pairs of chattering teeth.

Death may be mankind's great leveler, but water is surely land's. In the night, it conspired to make all terrains appear as one. High, low, sharp, blunt, near, far. Everything looked the same. Water seeped into my pores, flowed into my eyes. I couldn't tell if the rain was falling sideways or if I was charging at right angles. All landmarks vanished. Where was the factory? The black hut? Blood Hill?

Stumbling over a root, I slammed into the sodden trunk of a tree. It gave briefly and then snapped back upright to strike my face again. Strange tree, it stank of death. I spat its bitter taste out of my mouth and rinsed my face with rainwater. Then I saw: This was no tree. It was a man dangling from the branch of a tembusu. The body was brown, naked, hanging by its neck, twirling slowly on its rope.

The face was slack but unmistakable: Mina's father. I screamed until I was hoarse.

Though I had dreamed of punishing him, this was something else altogether: He was sliced open, chin to groin, like a fish. His entrails had become one long gray hose, spilling to the ground.

My body sprang into action without me. I felt my feet rising and falling, rising and falling, and my hands tearing at my face, rubbing, cleaning. My mind, meanwhile, remained frozen: that taint, that man. I had to get away from that taint, that man.

When the silhouette of Blood Hill appeared, with its smoldering, hissing tree line, both my mind and my body knew I was almost home. Only the dirt path to go.

I reached the front door, ready to collapse with relief on the bungalow step, but the door and all the windows were sealed shut. I was locked out of my own house.

"It's me!" I pounded on the door. "Let me in, dammit!"

My voice was weak, no match for the angry claps of rain. If Li and Robin were hiding in the back of the house, they wouldn't hear a thing. I picked up a rock and smashed it through a window.

The door eventually opened, slowly. As I pushed my way in, the sharp prongs of the amok fork jabbed at me but missed.

"Robin!" I snatched the fork from his unsteady hands. "It's me, you fool!"

His eyes widened as recognition flowed in. "Why, you're as wet as a dog."

"Has anyone tried to break in?"

"Not that I'm aware of," he said blankly.

The army should have been grateful to be spared of such a specimen. I slammed the door and locked it, tipping a chair against it as an added precaution.

"By the way," he said with a wink, "your brother's here."

Li was in the sitting room—and he wasn't alone. A comely Malay woman was perched next to him, drying her hair with a towel. *My* towel. Hatred shot through me. I was out in the storm on my own while he sat here, dry as a bone, playing hero to his Milkmaid paramour!

"To hell with you, Li!"

"What?" he said, acting innocent, enraging me further.

I tore off my ruined shoes and stormed to my room to undress, trailing prints of mud behind me.

Li ran along and grabbed my arm. "Are you all right? I was so worried."

"Then why are you sitting at home with your damned whore?"

"You told me to wait here! Anyway, I don't even know that girl. She begged us to let her in. Her name's Anim."

Anim? I dipped back to peer at her. He was telling the truth. This wasn't Zana. She was just another pretty Milkmaid, probably from his lobe. Doubtless his next conquest. Her skin was fair, silky—she didn't look like the type who did manual labor at all.

"She's really scared," Li went on. "You see, she's pregnant. And everyone around her was hysterical about the pontina."

"Pontianak—don't you know anything?"

He followed me to my room. I made him wait outside while I changed.

"Mina's father is dead," I said through the door. "Those savages murdered him."

No response. I opened the door and took a good look at Li's sullen face.

He snapped back, "Oh, stop acting like such a saint. You wanted him dead, too."

True then; not true now. I turned away before he could see my lips quivering. "Where the hell's Father anyway?"

"Still in Ulu Pandan, I suspect. Drinking."

No tears, not now. "Once this is over, I don't care what he says, I'm leaving."

"Where to?"

"I don't know. I'm tired of being ignorant. I want to learn things. I want to go back to school." That last part sounded like an unimaginable luxury.

Li squeezed my hand—a surprising gesture of solidarity. "Take me with you."

I knew this was his way of apologizing, for having wished me gone.

"You have your own two feet. I'm not carrying you on my back like a sack of potatoes."

He smiled. We both smiled. But I knew that what I needed to get away from included him. He was part of the history I had to flee.

There was a loud crash in the sitting room, followed by an extravagant groan from Robin. The man had fallen down drunk, no doubt. I rolled my eyes and we both relaxed, rescued just in time from discussing the future.

"I'm not helping him up," I said to Li. "I'm not touching that swine."

"I'm not touching him either."

We went to assess the damage.

Robin lay on the floor, whimpering gibberish, a strange look of stupor on his face as he stared up at the ceiling. The Milkmaid had her back to us. She was kneeling over him, trying to help. The end table was overturned, its legs in pieces. The fat oaf must have shattered it with his fall.

"Robin, you idiot!" I cried, but Li clutched my arm.

The images rearranged themselves before my eyes: The girl wasn't helping Robin. She was gouging into his belly with long, sharp nails. Blood sprayed everywhere. On the carpet, on the settee—all over her.

She turned toward us and screeched, blood dripping from her gums. Her teeth weren't teeth but little black fangs. Before we could move, she flew at us.

"Run!" Li pushed me out of the way and was pinned to the ground by the she-demon. Before my eyes, her flesh was mutating into gray, suppurating meat.

"Leave him alone!" I screamed in Malay.

She pressed her mouth onto Li's neck in an obscene parody of passion. He shrieked—in terror, I hoped, not pain. Grabbing the amok fork from beside Robin, I rushed to save my brother.

But as I ran toward her, the world slowed down, and the air thickened into a kind of glue. A second heartbeat began pounding in my chest, a shadow heartbeat that soon outpaced my own. Following this new, quickened pulse, the figures thrashing before me seemed to be performing a slow-motion ballet.

Li seized my ankle, and the second heartbeat ceased. "Help me!"

My senses rushed back.

Raising the fork high over my head, I plunged its tines into the pontianak's back. It felt like tilling hard-packed earth.

The creature unleashed a piercing scream that bore the fury of two women—one human, the other monstrous. She twisted her head to stare at me, her engorged eyes bulging as black as leeches. When our eyes locked, my second heartbeat resumed.

I killed my father, her dark pupils told me. *I know you understand.*

It was Mina, the dead Milkmaid.

I drank the blood you left me in the forest.

My blood?

Before I could speak, the fork whipped across my ribs, knocking me to the floor. The pontianak was coming for me now. I raised my arms to shield my face.

"Mina!" I begged.

She swiped at me with nails so sharp I felt only the slightest sting. I looked down. Five lines darkened along my forearms and the flesh around them split open like pods, disgorging blood.

The pontianak turned back to Li, twirling the heavy fork in her hands. Li closed his eyes, his lips shuddering in prayer.

But instead of impaling him, the creature used the fork as it was meant to be: She clamped his neck down. Then she circled him, making birdlike caws.

I had to do something. There had to be a parang somewhere outside the house, maybe in the tangle of shovels by the abandoned brick stove. I sprinted to the back door, unbolted it, and stepped outside.

The rain had stopped. The night possessed the wise, unhurried calm of the innermost rainforest, rich with the aroma of lilies, orchids, and frangipani. *Swish, swoosh. Swish, swoosh.* The sounds of leaves rustling in the breeze, perhaps the most ancient lullaby known to man. The trees beyond the estate swayed, their shimmering fronds dappled by the silver moonlight. All of the jungle beckoned, dark and deep, promising rest, comfort, everlasting peace. I craved escape into its velvet embrace.

"Ling..." Li's cry was watery, abstract, part of this forest dream.

My feet pulled me toward the jungle. After a few steps, something huge and black blocked my way, as if someone had cut a hole in the scenery. I could not see past this bullying square of pure absence. Quickly, the form grew depth—or rather, my eyes gave it meaning: It was the black hut. Somebody had moved it here. But why?

Its door was ajar, the big rusty padlock gone.

I kicked the door open. In the darkness was a lone parang, its blade as long as my arm. It stood poised on its tip, suspended in thin air. I groped around under and over it, even along its sides—there was nothing holding it in place. As I drew my fingers away, it glinted at me and didn't stop until I brought my hand back.

The instant I grabbed its handle, I heard my brother cry, "Ling!" as clearly as if he'd been standing next to me.

Li needed me—*now*.

Running back into the house, I saw that the pontianak had abandoned him for Robin. She hunched over him, a mad pianist about to launch into the blackest of chords, and threw her claws into his chest. Robin tried to scream but his cries thickened into gargles—blood had already filled his larynx. Bright red bubbles foamed at his mouth.

I came from behind the monster, pulled my arm back, but didn't have to swing—the parang had a momentum all its own. It was drawn, as if magnetically, to her neck.

The demon's head plummeted off her shoulders with one inelegant droop and rolled across the floor until it struck the leg of a chair. Its dead eyes stared back at me, and in that instant I experienced a weird foretaste of my own death. Emptiness engulfed me and drew me to the ground just as my knees buckled.

When I finally caught my breath, I looked over to Li. He nodded to let me know he was all right.

The pontianak's lifeless torso remained exactly where I'd destroyed her, held upright by the fingers still buried in Robin's gut. I pictured his blood spraying like a fountain if they were removed from him; I didn't move them.

"Save me," he pleaded in a whispery gurgle. But it was too late. Even his vacant eyes knew it.

I picked myself off the ground and went to fetch his bottle of gin.

"Help will be here soon," I assured him, putting on a brave, if dishonest, face. I poured the gin down his throat and watched it seep out of his wounds.

Li propped himself up on one elbow. His shirt was smeared with blood, and his neck and shoulders were covered in cuts. Seeing him in pain, I could no longer hold back my tears.

"She spat out my blood." He pointed to the crimson spatter on the wall and squeezed my arm to show he still had the strength. He forced out a smile. "She didn't want my bad blood."

"The workers were right, you know," I told him. "That was Mina."

Li looked startled. "Couldn't be."

"Why not?"

"Mina was short and dark." His voice tightened. "This one looked much more like . . . you."

The police finally arrived, with Father in tow. The workers' exodus had been sighted on the road into Ulu Pandan, and the station dispatched its only car to investigate.

The two uniformed men sat Father down. I could smell the toddy on him from the other end of the room. His eyes took in none of the blood and injuries before him. He remained locked in a narcissistic dream where tragedy favored him and him alone.

"What will I do?" he mumbled. "What will I do?"

I wanted to slap him, and then slap him some more.

The young Chinese officer accidentally kicked the pontianak's head across the floor and ran from the house screaming like a woman. His partner, a steadfast, bronze Gurkha—one of the Nepalese tribesmen the British had recruited in scores—shook his head and clucked, as if he dealt with decapitated demons all the time.

"I don't know how you did it, but you did a fine job," he told me, gesturing to the severed neck. He looked at my bleeding cuts. "And you don't seem to mind the pain." He was wrong—of course I did mind. But both Li and Robin were suffering far more.

Amazingly, Robin was still holding on. His cheek twitched and he muttered something to the Gurkha.

"Beg your pardon?" The Gurkha leaned in closer to listen. He pursed his lips and shot me a bemused smile. "He is telling me that you are a witch."

A witch? After I saved his life!

The Gurkha's smile grew conspiratorial, assuring me that he knew better. "Englishmen are all the same up-country. Their blood just cannot take it. They go mad, cause trouble, and get themselves killed."

He pointed at the weird Pietà of Robin and the she-demon. "We can fit him inside the car, but first I'll need to chop off her arms."

I searched for the parang—it was nowhere in the room. Out the back door, the black hut was gone. Gone, too, was the tranquillity and the cool, deep-jungle air. No orchid scent, no frangipani. The nightscape had reverted to its buzzing, irritated state.

Could I have dreamt the whole interlude?

With a handkerchief fastened over his nose, the Gurkha had already begun carving into the pontianak's arms with his kukri knife, the dagger of Gurkha warriors.

"Do you do this often?" I asked when he finally removed the pontianak's torso from the glistening stumps of her rotting forearms.

"Here in the countryside, we do all kinds of things. This is not even the worst."

I believed him.

"Don't say we never warn you," he said. "There are spirits here much older and more powerful than us people."

By the time he finished dismembering Mina, Robin Melmoth had joined the world of the spirits. But he looked calm, as if he were merely asleep. I half expected him to sit up at any moment and demand another sip of gin.

The Gurkha said a quick Hindu prayer and carried the two bodies—and the severed head—out to the Englishman's Jeep. We heard him tell his Chinese partner he would take the pontianak to the jungle and burn her, then deliver Robin to the Ulu Pandan morgue. But he announced his plan so theatrically that I wondered if Robin's body would ever see the morgue. The local police obviously had idiosyncratic methods.

The other officer drove us to the doctor, Li and I squashed in the back of the two-door Model B squad car, jerking back and forth with the bumpiness of the road.

"You were in a trance," Li whispered the next morning. Now that he felt better, his voice again assumed that pious tone. "What was going through your mind?"

"I wasn't thinking," I said. "There was no time. I just took the parang and—"

"What parang?"

"The parang I found outside."

He stared at me. "I was there. I saw you. There was no parang." The terror in his eyes returned. "You ripped off her head with your bare hands."

Of course, we were finished in the jungle.

The plantation was lost, even though some of our tappers had begun trickling back onto the estate, hungry for work. For a day or so, I felt the sweet reprieve of an impossible weight lifted off my shoulders. Absolution, almost. Then two mustached lawyers working for the Melmoth family materialized, mosquito-bitten and with complicated papers demanding payment for the Blood Hill fire, the runaway workers, and, of course, Robin's death, whether or not we had been directly responsible. Luckily, the Ulu Pandan coroner determined we were faultless: Robin Melmoth, it was officially ruled, had been mauled by a wild tiger. Still the lawyers persisted, and Father was fined for not keeping those beasts off the estate.

Our savings vanished in a flash.

Over the following days, we sobered up in our different ways. Father vowed he would no longer go into Ulu Pandan. Li avoided all contact with the Milkmaids. But I still had my own questions.

However the pontianak's head came off—Li had been delirious; his testimony was unreliable—I couldn't forget how her alien heartbeat had devoured mine, tying me to her, or was it the other way around? Who had colonized whom? One thing was certain: The jungle dead were not like any dead I'd known. They did not heed the same laws.

And though I refused to concede it at the time, Li was right: Anim did resemble me, not Mina. She had my eyes, my lips, my overlong arms, my knobby knees. What she told me was probably true. The pontianak had drunk my blood. The blood of my womb.

The thought made me shudder. I sucked down the rest of Robin's gin and tried to forget the whole episode. Without letting anyone know, not even Li, I quietly packed my bags. I knew I would never find peace in the jungle aside from the peace of death.

In bright noon light, I cycled through the plantation one final time. Blood Hill was charred bald, really the way it should have been kept all along. The corpse of Mina's father had been removed from the tembusu and cremated by the workers who had returned. The gargantuan tree itself was cut down and replaced by a small shrine—a simple wood crate smoldering with incense. The Melmoth estate was in shambles. Our family had certainly left its mark.

The black hut revealed no trace of itself, neither on the grassy knoll where I'd seen Li and his Milkmaid, nor behind our house.

At the hives, I bade farewell to my workers with cordial handshakes that startled most of them. Rani fled as soon as she saw me coming. It was a pity, as I'd intended to apologize. Following a quick shower, I grabbed my two canvas sacks and hitched a ride with the Gurkha policeman to Ulu Pandan, where I could find a bus that would take me back to the city.

Li followed a few days later. And then, unfortunately, Father.

If there's one truth about life I've learned in all these years of running, it's that there is no such thing as a clean escape.

Do I FEEL BETTER NOW—or worse? Thirty, forty years younger—or a good deal older? My mood shifts from one memory to the next, like a sick pendulum.

This bloodletting is double-edged—toxins exit, but so does vigor. My throat's dry. My muscles ache as if I'd run miles through jungle.

As I label my tapes, the telephone rings. I ignore it.

Chapter 1, chapter 2, chapter 3, chapter 4, chapter 5, chapter 6—the early years, the easy years. Juvenilia. Glad I'd stocked up on fresh tapes and batteries. I've always been ready for emergencies; I have the war to thank for that.

At long last, my answering machine intercepts the call.

"Ling," she begins, saying my childhood name as if she actually knows me. "I can tell you're there...Please pick up the phone."

"You missed a damned good beheading," I say to the room.

"I'm going to be a bit late. I'm being kept by...You remember our agreement? I had to make some final arrangements to fulfill my end of the bargain."

Our agreement. Of course, I haven't forgotten. Our agreement fires my every thought, my every memory.

"I'll make the wait worth your while, I promise. I won't disappoint you. So in the meantime"—she pauses—"percolate."

I pick up the phone. "Are you here to torment me or to save me? The dam has already broken. I've already begun. I can't stop now."

I tear the phone jack from the wall and walk straight to my window. I draw open the curtains, lift up the sash, and stare out.

"Who's there?" I call. It's only the night. My friend, the night.

I am telling this story to remind myself how brave I was in my youth. I took on a pontianak—and won. Why can't I be a brave girl once more?

I beat my fist against my chest. *Thump, thump.*

My heart replies, *Thump, thump.*

— 7 —

Wonder World

THE CITY HAD RESHAPED ITSELF between 1934 and 1937. It was taller, much taller, like a bean sprout of a boy who'd had a growth spurt over the holidays and returned in the new term a giant. I came back gaping skyward.

Even Bullock Cart Water hadn't been exempt from change. A fire had gutted our old row house soon after we left, snuffing out fifty in their sleep, just like that. It was torn down, leaving a gaping tooth on the block. Though all evidence pointed to arson, city officials refused to rule it as such, fearing copycats. A one-legged ghost stood at the site recounting the tragedy in a droning voice. I tried to ignore him but found I could not, so moved was I by his sense of duty and outrage. I'd like to think I'd do the same if I, too, had been so heartlessly killed.

Oh, to be back again in the city, where the dead spoke of their troubles rather than lash out in blood violence!

Our building wasn't the only casualty of passing time. The pavement barber was gone, as were the sadhu and the *karang guni* man. I never liked them much before, but now I missed them all.

Spring Street, the main thoroughfare, was now lined with apartment buildings eight or nine stories high. The neighborhood certainly needed them. It was swarming with new arrivals. Japan's invasion of China had pushed thousands onto our shores, and these lost souls aligned themselves according to whether they favored noodles (Northerners) or rice (Southerners). All of them chose Chinatown. I found myself looking for Mother and the twins in their midst, though I knew she'd be too proud to run to the city where Father lived. I kept a hopeful eye out anyway—if only for the twins. My eleven-year-old babies.

The refugees carried bad habits from the old country: prostitution, gambling, opium. Yet as before, the city did nothing when gangs came out with their knives; if no one scrubbed the blood off the pavement, it sat there blackening for weeks. In contrast, whenever a peaceful group of Chinese gathered to protest a shady Japanese business, the governor clamped down immediately, ordering curfews. Double standards in the colonial city we were accustomed to, but this protectiveness toward the Japanese was something new. Father surmised it was about face—and money. The Japanese were investing in shops, hotels, and restaurants and were so good at scratching British egos by mimicking them in dress, manner, and taste.

We lived on the top floor—the eighth—in one of the new apartment blocks on Spring Street. Though the rent was cheap, the upper floors remained largely empty. The night watchman told Father that most Chinese refused to live on the high floors because the local "singsong girls," or prostitutes, often used them as springboards for their closing arias, as the watchman put it, diving through the air to their crimson doom below. The properties, Father told us with a small shiver, were considered "very dirty."

"The eighth floor is popular for suicides because *eight* in Chinese, you recall, is a homonym for *prosperity*," he explained to Li and me. "Whether this leads them to fortune in the afterlife or not, we'll never know. What I *can* tell you is this: The Taoists believe that suicides make the most troublesome ghosts." I cringed to hear him use the word. "All right, I didn't always have time for this type of thing. But after the plantation, anything's possible. So, to be on the safe side, I urge you to behave yourselves. Don't do anything that might provoke them. And, here, keep these with you as an added precaution."

He handed both of us identical sets of trinkets—a Buddhist bracelet with orange prayer beads, a Christian crucifix on a chain, a medallion of the multiarmed Hindu goddess Kali, and a slip of paper with an Islamic tract in Arabic. I smirked but caught Li lowering his eyes in submission. The boy did like his charms; I knew these would join the desiccated toffee disk on his nightstand.

"I don't know what each of them means," Father said, "but they have to be kept together at all times. That's what the old woman who sold them to me said. I'm carrying a set myself."

"Oh no," I groaned with mock anguish. "We're missing a Star of David!"

Father glared at me, then glanced around the apartment. "This is not a joke," he hissed. "Do you want to get us all killed?"

The night watchman was right. The majority of the suicides on our floor *were* women. Most were either depressed taxi dancers, weary from hiring themselves out as dance-hall partners, or the neglected wives of opium-wracked rickshaw men. These unhappy souls somehow managed to sneak past the watchman and up to the open-air hallway of the eighth floor. Perhaps bribes were involved. The lazier singsong girls, however, rarely bothered to climb the whole way—they usually leapt off the fourth or fifth floor, and often survived. The ones who didn't survive lived with us.

There were five ghosts in our apartment when we moved in, six by the end of the first month. The irony didn't escape me that the dead dancers and prostitutes spoke to me, whereas their living counterparts, dolled up in rouge and sparkles, snubbed me as if I were the human equivalent of a bug—a girl who wore no makeup and loped around town in flat heels.

Over and over, the ghosts told the same stories: They fell for unreliable men and then—surprise, surprise—had their worst fears about them proven true. They moped around our apartment, repeating their pitiable sagas like defendants in a courtroom, proving yet again that death never consoled anyone with new wisdom, only regret. Frustratingly, I couldn't talk back or shoo them away; the channel of communication was strictly one way. Needless to say, Father's trinkets were worthless. Not that I would ever tell him. He was so much easier to get along with when he believed he was in control.

A few months after our return, in late 1937, the city opened an amusement park, like a miracle salve for everybody's woes. Wonder World sat in the no-man's-land between Chinatown and the docks and was the first social venue where the different races could mix freely, all in the name of fun and games—and, of course, vice. I tried in vain to remember what had been in that location before; Father thought it might have been a squatters' colony, Li a scrap-metal yard, but neither could recall for sure. Wonder World's presence was so pungently vibrant—a veritable lotus flower blooming in a muddy trough—that it wiped out all traces of what had come before.

Above its high vermilion walls, loudspeakers blared out its jumbled inventory: "Three cinemas! Two dance halls! Burlesque cabaret! Boxing ring! Silk underwear! Come and see live penguins! Come and taste our fish-ball soup! Beautiful Siamese girls! Beautiful Siamese cats! Two miles of games, three miles of food!"

The papers insisted that the honeymooning Charlie Chaplin had stopped by incognito—no mustache, no bowler—and on our first visit, a canny entrepreneur was already gaining from this unverified tidbit. He stood at the entrance, peddling souvenir cards in the Tramp's silhouette. Li and I watched him sell twenty in just five minutes.

It was from the gate that we had to observe all the fun. As Li and I wouldn't be allowed inside until we were eighteen, we gawked from the periphery as Father sauntered in, promising to return with presents. The sweet aroma of honeyed pork jerky wafting from within made us swoon. Salivating, we watched couples emerge dizzy with satisfaction, toting stuffed panda mascots the size of infants and drums of powdered milk— game prizes that seemed to suggest they should go home and instantly start making babies. We also saw drunken British sailors being shown the way out, but there would always be drunken sailors on the Black Isle.

When Father finally resurfaced after two hours, he smelled of cheap beer and even cheaper perfume. Not surprisingly, he was empty-handed.

"The ball-toss hoops are rigged," he laughed, forcing a tone of outrage. "They're all out of reach!"

Judging from the lipstick mark on his neck, the singsong girls were, alas, not.

St. Anne's had changed, too. When I returned to reenroll myself, I thought the old building had been torn down and replaced by a spotless, somewhat drab replica.

"It's the same old pile, minus the guano," beamed Sister O'Hara, the reading teacher I had once called a giraffe. "Sister Nesbit decided it was about time. A chunk of it fell off during the last Visitors Day and struck one of our donors on the noggin. You look disappointed. Don't you like it?"

The truth was the old version had more character. Thankfully, the nuns were as welcoming as ever. Aside from their equine body odor, they were almost supernatural—none of them seemed to have aged. The spring-footed headmistress, Sister Nesbit, was delighted at the return of the prodigal daughter, as she called me, and ushered me straight to class. She had always treated me with kindness, and seeing that old familiar smile, I found myself quite moved.

Although I'd dreamt of my return, I hadn't realized how starved I had been for knowledge until I reentered the school library. I devoured whatever I could lay my hands on. My new favorite was the saturnine Baudelaire, and I lingered in the stacks long past daylight hours, alone with books and ghosts.

There were far fewer of the latter at St. Anne's now, perhaps because Sister Nesbit had installed bright lights throughout the building. The writhing maidens of the toilet were gone—as was poor Dora Conceição. The hanging girl, however, continued to convulse from the fan during assembly, but I now found her presence weirdly reassuring.

On weekends, I followed my guides Hugo, Balzac, and Maupassant. They led me away from our narrow rooms to salons and factories filled with conversation and smoke. In my reading, I discovered some of the qualities that made the French great romantic figures but quite deluded colonials: They were short-term thinkers, impetuous, vain, thoroughly at the mercy of immediate, especially sensual, pleasures. While I loved the French for their style, I thanked my stars we had the British, who at least parlayed their stoical love of dull duty into constructing roads and schools.

In 1940, when I turned eighteen, Sister Nesbit delivered the news I'd been most dreading. I had officially outgrown St. Anne's, and unless I wanted to try for university—which I could not afford—it was time for me to leave. To soften the blow of my exile, she found me a position as governess to the Chew family, who lived in Monks Hill, a leafy neighborhood favored by bourgeois Peranakans. "See if you like teaching," Sister Nesbit said, "and if you do, apply to the teacher's college."

The Chews offered me room and board (dank closet and seat at the family table next to my ten-year-old ward). Happy for any excuse to avoid my family and the chatterbox wraiths of the eighth floor, I immediately accepted, though I resented the idea of being an equatorial Jane Eyre. I believed, with no evidence, that I was destined for better.

For his part, Li worked as an errand boy for a large family in the west of the Island. Though his job horrified me—he was essentially what that boy Cricket had been for us in Shanghai—he seemed disturbingly contented. I supposed his master's demands kept him too busy to feel anything more than passive numbness. Gone was his earlier spark. It was as if our up-country debacle had taught him it was hubris to dream or even desire. I felt that he ought to have been wanting more—and doing better. Doing what, however, I had no idea.

Hoping to enjoy what free time we had together, we steered clear of tricky subjects—Shanghai, the plantation, our uncertain future—and talked pleasantries. Going to the pictures suited us perfectly. On our days off, we would meet at the Rex, a salmon-pink Art Deco cinema near Little India, or at the Pavilion, which was more staid but had the crunchiest chili peanuts in town. I loved how American movie characters always spoke their minds, completely uninhibited. Bogart, Cagney, Astaire, Rogers—we liked them all, but our favorites were the best talkers: Katharine Hepburn and Cary Grant. *Bringing Up Baby* and *Holiday* we must have seen ten times, with undimmed pleasure.

After a while, I could detect in our voices traces of the luscious "transatlantic" diction spoken only on Hollywood soundstages. Li made a habit of tagging on "Say" and "Look" before he began a sentence, like a newsman pitching story ideas to his girl Friday. I never pointed this out to him in case he got self-conscious; I was just happy to know I wasn't the only one mouthing along with our heroes in the dark.

Away from the movie palace, I was far from a wisecracking ingénue. I made a terrible governess. Despite her mother's assurances that she was "bright" and "forthright"—meaning, of course, spoiled and rude—I hated the Chew girl, whose Christian name was Rosalind. The antipathy was mutual. She kicked me twice and called me a witch.

I resigned, having lasted all of five weeks.

Father, of course, was furious, telling me, "Teaching is the only honest work you'll find on this Island!" But quitting liberated my soul to new possibilities. At the tail end of 1940, I was glancing at a newspaper abandoned on the tram when a notice in an old-fashioned, genteel typeface caught my eye:

NURSE/COMPANION SOUGHT FOR AILING GENTLEWOMAN. GOOD PAY.

It was through this fortuitous ad that I would ultimately meet the man who would transform my life.

The old woman lived in a hulking mock Tudor in the Tanglewood estate, painted completely white. As my taxi approached, I felt certain I'd seen it before, perhaps on Father's infamous "bus" tour. Then I realized, with a mixed feeling, that this was the home of the philanthropist Ignatius Wee, patron of St. Anne's. This was where my education at his school had led me: to be his maid.

The grounds were crowded with Indian gardeners tending to the sprawling lawn, by hand. Backs bent over the grass, they made me think of the gleaners in Millet's painting, faceless and powerless. I might soon join their ranks—if I was lucky. It was a far cry from the plantation, where I was once boss. The thought of my decline filled me with anguish as I rang the doorbell.

An elderly Chinese butler led me into the foyer and vanished. I walked myself into the sitting room. The Wee family was Peranakan and possessed that tribe's weakness for all things European. Indeed, someone had gone through considerable trouble doing up the Wees' parlor in high Belle Époque style. Its puffy damask curtains and dragonfly-shaped Tiffany lamps verged on being over the top, but the slim-legged Viennese tables and chairs kept the room elegant—perhaps even too elegant for actual use. A mournful old crucifix (Peranakans tend to be Catholic) completed the scene with its bleeding Christ hovering above the ornamental fireplace, an eerie vision of suffering against all the opulence.

A gong went off, making me jump. It continued until I realized it was just a grandfather clock in the hallway chiming half past eleven. The sound only seemed excessively loud because it was deathly quiet inside the house. Had my client expired in the half day between my inquiry and my arrival?

I'd come prepared to endure a full interview. But the chief of the household staff, a delicate woman of thirty with aristocratic features, instantly smiled her approval when she entered the room and we exchanged our first words. She, too, was from Shanghai and eager to converse in our native tongue.

"Mrs. Wee is expecting you," she said. So my client was still alive. Was she Mrs. Ignatius Wee? I wondered.

The Shanghainese filled me in quickly. The Wees were an old family by Island standards, meaning that they could be traced back almost fifty years—the ancestral patriarch had been an inventory clerk with the East India Company. His grandson, Ignatius Wee, had his hand in many businesses, including a rubber brokerage, and chaired the local Chinese chamber of commerce. Nobody else in the family worked.

"Yes, I know, it's very quiet here," she stage-whispered as she took me along the echoing hallway and up the stairs toward the boudoir, where the ailing Mrs. Wee rested. "They desperately need the laughter of children in this house. But children are afraid to visit. You can't really blame them, can you?"

"What kind of illness does she have?"

"A tumor in her brain. It affects her vision."

Mrs. Wee's lair was the first room at the top of the stairs; it was as big as the downstairs parlor. The thick damask curtains were drawn, leaving it dark as night. I expected to find the old woman asleep. But a light clicked on and there she was—sitting upright in a wingback chair, awake and keen. She wasn't old either, at most sixty.

"Come here." Her voice was more forceful than I'd imagined.

I stepped forward.

"Closer," she purred, stretching out her withered hand. "I'm not contagious."

I obeyed, moving in until she could reach my face. She examined me with her fine, sinewy hands, her fingers running across my cheeks like tarantulas to massage my forehead and temples, her impervious eyes staring fixedly ahead. This was clearly a grande dame accustomed to having both looks and money; even with her infirmity, she was the most forceful woman I'd met—after Mother, of course.

Satisfied with her tactile inspection, she turned to me. "I'm not blind. Not completely, anyway." She said this defiantly, as if I would think less of her if she was. "Your forehead is quite high and slightly protruding."

I held my breath.

"It is an auspicious forehead," she declared. "And you have a Phoenix Pearl. If you don't know what that is, and I suspect you don't because you have done nothing to accentuate it, it is the swelling at the tip of your lips, just below the nose. It's considered very lucky to have one—if you're in the market for a husband. It more than makes up for your nose, which, though symmetrical, is too angular. Do you have any moles?"

"I'm not sure." Her directness perturbed me. I'd never been appraised like a leg of mutton before. "There's a tiny spot in the middle of my left cheek."

"Where? Let me see." She meant let her touch. I leaned forward and she felt for the spot. "Ah."

I froze.

"This is a mixed blessing. It means you will achieve some kind of social prominence. But you will care too much about this, and it will cause you much pain when it is taken away from you." She shook her head gravely. "Although you seem strong and confident on the outside, you have a fatal weakness: You derive your sense of worth from how others perceive you. You crave approval; you want to be adored. Therefore any loss of love or attention affects you aversely—even dangerously."

"You can tell all this from just one little spot?"

"My readings are never wrong. And besides," she added, softening, "I have that very same mole myself."

Indeed she did. But hers was larger, older, uglier. There was a strained silence. I had no idea how to respond; anything I said could be construed as a rejection or an insult. I decided to make myself useful instead.

"Would you like me to read to you, Mrs. Wee?"

"No, no. I don't care for stories." She waved her hand, and I suddenly realized that the Shanghainese had been standing in the room with us all this while. "Cancel the other appointments," she told the girl. "I'm too tired to be choosy. This one will do."

At once, the curtains were pulled apart by the Shanghainese, flooding the room with harsh tropical daylight. Mrs. Wee stared at me, studying my features, and I shivered when I saw her face. She was a dead ringer for Mother. Prettier and more weathered perhaps, yet the resemblance was un-mistakable. At least, from my fading memory.

"You can start today." It wasn't a question or even a request.

"What would you like me to do?" My voice wobbled.

"I would like you to go to bed."

"Now, madam?" It was not even noon.

"I know it's not your accustomed bedtime, but while you are working for us, it shall be. Your responsibility is to watch me sleep. Tonight and every night, until...well, until I no longer require your services." Now she was finished. "Little Girl will show you to your quarters."

The Shanghainese nodded and we departed.

"Why does she call you Little Girl?" I whispered to my compatriot as we descended the creaking stairway.

"I came here when I was seventeen, but because I was so malnourished, Mrs. Wee always insisted I was twelve." She laughed, a little wistfully. "I don't think she even knows my real name."

"Is she from Shanghai, too?"

"Oh no. Her family's been in the Nanyang for at least three generations. Why?"

"She looks a lot like somebody I used to know."

Little Girl smiled ruefully. "Of course she does. Everybody here looks like somebody back home."

She led me through the sweltering, cramped kitchen that had as its centerpiece an enormous stove with eight burners, two of which were actively boiling pots of bone stock. Four porcelain cups and an elaborate glass-tube contraption for brewing coffee sat on the counter waiting to be rinsed. A pair of pigtailed apprentice cooks squatted over day-old newspapers, grimly peeling a hillock of live, wriggling prawns while a wireless hissed out Cantonese madrigals of old China. The girls shuffled aside on their wooden clogs to let us pass, but neither looked up. Even though I was sure they couldn't understand Shanghainese, I waited for them to be out of earshot before I asked my guide the question that had perplexed me most:

"Why does Mrs. Wee want me to watch her sleep?"

"She's terrified of being alone at night, not that she'll ever admit it. That tumor affecting her eyes? It makes her see things that aren't there." Little Girl stopped walking and lowered her voice some more. "She thinks she sees ghosts. It's that old wives' tale, you know, about those close to death being able to see the other side. You must think she's a little unusual, not to say crazy, but—"

"I don't think that at all."

"The good news is you won't have to fight ghosts or anything like that." Little Girl laughed. "All you have to do is sit with her in the dark and reassure her that nothing is there when she wakes up hallucinating. She's just afraid of death, that's all."

"Why doesn't she ask you to do it?"

"I have to run the house, silly! Besides, she's too proud to let me see her in a state of panic." She smiled complacently. "She knows me too well. I'm almost like a daughter to her." Yes, a daughter paid a pittance to be her maid.

We stepped from the well-stocked pantry out into a Chinese-style court-yard. Poles were fluttering with fresh laundry—colorful cotton dresses, chiffon skirts, and tailored white shirts, some quite fashionable and none of which looked like anything Mrs. Wee would wear. She must have had many children, grown children—at least seven or eight from the number of garments I saw.

"How many children does she have?"

"Just two."

A floral-print skirt flew upward in the breeze, catching its hem on a wooden peg. *Rraahrrrr!* I had been spotted by a snarling Rottweiler. Even in its cage, it was threatening, and knew it. The beast was making a big show of its teeth, repeatedly leaping forward and bashing its snout against the mesh until the whole thing rattled.

"Agnes!" Little Girl shouted at the rotten thing, to no avail. The dog didn't like me. Dogs never did. "I'm so sorry. Agnes was trained to attack intruders."

We came to a small white stucco wing that looked as if it was once part of the house but had since been pulled off like a doll's arm and flung aside. The windows had uncompromising bars, which were painted black. They reminded me of the plantation hives—a more benevolent version to be sure, but still close enough to give me the shivers. I knew this was where I would sleep, like a lowly Milkmaid.

A young woman stood on the threshold of the open doorway, sporting the blue tunic and black pants worn by apprentice amahs from Canton. She was staring at us placidly, like the phantom that she was. Little Girl ap-peared not to see her.

"Do you believe in ghosts?" I asked Little Girl.

She gave me a noncommittal smile. "In the old country, maybe. Not here. The Island's too new, too innocent—and it's still mostly jungle. There hasn't been century after century of war and famine. Why would there be any ghosts here?"

"Why do you think Mrs. Wee is so frightened, then?"

Little Girl stepped over the threshold and through the ghost. I saw her shiver slightly and then dismiss the feeling with a shrug. "Sorry, what were you saying?"

"Never mind."

She led me to a room at the far end of the servants' wing. No stacks of bunk beds, thankfully. Just a single bed with fresh linens, a writing desk, and a surprisingly beautiful teak cupboard slightly scuffed from rough use, doubtless an exile from the main house. The room already had an occupant—an old Sikh, sitting on the floor in one corner. My cellmate. He saw me and instantly leapt out the window, through the prison bars.

"Have a good nap," Little Girl said to me as she closed the door. "I sincerely hope you're not afraid of the dark."

Unpacking, I found a yellowed Bible in the cupboard. I picked it up and thumbed through the Old Testament. Fires, plagues, floods—an endless catalog of earthly disasters. I'd forgotten how enjoyably sadistic these stories were. The sun had been down for an hour before I managed to drift off. It was a miracle I slept at all considering the lumpiness of the mattress and the fact that I ordinarily went to bed at midnight.

Three firm knocks on the door roused me at ten o'clock. Little Girl entered before I could tell her to wait.

"You're wanted. Mrs. Wee's about to go to sleep."

She escorted me past the barking caged Rottweiler and back into the moonlit house, where the only sound was the ticking of the grandfather clock.

"Don't expect me to wake you every night or chaperone you like this," Little Girl whispered. "Buy yourself an alarm clock and be ready for her at ten every night. She doesn't appreciate tardiness."

"Yes."

We passed a window that flooded the stairway with the fierce blue glow of the night sky. Little Girl stepped back and, with a cocked eyebrow, assessed my black blouse and matching skirt. "Are you going to a funeral? Why on earth are you dressed like this? She'll take it personally. Wear something less eccentric tomorrow. If you don't have anything, I'll lend you some. Then you're on your own."

"Very well."

"If she wakes up in the middle of the night and starts babbling about ghosts, just stay calm and tell her nothing's there. No matter what, your job is to keep her calm. I'll be honest, it can be terrifying when she starts wailing in the dark, but don't let it bother you. It usually doesn't happen more than, oh, once or twice a night. If she gets . . . difficult, her doctor has approved the use of spirits—cognac and the like. Offer her a few sips, no more. The decanter's on the bureau. Above all, *never* bring up the events of the night with her in the morning. She does hate being embarrassed."

"Not a problem." Strange, but nothing I couldn't handle.

"One final thing. Agnes roams the grounds at night, so I wouldn't leave the main house if I were you. We've both seen how she reacts to you. I'd hate to find you in pieces in the morning." She left me at Mrs. Wee's doorway with a sly smile. "The best of luck."

The room was pitch-black. It took at least a minute for my eyes to tease out the contours from earlier.

"Mrs. Wee?"

"Do you need a formal invitation, girl? Come in. Sit over here."

I was eighteen years old, and yet hearing her orders, I felt like a scared little girl all over again. Her silhouette emerged against the murky gray— she was in her bed and wanted me in the stiff wooden chair by her side.

"Can I give you a nickname?"

"Yes, madam."

"What about Shadow?"

"It's perfectly fine."

"Do you know why I chose Shadow?"

"No, madam."

"Because there's something negative about you, something dark. You know how some people have a radiance about them? Well, you're the opposite of that. You've made no attempt to smile or look cheerful whatsoever. I only took you on, you know, because you said you went to St. Anne's. I called Sister Nesbit and she told me I absolutely had to take you, that you were the brightest Catholic girl on the market and extremely discreet. By the way, I very much dislike your attire. I thought I told you I wasn't blind."

"I won't wear it again, madam."

"Well then, Shadow, I'm about to go to sleep. There's a tray of finger sandwiches on that little table next to your chair, in case you get hungry. But no water. I don't want you running off to the toilet during the night and abandoning me. Understood? All right, then, I'll see you in the morning."

She lay still for a few minutes. Her breathing soon settled into a slow, steady tempo. I'd never known anyone who didn't toil in the fields who could fall asleep so quickly, let alone a woman who was supposed to be in great pain. Morphine, perhaps? It was too dark to read, not that I'd thought to bring along a book. There was now nothing left to do but sit and wait for dawn, and once dawn came, sit and wait until Madam woke up. If this weren't wearying enough, I had to sit perfectly still because, I soon discovered, the wooden chair squeaked each time I shifted my weight, however minutely. Of course, this meant taking a nap was out of the question.

I could only stare at the outline of my new employer. She slept resolutely, flat on her back with her hands clasped over her rib cage, like one pantomiming the act of slumber. Only people in movies slept like this. As for me, my role seemed no different from a watchman at the morgue: I was guarding somebody who was effectively dead. My bored eyes combed the room.

I began to lure shapes out of the velvety black. The four posts defined the boundaries of the bed, the square blob was the dresser, the two squat men in conical hats were table lamps. Suddenly, out of the darkness came a low, ominous rumble. This went on for about half a minute.

Eventually, I realized it was my stomach. It needed food.

I sought out the low table Mrs. Wee had mentioned. It was so close by that I nearly toppled it by reaching out of my chair. Thankfully, she didn't even stir. On the table sat a platter stacked high with small rectangles, each as stiff as a blackboard duster. I picked one up and bit into it. Revolting! It was filled with margarine, ham, and cucumber slices, each layer staler than the one before. The lot of them had probably been sitting there for days. Yet I continued eating. I'd had no dinner, and come to think of it, no lunch before that. I only stopped when the crumbs got caught in my throat—no water—and reached for the decanter of cognac, again careful not to wake my slumbering client. I took a swig from the cut-crystal bottle. The liquor seared a fiery trail down my gullet, but I felt weirdly sated. I sipped again.

My eyes teased out more shapes. The bulging curtains seemed to be harboring silent children. There were about a dozen pillows on the bed, each like a dozing cat. I'd never known one person to need this many pillows, or cats. The grandfather clock gonged—sounding distant one time, intimate the next. Half past ten. Was it really only half past ten? Impossible! These hours were stretching out mercilessly. The job was proving worse than any night watchman's, who could at least enjoy the indelicate freedom to whistle.

Just then, a wave of coolness came cascading down my arms from above. I took it for a shiver of exhaustion. But the once-solid ceiling had suddenly become an open window, revealing an infinite blackness, like the night sky, save for the lack of stars. The edges of this rectangle began to snow. But it wasn't snowflakes that fell; it was numinous dust, akin to the pinpricks one saw after staring too long at the dark.

The dust glowed brighter, turning into sparks I was sure would land on my skin with tiny electric pulses. But as they floated weightlessly down, they vaporized into wisps of smoke that drifted toward the center of the room, forming a white, phosphorescent cross over Mrs. Wee. It was uncannily beautiful, like the precursor to a fairy godmother's entrance or a soprano's closing aria.

Illuminated by the glow, Mrs. Wee stirred like a horse shaking off flies but did not wake. A figure took form in the gathering smoke, directly above the bed. It looked eerily like Mrs. Wee, but younger, in her late thirties. This spectral Mrs. Wee hovered in the air, gazing down placidly. So seamlessly had I blended into the room that the ghost did not register my presence.

Or so I thought.

"Ah, the new girl." She said this without turning to me. Her voice was filled with echoes and sibilance, as if it were being transmitted by radio from far off.

"Stop tormenting yourself," I said. "Everything's fine. Go back to sleep."

It was clear she couldn't hear me. I tried again, lowering my voice into a whisper, to match hers.

"Go back to sleep. There's nobody here."

The spirit continued to hover, still not hearing me.

I tried several approaches until, exasperated, I drew in a long, deep breath. As I released the air from the very bottom of my lungs, my voice became slow, low, old, filling the cold room:

"Sleep, please..."

This time, I broke through.

"I have every right to be here, you know. This used to be my room."

I was so thrilled by my triumph that I almost laughed. But I continued to hold my voice steady, emitting it from deep down in my gut: "It still is, Mrs. Wee."

The spirit now turned to face me.

"Yes, I *am* Mrs. Wee, only not the Mrs. Wee you think. Not the aged Mrs. Wee lying in that bed below, so wracked with guilt she's not had a decent night's sleep in ten years. Oh no."

"You mean then you're her younger self."

The spirit scoffed. "This isn't *A Christmas Carol*, my little ragamuffin. I'm the *original* Mrs. Wee. The first, the true. Claimed by malaria ten years ago, only to find my old-maid sister getting chummy with my lonesome fool of a husband. Damn that Ignatius! What a drab gal she was, too. They married three months later, you know. And there I was, thinking poor Betsy would be alone for the rest of her life."

The dying Mrs. Wee's dead sister. "You've been haunting her since then?"

"Ten years and she never once noticed me. Then all of a sudden, hysteria. Poor girl must be on her last legs."

"Which is why you should leave her be. She's miserable." I tried placation. "Besides, you're in a better place than she is."

"How would you know? Anyone sent you postcards?"

I kept quiet. A sarcastic spirit. Did all ghosts cleave to their old ticks and quirks? If so, she was probably right: Hers wasn't a better place.

I closed my eyes to ignore the ghost—but she had plans of her own.

"How would you like to see an old woman scream?" she said brightly. "I find it can be quite bracing." She floated two steps back and threw her arms up high, preparing to summon her sister.

"There must be something I can do for you," I said as a last resort, "to help settle that score."

"Quid pro quo?" She lowered her arms. "Come to think of it…Yes, of course. Certainly. Could you give me my life back? My husband? My children? She despises my children, you know. Thinks they're spoiled rotten, which is true, but still I'd like them back. Think you can manage all that?"

I grimaced.

"Not so powerful now, are you?"

"Be reasonable."

"What makes you think *reason* has anything to do with this?"

I took a breath. "What else has she got of yours that you want returned?"

"My pigeon's blood earrings." She said this with a speed that seemed to surprise even herself. "Iggy bought them for me on a trip to Hong Kong. He wanted to bury me with them, but Betsy of course told the undertaker no. Said it would be a terrible waste. Not that she ever wore them herself. I think they clashed with her moles." She cackled sourly. "Anyway, there they are."

She hurled a cluster of sparks on Mrs. Wee's teak dresser. I tiptoed over and gingerly opened the top drawer. The exquisite earrings glistened, little cascading lanterns of cut rubies three inches long. They were laid out on a black velvet panel that flaunted their shimmer even more. In comparison, the rest of the jewelry in the drawer was dowdy—cultured pearls and generic jade teardrops.

"What should I do with them?"

"Use your imagination. Failing that, a burial in the back garden should do."

Easy. "Consider it done. Will this give you peace?"

"Beggars can't be choosers."

I grunted.

The ghost threw me a playful smile. "But it's the thought that counts."

Daylight was seeping through the cracks of the curtains. It was dawn. Though it only felt like minutes, I must have been negotiating for hours.

As more light poured into the room, I gazed at the stack of sandwiches. Each and every one was covered in a blanket of gray mold.

The courtyard was abuzz at dawn. Agnes the Rottweiler was in her cage, but this did not stop her from baying at me as I walked toward the servants' wing. It was as if she could smell the ruby earrings in my brassiere.

The Tamil groundskeeper, Subramaniam, was crouching by the dog with a flap of bloody sirloin. Evidently he also had the loathsome task of feeding the monster. Nodding to me apologetically, he said, "This dog, ah, very unpredictable." He extended his right hand and showed me the awkward dent where chewed-off flesh had been sewn up by a back-alley surgeon.

While Subramaniam's men tended the grounds, Saudah the Sumatran washerwoman rolled up her sleeves and began running water into two enormous basins. She and Subramaniam traded morning greetings—"*Selamat!*" "*Salaam!*"—and then she waved at me with a hand coated in suds. Happy to be included, I waved back.

The servants all seemed to get along, except for one notable exception: Issa the wordless Bugis chauffeur. He had just begun his slow daily ritual of washing and waxing the family's black Bentley. Issa looked at no one, spoke to no one, and yet seemed perfectly attuned to every exchange going on around him. The others left him alone. Just watching him lean across the car, with his warrior's physique and long, black mane, I understood why. He wore thick gold cuffs on both ears, proud emblems of his seafaring origins—pirate ancestors, undoubtedly—and his watchful, hooded eyes made it clear he did not wish to be disturbed. I thought I saw him take a fleeting glance at me but seconds later was sure I'd been wrong.

I scurried past the lot of them, the ruby earrings icy against my flesh.

The rose garden at the far end of the servants' wing was hidden and unattended. Using a trowel that had been left in a flower pot, I dug a small hole at the base of the reddest rosebush and buried the earrings. Red under red, for symbolism's sake.

Heading back to my room, I sneaked a peek at the caged Agnes. She was sitting on her haunches, quietly watching me. Good dog, good doggy.

The thing about civilized ghosts, I thought with enormous relief, was that they were reasonable—unlike the ones in the jungle with their irrational rage. And now, now I could *speak* to them!

Once in my room, I shooed away the harmless old Sikh. "Privacy, man!" I said in my new gut-whisper, and then fell into victorious slumber. I'd survived my first night.

Watching Mrs. Wee became a breeze. The ghost did not appear that night, the next night, nor the night after that. Burying those earrings had indeed brought peace to her dead sister. Emboldened by my success, I toted slim books, hidden on my person, as I reported to duty each night. Once my client fell asleep, I settled behind the damask curtains and read by moonlight. This way, I always had Baudelaire near and dear, his *Flowers of Evil* helping to soak up the lonely hours between ten and seven.

> *Sometimes I feel my blood is spilling out*
> *in sobs, the way a fountain overflows.*

After a week, Little Girl took me aside. She was all smiles as usual, but I sensed a touch of jealousy. Shanghai girls are skilled at camouflaging poisonous thoughts, but we're equally gifted at spotting them.

"I don't know what you've been doing, but it's obviously working," she said. "I haven't seen Mrs. Wee so calm, so refreshed in the mornings. You must work some kind of jungle magic."

After this barbed praise, she handed me my first pay envelope, the largest sum I'd ever held in my young life.

I celebrated my small triumph by taking Li out for a lunch of Russian shashlik at the Troika on High Street, in the heart of the shopping district. Russian imperial cuisine was all the rage on the Isle because it had been all the rage in Shanghai ten years before, and it didn't matter that the version we got here was prepared by Hainanese cooks who'd never once set foot in Leningrad.

The restaurant's circular driveway was filled with deluxe sedans—gleaming Cadillacs, Lincolns, and Studebakers—their Malay drivers chatting and smoking away in the shade of a banyan tree. Li and I slouched toward the entrance, feeling underdressed and underchauffeured. Once inside, the maître d's surliness did nothing to assuage our unease.

Li turned back toward the door. "Let's just scram."

I grabbed his arm. "I'm treating you to lunch and I say we stay."

We were seated at a romantic horseshoe booth, wedged awkwardly against the music stage. Two elderly, bearded Jews were perched on bar stools, strumming balalaikas as the lunch crowd chattered on, paying them no attention.

Minutes later, ironically, it was I who became eager to leave.

"I went to see him last week," Li said. "He needs us."

My stomach tightened. "Can we not discuss him until we finish eating?"

"Why do you hate him so much?"

"Why don't *you*?"

He sighed as if I were being childish. "You have to know what's happening."

"Can't it wait? We're celebrating."

But Li couldn't wait. He launched into a story that I only partially heard. "He's got a stall at Wonder World now . . . Takes water, melts rock sugar in it, then throws in some pounded-up agar. Calls it *bird's nest water* . . . has a sign extolling its virtues and all that. Profit's not too bad, but not great either."

"So?"

"Thing is, he's in debt. Deep in debt. He owes the Triads. Seems like everyone in Wonder World owes them something."

"That's his problem."

"No. It's ours."

"It never ends, does it?" I stopped a waiter passing by our table. "Please bring me your most expensive vodka. It needn't be any good—just the most expensive." I would sooner squander my pay on drink than give Father a cent. Li shook his head.

When my drink arrived—my first vodka and it was a generous double shot—I downed it at one go, my eyes fixed defiantly on Li. My throat burned worse than after Mrs. Wee's cognac. I coughed, annoyed at myself for showing weakness.

Li sucked in his breath, waiting to resume, and intensify, his lecture. So when the same waiter walked by again, I asked for more vodka. The waiter gave me a patronizing chortle, but I was determined not to be cowed. "Now," I barked.

Li leaned into the table. "At Wonder World they're hiring psychics, clairvoyants, that sort of thing. They're looking for girls who can talk to spirits—or who can act like they can." He looked at me significantly. "Pay's not bad. And it's not all that shady."

"*Not all that shady?*"

He pursed his lips. "We both know you . . . I mean, the pontianak . . ."

"You saw nothing. You were delirious."

When my second drink arrived, Li tried to snatch it away. I stopped him with my napkin and gulped the vodka down before he could do it again. The alcohol burned, even more harshly, but I was starting to like it.

"Why don't *you* volunteer?" I said. "Why does it have to be me?"

"Because"—he paused—"they want to attract male customers."

"You can go to hell!"

The balalaika duo stopped and the room went silent. I had shouted perhaps more loudly than I was aware of. I lowered my voice, and the musicians, after exchanging wry looks, resumed their plucking.

"I'm not doing anything for that man. He's brought this upon himself."

"At the end of the day, he's still our father," Li said quietly. "At least he's always predictable. Even in his failings. He never means any harm. He's not even asked us for any help. But I've seen him—I've seen how hard he struggles."

I reached into my handbag and slapped a handful of change onto the table. "That's all he's getting from me!"

As the waiter arrived bearing two sizzling platters, I sprang to my feet and pushed past the cabals of smug businessmen. The exit, to the exit. Once clear of the restaurant's driveway, I staggered breathlessly down the street until I caught up with the nearest tram.

On the East-West Express, a passenger at the back of the car peered at me strangely; I glared back at him. His forehead was stamped with a funny birthmark—pink and shaped like the male member, only partially concealed by his cheap fedora. I was reminded immediately of our servant boy Cricket. Little Girl was right: Everybody here did look like somebody back home.

It was only when I reached the Wee mansion and tumbled drunkenly into bed that I realized I'd abandoned poor Li with the restaurant bill.

In the middle of my sleep, Little Girl burst into the room. My head was throbbing. Reality was returning to me only in patches. It was still afternoon. I could hear Agnes barking furiously in her cage; farther off, Mrs. Wee was barking from hers.

"She says you stole her earrings!" Little Girl searched my face for telltale hints of guilt, anxious because she felt responsible for my hire. "You better not have!"

Seconds later, she was shunted aside by two aged Chinese servants

I'd never seen before, one male and one female, who began rummaging through my things, starting with the most intimate. They shook out my undergarments one by one. Neither stopped to address me. Little Girl ran out of the room with red-rimmed eyes, looking betrayed.

"So many white devil books," the male servant muttered to the female in the most toxic Cantonese. "What does a girl hope to do with this many books?"

"They warned us she was peculiar," she replied.

They found nothing, of course. When the ruckus was over, I was summoned to Mrs. Wee's lair. The familiar route up the staircase was now made strange by three new players lining the way, each eyeing me with varying degrees of skepticism. The family. Because we'd kept different hours, this was my auspicious introduction to the Wees. Here was gray-haired Ignatius Wee, the short, compact man I'd mistaken for a butler when he let me in on my first day, dressed now in shirtsleeves and possessing an air of strange detachment. Then his two children—a tall boy about my age whose lazy posture did nothing to diminish his striking good looks, and a younger teenage girl, plump and scowling.

The family had emerged from the shadows to put me on trial. It was as good a time as any, I told myself, to get acquainted with this invisible tribe. I was no thief, after all. They watched me walk into Mrs. Wee's room and followed, as if they didn't trust me not to pick their pockets from behind. Only the boy had the decency to seem embarrassed by all this. He shot me a lightning smile, then glanced away. Little Girl and the four house servants, all potential witnesses, trailed the family group.

"I trusted you, Shadow!" Mrs. Wee screamed from her bed. She was still in the silk pajamas of the previous night. "Where did you take my earrings?"

The proprietary way she said "my earrings" only made me dislike her more.

"Has the cat got your tongue? I asked you a question, girl!" She flung one of her frilly pillows at me, which the boy intercepted with athletic speed.

"Auntie Betsy," the boy spoke up, his voice surprisingly deep, "they found nothing in her room. You can't just accuse her like that."

"She's probably sold them," interjected the sullen sister. "These Shanghai girls are very cunning. She may even have a partner in crime." She glared at Little Girl, who withered visibly.

"Daniel, Violet has a point." Mrs. Wee gave the boy the evil eye. "If you were thinking with your brain and not some baser part of you, you wouldn't be quite so quick to defend this eel. She's probably taken my earrings to some pawnshop in Chinatown to pay off her father's gambling debt. Who knows, she may even be in cahoots with the Triads. Am I right, Shadow?"

I looked away, furious. I was prepared to resign, rather than face such indignity. The boy, Daniel, met my eyes again for a flicker of a second. I could tell he was on my side, but he didn't seem forceful enough to change anything.

The paterfamilias, Ignatius Wee, had been standing by wordlessly up to this point. Finally, he spoke. "Let's not fling about accusations." He sounded like an actor who was reading his lines, dutifully but without conviction. His accent was silky and posh, and the words seemed odd coming from the mouth of someone who looked as unassuming as a Chinatown rice merchant. "I'll make some phone calls to a few jewelers in town. If those earrings surface, they're sure to know. So let me go to work on this. Until then, let's all keep our heads about us. And by this I include you, Betsy. You really do need the rest."

"But my earrings," Mrs. Wee wailed, "you don't know how much they're worth!"

"I *do* know exactly," Mr. Wee said. "I bought them. Now, hush. Please." He mouthed the word *morphine* to Little Girl. She nodded in acquiescence.

I was escorted back to my room by the old servant couple. Little Girl appeared a few minutes later, her face tense.

"Mr. Wee has decided that you'll be barred from leaving the compound until the matter is resolved." She had taken on his stiff way of speaking—it let me know the order had come from the horse's mouth. "Obviously, you're not expected to watch Mrs. Wee."

"But you believe me, don't you?"

"Believe what? You stood there like a deaf mute, not saying a single word. How should I know what to believe?"

I heard my door lock behind her and the key withdrawn. Once again, I was alone.

Those "white devil books" helped to stave off my restlessness. And when reading proved ineffective, I tried to engage the old Sikh ghost in conversation. (The feeling wasn't mutual; he eventually fled for good.) Little Girl came by twice a day, at idiosyncratic times, bearing cold leftovers and bitter sighs, convinced I had ruined her good name simply because we'd come from the same town.

To my surprise, Daniel, too, came by to visit the sorry detainee. He brought cheese-flavored biscuits wrapped in silk handkerchiefs, which their oils instantly stained, and an adventure novel about American frontiersmen that bored me silly from paragraph one.

"It's one of my favorite books," he'd said. Here was a boy who'd never understand me in a million years.

In spite of this, I found myself looking forward to his next visit, cherishing the kind impulses and apologetic eyes that seemed to promise he'd be a stronger man someday—if only one had the time to wait.

In my prison cell, I had nothing but time.

— 8 —

Limbo

THREE DAYS OF WAITING, three days of indecision on the part of my captors.

Mr. Wee had heard nothing from his jewelry contacts, yet with a rich man's arrogance felt entitled to keep me locked up anyway. I had no choice. Were I to mention the ghost of his late wife, he'd surely have me carted off to the Woodbridge asylum.

I slept as much as I could, curled up facing the wall, refusing food, refusing drink, and finally refusing all communication, even with Daniel. I prayed for many things—escape, vindication, revenge—and day bled into night. For hours on end, I stared at a vertical crack in the paint, twisting and buckling like a tectonic wrinkle along a white and barren plain.

Finally on the third day, I was exhausted even from looking. I closed my eyes.

A tickle in my nose roused me. This became a burn. Liquid had filled my nostrils. I was breathing in water. The second I opened my eyes, raindrops, plummeting from the black sky like diaphanous bombs, blinded me with their explosions. My arms were heavy and cold—no, my *clothes* were heavy and cold, completely soaked through. The coppery smell around me was . . . earth. It was mud I was lying in, mud weighted down in rain!

I was being buried alive. I took a gulp of air and sprang upright to battle my undertaker. But there wasn't a soul. I was standing in the back garden somehow, alone.

Free.

Spotting the rosebushes, I knew the first thing I had to do. I reeled toward the reddest one and collapsed on my hands and knees, digging at its base with my fingers. The rain sabotaged these efforts, creating a swamp where I was expecting a treasure. I dug under a second bush, then a third, nearly uprooting them, and was ready to howl when someone—something—howled for me instead.

Agnes!

Five feet behind me, her bared fangs glistened a fair warning. Her black fur, slick in the rain, gave her the hauteur of a panther—a beauty she lacked in dry weather.

I knew that if I stayed very still, there was a chance she'd let me walk away. But in panic I chose flight. I threw a fistful of mud in her mean eyes and made a dash for the servants' quarters.

Her panting quickened behind me, right at my heels. Thirty yards had never seemed so far. I could almost feel her teeth tearing into my back. Then, all of a sudden, the sound of her footsteps were replaced by frightened whimpering. I kept on running.

The servants' wing had been transformed. Raindrops slid off its walls as if the building had been dipped in oil. But the door was ajar. I kicked it open and stepped into darkness.

The erasure of all sensations was instant and absolute. There was no Agnes, no rain, no roses. No temperature, even. My ears quickly grew used to the silence and began to pick up new sounds. I heard—or did I intuit?—the liquid whoosh of fresh blood coursing through my veins after a systolic kick from my heart. No, it was the boom and shush of ocean waves in the distance.

A light appeared far away and the ground beneath me began to rock, gently. My muscles, shifting weight to keep my balance, seemed to already know the rhythm.

The spot of light grew and a man stepped into it, celestial radiance flaring at his head.

"Hallo." He sounded as if he were at the end of an enormous, empty chamber.

The enormous and empty chamber materialized. Gilded in sumptuous Art Deco detail—blue peacocks everywhere—it made even the Rex cinema look shabby. I dragged my feet over the plush, endless burgundy carpet.

"Step out from the shadows . . . Pandora."

It all came back to me. We were in the ballroom aboard the SS *Prosperity*.

Mr. Odell walked steadily toward me in a gray silk suit and a sky-blue tie. On his feet were black leather wingtips. More suave than I'd known him to be, he also hadn't aged a day since our last encounter.

"Mr. Odell!"

I saw my reflection in the brass wainscoting. Alas, I had not traveled back in time. I was every bit my nineteen years, yet perfectly clean and dry.

"So you remember me."

"Of course!" Oh, the surging joy of this surprise reunion.

"I have to thank you for putting me in this suit." He tugged at his lapels. "It's a little Cary Grant for me, but I'll try my best to live up to it."

Before I could respond to this strange remark, I felt firm pressure against my right heel. This grew into a cold tightening around the ankle, as if a snake were coiling around it. I looked down and saw a green vine, thickening: The entire wall behind me was being engulfed by a botanical monster that was spilling and spreading across the floor.

I looked to Mr. Odell. "Where are we? What's happening?"

"Step away from the wall and come toward me. I have things to tell you."

"It's got my foot."

"Just walk."

He was right. The instant I lifted my foot, the vine surrendered its hold. The green swarm withered and began to recede.

"Don't look back. Just keep walking."

"Have I died?"

"Again with the morbidity! Oh, Pandora. You are not a ghost."

I stepped off the carpet and onto the polished, intricate parquet of the dance floor. We met in the center, beneath a hulking chandelier that looked like a tarantula made of crystal swords. The foot-long spears clinked against one another as the ship rocked. If any of them plunged, we'd be finished.

"They're not going to fall," Mr. Odell said, his eyes calm. "Trust me."

It was shocking how attractive I found him—effortlessly gallant, effortlessly wise, yet with no trace of sanctimony or arrogance. I couldn't have gauged it at the time of our first encounter, but he looked to be about thirty. Little crow's-feet around his eyes accentuated his smile, giving him an old-world type of grace I'd seen only in the movies, never on the Isle. He was the platonic ideal of a man at his peak—handsome, courteous, kind.

He extended a hand. Such a manly hand he had, too. This was the first time we'd actually touched. The faintest hint of a clarinet sounded, then a bassoon, then strings, emerging out of the waves. An orchestra had started up for us from some unseen pit.

"Shall we?" he said.

I took his hand and he glided me into a waltz. My first dance. He placed one hand delicately on my waist, palm first, followed by fingers, and I leaned in toward him until I felt the sweet warmth of his breath on my forehead. If I made a terrible partner, he gave no indication of it. We moved as if this was second nature, as if we'd danced together a thousand times.

"When you told me you saw little Rachel in the swimming pool, I realized we were kindred spirits. You see, some of us are born more sensitive than others."

"Sensitive?"

"Yes. That's what it essentially is. We *feel* things more deeply. We identify with those we have absolutely nothing in common with; we take on great causes, both noble and hopeless. We fall perhaps too willingly into love. Again, both nobly and hopelessly. To put it simply, some of us are compelled by what others like to dismiss as passion but that I prefer to call *humanity*."

I could have kissed him. Here was somebody who understood me without me having to explain myself. I would have swooned if the music hadn't slowed from andante to largo, and he relaxed his grip on my waist.

"In my case, it was hereditary," he continued, "a fissure or a fault, if you will, passed down through the generations like a goblet filled to the brim with wine. Once in a while, there are spills along the way. My grandmother was a seer, but she always took it as a curse. It was important for her to not stand out. She grew up in old Russia, you see." He laughed dryly. "They never much liked Jews there in the first place."

A gong boomed, drowning out the orchestra, and the music stopped. The chandelier jangled from the vibrations, glass swords clashing above our heads.

"Short dance, wasn't it?" He smiled. "Pity, I had so much more to tell you."

Golden rods of sunlight now shot through pinholes in the walls, and as more and more burned through, the holes blossomed and merged. Bathed in light, the peacock room began fading and wilting rapidly, its decorative papers curling and crumbling off the walls, revealing a jungle of vines. I held on to Mr. Odell as the dance floor bowed under our feet, spitting out wood splints with each new contraction.

"No!" I yelled, defiant that my will—or his—would overpower whatever was causing this. "Make it stop! I don't want you to go!" I clung harder to his arms.

And I kissed him.

His lips felt spongy, porous, and cold. Above us, the mammoth chandelier was disintegrating. Powdered glass poured down upon our heads like the most melancholy snow. His body, too, had turned spongy and porous, and soon my fingers were slipping right through him, as if he were made of sand. Tears of anger gushed down my face.

"Why aren't you fighting this?"

He smiled. "Control your emotions, Pandora. This is all happening in your mind."

My mind? "But how will I find you again?"

"As always." His voice grew faint, though his eyes were as vivid and sincere as ever. "I have tea at the Metropole with my wife... The last Sunday of every month..."

Vines, thick and green, sped across the room from the far wall and snatched him out of my arms in one swift tug, whipping him in the air as if he weighed nothing at all. My friend didn't struggle; he didn't even shield his face. He simply martyred himself to the unknown. The placidity of his surrender took my breath away.

"Mr. Odell!"

The instant he vanished into the bleached-out horizon, the room went black.

The chiming of the gong grew deafening, its mournful vibrations pounding through my entire body and making my teeth rattle.

Suddenly, I was awake—really awake this time, with all the earlier layers of wakefulness peeled away.

I was indoors, lying on my bed in the servants' quarters, curled on my side. I must have drifted off like this, staring at the fissure in the wall. Daylight had come, but only just, and the rain was gone.

The room was thick with the damp, monsoonal odor of mildew. It was an aggressive smell, one that seemed to crawl up my nostrils and down to my lungs. All of a sudden, I realized I was shivering. A chill ravaged me to the bones. I huddled under the bedclothes, watching my breath turn to mist and waiting for the tremors to subside.

Seconds later, the door opened: Little Girl. She stared at me with a mix of relief and cold suspicion.

"Mrs. Wee is dead."

I was too shocked to respond.

"Did you hear what I just said? Mrs. Wee has died."

She stomped toward me and yanked off my blanket, then leapt back with a gasp. "What happened to you?"

I looked down and was every bit as stunned as she. My arms and legs were clumped in muck, as if I had been crawling in a swamp on all fours. Mud coated the sheets like chocolate pudding.

"I was caught in the..." I couldn't finish that sentence without sounding like a lunatic. That crack in the wall. I looked at it again. Had it grown? Could I really have...

The gears in Little Girl's head shifted. "I tell you what," she said, glancing over her shoulder to make sure nobody was at the door. "Go and clean yourself up. I'll get rid of these filthy sheets. You have a major task before you this morning."

I wasn't sure I wanted to know her meaning.

"You are to clean Mrs. Wee's body before the children wake up."

Mr. Wee had in fact delegated the cleaning to Little Girl, of course, but she let the unwelcome task fall to me. It might have been blackmail, but I was thankful to be let out of my cell and given this opportunity to redeem myself.

When I had trouble lifting the pail of soap water and carrying it into the main house, I remembered I hadn't eaten in days. It must have taken me ten minutes to climb up those stairs.

Someone had stopped the grandfather clock to mark Mrs. Wee's passing. The house stood silent, suspended in mortuary time.

I approached Mrs. Wee's boudoir, and seeing her on the bed where she'd always lain, I felt a twinge of déjà vu. I half expected her to sit up and start hurling accusations, but of course there could be no more scolding, no more phrenological exams, no more moldy sandwiches. Light fell on her face from the pair of alabaster lamps that stood over her like watchful cherubs.

It was clear why Mr. Wee didn't want his children seeing their aunt—and stepmother—in this state. Her eyes were open and they stared skyward at the spot where her sister's ghost had been. Her mouth was agape, the purplish lips cracked with dryness. Could she have died midsentence?

Her body formed the shape of a cross. During her final moments, she must have kicked off the sheets. Her hands dangled over the sides of the bed. These were the hands that had examined my face, yet I'd never taken a clear look at them before. They were puny, shriveled little things, like the talons of some helpless bird.

When I brought her hands to rest at the center of her chest, I discovered that she was not yet completely cold. Her eyelids, when I pulled them down like window shades, still possessed the elasticity of life. In a few short hours, the disfigurement of death would claim her, but until that time, when the last drop of her blood turned black, she still belonged to our world. I swabbed away the tears drying into a film on her cheeks, but my many attempts to secure her gaping mouth failed. Finally I propped up her lower jaw with a leather-bound Bible, hoping it would stay closed when rigor mortis set in.

"There wasn't much pain in the end."

I turned. Mrs. Wee was behind me, sitting in the creaky chair that had once so tyrannized me.

I braced myself for recriminations, but she looked strangely relaxed, if very pale.

"You see me, don't you?" She clucked her tongue. "I knew I was right to call you Shadow."

"Are you . . ." I was at a loss. "All right?"

"Although I didn't choose the precise moment, it felt inevitable all the same." There was no trace of bitterness in her voice. "In the end, it was very much like falling asleep. No doubt you've heard this countless times, but really that's what it's most like." She stepped forward and looked down at her own body with the nostalgic tenderness of someone revisiting a beloved old doll.

"Mrs. Wee," I said neutrally. "Can I explain about the earrings? I didn't steal them."

"Oh, don't fret over those things. They're nothing—nothing!" She smiled for the first time, and I saw that she looked nothing like Mother.

She walked back to the chair and sat down, sighing, her face now bearing a sudden gravity for what I sensed was her imminent departure. Her eyes combed the room, taking in its contours for one last time, before returning again to her own lifeless form.

"Do you want me to convey any last words to your family?"

She mused for a second and said, with surprising finality, "No."

"Nothing?" I looked back at the body and thought of the unfinished sentence that had tried to escape her lips. "Are you sure?"

"It's all nothing!" She had already begun to evaporate. A twinge of regret crossed her features, but she waved it away. "None of it matters. None of it."

And then she was forever gone.

"Apology accepted," I said to the empty chair.

I turned back to the body. Her face seemed different—calm, even benevolent. I removed the Bible from her neck, and this time her mouth stayed closed.

The peace didn't last long. A fly buzzed in from the doorway and landed boldly on my late employer's nose. For some reason, this moved me to tears.

When Mrs. Wee was properly arranged, I went to Mr. Wee's study as Little Girl had instructed and knocked on the door. The widower was eating a slice of toast at the desk as he listened to an ominous report being read on the wireless. I thought his hair looked whiter than before, but this was more likely a trick of the morning light. Listening to the news and eating breakfast—was this how he mourned his wife? He looked up as I entered.

"The forecast is not good. War is coming down the Pacific. I can feel it." He spoke remorsefully, as if he had a hand in preventing damnation. He looked at me and sighed, perhaps about to apologize for my days of imprisonment. I cast my eyes away to make it easier for him, but he simply wiped the sides of his mouth with his napkin and stood up to hand me the breakfast tray. "I'll wake the children."

As he passed me in the doorway, he muttered, in a tone of sincere, if sublimely understated, gratitude, "Your help is very much appreciated."

Later, while I was emptying the pail of soap water into the courtyard drain, Little Girl came up behind me, disgruntled, refusing to look me in the eye. I expected yet more bad news, but no.

"Mr. Wee says you're free now," she said, then added in a poisonous key as she strode away, "even though you may still be a thief, for all we know."

My bitterness toward the old man vaporized. Once more I had the future to think about. I needed to speak to Odell: at the Metropole, on the last Sunday of the month! Why did it have to take a shocking hallucination for me to think of him?

"What's the date today?" I asked Saudah, the washerwoman.

"Tuesday, the seventh."

I dried my hands on my skirt and sprinted to my room. On my calendar, I marked out the special Sunday with a secret pencil dot. It was less than three weeks away.

That evening, after a full day spent making funeral arrangements, Mr. Wee invited me to join him and his children for dinner out. The news was again relayed to me by Little Girl, and from the way she spat the words out, it was obvious she had never been asked on such excursions.

To show my respect, I wore dark clothes and was startled to see that the Wee children had dressed exuberantly—not a stitch of black between them. Daniel shot me a bashful smile while his sister studied her unsightly, chewed-on nails, actively avoiding my gaze.

"I'm so glad you could join us," Mr. Wee said, gesturing for me to squeeze into the Bentley alongside his children. "We're going to my favorite restaurant."

Mitzi's was an unfussy eating house in Chinatown that specialized in boiled chicken and rice—food wholesome enough to be consoling yet not so extravagant that gossips could accuse Mr. Wee of celebrating his wife's passing. It was a place even Father could afford to go—that is, if he hadn't lost all his spare change to loan sharks and gangsters. Knowing that Mr. Wee liked eating at Mitzi's humanized him in a way that his odd reticence could never do.

Issa the Bugis chauffeur drove us in the silence that seemed to be his trademark. I was wedged between Daniel and the car door and felt a spark of static when his silk pants rubbed against my nylon stocking. With equally swift reactions, we quickly pulled ourselves apart.

At the crowded restaurant, I watched Mr. Wee's eyes scan the room. There was nobody here that he knew, and his mood relaxed. He sat back in the booth and sucked in the oily fragrance of chicken and ginger-garlic sauce that was swirling around us.

"In the grand scheme of things, what's one pair of earrings, right?" he said, urging me to dig into the communal platter of chicken. "There are more important things in life, like family and food."

I took the meal to be his apology.

Daniel kept shooting me little smiles when our gazes met. His sister, however, hadn't softened a bit. She spent the evening studying my every move with narrowed eyes, ready to see nefarious intent in every little thing I did.

The strange thing was that neither Mr. Wee nor his children seemed particularly upset by the loss of Mrs. Wee. Perhaps they had shed their tears in private and were now putting on a brave public face as a group, or perhaps the woman had been ill for so long that her death had come as a relief. Which it was, I couldn't tell.

I would later learn that this was how most upper-class Chinese—especially Island-assimilated ones—behaved in the aftermath of a tragedy; theirs was a cultural marriage between Confucian reserve and the British stiff upper lip. They had a pathological reluctance to show emotion in front of others and would sooner appear heartless than chance the smallest loss of face.

In spite of Mr. Wee's insistence that I take the most succulent piece of chicken thigh, I gravitated to the boniest parts—the wing tips and neck—not out of deference to my hosts but out of familiarity. They were what I'd always eaten. Violet watched my choices, doubtless suspecting me of calculated modesty, while Daniel appeared charmed by what he took to be my provincial ways.

"There's more than enough to go round," he said, putting a plump drumstick on my plate with his chopsticks.

Violet began muttering about her exams. She hurried her father to finish so she could return to her books. Plus there was Agnes. The dog had been having trouble breathing since morning.

"Bad things are happening all at once," she said, looking pointedly at me. "It's as if a plague is upon us. The Black Plague."

"Oh, stop it," snapped her father. "Now you're sounding like Aunt Betsy, God rest her acrid soul."

"Well," the girl replied, "*you* married her."

We arrived home to see Subramaniam's arm jammed down the throat of the whimpering, shuddering Rottweiler in the daredevil style of a lion tamer. Violet's scowl melted into worry and her eyes pooled with tears.

"The dog wheezing all day," Subramaniam told us. "I thought sure must be something stuck inside." With the improvisatorial zeal of a former plantation worker, he had force-fed her a chalky cocktail of Saudah's bleach while the family was out.

The poor beast had retched, and the first ruby earring materialized. Getting the other one was more work—its hook was caught in the flesh of her esophagus, and it was this that Subramaniam was now rooting for, his brows knitted in anguish as his fingers plumbed the mucilaginous well. When he surfaced with the second earring, hand and treasure both coated in slime, Agnes belched so loudly it even made me blush. Wearily, Subramaniam flung his find onto a white towel next to its vomit-encrusted twin.

Violet's face crumpled. "Who fed these to her? Agnes would never eat them!" She lunged instinctively to embrace the dog, then stopped herself, clearly not wanting to display any weakness while I was present.

"Actually, I remember seeing Agnes run into the house one afternoon," said Daniel. "It's quite possible she went upstairs."

"What? And rummaged through Aunt Betsy's drawers?" The indignation in her voice returned. "Agnes *never* goes inside the house. Even you know that."

"Vi, you weren't there, so you can't possibly—"

"Daniel," Violet growled, her eyes darting to me, "don't you be a fool."

"Vi, darling." Mr. Wee sighed. "Nobody cares about the earrings. They're back. No harm done. All right, my dear?"

"I'm not talking about the damn earrings, Daddy. I'm talking about the *truth*! Have you *all* gone mad?"

Her pride intact, Violet charged into the house, flinging off her patent-leather shoes like a petulant child.

"Don't worry, it's not your fault," Daniel said, and gave my elbow a firm squeeze. "My sister always overreacts; it's just her way. Aunt Betsy affected her more than she cares to admit. She'd been crying all afternoon. Besides, in the grand scheme of things..."

In the grand scheme of things, I had my reunion with Odell to look forward to—and the date was getting closer by the hour. But in the smaller, more immediate, scheme of things, my thoughts kept returning to Daniel's fib about Agnes and the way he had touched my elbow.

It was no accidental brush but a surprisingly hard squeeze, as if he had no idea how strong his grip was, or else he did and was trying to convey more with one caress than propriety allowed. That firmness, coupled with his deep, gentle voice—the voice that carried a chivalric lie in my defense—proved to be a seductive combination. As he removed his hand, his fingertips had grazed my forearm, leaving in their wake a trail of tiny goose bumps.

That night in bed, I imagined Daniel with me, unbuttoning my top and fondling my breasts. I let his hands run down my belly to the core of my longing. I felt his phantom lips lock with mine, the both of us gasping in tandem as our tongues probed and clashed. I hadn't had such craving in years; I'd forgotten how hungry I was, how starved for love. Li had been my first and only, and that misadventure had left me so confused that I tried to expel all such feeling, but it hadn't diminished my desires. On crowded trams and buses, brushes against good-looking men would reignite it in me, but they were mere sparks, always extinguished by the next stop.

With a single touch, Daniel unlocked my deepest need. I tussled with my amorous mirage all night, eventually drifting off as the blue shadow of dawn broke.

Hours later, a knock on my door woke me. I sighed, dreading the appearance of Little Girl and more of her sour insinuations. But it was Daniel.

"'Morning." His eyes lingered on my pajama top before turning bashfully away. "Oh, pardon me."

"It's fine. I'm awake."

"I have some good news for you, or what I think is good news." He turned back to face me, smiling. "Father said you can move into the main house. We have a spare room. Not Aunt Betsy's room, of course, but another one we keep aside for guests. You can stay there until you find new employment...not that there's any real hurry."

"Why's he doing this?"

"I'd hate to speak for the old man, but I think he feels terrible about the whole earrings debacle. It's his way of making it up to you. He'll also continue paying your wages until you're ready to leave."

This sounded overgenerous for Mr. Wee—or any employer. The rich were notoriously stingy here, and the Island was still recovering from the Depression. "You talked him into it, didn't you?"

"I didn't do a thing," Daniel said, his blushing cheeks belying his words. "Anyway, the room's ready, anytime you want to move over. It's the one next to mine." He turned to leave, and my books stacked by the door triggered a new thought. "There's a bookshelf, too."

"Thanks." I'd already begun mentally packing my things—and undressing him.

"Father means well, you know. He really does. We all do."

"And thanks for what you said about Agnes being in the house."

"Anything to calm Vi down. She can be a bit too much." He beamed me a look of affection, then quickly glanced away.

Once he was gone, I was mortified to find that my pajama top had been unbuttoned, revealing my breasts to Daniel in all their naked glory.

Seconds later, this shame grew into pride: I want that boy. I shall win that boy and change my life.

I moved into the house that afternoon. Over the following two weeks, defying the watchful suspicion of both Violet and Little Girl, Daniel and I grew close—if not physically, then magnetically. It was a mysterious evolution because we had nothing in common; a boy like Daniel really had no business spending time with a girl like me.

There were the obvious differences in class, but the personal divides were greater still. Unlike me, he was supremely gracious. I'd never heard him raise his deep, mellifluous voice against anyone. And except for his one white lie, which I carried with me like a verbal valentine, he was free of secrets and intrigue. One read him easily, not like an open book perhaps, but more like a weather vane. His thick eyebrows registered every little change in mood; his cheeks flushed at the slightest moral discomfort. Also unlike me, he looked like a movie star, a bona fide matinee idol. He had fairer skin than I did; deep-set, expressive eyes;

a high nose; and succulent, kissable lips. His head was crowned with lustrous hair that curled naturally at the ends, a prized coiffure in a society where most had hair that was dull, straight, and as black as the night.

Daniel cut a dashing figure doing the most mundane things—walking down the hall, nodding to the servants, even reading the sports page. He was a magnet for female adoration. I saw this in Little Girl and in the waitresses at Mitzi's—all the more so as he was oblivious to his own appeal. For although he looked the part of the *shaoyeh*, or a pampered young master in the old Chinese custom, there was an air about him that seemed distinctly unworldly. One could imagine that he might suddenly forsake everything and give himself to the rescue of Arctic seals.

With his stepmother gone and his father preoccupied with business, Daniel emboldened himself to pop into my new room constantly—the door always left wide open, in the proper etiquette—to discuss movies and music, even books. He liked Coleridge but found Baudelaire "too dark." Ditto on Mozart versus Wagner. I made myself amenable by always being around in a state of casual undress, nothing too provocative, just a few loose buttons and no brassiere.

Sometimes I was invited into his large, airy room, where he would serenade me with his guitar, singing sultry Spanish songs he'd learned phonetically from records, his eyes burning with ardor. I kept giving him opportunities to kiss me, but he was a gentleman through and through. By night, I brought myself to ecstasy repeatedly, thinking about my Prince Charming on the other side of the wall—a charming boy who could certainly afford to act a little less princely.

I knew I had to make the first move, and two weeks into being neighbors, I did. "Danny Boy" was playing on the wireless in his room, and I used the jocular excuse of the song's name to insist upon a dance.

I shuddered when I felt his hands upon my waist, and as we shuffled along, bumping into the furniture like two inseparable pinballs, the seducer became the seduced. I inhaled deeply to keep from flushing, or fainting and didn't notice when the song ended, only that my beau's handsome face was closing in on me.

He kissed me lightly, testing the waters. Instinctively, I threw my hands behind his neck and pulled myself up to him, parting my lips, inviting him deeper. He accepted with enthusiasm, and we edged toward his bed. His hands migrated down to my rump and squeezed me to him. His desire instantly hardened in his pants and I let out a moan.

He released me at once, blushing furiously as he pulled away.

"I'm sorry," he said. "I really didn't mean to."

"Didn't mean to what?" I ran my fingers up his arm. "Don't stop."

He grabbed both my wrists, and I felt waves of lust shooting through me.

"If we go on, I won't be able to control myself. I mean, my God, you're a very attractive girl…" His voice softened. "I think about you all the time. You haunt my dreams. You drive me absolutely cr—"

A door slammed, followed by approaching footsteps. Daniel quickly dropped my hands and pretended to fiddle with the wireless. Seconds later, Violet sauntered by the open door deliberately, glaring in at us with the grimmest and most disapproving scowl.

"Daniel!" she growled, and then was gone.

One particularly hot and listless afternoon, I decided to go to Daniel's room and play records while I awaited his return from swimming laps at the club. It was my first time there without an express invitation, but I knew he wouldn't object to finding me in his bed—languid and liquid with perspiration, like another pool to dive into.

When I heard his footsteps approaching, I plucked the needle off the record of Chopin nocturnes and leapt onto his bed, where I then arrayed myself in a manner resembling great carelessness—long hair loose and skirt hem shimmying up my thigh.

But, alas, it wasn't Daniel.

"What are you doing in my brother's room?" Violet looked ready to explode.

I covered myself and sat up straight for the inquisitive schoolmarm. "I was just listening to music. He said it would be all right."

She stomped over to inspect the record player. "Why did you shut it off?"

"Because I thought I heard him coming."

"But you just said he said it'd be all right."

"Yes, but he hates Chopin."

"Nobody hates Chopin."

"Well, then, maybe you don't really know your brother, do you?" I smiled, to sweeten those words.

She held on to her scowl. "What are you doing in our house? I mean, really? What do you want? What's your game?" Her expression darkened. "You and I both know you took those earrings."

I kept my cool. "But Daniel said he saw—"

"My brother was lying to protect you! I wonder why."

She took a few steps closer to me and studied my features. I saw on her the pillowy jowls of a joyless young girl who would mature into a joyless old spinster. God knows what *she* saw—worse, no doubt.

Narrowing her eyes, she hissed, "Who *are* you?"

Jaunty footsteps were followed by the appearance of Daniel's carefree face in the doorway—just in the nick of time.

"You girls having a secret powwow?"

"Daniel!" I cried, my voice aching with relief.

Violet broke out of her inquisitor's trance and retreated from me. "My dear brother," she said, squeezing out a smile for him, though not a friendly one. "I didn't know you hated Chopin."

"I don't hate Chopin. Who says I hate Chopin?"

Violet shot me a black look. "Stay away from this family! Everything was fine until you came!"

"Vi!" Daniel called after her, blushing with embarrassment as she stalked off. "Will you stop being so hysterical, please?"

Down the hallway, a door slammed.

Scratching his neck sheepishly, he walked over and sat down beside me on the bed. Underneath the fragrance of shampoo and soap, I could detect on him the medicinal whiff of chlorine from the pool, a scent I'd come to associate with him.

"Must be her time of the month," he said, leaning over to plant a kiss on my temple. "I hope she didn't upset you. You shouldn't take anything she says personally."

She had indeed upset me, but no matter. My consolation was here.

"Kiss me, Daniel."

He obeyed me, the good boy, cupping my jaw in his palm like a chalice and plunging his mouth into mine. He tasted of Orange Crush, his favorite postswim drink. I led his other hand under my blouse, then realized I needn't have guided him. Instantly he reached for my breast. We fell back across the bed and I rubbed my thigh against him, moving higher with each caress until I felt his urgent arousal pressing back at me.

"Close the door, Daniel."

He obeyed me, the good boy, and made a move toward the door. Then something in him turned, like a flipped switch, and he lumbered back to the bed with a pained expression. "We better not."

I led his fingers to the moisture between my thighs. He moaned softly.

"Daniel, we must close the door," I whispered.

"We can't."

"Then you can't have this."

I extracted myself from his muscled swimmer's arms and made for the hallway. He didn't stop me. Glancing back, I saw a handsome young man sitting on the edge of his bed, head hung low.

He was crying.

The following days, we were careful, kissing lightly and only at safe intervals—or perhaps I should say *he* was careful. He kissed me lightly, safely, even while professing his continued attraction to me. I didn't insist on more, not wanting to frighten him or confuse his pious little Catholic heart with my voluptuous desire.

I yearned for him to creep into my room and make love to me while the rest of the house slept, but of course this never happened. These days of frustration flew by, and suddenly we'd reached the last Sunday of the month. Thoughts of my new paramour gave way to memories of my old mentor. I had to see Odell. I had so much to ask him.

After a leisurely postchurch ham and omelet brunch, and a languid game of lawn croquet that Daniel had deliberately, irritatingly, tried to prolong with roundabout explanations of its rules, I excused myself quickly, trying not to betray my brimming excitement.

But it was Mr. Wee who seized my arm at the base of the stairs as I headed up to dress.

"I don't mean to pry, but how is the work situation coming along? Any luck?"

The job search. He certainly caught me by surprise. Distracted with the pleasures of the main house, I hadn't given my future employment any thought.

"I have a few leads." I smiled widely to cover my surging anxiety. "In fact, I'm just about to head out . . . for an interview."

"On a Sunday?"

"They're very busy. It's the only slot they had."

"I see," Mr. Wee muttered, just as the library phone began ringing. He abandoned me for it, already preoccupied. "Well, if you need any help in that area, don't hesitate to ask. I can always make a few calls."

"Thank you. I do appreciate it."

I raced upstairs, realizing with a glance at the clock that the croquet game had stretched overlong. We might as well have used flamingo mallets and hedgehog balls. I was going to be late.

I weighed my miserable choices: a drab button-down, sensible cotton dress in blue that might have me mistaken for the cleaning staff or a silky, low-cut red flapper dress I'd bought on a whim but was now afraid would make me look too available.

A knock on the door, and Daniel slipped in without an invitation. Ordinarily I would have been exultant, but this time he proved a nuisance.

"Father says you've got an interview. Why didn't you say something earlier?"

"It's just a stupid interview." I heard the defensiveness in my voice but couldn't stop myself. "It's no big deal. I probably won't get it anyway."

"What's the position?"

"Some secretarial thing."

"Where's it being held?"

"Why, are you planning to follow me?"

His eyebrows twitched. I'd wounded him. "It's just that it's supposed to pour this afternoon. Why don't you have Issa drop you off?"

The boy was genuinely concerned. There was no time to apologize for my short temper, so I gave him a quick peck.

In the end I chose the red flapper dress, and I did let Issa drive me. The afternoon had grown black as evening, with thick clusters of clouds huddled together like Mohammedans at Friday prayer. The commercial district was deserted. The few pedestrians on High Street were dashing toward shelter as the wind tore at their hats and skirts. I would have been one of these sad people had Daniel not offered the family car. The first drops of rain hit the windshield in startlingly loud clacks, prompting Issa to switch on his electric wipers and, to my astonishment, speak.

"Metropole." His booming voice stunned me. "Meeting a friend for high tea?"

"Yes," I said. "Sorry to trouble you like this on your day off."

"No trouble. There's no such thing as a day off for me. I'm on duty every day. Monday to Sunday. Nonstop."

Was he airing a grievance? It was hard to tell. There was no self-pity in his voice.

"I'm sorry to hear that," I said.

"No need to be sorry. Sorrow doesn't help anyone. There are so many poor people, so many hungry people in this world. Do you think your sorrow helps them?"

I said nothing. I was already beginning to miss his silence.

"So, who is this friend you are going to meet?"

"Just an old friend."

"An old *secret* friend." In the rearview mirror, I saw him crack a smile. "All right, don't worry. I won't ask any more."

"And don't wait for me. I'll find my way back."

"I'm sure you will."

It was my first time at the Metropole, and I instantly saw why Odell was drawn to the place. The lobby was done up in the style of a private club in 1920s Shanghai. Leather club chairs sat alongside rosewood benches. Birdcages in cinnabar red hung from the ceiling, each with its own carved canary. Scrolls of Chinese calligraphy flanked the black silk walls. This was an Englishman's Sinophilia run amok! Even the live band of poker-faced Mandarins played Dixieland jazz with by-the-book stiffness, rendering the music charmingly mechanical, exactly as it might have sounded in Old Shanghai.

The colonial era was feted here as if it were a lost age that had died centuries ago and not still chugging along around us. This aura of glamorous fatigue intoxicated even me. Faced with this worldly circus, I was relieved I'd chosen the silk dress—the cotton one would have had me looking like a schoolmarm lost en route to the Christian Reading Room.

A Chinese maître d' with a ridiculous pencil mustache and a practiced hollow stare met me at his podium. I watched his Adam's apple do a little dance.

"Reservation under...?"

"Odell." I peered past his shoulders at the room of wealthy European matrons biting into finger sandwiches and sipping black tea from bone china. The air smelled of Darjeeling and yeast, with an overlay of prickly heat talcum powder.

He looked at me quizzically. "Odell?"

"Is there not an Odell?"

"Of course there's an Odell. There's always an Odell. Once a month, as dependable as Big Ben."

The blood pounded in my temples. *He's here.*

"I'm probably not expected. I've come as a...surprise."

"Well, *I'm* certainly surprised." The maître d' smiled secretively, as if his discretion was some kind of virtue.

His expression went dead again as he shepherded me along the edge of the crowded tea room. Peals of laughter broke through the endless buzz of gossip. Many of the ladies were also guzzling champagne. We came to the back of the room and stopped.

"What did you say your name was?"

"Pandora."

"Memorable name." He smiled perversely. "Wait here while I announce you."

He knocked on a carved wooden door, then disappeared into its inner sanctum. Seconds later, he emerged with a different kind of smile—still wicked but now also cautious. He waved me through.

There was only one table in the windowless room. A gray-haired woman in a jade green cheongsam sat alone, though she was clearly expecting company. There were enough scones and strawberries on the tiered pedestal for two.

"Mrs. Odell!" I cried.

The woman looked up blankly from her teacup. I had expected her to be in her late thirties, but she looked fifty. The two strands of her pearl necklace hung off-kilter.

"You don't know me but..." I fumbled. "Your husband has told me about you...Pei-Pei? Mr. Odell and I met twelve years ago on the boat, I mean, ship from Shanghai."

The beginnings of a smile softened this still façade—of course she knew of the ship. The voice that emerged from her throat was filled with an aching nostalgia.

"The SS *Prosperity*?"

"Yes, exactly, that's it!"

Mysteriously, her smile vanished. Her face reverted to a melancholy stillness. As if I were no longer in the room.

"Mrs. Odell, is everything all right?" I glanced at the untouched place setting across from her. "Isn't Mr. Odell joining you?"

The maître d' cleared his throat to remind us of his presence. Fluidly Mrs. Odell raised one frail arm. I was sure she was telling him to leave so we could speak in private.

Instead, her face creased with anguish. "Make her go away."

"Mrs. Odell..." I was choking up. "You misunderstand me, ma'am. Mr. Odell—he told me to find you here."

"Remove her now, please!"

Hands dragged me out of the chamber. Mrs. Odell stared at me from her perch with a look that wasn't unsympathetic—merely exhausted. She tugged at her pearls.

And then I was out in the pouring rain, the back exit closing behind me. I banged my fists against the inhospitable barrier and shouted an oath through it, hoping it was loud enough to jolt the gilded tea drinkers. To my surprise, the door immediately flew open. The maître d' stood safely within its mouth, where neither rainwater nor I could touch him.

"I really shouldn't have let you in." His tone was gentle. "But I was curious to see if you could draw her out. You clearly did."

"What the hell do you mean?"

He winced, the first genuinely human expression to trouble his face. "They were my best customers. The most loyal, the most generous. Then, about fourteen years ago, on the ship to Shanghai, Mr. Odell contracted meningitis. Nothing could be done—he died. After that, Mrs. Odell lost her life, too, in a way. Her mind followed him out to sea. She clings to this tea date like it's the most sacred thing, and has been coming here alone now for close to fourteen years. They let her take the taxi from Woodbridge hospital once a month. After the first couple of years, she stopped needing a chaperone. She never strays." He bowed his head. "I don't know who you are or how you knew to find her here...Anyway, I apologize."

The door closed once more and did not open again.

I circled the city on the No. 3 tram, wet as a rag, bedraggled inside and out. With the silk dress clinging to my skin, I must have looked like a wrinkled red blister. Riders rushed on, filtered out, rushed on, filtered out. The sun retreated behind shops and hotels as the gas lamps flared on. After three complete loops, the elderly conductor begged me to go home. "The other passengers find you a bit unsettling."

I gave everyone a defiant stare as I stepped off at Wonder World.

Why there, of all places? I suppose I was lonely for a familiar face from the past, even if that face happened to be my father's.

There was certainly nothing consoling about Wonder World otherwise. In the three years since our return, it had allowed itself to become run-down and seedy through greed and overuse. The whole city, it seemed, had come hurtling through its crimson gateway demanding amusement. Rents had shot up and the old harmless game stalls surrendered to more profitable ventures: bars, lounges, exotic shows. The attractions had become very colorful, too florid, in fact, for my taste. Walking along, I saw Australian servicemen tumbling out of doorways clutching free beer in one hand and Thai prostitutes in the other. Nearby Filipino midgets played Cuban cha-cha on xylophones, dressed in nothing but silk pantaloons. The Westerners, of course, lapped all this up. Jean Cocteau, I later read, was a repeat visitor, praising its commingling of "the black, the white, the yellow, and the tawny" as only a French artist who saw all things in chroma could have put it. Had I been a large and hairy man, I, too, might have seen the fun in this unwholesome parade, but being what I was, a young Chinese female in a low-cut dress, I could have been mistaken for an extra in this Dionysian spectacle—cast in the role of vulnerable meat.

I was keenly aware I was the only unsmiling customer. The only one, that is, until I spotted my mirror—my brother—grim as ever. This was Li's day off and he'd chosen to spend it here, squatting by a tin barrel, diluting Father's "bird's nest" syrup with tepid water direct from a communal tap. It filled me with anger and pity that he'd rather sacrifice himself to duty than improve, or at least enjoy, himself. Where was the spirited, restless boy I'd once known and loved?

"Don't you judge me," he said. His insolence only brought more attention to the purple swelling over his left eye, a bruise that was causing his eyelid to droop. "Since you refuse to help, you have no right to judge."

"I haven't said a word."

"I can tell what you're thinking. You think I'm wasting my life because I'm not following my dream. Well, I have news for you." He looked up long enough to sneer, "I have no dream."

He had every reason to be cross with me—I hadn't seen him since abandoning him at the Troika—yet it was clear his resentment ran deeper than that. He had allowed the cold Confucian obligations of the old country to chase him into the warm waters of the Nanyang: Children were to stand by their father, no matter what.

I teased out a wad of bills from my purse, enough to cover the Troika incident.

"Keep your filthy money." He shut the tap off and began heaving the barrel back toward Father's stall. I followed close behind.

"Do you need a hand?"

"They called the police. Did you know that?"

"Who called the police? When?"

"That *bloody* restaurant, who do you think? They threw me in jail for two days until Father came up with the money. But, of course, you wouldn't know. Nor would you care. I hope this answers your question about why I don't hate him. He's the *only* person who gives a *damn* about me." He dumped the barrel down on the pathway with a grunt and rolled it edgewise to the back of Father's stall. "It's him you should be giving your filthy money to, not me."

Father was ladling out cups of bird's nest to a Burmese couple and hadn't even noticed my arrival—or at least, he acted as if he hadn't. Li stalked off into the crowd, leaving me stranded by Father's side. I waited for the customers to leave, then brought the money to his hand. His fingers closed around the cash without a word.

"Your brother's very bitter," he finally spoke. "He tried to join the civil service as a clerk, but they refused to take him. Didn't matter that his written and spoken English are both good. He's not European, not even

Eurasian. *Not even Eurasian*, they said." He shook his head. "I worry for him. This bitterness is landing him in trouble. Last week, he picked a fight with an Australian sailor at one of those new bars on the other side." He pointed to the far end of Wonder World, now chockablock with drinking holes. "If you hear of any good office job, please tell him. I don't want him to be a servant boy much longer—my son deserves better than that."

"He's not going to want any help from me."

"Surely Ignatius Wee has a friend who will hire him? Why don't you find out?"

"It's not that easy. I can't just ask my boss like that."

"Li is your only brother."

Li stormed back to the stall at this moment, carrying a big block of ice in a burlap sack. He flung the thing on the floor at the back of the stall and began attacking it with a wooden mallet. He was allowing me no opportunity to apologize or explain myself. I waved him a neutral good-bye and prepared to leave.

"We men have the odds stacked against us," he blurted out. "But you, on the other hand, could be making yourself useful." Smash—his ice block became two. "It'd be so easy for you to make three, four times what we make—just pretend to read them their stupid fortunes..."

"I'm not going to prostitute myself."

"As if you're not doing that already."

We stared at each other for an instant before I turned and walked away. There was no point in arguing.

"Go on, run away! That's all you ever do! You live in a dream world!"

I had hastened for the exit but found myself nudged and jostled by a whirlpool of elbows and thighs back into the dead heart of the park. All around me were hawkers pushing all manner of food and drink, hot and cold; hustlers shaking their cues at gullible marks; boxers, pimps, towkays, playboys, dandies, all of them strutting up and down the pedestrian boulevard.

An irate Hakka woman peddling bags of peanuts jabbed me rudely in the ribs. "You taxi dancers can go to hell with all that union nonsense! Those strikes cost me a lot of business! You girls should be grateful you can find work at all!"

I fled her, only to be accosted by a white-bearded Arab who pinched my bottom and winked as he passed. This was almost courtly compared to another, more odious ruffian who grabbed me by the waist and cooed in hillbilly Hokkien, "What's your rate, Little Flower? I don't have much, but I'm small and I'm fast. Maybe give me a discount."

I wriggled out of his rough brown hands and burst into the nearest bar— its theme was Wild West bordello. My bet was that this foreigners' drinking hole would intimidate my would-be suitor. It certainly intimidated me. A fat, wordless Chinaman in a sombrero poured whiskey at the candlelit bar, and I planted myself before him, fortifying myself with thoughts of my new favorite movie duo, Nick and Nora Charles, and how they drank and drank and laughed. I had to act casual.

"Give me a double, straight."

It was then that I noticed from the corner of my eye that the shadowy interior of the place was filled with uniformed armed forces men. Some bordello. Aside from me, there was not a dame in sight. I took my Scotch and drank it standing up, by the swinging saloon doors in case I had to make a quick exit.

A voice bellowed from the gallery, "Just when we fought all's gone to 'ell, a livin', drinkin' China doll!"

The speaker sounded young—a boy really, certainly no older than I was. I kept my shoulders squared and my eyes on the drink. Some of his mates chimed in with the squeaky rasps of schoolboys: "Bird holds down her drink betta than you do, Ron!"

"Bollocks!"

"*I'll* be 'avin' *her* wiv a squeeze o' lime, I will!"

"Aww, Musgrove wants to ficky-ficky!"

"Shut yer gob, Jonesy!"

Squealing chair legs told me at least two of the lads had peeled out of their seats, either to fight one another or to approach me. I trained my eyes on the counter while I paid the fake Mexican and strode quickly out of the bar with my head held high.

"Oy, come back 'ere! We just wan' a talk!" yelled one who had followed me out of the bar, his voice so new that it still cracked. "A li'l chat is all!"

I turned back to face him: He was at most fifteen, poignantly rosy-lipped and apple-cheeked, his freshly shaved sideburns beaded with sweat. My glance sent him scampering back into the bar. How did a child like this get let into Wonder World?

How did a child like this get into the army?

Again, I joined the shoving cavalcade as I sought the shortest route out of the park. The gate seemed no closer than before—if anything, the path seemed even more convoluted, even more elusive.

"Follow me," a voice boomed by my ear, with an authority so calm I could not ignore it.

Something caught my hand and pulled me deeper into the crowd, instead of out of it. I was as helpless as a fisherman being sucked into the ocean by a shark. Swimming against the human current, I saw the distinctive black knot that was Issa's hair and tried to break free, but his grip only tightened. We were at the gate in no time.

Yes, I was grateful for the rescue. But I wondered about his well-timed appearance. Once we were outside, I shook off his hand and saw the red marks on my wrist where he had fixed his grip.

"Did you follow me after dropping me off? Did Mr. Wee ask you to spy on me?"

Issa laughed dryly as he led me to the Bentley. "Mr. Wee has more important things to do than worry about you roaming around town. The *senior* Mr. Wee, anyway."

I didn't like what he was insinuating about Daniel, not because it couldn't be true, but because he had no business making such judgments.

"And no, Young Master didn't ask me either."

"Then what are you doing here?"

In the rearview mirror came a little smile. "You're not the only one with secrets, you know. One day, the two of us should have a little chat."

— 9 —

Where Have All My Ghosts Gone?

I DIDN'T CARE FOR THE SWIMMING CLUB. Dipping into the Olympic pool for the first time, I opened my eyes to gray torsos jutting out of the deep end, their arms flailing, eternal victims of drowning. It was the worst baptism. I never took a swim again.

But I will come out and admit it: I was seduced by the life the Wees had. The air-conditioned bedrooms; the freshly pressed, rose-scented laundry; the larder stuffed to the rafters with cans of abalone and hanging pallets of salt-cured duck; the lavish restaurant dinners that appeared to be a twice-weekly affair. Although Mr. Wee claimed that chicken rice was his favorite food, I learned that this wasn't quite true. Rice was a peasant starch—it rarely appeared at the Wees' dinner table, for if one could afford meat and vegetables, there should never be any need for rice; only the gauche asked for it. Mr. Wee, in fact, had an enthusiastic appetite for shark's fin, lobster, and buttery blocks of foie gras. The bird's nest I ate at his table was the genuine item, swallow spit retrieved in the Dutch Indies by nimble cave climbers, not the dismal agar impostor cooked up by Father at his stall.

Even more than the elaborate feasts, the thing I appreciated most about being with the Wees was the ease with which the past and the outside world could be sidelined, excised, dismissed. Neither Mr. Wee nor Daniel mentioned my job interview or questioned me further about my prospects; whether this was politeness, forgetfulness, or happy indifference on their part, it suited me fine. Even Violet and I arrived at some sort of a truce. Her disapproval of my friendship with her brother simmered down to a tolerable hiss.

"Shall we get out of here?" Daniel asked me one gray afternoon, as the Wee household was awash in an uncharacteristic dolefulness. Violet was cramming for her O-Level exams—ten subjects in which she could score no less than a B or be thrown out of Connaught Academy—and had taken to plodding up and down the stairs making distressing grunts and sighs. Mr. Wee was picking up and slamming down the telephone in agitated spurts, all the while riffling through stacks of Chinese tabloids with Little Girl loyally translating by his side.

I threw down my *Modern Screen* magazine, banishing the beaming face of Olivia de Havilland to the foot of the bed.

Daniel smiled. "I know just the place to take you."

Issa drove us in the Bentley. Issa and I hadn't spoken since Wonder World, and I treated him coolly, since any hint of familiarity would only give rise to questions. But I had nothing to worry about—in Daniel's presence, Issa was a perfect stranger.

As the rain trees and angsanas of the suburbs gave way to coconut palms and vine-draped banyans, I knew that Daniel's "place" wasn't going to be the botanic gardens or even his swimming club with its quartet of shimmering pools, but somewhere farther east. We passed Forbidden Hill, Jervois Swamp, even the power stations that kept the Isle electrified. On we drove, coming finally to a private turnoff. The lane was shielded on both sides by casuarinas, their pointy tops catching the breeze. In the distance, a lighthouse stood like a solemn cigarette.

Salt brightened the air. The conifers thinned as we went on, revealing a pristine stretch of white sand. Gentle waves rolled up in jade green, their foam edges as playful as chiffon trim on an evening gown. This beach was irresistible, yet nobody was on it, not even a ghost. Not since the jungle had I seen a place this deserted.

Mesmerized by the sight of water, I hadn't noticed our actual destination. Issa turned right into a narrow driveway about midway down the road and pulled under a porte cochere. We had reached what appeared to be a villa, Italianate in aspiration—salmon-pink walls, wrought-iron balustrades—but equatorial in modification: Like the homes of the rural Malays, it was raised five feet aboveground for ventilation. Daniel took my hand and led me up mosaic-covered steps to the verandah, which wrapped around the house.

"What a bizarre place," I murmured without thinking.

"It is, isn't it?" Daniel smiled. "My grandfather built it. It's very much a typical Peranakan villa, with a bit of everything. We're a hodgepodge people, as you know. But don't worry, it'll grow on you."

It already had. The villa was nowhere as large as the Wees' city house, but its idiosyncrasies made it even more appealing—for a start, it was less somber. The furniture was plantation-style rattan stuffed with brightly colored cushions. There were cheerful paper lanterns, orchid-print drapery, and even an upright Steinway in the main room, its lid left open and ready for an impromptu sing-along—though I couldn't imagine any of the Wees participating in such a thing.

"Do you play?" I asked.

"Nobody does. But Grandpa thought every country house had to have a piano. He must have read that somewhere. When he died, the house became my father's. Aunt Betsy did some redecorating, but Daddy insisted we keep the piano." His voice swelled with boyish pride. "This place will be mine someday."

The casualness with which he laid claim to such a luxurious abode brought a chilly quiver to my heart. I couldn't claim anything but a wardrobe of simple dresses and a shelf of dog-eared books. What different universes!

"How many other houses does your family own?"

"Just these two, and then there's the flat in Hong Kong, on the Kowloon side. But that's just a flat and I'm told that it's very small and dull because only Father uses it. No frills." He smiled, a little apologetically. "My father's not a man with many frills."

"But he's very generous."

"That he is. That he is." He paused, and I sensed a peculiar hint of disapproval. "Actually, if I'd gone to study in England like I was supposed to, there'd probably be a flat for us in London, too."

"You were supposed to go to England?" I hadn't known this. "Why on earth didn't you go?"

He banished the topic with a shrug and flopped down into an armchair. "Know what I like best about being in this house?"

"What?"

"No servants." He grabbed my waist and pulled me down onto him. This was the amorous side of Daniel that I adored, that I wanted more of. I curled up on his lap and we locked lips until he groaned under my weight.

Together, still entwined, we migrated to the settee, where I allowed myself to be pinned against the backrest.

Kissing Daniel was like coasting on air—light, pleasurable, slightly precarious. It was a plane we could have remained on indefinitely without either backing down or venturing any further. I wanted, of course, to venture much further, but each time I tried to slide myself beneath him, he pulled me upright again. I chaperoned his hand up my inner thigh, and though his breath grew heavy, he broke loose and planted his fingers on my head, combing my hair as one would a beloved Maltese. And so we merely kissed and kissed.

"But I want you, Daniel."

"I want you, too. But we can't."

After about two hours of pleasant but increasingly frustrating caresses, I insisted that we step outside for air. I ran barefoot on the white sand ahead of him while he ambled along in leather sandals, as if afraid of what sensual urges the beach might arouse on his naked feet.

The sand was soft and warm. The sea began a hundred yards behind the villa, and I pictured the water kissing the lip of the threshold at high tide.

"Does it ever flood?"

Daniel shook his head. "This is a strait. It's the most docile water imaginable."

Indeed. I thought of leaping nude into the clear turquoise water. There were no other houses for at least a mile in either direction. Far to the right, a villa perched on a rocky promontory like a pelican, and to the left was a limestone castle nearly hidden in a grove of coconuts. The singular lighthouse loomed yonder.

"You own this entire beach?"

"Not all of it," he laughed. "Just this two-mile stretch or so. Truthfully, I still prefer the swimming club."

"Why?"

"There are no surprises there. You know exactly how far it is from Point A to Point B—no sand, no waves, no jellyfish, no variables. After a good swim, all I want is a clean, fluffy towel, and the club has plenty of them. Cold drinks, too."

"But no islands." I pointed to the small atolls across the strait that appeared to be bobbing on the water's surface.

"Oh, those are the Spice Islands. They're Dutch. Cinnamon Bay is the one closest to us. My grandfather used to tell me it would be his one day. Sadly, not so."

I strolled to the waterline and let the waves wash up to me. Their cool foam nipped at my toes like hundreds of tiny mouths. Immediately I felt a giddy passion for the water and everything related to it, as if the fine sand between my toes, the wet breeze in my hair, and the faint scent of nutmeg in my nose were all part of my most natural state and that all of my previous life spent inland and without access to the sea was a travesty, an abomination. I wanted to live in Daniel's villa. No, not just wanted—I craved it.

We walked, holding hands, occasionally pausing to press our mouths together and brush away the hair that had blown into each other's eyes. We aimed for the black rocks near the lighthouse because I wanted to see what they were. To my surprise, Daniel had never wandered that far. As we drew nearer, I spotted an undulating speck on the beach ahead. Driftwood? Kelp? No, more likely a ghost. I said nothing and tried to act natural.

The closer we came to the thing, the more clearly I made out the shape of a head on the sand. It was vaguely humanoid and attached to a bulbous mass of deepest purple, perhaps the carcass of a sea lion. Each time the waves came up and lapped at it, the whole blob shook as if electrified.

"Do you see that?" Daniel asked.

My heart jumped. "See what?"

"That." He pointed at the creature. "Looks like a giant turtle or some-thing. Maybe a stranded dugong."

He started jogging toward it and I followed, relieved that it wasn't a ghoul I had to pretend I didn't see.

The truth was worse. This was no turtle or manatee but a beautiful woman, naked, on her back, being crushed alive by a giant octopus. Its legs were coiled around her fair torso and its slimy head—the size of two pil-lows—had pressed itself against her face, so close that they were eye to eye. The monster had trapped her so absolutely it was hard to tell if she was still breathing. We were twenty feet away when Daniel stopped; his head jerked back in shock.

"Mrs. Nakamura!" he gasped, then turned to me. "That's the lighthouse operator's wife. I have to do something."

I grabbed his arm. He would need at least a long crowbar to pry off the beast, and there wasn't anything like it near us.

"Mrs. Nakamura!" Daniel called out to her.

The woman did not respond but remained on the ground, motionless. We waited. When the next wave pulled in, all of a sudden she moaned in agony, an eerie bovine lowing, and the octopus went into a mad convulsion, tightening its grip on her and throbbing like one gigantic muscle. As it contracted and revealed more of Mrs. Nakamura, we discovered that the creature's mouth—an obscene beak at the base of its greasy head—was clamped over the poor woman's breast, leaving viscous trickles down her side as it sucked.

Daniel squeezed my hand. "It's devouring her!"

As the surf swept up once more, Mrs. Nakamura moaned again, this time a human-sounding moan. Daniel and I experienced a second wave of horror: Mrs. Nakamura was in ecstasy. We watched her hand clutch the creature's arm and guide it into the glistening crevice between her thighs, forcibly dictating its terms of conduct. With each thrust, she gave out a high-pitched whinny, reserving the shudders and moans only for when the cool sea foam drew up the sand and soaked her hair, her back, her legs. Her aquatic friend, too, was happy. As it closed its big cloudy eyes, the suction caps on its arms puckered up in unison and the tips of its seven remaining tentacles writhed in the air, each conducting its own lewd symphony. When the convulsions ceased, black rivers of ink flowed down the pale sides of the woman's thighs and into the receding tide. Before long, the cycle began again, both lovers goading themselves to a new state of exquisite tension until the next big wave.

"Mrs. Nakamura . . . ," Daniel murmured with strange wonder. Blushing furiously, he avoided my gaze.

We watched longer than we should have, confused and afraid. Silently, we continued our stroll to the cluster of black rocks. Again, looks proved deceiving. The rocks turned out to be massive prehistoric boulders, each rugged block propped against the other to form caves and catacombs. On an ordinary day, we might have worried about pirates hiding in them, but our day had revealed itself to be anything but usual.

We ducked into one of the alcoves to listen to the waves echo in its melancholy womb. The air was cool and smelled of the ocean. We found ourselves standing on a tapestry of seaweed—red, green, brown, maroon. Some of these spongy alveoli housed families of tiny crabs, three of which tried to climb up my shins.

"This is why I wear sandals," said Daniel, smiling as he plucked the little scramblers off me.

A flat rock near the entrance seemed the ideal spot to rest our tired legs. We collapsed upon it, lifting our feet off the sand. The tide must have rolled in across it for millennia and sculpted the rock face to its present smoothness. It was coated with algae, as feathery as down against our skin. When we realized our hands hadn't parted since finding Mrs. Nakamura, we laughed with jittery tenderness and kissed, first lightly, then with greater conviction. The cave amplified every sound, every scent, every touch. This time, Daniel didn't pull away but pressed himself insistently against me, acting on every amorous impulse he'd been holding back.

His eyes shone with a vivid new selfishness, that of a brute who wouldn't stop until he was satisfied—and this transformed him, made him even handsomer. The force and urgency with which he tore off my clothes thrilled me. I whimpered as he clamped my wrists down and thrust his tongue into my ear.

My back pressed against the green plane of our waterside bed, we did the most natural thing to be done by a boy and a girl bound by the unnatural mystery they had just witnessed together: We made love for the very first time.

After nineteen years of fits, starts, and multiple disruptions, my *real* life was finally beginning in earnest. To mark my rebirth, I decided to give myself a new name. Selecting one was trickier than I thought. I started with Pandora—but this was Odell's name for me, not one that I found for myself. It had to go. Then came Miranda and Cassandra, both ringing of hubris, and Scarlett (as in O'Hara), which on me would have sounded too significantly red, too crushingly Oriental. So I considered ordinary names—unobtrusive, forgettable names like Susan and Sarah and...

Exhausted by their drabness, I returned to Cassandra. Cassandra, the girl of Greek myth who saw things nobody else did. Since no one on the Isle knew much about the Greeks, I thought this could be my own little private joke. And lo, Cassandra I became.

Daniel liked it. In fact, he liked it so well he soon asked me to be the future Mrs. Cassandra Wee.

As expected, both Li and Father refused their invitations to our engagement party, offering the most unimaginative excuses. Both insisted they had to work. I was relieved. What if Li threw one of his tantrums? Or made remarks about "the rich"? But their tacit disapproval did weigh on me. I had cast off my old life—meaning them.

Daniel and I decided on a quiet, understated get-together at home because Mr. Wee felt that anything grander—a champagne-laden banquet at the Metropole, say—would be inappropriate, considering the anxious political mood. He had already begun to ration our restaurant feasts. We dined out just once a week, and only in private rooms, away from prying eyes.

Amidst talk that Japan was about to invade the Dutch Indies, our Isle was seeing an influx of blond settlers who'd fled their plantations in Batavia. They felt they would be safe from the Japs here—the place the British called their "indomitable fortress"—but our locals weren't so sure. Everyone had read about the atrocities happening in Nanking. To calm the nervous populace of Chinatown, the government held practice air raids. There were no bomb shelters, of course, but it was hoped that these calls for lights-out would keep the masses busy until the rumblings of war went away.

I barely noticed what was going on in the city, let alone the world, because there was another major change in my life, as monumental as my engagement to Daniel: I had stopped seeing ghosts. I didn't know exactly when the shift occurred, so preoccupied had I been with joy. I can only guess it was soon after he proposed.

Until I stopped seeing them, I never fully realized how much their presence had oppressed me. Privacy was something I had rarely taken for granted, even when alone. Until I could ascertain that no ghost was present—hovering silently in the corner of the bathroom while I washed or standing over my shoulder in the library while I read—I carried with me a constant, low-level awareness of being watched.

It might have been true once that seeing these souls made me feel less alone, but I was no longer lonely. I had Daniel. Now every excursion I made was filled not with quiet apprehension but unbridled joy—an adult innocence.

We took romantic strolls along the banyan-shrouded trails of Forbidden Hill, where not so long ago, I had seen the ghosts of two centuries. We spent nights in expensive old hotel rooms that a year before would have made my hair stand on end and found nothing there to impede our love-making but our own exhaustion. We even coupled in a Christian cemetery in the isolated west, the only visible creatures around us being sparrows, crickets, and butterflies. Bit by bit, I was reclaiming the benighted Isle, with pleasure as my beacon of light.

I burned to begin a new chapter as a conventional young wife. Mrs. Cassandra Wee. I believed that love had saved—nay, cured—me and I looked upon Daniel as the source of my salvation. Sweet, devoted, and refreshingly uncomplicated, he was the antidote to all the darkness that had come before. By earning his love, I had truly freed myself from my past.

At our garden party, we served tea, lemonade, three types of éclair, four types of cake, and champagne for the friends—Daniel's friends, that is—who knew where to look for it. I'd like to blame my peripatetic past for my lack of friends, but to be honest, after Dora Conceição, I had not cared to make any new ones. I had my books, my matinees, and my ghosts, and they seemed like more than enough.

About thirty or forty guests attended, mostly Daniel's old schoolmates and his father's colleagues, serious men who used the occasion to discuss politics as they distractedly pushed slices of chiffon cake into their mouths. Violet had been encouraged to invite her classmates, but she spent the entire afternoon sitting by Agnes's cage, alternately sulking and giggling at some private joke only she and the awful dog shared. She, too, as far as I knew, was friendless.

I wore a pale pink sheath dress—again, not too showy, at Mr. Wee's insistence—but Daniel's friends arrived in elaborate fashions imported from Paris and London, and eyed me with polite bemusement. None were unkind, yet I felt unsteady in their swirl. They were a tight, air-kissing clique who had been mingling since birth and ran with the same moneyed frames of reference. Had I seen the Italian leather pumps just in at Robinsons? Had I heard how disgracefully the sultan's son behaved at so-and-so's soiree? What's to become of the poor horsies at the Turf Club if the Japs rolled in? These bright young men and women chain-smoked and abandoned their plates on the bushes for the servants, leaving a trail of ash and crumbs as they sauntered from hedge to hedge. Daniel hadn't seen most of them since secondary school at St. Patrick's and, to his credit, moved among them shyly, like an awkward newcomer shaking their hands for the first time. One would never have guessed he was once rugby captain two years running.

Thinking that some champagne would help ease my nerves, I slinked into the library, where Mr. Wee had left a magnum chilling on ice.

A young man had beaten me to it. I caught him drinking straight from the bottle as he stared at the calfskin spines on the shelves, his nose almost touching them. He was wiry in the Cantonese manner, his features slightly epicene, and he reeked of hair oil; I could smell him all the way from the door. I cleared my throat loudly to make him jump. He didn't.

"Too much Dickens, don't you think?" he said coolly, flaunting an English accent that sounded freshly clipped. "Picturesque paupers, bene-factors with hearts of gold, funny names—we mustn't forget those funny names—all adding up to a formula of one hundred percent pap."

When I didn't answer, he raised the bottle. "Am I disgracing the vintage or myself by guzzling it like this?"

"A bit of both, I should imagine."

"Fair enough." He saluted me and went bottoms up again. Champagne frothed down his chin, but before I could worry about the carpet, he wiped himself on his sleeve. A provocateur, apparently.

"Who are you?" I demanded.

"The question is"—he smiled mockingly—"who are *you*?"

I was offended, and flustered. "Why, I'm Daniel's fiancée . . ."

"Only joking! Of course I know who you are." He snatched my hand and kissed it like a deranged knight. The drink gave his lips an icy, reptilian edge. "Felicitations. My name is Kenneth, Kenneth Kee. Dan's great chum from school."

Kenneth Kee? I couldn't remember Daniel ever mentioning him. But then Daniel hated talking about his childhood, which was another rea-son we got along—I didn't talk about mine either. Was it possible they'd really been "great chums"? I could hardly imagine two less similar boys. Daniel was all smooth predictability, and this Kenneth Kee was anything but. He moved as if he answered to a different, more restless god, as if he breathed in different air from those around him, myself included. And, strange in the tropics on a warm afternoon, this young man did not sweat.

"Why aren't you outside?"

He shrugged. "I don't mix well."

"Well, I grant you you've an outlandish accent."

"As do you. Been studying at Miss Hepburn's academy, have we, Cassandra?"

He hissed out my name like a snake, making it sound desperate and cheap, as if he were embarrassed on my behalf. I found his manner deeply irritating and thrust him my empty flute so he wouldn't try to finish the bottle on his own. He filled it to the brim, daring me to spill. I didn't, sipping steadily as he watched.

"I'm on loan to Oxford, on loan *from* Oxford...whatever it may be. Hence the aggravated lisp. God help me if I not only looked funny but spoke funny, too. You see, people over there have no imagination. Were I to speak with a foreign accent, they'd immediately assume I was unable to think or write intelligently in English. So in order to save myself the trouble of dealing with *my* fury about their lack of imagination, I decided to speak in the only way they understand, which is to say, like them. Does this answer your question, the one you're too polite to ask?"

"Y-yes...I think so." Silly me, I was stuttering.

"This would have been my third year if it hadn't been for the bloody war. Didn't Dan tell you? It should have been him who's over there at Balliol, but he sent me off in his place."

In fact, Daniel always refused to discuss why he hadn't gone to England. He'd never even struck me as the Oxbridge type.

"Why didn't he go?" I asked. "I mean, I'd like to hear your side of it."

"'Cause he's a timorous bastard, that's why." This provoked wild laughter in him and he took another swig. "Seriously, the boy's a sentimental fool. Couldn't bear to leave the old homestead. Though I suppose it's worked out all right for him. He caught you."

Our eyes met, and during that moment I thought he wasn't so bad.

"Lucky for me, then, he's a sentimental fool," I said.

"I keep telling him he should disappoint people once in a while. It'd make his life much more interesting. In fact, it'd make *him* much more interesting." He paused, realizing he might have said the wrong thing to me. "Bubbly?"

I let him refill my glass.

"Shall I show you what I brought him from England?" Reaching into his trouser pocket, he pulled out a tiny stack of cards held together with a rubber band. "He's going to be so cross with me. He's probably expecting either a hunting cap or a basket of jam from Fortnum and Mason. But I spent six months collecting this set, I did."

"What are they?" The cards were two inches long and an inch wide, and each sported a different drawing printed in color. Some had soldiers operating searchlights and dousing fires; others had civilians trying on gas masks.

"Cigarette cards. They put one in each pack of fags so fools like me would murder our lungs just to collect all fifty. It's a mania, I know. Once I found two in a pack and I was so thrilled I couldn't sleep for days. That's undergraduate life for you! But I told myself there's at least some philosophical value to this set. The theme is Air Raid Precautions—a little prenuptial humor." He laughed blackly. "The set with the blond bombshells I kept for myself."

I liked his sense of humor. I even liked the cards. But I doubted that Daniel would appreciate them—he'd have preferred the hunting cap.

"Well, I should get back outside," I said. "It was lovely meeting you."

"Wait." He plucked a random book from the shelf and, like a magician, brandished from behind it a green hat with comical earflaps. He cackled triumphantly—he had brought Daniel a hunting cap after all. "I, too, am a bit of a sentimental fool."

The peculiar boy decided to follow me outside and rejoin society. But one glimpse of Violet and Agnes from the doorway and his face turned ashen.

"Actually, I may stay inside for a bit."

I laughed. "Don't tell me you're afraid of dogs!"

"No, no, it's not Agnes that I'm afraid of... That horrible girl's been chasing me for ten years. She can be a bit relentless."

"Violet? After you?" This tickled me even more. "Well, she can be okay at times."

"I'm sure even Herr Hitler's okay *some*times. Please, don't even say her name in my presence."

"Violet! Violet! Violet! Shall I call her in here?"

"Stop it! You're too cruel!" He ran maniacally along the main hallway of the house until he spotted the folding screen in the far corner of the sitting room. Making a beeline for it, he reached behind the lacquered panels, grimacing until I heard the unlatching of a stiff bolt.

"Voila." He grinned, pulling the screen aside to reveal a hidden door to the garden. He clearly relished surprising me with his privileged information. I followed him outside and caught up with him on the flagstone path hugging the side of the house.

"When I was a youngster, I always made a point of visiting these." He pointed to the slabs lining the footpath. "I pretended each one was a tombstone for a forgotten pet. Dan always said I was being morbid." He went on one foot and hopscotched his way along a line of them. "Cat, cat, dog . . . rat, rat, dog. Goldfish. Hamster." The drink had compromised his balance and he tripped, giggling. Riding the momentum of his stumble, he careened like a fighter plane until he crashed into a rambutan tree. Flopping down on the grass, he emptied the last of the champagne into his mouth and set the drooling bottle upside down in a broken flower pot.

"So when's the big day?" he asked.

"We haven't quite decided. There's no hurry, not really. We talked about going on a holiday first. Maybe Paris."

"Paris? Perhaps, my dear, you've heard about the war?"

"I know. I said maybe. We'll go when it all ends." I giggled frivolously. The champagne had gone to my head.

I joined him in the rambutan grove, the massive house casting us in shadows. We watched the guests in the back garden, standing around in genteel little groups, not missing us a bit. Sunlight glinted off bracelets, necklaces, and luxurious Swiss watches. These people were as pretty as a postcard—more picture-perfect perhaps because I wasn't in frame to spoil it.

"Daniel must have had an idyllic childhood here." I'd only seen photographs. Here was hope that his old chum might tell me a story or two.

Kenneth smirked. "There was no way a happy childhood could have occurred in this house. His father was generous to a fault yet distant. Mother was temperamental and insecure, followed by a stepmother even more temperamental and even more insecure. Not to mention the hideously needy sibling with the name I shall not let pass my lips. On top of all this, our Dan's cursed with a ridiculous sense of guilt. I say ridiculous because, though he always felt miserable about lolling around in air-conditioned comfort reading adventure yarns while some of his classmates had to go to work, he never once lifted a finger to right the injustice. All he did was wallow in more guilt. In fact, guilt is the very essence of our Danny Boy's character, as you may or may not know."

"I'll bet you were just the same," I said with a bit of an edge. "Anyway, Daniel can't help his background, no more than *you* can."

"No, you're right. I can't help my background either. I grew up in an attap hut. Eight to a room, if one can call that a room. Worked at my father's fish stall at Ellenborough Market after school, every day for ten years. *Ikan bilis*, pomfret, stingray. Even today I can still smell them on me." He took a long sniff of his right hand. "Mackerel's the pits."

I now recognized the strained, slightly forced quality in his voice to be carefully buried anger. The arrogance, the knowingness—all of it was a cover. But I also felt a stab of instant kinship. He, too, had lived in more than one world; he, too, had known the high price of keeping those worlds separate.

The moment of confession over, Kenneth's cockiness returned. "I can proudly say that I've never spent a single night in an air-conditioned room in all my twenty-one years. Yet I'm no worse for it, am I? Look, I don't even perspire!"

"And why is that?"

He grinned like the Cheshire cat. "Because God made me special."

I hadn't heard any footsteps, but all at once, Daniel and three of his friends—two girls and a very spoiled-looking boy—appeared before us, bearing pink lemonade.

"That's where you've been hiding," Daniel said, a bit confused at our unlikely comradeship, since he hadn't introduced us. "Kenny. I didn't even know you were here. When did you get back?"

"Your father invited me," Kenneth said, as if that explained everything.

"Did you know each other from before?" Daniel asked us, still perplexed.

"*Before*? You mean from the fish market?" Kenneth pulled out a loaded smile.

Daniel laughed uneasily, and I suddenly felt the need to protect him.

"Kenneth was just telling me about life at Oxford," I said. "Apparently quite dull."

Daniel tried to smile, but it was more of a wince.

"Oh, Kenny," said one of Daniel's friends, a flirtatious girl with arms as thin as bamboo, "you speak four languages, you run, you swim, you're good at games, *reasonably* good-looking, and, I'm told, a magnificent dancer. What *can't* you do?"

"I'm rather poor at forgiveness," Kenneth replied without missing a beat. He shot a quick look at Daniel, who cast his eyes away.

"Heavens, Kenny!" exclaimed the other girl, even more affected than the first. She'd spotted the empty bottle. "What *have* you done with the champers?"

I had spent months avoiding Issa. It was all right when somebody else rode in the car with us—I usually asked one of the servants—and I arranged my chores so I never had to be left alone with him. Those looks he threw me in the mirror when nobody was paying attention, those insidious, knowing smiles, I dreaded them. It was as if we'd shared some terrible, sordid history, not just a chance encounter at a public fairground.

One day, the inevitable arrived. The tailor called for me to pick up my new collection of dresses, and I had to show up in person for the final fitting. It was a Thursday, which meant Daniel was swimming laps at the club. Violet was taking her afternoon nap, so I invited Little Girl along for the ride—Little Girl, who liked me even less after the engagement than during the earrings debacle. As we pulled out of the driveway, she decided she had some sudden chore to attend to and jumped out.

I was alone with Issa. Even the slick knot of hair at the back of his head repulsed me. He was male arrogance personified, with his long mane and silly gold gypsy earrings. It was a wonder that the Wees, such sticklers with the other servants, hadn't held him to a more orthodox dress code. But the rules didn't seem to apply to him, and his renegade status only gave him more cause to gloat. As we drove, I kept my sunglasses on despite the cloudy, overcast sky.

The journey to the tailor's passed in a taut, bearable silence. But once I had collected my dresses and returned to the car, the silence was no more.

"So, Cassandra," he boomed. "It's been three months. Our little chat. When can we have it?"

"We have nothing to talk about." I tried to be neutral yet firm, neither hostile nor evasive. Hostility would only make the ride—and all future rides—intolerable.

"You're wrong. You know you're wrong. We have plenty to talk about."

"So what if you saw me at Wonder World."

"Wonder World?" he guffawed. "I saw you that night in the rain. Near the roses. Digging like a dog."

My spine tensed for a long second. Issa's driving remained steady, hand over hand as he made deft turns on the winding road, giving no external indication that he'd said anything provocative. But I knew that he knew he had shaken me.

Was he the one who'd sprung me from the room that night? Was he expecting a reward?

"Nobody cares about those stupid earrings anymore."

"The earrings?" He laughed again. "You were dancing, inside the darkness." At the next stop sign, he turned his face to me. To my surprise, he looked concerned. "You see, we are not so different."

His smooth brown face brought to mind a warrior from another time and place, maybe Tongan, maybe Maori. Or perhaps an indigenous tribe that preceded the rest of us invaders, exiles, and immigrants.

"I saw it all," he said gently.

I froze. How could he know about my dance, my hallucination? Odell's visitation had only been a memory—*my* memory—and there was no way Issa could have witnessed any of it. Unless...

The car behind us honked twice, a Mercedes carrying a suite of anxious Europeans. The traffic policeman had flipped the sign to GO. With the tranquillity of the superior man, Issa pulled aside and allowed the car behind to overtake us. Then he drove us into a private residential cul-de-sac and switched off the engine.

"Trust me," he said. "I can help you."

What was he saying? That he, too, was cursed? Or was I reading too much into his words?

"I know you are scared. But I can teach you how to take control. I come from many generations of bomoh. Medicine men. Seers."

Witch doctors. Black magic was the last thing I wanted to hear about. I led a *clean* life now. That world no longer touched me.

"I don't need your help," I said. "And I'm not scared. Start the car, will you, and take me home."

"You think they are gone, yah? They are not gone. You can never get rid of them." His eyes creased with unearned intimacy. "They are still here, only they are waiting and waiting. And you can't blame them. Death is the most difficult thing we'll ever have to accept."

What did this shaman want? Why was he trying to subvert my new happiness?

"Do you want money? I can pay you."

"Oh no," he chuckled. "Money won't solve anything. You should know that."

He shot me a suggestive smile that made me chillingly aware of my vulnerability. I looked outside. We were parked in a dead end—nobody drove by. The bungalows around us were abandoned, empty shells slated for demolition, their lawns in disarray.

"Issa, I *order* you to start the car and take me home."

"As you wish, *madam*," he said, and very slowly turned on the ignition. Driving, however, did not stop his taunts. "Just remember they're waiting. Hell is going to happen, and all of them will be unleashed, the good ones as well as the bad ones."

"Then perhaps I should wish you the best of luck." Thank goodness we were approaching the resplendent rain trees of Tanglewood.

"If you don't believe me, I'll bring you a candle that's been blessed by a bomoh. Watch how quickly it burns and you'll know. Or the next time you look in the mirror, look closely. They are still here, hiding behind your shoulder. They are everywhere. They are just waiting for the gates to open . . ."

Our gates were finally here. I prepared to sprint from the car as soon as Issa rolled it to a stop. But before pulling up the handbrake, the pirate turned to me once more. "I am here. But if you come too late"—he pursed his lips—"sorry."

I slammed the back door and dashed into the house, nearly bowling over the servants who had scurried out to carry my dresses. I felt Issa's eyes burning into my back as I ran all the way upstairs and slumped into bed.

That night, when Daniel and I were alone in our room, I tipped the long antique mirror on its stand so we could see the both of us. Me, in the foreground wearing my new red silk kimono, Daniel behind me reclining on the bed, naked. Despite Issa's words, there were no ghosts. It was just the two of us.

"Take off your robe."

My coat fell to the floor with a whisper and Daniel eyed me like a connoisseur.

"Flawless." He smiled. "You're good enough to eat."

I must admit that, in the nude, we made a glamorous couple. I almost couldn't recognize my own reflection. There was a very handsome man in the picture, almost a Siberian prince, gazing at me with pure desire. And my face showed such joy. Amazement, even. I wanted to freeze this perfect tableau in a photograph—our bodies supple and eager, our eyes seeing only each other. In old age, we could both look upon such an image and marvel at our firm flesh, our immodest innocence.

Then I saw it.

A hand, yellow and sinewy. It reached up from behind the headboard and rested itself on Daniel's cheek, letting its long, bony fingers flail like a skeletal drape across his eyes. Daniel clearly felt nothing and saw nothing. I spun around, and it was gone.

Daniel lay stretched out in the same position, unchanged and untouched. He wore the lazy smile of a cat reclining in the sun, eager to be stroked.

"Come here," he purred.

I turned back to the mirror. Again, the yellow claw, caressing his cheek. Another unknown hand was reaching around his waist and running its fingers down his thigh. His flesh looked so defenseless, so soft, so human.

They are still here.

Issa was right. I hadn't outrun them.

"Stop admiring yourself." Daniel patted the empty half of the bed. "Come to me."

I tilted the mirror away from us and leapt into his arms, the strong, familiar swimmer's arms I believed had saved me from the darkness of the world. Rolling us over, he propped himself up on top of me. Our faces were inches apart.

"My dearest, why are you crying?"

It was then that I realized I was looking at him through a new veil—and not just of tears. Daniel was every bit as gorgeous, every bit as kind, every bit as loveable as before, but the enchanting quality that I'd attributed to him, the special sheen that had made him my knight and savior, *that* had vanished.

"I'm crying because I'm so happy." This wasn't a lie, but I knew now that this happiness couldn't last.

"You're even more beautiful when you cry, you know that? It's such an irony. Such a wicked irony." He kissed the corners of my eyes, and soon our kisses were mingled with the salt of my deep, unspeakable sorrow.

When he entered me, I held him so tightly that it seemed impossible two people had ever been closer. I clutched his face with both hands, reclaiming him from those defiling, monstrous claws. I kissed and licked his eyes and ears and cheeks, cleansing them of the horror that had tried to taint him. I wrapped my legs around his back and pulled us even closer, letting his every movement and every shudder reverberate through all of me. I wanted him to hurt me, to make me even more alert to the sacred intensity of the present.

"Bite me," I begged him. "Bruise me."

"No." He stroked my cheek and kissed me tenderly.

"Please, Dan, I want you to hurt me..."

"Absolutely not," he whispered. "I love you."

We made love through the night, drifting to sleep only to wake each other up every hour or so with a murmur, a kiss, or a caress. We had spent many nights together but never one with this kind of sensual compulsion. Yet, as much as I pleaded, he refused to mark my flesh with even the smallest nibble.

In the morning, I woke up the instant I felt Daniel pry my arms off his waist.

"Darling, you're holding me so tight I can barely breathe."

"Don't ever leave me." I hugged him tighter yet. "I couldn't live without you."

"I'm not going anywhere."

I nuzzled his arm with its dark, curly hairs and pores filled with the familiar, reassuring essence of Daniel: chlorine and Cussons Imperial Leather, musky with a full night of love. There was crust in his eyes and his lips were chapped—yet I had never seen a more alluring face.

"I want to bottle your scent," I said.

"Be my guest."

"Stay with me forever."

"That's my long-term goal." He smiled and kissed my hair. "As for my short-term goal, I want to take you back to the beach house. I want to make love to you in every room until the whole place smells like us. We'll bring bread and cheese and wine. We'll walk around naked for days and make as much noise as we like. We'll live like animals."

He had a dreamy, faraway look, the look of a boy speaking of dragons and snow-capped mountains, and I felt a surge of leonine protectiveness. I wanted to protect him and his fantasies; I wanted to protect us; I wanted to protect all the goodness in our world—for as long as I could.

"And we must go back to the cave," he said. "Our secret cave... That's where we should make our first child."

Our first child. Those words, that belief in our future, that faith in me. They struck me so profoundly I could no longer hold back my emotions.

"Hey, don't cry." He brushed away my tears with the kindest, gentlest hands I had ever known. "I know you're very happy, my dearest, but please, don't cry..."

That night, I found a red candle on my dressing table. A gift from Issa, no doubt.

When I lit it, the wick sizzled like a firecracker, leaving behind in less than a minute a scarlet pool of wax.

I STAND AT THE WINDOW AND INHALE. My breath is jagged from all this talking. The memories hit me harder still. I have never met a sweeter, more honorable boy than Daniel. He should never have been with me. Violet was right. He was too good for me.

How long have I been caught in this spell? A night and a day? Two nights, two days? It's bright outside, hardly the best time for a black reckoning. But I know better than to trust the face of things. The gnarl in my stomach has tightened again.

From the eighth floor in the clarity of noon, the city is one drab postwar Legoland, all crisscrossing telephone wires and boxy, rumbling generators atop each roof. But clear blue sky—no kamikaze crows. Miss Maddin is my crow, I suppose. She and I colliding; that would bring us symmetry, wouldn't it?

I'll take to my bed now and recharge. But quick, let me sweep up the bone dust I've strewn along the doorway. A fervent gesture at night, it looks ridiculous by day. Can't come across as a substandard housekeeper to my Professor Crow. First impressions can follow you to the grave. I should know.

THE DOORBELL. What timing. I've slept only, what, three hours. Not even that.

But she is here at last. My tardy savior.

My heart pounds.

"You certainly took your time," I say into the intercom.

No reply.

I buzz her into the building. Instead of the elevator, she takes the stairs.

Quick, steady footsteps echo up eight floors of stairwell, and before long, a middle-aged woman appears in my peephole. Obviously quite fit and determined to flaunt it.

I scrutinize her. So this is Professor Maddin. Certainly not what I've been expecting. She's not Dutch or South African or even European—she's Oriental. Should I be using the more politically correct term? Asian. Most likely Chinese, maybe Korean.

She leans in, the peephole turning her nose into a beige tuber. "May I come in?"

I creak open the door. She's tall and plain with an awkward smile, straight black hair. Under her navy blue blazer, she wears a white blouse and matching navy blue skirt. Business attire of the most generic, innocuous kind. No makeup, no jewelry. Should we compete at anonymity, she wins the gold.

She stands before me. I observe her short intake of breath as she registers my age, my stooped posture, my former beauty, such as it was, long gone to seed.

"Come in, come in," I say.

"Sorry for taking forever. I had to make some arrangements—as you know, every little thing has to be done in person in this country, and by hand. Japan..." A flicker of a smile creases her thin, pale lips. "What a paradox."

She steps inside. Her eyes dart across my little flat, comparing it to the image she's had in her mind.

"Did you have to travel far?" I look at her; she's empty-handed.

"Quite." She does not elaborate.

I follow her reptilian gaze around the living room. Can she see as I do? Or does she see even more?

"Please, sit down. Would you like something to drink?"

"No thank you," she says, too quickly. "I never drink."

Is this her idea of humor? Finally, we shake hands; hers are cold but not unfriendly. She has unusually soft skin for someone who's no longer a child.

She invites herself to my armchair.

"Please, don't let me stop you now." She gestures me toward the sofa, as if I were *her* guest—or patient. "Carry on. Lie down, if you like. Where were you?"

I stare at her. Who is she? *What* is she? She promised to bring me what I've been searching for. But would she?

"Ling, I have eyes. I have ears. I can see you're in the middle of a story." She pats the seat of the sofa. "Come on. Finish it and then we'll chat." She gives me her first real smile. "I'll meet you on the other side."

— 10 —

The Serpent in the Garden

I SENT INVITATION AFTER INVITATION, but neither Li nor Father came to see us. They hadn't the time, they wrote. They'd given themselves over to the volunteerism that was sweeping through Chinatown and spent their nights scanning for enemy aircraft.

"The rich sit in rooms and twiddle their thumbs," Li scribbled on a post-card of a tuxedoed dog tucking into a roast. "It's working men like us who will save the day."

I felt his words were extraneous; the card alone had made his bitter point.

China had been brought to her knees by the Japanese, and all across the Pacific, people were dreading a similar fate. On the Black Isle, we followed the worsening news with strange, morbid relish. Endowed with a deep sea-port and a steady supply of rubber and tin, we were an obvious target. It was inevitable that they would come. The only question was when.

I remembered reading in *Life* that German planes had rained leaflets along the uncertain boulevards of Paris: "Parisians, don't be afraid of bombs! Paris will be spared for the glory of Hitler!" That similar leaflets had not arrived from the Japanese elicited both relief and mounting terror.

To ease jittery nerves, the colonial guardians of the Black Isle herded up all the Japanese-born civilians they could find and housed them in barracks on the isolated western coast "for their own safety." I know that today such policies are thought inhumane, but I supported the internment wholeheartedly. Like everyone around me then, I feared and loathed the Japanese.

I pictured Mrs. Nakamura being ripped away from her octopus lover. If a civilian Japanese woman was capable of such perversity, it should have surprised no one that her compatriot soldiers were stabbing Chinese babies with bayonets and roasting them over open fires. Rumor had it some even ate them, doused in soy sauce. All across China, the Japs were rampaging, raping toddlers and grandmothers, hacking peasants in two with samurai swords, and razing villages that had been standing for millennia.

It was no longer just Chinatown that was outraged; it was the entire Island, the entire region, perhaps the entire world. Behind their elaborate pantomime of smiles, bows, and spoken pleasantries, the Japanese were showing themselves to be the most heinous savages on earth. Locking them up was the best thing our colonial leaders had done for public morale in years—crowds cheered as the aliens were trucked off. If only the government's other measures were as forceful.

The city had been dispatching Indian conscripts in small groups, each headed by a British supervisor, to lime-wash our roadside trees to help reflect headlights should electricity be cut off. Like most Islanders, I welcomed such preparations—until I saw the Indians chatting, then arguing, and finally dispersing after doing haphazard work. I quickly discovered why. After putting on a show for ten minutes or so, the white overseers disappeared.

The colonials, in fact, were vanishing everywhere. One by one, our neighboring bungalows became masterless domains. Robinsons, where their wives shopped for sundries, had become host to a sea of black hair. Li told me that the same was happening at Wonder World—no more foreigners all of a sudden, not even soldiers. It was as if a silent virus had come in the night and wiped them all out in their sleep.

Every day, droning voices on the wireless preached the sermon of preparedness, yet when it came time for crucial decisions, those in charge were nowhere to be found. It wasn't hubris, the excuse historians liked to use years later in maundering documentaries from the BBC. It was cowardice, pure and simple. Our rulers ran away. Looking back on it today, I would compare our situation to that of a play whose producers had decided in advance would fail and so made plans to be elsewhere on opening night. The Isle was doomed even before the curtains rose.

Money was no protection. One morning, I came downstairs to an inevitable development—breakfast in the Wee house had been compromised. The toast was bone dry. Violet instantly summoned the Hainanese cook.

"No more butter," the cook explained quietly.

"What do you mean, no more butter?" For once, Violet's indignation seemed justified.

"Fitzpatricks got no more butter. Margarine also coming to no more."

Fitzpatricks' big claim was if they didn't carry an item, then no shop or market for a thousand miles would have it. No butter at Fitzpatricks meant no butter anywhere, and no butter anywhere was terrible news indeed. The vanishing had become epidemic: first the colonials, now even plain old butter.

The cook disappeared into the kitchen for a minute and returned with a tray of eggs. Her expression was grave.

"What are you doing, Ah Koon?" Mr. Wee said, looking up from the morning paper. "What's going on here?"

The cook lifted the cardboard lid to show us two dozen eggs sitting snugly in their grooves. All of them were cracked. Peering out of each crushed shell was a bleeding little creature with obsidian eyes. Chicks, already half formed.

"Good God!" Violet cried.

Daniel swallowed and clasped my hand tight. "Dad, what should we—"

"Take those things away," Mr. Wee whispered. "Get rid of them at once."

"Bad sign," the cook said in Cantonese as she left. "Very bad sign."

I kept silent because I knew she was right.

After breakfast, Violet asked Issa to take her into town for groceries before supplies completely vanished. Daniel suggested I go along, and after a bit of resistance on my part, I gave in. This was as good a time as any for us to set aside our differences.

When we reached Middle Road, a roadblock at the junction of High Street kept us from advancing. Others like us, anxious women in chauffeured cars, were also out foraging—and failing. We watched five army lorries back out of Fitzpatricks' loading bay, honking repeatedly for clearance. Their green tarps bulged with goods—loot.

Violet shook her head. "Father told me they've been ordered to destroy the food, but I didn't believe they would do something like this. Aren't they supposed to guard us?" For a moment, she looked as if she would leap out of the car to protest, but instead she leaned forth and tapped Issa's shoulder. "To the Turf Club. Hurry!"

We raced back to the suburbs, arriving in time to see two lorries pull out of the Island Turf Club's winding, palm-lined driveway. I expected to see Thoroughbreds jammed in the backs of them, whinnying and blinking their big brown eyes, but they carried only soldiers, pale young boys with grim, spotty faces. I thought this was a hopeful sign—the horses hadn't been taken—but Violet gasped.

"Oh, God, no."

We sped toward the stables and passed the one remaining vehicle, an army jeep parked so hastily that it dislodged a whole bed of lilies.

Row after row, the fifty horse stalls were empty, the door to each left unceremoniously open. But the eerie silence suggested something other than freedom.

From the paddock beyond, we heard the exasperated cries of an Englishman: "Boy, go that side! You deaf or what? Not there, *there!*"

Requiring no instruction, Issa tore the car off the paved road and drove us across the grass toward the lone voice behind the stalls. We approached slowly, cautiously, inching toward a brown pyramid in the center of the muddy paddock. A uniformed British officer, evidently the one whose voice we'd heard, was shouting orders at two Indian jockeys as they clambered up and down the mound, splashing liquid from tin cans.

"You bloody buggers! Can't you hear me? You missed that one entirely!" The officer was so engrossed in his authority, waving his arms about, that he scarcely noticed our presence.

Fifty yards from the commotion, our car came to a halt and my stomach churned: I recognized the monstrous assortment of heads and tails. The beautiful Thoroughbreds, in the prime of their health, had been led out, shot, and stacked into this mountain of flesh. The coppery stench of death filled the air, and along with it, gunpowder and kerosene—the tripartite smells of war.

Jets of bright red squirted into the air each time the jockeys stepped on an open wound. The blood made for a slippery climb; both men lost their footing at almost the same time, slamming headlong against the faces of the creatures that until moments ago had been their treasured wards.

On the other side of the paddock, ten other jockeys stood frozen in a neat line, watching the scene in silence. A pair of baby-faced infantrymen had their rifles pointed at them, as if they were the next target. One careless sneeze on the jockeys' part could have triggered a hail of bullets.

Issa started the car again and drove us directly toward the pyramid itself.

"Issa," I said, "what are you doing?"

Violet buried her face in her hands. "The poor things...the poor, poor things..." She had a tender heart—when it came to animals, anyway.

"Issa, turn around and take us home," I said.

Pretending not to hear me, the pirate continued to drive. The British officer finally turned to see us, his head tilted in puzzlement. Nervously, he reached for his gun.

"Turn around *now*!" I barked.

Still, Issa ignored me. The officer had his gun out and his feet planted apart, poised to shoot. The boy soldiers, too, turned their rifles to our car.

"Issa!" I dug my nails into his shoulder. "If they don't kill you, I swear *I* will."

His eyes stayed on the road, but with the taciturn pride of a sage whose prophecies were coming true, he smiled at me in the rearview mirror and very slowly set the car in reverse.

"Learn to say *please*," he said.

Of course, even if I'd reported Issa's behavior, Mr. Wee had far more important things to do than scold a stubborn chauffeur. For weeks, he had been holding late-night meetings in the house, organizing—from what I could gather—a secret team of his colleagues to form a resistance should the Isle fall. He ran it along the lines of what he knew best, the chamber of commerce, and though his men didn't take to arms, they didn't "sit in rooms and twiddle their thumbs" (as Li had it) either.

Night after night, they arrived surreptitiously, some no doubt unwillingly, and convened behind closed doors. Mr. Wee had made it clear I was barred from the proceedings: This was man's work. Although he had the tact not to say it, I knew he felt that my loose—meaning female—lips could be a liability.

I was insulted, but I understood. Secrecy was paramount. As long as the British still ruled, such meetings marked Mr. Wee and his friends as anticolonial subversives. And so, the men came and went in the dark, wearing hats and scarves that kept their identities hidden from even the servants and, frankly, made them look ridiculous in the balmy tropical night. The tactic, if comical, was effective. I could never keep track of them, as only a handful were ever present at the same time and the roster constantly changed.

Daniel sat in on these summits, but reluctantly. He had little interest in politics—"It's all deceit, all the way," he always said—but felt obliged to give his father moral support. His job, he told me, was to sit by his father and nod and, when the need arose, carry in refreshments. I kept wishing he would absorb a few lessons about diplomacy and planning, but he remained resolute in his indifference.

The afternoon the horses were slaughtered, Lord Pickering, the colonial governor, made a surprise announcement on the wireless explaining that the increased presence of British soldiers on the Island was necessary because factory workers had been planning to go on strike.

It says something about colonial rule that, until the brink of disaster, I had never before heard the governor's voice. Because of this, I remember it distinctly. Lord Cecil Pickering II spoke as if he had a mouthful of caviar and couldn't let any of those fish eggs pop: "There are some on the Isle who are doing all they can to stir up trouble. I do not know if they realize it, but they are behaving as if the Nazis were their friends. I warn those people that I regard them as enemies and that I shall deal with them accordingly." He pronounced Nazis "gnat-sies." No mention of the Japanese. I imagined him, after the speech, reclining on a divan in a white toga.

All twelve of Mr. Wee's men were called together that night. I sat in our bedroom, tense, waiting for Daniel to sneak upstairs with a report. Two long hours into the meeting, the door finally clicked open to reveal the silhouette of my husband-to-be, hunched with worry.

"Father thinks the war's already begun, though nobody in government will admit as much." He hugged me to his chest, as much to give himself courage as to comfort me. His hands were clammy. "Someone said that Farquhar, the head of the general hospital, called an urgent meeting this morning. He told all the local doctors and nurses to be on standby. No one's to go anywhere. The same is happening throughout the civil service—travel freeze for all Asiatics—yet one of Father's contacts from the port said a passenger liner has just pulled in, obviously ready to ferry people away. They're trying to decide what it all means and what has to be done. I've never seen Father worried like this, and honestly, it scares me." He gave me a quick kiss. His lips, too, were cold. "I better go. I've told you too much already."

"Not nearly enough! Where's the governor now?"

"Nobody knows. They suspect he made that speech from abroad."

"Abroad?"

He hurried back to the door with an apologetic look. I waited about a minute, then crept down the stairs toward the library. As I passed the vertical coffin that was the grandfather clock, the library door creaked open. Out slipped a small-framed man who clung to the wall like a shadow.

He darted down the darkened hallway in a jagged, almost drunken manner. The shadow paused when he sensed my presence, tensed his neck like a squirrel scanning for predators, then took flight without a word. Of course: Kenneth Kee. Was he part of this cabal, too?

I made my move. I was close enough to the door to begin eavesdropping when a heavy hand fell on my shoulder.

I knew it was Issa.

"They are doing their best," he whispered. "But it won't be enough. They don't have what we have."

Without turning, without any hint of a concession, I said, "I want to talk to you. About everything."

"I thought so. Meet me by the car."

When I looked back, there was only darkness.

The instant we pulled out of the driveway, I started lobbing questions at him.

"Where are we going?"

"Forbidden Hill. Where it's safe to talk."

"Are you one of them, too?"

"Me?" He laughed. "What use would they have for a low-class chap like me? I have no money, no power."

"But that was Kenneth Kee, wasn't it? Why's he here?"

"No doubt he's one of them."

"But he's got no money or power. What do they want with him?"

"He's like a son to Mr. Wee. The son Mr. Wee would have preferred."

"What's that supposed to mean?"

"You have a gift for seeing hidden things and yet you don't see what's most obvious. Kenneth's a bright boy from a poor family, always first in class. Your fiancé—and I mean no disrespect—is rich but not so clever. It was a mutually beneficial arrangement: Mr. Wee paid for Kenneth's schooling so long as he let Daniel copy his schoolwork. For many years, Kenneth almost lived at the house. Mr. Wee even offered him the spare room but Daniel objected. Anyway, it was because of Kenneth's help that your fiancé managed to get a place at Oxford."

"But he didn't go."

"Of course not. If he went away for three years, who can say how his father's love would shift, correct? The prince must guard his place in the kingdom."

I held back my impulse to defend Daniel. Instead of making me think less of him, as was surely Issa's intent, these revelations filled me with a more ardent protectiveness: The boy couldn't even be certain of his own father's affections.

My questions about the Wees exhausted themselves quickly. Issa knew as well as I did that we had more dangerous things to discuss, not that I was ready to broach the subject: I didn't have the right words. He said nothing either and we drove on in silence.

The Bentley hurtled through deserted streets, reaching Forbidden Hill in fewer than ten minutes. Halfway up its south side, by the entrance to the cemetery, we left the car and began walking. The watchman had forgotten to lock the gates or had been bribed to leave them open—one never knew which on the Black Isle. We passed through them like spies from the world of the living entering the land of the dead. The change in the air was palpable—cooler, danker, the humidity clinging tighter to my clothes and skin.

"Don't be frightened."

"I'm not frightened." I was excited. The prospect of finally speaking to someone about the spirit world. My heart was racing.

"The dead are caught in an endless argument they can never win," he said. "The vast majority give up, but for some, this debate fuels them. It keeps them from having to accept the reality that, no matter how well they argue their case, no matter how *alive* they feel, it's already too late—they're dead. These are the ones you call ghosts." He gave me an enigmatic smile. "Come along."

The moon was full, a bright disk casting silver light on everything around us, everything except Issa's hair, whose blackness seemed immutable. Crows cawed and took wing as we passed.

I had assumed from the wrought-iron fencing that this would be a Christian cemetery. I was wrong. All of humanity was mixed up in this spiritual crossroads. On the gray slabs jutting out of the mossy earth like dragon's teeth were Taoist swastikas, Stars of David, Islamic crescent moons, even cherubim with plump cheeks blackened with mold. This was either neutral ground or a ring where all souls came to do battle.

We'd come seeking the quiet and had found it. Yet Issa seemed determined to drag me even deeper into the dark.

"Isn't this good enough?"

"Just follow."

We walked on until, suddenly, the world became so utterly silent and still that my ears felt hollowed out. No birdsong, no crickets, not even the faintest stirrings of a breeze. He stopped.

"Every cemetery has a sacred heart, where no sound and no wind can enter," he said. "We have reached the heart of this one. It is safe here. We will begin."

"Begin?"

He was not a man for small talk. He brought his palms together, crossed his legs, and lowered himself deliberately onto the damp grass. Thus arrayed, he nodded once.

"You and I are links in an endless chain of ghosts. The only difference between us and them is that we eat, we breathe, and we bleed." He gestured for me to sit, too. "They called my people the *Badjao* or *Orang Laut*—Sea Gypsies, the People of the Water. These names made us sound quaint, harmless, like simple people who spent their whole lives catching fish with their bare hands. But in the beginning, we had a title. We were the Royal Guard, the rajah's men. We were here for centuries before the rest of you came. We patrolled the seas. We kept the peace by keeping the invaders out."

In the moonglow, I saw him beam with racial pride—then instantly deride it with a sneer.

"But then our kings became greedy. They let in the outsiders in exchange for gold and silk. This one and that one, until eventually they all came. And now look at the trouble we're in. You may know us as the *Orang*

Laut, but we were never fishermen; we were never primitives. I want you to remember this."

"You were pirates."

His face twitched; then the equanimity returned. "We were *warriors.* We kept the peace by claiming what was ours. If you don't draw lines, you give in and give in until there's nothing of yourself left. But I didn't bring you here to talk about brigands. I brought you here to tell you about *ilmu*— magic. As the invaders came, my forefathers had to protect themselves and their livelihood. They turned to ilmu because magic is something nobody can take away from you. It is crucial that *you* remember this, when the war comes."

"You misunderstand me. I was hoping you'd tell me how to make them go *away.*"

"Miss Cassandra"—he shook his head—"you are gifted, a natural, and it needs you."

I froze. "It?"

"The Isle. Once all hell breaks loose, it will need as many of us as possible."

Again with his sorcerer's pitch. I'd never thought of my ability to see ghosts as being magic—much more a curse. "Tell me. You see them, too?"

"Yes." He smiled.

"Then how on earth can you think it's a gift?"

"How can it *not* be a gift? We can do things other people cannot."

"What if I refuse?" My voice grew louder. "What if I choose to be normal?"

"You will never be normal, Miss Cassandra." He began unbuttoning his long-sleeved shirt. Where the two halves of fabric peeled apart, I glimpsed his smooth caramel chest, covered with tribal markings. Two black serpents faced off in mirror image S's on his pectorals; below each of his shoulder blades was a black chrysanthemum rosette. As the white shirt fluttered to the ground, he flexed his muscles, showing off yet more: Black thorny vines crisscrossed up and down his biceps. I'd never seen these tattoos— he'd been careful to keep them hidden—and his priestly way of unveiling them suggested that we had embarked on some kind of a shared journey, no matter how unwilling I was as a traveler.

"Put your clothes back on."

But he proceeded as if he hadn't heard me.

"My grandfather painted me when I was twelve. Powdered charcoal, mixed with ground tiger bone. He believed it could ward off evil spirits. But evil is relative, isn't it?"

He rose to his knees, paused for a few seconds, and began digging in the dirt with his enormous hands. Before long, his palms were filled with fecund, loamy soil, graveyard meal fragranced with the humors of the dead. The recent rains had enriched the mix even more. I winced at the wriggling, blood-colored earthworms. He rubbed the black earth all over his arms, chest, and neck like the chieftain of an ancient rite, one that might suddenly turn violent.

"What are you doing? Stop that."

"Join me." It was an exhortation as much as an invitation. "We must dirty ourselves before speaking to the spirits. To earn their trust, we must be more like them."

"I came to speak to you, not the spirits!"

"Do as I say, Miss Cassandra. This is no time to be childish. I cannot show you the things I have to show you unless you do as I say. *Please.*"

I lowered myself and began plunging my fingers into the earth. The soil seethed as hot and foul as manure, moistened with the cadaverous fluids from six feet under us. But after slapping the first tentative pats onto my bare arms, my resistance eroded; the earth became a nurturing balm, a caress that heightened my sense of being alive. My mind leapt back to my nights alone in the jungle. I had been so powerful then, so alert, so fearless, and as much as I wanted to reinvent myself as clean, as ordinary, this warmth was proof that my flesh was inextricably bound to the earth. I crushed the dark salve all over my arms, more aggressively now, then on my neck, sparing no thought for the cotton dress that was my shell.

Kneeling on the grass, facing Issa, I could tell I'd passed some test. He smiled with no small degree of self-satisfaction, which instantly made me bristle.

"Don't look so smug!"

"Oh, I'm not smug," he said, still smiling, still superior. "Unlike you, magic did not come naturally to me. I had to acquire ilmu for myself, just as my forefathers did. There are several ways of doing this. One is through study, in which the seeker prays, fasts, and recites the Koran until he reaches a state of forgetfulness. Eventually, the magic descends on him. That was the way of my ancestors. My forefathers used ilmu to predict the rice harvest, the sex of a child, lucky numbers for gambling, but none of that interested me. I wanted something more powerful, something more... thrilling. And so I went down a different path, a path my forefathers warned me against.

"On a full-moon night like this, I went to the grave of a murdered man. I had been told that his enemy broke into his home and slashed his throat while he slept. Only at the grave of a murdered man will you find the restless spirit that is called *badi*. The badi is always searching for a better home.

"I sat on the grave. I took out my knife and started paddling with it, as though I were in a canoe." He mimed out the actions. "Left, right, left, right. After two hours, when my arms were aching and I was about to give up, the world... shifted. Suddenly, I was sitting in a canoe, a real canoe, in the middle of the horizon. The sky and the sea were both clear blue, divided by a white line. An old man appeared on this line and he began walking toward me, as if the water were solid. I knew this had to be the badi. When we came face-to-face, I asked the badi for a little magic. You cannot be greedy with spirits; you can ask for only a little at a time. Then the badi granted me everything."

There had to be more to the story. Restless spirits were not philanthropists—this I knew from experience. "What did you have to offer him? Your soul?"

"After a ritual like this, one is supposed to return the badi to a safe house, where it cannot do any more mischief. Usually, it's inside a monitor lizard or the heart of a tree. But I didn't. You see, my badi offered me a lifetime of ilmu jahat—what you people like to call black magic—in exchange for freedom. How could I say no? I was only thirteen years old."

I stared at him. With his upper torso soiled, he looked both grand and ridiculous—part guru, part child playing in the mud. In keeping with this image of him, I only half believed his story.

"If you possess such magic, then why are you just a chauffeur?" I asked.

"*Just* a chauffeur?" He grinned. "Why are you *just* a lady of leisure when you can be doing so much more with your gift? We do not evaluate success along such *simple* lines. Besides, being close to the powerful has its advantages, as I'm sure you've discovered for yourself. By the way, take a look around you now."

We were no longer alone.

The cemetery was peopled with the wandering dead, men and women of all ages, strolling past one another as if this were a town square, each of them caught in his or her own reality, oblivious to all else. *They are still here.*

He had tricked me! I stood up and tried to rub the taint from my skin.

"Make them go away! I don't want to see them! I told you I don't want anything to do with them!"

"But how will you command an army you cannot see, Miss Cassandra?"

He pulled a match from his trouser pocket and leaned over, striking it against the tombstone behind me. In its orange flare, I picked out Arabic script. We had been convening on the plot of a Muslim man.

"This is my father's grave." He paused. "He was murdered when I was young."

Murdered. The very word made me shudder.

I needed to free myself, get clean again. But the mud simply refused to be scraped from my skin. The more I tried to fling it off, the more it stayed on my fingers and spread all over my hands and clothes, everything I touched. This soil, darkened by a murdered man's essence, had encased me. My hands were shaking. How stupid I was to trust this loathsome pirate!

"Are you frightened, Miss Cassandra?"

"No!"

He stood up solemnly. "Fear is not a bad thing. We should never be afraid of fear. Because when you're afraid, you see the world in a new light. Everything comes into focus like never before."

With liturgical grace, he pulled out a dagger that was tucked under his belt, its jagged iron blade covered in wild floral engravings so fine they resembled fish scales. It was a *keris*, the sacred knife of the Malays. Only men of regal standing were permitted to handle one. Never women. And yet he was about to hand his over to me?

"Fear, rage, and evil roam freely in the world. To overcome them, you have to understand them..."

His grip tightened around the dagger. The curved blade of his keris dived down and slashed my left arm, above the elbow. Before I could feel its bite, the dagger was raised again, and in a flash my right arm, too, was struck. He was going to finish me off.

"Now you see what fear does? It collects you." His eyes were glassy, like an animal possessed.

"Please!"

"I'm not going to kill you. I'm just acquainting you with the truth." He pushed the keris into my hand and folded my fingers over its handle. "Do it. Row."

"What?"

"Use both hands. Imagine you are in a canoe. Row."

I glanced at the ghoulish red smiles on my arms. Warm currents of blood poured down to my hands, mixing with the mud until I seemed to be wearing dark, viscous gloves. Yet I recognized the cruel logic in his words, and having come this far, I now wanted his secrets. Wrapping my left hand over my right, I began paddling.

He continued. "You are angry."

"Of course I'm angry! How can I not be angry? You tricked me and then you cut me!"

"Good!" He chuckled. "Very good! Use that anger. Sink into it."

"Stop laughing. I could kill you!"

"Let your emotions collect you, Cassandra. Listen carefully: My badi was an old man, but yours may not be. The badi always takes the shape of someone you know. Don't be shocked when you see it. Concentrate your emotions, but control them. And be humble when you ask it for power."

I rowed hard. Left, right. Left, right. The ghosts of the cemetery were gathering around us, perhaps drawn in by my anguish.

An obese Tamil woman, her belly jutting out of her sari, her black mane sweeping the grass. A skinny old Chinese man in a moth-eaten suit. A small European boy in a pale blue sailor top, clawing at the pox on his face. I scanned at least ten others—a girl in a bridal gown, a Zoroastrian priest, a very tall Indian in a top coat. They kept arriving, and I smelled the fetor of their collective past: temple incense, curry, jasmine, sweaty underarms, stale coffee breath, formaldehyde, tobacco, and myrrh...

But these odors didn't disturb me so much as their vacant, needy stares.

I took my eyes away from them and fixed on Issa's father's tombstone instead. Left, right. Left, right. Left, right.

"Yes, that's the way," said Issa. "Ignore everything."

My arms had begun to ache, but still I rowed. And rowed. I found it easier to concentrate once I closed my eyes.

"Very good, Miss Ling..."

"Damn you, Issa, my name is *Cassandra!*" I opened my eyes.

I was surrounded by calm blue water. My eyes burned from the sudden brightness. When I reached up to shield them, my vessel began to list sharply from side to side. I was in a wood canoe—long, narrow, primitive. In my hands was a crude wooden oar. Water in every direction. No sight of land. I knew the only way to regain balance was to keep paddling in a steady rhythm. Left, right. Left, right.

It was just as he'd described—the sky and the sea, with nothing in between.

But wait. A black-robed figure appeared at the edge of the horizon, standing on the water. My eyes were grateful for this new focal point. The robe began walking, and with each step, it seemed to advance a mile.

In seconds, it was at my boat.

Somehow, as much as I tried, I couldn't look away from the magnetic darkness beneath its enormous cowl.

"You're my badi," I said.

"As you wish." It spoke Shanghainese, with a little girl's voice.

The black robe fell from her as if peeled off by some invisible hand. Underneath was my sister, five years old and pigtailed, in pink short-sleeved pajamas. She smelled like goodness itself: Florida water, talcum powder, and the faintest trace of fresh-baked almond cookies. Oh, the dimples on her cheeks! Oh, the little hairs on her arms! I longed to grab her and hold her to my chest.

But which twin was she? Xiaowen had the dimples, and Bao-Bao liked wearing pink...or was it the other way around? I couldn't remember. I couldn't tell.

"*Jie jie.*" She placed one tiny foot on the prow of my canoe and gazed fondly at me. "Look at me, *Jie jie.*"

I turned away. She—it—wasn't real. In real life, my twins were no longer little girls. They were teenagers. This was a trick by a graveyard sprite. A confidence trick.

"*Jie jie*, have you already forgotten me? Do you know which one I am? Am I Xiaowen or am I Bao-Bao? Can't you remember?"

My babies were never this solicitous. But the demon was right—I was guilty as charged. I'd let myself forget. The badi lifted her other foot onto the narrow, jutting nose of the canoe and perched herself there, knees bent in a squat like a little gargoyle. With her feet in place, she leaned forward, stretching out her index finger toward my chin. When she touched my skin, I felt the cold burn of an icicle.

"*Jie jie*, you're hurting my feelings. Why won't you look at me? I've waited so long to see you again. Don't you love me anymore?"

Her cold finger was strong. It tipped my chin up so that I gazed into her eyes, now very close to my face. I felt myself sinking into them. At the same time, she began to reek of damp earth, not the soil I'd been rubbing on my skin but something fouler and deeper in the ground, older, wetter, and sickeningly familiar…My invisible attacker at the plantation—he'd borne the same coppery odor. This same smell was in my lungs when he pinned me to the bed, when I thought I was going to die…

"Haven't you come to ask me for something?" the badi hissed. Up close, her babyish features took on a mocking hardness: Mother. "Or are you too proud to *beg*?"

I swung the oar at her.

Instantly the canoe rolled over, throwing me into the sea.

Cold. The water was bone-numbingly cold. I tried to swim but my feet refused to move. They'd become as heavy as anchors, plunging me deeper down the bottomless depths. My throat and lungs burned with salt water as darker and darker blues, then the blackest black, engulfed me. Even as I flailed with my arms, I continued to sink, lower and lower. I was being smothered, swallowed up by pure color.

When I couldn't sink any farther, a pair of rough hands seized me.

"What did you do?"

It was Issa, shaking me, furious. "Cassandra!"

I was back in the cemetery, collapsed atop his father's grave, clutching the keris. The ghosts were still there, watching my bewilderment with their impassive faces.

I despised them all.

"What happened?" Issa asked.

"I can't—" I picked myself up off the ground. Once the confusion subsided, once I realized the whole excursion had been trick upon trick upon trick, I hurled the dagger at his feet. "I never asked for this."

I ran. In just a few yards, I was out of the cemetery's silent heart. An explosive rip, then the noises of the real world: crickets, crows, frogs, wild dogs, and the night breeze, all crying for dominance, every voice shrieking. Plugging my ears with my fingers did no good. Every sound tore at me.

"Your hearing will return," said Issa, his words booming above the din. The disappointment in his voice was crystalline: "Wait for me in the car."

I staggered past the wandering ghosts of the cemetery, their bloodless lips rippling, murmuring indecipherable secrets. Together their whispers made a unified shushing, not unpleasant, like dead leaves being blown in the wind. Testimonies, apologies, prayers? They seemed to be gravitating toward a single point, every one of them—and I realized that the locus was Issa.

"What's going to happen to the badi?" I cried.

"Go to the car."

"Is there anything I can do?"

"I said, go!"

He turned to the ghosts. Two women, one in a sari and another in a bridal gown, were standing before him, expectant. He received them with raised arms, palms facing down, a pagan pope offering some kind of benediction. Both ghosts tilted their heads up as he lowered each palm to cover their faces. As he closed his eyes, his lips began to move, not quivering in the way theirs were but in a calm recitation of an ancient formula in an ancient tongue.

Watching Issa in action, I felt a surge of awe. So this was how powerful he really was. Until then, he'd been all braggadocio, all portentous guff. How wrong I was to assume he was *just* a chauffeur! I couldn't look away. I had to see what he could and would do. My curiosity was mainly selfish— I was thrilled to learn that I was no longer alone. That I wasn't the only one who *saw*, that I wasn't the only one who had to deal with *them*. Issa's strength gave me an enormous rush of relief because as long as he bore the burden of keeping the spirit world in check, *I would be free*.

Of his incantation, I caught just one word—*tidur*, which was Malay for "sleep." His hands continued to press down on the faces of the ghosts. Meeting with some resistance, he grimaced and his arms shuddered, but he didn't stop.

Both ghosts began to sink into the soil, feetfirst. Issa appeared to be sending them home "to sleep." Lower and lower they sank, until the pull of the subterranean vortex took over and he no longer had to exert any force. Soon there was no trace of the women. Two new ghosts had advanced from the group to take their place.

"Cassandra, go!" Already he was repeating the strange burial, palms raised.

"I heard you."

My ears stopped ringing when I reached the cemetery gates. I gazed down at my arms, wondering how I was going to explain away the cuts to Daniel. But both wounds had vanished, and my clothes showed no trace of blood. All that remained was dirt—the earth I had smeared all over my face and arms. The illusion of the keris was another effect of Issa's *ilmu*.

I waited in the car, drained yet exhilarated, monitoring the shadows cast by the wrought-iron gates. Nothing moved. Whatever exorcism Issa was conducting within the cemetery, none of the drama spilled out here. The ghost world was being contained by someone far abler than me.

I rejoiced. It probably sounds like the most feeble-minded response in the face of war, but the human heart will often react to crisis in the most inappropriate way.

That night, sitting in the car, I felt that for the first time in my life, after years of tolerating Father's weakness and Li's erratic behavior, I was in the care of wise and capable men—Mr. Wee in charge of earthly matters and Issa of spiritual ones. These strong, powerful men would make sure no harm ever came to me.

When Issa finally emerged, he was in his long-sleeved shirt. Somehow he had been able to wash off the mud. I felt a burst of pride at how stoic and regal he looked.

"Issa!"

He walked briskly to the car and, without a word, started the engine. The shirt clung to his skin, drenched in perspiration. As he drove, I tried to dry the sweat beading on the nape of his neck, but as my handkerchief neared, his skin bloomed with a million pale goose bumps.

"I thought you'd be braver than that," he said. "You always said, 'I'm not frightened; I'm not scared.' And I believed you."

His rage took me by surprise. It seemed unwarranted, considering how he had matters under control.

"Issa, I wasn't scared. I was angry."

He said nothing.

"So did you get rid of the badi?"

He swallowed but still said nothing.

"What about the ghosts?"

"They were supposed to be your army."

"Against who? The Japs?"

"Against anyone. Where human strength is not enough, we should seek *external* help."

Issa said nothing more and I didn't pursue the matter. He was seething. All I wanted was to go home and wash the filth off my body.

What I couldn't have realized at the time, of course, was that in abandoning the ritual, I had lost my chance to master my own gift, to alter the cruel course of history. It remains, to this day, the greatest sorrow of my life that I did not beg Issa's forgiveness and run back into the cemetery to complete what I had left undone.

It would have been that simple.

Because of my delusions, however justified or unjustified, because of my pride, however right or wrong, people I loved would perish in terrible ways. Of course, I cannot say for certain how many lives I might have saved, how many families I could have kept together, or how history would have been changed, but I do know that in the foolish complacency of a single night, in my choice of mediocrity over distinction, precious, innocent lives were lost. Oh, history.

I would never be clean again.

We cruised across the Edinburgh Bridge, the oldest suspension bridge on the Isle, arching gracefully over the Black River, gas lamps ablaze. Despite its name, the gray steel structure was constructed in Glasgow by convict labor in 1869 and then shipped over, grommet by grommet, chain by chain, and reassembled here. It was such a source of civic pride that policemen chased squatters off it every sunset. Tonight, under the full moon, carrying no one but us, the bridge looked especially desolate.

The surest sign of my remarkable shortsightedness must be that as we drove in silence along this overpass, all I could think of was how there was nothing lonelier in the world than an empty bridge in the night.

I had told Issa I wanted to be normal. But events accelerated the next morning, and in the merciless rush to keep up with them, normalcy became the first casualty.

Our breakfast was served out of tins: kippers, followed by peaches in syrup. Mr. Wee, Violet, Daniel, and I washed the food down with Earl Grey tea and gathered at the back door to watch Subramaniam and the gardeners. As Mr. Wee ordered, they had uprooted the rosebushes by the servants' wing, leaving deep holes in the ground that were then lined with clay tiles. Once they finished, the servants brought out the family's treasures—Fabergé eggs, china tea sets, and Mrs. Wee's old jewelry—triple-wrapped in burlap sacks and packed them into these subterranean coffers. When this was done, the gardeners began putting the rosebushes back in place.

I couldn't help but smile at how my affair with the ruby earrings had foreshadowed this current frenzy. No doubt the pair was experiencing a second burial. So much for the excessive drama of before. Now everybody was digging, scrambling.

"Careful," Mr. Wee cautioned the servants repeatedly. He called Little Girl over and unclasped the gold Rolex from his wrist. "Seal this in something watertight and bury it in a more secure spot. But make sure you remember where. This was a gift from my father. I'd like someday to pass it on."

She nodded solemnly, receiving the watch in both hands, impressed by its heft. "Do you want us to bury the big cross also?" She meant, of course, the crucifix in the sitting room.

"That?" Mr. Wee considered for a moment. "No, that should remain. Let it frighten the Japs a little."

As always, Mr. Wee possessed the dull gray, reassuring aura of someone who routinely erred on the side of caution. But my confidence wavered later that morning. He went into the kitchen and began rummaging in the drawers in search of something. Finally, he emerged with a pair of steel scissors, its looping black-painted handles bringing to mind the ears of a cartoon mouse. He held out the implement to Violet.

"Cut off your hair."

Violet's hands instantly went for her lovingly groomed bob. "But, Daddy..."

"Do it, Vi. We've already discussed this. Your hair will always grow back." He forced out a smile. "Be a good girl."

Her eyes filled up with tears as she took the scissors and, dragged along by mourning feet, slouched up the stairs to her bedroom.

"Cassandra." Mr. Wee turned to me. "You must do the same. It's for your personal safety. And put away your pretty dresses. We can never be too careful." Sensing my resistance, he clutched Daniel's arm. "Make her do it."

Burying the valuables was one thing, but Mr. Wee was behaving as if the enemy had already parachuted into Tanglewood and was marching up the street. Only hours earlier, he was Ignatius Wee the civic leader, hatching bold plans with his men. Now he seemed fatigued, as if he'd undergone a change of heart.

Daniel did as he was told. "Darling—" he began warily.

"I'll do it." What Mr. Wee said was true—the Japs were animals. "But I want a last look in the mirror."

"I'll come with you." My obedient fiancé curled one arm around my waist and directed me up the darkened stairway. He nuzzled his cheeks against my hair. "Know you'll always be my beauty, no matter what."

As the steps creaked under our feet, I told myself, *It's only hair, only dead cells.* But the pall of premature defeat...I felt a sudden urge to bolt.

"Come now, this is just a precaution." Daniel's grip tightened around me. "We can't be too careful. Better to be safe than—" He stopped, looking stunned.

At the top of the stairs stood Violet, body stiff, face tear-streaked and expressionless. Most of her hair, the best of her features, was gone. At first glance, she could have been a boy who'd been caught playing dress-up in Violet's things. But this was undeniably a young woman, with a young woman's soft hips.

She raised both hands mechanically. It seemed the act of butchering her hair had also sapped her will to live. In one hand, she held the scissors; in the other, dead clumps of black fell slowly to the ground.

"We've already lost, haven't we?" she whispered. "This won't make any difference, will it?"

I knew what she meant. After all, these were the beasts who tore into children and grandmothers.

"Vi..." Daniel eyed her nervously, unsure what to say. "Why don't you go back to your room?"

I broke free of his arms. "She's right, you know—this is surrendering. I'm not going to do it. I'd sooner die than be like that! I'd sooner die!"

"Darling, please! Don't you get hysterical, too!"

Mr. Wee came to the bottom of the stairs. "Let me be clear, Cassandra. I don't care if *you* die. But God help you if you take the rest of us down with your willfulness."

"But, Mr. Wee, this is like saying we've already lost."

"Arrogance!" His eyes flashed with an anger I'd never seen. "Daniel, take her to the beach house. We can't afford this here." Pursing his lips, he turned to leave.

"Father!" I cried, hoping to reel him back with sentiment. "Father, please!"

"Let's not get ahead of ourselves, Cassandra." He did not look at me. "Daniel. Go."

Pointedly silent, Issa drove us to the coast that afternoon. The sky was dark, not with storm clouds but thick marine fog that had blown inland and stayed, stranded. On the road in, it seemed like twilight—we could see neither water nor the beach. Yet this wasn't the only hint that the elements were awry.

The smell of the sea was magnified tenfold, as if we were breathing in clouds of rotting kelp. Even inside the house, with all the windows closed, we couldn't escape its salty, mineral reek.

Daniel paced the rooms, fidgeting restlessly, his fingers clasping the stack of cigarette cards Kenneth had brought him. He didn't take well to exile; without his father, he seemed lost. I'd never quite seen him like this.

"I wish you'd listened to Daddy."

"Your father was acting like everything's over. Remember how he said he didn't care if I died? I believe him, Dan. He doesn't care."

"But at least we'd all be together in the house."

I thought of what he'd said just days before, about spending a carnal weekend at the beach house. What a cruel irony that we were now here, alone as fantasized, but the mood was all wrong. Still, I slid up against him and began unbuttoning his shirt.

He brushed my hands away. "Darling, this is hardly the time..."

Let him sulk, then, I thought. I threw off my shoes and walked out to the beach.

The mist had begun to lift and pink-orange late afternoon light was gradually peering through.

It was low tide but the sand was barely visible. This time, it wasn't the fog. The shoreline was covered with parachutes—not down from the sky but up from the sea, each the size of a man's handkerchief.

Jellyfish, hundreds upon hundreds of them. The flat yellow sheaths were edged with petticoat frills, pale and ladylike, yet their gelatinous legs curled into long-fingered fists, symbolizing, even in death, defiance. They were everywhere, spanning the coast as swarms of buzzing flies descended on them.

The dead jellies alarmed me less than the few that were still pulsing, wriggling, advancing ever so slowly toward the house. Though it seemed impossible they would ever reach it, their invertebrate will was chilling; it was as if they were striving at all costs to reach us and deliver a warning.

"Daniel!" I burst through the back door and into the sitting room, just as he put on a record—"Blue Skies" by Josephine Baker, one of his favorites.

"What's wrong?"

I led him by the hand to the back verandah.

The instant we stepped out of the house, a cosmic switch tripped. A deep rumbling began at our toes, spread to the soles of our feet, then up our shins, our knees, our thighs. Immediately, a thunderous roar took hold, trapping our torsos in its cage of noise and shaking us until we weren't sure if we were being ripped from the earth or if the earth was being ripped from beneath us.

Our eyes scanned the sea. Even without speaking, we both knew what the other was thinking, fearing: A tsunami was upon us, a towering wave that would vomit from the bottom of the world creatures far worse than jellyfish...

I grabbed Daniel. "It's coming!"

But not from the water.

High above, piercing the fog and the gray clouds, were flying metal crosses, appearing one by one until they formed a V. As the planes passed over our heads, the red circles on the base of their wings stared down upon us like blood-filled eyes.

We became a single statue, frozen, unable to run. And in this moment, I felt something I never thought I'd feel: This wasn't how I wanted to die, clinging to a rich man's son, my own adventure barely begun.

We stood paralyzed until we glimpsed the tailfins of those soaring sharks. They were headed to the city—we'd been spared, at least for now. I unglued my beau and staggered inside on jellied legs. If he called after me, I did not hear him.

The house continued rattling with after-echoes. Every screw, every nail, every cup seemed to be bobbing, vibrating, alive. The Victrola needle jumped from groove to groove, striking random notes on the vinyl like a broken talking doll, yowling to be put out of its pain. The moment I flicked it off, a pencil shimmied off the dining table, hit the floor, and split into two.

When the rumbling finally ceased, I slumped into a chair.

Daniel appeared at the door. He looked at me with the forlorn expression of a child who'd done wrong yet didn't know what the wrong was. My face must have softened because he darted over and locked me in a tight embrace.

Caught in this awkward huddle, we both began sobbing, producing a weird harmony. In the distance, the bombs began falling, with long-tail squeals that lashed deep into our ears. We cried harder to camouflage the blasts. Six, seven, eight. What were they hitting? City hall, the esplanade, the tram depot? Nine, ten, eleven. Chinatown: Were Li and Father hit? Was everybody dead?

Air-raid sirens sounded in the distance, tragically late and tinny as the whines of desperate mosquitoes. The blitz, it seemed, was suddenly over.

A boom, this time much closer, shook us. Then another. Somebody was pounding on the front door. Were they already on the ground?

"Who's there?" Daniel shouted, his voice wobbly.

"It's me," came the unmistakable purr of Kenneth Kee.

Daniel instantly pulled himself away from me. The banging on the door began anew.

"I'll handle him," I said.

"Stop that, damn you!" Daniel cried at the door.

I let our visitor in. A mournful chorus of sirens trailed in behind him.

Kenneth looked as he always did—immaculately dressed, not a hair out of place, a manner informed by a reserve of reserve. From him came no hellos, no hugs, just a cold, unemotional order: "Put on the wireless."

I looked at him. "There's no wireless here."

"Then we have to settle for hearing the news firsthand." He went to the window and stared out. Together we heard a big blast followed by impotent antiaircraft fire, then sirens—round after round of sirens wailing from the city. Kenneth had on a strange sort of smile. I wasn't even sure *he* knew what he was feeling.

"That, my friends," he said, "is the sound of the British Empire, dying."

"What are you doing here, Kenny?"

"Your father told me to make sure you two were all right."

"Daddy? He sent us here in the first place. How did *you* get here anyway?"

"I drove."

"You drove?"

"I taught myself. At Oxford."

"Well, we're perfectly capable of taking care of ourselves. We don't need you."

Kenneth took a deep breath and slipped out the door wordlessly, but before I could chastise Daniel for his harsh words, he was back. Cradled in his arms were a kerosene lamp, a bale of blackout fabric, and a warm bottle of champagne.

"Let's keep calm till the morning," said Kenneth, carefully avoiding Daniel's eyes. "I'll take you both home then. In the meantime, let's not turn on any lights. And use this to cover the windows." He handed me the blackout material.

"What about food?" I said. "I'm afraid we may not have enough for three."

"She's right," Daniel jumped in.

Kenneth smiled lightly. "Don't worry about me. I don't need anything."

"You don't sweat, you don't eat. What *are* you, Kenneth Kee?" I asked him.

He shrugged. "A ghost."

None of us slept that night. The champagne hadn't helped; the sugar from it was buzzing through our veins. From our bed, Daniel and I could hear Kenneth prowling around the house, checking and rechecking all the doors and windows. He had taken it upon himself to be our watchman, and he did the job with more verve than mere duty.

"I know him. He's doing this on purpose," Daniel said. "To keep us awake."

But it wasn't Kenneth who was keeping me up. I couldn't stop thinking about Li and Father. Were they still alive after those bombs? I feared that their vigilante pride had put them on the roof of some Chinatown high-rise where escape would have been impossible. And then there were the ground troops. The amphibious Japs would soon find their way ashore, probably under the cover of night. An island, after all, is open in every direction, and we were trapped in a house, mere feet from the open strait...

With the house sealed shut, the air had become sticky and stale. I had grown so accustomed to sleeping in air-conditioned rooms that I found the humidity unbearable. Daniel and I had taken off our clothes and stripped the covers and still it was no use. I moved to the edge of the bed, fleeing the monsoonal warmth of our anxious bodies.

"Don't run away." Daniel rolled toward me and wrapped his arm around my waist, pulling me back into the inferno.

"It's too hot..."

He held me even tighter and pressed me facedown on the mattress, lifting my sweat-drenched hair to kiss the moist nape of my neck. "Don't let him affect us."

"What?"

"He barged in here, acting like a hero. Like we're helpless without him."

"I'm sure he's just doing what your father asked him to."

"That's the trouble—my father. Nobody asked Kenny to come back, yet ever since he's been back, he's been at those bloody meetings, behaving like such a great son. He's why I sit in—in case my father's friends think he really *is* his son. And I've seen the way he looks at you. I won't let him steal *you* from me as well."

His kissing grew more fevered, and when I tried to pull away from the heat of his lips, he gripped my arms with a new fierceness and pushed my legs apart with his knees. "Don't you...," he hissed into my ear. Before he could complete the thought, he had forced his way into me.

I was ashamed of my moans—Kenneth was just beyond the door, and I didn't doubt he had ears as sharp as his tongue—but Daniel did all he could to make me submit, and as loudly as possible. Biting my neck till I cried out, he plunged into me with such ferocity that the wooden bed squealed with every thrust.

"Say my name."

"Please, be gentle..."

"Isn't this what you always wanted? Say my name!"

I refused. He dug his fingers into my jaw and pulled my chin closer to his ear.

"Why won't you say my name? Say my name." He twisted my arm. "Come on, scream out my name..."

The sirens in the city eventually died down at four in the morning.

At dawn, the shore remained covered with jellyfish. No miracle had occurred overnight; no servant of nature had arrived to sweep them back into the sea and return the sand to its virgin state. Alas, what nature wrought was far less generous. The morning sky was darkened with a scrim—not fog this time but flies. Millions of them, from God only knew where. The jelly carcasses had browned with heat and rot, and their stomachs had ballooned, gas-filled and taut. The flies hovered over them, waiting and buzzing, buzzing and waiting, hungry for their day's feeding to begin.

A single jellyfish had made it to the bottommost step behind the house, tentacles shriveled in midreach. Its belly plumped like an over-yeasted loaf that was still rising, the skin stretched close to breaking point. I couldn't take my eyes off it. When this sac finally burst with a dull poof, I was thrown back by the shocking stink. Perhaps this first explosion was a signal that the rest should follow; across the beach, ripened jellies began popping, one by one, some flatly, others in piercing bangs. Flies and then flocks of gulls invited themselves to the feast, lured in by the putrid swill.

Kenneth came out and joined me, grimacing at the ruined shore. I imagined his mind whirring away on its ominous implications.

"Come on, it's time to leave." He tapped me gently on the arm, then

228

grabbed it, refusing to let go when he saw the blackening bruise above my elbow. "Does he always do that?"

I freed my arm from him and said nothing. The personal had to remain personal.

"And you let him?"

He didn't wait for my answer but walked away with a small, judgmental smirk.

Kenneth drove Mr. Wee's Bentley with the steadiness of an experienced chauffeur, one who knew that speeding was the surest way to unsettle his passengers. He kept below the speed limit.

Nobody said a word. I was still humiliated by Daniel's brutish behavior in bed and my response to it, and Daniel remained skeptical of Kenneth's every move. As for our chauffeur, we watched him pause at the crossroads just outside the city, pondering for a moment whether to take the shortcut that would plunge us into the devastation or the long detour, along the southern perimeter. Throwing a quick glance at Daniel in the rearview mirror, he chose the latter.

"Don't worry, Dan," he said softly. "I'll be out of your hair before you know it."

"I'm *not* worried."

The detour took us down narrow lanes that zigzagged through military barracks, then funneled us out alongside the port. Soldiers, mostly swarthy South Indians, were racing around helter-skelter, directing traffic, running along with sandbags and rolls of barbwire, seemingly without supervision. We smelled the burning fuel long before we saw the fat plumes of black smoke rising from the harbor and the wrecks of two titanic vessels, still blazing, turned on their sides like gargantuan steel whales.

"They got the *Prince*," Kenneth said, dismayed. "They've actually done it."

I leaned forward for a better look. So these were the glorious battleships, the HMS *Crown Prince* and the HMS *Resilience*, that were said to be guarding the Isle. A nauseating wave of pinpricks rushed through me and I reached for Daniel's hands—they were ice cold and of no comfort. Then our eyes met. His were swollen with tears.

Mr. Wee stood at the mansion door, as if he'd been waiting there all night. Perhaps it was a trick of light, but his hair had grown whiter since the previous afternoon. As we pulled up, Mr. Wee made a beeline for the car—and Kenneth's window.

"They got Pearl Harbor. The same time they hit us, they hit America."

"Daddy!" Daniel bounded out of the backseat and into his father's arms, almost knocking the air out of the old man with his embrace.

Kenneth turned back to me. "I can take you to Chinatown now, if you like."

I gave him a frozen nod and, filled with dread, slumped low in the seat.

As we pulled down the driveway, I heard Daniel's footsteps running after us. "Cassandra! Where's he taking you?"

"Let her go, Daniel," I heard his father say, steadying him back into the fold.

I didn't look back.

High Street was the busiest street on the Isle, but today there were almost no cars. I was embarrassed to be sitting alone in the back, with Kenneth playing my chauffeur, but he rebuffed all my requests to join him in front. Clearly, he didn't care what people thought.

I finally broke into his silence. "Is your family in Chinatown, too?"

"Perhaps." His jaw tensed. "They used to be. I haven't exactly kept abreast of their news. I haven't been the best of sons."

"So you haven't seen them since coming back?"

"Can't say I have, no."

"Then where do you stay?"

"Rooming house. Anonymous. Suits me well."

I wanted to ask if Mr. Wee paid for these accommodations, if his generosity had divided Kenneth's loyalties as it had divided mine, but I knew it was not my business.

"Are you worried about your relatives?" he asked. The gentleness of his tone surprised me.

"A bit." I laughed nervously. "Well, a bit more than a bit."

"I'm the same," he murmured. "You and I are just the same."

He stopped the car on Spring Street, which, except for pockets that had been reduced to rubble, looked eerily like its old self. Youngsters, darting from sidewalk to sidewalk, called for their parents and grandparents, and the street echoed with the wails of the filial, sounding as if they were all seeking the same few people: Papa, Mama, Ah Gong, Ah Ma.

A cross-junction away, our old eight-story tower block loomed, painted black to blend in with the night. In broad daylight, however, it looked to be the most inviting target. Yet for all its great height and funereal hue, it appeared to have survived. The neighborhood Pearl River cinema was not so lucky; its octagonal roof had caved in like an old pumpkin. The protruding ticket booth fared better, if one discounted its shattered window. The hand-painted banner for the current feature, a Cantonese-dubbed Abbott and Costello comedy, was singed but still fluttering.

I wanted Kenneth to drive us one block farther to the black tower and then go in with me to search for Li and Father, but the route was blocked by ambulances and rescue wagons. This was as far as the car could go.

People who a day ago had no inkling disaster would strike so swiftly sat dazed on the sidelines, their features made alien by grief. I knew that as soon as they noticed our car, we'd be overrun.

Sure enough, a band of women spotted us from a sheltered walkway and were now rushing toward us, waving their arms as if trying to hail a cab.

"You better go," I told Kenneth as I jumped out of the car. "Find your family."

He took a deep breath, then stretched his hand out the window. I shook it quickly. "Good luck, Cassandra," he said. It was the first time he'd spoken my name without it sounding sarcastic.

"I'll see you soon," I said, wondering if that were true.

"I certainly hope so, and in one piece."

I felt bereft as soon as the Bentley made a U-turn and sped away. I could have used Kenneth's company, even his odd, acerbic humor, while I searched for Father and Li. Why in the world did I let him go?

Looking around, I realized that this otherworldly landscape was in fact very familiar indeed. Kenneth had deposited me on the Spring Street traffic island, where I'd spent many an afternoon as a child. The stone bench was still here, as was the stump on which Mr. Singh the traffic man used to perch. I could have sat down and wept.

But I walked on. This was no time for nostalgia. All around me, I heard small, sharp explosions coming from the nearby high-rises. Sniper fire? From the erratic way they went off, with no enemy in sight, I began to suspect they were just gas cylinders blowing out windows. Still, every bang made me jump. Father's tower block seemed impossibly far away, and my legs were trembling so much I couldn't take more than a few limp steps at a time. Bit by bit, I told myself. I'd seen worse. I'd fought worse.

I approached the raggedy trio of women who'd tried to run to our car and called out to them in Cantonese, this being the lingo of the working class. "I'm looking for my family!" I gave them Father's name and Li's. "Do you know them? Have you seen them? You have to help me."

They stared at me; *they* were the ones who needed assistance. The middle one had a foot-long gash across her shoulder, with blood seeping down her pale blue tunic. She was nearly unconscious, and the agony was dangerously absent from her broad, rustic features. Her two younger companions—daughters?—propped her up, whimpering as much from her weight as from fear.

"Why did you let that car go?" one of the girls shrieked in Mandarin that came straight from the icy steppes of the North. "Why?"

"Please, help us," the other one moaned. "A wall fell on top of our mama."

Before I could reply, the rumbling beneath our feet started again, and the women began to scurry away. I gazed skyward. The planes were returning, but they were smaller, spryer ones this time: two flying specks tilted toward the area like birds of prey.

I saw something else. High up on the roof of the black tower, a man's silhouette poked into view. He'd emerged from a crouching position to stand at full height. In his hand was a small object, an object he was pointing at the planes. A pistol! I felt certain it was Li; such quixotic stupidity was just like him. The first shot rang out, followed by echoes that reverberated through the concrete valley. All the way down the street, I could hear the shooter's deranged yodels, the mocking hoots of a madman. No, this couldn't be Li; this fool was much crazier than my brother. Or so I hoped.

And then the planes were upon us, zooming over Spring Street, clacking like the world's noisiest lawnmowers, so primitive-looking it was a wonder they could even fly. I knew I should have run, but I was riveted to the spot, like a spectator waiting for the movie to unfold. I had to make sure it wasn't Li who was demanding his close-up.

High above the black tower, the gunman fired at the planes—four, five, six times. I was watching a child spit at a storm. This chap wasn't just mad; he was suicidal. I kept expecting him to crumple into a heap. But the enemy paid him no heed. Protruding barrels at the rear of both aircraft locked into place, and suddenly the ground around me was dancing—sand, gravel, stone, leaping into the air like fountains of dust. The earsplitting cracks of the gunfire came afterward. Crouching to take cover, I saw that the ambulance by me was riddled with holes: It had been the target.

The planes whizzed by and we were given a moment's reprieve. Frantic civilians emerged from nearby buildings to push by me, hundreds of them, racing toward the city's colonial core with nothing but the clothes on their backs. The poor frightened souls; they still believed the Brits could save them.

And it was on the backs of these terrified runners that I saw the dark shadows announcing the reemergence of both planes.

This time, the gunman on the roof got what he wanted. The first plane came for him. Having run out of bullets, the rebel stood fast, screaming taunts. The jet responded with a torrent of its own. The man's body twisted as if each hit was a quick tug of a puppeteer's string; his silhouette crumbled from view.

The other plane dived low, as if to scoop up the fleeing crowds. The wind from the passing plane pulled at me, even as I hugged the ground. Seconds later, the people running ahead began dancing themselves—puffs of red smeared their backs just before they fell, their flesh hitting the asphalt in sickening wet thuds.

Even over the din, I heard mad giggles from the sky. I thought it was my imagination at first, but I'd made no such mistake:

"*Banzai! Banzai! Banzai!*"

An eerie silence took hold as the planes vanished from view. I stood up again, hypnotized with disbelief. The street's population was doubling before my eyes. The ghost halves of the newly dead bloomed into view and began stumbling around their former shells. Some wailed, piercing the hush, but most were simply too stunned.

A hand grabbed me and pulled me toward a dust-covered row of shops.

"Are you crazy?" It was one of the girls with the injured mother. "I'm surprised you're still alive, standing there like that!"

She dragged me into a debris-laced watch repair shop, its glass window bashed in by looters. The display cases were shattered and empty; yet we were surrounded by a cacophony of ticks and tocks, as if the shadows of the missing timepieces were still here, declaring their presence. It didn't take long to realize that the ticking was coming from a row of grandfather clocks in the middle of the shop, evidently too bulky to steal. Behind this row, the girls' mother was lying on the floor, in a spot cleared of broken glass. Her eyes were open but registered little. The other daughter held her hand and sobbed. The girls, I discovered with a jolt, were identical twins.

"We just arrived from Hebei Province," the first sister told me, finally releasing my arm. "We don't know anyone, and we don't speak a word of English. Please, miss, you have to help us! Mama needs the hospital."

There was no telephone—it had been taken. I went behind the shop counter and rummaged through the drawers. All empty.

"Have you checked the storeroom?" I asked. Both girls shook their heads.

I dashed to the back of the shop, where a door was ajar. Inside the tiny space were a desk and a chair and multiple upturned boxes spilling order slips and other documents. Wedged behind the desk and the wall was an ancient, rusted bicycle. Pegasus brand. Nobody had thought of stealing this. I eased it out and wheeled it into the shop, its wheels squeaking as they rolled.

"Where are you going?"

"To get help."

"But the planes may return."

I was moved by her concern for my safety, as her own mother lay dying. She was right. I could hear a bomber circling back.

"What's your name?" I asked her.

"Our family's name is Liu. I'm Liu Shanling." She shook my hand. "My sister's name is Shanmin."

The rumbling sent us hiding behind the counter. We hunkered wordlessly as the plane dropped two shrieking presents onto Spring Street that left the entire shop rocking. Liu Shanling and I both knew, in the day's deepening gloom, that her mother wasn't going to survive. Neither of us needed to voice it.

When a graveyard silence blanketed the street outside and the ticking of the grandfather clocks became suffocatingly loud, I rolled the bicycle toward the door. Liu Shanling grabbed my arm again.

"Promise me you'll return for us."

"I promise." She released my arm. I looked over at the dying woman. "I'm very sorry about your mother."

"Hurry!" wailed the quieter twin. "Please, whatever you do, hurry!"

All along Spring Street, the ghosts of the newly dead called out to me in a Babelian crush of dialects: Hokkien, Mandarin, Cantonese, Shanghainese, Teochew, Hakka, and smatterings of other tongues still more obscure.

"What happened? Will you tell me what happened?"

"Why can't I move? Why can't I move?"

"Look at me! Why won't you look at me?"

"My whole body's on fire!"

"It hurts! Oh, it hurts!"

"Save me!"

The black tower loomed before me, its top floors burning. Despite my promise to Liu Shanling, I had to check on my own family first. But just outside the building's entrance, medics had set up a roadblock. Khaki-clad volunteer troops were unspooling thick bales of barbwire and police were turning people away. A Gurkha guard pointed up: The top floor looked ready to crumble, like the chalky corner of a block of cheese.

"Is anyone up there?" I cried.

"No idea! But we're doing our best! Come back tomorrow!"

I was about to argue when a section of wall, complete with glass window, came plummeting down the side of the building. We all ran. The white lace curtains on the window frame billowed in the air, almost balletic, but when the crash came, there was no grace at all—just rubble, dust clouds, and heart-stopping screams.

I fled. With its dented front tire, the Pegasus made for a wobbly ride, but given the devastation around me, I had no complaints. I pedaled toward home.

The colonial district was deserted except for the dead. Here, too, some buildings were flattened while others were curiously unscathed. From three streets away, I could see Robinsons, that great department store, blazing like a matchstick mansion. But city hall, with its friezes and Corinthian columns, looked confident as ever. The planes had targeted the concert hall next door instead, having reduced its Victorian clock tower to a smoldering cairn.

Hanging from city hall's largest windows were the banners of surrender—light-colored flags improvised from tablecloths and sewn-together shirts—but it was unlikely that these were what had saved the building. Instead I sensed in the bombers a more demonic perversity.

You see, city hall faced the large rectangle of green known as the Padang, or "open field" in Malay. To the flying killers, it must have seemed a grander canvas. Cricket and rugby were played here, Europeans only, except on parade days when members of the lesser races were asked to dress up in their "national costumes" and exhibit themselves as part of some colorful marching block. But now, as I glimpsed the white bodies strewn across the grass like abandoned rag dolls, I knew more than ever that the Padang's exalted green was just like any other green—all it took was a single blast from a cheap Jap bomb to form a perfect crater in the center of the field.

I cycled on. The reek of alcohol smacked me as I approached the Cricket Club, a Georgian pile at the Padang's north end. Shattered glass glittered across its concrete front steps, but not from any enemy bombardment. Weeping, ruddy-faced sots were gathered at the upstairs windows, letting bottles of gin slip from their hands and smash to smithereens on the ground below. Inside, a piano pounded out "We'll Meet Again," accompanied by an off-key chorus. The Union Jack, meanwhile, hung clammily on the flagstaff by the main door—it had never seemed more irrelevant or forlorn. Kenneth had been right: This was the death of the British Empire.

I paused there, horribly enthralled by the waste. Most of the sacrificial bottles had not even been opened.

But home, I had to get home to Tanglewood. I forced myself to concentrate as I pedaled, as if picturing the Wee mansion would bring me there sooner. My clothes were soaked with sweat and dust and the smell of death; my leg muscles ached with every rotation of the wobbly wheels.

After an eternity that was only three miles, I left the city limits and turned down the long road into the suburbs. The crickets chirruped hysterically in the banyan trees, threatening to drown out all thought. Perhaps not thinking was better, but I had to remember my mission. I murmured the names of the twins as I chugged along, feeding steam to my engine: "Liu Shanling, Liu Shanmin...Liu Shanling, Liu Shanmin..."

My legs gave out when the rain trees of Tanglewood finally came into view. I had to push the bicycle the last hundred yards, reminding myself what I had to do: Ask if Kenneth was all right, let Daniel know I was all right, enlist help finding Father and Li, get aid for Liu Shanling's family. What I actually craved was food, water, and a long cool bath. But those, of course, could wait.

The Bentley sat in the driveway, unscathed. I relaxed—Kenneth had made it back. I let the bicycle fall in a rusty clatter and ran the rest of the way to the door.

"Stop!" A stout man emerged from the side of the house, his face concealed by a khaki cap and large black kerchief. He pointed his rifle at my face and added in Mandarin, with a Shanghai accent so thick it pricked up my ears, "Identify yourself!"

I raised my hands but said nothing. Was he a looter?

"Identify yourself, I said!" He closed in on me, pressing the rifle tip against my throat. Then I saw something in his beady eyes shift as he studied my face, and from his unseen mouth came a shrill whistle, perhaps some kind of a bandit's signal. Running footsteps quickly ensued.

A reassuring face materialized at the door.

"Kenneth!"

Kenneth gestured for the gunman to release me. "She's the young master's fiancée. She lives here." He turned back toward the house without so much as a hello or glance in my direction.

"Did you find your family?" I asked.

"No," he said curtly.

"Did you even try?"

"Look, I have to get back to the meeting. Mr. Wee is waiting." At last he met my gaze. "Glad you're fine."

With Kenneth gone, it was just me and the masked gunman at the front step. Now it was my turn to question him. I used our native dialect.

"Who are you? Show me your face."

"No." He stepped back.

"What are you hiding?"

"My identity is meant to be secret. I work for Mr. Wee."

"Which means you work for me, too. Now, off with your mask and your cap."

With one reluctant tug, the black bandanna fell, revealing a rubbery, sullen face that looked oddly familiar. Then, as he lifted the cap from his spiky, sweat-matted hair, I saw the distinctive pink birthmark on his forehead.

I had been right—I *had* seen him on the tram.

"Cricket!" My delight equaled my astonishment. "It's you, isn't it, Cricket?"

The chunky young man averted his eyes. "I don't know what you're talking about, miss. Now may I put my mask back on?"

I felt my lips quivering at the coincidence, and at his denial. I didn't know whether to embrace him or pound him with my fists.

"You worked for my family in Shanghai! Don't pretend you don't remember. We were twins, my brother and me. You were our cook's godson. You kept spiders. And that birthmark. Sister Kwan always said it looked like a—"

"You're sadly mistaken."

"No, I'm not. Tell me! Do you know what happened to my mother and my sisters? Did they leave Shanghai?"

The fleeting look of panic that crossed his face made me feel sick.

"I don't know anything, miss." He scrunched up his features, feigning irritation. "I don't know you at all!" Then something rose in him. A conscience? He realized he couldn't maintain the charade any longer and heaved a sigh. "All right, all right. I may be who you say. But I don't know what became of your mother. I fled as soon as the Japs arrived. The irony is that I came here, and now they're here, too."

"But surely you heard news from . . . the cook?" I'd already forgotten her name.

"Everybody fled. We took our things and we ran. All of us, except . . ."

"My mother."

He nodded, painfully. "And your sisters. Your mother wouldn't leave the house, and she refused to let us take the little ones."

The little ones. My babies who were no longer babies. I shuddered thinking about them trapped in those dark rooms with the Gorgon while bombs fell overhead. Tears began streaming down my cheeks.

238

"I'm sorry," he added with a new softness. "I really shouldn't have said anything. I've been dreading this day ever since I came ashore—running into you."

"Was there any chance..."

"Miss, I really can't tell you any more. I simply don't know."

Kenneth reappeared at the door, puzzled to find me still standing there.

"Cassandra? Dan's been waiting for you. He's beside himself with worry." He cast a stern look at Cricket. "Zhang, where's your mask?"

Cricket seemed relieved to be given the order to cover his face. I turned to enter the house, still shaken by the unexpected visitation from the past. Cricket...Oh, how the walls were tumbling down! In the chaos of war, I could feel my various, separate worlds begin to collide—past, present, rich, poor, dead, alive.

Kenneth grabbed my arm in the doorway.

"Cassandra, before you go in..." He paused, trying to find the right words; then he whispered, "This may seem forward of me to suggest, but Zhang and I will be leaving for the jungle tonight to join our camp. Issa, the driver, is already there."

Issa, too?

"I was thinking that you might want to come with us. I know you have your obligations, but dammit, it's your *life* we're talking about. One can argue about loyalties later. You'll be safer there. The Japs won't ever find us, and we're armed to the teeth."

I was beginning to understand. Kenneth Kee, present at all the secret meetings. Kenneth Kee, always sure of what to do in a crisis. Kenneth Kee, who spoke so casually of arms. I stared at him.

"What are you? The Resistance?"

"Officially, we're Communists. Unofficially"—he smiled—"we're survivors. Think about it. We leave at midnight. And, please, I beg you, not a word to Dan."

Of course, I breathed none of it to Daniel. After an artificially cheerful meal eaten out of cans and lit by candlelight, we went to bed that night, chastened and a little embarrassed by the previous day's drama. Daniel was not one for explosive emotions. From his gentle caresses, I could tell he was quietly apologizing for his violence of the night before.

"Don't worry. Daddy will help you find your relatives tomorrow."

While he spooned me and anointed my back with kisses, I gazed at the bedside clock and pondered Kenneth's offer. It was ticking toward eleven. But how could I give *this* up? Would I throw away all the security I'd worked for by joining a band of outlaws in the muck? I saw Kenneth's intelligence and knew firsthand Issa's powers. But who could put faith in any of that during wartime? Mr. Wee's plan of diplomacy seemed the wiser, safer way. At dinner, he'd seemed utterly convinced that our house would be spared by the Japs—the result, no doubt, of complicated negotiations he'd made. If I remained in Tanglewood, I would have bed, board, a clean bath. If I went into the jungle...It wasn't a difficult choice.

Nevertheless, when the clock struck twelve and I heard a car drive off, I felt a sharp twinge of regret.

I fell asleep in Daniel's arms out of sheer exhaustion and anxiety, only to be woken before dawn by the rumble of planes.

"Shhh..." Daniel held me to him and kissed my neck. "We'll be all right. Daddy said our house will be all right. There's no place as safe as home."

We heard the air-raid sirens wailing from the city, followed too soon afterward by bombs. Even miles away, the walls of our room shook.

I sat up, ice-cold. In the excitement of returning home and seeing Cricket, I'd forgotten all about the Liu twins and their mother!

"I left them in that place. With no food, no water." I wept. "Oh, Dan, I promised I would save them! I promised!"

He clamped his arms around me, somehow fearing I would bolt into the night. "Calm now. I'm sure they're okay. We'll find them in the morning. Daddy can help. There's nothing to be done now. There's nothing to be done now but rest."

I couldn't rest. I jumped out of bed and began dressing.

"Wait."

Another ten minutes passed as Daniel got dressed. In the hallway, at Daniel's insistence, we waited for Mr. Wee to get dressed. Another five minutes. Through the half-open door to Violet's room, I glimpsed her still asleep, sucking her thumb like an infant. It still shocked me to see her hair looking so short and ragged. After what seemed like half an hour, we finally walked down to the Bentley, whereupon Mr. Wee slipped into the driver's seat.

"Where's Issa?" Daniel asked his father, his sense of order violated.

"He wanted to join his family. So I let him."

"In the countryside?"

"Yes, Dan, something like that."

The streets were deserted. The only vehicles about were either military or medical, and these drove urgently, ignoring all traffic signals. We found the watch-repair shop on Spring Street with some difficulty, between a mountain of rubble that had once been a cafe and a black hollow that had been a provision shop, neither of which I'd registered in the madness of the previous day. The watch-repair shop had not been spared. Seeing through the debris of the shop, I found beige glimpses of what remained—two young bodies wrapped around their mother, the three of them buried under tons of plaster and stone. The Liu women had waited loyally for my return, when I'd given them no proof of my worth apart from my word. Country girls. Decent, trusting country girls.

I covered my eyes in case I saw their ghosts and wept so hard that even Mr. Wee was moved.

"Let's go home," he said, his whisper echoing down the desolate street.

Look down on yourselves from the stars, I cried,
Look down on yourselves from the stars.
They heard me and lowered their eyes.

WISŁAWA SZYMBORSKA
"Soliloquy for Cassandra"

PART TWO

The Haunter

O<small>H, HOW I PINE FOR YOUTH</small>, even the unpretty parts. Even as this intruder sits in my room, hanging on to my every word.

I was young; now I am old.

My stupid hands. They're shaking again. How many little tapes have I filled? Ten now, each nicely numbered. I crown the existing stack with the newest one. It clatters when it strikes its sisters. Slight wobble.

In the darkness of my sitting room, the professor applauds.

"Original." She sounds amused. "This is the first I've heard of the jelly-fish invasion. And I've combed those beaches in my studies, so to speak."

Does she think I'm lying?

"But no, I don't doubt you for a second. You were there, with your very unique way of seeing. It's refreshing... your empathy with the natural world."

"Stranger things have yet to be mentioned, Professor."

"And I look forward to hearing about them. About everything, actually. Warts and welts and all. Spare no detail."

I don't see her smile but hear it animating her voice, giving it a forced note of intimacy. Suddenly I'm seized by a feeling of dread. She is, after all, a complete stranger.

I look around my apartment. This woman and I are sitting in the shadows when we should be greasing our knuckles in a well-lit ring, the better to see what the other's got. Damn the winter. It's just past four and already black outside.

I get up to turn on a lamp.

"Don't bother with the lights," she says. "I'm not afraid of the dark. And I can't imagine you are either."

"No, I'm not." Truth be told, I feel better not seeing her face. Faces can be extremely deceiving. In the quiet, my stomach rumbles, juices roiling in the void. "But tell me, Professor. Do you see as I do?"

"What do you mean?"

"See."

"Oh! No," she says. "I wouldn't be in academia if I did. Why?"

"Because not long ago, there was a ghost in this apartment."

She is quiet for a while. Then, very timidly, she whispers, "Is it still here?"

"I honestly don't know. I was hoping you could tell me."

Again, silence.

My gut betrays me again with another round of gastric purring. I blame the night for taking a slightly sour turn.

"Do you need to get something to eat?" she says, surprising me with her concern.

"No, no, I'm fine. I prefer to carry on. May I?"

Again, I scan the darkness for him, my ghost. I hope he will linger long enough to hear my side of the story, to forgive me for what I had done. But him and the professor—what is their dark connection?

Dear fiend in the shadows, are you listening?

— 11 —

Turnipheads

I'D FORGOTTEN ALL ABOUT CHRISTMAS. But on the tram three days after the air strikes, I saw the fairy lights strung across High Street, each parabola anchored by a lone blue star.

The lights caught my attention because they had been left on in broad daylight, eating up precious energy. This small disorder unsettled me as much as the ruins I had seen—it hinted at a much deeper chaos.

After I'd spent days convinced my family was dead, Li had telephoned to say that he and Father were fine. Naturally, when I begged him to join us, he refused. "They've already hit Chinatown twice; there's no way they'll hit us again." These lights—uncannily optimistic, spookily wasteful—reminded me of his cocky tone of voice.

I spent an hour haggling with one of Mr. Wee's contacts, a seedy Cantonese named Fatty Wai whose black-market operation was located within a halal butchery near the Balmoral Hotel. Mr. Wee had asked me to buy chicken breasts; Fatty Wai gave me only heads and necks. Mr. Wee had asked for a tin of corn oil; Fatty Wai said he could spare only used, blackened grease of indeterminate origin. His attitude improved when I waved a hundred-dollar note at him, but this didn't spare me a new round of negotiations. By the time we closed the deal, I was ready to collapse.

The tram took longer than usual to appear. There were four others waiting with me in the shelter, all women—though one had her hair shorn to resemble a young boy—and all nervous. We had each come from Fatty Wai's or an unregulated shop like his. Staring at the deserted street, we clutched our groceries, disguised under burlap sacks and newspaper as refuse or household items we were trying to hawk. I guessed that the others were either high-class servants or unloved daughters-in-law. None seemed accustomed to taking the tram. But with few private cars traversing the roads, public transportation was the best way of remaining discreet.

Finally, I heard a light, metallic rattling in the distance and felt my companions' relief: Our ride was approaching. Except, of course, I was the one person familiar enough with trams to know that this wasn't one.

The noise grew closer. From around the corner washed a great wave of bicycles. Hundreds of young Japanese men, maybe even thousands, decked out in short-sleeved shirts, khaki shorts, and canvas sneakers, were pedaling in silence down the unobstructed street. None appeared to be armed. They could have passed for local schoolboys were it not for their stiff, expressionless faces and the white strips they wore on their foreheads emblazoned with the bloodred Rising Sun.

"They look like they're here to bring peace," murmured the girl beside me, the slight creature whose hair was shorn. Her eyes stared with a dangerous optimism.

"Don't be fooled," I whispered.

The bicycles vanished. Minutes later, we heard stuttering blasts of gunfire echo from the colonial quarter and Chinatown, all the way perhaps to the river.

By the time the tram finally arrived, an hour late, the five of us were in jitters. One of the girls decided to walk after all, fearing ambush. The rest of us got on and prayed to get home alive. We closed our eyes when our ride passed Wonder World. It rang with screams, followed by the soulless *rat-a-tat* of machine guns.

The next day at high noon, the Japanese infantry marched through Tanglewood, their senior officers trailing behind in jeeps. The invaders weren't alone. They had Westerners in tow—a few soldiers but mainly civilians. Most of these prisoners were dressed in nothing but shorts and negligees, clearly rousted out of bed with no grace or warning, and not even permitted a minute to put on their shoes. The harsh noonday sun laid bare their once-white feet, now dark with dirt and cuts, already brown, already red.

There was no triumphant fanfare, only clattering engines, synchronized boot claps, and the fearful whimpers of the captives. The Japs had infused this victors' tattoo with their famous quiet restraint. But I wasn't fooled. Such understatement was a conscious choice. It was their way of boasting.

You've got the wrong whites, I almost shouted. *These are not the powerful and the vain. These are drunks, innocents, do-gooders, pacifists even—the ones left behind.*

Daniel, Violet, and I watched the procession from the sitting room window, while Mr. Wee stood in the open doorway. His hand rose to his brow in a salute when one of the jeep-riding toads aimed a squint at him. I was mortified at his easy submission. But I supposed he had no choice.

"They're marching them to Shahbandar," Mr. Wee said.

He didn't need to say any more to bring a chill into our hearts. Shahbandar Prison was more than ten miles away, and if the parade had taken this detour along the winding three-mile vein that was Tanglewood, it would also surely go through other enclaves where the Europeans once lived and played. The prisoners would have to walk twenty more miles before they reached the dank, rat-infested cells of Shahbandar, the Victorian jailhouse formerly assigned to the criminally insane, notorious for its midnight wails, heard for miles around.

"Serves them right, red-hair pigs!" Little Girl blurted from the gloom behind us.

Mr. Wee turned and glared, and her smile faded.

At the tail end of the cavalcade, two skinny soldiers, no more than sixteen, leapt from the back of a slow-moving jeep and scurried to our house bearing a cloth package. The grimmer of them presented it, with both hands, to Mr. Wee. But this was no gift. It was the flag. The boy soldiers pointed at the upstairs balcony: display it.

The Japanese reserved the pomp and circumstance for a radio address that evening by a certain Lieutenant Colonel Jodo, a limp-voiced man who announced that our isle was henceforth to be known as Lighthouse Island.

"Dear Islanders, I am honored to deliver the good news: The great nation of Japan has established the East Asia Co-Prosperity Sphere in which Lighthouse Island will play a key role. Japan has come to free your people from the yoke of the degenerate West, as Moses once freed the Jews, as the Buddha once redeemed the poor. You will no longer be enslaved, my friends. You will no longer suffer in silence and indignity under the white man's command. Stand up, Islanders, as we appreciate our beautiful national anthem. May the emperor's reign last ten thousand years."

His voice was replaced by the hissing of a record, which bled into a prelude of drums and cornets. The anthem itself, sung by a male alto, was composed of tuneless ee's and oh's. When he was done, a choir of young children repeated the ugly song; it was no improvement.

As we listened to this in the living room, Mr. Wee gazed at the bleeding Christ over the mantel.

"Well, they're certainly efficient," he said. "We have to give them that."

There was a knock on the sitting room door. Little Girl poked her head in. "The men are here, sir," she announced in the stiff, official voice she used with him.

Mr. Wee nodded and turned to Violet and me. "Ladies."

We understood. He wanted us out of the room before his VIP cabal could be led in. Violet took her needlepoint sampler and stood up quickly. She'd been steadying her nerves by sewing aphorisms all week—today's was *No coward soul is mine*, by Emily Brontë—and knew herself well enough to admit that politics ruined her equilibrium. I, meanwhile, lingered, waiting until she left before I spoke.

"Mr. Wee, I have relatives in Chinatown. If you let me into your plans, I can alert my brother. We can help you organize. I mean no disrespect, but it really does help to speak Chinese there. I know Mandarin, Shanghainese, and a few other dialects..."

"Cassandra." He raised a hand, vexed. "I have enough to worry about as it is."

"You know you can trust me—"

"Listen to Daddy, dear." Daniel remained by his father's side, drawing strength from this manly consolidation of opinion. "Go upstairs. I'll join you in a little bit."

As I ascended the stairs, the shadowy figures in the hallway below filed into the sitting room. I felt an unexpected hollowness when I remembered that Kenneth was not among them.

The next afternoon, which was dreadfully overcast, I bicycled along backstreets to Li and Father's temporary lodgings not far from Wonder World. On the telephone, Li had described it to me as a large rooming house. It turned out to be a slum—corrugated tin shacks pressed together to form a makeshift village.

Everybody there seemed to know them as Camel and Bitter Gourd.

They'd apparently made themselves useful, if not exactly beloved. Father—that is, Camel—sold cups of bird's nest without inflating his prices, which was considered honorable, while Li became the slum's unofficial warden, doing rounds at all hours wielding a parang. Through these small acts of community, Camel and Bitter Gourd had ingratiated themselves enough to Mr. Sun, the unofficial chieftain, to secure a shared sleeping berth in his shack.

When I arrived at Mr. Sun's hut, Li was alone, tying a bandanna around his forehead in the Japanese style, except that his displayed a hand-drawn Taoist yin-yang symbol. The dark rings under his eyes told me that his anemia had returned, but he was buzzing with nervous energy, perhaps fueled by coffee or, I feared, some less benign drug. The sight of him made my tears well up. The sun had tanned his skin and bleached his hair so they were now almost the same shade of brown.

"Why are you here?" he said coldly. But I could tell he was moved because he refused to look me in the eye.

I flung myself at him. My boy was all skin and bones, and his flesh smelled like old rain.

"Li, you have to come with me."

"What are you talking about? I belong here."

I glanced at his soggy surroundings. The morning's drizzle had not yet dried and another storm was already due. Chicken mesh stood in for a window, and rusted soup cans caught the rainwater that was still trickling down from the roof. The bunk he shared with Father was nothing but a bundle of blankets laid out on a wood pallet; my back ached just to gaze at it. The whole shack could so easily collapse on them, just as that shop had crushed Liu Shanling and Liu Shanmin.

"Don't judge me," he said softly.

"I'm not judging you. I want to save you."

"*Save* me? Now you sound like *them*."

I tried another approach. "Guess who I saw the other day? Cricket, of all people! He was at the house. Imagine that!"

"Who's Cricket?"

"Our errand boy, from Shanghai. Remember?"

"Nope. Everything from back then has vanished. If Mother were standing here in front of us, I doubt I'd recognize her."

I noticed the lump on his forehead he'd been trying to conceal behind the yin-yang symbol of his bandanna.

"What's that? Are you hurt?" I reached for the cloth.

"Don't touch it."

"Come on, let me have a look."

Li plucked off the bandanna. A gold disk fell into his palm. It was the toffee medallion from our day in the park, all those years ago.

"I can't believe you still have it."

"It's my only souvenir," he said. "Aside from you and *him*, of course." He caressed the disk and slipped it into his pocket.

A flurry of footsteps raced past the tin shack, bodies scraping against a wall and making the whole hut rattle. Li's attention, like a dog's, instantly shifted.

I grabbed his calloused brown hands. "Listen to me. Stay with us. You'll have your own room and you can take baths. You can protect these people from there."

"Protect the slum, from a mansion?" he scoffed. "Even if I wanted to, I—"

More fleeting figures passed the shack, along with anguished cries of *"Lopak-tau lei lo!"*—the "Turnipheads are here," *Turniphead* being the slang for a Japanese soldier.

Li moved his sleek frame to the doorway and peered out. His jaw tightened when Father appeared, panting.

"They've come in!" Father said. He didn't register my presence. "They're asking for healthy Chinese men. Nobody knows what they really want."

Li picked up his parang.

"They have guns, my boy," Father cautioned. "The slum is surrounded."

"I don't care. I'll go down fighting."

"You'll get everyone killed," I said.

Father finally turned to me and the blood drained from his face. "Oh! My little girl."

"I want you both to come with me," I told him. "Before it's too late."

Father threw a helpless look at Li, as if he'd given up his own free will and ceded all decision-making to his son.

"It's already too late." Li's words remained absolute, even as doubt began to cloud his eyes. "You better go home. I can take care of myself."

I embraced him once more, my fingers slowly easing the parang out of his grip. This was the most I knew I could do. I whispered into his ear, "If they try to take you, tell them you're Malay."

He put his face next to my cheek and sniffed at the air—or rather, he inhaled me so deeply that I felt my pores quiver. I knew what he was stealing, what he was trying to capture forever in a lungful: the scent of shampoo, perfumed soap and fresh towels, relics from a world now lost to him. He brushed his lips against my skin as if I were an exotic flower to be savored, not kissing me only because Father was present. Then he did it anyway—right on the lips. His lips were every bit as soft as I remembered.

"China man . . . China boy! China man . . . China boy!"

The refrain being bellowed up and down the alleys grew louder as the soldiers waded deeper into the pitiful maze at the very center of which we stood. They were closing in. Their calls reminded me of the old *karang guni* man from Bullock Cart Water, the one Li and I hid from as children. Only there was no hiding to be done now.

"China boy!" This voice was curt and close and accompanied by the sudden glare of a flashlight. I froze, expecting gunfire. Through the doorway, I saw a soldier's muddy boots and the glinting tip of his bayonet.

Li gently withdrew from my arms and nodded at Father, who gave me a wince of apologetic regret—*he* wanted to come with me.

"Let's see what they want," Li said. Before I could say or do anything, he and Father surrendered themselves. When I ran to the door to look, it was as if they'd been devoured by the disembodied voice. They had already disappeared.

Winding my way out of the slum, I saw lorries roar away from the cluster of shacks, bursting with human cargo. The men were penned in like pigs, watchful and passive, holding on to each other to keep from falling off as the lorries rocked along the bumpy, unpaved road. I'm sure that if I'd seen Li among them, I would have run after the trucks, screaming like a banshee. In the past hour, the roiling clouds had grown denser, darker. I pictured Li and Father in their open lorry bed. Soon, the deluge would soak them completely.

As I got on my bicycle, a little boy raced across a muddy field toward me. He was about six years old, his delicate round face stained with dirt and tears.

"They're going to kill them all," he shouted.

Then he, like Camel and Bitter Gourd, vanished, just as the first drops of rain came plummeting down.

Back at the house, my legs could feel no sensation. I couldn't eat. I couldn't contain my heaving sobs.

"But what on earth were they doing in that awful place?" asked Mr. Wee.

Mr. Wee, it turned out, had known beforehand about the raid on the slum. What he hadn't known, and found inexplicable, was that Father and Li had chosen to live there. Of course, I'd been too ashamed to tell him, or Daniel. Trying to be kind, Mr. Wee vowed he would work on extricating my people, as he called them, from Queenstown Prison, where thousands of Chinese were being "processed." Then he ordered me upstairs to bed like an invalid child.

"It's not that I don't trust you, Cassandra," he said, "but my colleagues are very particular, and I must respect their wishes. Every little misstep these days is the difference between life and death."

I trudged upstairs, still shaken by the little ghoul's words at the slum. Daniel came to the bedroom a few minutes later and was no more consoling than his father. He carried a glass of water and a sleeping tablet and placed them meaningfully by the bed.

"Get some rest, dearest," he said.

"You were there at the meetings . . . You must have heard about the raid. Why didn't you tell me anything?"

"Hundreds of things are said; one can never keep track of what's what. Mostly they turn out to be rumors. The men are mainly concerned with keeping the power stations and water supply free from tampering, and their own families safe."

Self-interest—but of course! I'd seen no evidence of any organized resistance against the invaders in the city, and it suddenly dawned on me that Mr. Wee and his gilded chums might have been playing it both ways: accommodation—that is, *collaboration*—by day, subterfuge by night. Hence the obsessive secrecy, hence the paranoia, hence Kenneth's and Issa's hasty departure to the jungle. At least Li and Father had stayed true to their principles.

"You don't understand, do you?" I cried. "If *I* had been at those stupid meetings, I could have saved my family!"

"But you never said a word about them. So how can you possibly blame us for not knowing!" Daniel was losing his temper. He took a deep breath, calmed himself. "I know you're very cross. But give Daddy time and don't ask too many questions. He's doing all he can to make sure we're safe. He'll solve things. I promise you he will. And anyway, remember—*we're* your family now."

"I wish Kenneth were here," I heard myself say before I could stop it.

The color seeped from Daniel's face. "Why?"

I shook my head. I had lashed out thoughtlessly, cruelly, when it was my own propensity for keeping secrets that had led us all to this. I embraced Daniel and prayed that it was apology enough. It took him a few minutes to forgive me.

I cultivated my little corner of freedom. I was sent to Fatty Wai's shop three times a week, and three times a week, I decided to make the most of my time away from the house. At this point, the city's dead harassed me more than the soldiers did. I'd mastered the art of dressing drably and looking inconspicuous with my wares, so the guards never paid me any mind. The spirits were a different story. They rushed up with missing limbs, pressing their bleeding bellies against me, shouting demands—revive them, find their relatives, locate their disintegrated bodies. They weren't malevolent— far from it. Their situation was only grotesque because their lives were finished and they couldn't accept it. If only I had completed my lesson with Issa. I might have known how to bring them peace. As it was, all I could do was look away.

To avoid them, I took a route that passed through the checkpoints. Instinctively, the dead stayed away from the enemy. The young soldiers were usually too busy fiddling with some stolen toy or another to bother me. The quieter ones even read books.

One morning, things changed. As usual, I had asked the shifty, sweat-soaked Fatty Wai for chicken, but today all he would give me were two odiferous, wriggling slabs he claimed were horse mackerel but were certainly live eels and a weeping block of tofu. These meant I'd have to make my way home as briskly as possible.

As luck would have it, the checkpoint guards were absent that morning. Enemy-free, the dead swarmed, grabbing at me as I headed to my tram stop. Cursing the soldiers, I elbowed my way through the throng of mendicant dead, hardening my heart with every step, closing my eyes to their open wounds. *There's nothing I can do for you, Uncle. Madam, please, I don't know how to help you.*

Approaching the tram stop, I discovered it was where the soldiers had gone. Ten or twelve were gathered around the shelter, locked in some new excitement. One of them, a bespectacled boy I'd earlier seen delighting over a pocket watch, was playing with a toy of a wholly different kind: a girl.

And not just any girl. She was the one with the shorn hair I'd met just a few days ago, the one who thought the bicycling soldiers were here to save us. I thought it couldn't be—the irony was too harsh—but indeed it was that same girl with her big, naïve eyes. She'd been stripped naked and was being spread-eagled on the wood bench by four giggling soldiers her own age, about seventeen, while their bespectacled leader unwrapped her shopping, layer by layer, with his pale, skinny fingers. From the slime-soaked newspapers, he pulled out a drooping eel. The girl had clearly been to Fatty Wai's, too.

In a show of encouragement, his enablers yelled, "Banzai!"

Unlike his accomplices, Bespectacled Boy did not laugh. With frowning, almost bookish devotion, he gripped the eel's head and rammed it into the crevice between the girl's thighs. She screamed hoarsely, retching a dribble of white froth down the side of her mouth. The boy continued to feed the eel deeper inside her until his hands were coated in blood. As the girl began to choke on her vomit, he shut his eyes, luxuriating in the effects delivered by his sexual surrogate.

I turned to run, fearing his friends would spot me—and discover my own eels—but fate intervened. A band of Chinese men burst out of a nearby shop house wielding rocks and knives. A brick whipped through the air and cracked Bespectacled Boy square in the head, knocking off his glasses and sending him sprawling to the ground. The other soldiers released the girl and reached for their guns. These looked like children's toys until one of the boys raised his and fired a crackling shot.

This was a call to arms. Yelling like men possessed, the Chinese militia rushed past me and fell on the soldiers, swinging their weapons. More shots rang out, and bodies fell on both sides. The battle then spilled onto the tracks. In the midst of this, I heard the clanging of the approaching tram. I rushed forward, preparing to hop on. But as the driver slowed down, repeatedly sounding his bell to warn those fighting on the rails, the violence spiraled instead onto the tram. Both sides leapt aboard and began clashing anew, forcing the driver to abandon ship with his hands in the air.

"Miss..." Somebody reached for my waist.

I panicked. Without glancing back, I sprinted down an alley that I knew to be infested with souls. My assailant quickly caught up and netted me in his arms. I struggled, heart pounding, but couldn't break loose.

"Shhh...Don't worry," he cooed in English. "I'm not part of that fracas."

Nor was he one of the dead. He was obviously a civilian like myself, caught in the crosshairs. When he released me, I was grateful for his company, as the ghosts around us scattered. I turned around to look at him. Not only did my rescuer possess a regal Oxonian accent as startling as Kenneth's, but also he was tall and broad-shouldered, with thick brows and a light beard—not a man to be trifled with.

He bowed his head slightly. "Forgive me if I frightened you."

I examined him more closely. He was fair-skinned, rather Northern Chinese in his features and old-fashioned formality. I sensed Peking in him—genteel, gold brocade Peking, not the Peking of bureaucrats and petty civil servants.

"I worried that you'd be caught in that fray. And I couldn't not intervene."

"Thank you." I was still panting. Gazing down quickly at my package, I discovered that the wrappings had come loose. The smelly, slimy pieces of eel were now sloshing around the bottom of my market bag.

"You're carrying fish," the man said matter-of-factly.

"It's not fish and it's not mine. I'm carrying this for somebody else."

"Lucky them." He smiled. "May I offer you a lift somewhere? My car is just here." He pointed out a black Ford, parked on the side of the road. "The tram's obviously not a wise choice today."

"Oh no, I couldn't." Of course I could—the eels even demanded it—but his chivalry felt too good to be true. "Were you following me?"

He blushed, and my fears were somewhat allayed. "I didn't intend to," he said. "But once in a while, a beautiful woman comes along and takes my breath away. My only regret is that I didn't act sooner, so you needn't have seen what those monsters did."

What those monsters did.

"Please accept my offer. It's not safe for a girl to be walking around like this. I'll drive you to your destination and shan't bother you after, charming though you are."

I looked at the car, mere steps away, and then back at the man, with his kindly, gentle eyes. The heavy, disgusting eels, for which I had paid Fatty Wai a small fortune, eventually decided things for me.

"Thank you."

As we drove, I marveled at his calm. He clucked at the sight of armed soldiers guarding Wonder World, whose tall red walls the Turnipheads had turned into some kind of a fortress. But other than these mild objections, my new friend showed little distress over what had become of our city, even as we drove around intersections blocked by blackened buses and fallen walls. His detachment reminded me again of Kenneth; he simply refused to let the horrors overcome him.

Once we emerged from the city and plunged into the leafy suburbs, with their scent of orchid and fern, I relaxed.

"Did you study in England?" I asked. "I have a friend who studied at Oxford. You sound a bit like him, actually."

"England?" He chuckled. "Oh no. But I had very good teachers."

"Where did you study?"

"Japan."

The back of my neck went tight.

"How . . . interesting," I said carefully. "How long were you there?"

"All my life." He threw me a dashing smile. "Perhaps I should have introduced myself. My name is Taro. It means 'boy.' I was the baby in my family, you see, with two older brothers. My parents called me Taro because they never wanted me to grow up. Unfortunately, I had to disappoint them."

Now I was speechless—and frightened. Why was this Japanese man helping me? We cruised up the lush green lanes of Tanglewood, all of the properties shabby with untended lawns, before he spoke again.

"How long have you lived here—I mean, delivered fish to the people here?"

"About a year."

He cast me a look of strange tenderness and continued giving me little smiles until my cheeks began to prickle. It was clear he'd seen through me. But instead of pointing out my deception, he stepped very gently on the brake, as if this slowing down would be a prelude to some sort of courtship, perhaps even a kiss.

Home was just fifty yards away now, the driveway packed with cars. I grew nervous. Mr. Wee's secret friends were here. I looked at Taro, but nothing in his expression changed. He didn't seem to find the cars unusual, thank heavens.

It was then that I heard a *vroom* and saw a military jeep pull up alongside us. In that moment, a chill ran through me. Taro remained calm; he gave the driver a solemn, respectful nod and waved for it to overtake us.

I relaxed. But only for a second. Swerving suddenly, the jeep crashed through the Wees' gate, speeding over the lawn and screeching to a halt in front of the mansion.

Taro placed one firm hand on my wrist. He watched, smiling, as four soldiers spilled out of the vehicle and barged into the Wee house—two through the front, two through the back. When I tried to bolt, his fingers tightened into a vise.

"You bastard!" I cried.

"That's not a very ladylike thing to say."

He drove us up the driveway in time to see Daniel and Violet stumbling out the front door, hands on their heads, tears streaming down their faces. A soldier followed close behind them, his rifle pressed against Daniel's back.

When Daniel saw me, he gazed at me with eyes that were less accusing than hurt. Betrayed.

"Cassandra!" he cried. "Why?"

Taro glanced at me. "Your name's Cassandra? Yet you didn't *see* this coming." He whipped out a pair of handcuffs and locked my wrist to his with a decisive click.

"Daniel," I wailed, "listen to me! I didn't know! I really didn't!"

"I always knew there was something wrong about you!" Violet hissed, her venom rising to the surface. "I saw it first but none of them believed me! You're evil! You're pure evil! You've destroyed *everything*!"

Taro chuckled. "I think this one likes you."

The soldier jabbed the back of Violet's head with his rifle, nudging her and Daniel to the side of the house.

More prisoners were marched out the front door, six men in shirts and ties—Mr. Wee's cabal, meeting in the afternoon for a change. These "conspirators" were brought out under the bright sun and displayed, I realized, for Taro's benefit. Without their scarves, dark glasses, and the cover of night, they looked utterly ordinary and vulnerable, squinting in the light, white singlets showing through their thin cotton shirts. They were all on the short side, balding and paunchy, each the very picture of the typical Chinese towkay. There were no Resistance heroes here, only small, nervous men wearing bright rings and expensive watches.

Taro nodded quietly, registering each of their scared faces. Finally, the pièce de résistance was brought out in handcuffs: Ignatius Wee. He was followed by a soldier holding up a stack of papers and an intricate map, evidence of subterfuge, perhaps. Taro nodded again. Mr. Wee's face was red with frustration. He couldn't resist glancing at the confiscated map, like an inventor forcibly removed from his life's work before he'd made his breakthrough. His eyes filled with shocked dismay when he spotted me in the car; this turned into a kind of dark puzzlement when he recognized Taro.

"Officer," he said, clearly trying to keep his calm. "Lieutenant Colonel Rukumoto, I'm afraid there's been a misunderstanding. I've been working with Colonel Nagata. Please call him. My friends and I were just discussing your plans for the factory. We were hoping to—"

"There's no misunderstanding, Ignatius-san," Taro replied coolly. "I'm sorry to break up your little tea party, but you know very well you were not to share these plans with anyone, not even your wife—were she still alive. 'Not even the Pope' I believe were Nagata-san's exact words. Well, Colonel Nagata always said he trusted you because you're such a quiet little man; I didn't because you seemed *too* quiet, *too* obedient. I like to think I have a good nose for treason, and I'm always delighted when my suspicions are proven correct. So, *arigato*—thank you."

Leaning his head out the car window, he gave orders to his men in gruff, guttural Japanese. The soldier watching over Daniel and Violet instantly began pushing them, using the blunt force of his rifle butt, toward the jeep. Another soldier leapt into the driver's seat and waited for the two captives. As brother and sister passed in front of Taro's car, Daniel cast his eyes away from me, whereas Violet shot me a glare boiling with the promise of vengeance.

"Daniel!" I couldn't bear him thinking me treacherous. "I love you!"

At this, Taro turned again to me, diabolically tickled. "Tell him you'll send him chocolates."

Mr. Wee ran to Taro's window, his face melting with panic. "Please, Lieutenant, I beg you. Don't take my children. They have absolutely nothing to do with this. Nothing! Please, Rukumoto-san, have mercy. I'll give you anything. You can have the house! Take my beach house as well. Just, please, leave my children. They're completely innocent. They know nothing! I beg you!"

Taro waved, and instantly a soldier struck the back of Mr. Wee's head with his rifle, knocking him to the ground. The poor man crawled on all fours as blood trickled darkly down his collar. The soldier yanked him up with one hand, slapped his face, and then, as Mr. Wee was still stumbling to find his feet, kicked him toward the back of the house.

Daniel and Violet were loaded onto the jeep, sobbing violently at the sight of their father in pain. I felt equally sick. This had all happened because I had placed my trust in a handsome stranger. Not true, of course, but it was how I felt at the time.

Violet shrieked her battle cry: "Cassandra, I'll hunt you down!"

Taro raised his eyebrows and smiled.

"Where are they taking them?" I asked him. I was startled by how small my voice sounded.

"Where the children of traitors belong."

"But they had *nothing* to do with their father's dealings. I swear to you. Please!"

My words meant nothing. The jeep's engine started with a jolt that nearly threw the driver off balance. Then it took off with Daniel, Violet, and their armed guard in the back.

As they disappeared, I realized all this business had been conducted by the lieutenant colonel without any show of force, without him even raising his voice or emerging from the car. It was his calm, not his men's violence, that was most chilling.

Finally, he decided to step out of the Ford. I climbed out through the driver's side after him, as we were literally chained, and followed him inside the house. Stepping into the foyer, he looked around with an exaggerated air of wonder, like a homebuyer come to claim his new manse. He closed the front door behind us.

"What a pleasant house," he said. "Good bones."

As we walked by the parlor, the large crucifix caught his eye. He raised his brows again but refrained from comment. In any case, it did not alarm him, as Mr. Wee had hoped. If anything, it only amused him.

I counted six discrete gunshots from the driveway, each louder and more appalling than the last. Six. This meant there was still a chance that one of the men, Mr. Wee, had been allowed to live. Then, as if to shatter my tiniest hope, Agnes began to bay in the courtyard behind the house.

"Come on, darling," Taro said as he drew me up the stairs. "It's about time we got better acquainted."

He didn't touch me that afternoon. What he did was odder.

"Where do you sleep?" he asked.

I showed him the bedroom Daniel and I shared. He instantly began looking through the wardrobe and drawers, fingering my undergarments one by one, pausing only to gaze at me with the same tenderness he'd given me in the car. Was he willing me to fall in love with him? Trying to convince me of his love? In either case, he sought my complicity. When he finished going through my things, satisfied that I'd hidden no weapon, he unlocked the handcuff binding me to him.

Immediately, I made a run for it. But he shut the door and leaned into it. When I rushed to the open window, he whipped out his revolver and aimed it at me.

"Do you really want to die?" he asked. "Because I will shoot you, you know, before you can even jump."

He stood before our full-length mirror, and I peered at it to see if there were others in the room, encircling his body as they had once Daniel.

There was nothing; we were completely alone. Even the monsters had fled.

"What do you want from me?"

"I would like you to be yourself," he said. "I would like you to behave as you would on any other ordinary day. Like an ordinary housewife."

To behave as I normally would—at gunpoint? In front of the enemy?

I wanted to scream but my body betrayed me instead. A warm stream flowed down my legs, and the silk carpet beneath my feet grew soggy.

Taro clucked. "Is this what you call acting like yourself, Momoko?"

Momoko? Was this a term of hate?

He put away his gun and folded his arms. "Clean yourself up. Remember, we're civilized people, not monkeys."

He sat by my bath. There was no hint of lasciviousness when he watched me, although his eyes were fixed upon my body. He observed me as a physician or tutor might—with curative, instructive intent, rather than as a man. I learned very quickly from this, and from the way he'd given orders from the car, that he was not one who liked to dirty his hands. If he wanted me dead, he would have a lackey do the deed; as long as we were alone, my life was unlikely to be in danger.

"What have you done with Daniel?" Just saying his name left me shuddering.

"As long as you're good to me, Momoko, you will see him again."

"What about Mr. Wee?"

"Momoko..."

He persisted in calling me that word, that name, which sounded like something one might call a child or a pet.

When I emerged from the bath, shivering though the day was warm, he picked out a red silk cheongsam from my wardrobe and laid it out on the bed. As I dressed, the smell of Cantonese cooking wafted up the stairs: soy sauce, sesame oil, rice wine, braised green onions. The servants! Were they still in the house?

He escorted me downstairs with his arm wrapped firmly around my waist, like a man leading his fiancée to a ball. Nothing about him looked threatening, let alone murderous, and this was precisely his most unnerving aspect. He had mopped his face and neck with a wet towel as I dressed. Now, with his hair moistened and combed down and his shirt crisp, he looked polished enough for supper with royalty.

The dining table was set for two and lit with candles. No sign of the servants anywhere. Yet fluffy white rice filled our bowls, and a main platter held two fatty eels, braised in the cook's recognizable style with chopped scallions as garnish. Just seeing these creatures, their heads still intact with cloudy eyes and serrated teeth, turned my hunger to revulsion. That poor girl at the tram stop...

"Won't you dine with me, Momoko?" He sat me down first, then took his place across from me. I noticed the absence of knives, forks, or chopsticks.

"What have you done with the servants?"

"I've done nothing. They cooked and then they left." He tipped an open bottle of red Bordeaux over my goblet and poured, then clinked his glass—pointedly empty—against mine. "Chin, chin."

"But you aren't drinking." It could be a fatal mistake if I didn't make him taste the wine first.

"Wine doesn't agree with me. I prefer sake."

I retracted my hands. "Well, I won't drink alone."

"Fair enough." He poured himself a glass and took a big gulp, wincing with distaste. "But you ought to have gathered by now that I mean you no harm. Quite the contrary, Momoko."

Smiling, he pushed the serving spoon into the belly of an eel. Instantly, the creature's gills flexed and fluttered. It was still alive.

He placed the juicy fillet atop the rice in my bowl.

I tried to contain my horror. "After you," I said.

"Thank you, but Chinese food..." He wrinkled his nose.

"Then why all this trouble?"

"Because I wanted to give you a final taste"—he cast me a smile that conveyed a galaxy of nostalgia—"of your old life. Isn't this a classic Chinese delicacy? I was served a dish like this in Shanghai once—the body cooked, the head left alive. The chef very proudly said it proved that the fish was fresh, and I thought, 'Barbarians.' Now, eat."

I did as I was told, spooning rice into my mouth without really tasting it. When he told me to have more wine, I did that, too. I sought oblivion, and the wine helped. Glass after glass, I drank it all down until my cheeks were burning.

I kept my eyes on the eel, hoping it would finally be still. But its gill continued to twitch.

Taro stood up theatrically, and with his eyes fixed on me, sauntered to my side.

I tried to appear calm. "Why do you call me Momoko?"

"You remind me of a girl I once knew named Momoko. The similarity is uncanny: the same penetrating eyes, the same stubborn jut of the chin, the same eagerness to flirt one moment and to scold the next. It's as if you were put here to torture me with memories of her." He paused. "Momoko was the love of my life. Every time I touched her between her legs, she would be silky wet. It was like stroking a live oyster." He smiled. "Once upon a time, I was going to marry her."

"Did she die—of disgust?" I used the bluntest words I could.

"No, no, she's quite alive. She just . . . didn't wish to be with me, that's all."

"I'm not surprised."

"Look at me," he said, his voice suddenly sterner. "Momoko."

Standing before me, he pushed hard on the backrest of my chair, and it tipped backward, taking me with it. My surroundings did a cartwheel, and the chair landed with a loud crack. I braced myself: This was it. This was the part where he avenged his shattered ego by slicing open my throat.

With quick hands, he pitched the chair out from beneath me and flung it to the side of the room; it clattered across the wood floor and struck the wall. Then he leaned over me, possessive yet not wholly certain of his power, like a tiger surveying his prey.

"Momoko," he murmured, gazing at me with wretched torment.

Saying her name galvanized something within him. In a second, his hand moved under my skirt. I felt his fingers probing between my thighs.

I struggled, trying to push his face away, but he held me down. It wasn't just him I had to fight off—the wine had fogged my head, paralyzed my reflexes.

I succumbed.

The next day, I awoke, alone in bed, a little past noon.

It seemed like another universe—calm, free of air-raid sirens and the sounds of gunfire. Had I been freed?

I descended the stairs cautiously, groggy from last night's drinking. The aroma of soy sauce and sesame oil clung to the air, along with a sickening marine tang. Otherwise, all was clear; it seemed I was alone in the house.

On the dining table sat the evidence of last night's feast—spent candlesticks, my rice bowl with its crown of oleaginous fish flesh. The chair remained on the floor, turned on its side, against the wall.

Ravenous, I decided to grab myself a bite of rice. As I reached for a spoon, I saw that both eels, sitting in a congealed puddle in the center of the table, were missing their bellies. Their eye sockets played host to colonies of flies.

Just then, a black cat, mangy and yellow-eyed, leapt up from one of the chairs. It began padding around the eels, hissing at me.

"It's all yours, kitty. All yours."

The front door beckoned. I burst out of the dank corruption of the house and into the embrace of the outside world. Fresh air ought to save me.

It was blazingly bright outside, the air filled with birdsong and the chirrups of crickets. But the view was terrible. Suspended from the porte cochere were two carcasses—man and dog, except neither was wholly man nor wholly dog. The heads of Mr. Wee and Agnes had been severed at the neck and exchanged. The two bodies were strung horizontally, limbs pulled aloft. Blood pooled on the drive below, the edges already blackening to a crust.

A scream tore loose from my throat.

As he'd done once before, Taro rushed from behind me, scooped me up in his arms, and kicked the front door shut behind us.

"They weren't meant for your eyes," he said.

Looking at him, I recalled the kind face of the man I was supposed to marry—my real fiancé, not this impostor, not this murderer.

"Daniel!" I shrieked as loudly as I could, in case he was near and able to hear me, in case he'd been held in the storeroom or the servants' wing, in case he could still detect the love in my voice.

The back of Lieutenant Colonel Rukumoto's hand lashed across my face.

I don't remember the rest.

Weeks passed. Maybe months. I couldn't tell. The monsoons had arrived sluggishly and washed away just as sluggishly; then the new year had come and gone. I only knew about this passing of time because there had been endless, sticky days with biblical torrents of rain, and there had been fire-crackers—then, before long, no more of either.

What concerned me on a daily basis was flesh. My flesh kept me alive. Not my intelligence, not my pluck, not even my ability to see ghosts, which, incidentally, was meaningless in a house where ghosts feared to tread. During the day, Taro kept me locked at home with his silent goons. I was free to spend these hours as I chose, so long as subterfuge and contact with the external world were not involved. And every evening, like an old-fashioned businessman, he returned to me, the house, and his waking dream of middle-class domesticity. I was how he numbed himself; I did for him what ten bottles of sake could never do.

I, in turn, began to look forward to his return, just so I had somebody to talk to. Of course, conversation came with a price of Taro's asking, and I soon adapted to this barter in skin. Sex became a way for me to crush the hours, to escape from the present and forget, forget, forget. I fled into my body.

It was also how I survived. Every night, the mindless act of removing my clothes bought me—and poor Daniel—another day away from prison or death. Whenever I did not submit as he pleased, my captor brought up Daniel's name—casually, of course, because all he'd need issue was a casual order and Daniel would be no more. With these tart little reminders, he ensured my compliance. But he wasn't always a brute. No, he was often startlingly gentle, exemplary even, and on those monthly days I was un-available to him, he was content to watch me eat, sleep, bathe—in effect, study me as I carried out the ordinary acts of life. He had no interest in my desires, never solicited my opinions; to him, I was a specimen, a pet, a thing.

The more mundane my activity, the more pleasure he derived from it. I learned not to panic when he stole into the bathroom to observe me brush-ing my teeth as if it were the most enthralling demonstration on earth.

He called me his wife. To the junior officers who frequented the house, I was also unofficially acknowledged as such, although they called me *Okasan*, which meant "Mother." I was never paraded out in the world or showed off to Taro's superiors at parties, because as a self-avowed traditional man, he believed that the world of the home and the world of the work-place should never mix. In fact, so convinced of his own dictum was he that I was never let out beyond the courtyard of the house, and even then, not without the supervision of some expressionless uniformed cretin who kept his hand on a pistol.

I consoled myself with the thought that I was experiencing a parallel confinement to Daniel, to Li, to Father, trapped in their respective cells, though there, of course, the similarity ended. Yes, I worked like a slave cleaning the house, but Taro gave me all the creature comforts he could gather during wartime, short of diamonds and foie gras. We had air-conditioning; we ate beef. He plied me with wine and, even better, cognac, chocolate, and books, trying to prove to me that he had a soul. I was not even expected to cook. One of his flunkies, an eighteen-year-old from Kobe whose family had run a tavern, became our chef. My epicurean offerings were required only in the boudoir.

Yet not one day went by without me thinking about Daniel, Li, and Father. I even worried about Kenneth, with his band of merry men in the forest. How could these fighters, mere flesh and blood, do battle with bombs? Of course, as Taro's "wife," I knew better than to bring up my fiancé's name. Already each time I mentioned Father or Li, asking to see them, he met my words with an icy silence, as if I'd uttered something so vile that he couldn't even bring himself to respond, that with my thoughtlessness I had violated the sacred rules of our union. He would use this as an excuse to get drunk. And when Taro was drunk, he was not a man worth negotiating with. He did not appreciate conversation, and he got very, very rough.

Several times each day, I gazed into mirrors, checking for ghosts. They were never there. I found myself praying for their return—even the spirit of Mr. Wee, who had cause to hate me—so I could glean from them news of the outside world or coax them into frightening my captors. I wanted my allies—my *army*, as Issa had put it.

Oh, Issa. I'd been afraid of the wrong things. The horrors I had witnessed far eclipsed the ghouls of his graveyard. But how could I right my cowardly wrong when I was no longer free to cross the street, let alone find my way back to Forbidden Hill?

An idea popped into my head one morning during my prisoner's constitutional—that is, my daily laps along the rim of the courtyard. I had the post-rain redness of the roses to thank for this bit of inspiration. They made me think of the gated rose garden in Shanghai and the dead children whose blood, Sister Kwan told us, gave the blooms their glow.

"Of course," I whispered when the inspired kernel took root.

My two young wardens eyed me cautiously.

"Okasan?" the shorter and softer of them said.

"Stop calling me that, will you? I'm not your bloody mother."

"But, Okasan..."

I kicked off my slippers and stepped away from the concrete, onto the soggy muck. The soldiers exchanged anxious looks, trying to second-guess my next move. I'd never strayed before, nor had I ever spoken to them.

"What are you doing?" said the taller, sterner boy, hands at his waist.

I leapt onto the most freshly heaped mound of dirt behind the rose-bushes, the sure sign of a recent burial. The soil was still springy beneath my feet. "Won't you join me?"

From their horrified expressions, I knew my instincts had been right— the murdered men lay below. This wasn't the sacred heart of any cemetery, nor did I know the words to Issa's chants, but improvisation was better than inaction, and I had nothing to lose. The two boys conferred in quick-fire Japanese as I unbuttoned my blouse.

The sterner one, feeling the strain of Taro's dictum to not hurt me, spat out his distaste. "Okasan, stay on path! We do not want you to have accident!"

"Accident? You mean, like this?" I flopped myself down on the sickening earth, the mud smearing all over my skirt and shins. I folded my legs as Issa had done and threw my blouse aside.

The sight of me in my brassiere, covered in mud, sent the boys into a panic.

"Okasan, obey!"

Using a twig, I began loosening the clods around me; then I rubbed the muck on my face, neck, arms, and chest. The mineral, *living* smell of the earth and the thought of the bodies beneath me made me want to retch, but I played at harmless high spirits, like a child making mud pies. I had to. "Come and join me!"

I continued in this manner until the humorless martinet stormed away, presumably to telephone Taro, leaving his comrade to watch over me.

"Please, Okasan," the nicer boy begged. "You must stop. Isamu-san says he wants to shoot you with gun."

My stomach turned but I continued to smile.

"We are forbidden to touch you, Okasan." He kept a safe distance on the edge of the concrete, as if the plant bed were molten lava. "We only watch you. For safety."

I closed my eyes and tuned out the world. I had to act fast, even if it was unlikely that Isamu would shoot his superior's wife for mere horseplay. I grabbed the twig in both hands and began rowing. Left, right, left, right—just as I had rowed on the grave of Issa's father. I realized the precise elements were lacking, but I had to try, just as I'd improvised on the plantation and then again with the ghost of the first Mrs. Wee. No longer could I witness this war as a passive bystander.

It was time to round up my ghosts.

"Forgive me," I whispered to the bodies below.

Not knowing Issa's Arabic chants, I called upon prayers from every cob-webbed crevice of my girlhood, murmuring and repeating this motley catechism with the hope that they would cede their customary meaning and take on the watery lingo of trance. This was harder to achieve than I'd supposed because, aside from me not being in the silent heart of a ceme-tery, my guard was continually barking, his voice warped with rising panic.

"No, Okasan! Please stop . . ."

I blocked him out.

Left, right. Left, right. Amitabha, Amitabha. Om, om, om. Our Father, who art in heaven, hallowed be thy name . . . Lead us not into temptation, but deliver us from evil. Left, right. Left, right. Left, right. Allahu Akbar, Allahu Akbar, Allahu Akbar . . .

I rowed and I rowed, faster and faster. I chanted and chanted, faster and faster, pressing my eyelids shut, blocking out the world. I had only mere minutes before Isamu returned.

I concentrated. I thought of the murdered men beneath me, savoring their outrage, their shock, their fear. I knew I could feel their pain like no other living girl could.

Left, right, left, right, left, right . . .

Sooner than I expected, the earth began to tremble. Or was it waves? The sea?

I opened my eyes.

"Okasan!" The boy soldier was still rooted to his spot, staring at me with terror. His hands stretched out before him, ordering me either to calm down or to stay away from him. The tremors continued in the earth, but where was the water? Where was the badi?

I tried to stand but slipped on the damp earth and fell back on my rump. My legs were soft, weak, and wracked with pins and needles. Heat was rising through the topsoil, the steam becoming visible in streams.

Something was happening.

Mere yards before me, fingers and then a hand reached out of the muck, the nails blackened by death, the flesh gray. The sight repulsed me but I was also thrilled: My summoning had actually worked.

Now more fingers and a second hand. The matching pair, finding their grip on the surface of the earth, flexed, consolidating their power. Two hands are better than one. With a muscular push, the ghoul's head and shoulders emerged.

But this was no dead man. This was the slick black head of Agnes—atop Mr. Wee's torso.

I screamed. I was witnessing an unholy birth—disgusting and exhilarating at the same time. Could it be that Agnes was my badi?

The monster slowly pulled itself out of the soil and stood on all fours, its clothes filthy with worms, moss, and amniotic mud. As it became aware of the sunlight and the air of the living world, it peeled open its fur-lined obsidian eyes to examine me. No animus, but no recognition either.

The mouth of the beast opened wide, wider than was possible for any living beast. Its teeth were not canine but human, blunt and square and lined with brown mucus. Its tongue glistened black.

"Agnes..."

That name stirred something within the creature's core. It closed its massive jaws and sat down on Mr. Wee's legs, suddenly more man than dog.

"Are you the badi?" I asked it. "Will you help me? Please? I beg you."

It tipped its head sideways, as if it wanted to understand me but could not.

"We can win this war. Help me, Agnes."

The beast leapt back at the name, snarling, insulted. It retreated behind the rosebushes, where it stood with its arms folded, like a disappointed schoolmaster.

"Momoko!" came the familiar voice.

I turned to see that my "husband" had arrived. Taro peeled away from his young wards and stepped briskly onto the mud.

I called out to the dog-man, "Stop this man for me, Agnes. Please!"

The creature had begun skulking away. It wanted nothing to do with me now that Taro was here.

"Agnes, don't go!" I turned to Taro. "Do you see that thing?"

His hand lashed across my face: No.

I split my attention between Taro and the spirit, one coming, the other departing, feverish about how the scene might play out. Anything could happen now that my badi was here. There was still hope; there was still time. I could salvage everything.

"Agnes, come back. Please!"

Taro threw another hard slap across my cheek. The dog-man sprinted away on all fours and bounded over the back wall of the property, disappearing for good.

The experiment had been a complete failure. Instead of raising an army, I had set loose a spirit, a monster, whatever it was. I didn't need a bomoh like Issa to tell me there would be repercussions.

"You're worthless," I said to myself. "Worthless."

Taro agreed.

"You shame me," he said. He caressed the spot where he'd struck me and took a more soothing tone. "The boys were worried you'd lost your mind. From now on, just to be safe, no more walks for you."

One evening, we had guests. Until I was told the occasion was related to the autumn solstice, I had no idea that ten months had gone by, since the Black Isle saw no seasons beyond rain and no rain. I had endured ten months' shame.

Taro stayed close by my side, as he often did when others were present, in order to explain to me yet another of his countrymen's customs. Their traditions often struck me as corruptions of Chinese ones, made more rigidly ceremonial, more fanatically devoted to hierarchy, and much more obsessed with death. This one was no different.

Arrayed around the sitting room, on every conceivable hard surface, was a constellation of lit candles. Seated on the floor, facing the center, were twenty soldiers in uniform, their boyish faces made even smoother by candlelight.

"This is an ancient storytelling game," Taro whispered into my ear. "The boys have been begging me to let them do this, but I made them wait for a moonless night. More atmospheric, you see."

We moved to the doorway, where we could view the action discreetly. The boys were starting to titter, perhaps experiencing second thoughts as they gazed up at the bleeding Christ over the mantel. Too late. The ceremony was about to start, and Taro—if not Christ—was going to judge them.

"The game begins with a hundred candles. Each boy will tell an old ghost story, a short one, like Aesop's fables without the moralizing; then he will blow out a candle. And so on. The legend is that when the last candle is blown out and the room is completely dark, a ghost will appear."

A ghost? Aside from my botched summoning, the dead never visited anymore—they were too wise for that.

"Do you believe in ghosts?" I asked him.

He smiled. "Don't spoil the mood."

A thin boy with the pinched, self-serious air of a head prefect cleared his throat and the chatter around the room ceased. He took the honor of being first speaker earnestly, intoning his story with the gravity of a village raconteur. Taro smiled and shook his head but did not bother to translate. Once he was done, the boy sucked in his breath and puffed out the candle closest to him. His comrades applauded politely.

"What did he say?" I asked Taro.

"A myth about an old woman who flies around searching for her missing arm, from a Noh play. Quite childish, in my opinion."

The second and the third boys told their tales and blew out respective candles. Again, Taro didn't translate them for me, and I began to feel impatient.

"*Botan Doro,*" he said just as the fourth boy began. "He's telling the story of the Peony Lantern. Do you know it? It's Chinese in origin. Shocking, but quite poorly structured, like most Chinese tales."

The fourth candle went out. The night was going to be long indeed if Taro refused to do any translating. I made a motion to retreat upstairs, but he grabbed my arm.

"Wait," he said, and listened as the fifth boy began. This one earned a smile of approval from him. "The story of Kiyohime." A tremor of excitement shot through the room. The audience, likewise, was energized.

"Kiyohime was the daughter of a village innkeeper," Taro explained. "Every year, a handsome young monk named Anchin stopped at the inn while making his annual pilgrimage to a shrine, and every year Kiyohime fell more in love with him. Finally one year, she was so overcome by her emotions that she confessed them to the monk. He was terrified—he was a monk, after all. He immediately fled from her, back to his monastery. He had seen the mad lust in her eyes. Furious, Kiyohime chased him for miles but found herself stopped at the Hidaka River, which he had crossed in a boat. Her rage grew and grew until her lower body transformed into a sea serpent, and she swam across the water. When the other monks warned Anchin that she was approaching, he hid under his temple's large bronze bell. Possessing the instincts of a snake, Kiyohime found him all the same. She coiled her snake body around the bell, and so intense was her fury that she melted it, killing them both and melding them together forever."

Taro applauded the loudest at the end of this tale, causing the storyteller to blush and bow his head. The others turned to glimpse the rare sight of their lieutenant colonel showing approval. I myself knew how uncommon this was.

"You may go now, if you like," he told me as the sixth storyteller began. "I'm staying to see which of my boys starts wailing like a girl before the end."

I went upstairs and prepared for bed. Every four or five minutes came the clatter of applause from downstairs. I waited for the mewls of panic but guessed we'd have to be deeper into the night for any to emerge. I fell asleep before Taro could join me.

Sometime later, I jolted awake. I was alone still. The room was black, no moonlight. Not a peep from downstairs either. Was the game over? I flicked on my bedside lamp.

There was a man in my room. He sat cross-legged on the floor, startlingly gaunt.

Father!

He was close enough to touch me with his bony hand and I dreaded that he would. I didn't want to feel just how frail it was, how unlike the hand that once possessed the vigor to hurt me. Had Taro brought him here to see me? If so, my separate worlds were colliding again.

"My precious daughter," he said in the musical Shanghainese of our lost world. He spoke it as if it were our own private language, partaken by nobody else, but his voice had a terrifying hollowness. "I have died."

The meaning of his words quickly took hold.

"Don't cry, my girl," he said with a kindness I hadn't seen since childhood. "I know you did your best, and I'm relieved that I've found you again."

"What did they do to you?"

"The afternoon you saw them take us, they threw us into Queenstown Prison. They'd heard that Chinese rebels were living in our slum—and yes, those rumors were true. Your brother was one of them. Brave boy. But nobody would talk so they blindfolded us and took us away. I only know it was a beach because I could smell the sea and feel the sand between my toes. The waves were very quiet, very calm, like the whispers of children who knew not to interfere while grownups were talking. And then they ordered us to wade into the water. I thought they were going to make us swim until we drowned, but that would have been much too slow. I felt the water rise up to my knees and...they shot us."

My stomach lurched. "Was Li with you?"

"That's what I've come to tell you. They didn't take him. As you saw, his skin had become quite dark. And he remembered many phrases from our plantation days. He convinced them he was a Malay, clever boy, and they let him go. It is strange how what shames us can sometimes return to save us."

Thank heavens, Li had heeded my advice after all.

"There are so many things I want to tell you but my energy is nearly gone. So let me hurry: Li's survived so far on his wits but his luck's run out. Last week, two soldiers caught him stealing a bao. A *bao*! You know how he needs his nutrition. They've locked him up at Shahbandar and his anemia has gone from bad to worse. You must save him. At the very least, visit him, feed him, make sure he's all right."

"But I'm trapped here, Father! Can't you see? I'm a prisoner, too."

"I beg you. You're his only hope..." His voice trailed off. "Our family..."

The bedroom door clicked open, and as I turned to look, Father vanished—without any kind of good-bye. Now I wished he *had* tried to touch me with his bony hand. In death, he was gentler and more compassionate than he'd been in years. I felt abandoned, robbed of our final words.

Taro stepped into the room, reeking of sake. He'd begun to undress when he realized I was awake and that the light was on. But he barely noticed my face or he would have seen my tears.

"Can't you sleep? Did the talk of ghosts bother you?" He flopped into bed with a sigh, hurling his shirt onto the floor. "I hope you don't believe in that rubbish, a sensible woman like you. Now, turn off your light."

I did as I was told and scanned the darkness for Father. Nothing.

"How did the game end?" I asked.

"Of course, nothing happened, but it didn't stop them from acting like terrified sissies. One of the boys, Takara, claimed he saw a cloud of white smoke rushing up the stairs. 'Like cotton wool?' I asked him. 'No, sir,' he said. 'Like your breath on a cold winter's night, sir.'" He paused for a moment, then added, laughing, "Tomorrow, I'm assigning that fool to sentry duty in the jungle—alone!"

I waited till he was settled against his pillow before I brought my fingers to his waist and caressed his beef-fed, sake-filled belly.

"Your hands!" He flung them away. "They're as cold as a corpse's!"

I rested my head on his chest instead and let my tears pool on his skin.

"What's the matter now?"

"I miss my brother."

"And what's inspired this mawkish display?"

"It's been much too long. He needs me."

He gave a lascivious chuckle. "*Needs* you?"

"He's not just my brother; he's my twin. You can't really understand unless you have a twin. Couldn't he stay here with us? He's good, very good, I promise."

"How good? Should I consider corrupting him?"

I clutched at his arm. "If we're kept apart for too long, we fade."

"I see you've let those stories go to your head. People aren't ghosts, Momoko—they don't *fade*." He turned on his side and yawned. "I'm tired. We'll discuss it in the morning."

As I feared, there was no discussion in the morning.

Taro decided that a change of scenery would cure whatever ailed me, and I was whisked away to the beach house. Yes, he had accepted Mr. Wee's "offer" and had wasted no time in claiming the place as his own, having revamped its interior so that it now resembled a rustic Japanese cabin: floors covered wall to wall with tatami mats and funerary white paper lanterns strung everywhere. The Wees' expensive chairs, tables, and settees had been thrown onto a bonfire and the orchid-print curtains replaced by bamboo shades in the same sickly hue as the mats. The house that had once felt like an idyllic refuge was now an austere, bare-bones penitentiary, devoid of anything soft or luxurious.

Through the windows, I saw that hundreds of papayas had fallen, overripe, from their trees, splattering puddles of orange vomit on the grass. Taro must have felt that tropical fruit was beneath him and ordered his men not to touch them. I burned with rage at the willful waste—elsewhere on the Isle, good people were starving.

"Enjoy your rest," Taro told me before leaving me in what used to be the sitting room but now contained nothing to sit on. "I'll collect you when you're recovered."

"How long do I have to be here?"

"That's entirely up to you, Momoko."

He strode back to his car as four blank-faced underlings created a human wall between us. Without once glancing back, my "husband" drove off. The quartet of young soldiers didn't move a muscle until the engine putter of his car was drowned beneath the crashing of waves. But once he was gone, these tin soldiers sprang to life, throwing off their hats and boots, unbuttoning their shirts, and prancing through the house with the single-minded vivacity of children. They didn't pay me the slightest attention.

Following them out to the back verandah, I watched them race one another toward the surf, stripping down to diaperlike jockstraps. Months had passed since the beach had been draped in jellyfish, and I wondered if these boys had been the ones who'd disposed of the mess or if nature had done her own housework. Whatever it was, the strand was as good as new.

The four boys approached a line of men already at the water's edge. There were about thirty of them, dressed in civilian clothes, soaking their bare feet along the sea foam. I wasn't the only prisoner being held here, after all.

However, I was the only living one: The men on the beach were ghosts.

I looked for Father among them. No luck. There must have been other beaches where countless other men had been gunned down. The lost souls here faced the blue yonder with waves lapping at their calves, stoic memorials to their own murders. For *whom* they stood, I had no clue, since their martyrdom would go unnoticed unless more people started growing eyes like mine.

Their isolation moved me. Death for no reason, death with no legacy.

I returned to the boys. Once cooled by the water, the four near-nude soldiers began culling, scooping, and pushing wet sand with their bare hands up the drier slope. Away from the watery tongue of the waves, they molded shapes in the sand. When the sand got too dry, the sculptors ran back to the water and imported new moisture in their cupped palms. Soon, towers and turrets took shape, then the lank limbs of beasts.

Life-sized women gradually rose from the sand, each in a different pose. All four of the sand models appeared anatomically correct, apart from their enormous breasts—the products of outlandish fantasy—and as their features got more detailed, the boys grew sexually aroused. One had his sand maiden cup her hands behind her head; another gave his a vulgar, gaping mouth. Two of the nymphs sat and two reclined, but all four had their legs shamelessly splayed.

The boys waited for their slowest comrade to put the finishing touches on his creation before they all stood up and judged their harem together. They critiqued one another's artistry with studious dedication, but when one of them—the one who appeared to be the leader—licked his middle finger and pushed it into a reclining female's crotch, all discussion ceased.

They silently removed their underwear, and a meditative, even religious, mood descended upon them as each boy fondled himself to his fullest extent. Each soldier selected his own girl and lay atop or astride his impossible lover. Three of the nymphs withstood just a couple of thrusts from her suitor before her thighs crumbled back into the sand; only the reclining beauty who'd been anointed with the finger stayed intact—she was made of wetter stuff. Within minutes, however, even she was felled. This didn't stop the boys from kissing and fondling whatever was left and bringing themselves to loud, shuddering climaxes in the sand.

That evening, after dinner, one of the boys sprinted into the house with sand-covered feet, exclaiming. The others followed him back to the beach with dubious expressions. For a second, I wondered if their sand nymphs had come to life. But as soon as I stepped outside, the commotion became all too clear: The octopus had returned.

There was no mistaking it—this was Mrs. Nakamura's maritime love, brought back by the rising tide. The poor suitor crouched, heartsick, on the remaining shoreline, more gray than purple despite the pink glow of the setting sun. Its many arms flexed and throbbed, dragging its muscular bulk in slow motion across the sand while the saucer eyes on its head roamed the coast for one beloved silhouette. How steady its devotion, how uncowed!

The boys, flush with adrenaline and shouting to each other, ran back into the house. They reappeared hugging rifles, their bayonet tips gleaming.

"No! Please, no!" I shrieked while they marched back down toward the sea. But they ignored me again, yelling, "Banzai!" till their voices squeaked and croaked.

The octopus screamed, too, like Caesar, as the four blades disappeared into its flesh. It made a high-pitched whistle, the cry of a freight train in the night—desperate, unstoppable, gloomy with distance overcome and distance it may never yet see. Here was another romantic, reduced in a matter of seconds to shreds and a jelly mass. Its corpse leaked black lines toward the water like a love letter written in the sand, but the ink vanished as soon as it joined the martyrs still standing waist-deep in the tide.

Eventually the sea claimed everything. It swept over the ghosts, the octopus, and, of course, the harem made out of sand. Above the waves, nothing left a trace.

But I remembered them all.

Taro returned, without warning, two months later. There was a spring in his step, as if his time away from me had revived his spirits.

"The fresh air has done you good," he told me in the car. "Did you miss me?"

This was a trick question. But I knew how best to answer. "Yes."

"Do you miss Daniel?"

The name felt like a stab in my heart.

"Well, do you miss Daniel?"

"No."

"Are you being truthful with me?"

"No."

We drove on for a few miles before he spoke again.

"I've been thinking about what you asked me, before you left. About your brother."

I sat up. "What about my brother?"

"You said you missed him. A lot. Well, who would you rather see— Daniel or your brother?"

An even trickier question. I couldn't answer this one.

"I'm thinking about taking your brother out of prison. But freedom won't suit him. I think he's one for routine. There is a wildness in him that needs taming."

"You've met him?"

"Oh yes. You had me very curious. I thought he had to be something *magical*."

"Can't he stay with us?" I regretted my words as soon as I blurted them.

"I will take him out of prison. That's all I can promise for now." He pursed his lips. "And I will do it not because I think he deserves it but as a concession to you. The boy has a lot of fire. He sat there looking all thin and sickly, but the moment I approached him, he jumped up and spat in my eye."

"I'm sorry. Please forgive him." My lips burned at my own servility.

Taro turned to me and grinned, as if struck by an amusing idea. "How well do you think he gets along with Indians?"

Li was assigned to the Rat Brigade—the lone Chinese boy among sixteen Indians, all from poor, tenacious backgrounds that had toughened them and made them ruthless. Their task was to comb the city for rats and take them back to an old opium warehouse by the Black River. The work was simple enough as there was no quota, just whatever the boys could find, but a fierce competition developed between them to outdo one another in the number and size of the vermin they caught. The winner of the day's contest earned himself a glass of soybean milk—lunch.

In order to capture the biggest and best rats, the young hunters of the Rat Brigade danced through alleyways, dived down rubbish heaps, and crept into the most rotten slums they could without getting themselves hacked up by Chinese cleavers or Malay parangs or torn to pieces by wild dogs. Luckily for them, not many dogs roamed the city—the starving locals had turned most of them into supper. At night, after a long day's foraging, the boys returned to shower, eat, and sleep in a military-style dormitory next to the old opium godown. They were, after all, almost soldiers.

The Brigade was Taro's brainchild, invented, he said, primarily to take Li out of Shahbandar. Yet he remained determined to keep us apart. He took me to examine the cleanliness of the dormitory, which was also ghost-free, though I was barred from setting eyes on Li.

"I appreciate your generosity," I said, choking back my bitterness, "but couldn't you find him a desk job? Why not put him to work at our house?"

"Out of the question! I don't want him anywhere near me. Or you."

"He's not contagious, you know. It's just anemia, for God's sake."

Taro shook his head. "Anemia's nothing. It's rats. It's as if your brother has a sixth sense . . . for filth. Today I was told he collected thirty-five rats. That's a record."

"But what do you want with the rats? Feed them to your troops?"

"Don't be obtuse." Taro sniffed. "We're not savages. We use them for science."

A week or so later, Taro came home smiling.

"I thought you were being metaphorical, but your brother *is* fading." His smile grew wider. "And by the way, I found him a desk."

The next morning, one of his drivers dropped me off at the hulking old godown at the mouth of the Black River. The warehouse once housed trillions of pounds of Indian opium, cargo that turned civil servants into lords overnight and made Britain the wealthiest country in the world. When I was at school, the nuns always spoke reverently about this very building, but it wasn't until I stood there—a prisoner of history—that I finally grasped that it had been, in a way, the heart of the colonial world, the spine of the Empire's spine. An enormous Japanese flag now hung from the roof, covering most of the sun-bleached letters painted across its widest wall, words I was almost sentimental about, if only because they were not Japanese: EAST INDIA CO., UNITED COMPANY OF MERCHANTS OF ENGLAND.

Along the river, life was at a standstill. The remaining handful of bum-boats and sampans were empty, bobbing nakedly on the muddy water, their noses nipping and scraping against the banks. The wide fish eyes painted on each prow stared lifelessly at me. They had only seemed sentient when coolies were running along their backs.

The only thriving vessel was an unmanned boat with a slow-puttering motor and eyes that had been painted over with black—symbolically blinded. A rope bound it to a gangway leading to the back of the godown. For one delectable moment, I daydreamed about rescuing Li and stealing him away in it, but the idea was laughable. In a war-torn world, where could we possibly go?

Two armed guards escorted me into the warehouse's interior, which was nothing like the cramped dormitory Taro had taken me to see. This was a cavernous, windowless hangar large enough to house a zeppelin. But in-stead of smelling like the smoldering metals of an aviator's workshop, the warehouse stank of mothballs and formaldehyde.

On the ground, the hall was divided into separate little areas by house-hold folding screens obviously pilfered from middle-class homes. Some still boasted full-length mirrors, which multiplied the number of workers I saw. Most of the employees—if they could be called that—were grim-faced Ja-panese in white lab coats. Three Indian youths in the khaki uniform of Cub Scouts half their age volleyed between the sectors; these had to be Li's Rat Brigade colleagues. I was relieved that they did not look mistreated.

Under the low buzz of industry, I heard a steady, unmistakable squeal-ing: rats.

I was pointed to the corner where Li was stationed, cut off from the others by a series of wood partitions. Had Taro isolated him out of cruelty or kindness? With him it was impossible to tell.

On a stool, leaning over a worktable with his back to me, was a living skeleton in khaki. I ran over silently and embraced him, squeezing him un-til the shocking contact with his rib cage impelled me to let go.

"I've missed you. They wouldn't let me see you."

He stared at me with dead eyes. I'd first seen that hollow look many years ago, on our fateful seventh birthday. Now, as then, he carried on him the wear of a man many times his age.

"They killed Father."

"I know."

He gazed at me, puzzled as to how I would have heard, but that thought floated away and another took its place.

"So it's true—you're his mistress." He spoke this as fact, not accusation. His spirit was too weak for that.

"I'm his prisoner."

Li ran his eyes over my freshly laundered dress and the floral silk scarf at my neck. "Yet you've gained weight."

I blushed, mortified. It was true. While others starved, I ate. I was lucky.

I feared he would say something else cutting that would make me regret my visit, but instead he leaned close to my ear and whispered, in the Shanghainese of our long-ago childhood, "I know what you did. Thank you. Seeing you, I already feel stronger."

He turned back to the work awaiting him on his long, aluminum-topped desk. "I have to finish my quota or they won't let me eat today."

I recoiled when I saw his "quota": a line of five rats, each about a foot long, not counting its tail. Thankfully, all were lifeless.

"Did you kill them?"

"They're just asleep." He flicked on a task lamp and, with an effort that seemed too great for his frail arm, craned its folding neck to shine on the pests. The light turned their black fur silver. "I have to work fast before they wake up. Or else..."

With one hand, shaky with exhaustion, he picked up a pair of rusty tweezers and leaned in. With the other, he rooted in the creatures' hairs, searching.

"What are you looking for?"

"Fleas." He glanced back at me. "I wouldn't stand so close, if I were you."

He spotted one almost immediately and carefully liberated it from the rat hairs. The tweezers looked heartbreakingly heavy in his bony hand, but the flea was inert, which simplified his job. He dropped the black dot into a lidded glass jar, where it joined at least a hundred others.

"Are all those dead?"

"How many times do I have to tell you? They're just *sleeping*."

"But what are they for?"

"Don't know," he said. "I stopped asking questions. Not knowing makes life easier."

I stood behind him while he continued his assignment, cursing whenever he dropped a flea with his trembling hand. When he was done, he put the lifeless rats away in a metal cage and locked the trapdoor. Finally, his gloves came off.

"My head aches. My eyes burn. My hands shake. Everything feels like hell."

I enveloped him in my arms again, and this time, without his gloves, he responded. But his hold was feeble. My brother was a dying man.

I examined his emaciated face. For all our mutual bitterness, nobody knew me as well as Li did. Beneath the sun-scorched skin, the exhaustion, the rage, and the disappointment, he was still the same boy, my spiritual half who had crossed an ocean with me and endured the same demons by my side. Hugging him, I felt a monumental loneliness at all the times we had spent apart.

"Don't kiss me," he warned.

"Wasn't about to."

I turned around. Nobody could see past the wooden screens surrounding our little corner. From my handbag, I pulled out a steak knife sheathed in antiseptic cloth.

Li pulled back. "You've come to kill me."

"No," I said. "The opposite."

I drew the sharpened blade along the soft inner flesh of my left arm. From it, crimson liquor began to weep. I didn't think about pain; I thought about life.

"What are you d—"

I pushed my wound against his lips, staining them bright red. He bucked back like a wild mare.

"Drink. It's our only chance. If you want to live, Li, drink!"

His terror slowly faded and he gave me the subtlest of nods. When he took my arm in his hands, his grip was unexpectedly firm, as though he feared I might change my mind and back away. Together, we looked at the new blood blooming like a mushroom cap on the surface of my skin. Before long, it would spill down to my elbow.

He pressed his mouth to the slit, first licking around the wound so no drop would be lost. A grimace of distaste flashed across his face, but it was his body that craved the stuff, and the body quickly won: A familiar look of concentration overtook him, driven by a primal need for sustenance, escape, transfiguration. His inhibitions fell away. He began not only to drink, but also to suck.

I leaned back against the table for support. For five harrowing minutes, I feared he would never stop.

Afterward, I wrapped the antiseptic cloth over my wound and pressed it tight to stem the flow. I could feel my blood pulsing just beneath the surface, now in the habit of bursting free. Li slumped onto the floor, panting, his teeth and gums lurid red. He seemed even more exhausted than before, and I was terrified I might have made things worse. Quietly, he raised his hand to tell me to stop worrying. And what I saw gave me hope: His hand had stopped trembling.

"I'm a monster," he whispered.

"No, no, you're not." I joined him on the floor and rested my head on his shoulder. "It's not your fault. You can't help what you have."

He thought for a moment. "What if it *is* my fault?"

"What do you mean?"

He said nothing. I prodded him with a gentle kiss on his cheek. Finally he spoke, again in Shanghainese. "I have a confession to make."

I felt a numbness beginning in my wound, reaching all the way to my heart.

"Remember our seventh birthday? Remember the old man in the park?"

I nodded slowly.

"I knew he would be there. Which was why I insisted on going. The night before, I prayed and begged to whoever or *whatever* was out there. To this day, I'm still not clear who or *what* I prayed to, but when I saw the old man, I knew he had heard me.

"I prayed for freedom. Escape. Mother favored me, but I hated it. I hated that we were subjected to all her fears, that she was instilling terror in us so we'd become like her and keep her company in her living tomb. But as a child, what power did I have besides prayer?"

He began to weep. Once again we were revealed to be synchronous, through and through, in our childhood desire for freedom—especially in our preternatural ruthlessness. I kissed his shoulder.

"As long as I could escape," he said, "I didn't care what they wanted in exchange. And so, in the park, I gave the old man my health."

"When he asked you to kill the kitten."

He winced at the memory. "I have nobody to blame for my illness but myself. I try to fight it by keeping busy, but it doesn't do a thing. My hunger never goes away."

His confession appeared to comfort him. When I looked at his face again, the ruddiness of life had returned. My blood had nourished him, and for this I was supremely grateful. Whatever happened in that park happened a long time ago, in another universe. Whether it was a supernatural pact he'd made or just pure happenstance, at least I'd made him stronger again.

"You look better. Do you feel better?"

"Much." He looked me in the eye. "Thanks."

"We'll survive this, Li. We'll outlive this war together, I promise you that."

I embraced him, and then, just as I was about to be engulfed in waves of sentiment, when I feared letting go of him would mean losing him as I'd lost Father, I forced myself to release him and stand up. I didn't dare risk staying too long. It tore at my heart that I couldn't just bring him home and nurse him back to proper health.

Li remained on the floor, his face crumpled to see me go.

His hand disappeared into the left pocket of his khaki shorts. It emerged with his weathered talisman, the gold toffee disk, which he held out on his palm. In these circumstances, it shone like an old friend.

"Take this away from me. Too often, I've been tempted to break this open and eat it. It came from that old man, you know, so I suspect it would end our pact, once and for all. But I fear it. I truly, truly fear it because I don't know what it is."

He forced it into my hand, and I knew I couldn't reject it. I closed my fingers around the tiny little thing. Hardened over the years, it now felt less like a sweet than a coin—one-way fare for the boatman across the Styx. But its wrapper was sticky, reminding me that, for all of Li's elaborate fears, it was probably nothing more than a harmless lump of sugar.

"I have to go," I said, and kissed him on the forehead. "But I'll come back."

"You promise?"

"I'll do everything I can for you. Please know that."

As I walked away, I passed a wall of wood screens and, in the corner of my eye, caught somebody's gaze in a mirror. There was a grim, sallow woman staring at me. When I looked again, I realized the phantom was me.

— 12 —

The Rat Brigade

THE BLACK ISLE WAS FROG-MARCHED INTO THE FUTURE. Our clocks were set forward two hours, to match Tokyo's. Even today, I sometimes find myself wondering where my two missing hours went.

Those lost hours, however, were a drop in the proverbial ocean compared to the three years I served as Taro's "wife." I spent 1943 and 1944 as his property. I existed solely on his terms. But having read enough testimony from that grisly period, I should not complain. A mock marriage was preferable to death.

As with any other evolving couple, our marital quibbles had shifted from such quotidian concerns as food, clothing, and sex to questions of fate, history, and the future—of which my "husband" held many strong and misguided opinions.

Our war of ideas reached its peak in 1945. Only in hindsight does it seem I'd been mad to even think the man was worth reasoning with. But this was my first real taste of marriage, not counting my engagement to Daniel, and so I did what I thought any sensible wife should try to do— hold my own.

Let me paint a quick picture of our domestic life. Two adults at the dinner table, talking. What passed for conversation between man and wife in the year 1945 went something like this:

"Your people were blind to the oppression!" says the husband. "Isn't it telling that the finest buildings on the Black Isle are the Supreme Court and Shahbandar Prison?"

"The British also built roads and schools," the wife retorts. "What has *your* great nation done for us? I'm not saying that the Brits were gods. But life has only gotten worse since your occupation."

A year or two earlier, the husband would have slapped her for that remark. Not anymore. It was, in its way, love.

"It depends on one's definition of progress, doesn't it?" He collects his thoughts, preparing another lecture. "According to the Western model, perhaps we are failing. But the Japanese ideal of harmony is built on the notion that there is darkness in the world, that the truth is more often than not made up of shadows. The sublime quality of a Japanese home—which you have yet to appreciate—is built on the mystery of shadows. Shifting darkness and shifting light. We thrive in dark places: Our food looks better, our art looks better, and above all, our skin looks better. Westerners, on the other hand, are like children who are afraid of the dark. To them, shadows represent what's unknown—and perhaps unknowable—and they genuinely fear it. They cannot imagine how one might tame the darkness by contemplating and *accepting* it.

"That's why, while the Americans and the British are busy trying to eradicate what they perceive to be shadows in the world, we yellow skins, who have lived amidst the darkness, will rise up. By the end of this century, Japan will topple the West." Husband shoots wife a withering smile: "By AD 2000. Mark my words."

By early 1945, Taro trusted me enough to allow me monthly visits to Li. During these furtive reunions in the old opium warehouse, I always brought out my knife and fed my starving brother.

Each month, even as my driver kept to his regimented route, I took in how the city was changing—and how it wasn't. Instead of seizing upon the building frenzy that had transformed the Isle before their arrival, the Turnipheads brought all construction to a halt. No matter how glowingly Taro spoke of progress, order, and triumph, ruins stayed ruins; looted shops and restaurants remained shuttered and bare, like the pitiful crumbs of Pompeii. They had saved the best buildings for homes and offices: the Balmoral Hotel, the Teutonic Club, even the old St. Anne's compound.

Wonder World had become a fortified brothel where servicemen went to seek comfort. Reels of barbwire curled atop its red walls to discourage its courtesans from even fantasizing about escape. The higher-ranked Turnipheads frequented what was once known as the Millionaire's Club in the Flower District of Chinatown, which offered kimono-clad consorts of a more specialized order: girls not just younger and more pliant, but who were trained in serving opium to those so inclined. On the nights Taro failed to come home, I felt pangs of jealous fear knowing he was probably there, possibly auditioning my replacement. Whenever I was driven past the club's Italianate façade, I would close my eyes and think of wasps.

The rest of the city regressed. The major thoroughfares were clogged with soothsayers, interpreting dreams in Hokkien, Teochew, Cantonese, Malay, Tamil, and in the most enterprising of cases, Japanese. On old Edinburgh Bridge, black-market touts hawked bottles of soy sauce and cans of baked beans, and no one ever came to chase them away as the British once did. The Isle was a shambles.

But no matter what anyone was selling or yelling, whenever a Turnip-head soldier approached, everyone was expected to bow low, no matter how young, stupid, and drunk the soldier might be, nor how long he maliciously lingered. Disobedience carried a heavy price. Once, en route to Li, I watched an old woman being assaulted by a soldier who could have passed for her grandson. She lay limp on the pavement as he kicked her head, again and again. A small crowd gathered but nobody dared to help her. On my way home, I saw her body twisted by the side of the road. Nobody had dared to move her either. Her soul stood by her corpse, shaking with rage and swearing in the foulest Cantonese at all who passed.

Still, the occupation's most unexpected outcome had been the mass confiscation of air conditioners. All across the city, I saw gaping holes and shadowy stains in office buildings where cooling units once sat. No doubt this had been done to break the spirits of those accustomed to chilled rooms, but where those thousands of units disappeared to remained a mystery.

When I arrived to visit Li in February 1945, he was not at his desk. The sight of his empty stool sent my pulse racing. I had been so accustomed to our routine—*all* routines—that any small variation had the power to derail me. Surprises never meant good news during wartime. Yet I had no choice but to wait for him in his cubicle. When he finally appeared, he wore a look of bewilderment. His khaki uniform was spattered with dark red dots.

"My friend Samy," he began. "They took his arm..."

"What are you talking about?"

"They cut off his damn arm! We were carrying our fleas to them in the back. One of the rats escaped and bit him on the finger. Usually they don't care about this kind of thing—I mean, look at me." He brandished the old puncture marks on his hands. "But for some reason, they grabbed Samy and...they just sawed off his entire arm, with no warning! I saw the whole thing. It was...I don't know...so quick."

Li slumped onto his stool, still in a daze. I, too, felt queasy.

"This happened in the back of the hall?"

"Yeah, deep down there, where there's a whole warren of rooms."

"And where's your friend now?"

"I don't know." He shook his head. "He fainted from the pain. The worst part is I was so shocked I couldn't move. So I saw everything. The blood...the muscle, the bone...I was afraid I was going to be next but my legs refused to move. Finally, they just kicked me out of the room and closed the door."

It sounded at once logical and nightmarishly excessive. They—whoever "they" were—must have feared that the rat carried some kind of infectious disease. But even that could not explain their drastic measures.

I whispered, in Shanghainese, "Who do you mean by *they*?"

Li's eyes darted around nervously even though no one was remotely close. He replied in Shanghainese, "The ones in white, of course."

"Doctors?"

He refused to elaborate. Then he added with a shudder, "It's cold in those back rooms. Very, very cold." He took one glance at my left arm and gave me a look of incredible sorrow. "I don't think I have the stomach to drink today."

Taro was barely in the door when I began pelting him with questions.

"Who are the men in white? What do they do?"

"Calm down. I won't entertain a madwoman, let alone a mad wife."

He undid his laces, removed his boots, and nestled them at the foot of the stairs. After putting on his slippers, he went to pour himself a glass of Armagnac, deliberately moving at a snail's pace. I waited as he strolled over to the icebox and, with a smile, dropped three cubes into his tumbler. Finally, as he settled into his favorite chair, he gave his drink a little shake and took a long sip.

"By the way, *this* is supposed to be your job: boots, slippers, drink. I must be the most liberal, most browbeaten husband around. My mother would be ashamed of me."

"And she should be, seeing that I was meant to be somebody else's wife."

A flicker of rage crossed his face. "Now what was it you wanted, Momoko?"

"What do the men in white do, at the warehouse?"

"Which warehouse? You have to be more specific."

"You *know*, the *one*."

"I told you a long time ago. They're scientists."

"In what field, exactly?"

"A sudden interest in the sciences, my Momoko?" He smiled his warden's smile, one that was supposed to quash me with its effortless contempt.

"Those 'scientists' cut off a boy's entire arm today, right in front of Li."

"Perhaps I should have you stop seeing him. These visits clearly upset you."

"That's *not* what I meant!" I cried, then forced myself to rein in my outrage. "I'm just curious. I want to know what it is that they do, that's all."

"Oh, that's all, is it?" He finished off the Armagnac and began his long march to refill his glass. "You do realize that I've been giving in to you time and again. You ask me to pardon your parasite of a brother, find him a desk job, and I do. You ask to see that little worm, and I let you. And now, what is it, you want me to hand over military secrets in order to satisfy your *curiosity*? And if I did that, would you perhaps want to tell me how to deploy my men, how to secure my borders, how to shake hands with my own bloody generals? Momoko, does your pride know no bounds?"

I waited for him to construct his drink. This time he left the ice tray out on the dining table to melt—not intentionally but, I guessed, because he was getting annoyed.

"I had a very good day at work today," he said, sitting down again. "But instead of asking me about my day and bringing me my slippers, like any other normal wife, all you can think about is yourself and your *curiosity*."

"You never want to discuss your work. You've made that clear."

"Ah!" He chuckled. "On that count anyway, you've been unfailingly obedient."

"How was your day, my darling?" I forced out a saccharine smile and a genuflection so false even he had to laugh.

"My day, dear wife, was very fine indeed," he returned in an exaggerated pantomime of husbandhood. "We made a significant victory today. You see, a few days ago, my boys chanced upon a camp of very angry Communists in the jungle. Two hundred, maybe three hundred of them, living in the swamp like rats, very angry rats. There was a series of skirmishes, and this afternoon, my boys brought the surviving fighters down to Shahbandar. All twelve of them—eleven, actually. One died en route and they had to toss him out of the jeep...Oh, as soon as the body landed, a tiger jumped out of the bushes and ripped off his head!"

His hyperbolic glee seemed specially designed to needle me. But even as I knew this, I couldn't help feeling sickened: Were Issa and Kenneth dead? Ken had always struck me as a man with a greater destiny than this, yet history has a way of subverting destinies, especially the most promising ones.

"You're very quiet," Taro said, suddenly more sober. "Are you thinking about another fiancé or brother in that band of rebels? I know some of them were Ignatius Wee's associates. But these were the naïve friends, the friends with no money or power who went to fight in the mud while Ignatius-san and his cronies sat in air-conditioned mansions eating our steaks and plotting against us. Actually I admire these Communists. They have guts and conviction. Fighting spirit. Of course, this doesn't mean I won't be locking them up in Shahbandar and putting them through some fun and games. So is there anything I should know about any of them?"

I shook my head, my eyes burning. Mentioning my friends, were they still alive, would only single them out for worse treatment.

I prepared to go upstairs. No way was I going to display any more emotion for my tormentor's satisfaction.

"They were quite audacious. The two hundred of them actually thought they could outfight us—with their antiquated Soviet weapons, no less. And while we're speaking of numbers, I should mention the landmark figure we reached today: one hundred thousand."

I started up the stairs. I didn't want to look at him. I didn't want to know.

"Where's your fabled curiosity now, Momoko? Aren't you curious one hundred thousand *what*? Dollars, monkeys, tigers, bananas?"

I was at the top of the stairs when I heard him bellow: "One hundred thousand dead Chinamen."

It took several months for Taro's mood to lift again, just in time for Obon, the Japanese festival of the dead. As I'd noted many times before, nothing cheers up the Japs like thoughts of death, save for perhaps the festivities surrounding their Foundation Day, which commemorates the special morning in 660 BC when a wiry little man fell out of the sun and declared himself emperor. Of course, I am distorting their history, but no more than they had distorted mine.

In an odd twist of fate, the night of Obon also happened to be my twenty-third birthday—August 3, 1945. But this wasn't the only reason I would remember the night forever.

Taro and I ate a light ceremonial dinner of grilled sea bream and miso soup, after which we lingered at the table. He had a shallow sake cup poised on his knuckles, filled to the brim, and none of the liquid rippled or spilled. It was his sixth cup—the point of the demonstration being to prove how steady his nerves were, even under the influence. Finally, he glanced at me.

"Do you want to see that old friend of yours? The prince of Shahbandar—he's asked for you."

I leapt to my feet. His words were abundantly clear: Kenneth was still alive.

"Of course I want to see him!"

Taro, in theatrical mode again, winced. "Ah, if only you showed *me* such interest, Momoko. Oh, how times have cooled us..."

I had to keep him from going off on a tangent. "So, when can I see Kenneth?"

"Kenneth?" He looked startled.

I realized my slip. But the best response now was silence.

"Don't you mean Daniel, your betrothed? Or has he also fallen by the wayside, like poor me?" He smiled slyly. "But yes. I do have a man at Shahbandar named Kenneth. Kenneth Kee, actually. But I doubt he's your type—crude, ugly, low-class, swore like a sailor when my boys captured him. They found him in the swamp and perhaps they should have left him there. Your Daniel, on the other hand, has been faultless. Most obedient prisoner we've ever had. Says 'please' and 'thank you' for everything. That's why they call him the Prince. I thought it only fair that I reward him with a visit from an old friend—that is, if she hasn't already forsaken him."

"I haven't forsaken him." Dampening the hope of seeing Daniel was, unfortunately, my new worry about Kenneth. As if the hell of Shahbandar weren't enough, I'd further endangered him by mentioning his name.

"Good, good. Because I promised your Daniel he would see you." Taro leaned forward to kiss my ear. "And you know how I hate to go back on my word."

At ten that night, he took me to an Obon celebration with some fellow officers. This was the first time I would be seen by his peers, and I couldn't tell whether this sudden change in policy reflected a change in his attitude toward me or if the kitchen simply needed an extra pair of hands.

The gathering was held at the beach house, its driveway newly lined with square paper lanterns, creating a catwalk of muted, glowing footlights. I can't deny it—there was a serene elegance to this backdrop, reminiscent of Hokusai's woodblock prints. The four tin soldiers who had been stationed there were nowhere to be found—perhaps their indiscretions had been discovered—and the illuminated house felt like a set readied by a team of spectral stagehands who vanished as soon as the players arrived.

Gazing upon the lovely scene, I was reminded that the Turnipheads were not without a fine aesthetic tradition; it was just that they had a remarkable propensity for subverting grace in the service of evil. As a result, I mistrusted their displays of beauty. What other modern society venerated stones and built shrines for wood sprites while at the same time encouraging—even celebrating—the thirst for human blood?

Of course, entering the house on Taro's arm, I had no idea that the events of this night would return to debase me in the decades to come; otherwise, I might have found something sinister in the pile of samurai swords parked by the door. But I had become inured to such Turniphead habits and instead continued to make snide private jokes: Surely Taro's friends were overcompensating for some manly lack?

I had worn my favorite red dress, the one with the silk spaghetti straps, copied from something I'd seen Myrna Loy model in a magazine. It was my birthday, after all. A red silk bow bloomed at my waist; I looked like my own birthday present. If Taro's ego needed to be stroked in front of his superiors, I would submit to my wifely chore just this once and save myself the regret. The man had promised me Daniel as my reward.

The Turnipheads liked their drink. That fact had already been well established, if not by my eyewitness accounts, then by a long tradition in art, literature, and the annals of civil misconduct. Taro had invited ten colleagues to this drinking party, and they all showed up wearing their olive-green uniforms like a troop of overexcited Brownies. They ranged in age from Taro's thirty to about sixty, and what united them, beyond the love of sake, was that they all looked more like buttoned-down bank managers than engineers of death. They seemed born to file paperwork behind drab desks and, on weekends, jostle fat babies on their knees. Although I'd expected to meet and greet their "wives," with whom I could compare spouses and extrapolate rumor from fact, none had been produced.

Most of the officers had as many as three white sakuras—patriotic cherry blossoms—woven onto their striped shoulder boards. Despite being host, Taro had the fewest, just one. Given the national obsession with face, this struck me as comically poignant. It meant that all of his friends were higher ranked: commanders, rear admirals, and such who went to war emboldened with the promise of reincarnation as flower buds. As the night progressed, Taro's low rank turned out to be a saving grace. As if to illustrate my treatise on the Japanese penchant for annihilation, the more sakuras an officer had, the more sake he was obligated to drink.

Exempt from this contest, Taro watched his friends drink. I played the docile hausfrau and served them with backbreaking devotion, pouring chilled sake from rustic clay bottles into their little cups, which they held out to me while seated cross-legged on the tatami. Part of me felt the occasion wasn't quite real, that I was hosting a tea party for teddy bears, filling their dainty cups with water, except that my dolls were becoming ever more animated with each sip. Over the hours, as the room grew thick with tobacco smoke, their faces glowed red and grotesque; some even stood up to dance to the *shamisen* string music playing on the Victrola. As they stomped and skipped and crumbled onto the mats, gurgling with coughs and laughter, they seemed at last to be truly happy. Yet something was amiss—where were the geishas and the dancing girls?

Taro observed his superiors' descent into silliness with a strange, detached grin. He pulled me gruffly down on the mat by his side, and for an instant, I almost believed he was going to confess that he'd poisoned the drink. Instead, he grabbed my wrists and kissed me in front of his muddled comrades, not releasing me until someone exclaimed that sake was spilling from the bottle in my hand.

A white-haired Three-Sakura roared his approval and applauded for an encore. *"Ankoru!"*

The others followed suit, and Taro made a grand show of modesty, standing me up with him and bowing effusively. Then, very suddenly, he whacked the back of his hand against my cheek. I was caught unawares and pitched to the floor, dropping the sake bottle entirely. The men howled with laughter, and it began to enter my mind that the night's entertainment was only beginning, that *I* might constitute part of the show.

Taro tore off his uniform shirt and flung it aside. His fury took me by surprise because, until this moment, I'd assumed he was in a good mood. Now, it was as if he'd found a way to funnel his anger and contempt for me into one bullish gaze. His comrades had retreated to the sides of the room, leaving Taro and me in the center of the arena. The lights began to dim so that instead of men around us there was only smoke and shadows.

As soon as I pulled myself off the floor, Taro charged at me. Some of the men gasped. This time, I ducked and avoided being slapped. I rammed my foot into what I knew to be a sensitive spot in his knee, causing him to grimace in pain and rage. I tried to run free, but I'd taken only three steps when I was shunted to the ground, face-first, with Taro pinning me flat with his weight like a sumo wrestler.

With the men applauding cheerily, Taro whispered in my ear, "Be brave, Momoko. Think of Daniel. Think of your friends. These men have power over their lives. We must make them happy." His voice, unlike his act, was coaxing rather than stern. "Ignore them. Do as we always do. Submit to me."

Before I could lodge my protest with a backward kick, he lifted me into a standing position and began ripping apart my red silk frock from behind so that my nakedness was unveiled to the audience, parcel by parcel, like a steer placed on auction for parts. My face, my neck, my belly, my loins—every piece of me was feverish with shame, yet I knew I had to endure. Lives were at stake. But Taro wasn't just stripping me. He fondled me, caressing my tender flesh as each new patch of skin was freed; there was no difference in the way he touched me here and when we were alone in bed.

Finally, when the last of my dress fell to the floor, he unhooked my brassiere, let it drop, and cupped his hands beneath my trembling breasts.

Leaning in to my left ear, he breathed dreamily, "Close your eyes."

The shushing of the waves on the beach, the rustling of the breeze against the shades, the plucks of the ancient *shamisen* and the sighs from the black-ened edges of the room: All the sounds of the world quickly faded into the dark.

It was just Taro and me now, and the sounds we made. My open expression of pleasure was my way of encouraging his goodwill, to save his face in front of his superiors, and above all, to protect my own life and those of my loved ones.

I quickly discovered the advantages of the tatami—instead of limiting ourselves as on a bed, we had a play area that was vast, and there were no obstructions. The floor emboldened us. After coupling in our usual positions, we tried new arrangements. Gone was the anxiety about falling off the mattress. Gone were all our inhibitions. I rode astride him, taking him to the edge of rapture before he lifted me and flung me onto my back. I opened my eyes. *No, not so soon*, his avid pupils told me. *I want to satisfy you first.* He plunged three fingers into me and, unlocking my most sensitive spot, brought me to a maddening climax. I knew he was showing off, that I was an instrument only he had the privilege to play, but this did nothing to diminish my pleasure. He brought up his fingers, glistening clear with our married juices, and sucked on them.

Thirsting for more, he hunkered low and raised my thighs to meet his mouth, latching my calves against his shoulders and back, and proceeded to lap at the secret me with his probing tongue. Inch by inch, he backed himself up so that I was tilting upside down from him. As I screamed and shivered, the blood and adrenaline rushing down to my head, he gripped my waist firmly and drew me rhythmically toward his hungry mouth until spasms of ecstasy engulfed me so many times that I lost all count. Whenever I surrendered, the world vanished, the war vanished. It was at once my freedom and Taro's ultimate proof of ownership over me.

We collapsed onto the tatami to retrieve our breaths, both of us covered in sweat. My muscles were limp, but knowing Taro, I knew we'd hardly even begun. Waiting for the sea breeze to cool us, I gazed over at him, and he shot me a heartfelt smile with his watery eyes. With great tenderness, he mouthed, "Momoko." For a moment, I felt I was staring into Daniel's loving eyes. Daniel, whose life I was preserving with this betrayal.

Taro's member was a beast of erotic majesty, grand and aloof. I was magnetically drawn to pay it my respects. As I crawled and licked and nibbled my way down the hairy center line of his torso, gasps escaped from the dark sides of the room. Those gasps were the last things I heard before I succumbed to a familiar fever dream. When his moans grew jagged and I felt him begin to buckle in my mouth, he pushed me away brusquely, and I fell flat, the hard straws of the tatami striking my back.

He smiled: *Not yet.* My lips were tingling—they ached to be kissed, slapped, even bitten. My mouth yearned for a further taste. What I needed was yet more intensity, intensity that would heighten *and* obliterate all my senses, and he knew this. I picked myself up and we charged at each other like hungry animals.

He kissed me deeply while I kept my eyes closed and spread my legs for him, lusting to feel him fill me again. But instead of taking me, he withdrew and there came a sharp crack that left my cheek stinging. From experience I knew it wasn't his hand but some flat-edged belt. Wet, salty warmth dribbled from my lip, but before I could touch it to see if it was blood, he spun me around and bound my wrists behind my back with his leather belt—this was what had struck me. I wasn't shocked. There always came the inevitable point at which he decided to claim as much pleasure from me as he could, on his own terms and not necessarily mine.

I opened my eyes to meet his, black and devouring, close to my face. *Trust me*, they said.

At some point, the dream ended. There was a rustling in the shadows, a rustling like lascivious flesh rubbing against the woven grain of the tatami. Evidently one of our spectators had grown agitated. For the first time that night, I worried that a hoary old officer might leap out of the dark and force himself on me, wielding a three-sakura authority that none of the others would dare defy.

The moans and scratching sounds on the tatami grew increasingly incensed, yet nobody paid them the slightest heed. I broke out of Taro's embrace and gathered up whatever shreds of my clothes were left. I was blushing, deeply, ferociously mortified.

Taro wore a quiet grin, studying my response to the intrusion, amused at my inability to get dressed. I had nothing to wear. He threw me his uniform shirt. I half expected to find a new sakura sewn on his epaulette, awarded like a merit badge for his performance. But there was still just the one. He took his own sweet time pulling on his underwear and trousers, eyeing me all the while. His gaze filled me with mounting dread. Something wasn't right. Meanwhile, the commotion in the dark continued.

"Make that pervert stop!" I hissed.

"I wondered when you were going to notice him," Taro said, straightening my collar.

He muttered a few words to his colleagues in the shadows, and somebody brought on the house lights. I dreaded what my eyes would find once the darkness was lifted, but nothing I feared could have topped what was there.

Behind the row of officers stood a pair of shoji-screen sliding doors, installed as part of Taro's Nipponification of the house. Between the doors was a gap of about an inch. Widened eyes stared sideways through the slit. My legs grew weak, as if this extra spectator tipped the balance of decency, exposing just how grotesque our display had been. This shame was followed, oddly enough, by outrage. The man was a stowaway, an unknown quantity.

Marshalling whatever dignity I had left, I rushed to the screen and pulled it open.

"Daniel!"

He lay on his side, bound and gagged, his bulging eyes terrified to see me moving toward him. One of the tin soldiers was laboring to hold him as he struggled, bucking backward. I knelt down, and cradled his head against my bosom. Even then he continued to fight me. I shushed him as best I could, eroding his resistance until his entire body was overrun by a river of sobs. Holding him, our past came rushing back at me. Our pure, uncorrupted past.

"I had no choice." I covered his forehead in kisses. "He gave me no choice. I had to so I could see *you*, Dan."

He turned his face from me, shaking his head and wailing into his gag. He was trying to tell me something, and I was afraid to hear it. On and on he struggled, twisting and roaring, until finally I undid the sackcloth covering his mouth. The boy soldier scuttled away, as if by freeing Daniel's mouth I had set off a ticking bomb.

"Vi was right—you're a whore," Daniel gasped, his voice heartbreakingly weak. His eyes searched me, as if there were one pressing question he'd been waiting to ask. "I *have* to know. Aunt Betsy's earrings...You stole them, didn't you?"

"No!" I cried. This was what he wanted to know? "Of course not!"

He shook his head again. "The truth."

"Dan...I'll explain later. It doesn't matter now."

He stared at me as if my answer confirmed some deep suspicion he'd tried to hold at bay. "Of course it matters!" Somehow he had found the energy to shout. Then, going limp with sorrow, he turned his face away. "I was so *stupid...*"

"Dan, trust me..."

A hand clutched my shoulder. I looked up to find Taro standing behind me, the proud engineer of the night's puppet theater, marveling at his marionettes. We had hit our marks for him.

"Bravo," he said in a stage whisper, and launched into clopping applause—ostensibly for us but really for himself. His colleagues followed his example, enthusiastic if slightly perplexed. Taro, feigning the modesty of a master, turned to bow.

I watched him, the very emblem of how his diabolical nation had fought this war: arrogance and base depravity posing as art, as high culture. For too long, I'd submitted to him. For too long, I'd let him manipulate me like a toy. Now this.

Copying Taro's solemnity, I rose, curtsied, and, as he cast a knowing look at his peers, thrust my foot with great force into his crotch. I didn't glance back for his reaction. I rushed to the door, where the guests had deposited their swords.

I snatched the nearest one and felt a surge of courage. I couldn't just run now—I had to use it. Holding it with both hands, I charged at Taro. The officers gasped as I angled the blade at his neck. The air shrieked as I sliced into it. With one startling whip of his arm, Taro knocked the sword out of my hand. Its blunt edge nipped his elbow, drawing blood, but his neck, alas, was spared. His next move was equally swift; he locked me in a choke hold within the crook of his arm, poised to crush my neck at will.

Two of the officers clapped, then stopped when they grasped that this was part of nobody's cabaret.

"Momoko, it was all going so well," said Taro. I could feel his rage bubbling to the surface once more. "Why did you have to spoil things?"

I tried to steal another glance at Daniel but Taro held my head tight. All I saw before me were the stony, hostile faces of the Nipponese officers.

Taro's arm tightened over my throat. I tried to cry out one word— "Daniel"—but the air in my lungs disappeared.

I may have died. I should have died. But my despair was not yet done; history was much crueler than that.

I woke to find myself enshrouded in darkness, my nostrils packed with the scent of mold and wet, mashed-up rot. My body was penned in on every side, not by hard walls but by soft, clayish barriers that yielded to my touch and oozed a warm, foul-smelling stew. My body ached, too weak even to panic. My thoughts swam round in ever-diminishing circles: So this is the end...the end...the end...

Hours later—or was it days?—pairs of unknown hands plucked me from this ditch and threw me onto a stretcher. With whatever vague sense of reality I had left, I saw that I had been sleeping in a communal grave— sharing the hole not only with human remains, but also dogs, rats, and things in between.

I was ferried back to the Wee mansion and given a bath. I remember only that the water was scalding and that afterward it drained brown. That evening, wrapped in a towel, I was presented to Taro, who was perched in his favorite armchair holding a tall, sweating glass of lemonade. He rocked the glass and it trilled with ice cubes and loose floating pulp. My mouth was bone dry and yet, hearing the ice clink, it began to water. But I barely had the strength to stand, let alone grab his drink.

"I'm impressed," he said. "You simply refuse to die. Your determination is almost...Japanese."

I gestured feebly at the lemonade. Instead of offering it to me, he brought the glass to his own lips for a long, satisfying quaff. When he saw how I craved the nourishment, he took a few gulps more. His shoulder board was different—there were now two sakuras. He'd been promoted, no doubt thanks to our obscene Kabuki.

"We humans are buoyed along by fantasies, and these fantasies can give us astounding tenacity. For example, at this very moment, you're hoping for a sip of my lemonade. You think that based on our past... mutual understanding... there is a chance, even if a small one, that I will offer you a sip of my lemonade. Isn't that right?"

I resisted the temptation to agree or disagree.

"In the same way, I suspect that the merest glimmer of a dream to see your friend Daniel again has kept you alive. Hope is such a touching conceit." He smiled. "But what if I told you that you can't have my lemonade?"

Tightening his grip on the glass, he drained the cold, restorative nectar, his Adam's apple bobbing up and down with each gulp. When he finished, he rattled the ice cubes, sucked down the last dribble, and handed the glass to a young soldier, who instantly whisked it away.

"What then?" He smiled. "What happens to that hope?"

"Where's Daniel?" I said, my voice raggedy and weak.

"Ah, and here we are. Back to your old friend." He paused theatrically. "I've handed him over to Unit Seven Thirty-One."

"Where?"

"I think the question is *what* rather than where. Unit Seven Thirty-One is a research institution with very long arms—with fingers everywhere. In fact, you've been to one of its outposts more than once: warehouse, river, rats..."

"The point..."

"The point, Momoko, is that your friend has been donated to science. At Unit Seven Thirty-One offices around the world, our doctors test the limits of human endurance. They conduct experiments on how the body responds to electricity, frostbite, burns, all kinds of things. For if we want to conquer the world, we have to know how this breakable vessel of life reacts to different conditions. You should see the Korean we've preserved in a tank of formaldehyde, cut in half lengthwise while he was still screaming. He gave me my first true glimpse of a broken heart—quite literally. Then there's brain surgery practice, which I know sounds like a terrible joke. But surgery is an art, and how should artists improve except through practice?

"Sadly, at our local cell we don't have the equipment for such flights of fancy. We do our best with what's available locally, and that means we play with sand, knives, fireworks. And rats. Thanks to the work of boys like your brother, we've been able to develop very valuable pathogens. Know what those are? Germs. In villages all over China, our doctors have been handing out germs to starving children in the form of milk and noodles. It's startling how easy it is to break down barriers with a smile and a few compliments—as you know from your first meeting with me. Less startling perhaps is how effective old-fashioned diseases like the plague still are. They never seem to go out of style.

"If you'd wandered deeper into the cold lockers of the warehouse by the river, if you'd simply been *curious* enough, you would have witnessed frostbite studies in action. How does a pregnant woman in wet clothing react in zero Celsius? How does her fetus respond? What about minus ten? At which point does the human body begin to freeze? At which point does the body cease to feel pain when fingers and toes are cut off? What about the arms, the legs? These are all legitimate, scientific questions."

Taro spoke on and on, but my mind had become a blank. Every thought vanished. I didn't ask "Why?" or "How could you?" for those were the queries of a steady mind under reasonable circumstances, and neither were present.

I sank to my knees. Had there been any substance left in me, I would have retched, emptying out the crawling sickness curdling in my guts.

"Daniel Wee was an interesting specimen," I heard him say. "Unlike you, he had a weak spine..."

"Stop..."

"Not literally, I mean." He smiled. "I'm not *that* scientific." He paused and grew more solemn. "He begged us to blind him. And we respected his wishes. I never imagined it was possible to die from blindness until I saw him. How he screamed."

Taro shrugged, as if the man I loved had been nothing more than a fly.

"We gave the two of you a romantic burial. Side by side, like Romeo and Juliet. Maybe you recall waking up next to his body..."

There was nothing left. I had nothing left. No hope, no fantasy, no future. Nothing left to say, nothing left to do.

I had met and fought haunted spirits and bloodsucking demons, but nothing had prepared me for the heinousness of living, breathing human beings intent on destroying their fellow man. With Father and Daniel dead, Li reduced to an unthinking skeleton, and Kenneth almost certainly meeting a fate just as barbaric, I saw no point in fighting on. In the papers and on the airwaves, every report boasted about how Japan was winning the war and conquering the Pacific, that its troops were preparing to invade the United States. How could one person stand a chance against an entire nation of the insane? I was no warrior. I'd been the enemy's enabler, partaker, even wife.

My puppet theater was done.

I was led up the stairs as though to the gallows. The guards knew I needed no handcuffs. If my lifeless eyes didn't tell them this, then it was my leaden feet, which took every step as if it were my last. I climbed the final stairs on all fours and had to be lifted by two sets of hands into the bed chamber.

But I had a burst of life left in me. The second I heard the door lock, I rolled myself off the bed and began crawling, not stopping until I reached the jewel box on the dressing table. I avoided looking at the mirror, fearing that the sight of my face might cost me my nerve.

Hidden beneath strands of pearls and diamond brooches sat Li's old toffee disk. I dug it out and paused to admire it for a moment—not for its tarnished gold wrapper, whose beauty had long since dulled, but for its unknown power. This little thing had held my sweet brother captive since we were seven years old.

It had to be poison. What else could it be?

The wrapper came off with some difficulty. Tiny specks of gold foil clung to the ancient brown coin. Traversed with intricate fault lines and ridges, it had obviously melted and grown solid again. It had its own topography—even history. This seemed to me apt as it would probably take one world to obliterate another. *Poison, Poison, work your dark magic now . . .*

I eased the toffee onto my tongue and braced for a wrenching bitterness. But what I tasted was only a familiar buttery saltiness, followed by the concentrated smoky-sweetness of burnt sugar. The disk crumbled into powdery clots as soon as my saliva seeped into it.

I chewed on these gritty, desiccated pieces, bracing for pain to settle into my organs. It was like eating honeyed crayon.

I lay flat on the bed and waited to die. But there were no pangs, no eradication of the senses, only more thirst. Already parched, I now craved water to wash down the cloying sweetness lining my mouth. Waves of exhaustion engulfed me, and I gave in to them, relieved. I glanced at the clock: It was 11:05 in the morning. I didn't even bother to say good-bye.

I was jolted awake by the great clatter of a motor racing up and screeching to a halt.

I was still in bed. I hadn't died. And the world, it seemed, hadn't died either.

Had I dragged myself to the window and peered out, I might have seen a jeep in the driveway, its noisy engine puttering. But my body was still weak, and I chose to remain in bed. I heard rushed footsteps, then an urgent banging on the front door. The commotion moved indoors. Under the floorboards, an agitated volley of questions sounded. But there came no answers. As quickly as it had come, the jeep revved its engine and sped away, tires squealing as it nearly lost control at the gate.

The ensuing silence hung tensely in the air.

Moments later, loud footsteps clopped up the stairs. They were unmistakably Taro's. He entered the room, wild-eyed, his gaze locking onto any object that might give him his bearings—anything but me. He closed the door and began pacing with the fretfulness of a beast that had been cornered but was not ready to surrender.

He looked stunned. The sadistic glee of not so long ago was replaced by the bewilderment of a boy who'd just been told his parents were dead. Tears flowed down his cheeks as he fought back a wail. Knowing his moods, I felt sure that rage would erupt in a matter of seconds, if only to cover up the embarrassment of these tears.

But no.

"Hiroshima," he whispered to himself. A high-pitched sob trailed his words, and he gave in to it, his entire body shuddering. He turned to me, incredulous, and repeated that strange word, now in the form of a question: "Hiroshima?"

From downstairs, pistols began firing, every bit as loud and sickening as the shots years ago when Mr. Wee and his friends were lined up and killed. Only now the bullets meant something different. From his grief, I knew Taro had given his soldiers the immediate order to die. Round after round, a young voice screamed out some kind of oath that was silenced with a heart-stopping bang.

Death brought Taro no joy this time. He jumped at each individual blast, murmuring with tenderness the names of his dead boys.

The Americans dropped the atomic bomb on Hiroshima on August 6, 1945, instantly killing a hundred and forty thousand people on the ground. On the morning of August 9, they dropped another bomb on Nagasaki, which snuffed out eighty thousand more.

I will leave the historians to make noises about the disproportionate numbers of Japanese civilian lives lost. But nothing about this brutality surprised me. Under the cover of war, human beings are capable of greater monstrosities than any natural—or supernatural—force. What's pertinent to my story is that these bombs ended Japan's thirst for war. The Imperial Army was forced to surrender.

On the Isle, however, nothing really changed; in many cases things got worse. Die-hard soldiers, fancying themselves *ronin*, went on last-minute rampages at schools and hospitals. Islanders caught removing Japanese flags were gunned down.

I continued to be a prisoner. Taro had quickly regained his calm after the suicides of his boys and gave no hint of what he intended to do with me. It would have been as easy to kill me as to let me go, and both options must have tempted him; he chose neither. Even after the war had effectively ended our "marriage," he kept me in bed with him. He continued to sleep next to me, though sleep was all he did. I thought of escape, but he watched me like a hawk.

The night before the Imperial Army's official surrender, Taro decided to throw a party. Everybody was to gather for one final drink at the beach house.

"Don't worry," Taro said as he led me to the car. "We're not going to make you perform this time."

The house looked desolate. The tin soldiers were nowhere. I could only guess that each had embarked on his own afterlife of cherry blossoms. These valets absent, I was ordered to help lug in cases of sake, cognac, and champagne. From where these bottles had been pilfered I had no idea, but the supply appeared to be bottomless. There was enough alcohol to give cirrhosis to an entire battalion, let alone a group of ten.

Before the guests arrived, Taro pulled me aside with a rigid formality I found portentous and recited a Japanese poem from the fifteenth century, supposedly uttered by a military scholar just after he'd been stabbed:

> *Had I not known*
> *that I was dead*
> *already*
> *I would have mourned*
> *My loss of life.*

Here was the first overt indication that the ceremony would not be a happy one. The next sign was that, like Taro, the ten guests arrived in formal regalia, complete with medal-encrusted sashes and polished brass buttons. This time, they had also brought along their "wives," whose condition disturbed me even more: Every one of these pretty young girls staggered around with lifeless expressions, barely able to cross a room without being escorted by hand. Not one could carry out a conversation.

"Do you think they'll free us tomorrow?" I asked the most lucid-looking of them.

She nodded vaguely.

"Where will you go?"

She frowned, then nodded again.

Nobody was expected to play waitress tonight. The party was a free-for-all. Unopened bottles lined the sides of the sitting room three or four rows deep. Every man grabbed his own favorite or two and guzzled it straight from the lip. Despite their professed chauvinism, when given the choice of Dom Pérignon or sake, all of the officers chose the champagne.

Yet regardless of the loosening brought about by drink, the men continually stole glances at their watches—ever mindful of their remaining minutes. The anxiety was most transparent in Taro, whose grinning only emphasized the tightness in his jaw. As the midnight hour neared, a hush fell upon the room, as if the haze of drunkenness had reached its logical extreme and come out the other end—as clarity. The men poured champagne down their throats, hoping to recapture a happier state of oblivion, but no matter how much they drank, clarity refused to leave them.

My body sensed it: Death was coming. I didn't know how or when it would arrive, but I wanted no part of it now. I edged my way toward the rear of the house, hoping to make a quiet getaway.

Taro intercepted me in the kitchen. He was standing by the back door, all alone, holding a bottle of Russian vodka in his hand.

"Where are you going?" He seemed calmer than his friends, but this did nothing to reassure me.

"I have to use the toilet."

"Well, this is not the way to the toilet, is it?" He knocked back a swig of his vodka, his eyes trained suspiciously on me. "Give me your shoes."

I surrendered my ballet flats. To further reassure him, I grabbed his vodka bottle and threw back a gulp. I strode briskly toward the toilet, and when I turned back, I saw that Taro had craned his neck to eye me the entire way.

Safely inside the bathroom, my pulse was racing. There could be no doubt—something was to happen at midnight. I glanced at the round-faced electric clock on the bathroom wall, its motor issuing a chiding *chick!* with each passing second. Four minutes to midnight.

It was now or never. I pushed open the window as wide as it would go, climbed onto the sink, and squeezed myself out limb by limb, scraping my arms bloody.

There was no ledge to lower myself onto. The ground was eight feet below me.

I jumped. I landed clumsily, the wiry grass scratching my hands and bare feet. But this was no time to fret about bruises. Without looking back, I sprinted to the surf's edge. The martyrs were visible in the dark water, their heads protruding above the high tide like a long line of stepping stones.

"Help!" I called out to them. "Help me, please!"

None of them turned, of course. They remained forever imprisoned in their own heroism, their own doom. I had only one hope. I ran for the shelter of the old rock boulders. I knew I could stay there overnight, maybe even until the British were restored.

I was halfway there when I felt my feet being lifted off the ground. The air was hijacked by an enormous explosion. Sharper and louder than any gun. As I flew forward onto the sand, ears ringing, the world around me shook. Had I been hit? I patted myself, searching for wounds. None. I looked back. A sandstorm came swirling toward me, whishing into my eyes like a solid mist.

When it finally began to settle, I saw the beach house. Greedy orange tongues shot out of every orifice, melting windows and doors. They licked up and down the exterior walls, lashing out at the black night. I was grateful for the blaze's thunderous crackle, for it spared me the cries of those within.

As much as I wanted to escape him, and as much as I hate to admit it even today, I wept. Taro was in that burning house. All I could think about was what excruciating pain he was suffering. When it came to embracing death, Taro had been most un-Japanese. It was hard to picture him stoically giving in to the flames like a Hindu sati on her dead husband's pyre. So how did he face his doom? Screaming in fear?

My heart was pounding. Had I been any slower on my feet, I'd be in there myself, reduced to clumps of ash, indistinguishable from the very men who'd made me a slave. Trembling, I forced myself to stand up and continue running to my black old cave. I'd search for Taro's ghost tomorrow.

When morning broke, I brushed off the dusting of sand that had settled on me while I slept and walked along the shore, keeping my distance from the smoldering mouth of the beach house. I didn't want to see the bodies; I was after their ghosts—and of course there were ghosts. Four stood in the blackened ruins, wailing. No Taro. Yet, having lived with him, I was positive about one thing: Taro would have a ghost. That man deserved a haunted fate.

Incredulous, I combed the beach for him again before sluicing inland, dismayed and unfulfilled.

Already the sun was beginning to bake the roads; they burned like coals against my bare feet. About two miles in, I came upon a man's corpse, facedown on the side of the road. My heart leapt, but it wasn't Taro. All the same, I took his shoes. The loafers were at least two sizes too large but better than nothing. I thanked his spirit, who sat by his body holding a silent vigil, and walked on.

The walk to the city was fifteen miles. Never before or since have I experienced the Island as intimately as I did that hot August day, going on foot from its salty east coast to its southern-central commercial heart. The landscape wasn't picturesque, and beneath the dull equatorial light, not a single vista charmed my eye. Yet after years of confinement, I felt something in me stir.

You can learn a lot about which parts of your country are favored by the powerful just by looking at its roads, signage, foliage, and the virulence of its mosquitoes. The British had cared nothing about Little India and Kampung Klang, where the Malays lived, and only a little more about Chinatown, whose denizens were thought useful. In all three areas, there were few trees, uneven roads, and drains fetid with waste. I'd known all this, of course, but on this day—a new day of freedom—I had an awakening. I believed I could help things get better, or at the very least, fairer.

As my blistered feet brought me closer toward the city, it seemed as if my surroundings were gradually progressing, pigment by pigment, from a world of black and white to a universe of color. Wonder World was the turning point. Its bright red battlements seared their way into my consciousness. The gates had been flung open, and throngs were clamoring to get inside the walled city, some no doubt out of prurient curiosity, but most simply because they now could, and freely. Having entered, they then pushed to get out, their faces darkened by the sight of the desolate barns where the Isle's wives, sisters, and daughters had been imprisoned and raped.

Now it was everywhere else that felt like an amusement park. Men and women jammed High Street, crowding the sidewalks as they spat at Japanese signs and competed to tear them down. Tooling along, cars honked, skidded like bumper cars, blithely ignoring the rules of the road.

High above Forbidden Hill, fireworks boomed. Nobody knew whose treats they were, which only made their appearance more thrilling.

When I reached the Rat Brigade warehouse, or Unit 731 as Taro had called it, I realized how careful the Japanese had been about leaving no trace of their work. The complex had been emptied of its infernal paraphernalia. Squatter families now occupied the work stations and dormitories, their ripe, unwashed bodies replacing the smell of mothballs and formaldehyde. Even the cold rooms in the rear had been stripped and scrubbed. Except for blood blackening the grout between the tiles, there was little evidence of what had occurred there before.

The dead huddled by the dozens in these cold back rooms, still shivering, still bewildered, long after their mutilated bodies had been turned into landfill. Li, however, was nowhere to be found, either among the dead or the living.

I sat on the ground and wept for all that had been lost. I thought of Father and Li, Mr. Wee and Daniel. And Kenneth—surely he was gone, too. I even thought about Violet Wee, though we'd never been the best of chums.

That night, pushing through the crowd, I encountered only strangers.

Penniless though I was, I didn't take shelter at the Wee house. I had thought about it, but my memories were still raw; a freed prisoner doesn't instantly think of returning to her cell. Besides, at that moment, I didn't feel homeless. Rather, a new notion of home had dawned on me during my long walk: Home for me was *all* of the Black Isle—every inch of it, from the jungles of the untrammeled north to the bustling harbor in the south. I loved the Island. This epiphany overwhelmed me and I began laughing and crying, not knowing if I was happy or sad or if there was a difference.

I wasn't the only one who returned to the city that day. As soon as the Japs left, the dead poured back in, just like me, to reclaim their home sweet home.

— 13 —

Quartet

THE BRITISH CAME MARCHING BACK through town, singing their anthems to king and country. But once the parade was over, our euphoria crumbled. Civil service functionaries popped out of the dust clouds and began handing us Union Jacks: Raise them high.

I can still smell those flags. Mildew, tobacco, and cloves. I remember wondering in whose cupboards they'd been stowed and at which far-flung edge of the empire—Rhodesia? Cairo? Calcutta? My mind was flooded with images of minarets, barefoot children, and dusty courtyards. But these romantic musings were quickly dashed.

"Chop, chop!"

Our self-appointed supervisors began to hurry us in their insulting pidgin, as if every second suddenly mattered. *Chop, chop*, as if we were mindless servants or dogs. *Chop, chop*, as if they had no idea, no concern, as to what we'd gone through in the last few years. *Chop, chop*, and they turned back the clock to 1939.

One of the first actions the British took upon returning was to expel the desperate families huddled inside the Balmoral Hotel and restore its policy of "Europeans Only." Even before visiting hospitals or feeding the poor, they chose to remind us that we were second-class boarders in our own land.

Only days before, I had joined thousands in merrily ripping down the Japanese insignia covering the city. Fueled by songs like "It's a Long Way to Tipperary," we tore at them until our hands bled. Such optimism! But as soon as these colonials began shouting orders, we experienced a united shudder of déjà vu.

The musty old stench had returned, and it permeated everything. Most of us abandoned hope, and with it the Union Jacks. We let them be trampled on streets, drowned in drains, blown aside by the wind. The British overseers gaped, incredulous that their orders were being openly defied, but they could do nothing. There were just too many of us. And now *we* knew it.

I sought work at the General Hospital on Alexandra Road, a rain tree–lined avenue close to the harbor. They were desperately shorthanded and I was desperately poor. Like hundreds of others, I had been sleeping in the boarded-up corridor of a High Street shopping arcade. My days of savoring chocolate, cognac, and books were a distant, fantastical memory.

I could have gone to the back garden of the old Wee mansion and dug up some of their buried heirlooms, but I dreaded the horrors I might uncover once I began digging.

The hospital's reception desk was next to a pillar pocked with bullet holes. As I approached, nurses, patients, and ghosts gathered around a wireless, listening to a testy British general being interviewed:

"No, no, it wasn't that they were better *soldiers,"* he corrected the interlocutor. *"That's utter rubbish! One British soldier is equal to ten Japanese— but unfortunately there were* eleven *Japanese. I tell you, it all boiled down to numbers..."*

Somebody jeered, but nobody lifted a finger to turn the radio off. It was such a relief to have the airwaves filled with something other than hectoring Japanese brutes, and the listeners were addicted, rapt, greedy even for myths. Tired of the general's lies, I left the building without a soul—living or dead—turning to watch me go.

Next, I tried Woodbridge, the mental hospital next door. The Isle had long been home to a disproportionately high number of such places, catering to all from the wives and daughters of colonials who'd failed to take to the tropical torpor to the hordes of overworked laborers from India and China who feigned madness to grab a few nights' respite from their filthy, overcrowded quarters.

Woodbridge was the grand-nanny of them all—the largest, newest, and most efficient at keeping its population in line. Its establishment in 1935 rendered all of the Victorian madhouses obsolete by culling the Island's lunatics under one roof and freeing the older buildings for new lives as schools, libraries, and hotels—all of them very haunted. Though devotees of British colonial architecture had complained about its bunkerlike starkness, I was grateful for its lack of gloomy filigree.

The institution took me on instantly as a receptionist without asking for any credentials. What they did do was glance at my hands; although they were scuffed, I had all my fingers, and this was enough to make me a good hire. The staff was overwhelmed with new patients—the Indian head nurse scowled when I called them *inmates*—and needed all the help they could get. Most of the influx had been transferred from overcrowded hospitals and weren't actually insane. "Not yet, anyway," the head nurse, Miss Joseph, muttered darkly, gesturing for me to follow her.

She took me on a brisk tour of the wards, which radiated the smell of cheap disinfectant. The patients ranged from textbook loons, baying as they sat strapped into chairs, to docile crazies who smilingly smeared food on their hair yet knew each nurse by name. They were housed by level, with the most violent in the basement, the more sedate on the second and third floors, and the harmless ones at the top.

My heart almost stopped when, on the fourth and highest floor, in a quiet ward reserved for "sleepers," I saw a familiar face, sitting up in his bunk while all around him everybody slept.

It was Li.

At first, I doubted my eyes because when I called his name, his face offered not the slightest trace of recognition. But when I stepped closer, I knew: It was indeed Li, my Li, in Woodbridge's standard sky-blue pajamas. After a few seconds, he looked puzzled, like a little boy just rustled from his nap. He knew he was supposed to recognize me, but try as he might, he did not.

"Don't make eye contact, Cassandra," cautioned Miss Joseph. "Leave that to the professionals."

"Can you tell me what happened to him?" I couldn't keep my voice from wobbling. "That's my brother."

Miss Joseph gave me a look of surprise; her eyes softened. "Wonders never cease." She strode to a metal pocket at the end of the ward and pulled out a battered-looking ledger. "Ah, yes. He's not one of the transfers. A Jap walked him in personally very late one night when it was raining like crazy. Both were drenched from head to toe. I was on night duty, doing reception, and I remember thinking how weird it was. Gave me goose-flesh, actually. The Jap didn't give his name and I didn't ask for it, naturally, but he was quite tall, no-nonsense, about thirty, thirty-five. A Jap helping a Chinese—you didn't see that very often, and this was even before the surrender."

Tall, no-nonsense, thirtyish. The Japanese man might have been Taro. But why would he have done this good deed—without telling me and taking credit for it?

I looked over at Li, who only appeared to be gazing back; his line of vision drooped midway between us.

Miss Joseph frowned at the ledger. "Says here the boy stayed quite lucid, but then, a few minutes after Hiroshima, he suddenly went into convulsions and fell into a coma. That's why he was sent up here. Seems he's been unconscious until this morning, in fact. Now he's in what we call the settling-in period, when he will slowly readjust to the world around him. If he's lucky."

A few minutes after Hiroshima—did this have to do with the toffee?

The nurse patted my arm. "He won't be going anywhere soon. Make all the eye contact you want."

After she showed me what I'd be required to do, mainly reception desk duties because of my fluency in languages, she took me to my lodgings in a hostel behind the hospital—a relief from the shopping arcade walkway. I thanked her and raced back to the fourth floor, two steps at a time. I was terrified that Li might have somehow vanished, that my earlier glimpse of him had been nothing more than a hallucination. But there he was, the only one awake in a ward of thirty or so slumbering souls, sitting as alert as a meerkat. He pointed his index finger straight at me.

"I know you," he said in Shanghainese. His voice was hoarse.

"Of course you know me."

I hurried to his side and embraced him tightly, the tears now falling freely down my cheeks. The nurses, thank God, had been feeding him intravenously—there was flesh on him—but he kept his arms lank by his sides the whole time. After clinging to him for several minutes, hoping he'd remember the warmth of my body or my scent, I sat on the edge of the bed waiting for him to speak again.

"I know you," he repeated, "but I don't know *who*. I'm all mixed up."

"Take your time. The war's over. The important thing is that we survived, Li. You and I." I hugged him again. Again, his arms didn't respond.

"The *war*?" He screwed up his face and pondered. "Are you my mother?"

I wanted to sob. But I laughed, for his sake.

"I'm your *sister*, your *twin*. We're the same age, to the very day. We were born in Shanghai together. We came to the Black Isle together. On a boat. With our father. Do you remember Shanghai at all? Bullock Cart Water? The plantation?"

Li closed his eyes, concentrating.

"Do you remember the toffee?"

His eyes popped open, and with an expression of childish glee, he cooed, "Shanghai!"

I squeezed his hand. He wasn't completely lost to our world after all.

"And toffee." He grinned. "I like toffee. Did you bring some for me?"

"No, not today. Maybe tomorrow. But tell me, Li, do you remember your special toffee, the one you carried with you everywhere?"

He shook his head, growing annoyed that I seemed to be testing or tricking him. Then all of a sudden, his eyes sparkled.

"I remember, yes!" he exclaimed. "Twins! The babies. They had furry arms. Are they here? I want to see them. I want to play with them."

"They're not here, Li . . . We didn't take them with us."

"How could we leave without them?"

He was right. How could we? My eyes filled up. "It was a very long time ago."

"But I want to play with them." His voice had taken on a childish whine.

Before I could calm him, he exploded into violent tears, bawling like an infant who wanted his mum to put things right.

"I want them here *now*!"

A Eurasian nurse came running into the ward light-footedly, glancing around to make sure Li's wails hadn't woken the others. She had a syringe poised in her hand, ready to plunge its mollifying sap into Li's flesh. Seeing her, Li gave a series of nervous whoops before the needle descended into his thigh. A second later, he was limp.

"What did you do to him?" I cried.

"We don't tolerate screaming here. Twelve hours of sleep ought to calm him."

"But we were just talking."

"Please leave," the nurse said, glowering, "unless you'd like one of those, too."

At daybreak the next morning, I returned to see Li. His so-called settling-in had made little progress. All he remembered began and ended with Shanghai; all he loved began and ended with the twins. I tried to jog his memory by mentioning the name of his school, his favorite playmates, the *karang-guni* men who frightened us, even the pontianak. But nothing. It was the same the next day and the day after that, and even after he was moved from the coma ward to another that allowed him movement.

No matter his new freedom, Li remained trapped in the past. It was a tune he couldn't shake, but it was the only tune he knew. I told myself, *At least he's alive. We have time—give him time.*

Although I fought against it, Li's preoccupation with our past filled my mind with ghosts.

I didn't know how or where to begin looking for our sisters. Certainly, the British authorities wouldn't help. I would have had to cultivate friends with ties to China, who would then have to be willing to write letters or make inconvenient journeys on my behalf. The process could take months, even years. And in all honesty, I didn't want to start a search that might produce an answer I wasn't prepared to hear. It seemed more important to find my own bearings first, to recalibrate my here and now.

Several weeks after their return, the British held a ceremony on the Padang for the Isle's civilian war heroes. The whole island was invited, but the grounds still held the stigma of exclusion for too many; only two hundred showed up. The spectators, mainly Westerners, clustered around the steps of city hall. The organizers had expected thousands to spill onto the green. As it turned out, bullhorns were barely needed.

I told myself I was going only because I had nothing better to do, but this wasn't wholly true. I felt entitled to go, as a survivor and an Islander. I was curious to learn who the government was going to reward. Would they acknowledge the local heroes or anoint only their own, members of the Europeans-only civil service?

Predictably, they began by bestowing medal after medal on British men and women—a few seemingly unscathed by the war, others permanently shattered by their years at Shahbandar, so broken they had to be helped up the steps. I pitied them but felt no kindness whatsoever toward the committee to whom natives did not matter and native heroes certainly did not exist. They made no attempt to conduct the event in any language other than English, and I watched a family of Malays, dressed in finery for the occasion, storm away. They had grasped no more than a clutch of words. I, too, eventually broke from the crowd and worked off my irritation by walking onto the Padang, where one of the earliest and biggest bombs had fallen.

The central crater had been filled in with soil but remained bald: The grass hadn't grown back in four years. Strange, for there was a saying on the Isle that if you stuck an ice cream stick in any field, you'd have a tree the following day.

I soon found out why. As I neared, a group of European boys and girls materialized, running along the rim of the enormous dell, stamping their feet. They were their own grave tenders, trampling on any sprig of green that emerged from the bomb site, their death site.

"I don't want them to forget us," a boy with pale lashes told me.

I was about to console him with a platitude when my ears perked up. At last, non-Western names were being announced on the bullhorn.

"Mr. Zhang Ming...Mr. Iskandar Ibrahim...Mr. Kenneth Kee..."

Kenneth? Could he still be alive? I began sprinting back.

I arrived to see three very familiar figures descending the steps, bedecked with red sashes and brass medallions. I was smiling so wide that my cheeks ached. There was Cricket with his pink birthmark; Issa, shorn of his long hair; and the one and only Kenneth Kee. The odd triumvirate smiled demurely at the crowd, grateful yet not exultant.

Prison had made all three startlingly lean, especially Cricket, who had been chunky from youth. But far from looking weakened, Kenneth was muscled, more sleekly defined.

I rushed to meet them at the bottom of the steps, expecting to find them surrounded by proud, weeping relatives. But they were alone.

Kenneth was the first to notice me. Naturally, he acted blasé, as if he'd expected me all along.

"I feel faintly ridiculoush, like I'd won the bronze for shot put or javelin." He lifted the brass medal embossed in cursive: *For Gallantry*. "Not quite the Victoria Crossh, ish it?"

His voice was strange. He now had a clenched-jaw kind of lisp, as though he had missing teeth or a swollen tongue. Although I wanted to, I didn't dare embrace him. I'd never done it, for he always struck me as one who'd disdain such intimacy. Instead it was Cricket who walked over and surprised me with a hug.

Kenneth placed a reassuring hand on his comrade's shoulder.

"Enough, Zhang," he said, "or they'll demand your medal back."

Now it was only Issa—Iskandar Ibrahim in name, if the announcer had got it right—who kept his distance. Not only were his gold earrings gone, but also his right hand was disfigured; like an unfinished sketch, it was missing its thumb. Still, the aura of a shaman hadn't been wholly stripped from him. His cosmic arrogance had outlived the war. He stood apart from us, arms folded, finally deigning to give me the minutest of nods. With him, I knew I had to make the first move. He hadn't forgotten that I had wronged him, cast away his advice. Nor had I.

"You look younger without hair," I said. Foolish words, but they were all I could think of at the time.

He grunted, and then in a tone that wasn't entirely unfriendly, said, "You don't look too bad yourself, Cassandra." He had pointedly dropped the "Miss." He was no longer my servant. Fair enough.

With that, a fragile peace was forged.

"I'm starved," Kenneth declared, and the four of us strolled away from city hall, not even waiting for the ceremony to end.

All three men had buried their medals in their pockets by the time we reached the side street. Kenneth led us to an Indian-Islamic roadside stall, where we sat on stools and wolfed down curry-dipped *pratas*, the tastiest of the Isle's flatbreads. I dodged their questions about my wartime years, simply saying that I considered myself lucky. On their part, they didn't recount the horrors at Shahbandar either. What nobody needed to say was how close they'd become. From the way they shared their food, like brothers in a poor, teeming family, it was clear they'd disavowed their prewar lives and the class differences that came with them.

In the joy of our reunion, we'd ordered enough for six and ate till our bellies nearly burst. But Kenneth was not one to let anything go to waste. While Issa tipped his leftovers on the street for a knot of hungry neighborhood cats, he took over my unfinished bowl of curry.

"I'll eat it," he said. Mimicking the cats, he lapped at the sauce.

For the briefest second, I glimpsed his diseased tongue. It was black and forked, split from the tip down.

He caught me. "Are you horrified?" he said, pushing the bowl away.

"No," I lied.

"Quite all right to be, you know. I would be, too, if an old friend I hadn't *theen* in a while *thhowed* up looking like a bloody *thnake*." He laid it on thick to make his point. Then the venom faded. "Creative people, the Japsh. They *thnipped* it down the middle with a pair of *thcissors*."

Oh, Kenneth. That he could be understood at all was clearly a supreme act of will, the result of rigorous training and the skilled avoidance of certain problem words—my name, for example.

"I've seen far worse," I said.

"No doubt." His eyes flashed with a sudden fierceness. With one ruthless, penetrating glance, he told me that he knew all about my years living in air-conditioned rooms, taking hot showers, eating square meals, and sleeping night after night with the man who'd not only murdered Mr. Wee, our mutual benefactor, but also Daniel, his friend. But how *could* he know? I'd said or done nothing to give myself away.

My cheeks prickled. It was Cricket who came to my rescue.

"So, should we tell her?" he asked Kenneth. It was strange to hear Cricket speaking English—stranger still that he spoke it so well.

Kenneth sucked in his breath. "I'd hoped to wait till teatime, but now that you've brought the matter up, fine." He glanced around for eavesdroppers and, finding none, turned to me. "We are regrouping, like vermin, like bacterium. The war'sh not really over, not yet, and I think you know what I mean. They think they can buy our favor with a coin, a medal, like we're children. We're ash much children as Mohandash Gandhi, Chandra Boshe, or all the othersh they're worried about in Burma, in Egypt, in Paleshtine. We're all marching to the same deshtiny.

"You know I'm no romantic, sho don't take me for one when I tell you that it'sh deshtiny you were there today, that we met again. The fact that you're alive ish proof of your durability." He spoke this last word, I thought, with a tinge of bitter irony. "We could do with a woman like you—with your unique outlook."

I glared at Issa. Had he told Kenneth about my eyes? Issa gave me the subtlest of winks, assuring me he hadn't betrayed the secret we shared. All right. Then did Kenneth know about Taro? Taro—my shame and sorrow. I felt a knot tighten in my gut.

"Do you hear me, Ca— Are you paying attention? I'm inquiring if you'd like to join me. Join we three."

I was so stunned that I remained mute. A stream of what-ifs flooded my mind, ruthlessly stirring up all the questions I'd long tried to still: What if I'd gone up-country when Kenneth made his first offer? What if I'd worked with Issa to raise up armies of ghosts? What if I hadn't met Taro? What if Mr. Wee and Daniel were still alive? Would I still go with Kenneth now?

"Yes, of course!" I nearly shouted. I was being given a purpose, a second chance. I wouldn't let it slip by this time. And then, like a shot in the heart, I remembered Li.

Again, Kenneth was quick to read me. "Ah, but you have doubtsh."

"It's her brother," Cricket murmured.

"Believe me," said Kenneth with the soothing tones of a longtime preacher. "Family is patient. History is not."

History also needed money. After wrestling with my conscience for a few days, I told Kenneth about the buried treasures at the Wee house. Was it immoral to steal from the dead? Who can say. All I knew was that the cause had to have funds.

As the four of us drove up to the old address, I asked Issa—behind the wheel, as ever—to let me out at the gate. Unlike the others, whose emotional ties to the place had either been extinguished in prison or never really existed at all, I couldn't bring myself to enter the estate.

The jungle had reclaimed it. Grasses grew wild, and rustling unseen were snakes, toads, monitor lizards. These invisible residents didn't disturb me as much as the ones I *could* see: faceless, anonymous ghosts wandering the property. Some must have been Mr. Wee's associates and some Japanese soldier boys, but from where I stood, beyond the gate, it was impossible to distinguish between the two.

I was most terrified of encountering the dog-man. Whether it was a badi or just a restless spirit, it was proof of my failure. Another secret shame I wanted to forget.

"No need to worry about the gendarmerie," Kenneth told me when I said I'd be the lookout. "They don't bother to patrol here anymore. Now we watch for lootersh."

Cricket nodded and handed me his loaded rifle, which only made me more anxious. I looked over at Issa, who gave me a sympathetic nod—he alone understood how disturbed I was by the ghosts I was seeing. Whether he had any intention of "putting them to sleep," as he'd done the spirits of Forbidden Hill, I couldn't tell. And I was in no mood to tell him about the dog-man.

"Under the roses" was all I needed to say. Issa knew exactly where to dig.

In a flash, the trio disappeared into the dark carrying shovels and gunny sacks.

Aside from the mating calls of cicadas and toads, the whole of Tanglewood was cloaked in an acquiescent muteness. I could hear my every breath, punctuated by the sounds of shovels striking earth.

I told myself that Mr. Wee would have wanted his things to go to his surrogate son. If not, the colonials were sure to raid the unclaimed goods in any case. But even as I parsed these thoughts, I still felt like a thief.

One agonizing hour later, Issa's silhouette emerged from the dark. Kenneth and Cricket followed close behind. They all carried bulging sacks, and when they brushed by me, I smelled the coppery scent of wet earth. At night in the tropics, especially after a full day of pounding rain, the soil always smelled of old blood.

Wordlessly, the three began squeezing their gunny sacks into the back of the van that Kenneth, ever resourceful, had talked a factory watchman into lending him. Their faces, particularly Cricket's, were grim. I knew they had come upon bodies.

Cricket, his hands shaking, dropped his shovel on the driveway. It made a loud clang. We froze, but except for a barking dog going crazy in the distance, the world didn't care.

As we sped away, I saw that Kenneth was wearing Mr. Wee's gold Rolex, its dull shine illuminating the cab's dark interior. It sat a little loosely on his wrist, but he wore it with delicate pride, as if it'd been his to own all along. He made no big show of it, but I could already tell that he regarded this watch, and not the brass medal, as the true reward for his gallantry, the real compensation for his mutilated tongue.

Kenneth had been right about himself: He wasn't a romantic. He was a pragmatist. He believed in fairness, equality, and, above all, payment for work done.

"We're not thieves," he said resolutely as we stole into the night.

I continued working as a receptionist at Woodbridge, visiting my brother every day. By night, I went to meetings with Kenneth and his friends, preparing to adopt the life of a freedom fighter.

Li was still trapped with the mind of a seven-year-old and was prone to a seven-year-old's tantrums. Whenever I pushed him to recall anything beyond Shanghai, he would either wail or descend into a hostile silence. Again and again, Miss Joseph advised me to give him time.

Always that word: *time*. It is a convenient illusion, beloved by so many, that time—meaning patience, meaning passivity—is able to heal all wounds. What people fail to reckon is that time is the sore itself, a greedy, devouring mouth.

I was twenty-six when I left Li and Woodbridge to join Kenneth and his group. Up-country in 1948 was no longer the untamable mass I'd known. I had somehow expected the jungle to remain vast and eternal, not realizing that while the jungle was content to remain as it had been for millennia, progress had expanded and encroached. Rubber plantations now covered twice the area they had during my days on the Melmoth estate. The Japanese, who'd invaded the Isle ostensibly for its strategic location, had also set their eye on its rubber. So, far from being dismantled, the Isle's plantations had grown fat during the war. After the war, planters— mostly British—did their math and grew even more rubber, flattening the township of Ulu Pandan to make way for groves. Rubber had become the government's largest source of income—and destroying the plantations Kenneth's obsession.

When I first arrived, his camp was more precarious and exposed than I could have imagined. It sprouted in a clearing that had once been a Malay family farm.

His recruits had laid down running paths and shooting ranges over old tapioca beds. The kitchen and storehouses were improvised out of coops and barns. The thirty of us slept in tents, ready to pack up at a moment's notice, which we had to do every few months.

Kenneth may have claimed allegiance to Communism but I never once saw him toting around the books of Marx and Engels or heard him proselytize. The only Russian works I ever saw him read were novels—*War and Peace* and *Crime and Punishment*. Communism, I quickly grasped, was a convenient banner under which to unite his disparate recruits. His populist goal was actually more basic and, at the same time, grander: independence. This was our only real religion, and we kept the faith zealously.

Much of what we did in pursuit of independence has a poor reputation today, and I am slightly embarrassed to recount our activities in detail. Suffice it to say that many in Kenneth's camp studied maps, made blueprints, shot guns, and built bombs.

Not Cassandra, however. Kenneth excluded me from this training, assigning me instead to "domestic" tasks. Like the five other female recruits, my duties were to cook and clean, raise fowl, and grow vegetables, in service of the men. I bristled at the role but couldn't complain. We saw fighters returning from raids bloody and in pain. A youth named Samuel Lee died from an attack by guard dogs, his mutilated body left behind on enemy land.

We kitchen hands knew whenever something terrible happened. Dinner passed in a grave silence, the food hardly touched and the whisky soon gone. Cricket became my gauge: His trembling hands spoke volumes. And in washing the men's clothes, we witnessed the private evidence of fear staining their undergarments.

I also reacquainted myself with the jungle. I became intimate with its plants and creatures—our stomachs depended upon its offerings, after all. I couldn't bear the thought of our men risking their lives on a daily basis only to sit down to a supper of boiled yam and grass soup. Subsistence didn't have to be drab. Not when mangos, bananas, coconuts, and passion fruit proliferated around us. For our men, I cooked stews with jungle fowl, slow-simmered with pepper and clove, stolen in fistfuls from nearby plantations.

For three years, this was how I lived—my voice hushed, my head low, grateful to have a purposeful life, where my work bore visible results: full bellies, clean clothes, brave men.

As it happened, the Melmoth plantation sat next to our fifth and final campsite. It had never quite recovered from the trauma of my family's care-taking, but its dilapidation proved ideal. Kenneth used its weed-covered lobes as a training ground for his unit.

Posing as a traveling salesman, he had met its current owners. They were a fresh-faced English couple named Manning, who'd purchased the estate for next to nothing, taking it on as more of a romantic experiment than a proper commercial enterprise. Armed with pickaxes, they had tried to revive the remaining plant stock without any hired labor—which would have been a tragic mistake if they'd actually been serious. Kenneth quickly grasped that the Mannings would never be able to keep up with the jungle, nor did they have any genuine desire to do so. Ironically, it was their indif-ference that kept them safe from his plans. He loved the way that, instead of the Union Jack, they flew a Jolly Roger on the rusty old flagpole in front of the house.

The Mannings would have been easy to finish off, but Kenneth des-perately wanted to believe that they were special. From the clattering typewriter sounds he heard emerging daily from the caretaker's house, he decided that they were poets. When he wasn't speaking of annihilating the enemy, he brought the Mannings to life with loving descriptions: Mr. Man-ning was curly bearded and walked around in batik shifts, his nose deep in books, while the blond, ethereal Mrs. Manning liked to play tunes of her own devising on a pan flute. "Bucolic pagan reveries," Kenneth called her compositions, "evoking wood sprites on a midsummer's night."

"They remind me of many good people I knew up at Oxford," he once declared over dinner, in a tone that verged on Wodehousian parody. "I do like those two. They make such handsome mascots."

Cricket made his own forest friends. Although hard to reconcile with his trembling hands, it was well known in the camp that he was Kenneth's best killer, not just a formidable shot but a stealthy hand with a bowie knife.

Every now and then, to soothe his nerves, he returned to the insect love of his youth. I sometimes saw him striding out of the bush at dusk with bright green stick insects, red moths, and monarch butterflies clinging to his hair and clothes. In those moments, he looked majestic, peaceful, and his colorful discoveries brought much-needed bursts of optimism to our bandit camp.

It was in the camp that I watched Kenneth the Leader begin to flourish and my old friend Kenneth slip away from me.

Not only had he sentenced me to a segregated life, far from the center of action, but also he deliberately distanced himself. Instead of being inducted into the charmed circle, I became for him, as soon as I arrived, just another recruit with whom he shared no history. He rarely spoke to me alone, and when he did, he conveyed only kitchen orders or complaints in his damned neutral tone. Though I saw him almost daily for three years, I learned less about him than I had from our rushed conversations in hallways during those first crucial days of the invasion, when he barged his way into my life with Daniel.

So what kept me there wasn't altruism. It was something more complex, more elusive. After all, it was I who'd led Kenneth to the Wees' treasures. Every Sunday, when the camp sat down to its communal supper, I pictured the pawned jade brooch or silver teaspoon that had paid for the meal. Each time a bomb exploded, Mrs. Wee's diamond rings came to mind. No doubt these thoughts occurred to Kenneth, too. Whether or not we shared a spiritual connection, the gold Rolex he wore even on the most sweltering of days was surely a constant reminder that he and I maintained a material bond.

For three years, I watched him devote his energies to secretive planning, taming both body and tongue—his diction had regained all of its original luster—and living in what appeared to be fastidious, monastic solitude. Not that he was a Zen master. There were many days when he wore the aggressive loneliness of the banished child, ready to hurl rocks at his friends.

His remoteness made me all the more determined to win back his affinity, or at least our prewar cordiality. Gaining his attention, however, was another issue. Increasingly, he lived in a bubble of his own making, with Issa and Cricket guarding him like sphinxes. He was shielded from the rest of us. Even when by chance he ended up next to me at one of the Sunday feasts, he never addressed me except to say, "Pass the salt"—a criticism, by the way.

Many in his position might have used it to procure lovers or companions. Not Kenneth Kee. As far as I knew, Kenneth always slept alone.

After we firebombed the first few plantations, the British began fighting back in earnest. They built high fences around their estates, armored their vehicles, and hired mercenary commandos to comb the rainforest, searching for us.

We had no choice but to keep moving around like fugitives. Even as our opponents grew stronger, Kenneth was determined that we not give up. It was a sour irony indeed that both sides had been toughened by their loss to the Japanese.

One night in early 1951, after several dispiriting weeks in the rain-pelted wilderness, Issa gathered the remainder of our group, halved to a mere fifteen, around a small fire. It was the first time this hater of public speaking addressed us. Naturally this brought me a feeling of dread.

"We have reached a turning point," he said, his voice growing graver. "I was in the city this morning. A state of emergency has been called. Chinese students have been holding boycotts, protests, just like in China. All the schools have been closed for weeks now. I saw police charging into Chinatown, waving their truncheons. And they weren't afraid to use them, even on children. But it's not just Chinatown that's in trouble. Factory workers are on strike. Bus drivers are on strike. Everybody's on the street, all the time—cops, looters, troublemakers. Everybody's restless. It's like the old days, only now there's no longer the same old fear. It's *complete* chaos."

Recruits whispered among themselves. Without saying it, Issa had stirred up the doubts we'd been quietly harboring for weeks. By being in the jungle, were we fighting on the wrong front? For once, I was grateful that Li remained confined in Woodbridge, and not free to raise hell on the streets.

Issa waited for the murmurs to subside. "I strongly believe we should return to the city and join in the struggle there."

"Nonsense," Kenneth cut in. "Let the schoolboys make noise. Up here is where we stand a chance of victory."

Issa did not argue. He had registered his point—that was all he'd wished to do. Quietly, he nodded and receded into the darkness.

The group, including Cricket, trickled back to their tents, until only

Kenneth and I were left standing by the dying fire. In the glow of the embers, I saw how tired he looked, how gaunt. He was in dire need of a good night's rest and, I felt, a friend's good faith.

"Ken—" I began to say.

He turned away, perhaps shunning me, perhaps daring me to come closer. I couldn't tell what he wanted. After a few minutes of his impenetrable silence, I left him alone.

That night, I went to Issa's tent. He jerked up, grabbing his keris. Seeing me, however, did nothing to subdue the look of trouble on his face.

"I need your help," I whispered. "I can't do this on my own."

He understood instantly. Our conversation had been interrupted years ago, and it was time that we saw it through to the end.

I followed him deeper into the jungle, feeling a surge of déjà vu when I realized that his hair had regained its original length and luster, although most of it had turned gray. But he no longer intimidated me. His footing was not always sure, and in his withered right hand, which could no longer make a proper fist, I saw the abominable effects of torture. He was now less a ruthless pirate than an aging chieftain, long abandoned by his tribe.

After we had walked about a mile, he abruptly stopped. "Do you know the nearest burial ground?"

I, too, understood instantly and assumed the lead. I took us through the darkened wood to Blood Hill on the old Melmoth estate.

Since the poetical Mannings had never bothered to put up barbwire or even keep dogs, we simply walked onto their property. The caretaker's house was dark, and it was safe to assume that the young couple was asleep. Of course, if either had come running out with a loaded rifle, Issa and I would be finished. We only had parangs with us to slice at the bush and fend off beasts.

"There's something I've been meaning to ask you," I said, and came to a halt. "Why did the Wees call you Issa if your name's Iskandar Ibrahim?"

The moonlight glistened off his smile. "I have no idea. I suppose it's easier to say, and I never bothered to correct them. At least they didn't call me Ahmad, which is what they called every other Malay—including my father, whose name was in fact Abdullah."

He had none of his old bitterness, and this surprised me. But as we walked, I realized I had better warn him about my past in these woods.

"Years ago," I said. "When I was a girl here, I . . . met a pontianak."

"You *met* a pontianak?" He paused. "Did you *meet* a bomoh, too?"

"Yes, a sinister one."

"And were you by any chance having your—"

"Yes, yes, it was that time of the month."

"Well, then. Blood and black magic. A very dangerous mix. Playing with corpses is not exactly my territory, nor should it be yours. I hope that episode ended well."

"I think so."

"And you're not by any chance now—"

"No," I assured him.

He drew in a deep breath, not wanting to let uncertainty enter into the mix. "All right, we have to keep walking, Cassandra, if we want to complete our task before the sun comes up."

"What about badis?"

"What about them, Cassandra?"

I was about to confess my botched summoning, but his tone—nurturing and impatient, all at once—made me too ashamed. Why bring up that old embarrassment? We were about to go and mend things now. Clean slate.

"You're right," I said. "We should keep walking."

Blood Hill was every bit as bald as I remembered. We climbed up its grassless slopes and stood atop its crest, surveying my old dominion. Even in the moon-silvered dark, I could see where the twin lobes ended and the jungle began. How small my universe had been.

"Kenneth is not doing well," Issa said when we finally sat on the dry, hardened soil. "Mentally, physically. Independence means too much to him. He thinks it's his way of correcting history."

"What do you mean *correcting*?"

"Ever since Shahbandar, he replays the past in his mind, over and over. When some people do that, they learn from old mistakes. Not Kenneth. He dwells on them." He took a breath. "You see, Daniel was also at Shahbandar."

Of course. The thought sickened me.

"Don't worry. Kenneth blames only himself. But if you hadn't agreed to come up with us this time, I really don't know what he would have done." He stretched out his arms and looked around us. "You don't see many ghosts in the jungle, do you?"

Good—change of subject. "Even when I was a child, it was quite *clean* here."

"But do you know why?"

"Fewer unhappy deaths?"

"If only. People have been dying here for thousands of years, and I assure you most of those deaths were not happy. No, it's quiet here because the spirits of the jungle live inside the trees. In my ancestors' time, we had bomohs dedicated to putting them there. When one starts seeing spirits in the jungle, it's time to get worried—it means that every tree has been occupied." He touched my right hand with his withered one. "Tonight, we'll have to call them out. And a graveyard is always a good place to start."

Goose bumps scurried along my arms. Even in the moonlight, his hand repulsed me. It looked and felt like a mummified rat.

"You must understand, Cassandra, I don't believe in using spirits for personal ends. They're not toys. Once we've called them up, we can try to make them obey but ultimately, they're just like people—it's up to them. But Kenneth's plan . . . Sooner or later, the Brits are going to find us. I won't survive Shahbandar again . . ."

I nodded slowly, pondering the implications of my agreement. I knew its dangers.

"Do you sense evil on this mound?" he asked.

"No." That was the truth; it felt clean. "When I was young, people said unwanted baby girls were buried here. Or wives accused of adultery. In any case, they were all victims. I doubt these spirits will be malevolent or hard to control."

"We better hope not. Things can go out of control very quickly." He paused. "How many souls are buried here?"

"I honestly don't know. Ten, at most?"

Issa was already unbuttoning his shirt. Where I expected the black tattoos of snakes and rosettes, I saw a living map of whitish welts and pink scar continents.

"As you can see, I'm not what I was." There was no rancor in his voice, no accusation. "The Japs didn't do this. I did it to myself as soon as they invaded. I didn't want them skinning me for my secrets."

A dense bank of clouds sailed across the moon, and for a few seconds, the light vanished completely.

"Do you want me to begin?" I asked. "The rowing?"

He nodded, pleased that I hadn't forgotten the ritual. Locking his eyes on me, he dug his fingers into the earth and lifted up crumbs of dirt, rubbing them over his face and chest. I followed suit. The soil on the mound was strangely dry and odorless. Free of plant roots and insects, it resembled virgin earth, if there'd ever been such a thing—earth that has never been used. Unlike the warm sludge of Forbidden Hill, it felt cool on my palms.

"Just empty your thoughts, my child, and concentrate. Remember, prepare for the unexpected. Stay calm when you meet the badi."

I cringed. The word made me think of the dog-man.

"Do not succumb to his temptations, no matter what they may be. And above all, be brave."

He handed me his keris and began an incantation. It had been years since I'd heard Arabic and was startled to remember how soothing I found its cadences. Gripping the handle of the keris, I closed my eyes and began rowing.

I would do it for the Isle. I would do it for my own freedom.

I rowed for what had to have been hours. Even though I'd anticipated the effort, I'd forgotten how endless the time would feel and how quickly my arms would lose their vigor. Just when I thought I could row no more—

Salvation. My ears picked up the liquid strum of moving water, of waves. My eyelids twitched, and in rushed streams of sunlight.

It was day. I was at sea, in a canoe, and all was calm. The experience was reassuringly familiar. I scanned the horizon for the badi. Indeed, there it was in the distance, its black-robed back turned to me. I waited, yet the badi did not deign to pay me any attention. I wanted more than anything to shout to it but stopped myself. This time, I would follow every rule. I continued rowing, the blazing sun scorching my hair and skin. With each pull of the oar, bolts of pain dug into my shoulders and back. A stabbing cramp set in at the base of my neck and grew.

Just when I'd pushed myself to the limits of endurance, the caped figure turned.

Who would it be? Father? Mother? Daniel? It began its approach. Not the dog-man. Please, not the dog-man...

Twenty feet away from me, the badi dropped its cape.

"Why, Cassandra," it said.

Standing on the waves, the warm breeze fluttering through his hair, was someone who looked completely at ease walking on water: Kenneth Kee. Not the conflicted, up-country Kenneth, but the prewar, Oxonian Kenneth—warm, unfettered by doubt, amused by folly. The smiling Kenneth.

Steady, I warned myself, *steady. It's only an illusion.*

The badi sauntered across the glassy water until he came to the tip of my canoe.

"You can stop rowing now," he said. "Release the oar."

I didn't believe him.

"Trust me," he said, and planted a foot on the prow to keep it from moving. "You're not going to topple over while I'm here. I won't allow it."

I dropped the oar. My arms felt numb, almost alien, no longer part of me.

"See? You can trust me."

I wanted to believe him. He filled me with a longing for the Kenneth I once knew: young and confident, the world at his feet.

"You look so happy!" I blurted out.

He smiled. "I *am* happy. The question is, are *you* happy?"

I built up my nerve. "I would be happy if you freed the souls of this burial ground. I'd like to borrow them for just one night. If you please."

He laughed. "And here I was thinking you'd want me to help you turn back the clock and bring back your beloved Daniel."

I kept quiet. The badi was tempting me with impossibilities, just as Issa had warned. Impossible wishes for which it would exact an even more impossible price.

"If that's all you want, then good for you. You've certainly learned your lesson. Bravo." He applauded. "And what do I get in return were I to oblige?"

I looked at the badi's youthful glow and again compared it to the dour, grim Kenneth of today. "I want you to be happy."

"What's this fixation of yours with happiness, Cassandra? Don't you know that happiness is not a prize one attains after hard work, like a medal or even, as Charlotte Brontë once put it, a *potato*? There's no baccalaureate of happiness. Happiness only exists in the pursuit, in the fight. It can't be bought; it can't even be earned. It has to be *lived*. So don't taunt me with happiness. Offer me something solid, something I can hold, something I can use. Like your body."

He climbed onto the canoe and sat facing me, his shoes dangling into the deep blue sea. His skin was radiant, tanned. He'd never been so charming.

"Come now, Cassandra. We're soul mates. We both know we are. And we both know that you've always wanted me. All those lonely nights in the jungle. You knew I was alone, yet never once did you come and find me. Was it shyness? Fear of rejection? Well, lie to your loins no longer, my friend. We both know what a creature of lust you are, how much you're defined by your animal appetites." He pitched himself forward so that our faces almost touched. "How wet you get in the dark thinking about the two of us—fucking."

He reached for the pin holding my hair up in a knot and with a quick tug freed it, sending my locks tumbling down my shoulders. I held steady, reminding myself that all of this was a projection of my mind. No matter what this impostor said or did to me, he wasn't real.

Rising to his challenge, I began undoing my top, a white blouse with a seemingly endless queue of small buttons. Impatient, I yanked it over my head and tossed it into the water, where it was instantly carried away by the current. I unhooked my brassiere and did the same.

I waited for him to reach for me, but instead he pulled back and kept his distance. He eyed my body coolly, scanning it for imperfections. Then he twirled his finger.

"More."

I lifted myself gingerly, careful not to let the canoe list from side to side, and pulled off my skirt, dropping it, too, over the edge. Then finally, my cotton knickers, which bobbed away like a paper boat. I tried not to flinch as the fiend stared at me.

"That'll do," he said with a peremptory chuckle. "A little too fleshy here, *much* too wobbly over there. And I hope I'm not the first to mention this, but you're frightfully...asymmetrical. Not my type, I'm afraid."

I gazed at my clothes. The waves had already carried them far away.

The badi hoisted his legs up from the water—somehow his pants remained immaculately dry—and hunkered like a gargoyle on the canoe's prow, facing forward. I burned to push him into the water.

"You cannot force these things, you know," he said, leering back at me. "The romantic impulse cannot be engineered."

"It's all right."

He stood up and stepped onto the surface of the water. It gave slightly under his weight, then buoyed up his feet like springy foam. Making a show of tidying his clothes and hair, probably to needle me some more, he began walking away.

"Wait!" I said firmly. "I haven't given you the permission to leave."

He turned back with a look of mock surprise.

"*I* called you up. I get to decide when you go. You're not leaving before you fulfill your end of the bargain. Lend me the girls."

He furrowed his brow. "Haven't the faintest idea what you're on about."

"The women buried in the bloody hill."

"Relax, I was only joking. 'Course, I know the ones you mean—even if you don't. The *bloody* part, however, will cost extra." He began making his way across the water, away from me. "They're already waiting." Tilting his head back one last time, he boomed, "I've left you high and dry, haven't I, Cass*h*andra?"

Then he ran like the wind.

With the badi gone, I stared down at my naked body. My clothes could not be salvaged, nor my dignity.

But before the waves of self-pity could wash over me, the world began swirling in a clockwise direction, as if under the influence of some diabolical magnet. Without oars, I was helpless in the canoe. I could only surrender and watch the horizon go round and round and round. *None of this is real*, I reminded myself. *None of this is real.*

The circling grew faster, tightening, and everything, from the canoe to my clothes bobbing away in the distance, was pulled along with me, descending into a watery spout.

Deeper and deeper I sank into the vibrating valve, twirling so fast that all I could see of the sky was a shrinking patch of blue. The air turned freezing cold as the dark liquid walls closed in. Just as the water touched my skin, darkness swallowed me up.

Everything remained black until my eyes began to tease out gradations of light and shade. I found myself cross-legged on top of Blood Hill, Issa facing me in the moonlight, exactly as before. Except for one thing: I was completely naked.

"Cover yourself." Issa handed me my clothes, clumped on the ground next to me. He kept his eyes tilted away.

We weren't alone.

All around us were prepubescent girls—maybe a hundred of them, their lips reddened with cinnabar, their eyelids darkened with kohl, giving us the apprehensive stares of underage brides. Solemn, even stately, they wore ceremonial robes of gold and silver. But they were eerily bald—every one of them, cleanly shorn. They didn't even have eyebrows.

The innocents buried in the hill. It had worked! But how wrong was I to guess there'd be only ten.

"Welcome back, Cassandra," said Issa. His tone of avuncular affection was new. I had made him proud. "I've been speaking to our young friends. The rumors were only part true. They weren't disappointments to their parents or their husbands. They were all beloved daughters, and that's why they were chosen—to be sacrificed. It was the custom to appease ancestral spirits with virgins. Unfortunately, the ancestors had asked for nothing of the sort. So these poor girls died in vain."

I was still trying to catch my breath. I tried not to think about the terror they must have felt at the moment of their murder. And the sense of betrayal.

"There are two new complications," said Issa. "First, there are more of them than previously expected..."

"I can see that."

"Secondly, *you* are more powerful than previously expected. We'll have to hope that the two things will cancel each other out and keep our situation under control."

"Have you told them"—my voice shook—"what I'd like them to do?"

"Yes. You were away for hours."

The girl closest to us, who looked no more than eight or nine, had gray skin with the serious, unblinking eyes of a very old woman. She placed her tiny hand on Issa's shoulder and spoke softly to him in an ancient-sounding tongue I didn't recognize, a series of low rasps, all sibilants and air.

"She says they will do our bidding tonight, if we let them go in peace afterward."

I nodded. "She has my word. Tell them I'm extremely grateful." And deeply saddened, I wanted to add, but this was neither the time nor place for condolences. We needed to harness their outrage, their wrath.

The little girl and Issa began whispering. I gazed at my soldiers. They wore silver bangles and filigreed earrings that must have been acquired at great expense. These were truly the prized daughters of some vastly misguided people.

"The girl says we should sleep now," Issa said, "here, on this hill. They will complete their task while we sleep. It will be very quick."

"Sleep *here*?" For all my triumph, I couldn't imagine letting my guard down atop any burial ground, let alone one where the spirits outnumbered us.

"We have no choice, Cassandra."

The girls pushed in closer to us, tightening their circle until my lungs were thick with their scent of damp mold and earth. The ones in front reached for Issa's hair, running their gray hands through his gray locks. He received them passively, his eyelids already drooping, heavy with sleep. I felt tugs at my own hair and realized they were doing the same to me, rubbing the strands between their palms, washing their hands. Their flesh was as cold and scabrous as wintry twigs.

"Give in to sleep, Cassandra."

"Issa..."

I reached for him. But we were too far apart, and he didn't reciprocate.

"Give in," he murmured, "give in."

— 14 —

The Night of the Burning Trees

I OPENED MY EYES to see snow. Snow falling all around me.

But these weren't the big innocent flakes of Bing Crosby and his winter wonderlands. They were dusty, warm to the touch, and when they melted, they turned gray and then black, impossible to wipe off. My mouth was dry, clotted with the flat, unremitting bitterness of ash—the taste of the end of all things.

Issa was still asleep a few feet away, covered in the weird snow. He looked like a stone memorial, one darkening by the second. As the flurry thinned, the Melmoth plantation came into view.

Even during its decline, the estate had had thousands of trees. Not one survived. The lobes were decimated, as if a hundred lightning bolts had ripped through, leaving only charred stumps. Standing on the hill, I could see to the floor of the plantation.

I shook Issa. He lurched awake. To judge from his wild eyes, he was as mortified as I was, as if we'd gotten deliriously drunk together and shared a forbidden passion.

Seeing the devastation below, his panic erupted. "Those two!"

Without another word, we raced down the hill.

At the end of the straight dirt road was the caretaker's house, or what was left of it: a roofless box with blackened walls, looking ready to crumble at the slightest touch.

We didn't have to kick in the front door. There was no door; nor did there remain any windows. The roof appeared to have been ripped off by some tornado's hand, but a tornado would have been kinder and left the rafters out of mercy. Nearly all the furnishings had been reduced to powder. Only random metallic things were still recognizable—an iron stove, a brass bed frame, two desks with blistered typewriters. These all seemed like sculptures made out of black sand.

"Hello?" I yelled, hoping for a miracle.

No answer.

"Maybe they saw the flames coming and drove away," I said.

This wishful scenario, too, went up in smoke when we reached the back of the house. A Chevrolet truck, burned black, sat spent on the dirt drive-way. Its tires had melted into gummy paste.

Issa looked around cautiously. "They may still be around. Check the lobes."

We ran back to Blood Hill, Issa slowing from the exertion. Where the path forked, just beyond the mound, we found the young English couple.

Or what remained of them. They were mangled and black, as if some-one had taken two shop mannequins, twisted them into poses of agony, and dipped them in tar. Had I seen them from the hill, I might have taken them for tree branches. Up close, there could be no mistake. They smelled like cooked meat—with a rancid, sulfurous overlay. I covered my nose and backed away.

"How could you let the girls do this?" Rage was strangling my voice. "Didn't you give them proper instructions?"

Issa stumbled back, startled by my fury.

"I asked them to destroy the plantations. Just the plantations." He shook his head. "But there were more of them than I expected. I've never been able to call up this many. I never expected you...a woman's power...to be so...I should have known better."

His shoulders slumped in defeat. The great Issa was suddenly lost, helpless.

"Forgive me, Cassandra." He sank to his knees. Tears streamed from his eyes, two black rivers flowing down his ash-covered cheeks. "I'll find their souls. I'll bring them peace."

Weeping myself, I helped him to his feet.

"No friend of mine should ever have to kneel," I said, and clasped his withered hand in both of mine. "Do what you must do, Iskandar."

I set off through the blizzard of ash. It had picked up one last burst of in-tensity as the winds changed. But the falling flakes were no longer white—

humidity had turned them all gray—and the day spread out before me as dark as twilight.

I ran through swaths of burned plantation floor, the embers hissing as I stepped on them, singeing the soles of my shoes and releasing little black puffs of acrid smoke.

Through the silence, Issa's cry resounded in the distance:

"Don't tell Kenneth..."

I wouldn't have to tell Kenneth a thing. Even the blind could have sensed the vastness of the damage. What I saw filled me with mortal horror. But I would be lying if I didn't also admit to feeling awe at my own strength. Issa was right. It was *my* power that had caused this dreadful, eerily beautiful apocalypse. My doing. If only I had called them up during the war...if only I had set them upon Taro...

Melmoth wasn't the only estate to have been devastated. Gone, too, were the grand British plantations and the thriving ones owned by the great American tire companies, Firestone and Goodyear—and frankly, we had nothing against the Americans. In the distance, the jungle wilderness remained richly verdant, but here, the world was charcoal black. I sprinted across acre after acre of charred fields where only a day before there had been thick skeleton armies of rubber trees. Now, nothing moved, nothing lived. Aside from my own footsteps and panting, I heard no other sound—no hint of people, animals, or even birds.

Had my girls slaughtered every living being?

I kept going. My eyes burned; my lungs heaved ashy dust. The air felt sinister, as if I were running through an endless thicket of cobwebs. So much soot had collected on my hair and skin that the more I ran, the more I must have resembled a kind of ghoul.

By the time I caught the first signs of human life—Malay tappers salvaging what they could from smoldering barracks, a European family packing into an armored Ford—I was filled with too much anguish to stop and savor my relief.

I fled the blackened wasteland.

At long last, I reached the moist green jungle and tripped over a crow with a tattered wing, hobbling to get out of my way. I knelt there, panting. Trembling in the undergrowth were other injured creatures—frogs, field mice, lemurs, pangolins, all in a state of shock. The poor things were gasping for air, their big round eyes staring back at me through foliage. I had to watch my every step to avoid crushing their tiny feet and tiny tails.

"I'm sorry," I gasped. "I'm sorry."

I didn't know where I was going, but I had to get up and keep running.

Perhaps a mile later, I rounded an ancient cycad with a gigantic fountain of fronds and—smack!—slammed into someone, knocking him to the ground.

"Cassandra."

I jumped. It was Kenneth, his voice every bit as raspy and hollow as that of the dead girl on Blood Hill. He was stunned and exhausted, but I also sensed his enormous relief. I helped him to his feet. Above our heads spread the vast canopy of a banyan tree that looked to be a thousand years old, its wise dangling roots furry with ash.

"I'm sorry," I said, more out of reflex than anything.

We stood motionless for a while, two old friends shrouded in many kinds of fog, our hair prematurely gray, our skin already turned to dust. Without thinking, I gave him a hug. Just as spontaneously, he returned my embrace, holding on for a long, long time.

"We won," he murmured. "I think we won."

We returned to a city that was in a state of emergency. Riots broke out day and night.

One of Kenneth's cellmates from Shahbandar ran a rooming house and allowed him, Issa, Cricket, and me to stay there until we were sure we weren't wanted by the authorities. Until then, we kept a low profile, moving only within trusted circles in Chinatown where the Brits had no intelligence. It appeared that nobody was hunting for us, but we couldn't take our anonymity for granted. Desperate to arrest anyone related to the up-country chaos, the government had posted huge rewards for tips. And betrayal is, after all, one of the great leitmotifs of revolution.

My handiwork stayed front page news for weeks, as did the terrible numbers: thirty-six planters and more than a hundred workers dead. I didn't regret the loss in property, but for the lives lost, I prayed for every one of their souls.

Somewhere along the way, an editor at the *Daily Monitor* came up with

"The Night of the Burning Trees," and this colorful title gave the holocaust a second explosion of life. Months after the fact, eyewitness accounts still flooded the tabloids. Surviving planters spoke of "mists" moving across the up-country darkness, told tales of gold and silver "flags" shimmering in the trees. Their wives reported footsteps and the "shrill, wicked laughter of little girls at play." But the Malay and Tamil tappers who slept closest to the crop provided the most chilling testimony. They said they saw lightning flashes that "shot out of nowhere," sparking huge flames that only the swiftest could outrun.

In the city, everybody had an opinion about what had happened. The official government line, as always, was to blame the Communists. In Chinatown coffee shops, I listened in as shopkeepers and clerks, red in the face with conviction, insisted that the British had planned the sabotage themselves. In the wet markets, nervous housewives blamed the Island's unseen forces, saying, "It's very, very dirty."

I'm sure Kenneth had his own convoluted theory, but he never voiced it. With his usual nose for history, he'd been right to declare our victory in the forest. We *had* won—at least up-country. Most of the colonials abandoned their plantations, many leaving the Isle altogether. But whether he felt that the fire had been an act of God or the result of human error, I had no clue. He remained, as ever, a cipher as he scanned the daily headlines, lingering only on the numbers that he cared about: the financial toll of the destruction, the steep decline in the government's popularity. As to the other figures—the human figures—he displayed no discernible interest.

He didn't learn of the Mannings' deaths until he read it in the papers one evening, at a Cantonment Road newsstand. The color drained from his face and he propped himself up against a rack of Hindi film journals.

"Good God...," he gasped. Three months after the fact, the tragic, human dimension of the Burning Trees finally touched him. "I'd hoped to become friendly with those two, you know. Eventually, I mean, when things boiled over. I'd never come across people who read and write for pleasure, not on the Isle. It may sound crazy, but I felt they were the kind of people who might understand me, that we could and would become friends, comrades, equals. That we'd go to shows together, have serious discussions about books and ideas over supper and drinks, that maybe I'd even visit England with them, bicycle around the countryside with scones and clotted cream in our picnic baskets, and talk and fish and read and dream..." He clutched his head in disbelief. "I've never seen Issa crack open any book aside from the Koran, and that doesn't exactly count. As for Zhang, he's so thick sometimes I wonder if he can even write his own name."

He sputtered on like this, tears welling in his eyes. What seemed clearer than ever was his sense of isolation. His loneliness had reached its limit and was pushing through his cool exterior to emerge as spite and whimsy. Scones and clotted cream? Kenneth Kee was having a nervous breakdown. To keep from crying, he peeled off a random magazine and began crushing and twisting it into a ball.

Watching him succumb to his emotions, his unfamiliarity with them making the outburst all the more awkward and childish, I suddenly grasped how powerful I was compared to him. I, a penniless, unconnected girl, could do secret, invisible, mighty things that the brilliant war hero Kenneth Kee could not.

"Would you like to get something to eat?" I finally said.

"I'm not hungry."

"Come on, now. Even Mao eats."

I took him for chicken rice at Mitzi's, a favorite of mine since my days with the Wees. It was the first time Kenneth and I had really been alone since our long embrace in the jungle, a display of feeling I suspected embarrassed him as much as it surprised me. We chose a booth in the corner of the boisterous dining room and drank hot pu-erh tea as we waited for our food.

"I hate this place," he said. "I've always thought of it as a place the rich went whenever they wanted to pretend they were of the people, or to remind themselves what real people ate. Because in truth, 'the people' never eat here. We all know this is the preserve of the rich, where philanthropists bring their mistresses on weeknights and their families on Sundays. Real people eat at the nameless canteen across the road, where everyone has to share tables and the tea is always cold. That's where I take *my* chicken rice. And by the way, did you know that this was one of the five or six restaurants on the Isle that went on, business as usual, for the duration of the war?"

"This was Mr. Wee's favorite restaurant."

"Then you know exactly what I mean." He took a long draft of his tea. "I hope you don't feel I'm being ungrateful."

"Kenneth, we're just here to eat dinner. It's not that complicated. You don't owe me a thing."

"I didn't mean to you. I meant to him. But honestly, it's much easier to give than to receive, don't you think?"

What exactly was he saying? For the briefest moment, my gaze fell upon his gold Rolex. Of course he instantly seized on this, his brain whirring afresh.

"Do you hate me, Cassandra?"

"Hate you?"

"Yes. Is that so odd a question? After all, I hated *you* for years." He watched for my response.

"Those years were hardly voluntary. I had to survive, Kenneth."

"No, no. It's not your years as a whore that I hate. Those I don't like but I understand. What I hate is that you engaged yourself to that useless spaniel Daniel. You see, that convinced me that things would never be fair, that even someone who should know better would always choose wealth over synchronicity."

What was he talking about? Was he actually accusing me of choosing Daniel over him or simply making a general point about class?

He let out a growl, sounding like a child who's unable to stop himself. "He was so bloody *good*. So ineffectually *good*. I mean, how deeply boring can a person be? Good God, how I *loathed* his puppy-dog eyes! What a bloody princeling!"

Just then, aromatic platters of chicken and rice arrived at our table on the arms of a nervous young waiter.

"Stop it. You're frightening this poor child," I said, forcing a smile at the boy, in whose palm I placed a few extra cents as tip.

"Cassandra, I don't care who I scare. I'm telling you the truth, at long last. And if I can't speak my mind to *you*, then..." He squeezed out a tight giggle so I'd think he was joking. "Sure, Danny boy was *nice*, but dolts are often nice. He took everything for granted. And he tainted everything he touched."

"Including me?"

"Absolutely." He smirked. "Perhaps the worst of all."

I pushed my plate away. "Look, you snake, how dare you talk about Daniel like that? He brought you into his family and treated you well, even when you didn't deserve it. Just so you know, I'd much rather be sitting here with him today than with you. It's too bad that he's the one who's gone and not you. Because, honestly, if we were to talk about *fairness*, you owe him everything—and not just that stupid watch!"

I stood up to leave. He looked surprised that his barbs had so offended me.

"Don't you, too?" he asked.

"What?"

"Owe him." He gazed at my plate. "You're wasteful to boot. You might as well finish it. You've already paid."

I should have left. My story could be happier if I had. But I just stood there.

Kenneth was infuriating. I'd begun the dinner on *my* terms, in a position of strength, yet he'd managed to rile me until he was back in control. If I walked out on him now, it was admitting defeat. Finally, hunger decided. And in the moment that I sat back down, my fate was sealed. Because a plate of chicken rice had beckoned to me, because I had nothing better to do, and perhaps most of all because I'd seen him cry, I failed to flee the sticky threads of Kenneth Kee's ever-spiraling web.

We finished the meal in silence. We were both ravenous—the boiled yam dinners at the boarding house had been uniformly atrocious. With each mouthful, I was sucked back into Kenneth's dominion of pregnant pauses, doublespeak, and roundabout thinking.

"Do you think things will ever get better?" he asked when the last bite was gone. His voice was calm, as if we'd been chatting amiably the whole time. "Do you think what we've gone through has been worth it?"

Despite myself, I was touched. He was, in his willfully opaque way, asking to be reassured.

"Absolutely," I said.

"Good." He smiled. "I thought so, too, but I wanted to hear it from you."

We wandered slowly back to our boarding house at the edge of Chinatown, now a labyrinth of cheap rooming houses, many of them also serving as bordellos. The zoning laws had been relaxed, as part of the government's last-ditch effort to quell the restless natives. Ludicrous as this might sound—using prostitution to quash dissent—the lawmakers were convinced it would work. And perhaps it did. In the past weeks, there had been next to no rioting.

The curfew was nine o'clock, so although it was only half past eight, men of all ages on our street were kissing their escorts good night before scurrying to catch the last ride home. Kenneth eyed them dispassionately, as if they were anthropological specimens placed in his path expressly for his study. I expected him to say something caustic about the aging courtesans or the resilience of the world's oldest profession, but he remained quiet all the way to our ramshackle house.

We both had rooms on the third floor. When we neared mine, I said good night.

"Good night?" he asked, smiling oddly.

He reached over and pulled me into the clumsy embrace of a man unaccustomed to giving hugs. All his weight shifted onto me, and I had to lean back against the wall to steady myself. It was like holding up a collapsing suit of armor. But the instant I relaxed and gave in, his embrace turned eloquent. He thanked me for the meal, apologized for his eruptions, rejoiced that our jungle days were over, and worried about the fate of our beloved city. Anyone who saw us would have thought we were conducting some kind of strange communion in the hallway.

They wouldn't have been completely wrong. When Kenneth's garlic-scented mouth brushed against my ear and neck, I realized that his outburst at Mitzi's had indeed been personal.

It was a lamentable seduction. More an attack than a wooing. Nevertheless, I unlocked the door to my room and removed us from the view of potential gossips.

Given all that would happen, it seems incredible that I remember nothing else about my first night with Kenneth Kee. I'd never thought of him as handsome or erotic, and I'm certain that even as he lay in my bed that evening, I did not think of him in those terms. Truth be told, Kenneth had only ever struck me as alluring when he was animated by the badi, who, drawing on my own nature, knew how to arouse me. Inhabited by his own self, he was an odd collection of angles, a bit sharp-jawed and narrow-featured for my taste. His eyes were too close together. He reeked of Brylcreem. To top it all, he was short—no taller than me. I continued to see all the faults I had noticed in him the first time we met in the Wees' library.

Nor do I remember much of our subsequent trysts.

What I do recall, and clearly, is that some other dynamic force drew us together, free of the usual conventions of physical attraction. Not since my cavorting with Li in the old plantation house had I felt such an intensity of shared understanding, such a mutual eradication of soul-loneliness. We canceled out each other's alienation. Together, we felt radically normal. Well, *I* did, at any rate.

Normalcy can be an addictive drug in any age, and during the edgy days of the emergency, when the streets were darkened with armed police, its hold was especially strong. I say this not to excuse myself but to help explain my otherwise inexplicable attachment to a capricious man I often found repellent.

We coupled a few times a week, always in my room and always in secret. I knew that he didn't want Issa or Cricket to find out about us; this was one of the myriad things he never needed to say but that I immediately sensed. I worked hard to keep our affair quiet, even though it made me complicit in his shame. For what else could it be but shame to be sleeping with a tainted courtesan, a dead man's bride?

The frequency with which he told me he hated me would have sent feminists up in flames. Early on, he said it with a wounding glee, later with irony, and finally as an incantation, until the word *hate* lost its original sting and meaning and became a kind of perverse mating call. I suspected he used that word only because he couldn't face uttering its opposite.

Very occasionally, however, he did indulge in bouts of expansiveness, and during these moments by his side in the dark, I savored my glimpses inside this very guarded man. I heard how he'd learned to drive at Oxford, where he worked as a chauffeur to several dons to help subsidize his studies. I learned, too, that had Mr. Wee not died, Kenneth would have gone back to finish his degree. He'd made good friends at Balliol, many of them students from Africa and the Middle East who, poetically enough, had been at Oxford to learn how to overthrow the Brits. If he'd graduated, he would have been the first in his family to have done so. Not that he was close to his family. The closest he ever came to talking about them was to say he rarely saw them. Instead, he stuffed the cash he made from odd jobs into a brown envelope and slipped it under the door of his parents' house on the first of every month.

Although none of his "secrets" were particularly intimate or illuminating, he had a way of making them seem like profound confessions, and I felt pressure to reciprocate.

But when I told him, sobbing, about my lost sisters, he said nothing. When I admitted feeling conflicted that my trinity of pleasure—chocolate, cognac, and a good book—had been introduced to me by Taro, he only smirked. Then late one night as we lay in my bed, watching shadows from the street below crawl across the ceiling, I revealed more of myself than I perhaps ever meant to.

"What do you know about ghosts?" I lit up a Red Lion cigarette to act casual.

"I know I have a lot of them," he replied, using the glowing tip of my cigarette to breathe life into a smoke of his own. "Why? Would you like to compare notes?"

"I don't mean it metaphorically."

"But those are the only ghosts worth our time. The other kind's for cuckoos."

Cuckoos? Here he was again, dismissing something he knew nothing about. Why did I even bother?

"Oh." He paused. "You *do* mean the literal kind, don't you?"

I kept mum.

"Why, do you see them or something?"

Slowly, I said, "Or something."

"Ah"—he took a long drag—"I thought as much." Whether this was true or he was bluffing, I couldn't tell. "Go on, then. Don't make me beg."

"And show myself to be cuckoo?"

"Oh, don't be so sensitive." He handed me the ashtray and sat up, looking directly at me. His eyes gleamed in the dark. "So it's true then?"

"Since I was seven."

"And are they all around us?"

"Always."

"What about right here, right now? In this room?"

My eyes darted to the old coolie squatting in the corner. He'd been in the same spot since the beginning of my stay but had never posed a hindrance.

"There's one."

"Thought so." He smiled, sitting up even straighter. "You know, I can see the ghost of the ghost in your eyes. Go on—describe him."

"Chinese, about sixty, skin and bones. Probably a coolie. He just sits there. No fuss. He's looking at us but I don't think he understands English."

Kenneth gazed at the corner. "So he was here, while we were . . . He saw it all?"

"Yes, but don't worry. He doesn't participate."

"You *are* cuckoo, you know. Just not the way I meant." With a wide, incredulous grin, he hauled the bedcovers off, flopped onto his back, and directed a long sigh into the musty night air. "Blimey." He drained the cigarette and lit up another, and then embarked on a kind of muttering monologue. "You'd better not be pulling my leg, I tell you." He turned to squint at the corner again and then looked back at me. Puff, puff. "Bloody hell." Deep suck and jagged exhalation, punctuated by a gleeful cackle. Fumes spewed from his nostrils and mouth. "All this time. You're good at keeping secrets, I'll say." Another puff while his mind whirred. "Have you told anyone else?"

"No." I glanced away, not wanting him to discover Issa in my eyes.

"You never told Daniel?"

"No."

"Not ever?"

"You're the first, Kenneth."

He chuckled deeply, irrationally pleased. I'd felt an initial rush of relief from sharing the secret, but now his enthusiasm unnerved me.

"Bloody hell," he said again, laughing and displaying for me the length of his left arm. "Look at this. Goose bumps. I haven't had these since I don't know when."

I ran my fingers along the cool, scaly patches of his biceps—unlike me, he really did not sweat—and beneath my touch his skin sprouted yet more grains.

"Do you like it?" he asked.

"Your lizard skin?"

He smacked my hand for being deliberately obtuse. "Having ghost eyes."

"Not really, no," I said. "But it's never been a choice, so I can't think of it in those terms—or I can't *let* myself anyway. There've been times I fought it. For years. But one grows up and adjusts to what's there. It's like a deformity. One adapts."

"A deformity?"

I watched him squeeze his lips into a thin line; his mind was springing into action yet again. He tipped me back onto the pillow and pressed his lips to mine. I felt his tongue push in, overwhelming me from top and bottom, as if he had two tongues.

"You're a very strange girl, Cassandra. A very odd bird indeed."

One had to give the politician—or the reptile—in Kenneth full credit for playing it cool. He waited two more nights before mentioning what must have struck him the instant he heard my secret. Coolly, too, he chose the perfect setting to continue this discussion. For the first time, I was invited to *his* bed.

His room was spare and tidy, as if he'd moved in only days ago and hadn't properly unpacked. In fact, he owned too little to produce any clutter—a stack of dictionaries and a mug of sharpened pencils were all he had on his desk. His bed was a picture of monastic austerity: white case, white sheets, a single hard pillow that made my neck ache. So immaculate was the room that, unlike mine, it was even ghost-free.

"Have you ever thought about utilizing this 'deformity' of yours?" His tone was light and casual, offhand. "I mean, in a way that might make you value it, rather than think it a burden?"

"You mean, to get rich or save the world?"

"So you have considered it." He picked a bit of lint off my clavicle. "Ever spent much time with Issa?"

"Not really. To be honest, I find him a little frightening."

"Well, maybe in the old days. He's more like a shriveled old scarecrow now." He sat up and handed me a smoke. "During the war, when we were holed up in the jungle, he used to go on about his grandfather or great-great-grandfather being a kind of South Seas shaman. I always dismissed it as guff—never could stand people who boast about their forebears—and I chalked it up to bitterness over his people supposedly losing their land, their water, what have you. But as time passes, I'm more of the mind that maybe he did, or does, have some, I don't know, connection to the spirit world. Like that Night of the Burning Trees. I've always had an inkling that Issa had something to do with it."

"Suppose he did," I said carefully. "Wouldn't he tell you?"

"'Course not. Would a player reveal the ace up his sleeve? He's not as stupid as he looks."

Was he implying *I* was stupid to have told him about my ability?

"Issa's one of your closest friends," I said.

"He's a *comrade*...for now." He registered my dismay. "Don't act naïve, Cassandra. It doesn't become you."

"I'm far from naïve, Kenneth."

He lit a cigarette.

"Back to using your talent for good." He looked at me with tenderness. "This is merely a suggestion, but perhaps you might consider getting to know Issa. Maybe you two could, I don't know, collaborate."

"On what? Holding séances?"

"There are people in this city who need to be scared into putting things right, and you know exactly who and what I mean. If we could *accelerate* the process, I don't see why we shouldn't. God knows our people are restless. We can't afford to let this momentum pass." His eyes suddenly turned sharp and cold. "Obviously, I hope you two will have the courtesy to consult me before you do any unnecessary damage *this time*."

The next afternoon, I paid my monthly visit to Woodbridge—not as often as a doting sister might have gone, perhaps. Then again, time stood still for Li. When I had rushed to see him after my years in the jungle, his nonchalance made me realize: He hadn't even noticed I'd been gone.

He was the antidote to Kenneth's mercurial moods and secret agendas. As long as I didn't provoke him to remember what he couldn't, he remained a boy of seven.

I found him traipsing around the garden in the hospital's blue pajamas, sniffing at the hibiscus shrubs as if they were roses, when of course hibiscus gave off no scent at all. As always, my first glimpse of him was unnerving— a child's exaggerated tics affixed on a grown man's face. But I had trained myself to readjust my expectations, even to welcome his simplicity.

When he spotted me, he rushed over.

"I passed with flying colors," he announced, flapping his arms like a bird. The armpits of his pajamas were drenched in sweat.

"Did you take an exam?"

"The test, silly!" He rolled up his left sleeve and showed off the bandage on his arm. "Miss Joseph says I'm not sick anymore. I have good blood now."

I wondered if this was true or another of his fantasies. "How do you feel?"

He did a little soft-shoe, all elbows and two left feet, and spun a sloppy cartwheel that had him nearly crashing into three catatonic women in wheelchairs. He landed in a hedgerow of ixoras. A middle-aged nurse came running over, gesturing with a half-eaten ham sandwich.

"I can't leave you alone for even one minute!" she barked, and then turned to me. "This one's got so much energy we should be putting him to work. Always running all over the place. At night, when we do our rounds and don't see him, we'll come outside, and sure enough, he'll be sound asleep on the grass."

"Sorry, Missy," Li told her, holding his hands behind his back, barely able to contain his mischievous grin. He called all the nurses Missy because it was what the older Cantonese patients called them—and because he knew this nurse in particular bristled at the term.

"Did he really take a blood test?" I asked the nurse.

"Yes, spectacular results. His blood count's better than anybody's. Probably explains his incredible energy."

Li grinned. "I told you!"

The nurse gave him a pat on the back and went off to finish her lunch. I sat down with Li on a stone bench in the low-hanging shade of a rain tree.

"Oh, oh, oh!" Li leapt up. "I almost forgot to tell you. I talked to the twins." He crinkled his index fingers. "Xiaowen, Bao-Bao, Xiaowen, Bao-Bao, Xiaowen, Bao-Bao."

Those names. I hadn't heard them in years.

"They came to see me." He pointed at the gap between two red hibiscus bushes. "They were there!"

There was nothing there. But the space was just wide enough for two little girls.

"When did you see them?"

"I don't know." He shrugged. "I was sleeping and they woke me up. I was sleeping *inside* but they woke me up *outside*. They told me to tell you not to worry. They said they're happy because they're together."

"Li..." I tried to tread gently. "Were they ghosts?"

"No!" He shrieked with laughter. "How can you say something like that?"

"How old did they look?"

He thought for a second. "Like you. They look just like you." He nodded, reinforcing the memory. "Their arms are still furry, like when they were babies."

"Did they say anything about Mother?"

"They built her a big, big house. It's all completely white and there's a rose garden and big, big fields and a maze. They said when we go and visit them, we can stay there. But they're very busy now because they have to shake hands with everyone."

"Did they shake hands with you?"

"Of course!" He heaved a grandiose sigh at my expense. "Don't tell me you still think they're ghosts. Only mad people can see ghosts, *jie jie*."

He showed me his right palm—it was stained bright red with the juices of some stubborn alien bloom.

I couldn't wait to talk to Issa, but ever since we returned to the city, he'd grown distant. Within a few weeks, he moved out of our Chinatown boarding house and into a hostel in the Islamic quarter at the other end of the city, saying he felt more comfortable being "among his own people." Had this to do with the Night of the Burning Trees? Even Kenneth never seemed to know what he was up to half the time. Curfews and roadblocks made traversing the city an ordeal we all tried to avoid.

After several calls, Issa agreed to meet me in the Kandahar coffee shop by the white-walled Sultan mosque. His lodgings, he said, were close by. The colonials never came to these narrow, cobblestone streets, not even to gawk at the gold minarets and jade floor tiles of the celebrated old mosque. The lanes weren't wide enough for cars, and colonials didn't like being on foot in strange neighborhoods. Once here, I understood completely.

It was Friday, just after afternoon Jumu'ah. The curry and spice in the air made the day seem even warmer and stickier than it was, yet the men emerging prayer-fresh from the mosque wore long white robes. When several of these pious gents, many wearing the white skullcaps of the hajj, cast me poisonous stares, I realized that the streets in this section of town were segregated along gender lines; women were unwelcome on this one.

Their looks were still less hostile, however, than those from a quartet of Gurkha policemen stationed at the nearby cross-junction. Cops had become ubiquitous around the city since the emergency began. The four had their hands on their pistols, somehow perceiving my presence as a threat.

Before any of them could make their way toward me, I spotted in the crowd Issa's long, gray mane and the pink scars on his upper arms. It was the first time I'd seen him in a short-sleeved shirt. He still looked like a pirate or genie, but Kenneth was right, there was now a bit of the old scarecrow about him, too.

"Iskandar!" I called.

He turned and smiled. "Welcome to the ghetto."

What did the policemen and the devotees think of me now? Was it better or worse that I'd come to meet a man? Issa led me into the dark cave that was the Kandahar, taking a table in the corner.

"He knows," I said when we sat down.

Issa nodded. "I suppose it was inevitable."

"He wants us to work together."

Issa laughed. "He wants to play us off *against* each other."

"It's nothing like that. We all want the same thing—the world wants the same thing. Let's drive them out. They're already itching to leave. They just need one final push. Small-scale, minimal fuss, maximum impact. It's the time, Issa."

We let my proposition hang in the air. He sipped his milk tea and I sipped mine.

"Tell me," he said, "are you in love with him?"

The question took me by surprise. Was I? In any case, it was certainly none of Issa's business, and I wasn't going to let him change the subject.

"Don't you want to take the Isle back?" I said. "I thought we want the same thing."

He smiled. "Where you are correct is that I'm worried for the Isle. But what concerns me, perhaps just as much, is how you seem to have given him authority over you, letting him send you on little errands like this."

"I'm here of my own free will."

"He knows where I live. He knows how to find me. In fact, this is where he and I meet once a week. We were here just yesterday—at this very table, talking this over."

So Kenneth had already arranged everything. Why, then, had he sent me here?

"Look," Issa said. "I'm too old for his games. When I first met you, you were the most confident, headstrong young woman I knew. Very stubborn, I should say. And now..." He gazed at me with tender concern.

"I was a stupid child. Now I've found a cause greater than myself. Now I've found a way to be useful."

"Cassandra, *you* are the one with the power, not him. Don't ever forget that."

We sat quietly for a moment. Once again, I was struck by how Issa seemed to have changed—from enigmatic, dangerous foe to sage uncle.

"Of course I'll do it," he finally said. "I've already told him I would."

I must have smiled too happily, because he added, "It's not something I agreed to lightly. And despite how he sometimes acts, I'm not his Caliban. So I want you to fully understand what you're putting yourself into. You're a commander, not his soldier. We'll finish what we started in the jungle, but we can't make the same mistakes. If we knowingly take innocent lives again—even one—we'll pay for it later with our souls. We will become ghosts. Remember this."

The thought sobered me up fast.

"It was arrogance on my part to have thought of the spirits as an army: They're our equals. Yet when it comes to paying the price, it'll be only you and me—not Kenneth—and it'll be quite a price. As you know, things can go wrong. Many bomohs don't survive more than one summoning in their lifetimes. We're about to attempt two in less than a year.

"Assuming all goes well, you and I will be physically, mentally sapped for years. Years, Cassandra. Not just one or two, but five, six... I've seen men sleepwalk through *ten* years of their lives. You probably won't be the same again. Your reflexes will slow; your mind will dull. It will age you. All that if it goes *well*. And if it goes badly, we die."

On that bleak note, he shot me a quicksilver smile.

"Then, there's the other price. Kenneth's a very clever man, but he doesn't have what you and I have. He could never do what you and I can do, and ultimately what he'll feel, if we succeed, is that he owes us an enormous debt. And this will weigh on him. You know it will."

I knew he was right. Already the Rolex around Kenneth's wrist was a daily reminder of how much he was still in the Wees' debt; it was his golden handcuff.

But could I live with myself if I let opportunity slip by, as I had before the war? The Isle needed me. The independence I'd fought all my life to win was now tied to the Black Isle's fate. If I could bring freedom to all my fellow Islanders, what was losing a few years of my health? I would have lain down my life if it meant the Isle could finally be our own.

"Are you ready for the consequences, Cassandra?"

"You were just telling me not to forget how powerful I was." I took his hand. "Teach me your chant."

When people's deepest instincts drive them to do something, it takes almost nothing to remove that last hurdle. The British yearned to leave. You could see it in their faces as they sat nursing their gin in coffee shops at noon, in the way they clutched their children at the taxi ranks. Who were we to make them stay?

There would be sacrifices.

There would be regrets.

But everybody stood to gain—Islander and British, living and dead.

A fortnight after our meeting, Issa and I defied the evening curfew and took the last trolley to Forbidden Hill, the site of my unfinished lesson years before and soon to be the new home, if the British had their way, of a luxury hotel.

Having discussed everything with Kenneth beforehand, I knew exactly the favors to ask of our underworld allies. Terrify the British, not kill them. Spare the children. Because the Brits were already jittery, grand gestures were unnecessary. Restraint was the key—cold spots, strange miasmas, displaced objects, doors and windows opening and closing on their own, things that might make them question their own sanity. We wanted to give the colonials a little push, but they had to believe they came to the decision to leave by themselves. We had to give them reason—and face.

I spent weeks perfecting Issa's Arabic chant. He called it "singing," and it was soon clear why. The "song" began as a Sufi incantation known as *dhikr*, composed of the various names of the Muslim god, which were joined by names of the saints and magical forebears from Issa's Bugis ancestry. The recitation was for me less a test of memory than a test of will, because specific emotions had to be attached to each cycle of names—joy in the glory of life, grief at the transience of life, passion as a seeker, humility as a seeker. The goal was to repeat the cycle in such a seamless succession that they ceased to sound like names but full-bodied, poetic sentences, sentences so alive with feeling they would draw me into a trance.

"Think of each line of names as a fragrant garland," Issa told me as I closed my eyes and began really seeing what he described. "Lay the garland of sorrow over the garland of joy, the garland of humility over the garland of pride, until you have a tower of wreaths high enough for the tomb of a king."

My enchanted tower of wreaths was as real to me as any made of brick and mortar. And soon, before me, an avenue of more towers bloomed, the fragrant garlands proliferating without the slightest effort. I saw myself, tiny and inconsequential, in this floral corridor, and as I began walking, waves of emotion swept through me. It was not merely joy at the vibrant colors and smells of the flowers but an overwhelming awe at the beauty and the variation—the greatness—of life. This was followed by a supreme alertness to any petal or bud that was fading or had fallen to the ground, the sight of which drew me into a deep, aching sadness: Splendor can never be prolonged; the end always comes. To tame this grief, I had to bow to a higher level of awareness. My thirst for beauty and permanence turned at this point into a spiritual hunger, one that only knowledge of the truth could satisfy. Wisdom, when it arrived, was harsh; it told me to accept my own insignificance in the schema of all life. At this, I was once again in awe at the towers of wreaths before me, stretching out now in all directions.

After my lessons were done, Issa handed me a vial of what was clearly bone dust.

"As soon as you reach home," he said, "sprinkle this across all entry points—doors, windows. This will keep them out."

"Dare I ask *who* this was?" I said, examining the bottle.

"No"—he smiled, serious—"because I dare not tell."

At the cemetery, I began chanting as soon as we arrived. There was no need to row or endure the badi and his games. I simply chanted for hours, until my throat was raw. With Issa by my side, I felt no worry.

Under the moonless night, I watched the spirits gather around Issa and me, entranced by the cadences of this ancient song. As before, I was struck by the mix of ages, races, and faiths of the dead, and the way they all lived side by side in this gloomy, gated plot. When all rose who could have been risen, I felt calm, completely at ease. I made my vow to my diverse constituency, repeating my message in the five languages I knew—English, Malay, Shanghainese, Cantonese, and Mandarin:

"My friends, your eternal home will be in jeopardy if the British remain. They plan to flatten Forbidden Hill to make way for a hotel. In exchange for your help, I promise that you will have a permanent home here on Forbidden Hill. I'll make sure you will *never* be disrupted from your rest."

As I explained their side of the bargain, my army stood listening, their eyes blank, uninspired. Did they understand what I was asking of them? I looked at Issa, whose face showed only calm.

After the ghosts dispersed, their lips quivering their weird prayers, I could only wait and wonder. But one thing was already clear. Issa had been right. Calling forth the dead nearly killed me.

He had to carry me down Forbidden Hill and put me in a taxi. I wanted nothing more than to take to my bed, which I did—for seven full days and seven nights. I felt as if I'd caught the flu, and indeed the symptoms were similar: fever, migraines, muscle aches, the loss of energy and appetite. But this was no flu—unless it was a flu whose symptoms lasted not just days, but months.

Sadly, out in the world, nothing seemed to have changed.

"Maybe we need to do more," I told Issa one night when he came to visit.

"You've already done more than your share; anything further would be testing fate," he said. He, too, had been weakened, though far less severely. The chanter always suffered most. "The dead cannot be hurried. The Night of the Burning Trees was a rare exception. The youth of the girls made them impatient. Too much so, in fact."

But *I* was impatient. It enraged me to think I'd sacrificed my health to no result. I could still see the passive, blank faces of my constituency at Forbidden Hill. Did they feel no obligation, no urgency to protect their own resting ground?

As soon as I recovered the strength to walk the streets on my own, I sought out two smaller resting places—a Taoist mausoleum in Chinatown, packed with the cremated remains of lonesome amahs, and an overgrown field in Little India where Indian convict laborers had been thrown into mass graves. There, without Issa, I chanted again and asked for volunteers in ridding the British.

In the days after, I obsessively followed the news, looking for signs.

The first one came at the Polo Club. One morning, during the Anzac & Friends tournament, horses from both the Island and Kiwi teams began bucking violently for no apparent reason, throwing off all their riders. Island captain Killian Ross lost his helmet and was trampled by his own horse, costing him his right eye. Several other players suffered broken bones. Nobody could explain the accident but it was quickly forgotten—horses were just animals, after all.

Less easy to dismiss were the events a fortnight later. The aptly named Cyril Cunning, the councilman who'd first suggested flattening Forbidden Hill, woke to find his eyes sewn shut with red Taoist thread. His wife began packing for England that same afternoon. The next day, just before lunch, the notoriously awful magistrate Alan Topper was set upon by his paperwork. The sharp edge of a lucrative engineering contract blew toward his eyes, slicing open his lenses. He ran from his office, blood streaming down his face as he screamed, "I can't see!"

The eyes. I had to smile. The ghosts were targeting the colonials' blind spots.

Two weeks later, yet more mischief. In an overgrown training area not far from the polo fields, night sentries reported seeing bare-skinned Tamils roaming the grounds. When ordered to stop, they simply vanished. When fired upon, bullets seemed to pass through their bodies. Entire squadrons of Gurkhas, bold warriors who had served as peacekeepers during India's bloody partition, resigned, fearing for their lives.

After this came a long and desolate lull. Months went by with nothing out of the ordinary being recorded. I feared that, like me, the dead had worn themselves out.

Then one afternoon, I took a trip to the newly opened Van Kleef Aquarium, a large modernist cube not far from city hall. I was feeling depressed, hobbling around on a cane at the age of twenty-nine and unable to concentrate on a book for more than minutes at a stretch. I ruined my health, and still the Brits were hanging on.

As luck would have it, I'd picked the worst possible day to visit. It was May 24, Empire Day. Schoolchildren had the day off and the building was packed with a fleet of pint-sized, fair-haired delegates in the sickly green uniforms of the British Council kindergarten. Because of this group, the ticket seller had closed off the place to all other visitors but me—perhaps she felt sorry for the poor limping creature that I was.

Squeezed into the lightless, tank-lined passageways with a hundred children, I told myself I could shoo away the rowdy ones with a firm tap of my cane, but such measures proved unnecessary. They walked hand in hand, twenty charges in lockstep with each teacher, everyone sporting a paper crown to honor Queen Victoria's birthday. Tunnel after darkened tunnel, the tiny monarchs traipsed in a hushed, bug-eyed state of wonder—impressively, not one of them sniveled. At their age, I would have been scared stiff by the expressionless orbs flitting and flying across the violet windows.

Finally, after eyeing these exhibits of modest anemones, sea stars, and unflappable fish—all locally caught, the signs proclaimed—we came to the hall containing the Van Kleef's pièce de résistance: the Great Blue Yonder. The tank, the grandest in the Orient, was a glass chamber two stories high in which swam an undersea menagerie culled from far-off waters—coral, moray eels, and octopuses from the mid-Pacific, and four Australian great white sharks, each the size of a canoe.

Yelping in excitement, the children pushed ahead of me until I stood waist-deep in a sea of little crowned heads. They pressed their faces against the glass, even as their teachers warned them to stand back. But it was hard to fault their curiosity—this blue room was amazing. It pulled us all to the bottom of a fictional, harmonious ocean where sharks and octopuses were the best of friends.

The beasts, however, were unnaturally still. They seemed to have been hypnotized. The sharks floated in suspended motion instead of firing ahead, as they are wont to do. Only their gills shuddered.

The children were transfixed. Here were harmless sharks and spongy octopod arms that would give you a nice hug. They bustled by me to push closer to the glass, seeking authentication: Were these puppets or the real things?

I gave way to the anxious cohort, moving to the back of the hall. This was when I noticed the black nests of kelp in the tank beginning to move. They rose from behind the sharks like sentient weeds. As they swam toward the glass, I grasped that these were no fugitive plants, nor even fish, but the undulating Rapunzel locks of two creatures that had no business being there.

The ghostly pair showed themselves to be lithe, demonic maenads, all flowing black hair and naked flesh. They had the white eyes of the blind. But they could swim, and very well indeed, producing hoops of air bubbles around the somnambulistic sharks.

Now the madness began.

The two maenads grew rigid and torpedoed toward the glass. They banged their heads against the transparent wall, with a dull, sickening *thump*. Instinctively I looked to the exit. But no one else reacted. Hadn't they heard it?

"Keep away from the tank!" I shouted to the children.

A curly haired boy turned back to look at me, quizzical, but my cry only inflamed his friends' curiosity. They crowded in still closer to the glass.

The maenads swept back for a second, as if put off by all the small faces. Then, with a swift flap of their gray arms, they pitched themselves forth and again struck their heads on the glass. *Thump!* This time, the impact was loud enough to make the children jolt back. But none of them knew what to make of it. The curly haired boy walked toward me, throwing frightened glances at the tank.

"Tell the children to move away!" I cried to a nearby teacher, who seemed mesmerized by the static sharks. She didn't move. "Hurry, children!" I led by example, grabbing the hand of the curly haired boy and pushing toward the exit. "Come with me, everyone! This way!"

The maenads stepped up their attack. They rammed their heads at the glass once more, this time producing the recognizable crunch of breaking glass.

I didn't hear the glass shatter—it was drowned out by rushing water and shrieking children. The gargantuan tank tore across the center like a cellophane screen. Water rushed in to fill every pocket on the floor in one continuous wave. Even at the exit, water washed up my shins. Fish and glass followed in a violent whoosh. Behind me, the great hall had turned into a lake, the cold water swallowing up children too stricken to run. My God, they might drown!

What happened was even worse. Freed of the tank, the sharks sprang out of their coma. Each white beast splashed its way to a child and greedily flexed its jaws. But this wasn't just hunger—it was mania driven by plenitude. Blood squirted from the soft bodies as the frenzied sharks ate their way around the hall, sampling the arm of one, the leg of another, spitting out a chunk when they saw something better, juicier. The water churned, a frothing fountain of reds and pinks. No doubt the eels and octopuses would divide up the rest.

All this happened in seconds. The shock giving me new strength, I forced open the emergency exit—sounding the alarm bell—carrying the curly haired boy with me. Immediately a torrent of water gushed out with us. As the red river drained, I set my shivering ward back on solid ground.

"You're a brave one," I told him.

I turned back and saw the maenads standing in the empty tank. Their grins told me everything. This was the high price exacted by delinquent ghouls—the ones who, like me, didn't always abide by the rules.

The aquarium nearly finished me off. Although it sounds melodramatic to say it, I was never the same again. It was one thing to read about nefarious men getting their due and quite another to watch children being savaged before my eyes. Morphine barely lessened the nightmares that followed; it only kept me asleep longer, replaying the horrific scene again and again. I couldn't leave the rooming house for weeks.

"Never let me have *anything* to do with the spirit world again," I begged Issa. "I'd rather die than cause injury to another child."

To my astonishment, Issa remained calm. Too calm.

"All riots burn themselves out," he said. "Once they're sated, the spirits will eventually return to their graves, even the unruly ones. We have to look at it this way. At least none of the children were killed."

"They'll be scarred for life!"

"Blame yourself if you like. But we can't win every battle, Cassandra. Let's just be content with winning one."

He was right—about that battle. As much as the government-run *Tribune* tried to play it down, evidence of the exodus was everywhere. Taxicabs cruised along High Street empty. Both the Balmoral and the Metropole hired Chinese and Indian touts to solicit local custom for their restaurants and bars. One Monday night, Fitzpatricks, the hundred-year-old grocery that had fed generations of homesick Brits, shuttered its doors for good.

Change came officially, many months later. The civil service was forced to make up the loss of British personnel by taking a drastic measure: non-Europeans were welcome to apply. Naturally, Kenneth was first in line in May 1954.

The night his application was accepted, my energy made a miraculous comeback. After two long years of exhaustion, I felt stirrings of my old self again.

Kenneth and I celebrated in our usual way—in private. He booked a room at the Balmoral, which had opened its hallowed doors to Asiatics, albeit at inflated rates.

"Who did you have to rob to pay for this room?" I asked him when he met me at the entrance.

"Nobody." Kenneth showed off his watchless wrist. "I'm free at last."

Much to my surprise, the hotel didn't come close to living up to my fantasy of it. Its high-ceilinged lobby lounge was airless, even with the electric fans rattling at full speed. The interior was a monotonous study in white, from the Indian porters' uniforms and the rattan settees to the plastered walls and the marble floors. White might have been de rigueur at the grand seaside hotels of Brighton or Hastings, but it was hardly ideal for the tropics. At the Balmoral, the hallways were patterned with green, yellow, and gray corsages of mildew and rot. Not wanting to burst Kenneth's bubble—after all, he'd pawned his prized Rolex for this—I kept these observations to myself.

Our room, lucky number thirteen, had a four-poster bed and a balcony overlooking a pleasant courtyard, but the carpet—once white, now verdigris—smelled like a wet dog.

"Now that you're in," I said, settling on the bed, "we can't forget the spirits. They put us in this room, on this bed. We have to make sure Forbidden Hill stays untouched."

"I'll do what I can." Kenneth joined me, and the springs on his side of the mattress began squeaking, as if to discount the solemnity of his vow.

"Seriously, you promise?"

"Yes, yes." Again the bedsprings squealed.

"Should we ask for another room?"

"If we did that, we'd look like bumpkins. The English live with their discomforts. They *relish* them."

A bottle of champagne softened all of the room's flaws. It made them amusing, even educational, as if we'd lifted the veil to an emperor's chamber only to find it filled with hay. The champagne provided a corrective in other areas as well. That night, Kenneth struck me for the first time as handsome. His swagger had returned. He fastened my wrists to the bedposts with two of his neckties and did what he claimed he'd wanted to do to me on the day we met in the library.

For the first time, I let myself yield to him completely.

"Did you ever come this much with *him*?" he asked as we lay there, still in the glow of the moment.

"Don't spoil it, Ken."

"How many times?"

"Stop it."

In the moonlight, through the open French doors, I studied his future statesman's jawline and the ambition sparkling in his eyes—ambition every bit as raw as his lust. I kissed the dimple on his cheek that I knew would one day enchant old grandmothers and enjoyed the fighter's grip that would astonish his enemies when he shook their hands.

Though we had slept together countless times before, this was the first night I can recall in any detail. Perhaps this had something to do with the elation of being in a hotel room with luxurious, orchid-scented sheets and ordering room service champagne without a care. It all felt very *adult*, being able to afford our own extravagances.

Or perhaps I remember it because deep in the night, with my ear pressed flat against his chest, listening to the weirdly slow beats of his uncertain heart, I told Kenneth Kee that I loved him.

Y<small>OU LOVED HIM</small>?" Mary Maddin asks. This is the first time she has broken her silence in hours.

"Well, I am human, you know. *Was*, if you prefer."

"Cassandra," she says, speaking my new name as knowingly as she had the old. "We agreed on the truth. Our contract is void if you sugarcoat things."

"Sugarcoat things? Did you not hear me when I told you that thirty-six planters and a hundred workers perished in that fire? It was *my* fire." Recalling this, I begin to shake. I have to stop shaking. "Likewise, I admit that I told Kenneth I loved him. I'm not proud of the fact, just as I'm not proud of many other things, but it's what I did. The *bitter* truth."

She says nothing, and in the darkness of the sitting room, I hear her fidget with her jacket. It sounds like she's trying to scratch out some old food stain with her nails. After several long seconds, she breaks the tension.

"Then you lied to him, you misled him. Because there's no way you could have loved him, considering what you did to him later on."

Her words make me sit up. "You know about what came next?"

"Everybody knows what happened next. It's in all the history books."

"So remind me again why you're here, Professor."

"For all the parts that *aren't* in the history books. Were *never* in the history books."

"Then let the record, the *new* record, show: Yes, I loved Kenneth Kee. Even a woman with special eyes can be shortsighted when it comes to matters of the heart. You'll allow me that, won't you?"

I can hear her taking deep breaths. Or is that my ghost?

Finally, in a near whisper, she gives me the go-ahead: "Yes."

— 15 —

A Sorcerer's Work Is Never Done

BY 1957, FREEDOM WAS CLOSE AT HAND. The British were set to leave by the end of 1959, and the Isle was poised to be its own place, an island republic in a sea of other orphaned lands.

But the British, unlike the French or the Dutch, wished the world to know that they'd tried to be reasonable with their little colony. Before letting go, they set forth a series of tests for the new leadership. If the Isle passed, they could leave with a clean conscience, their ward having proved its maturity. If it failed, they had the perfect alibi for their retreat: We tried to civilize these people, but in the end... goodness gracious!

Or at least, that's how Kenneth saw our situation.

Since entering the civil service, he'd built a popular following on his uncanny ability to gauge the mood of his public. Though only a junior officer in the Ministry of Social Affairs, he was a rising star who had for three years distinguished himself as a kind of walking bellwether, spending his lunch hours in the crowded alleyways of Chinatown, Little India, and Kampung Klang, and emerging with a sense of what needed to be done to improve people's lives. His superiors were stunned by the ease with which he moved from doorway to doorway, soothing the anxieties of everyone he met with the firmest handshake in the land.

The colonial big shots who'd hurried through these same neighborhoods on their walkabouts had never shown any interest in shaking any Islander's hand, let alone the blackened, greasy palms of illiterate auto mechanics or pail carriers in the dwindling night-soil trade. Yet Kenneth sought out these filthy, working-man's hands—the lowlier the trade, the more resolutely he would take their palm in his. And he always looked each person in the eye, as if collecting his or her face for the growing tapestry of humanity that was slowly and meticulously being woven in his mind. At the news of a Kenneth Kee visit, throngs would issue forth from the overcrowded tenements and shantytowns, their hands outstretched in wait. Even infants pulled away from their mothers' arms to graze their tiny fingers against Uncle Kenneth's sleeve.

I'd heard that in private gatherings, the remaining Brits called him the Chameleon—not kindly, of course—but this was an erroneous impression. As somebody who'd accompanied Kenneth on his rounds during my own lunch hour from Woodbridge, interpreting for him some of the more obscure Chinese dialects (between Cricket and me, we just about covered them all), I knew him to be less a chameleon than a ventriloquist. His attitude never changed; instead, he listened to workers and residents as they articulated their hopes and dreams, then repeated these back to them using his own words, quietly incorporating what *he* felt they should be aspiring to. He left people wishing for things that, as soon as they heard them, they felt they could no longer do without: hot water, street lighting, cheaper bus fares, safer streets. Precisely because he gave shape and voice to their unknown desires, they adored him as a kind of savant, though of course they'd never use that word.

What they never suspected was how, after each walkabout, he dashed to the nearest sink and scrubbed his hands. I carried his vial of Lysol; Issa carried his nail brush.

As independence loomed, Kenneth Kee, feared and admired by the old guard for his popularity, was asked to design the young nation's flag. We knew from the beginning that this test was double-edged. The flag, if designed well, had the potential to unify the disparate groups of the Isle but if done poorly could turn the new state into an international laughingstock.

Late one night, mere hours before Kenneth was to unveil his work, the phone woke me.

"I need you," Kenneth said, and hung up before I could reply.

I rushed over to his apartment, just a few blocks from mine on quiet, suburban Clemenceau Avenue. I had rented a walk-up flat in this placid neighborhood as an antidote to my hectic new post as the chief of Woodbridge's nursing staff, and hearing how much I liked the area, Kenneth had done the same. One benefit of suburban life was that I never had to worry about being seen, even if I happened to be running around in my night-dress—as I was doing that night. I'd long ceased to care what the dead thought of my looks, and as for the ancient Sikh security guards along our road, they were all, predictably, asleep at their posts.

When the door was opened by Issa, I gasped. I hadn't expected to find him in Kenneth's cramped little one-bedroom apartment, nor had I expected Cricket, who stood in the middle of the smoke-filled sitting room, clutching a tumbler of Scotch. Both looked worn down, as if they'd been holed in for hours, smoking Dunhills and arguing.

Seeing me enter in my nightclothes, hair uncombed, they exchanged a glance, confirming their suspicions that Kenneth and I were more than mere colleagues.

Kenneth, who sat hunched over papers at his tiny dining table, had more pressing matters on his mind.

"Hurry up." He waved at me. "We don't have much time."

Next to an ashtray brimming with stubs were about a hundred sketches of flags, finished in crayon. A few were plain, but most were crowded with eagles, lions, tigers, even unicorns—outmoded Anglophile symbols of her-aldry that Kenneth must have found impressive. I suppressed a smile.

"I'm at a complete loss." He shook his head and picked out the most promising ones for me. "I might have to start again from scratch."

"Just include a crescent moon," Issa said.

"Fuck your moon! I've had enough of your damned moon!" Kenneth reached for the glass in Cricket's hand. He took a long draft and turned to me. "As you can see, it's impossible to do anything by committee. Every-body and their dog wants their say."

"But that's democracy, no?" I said.

He snorted. "First the flag, then we can talk democracy. But we have nothing if we don't first have the flag." He waved Cricket and Issa away. "Go. We've exhausted one another. Any more arguing and my fangs may begin to sprout."

Cricket offered a final bit of encouragement. "Keep it simple."

"Simple?" Kenneth didn't even look up from his sketching. "Don't tell me what to do, you Chinaman. What do you know about my country?"

Issa and Cricket took the abuse astoundingly well; like family, they absorbed the bad with the good. At the door, they looked thankful I was there to pick up the load.

"Whatever you do," Cricket whispered, "don't let him drink anymore."

I didn't. Kenneth and I talked and sketched flags the rest of the night. He never apologized for waking me and I didn't expect him to. Nor did he seem annoyed that I'd shown up in my nightclothes, thereby exposing our intimacy to his friends. Maybe he was relieved, as I was, that our longtime secret was finally being let out.

My chief contribution that night was to suggest that the flag contain the color red, since, on a visceral level, it symbolized the life force that coursed through every Islander's veins, no matter his or her background. Secondly, I persuaded him to include a crescent moon, despite his fierce personal resistance. I understood Issa's point. Muslims made up a good third of the population.

"You do want their votes, don't you?"

He did. To be fair, the rest of the design was cooked up by Kenneth, with me by his side, making him coffee and kissing his furrowed brow. In the end, the flag proved democratic after all. He even heeded Cricket's words by keeping it clean and simple.

"For the sake of schoolchildren, flag-printers, and the not-so-bright, I shall exile my galloping unicorn," he sighed, half jokingly. "So long, too, snake and scepter."

At daybreak, the flag of the Black Isle was born, a minuet in red, white, and blue.

The Isle's first national day was declared on August 31, 1959, and the weather turned out to be drizzly, a perfect morning for sleeping in. But thousands poured onto the Padang to watch the new flag being raised for the first time. When it peaked, I reached for Kenneth's hand.

We held on tight, the proud, discreet parents of a shared secret. The flag's creator would never be named. It had been decided by the ex-governor that it should spring to life in a miraculous birth, unencumbered by history or memory. But when it came time for everyone to sing the new national anthem, played by a marching band in bright yellow raincoats, Kenneth and I were at a loss for words. We weren't alone; only a learned handful could even follow the lyrics printed tightly on the programs. In a belated sop to the indigenous population, the British had commissioned it to be in Malay, and not the market Malay that many of us used, but the archaic, courtly Malay that nobody spoke.

We had to have faith that the tune, neither British nor Asian, would eventually grow on us, maturing as our nation matured. Luckily, this faith had already taken root. I saw tears in every eye, even Kenneth's.

The doddering governor Lord Pickering had just begun his speech when the drizzle seemed to explode, becoming a full-fledged storm. His words were rendered incoherent. Was this a eulogy or a christening? When sudden flashes of lightning lit up the sky, squawking bullhorns called the ceremony to a premature close. All but the most ardent dashed for shelter, holding soggy programs over their heads.

Kenneth and I were the only ones to remain on the steps of city hall, drenched in our expensive new tailored clothes. In addition to my silk dress and leather pumps, I'd bought myself a permanent wave in the best salon on High Street. Now I could only touch my flattened curls and laugh. Unable to get any wetter, we sat down on the watery steps and watched the rain cover the grass of the Padang like multiple sheets of vibrating glass. Kenneth was laughing, too, but in a different spirit. He stared at the flag high above us, too sodden with rain to even shudder in the breeze.

"If I'd known the anthem was going to be in Malay, I wouldn't have put that crescent moon on the flag. Now it's a permanent stain."

"It's not a stain. Besides, the governor liked it."

"*Ex*-governor, overcompensating out of guilt. Now the whole world will think we're another volatile splinter nation. Another Pakistan."

"They won't." I took his hand. "Anyway, the flag's quite handsome."

"That it is not. The moon's a mouth, laughing at us."

"Nobody will see it that way but you."

"But I will *always* see it." He grimaced. "I suppose our national outlook has always tended Anglo-Chinese. We have both British indirection and Chinese cunning in our veins. It's a potent formula, if we can keep it this way—and there's no reason why we shouldn't keep it this way. I'll just have to tell myself the moon's a decoy."

We watched the rain for a while longer. As the mud rose from the grass, the Padang turned into a lake of chocolate milk. Frogs began croaking a raucous symphony normally reserved for night.

"God, I hate the tropics," Kenneth finally said. "I wish the Isle could just pull up its anchors and sail off to a better neighborhood. We deserve better than this."

For all his reassuring handshakes, there was one fear Kenneth Kee could not subdue. After the Burning Trees and the mysterious incidents leading up to independence, our citizens had become obsessed with the dead.

"This is a time when our minds should be fixed on the future, not the past," he said to me. "You're the one who sees them all the time, yet you're not half as obsessed as they are."

"It's probably *because* I see them that I don't find them half as interesting."

Newsstands were now filled with supernatural novels, and for those who couldn't read, there were horror stories in various languages on the radio. Even if one never consumed any of these fictions, the taint of superstition was impossible to avoid. Self-proclaimed psychics sprang up along respectable shopping streets, promising, in gaudy signage, to ferry news to and from the beyond. Even the stodgy *Tribune* had begun carrying articles on ghosts, propagating a rumor that the ladies' toilet of the Rex was haunted by a weeping woman—no matter that this was true.

Naturally, this frenzy clashed with Kenneth's rational views. Having used them once, he wished to have nothing more to do with the spirit world.

"People around the world are going to think we're all fools—or worse, witch doctors," he groaned. "These are the crucial, formative years, when the Isle's reputation is being forged. We can't afford to be thrown into the wrong club."

For the Black Isle to make the sprint from independence to respectability, gears had to shift once more. Kenneth's brain whirred and whirred.

In August 1960, almost a year after independence, Kenneth took me to celebrate my thirty-eighth birthday at the Ship, a venerable restaurant built along nautical lines and best known for its steaks. While I preferred to ignore these annual milestones, Kenneth, with his head for numbers, always kept count.

I arrived at the restaurant trying to subdue the hope in my heart that he'd offer me a different kind of present this year. We had lived separately for the eight years of our liaison, as was normal for unmarried people at the time. But Kenneth never brought up the Likely Next Step, and I'd tried to accept that such a step might never happen.

Was marriage all that important? Today's women might roll their eyes at me, but back then it meant securing Kenneth's heart. Of course, it's not as if I were a simpering Victorian heroine in a frilly pinafore, waiting for Mr. Darcy and his sachets of gold. I was a strong woman who could summon forth spirits and accomplish in weeks what Kenneth couldn't begin to do in years. Even so, when it came to making the first move, I was still only a woman. And in those days, in that benighted part of the world, women didn't propose. That was strictly a man's job, no matter how enlightened the beau or brave his girl. If Kenneth didn't want it, I wasn't going to risk pushing him away with my eagerness. Had the notion even crossed his mind once, he'd had ample opportunity to ask. We were, after all, the best of friends.

"There's a contagion of sentimentality about," he said, cutting into the medium-rare beef Wellington we both ordered. "I know we've been through a lot of drama and uncertainty—occupation, emergency, independence. But *life* is full of uncertainty. People can never progress if they refuse to confront this. It demeans them. It turns them into children."

He'd said such things before, but on this evening, I sensed a double meaning, as if he were offering a critique of my lingering romantic expectations—or what he perceived as such. The waiter refilled our champagne flutes and we sat back, gazing at each other in our corner alcove—the make-believe captain's cabin. Since becoming a public figure, Kenneth would only go to restaurants with private nooks where he could dine, hidden from view. At first I assumed he was self-conscious about his tongue; later I realized that he feared his image as a working-class hero might be compromised if people discovered his fondness for fine food and, worse, expensive wine.

He always ordered champagne on birthdays. But over the years, I'd come to learn that he was far more enamored of the idea of champagne than its taste. He gulped it down and got drunk far too quickly.

Already more than a little tipsy, he suddenly leaned into the table. "Listen. I have two proposals I'd like to run by you tonight."

I knew not to get hopeful; as usual, Kenneth was just having fun with words.

"What's that term again, the one you use to describe a ghost-free area?"

"Clean," I said, sipping my drink.

"Right, *clean*. I was always fond of that term. It's concise, unfussy. Conveys everything, really. I've been thinking quite a bit about how to get the Isle *clean*. It's almost as if we have to *rip out* the sentimental, backward-looking lobe from people's brains so they'll stop their blasted fixation on those awful things."

"Ken, I really don't think it's sentimentality. I think it's fear."

"Whatever it is, it's crippling us. I have two solutions. To start with, in any case."

I nodded. He smiled and took a big swallow of champagne.

"I was appointed deputy minister today."

This good news took me aback. He'd given no hint of it and had seemed, until this moment, almost peevish. The appointment had loomed as a possibility, but I never imagined it could happen so soon, especially when older generations of grassroots leaders, the kind who hated educated elites, were still holding the reins. As deputy minister of Social Affairs, he'd be in contact with factory workers and captains of industry, and this mobility was what he'd always craved.

"That's wonderful!" I took his hand.

"Yes, they, too, like my handshake." He gave my palm a good, hard squeeze. "And though they'll never admit it, it's because I shake hands like an American."

"So when will the news be out?"

"Press release goes out tomorrow. Which was why I wanted to celebrate with you tonight—in addition to your birthday, of course. I haven't even told Issa and Zhang yet." Another smile. "And you thought you were the only one who could keep secrets."

I brought his hand to my lips and discreetly kissed it.

"So, my proposals," he said. "I will share one with the public tomorrow. The other's strictly between you and me."

I returned his hand to show he had my full attention.

"First proposal: I'm going to suggest a master plan for lighting up every last dark corner of this island. We'll begin with the city, of course, putting lights in alleyways and lights in the slums; then we'll move outward, expanding to the suburbs until we get to the rural areas. Bright, electric streetlights by kampungs and shantytowns, anywhere ignorance might breed. Eventually I want *all* public areas, roads, reservoirs, cemeteries, and open fields to be lit so that everyone can feel free to roam about at *any* time, without fear." He cracked a smile. "If we can't control the minds of these ninnies, why not illuminate the hell out of them?"

"It'll have no effect on ghosts, you know. They exist regardless of light or dark."

"Ah, but it'll have an impact on *people*. I'm not planning for the ghosts at all—they don't vote. But if we can liberate people from the habit of superstition, think of all the things we can achieve! Think how productive we could be if everyone spent less time on prayer and idiotic rites. They're all incredibly wasteful—of time, of energy, of material." His voice grew subdued but his conviction was no less strong. "I know that for you, ghosts are real. But to everyone else, they needn't be. And this is where my second proposal comes in."

"The one that's between you and me?"

He nodded slowly. "You will set up a ghost-hunting business."

I couldn't tell if he was actually being serious. "Like pest removal?"

"If you like." He smirked, but his tone remained earnest. "I say 'ghost-hunting' only because it sounds more scintillating. I will supply you with your clientele. They won't be just any old Tom, Dick, or Harry but important people who need such services and don't want their names known to the world. There's a demand for this, I tell you. I can send you four or five names as early as tomorrow. People who'll pay *beautifully*. The only thing is you must leave absolutely no trace. It's entirely sub rosa."

"Ken"—I lowered my voice to a whisper—"don't you remember last time? I was almost killed. It's not a game."

He seized both my wrists. "Cassandra, I am asking you to make them *go away*. It's the exact opposite of calling them up. I'll work in the light, you'll work in the shadows, and together we'll make this filthy little island *clean*."

He was proposing I become his spiritual housekeeper. Even the language he used was insulting.

"Let me think about it," I said, wringing his hands off me. But I already knew I wanted no part of it.

"What's there to think about? It's you and me, Cassandra. Just you and me."

I looked into his eyes. Despite the boldness of his plan, the grandness of his ambition, there was not the faintest trace of the fevered visionary about him. Kenneth had never looked more sober, more calmly convinced about what would be good for me.

Kenneth had called it a proposal, but for him the plan was already set in stone.

The moment I entered work the next morning, I was greeted with Arctic coolness by Miss Joseph, the head nurse who'd become a sort of grande dame at Woodbridge. Over the years, her detached mien had hardened into an icy armor, inspiring fear in patients and nurses alike. She held a special distaste for me, regarding me as the poor, bedraggled thing she'd taken in years ago, only to have me maneuver my way up into becoming overseer of *her* nursing staff. This was her version, of course; the way I saw it, I'd put in long, hard years at the front desk and was promoted for my diligence and, unlike her, my comfort working in the wee hours, all alone in the dark.

"You got your wish," she said, her eyes glued to her coffee mug.

"My wish?"

"Oh, don't act coy."

She fished out a letter from a register close to her, smoothing out its two fold lines, and thrust it in my face.

I saw the gleaming red imprint of the hospital's official chop—"Approved"—and began reading. It was a neatly typed letter of resignation, in eloquent, lightly condescending prose, about my accepting an offer from an employer more appreciative of my skills. At the base was my supposed signature, made in Kenneth's hand.

He was waiting when I came home—perched in my armchair, legs crossed, reading the *Tribune*.

"I forgot your presents last night." On his lap sat a leather-bound book, a bar of chocolate, and a small bottle of cognac. "Happy birthday, toots."

"How dare you!"

I ran over to slap him. He moved his head, and I missed.

"A simple 'thank you' would have sufficed." He smirked. "Book, chocolate, cognac—still your holy trinity, I hope?"

"Who do you think you are? You made me look like a bloody fool! I never said yes to your proposal—I said I would *think* about it! Don't you care about what *I* want?"

"It's because I care that I did it. You're better than that hospital and you know it."

"I can't afford to make enemies at Woodbridge. Li's still there."

"So take him out. There are better places in town. And soon you'll be able to afford them."

He pulled out a folded slip of paper from his shirt pocket and handed it to me. It was a list of five names, complete with telephone numbers and addresses.

"As promised. Should be a year's salary right there, if not more."

The names were familiar. I'd seen them in the papers—G. B., the owner of Robinsons department store; Dr. S. Y., the chief surgeon at Mount Alvernia Hospital; W. K. B., the president of the Green Spot bus company; and a couple of prominent housing developers. I could understand why these men might feel they needed the assurances of a state-approved "psychic." Most of the Isle's construction projects sought the blessings of a geomancer, but they were a famously shady bunch, so to get one vouched for by Kenneth, who everyone thought the coming man, probably made all the difference.

The money would certainly be helpful to me—and Li. But did I want to deal with that world again? I remembered all too well what it was like when things went wrong: jungles of snow, rivers of blood, a physical and emotional toll that might well kill me.

"Aren't you supposed to be at work?" I finally spoke. "You said the news was going out this morning."

"It did go out. I want to let the excitement die down a bit before I make my entrance. Not everyone there likes me, you know. And I didn't want to go in without the knowledge that I have this *consolidation* in place." He peered briefly at the list in my hand. "I've sorted them according to importance. Importance of the requester, not of the situation. For all I know, they may need nothing more than a plumber. Or a podiatrist. But you're discreet. You won't make them feel like fools. And if there happens to be some ghosts..."

"Ken, this doesn't change anything. I still need time to think about it."

He stood up to leave.

"Then this should help you think." Lifting the book that was his present to me, he rapped his fingers on its gold-embossed cover: *Jude the Obscure* by Thomas Hardy. He smiled. "Best book ever written about missed opportunities."

Three weeks later, I saw my first client, G. B., owner of the Robinsons department store. We met at his private, unlisted club, on the second floor of an innocuous office building on D'Almeida Street. The moment I stepped inside, I realized this was less a watering hole for the elite than a collection of waiter-serviced conference rooms, a venue for towkays to hold meetings they wanted neither the home nor the workplace to find out about. The largest room could fit up to twenty comfortably, but most had tables just for two. We took one of these small chambers. Little did I know then that over the next ten years, I would return to these rooms time and again.

G. B. was a corpulent Eurasian with an oily toupee, exactly as he appeared in news photos, but to my surprise, he had the gentle manner of an old dowager. He took a lot of sugar and cream with his orange pekoe and held the teacup with his pinky aloft. After a bit of polite chitchat, he handed me a slip of paper with an address.

"My mannequin warehouse," he said. "We use them in my store. They're high quality, imported from Czechoslovakia, not like the cheap ones my competitors use. Anyway, my dolls have been doing a bit of dancing at night, on their own." He eyed me carefully. "You don't think I'm being fanciful, do you?"

"Has anything been stolen or vandalized?"

"No, no, it's not like that. After the fifth time, I knew it couldn't be some kind of a prank, because no joker is that committed. It would take hours. You'll see."

He handed me a stuffed envelope, the contents of which had been previously negotiated by Kenneth: Six months of my old wages. I tried not to gasp when I saw those crisp new bills. G. B. and I signed no contracts; in those days, grown-ups knew how to trust each other and keep their mouths shut.

At nine that night, I went to the warehouse. It spanned the length of a short street in the southwest corner of the Isle that, only a few years before, had been entirely swampland. I wasn't alone. As G. B. had promised, a band of freelance Gurkha guards stood watching the property, shirtless and smoking aromatic clove cigarettes. G. B. had also offered dogs but I politely declined—canines never liked me.

With my hair pulled back into a severe bun and my grim ensemble of black blouse, black shawl, black skirt, I made the guards a little nervous.

"Good evening, madam." They put out their cigarettes and bowed to me. I nodded mysteriously in return.

It was a bare-bones warehouse, with moonlight leaking through ventilation slats in the walls. I entered on my own. Stealth was key. I resisted turning on the lights. They would only send the culprits—I hadn't ruled out human mischief—scattering into the shadows. In the silvery dark, I could make out the assembly of five hundred mannequins—bald, naked, grinning. All female. They stood in neat rows, ready to be activated, like a mechanical concubine army.

I moved to the darkest corner and sat down.

Nothing happened for hours. No noise, no motion, not even the scurrying of rats.

Then, around midnight, it began.

From the back of the hall rose a piercing squeal—the sound of a mannequin's limb joint being turned. It was followed by another squeal, closer to the center. I stood up slowly, then, hearing the next sound, darted to its source. There I found at the front of the hall a dummy trio facing one another, their arms stretched out to join hands.

A patter of quick footsteps, from the deep center of the hall. A dark shadow flitted between the dolls, humanoid in form yet much too swift to be so. My client's suspicions were right. This was no common thief.

There was no choice. I had to enter the mannequin maze.

The gaps between them were narrow, just enough for me to squeeze through. I inched along this beige forest, feeling the hard plaster arms grazing my sides. Gooseflesh sprouted all over me. Each of these bald women was identical—blue eyes, dark Slavic eyebrows, ruby lips, breasts without nipples—and they were all six feet tall. What outlandish fantasy was G. B. encouraging with these models? No housewife on the Isle looked remotely like them.

An earsplitting series of squeaks scattered my thoughts. I stopped moving.

Suddenly, the squeaks were replaced by rumbling that grew louder as it neared. One after another, beginning at the back, these Amazonian women had begun to tumble, face forward, like dominos. When the one before me came bearing down, laden with the shocking weight of her sisters behind her, I was pinned beneath her artificial grin.

She was as cold as ice. I screamed.

The warehouse grew eerily quiet.

"Who is it?" called a young girl's anxious voice.

"A friend," I said, freeing myself from the doll that had crushed me. "And *you*?"

Astride two felled bodies, at the back of the hall, stood a girl of twelve or thirteen—Indian, wrapped in a sari that glowed pink even in the dark.

"You can see me," she said.

"I can hear you, too."

I stood and showed myself. She advanced toward me, stepping on the dummies as if they were her bridge. This was a fearless child.

As she neared, I saw the blackened welts on her cheeks and neck: small-pox. The sight of her—so young, so spirited, so dead—brought a lump to my throat.

She eyed me. "You didn't turn on the light. They always turn on the light when they come in."

"I thought you might run away if you knew I was here."

"Aren't you afraid of me?" The boastful little thing.

"Frankly, I'm more afraid of them." I gestured to the fallen women, some of whose arms and legs had popped off at the joint, their faces still placidly smiling.

She laughed, the bright laughter of a quick-witted girl. "But they're so pretty! I wish I could look like them. But with hair, of course. And clothes. Not a stupid sari but nice, modern type of clothes. Like in the departmental stores."

"I don't understand. Why do you toss them around? Is it fun?"

"I can't sleep!" She gave the nearest doll a firm kick. "It's so unfair. I have a soul but obviously I have no body. And here are these bodies, and they have no souls!"

Again she laughed, but this time her eyes surveyed the mannequins with a mixture of longing and sadness.

"We can't have everything, you know, dear," I said gently.

"I'm not asking for everything. I've got *nothing*! I had nothing in life, and then in death, *nothing*! I mean, look at me!" She bared her arms and legs, darkened and deformed by disease. "All I want is a pretty body to go to sleep in, that's all. If I had one, just one, I'll finally be able to sleep."

"So why don't you choose one?"

"I can't find the right one."

"But they're all the same."

"*That's* the bladdy problem!"

She cackled, shrill with frustration now. With a balled-up fist, she punched one of the mannequins near her, sending it flying several feet. "I hate you!" she yelled after it.

I longed to comfort her. *But wait*, I warned myself. *The girl doesn't want my pity. She wants my help.*

"What if I chose one for you? Would you accept it?"

She looked at me, surprised by my offer.

"But how will you know which one to choose?"

I pointed at a random doll. "I say this one. She's a bit prettier than the others."

The girl stared at the mannequin, skeptical. Protectiveness took over quickly. She leapt to its side and examined her potential shell from head to toe.

"I still can't tell," she said. "What if she's the wrong one?"

"You asked me to choose, and I think she's the right one." I removed the black ribbon from my hair and tied it around the doll's left wrist. "See, I've marked her. Now she's not like the others."

The girl nodded and lay herself atop the dummy, fidgeting until she locked into a favorable pose, her knees around the mannequin's waist, her arms around its neck. Mother and desperate, clinging child. It didn't look very comfortable but the girl yawned, and within a few minutes, began to fade. Her staring eyes were the last things to go.

I quarantined the occupied mannequin, carrying her outside and leaving her against the warehouse door. The Gurkha guards moved themselves away from her, afraid even to glance in her direction.

The following day, I met G. B. at his club and gave him instructions: Get the doll a good wig, find it the most fashionable dress from his store, and take it to a Hindu priest to have a traditional death rite conducted.

"The days of your dancing dolls are now over," I assured him.

A single tear rolled down my client's cheek. I still remember it vividly—satisfaction always made me very happy.

I filled my wardrobe with black clothes—smart and stylish, rather than drab and funereal.

Most times when I was called in, once or twice a month, I could have offered a diagnosis in a matter of minutes, but had I done so, my judgments would have been valued far less. My clients were captains and overlords who watched over buzzing personnel. They needed to believe they were paying for detailed analyses from an expert who took weeks to close each case, not snap judgments made by a dilettante, however highly touted, to whom it came as no effort.

I worked up an act. In a pantomime of precision and thoroughness, I would walk gravely through proposed building sites for hours, even days, poking my fingers into the soil, sniffing the air, caressing door frames. "Dirty," I would say, shaking my head. "Very dirty." While this was in part theatrics, I was no charlatan; I always gave my clients exactly the information they sought, including the sad truth: Male ghosts of an older generation did not welcome expulsion by a woman like me. They required extra cajoling—and additional threats, trade secrets I shall take to my grave.

Only once did I absolutely forbid anyone from setting up shop. The self-made "Tour-Bus King," L. W. T. wanted to establish his "hotel with a view" atop Forbidden Hill. The location was first-class, to be sure, but I had promised the spirits there an eternal home. I told Kenneth, and he grudgingly acceded to my verdict.

Usually, I spelled out the relevant risks and left the ultimate decision to build or abandon up to the client. I was merely a facilitator. My job was to reduce the possibility of conflict and inconvenience to both parties, living *and* dead. And I never, ever forgot to keep an eye out for the dog-man, my fugitive badi. That we hadn't met again in all these years meant he preyed on my thoughts more than the ghosts I did see.

Because the Isle *was* dirty, work was steady. When I finished with one job list, Kenneth promptly furnished me with another, always incanting, until it became a cliché, "A sorcerer's work is never done."

I deposited the cash in my savings account and watched it grow—six years of my old salary in less than a year—withdrawing only the amounts I needed to get by on and for occasional indulgences like cognac, chocolate, and leather-bound editions of my favorite books. With the memory of poverty still close, I didn't spend my earnings all at once but instead luxuriated in the dreaming—Italian handbags and shoes, dresses from the pages of *Vogue*, dinners at the Ship.

Though it had taken over a decade, I had finally pulled myself out of the postwar inertia. My destiny—and the Isle's—was finally blossoming.

With my secret guidance, buildings were rising everywhere, ten, twelve, fifteen stories high. Thanks to me, there was clean land for the Balmoral Hotel's expansion, accommodating new package-tour clientele from England, America, even Germany. But I was proudest of my contribution to Holland Halt, a low-cost housing estate that has continued to put roofs over ten thousand heads ever since its completion in 1964.

Kenneth proved to be less thrilled about my success than I thought he would be. The shadow, he decided, was getting too grand for its master, even as the master took credit for everything the shadow did.

"You're gloating!" he said to me one night in my bed. "I saw your new shoes."

"I'm not at all gloating. It's just two pairs."

"And both Christian Dior. God knows what else you've got hidden away."

"You should talk. You're the one who now plays *golf*."

"Don't change the subject. These assignments are supposed to be secret, Cassandra. *Sub rosa*."

"And they are—I've not told a soul. And my clients, *our* clients, certainly aren't going to be blathering about me around town. They're always incredibly embarrassed by their problems. Sometimes I feel like a sex doctor."

"I'm sure you do. I've heard the way they talk about you afterward. So sated."

"Don't be an idiot."

He grew quiet. "I'd like thirty percent. Finder's fee."

"But you already skim the cream off the top...don't you?"

He said nothing.

"Ten percent," I said.

"Twenty-five."

"Fifteen."

"Done."

On the night of Kenneth's forty-second birthday in 1962, we celebrated quietly in his apartment. I brought him a Black Forest cake from the Balmoral's bakery and, of course, a bottle of his esteemed Dom Pérignon. I could have invited Issa and Cricket, but it had become an unspoken custom with Kenneth that we celebrated our birthdays as a couple.

"Enjoy the view," Kenneth said cheerily as we tucked into the cake at his wobbly excuse of a dining table. "Because very soon, all this will be no more."

"What, your girlish figure?"

"Alas, no." He smiled, his upper lip smeared with cream. "I mean this measly flat with its measly rooms and measly walls and measly cooking smells from the measly flat below and the measly old Sikh asleep in the measly guardhouse no matter the time of measly day or measly night."

I burst out laughing. "Are they knocking this measly place down? I mean, I've a measly right to know. I live practically next door."

"I'm moving at the end of the month. Found a nice new place by the Gardens. Two bedrooms, two baths, wraparound balcony. All mod-cons, as they say. And I'm buying, not renting."

"Oh." I tried to keep the wariness from creeping into my voice. "You never said a word. It sounds expensive."

The area around the Botanic Gardens had been a highfliers' enclave since the days of the British; it was still the dominion of diplomats and politicians, and their black-and-white mansions. Evidently, new apartments had been put up for arrivistes, though not under my advice.

"Expensive it is, but the down payment's doable. I know, I know, I should have asked you to suss the place out before I signed all the papers, but"—he shrugged—"I suppose I got smitten. Didn't want anyone telling me about the headless sadhu stationed in my kitchen or whatever it might be. You know how it is."

"I wouldn't tell you anything you didn't want to know."

"Ah, but I can always see it in your eyes." He squeezed my hand. "The ghost of a ghost, ever visible."

I let him finish his cake before I spoke again.

"I had no idea you were looking. This is secretive even by your standards."

His eyes grew glassy, almost sentimental. "I ran into an old friend the other day, from prehistoric times. And it got me thinking, you know, about growing older, about having to grab hold of things. I mean, I'm forty-two. High time I made the commitment, don't you think?" He gave me doe eyes, but as ever, he looked more wolf than doe.

"Who's the friend from 'prehistoric times'?" For some irrational reason, I thought of Taro and felt slightly ill.

He deflected my question with a spirited jangle of his keys. "Do you want to see the flat or not? We can take a quick drive over there right now."

I shook my head.

"I've spoiled the mood, haven't I?" He sighed. "I hoped you'd be happy for me."

"I am, for *you*. But...I like having you near."

He walked over and hugged me in my chair, stroking my head as he pressed my temple against his chest. I had seen him administer this same embrace to terminal patients in the cancer ward; he later explained it was so he didn't have to look them in the eye.

"There, there," he said.

I broke out of his arms. "If you wanted to get away from me, if you wanted for us to end, all you had to do was tell me."

"For us to end?" He looked astonished. "I want no such thing. What would I do without you? What would the Isle do without you? We've been through thick and thin together. You and I, we're a team."

A team. That was stunningly unromantic, even for Kenneth Kee.

"Look, why don't we go out for a drive? Some fresh air would do us good. This Black Forest cake...maybe there's a reason why Germans are always in a foul mood."

"I told you. I don't want to see your bloody apartment."

"Nobody's going to make you. Let's just take a little spin." He smiled, his cheeks flushed from champagne. "Humor me."

Kenneth led me to his car, a three-week-old 1962 MG convertible in seaweed green. He adored it more than anything. Perhaps I should have taken its purchase as a portent of changes to come, but having no interest in motoring, I'd only seen his car as a car and little more.

"Where are we going?"

"You'll see."

"That's what the scoundrel always says before flinging his fiancée off a cliff."

"Hah!" he said happily. "It is, isn't it?"

We sped with the top down, headed not toward the Gardens but east toward the sea, the car radio blasting "Bali Ha'i" from *South Pacific*. It was an apt anthem—an incantatory ode to the tropics, all trilling flutes and lush, watery harps mimicking the wind and the waves. The best part, of course, was the unearthly banshee chorus: *Here am I, your special island, Come to me, come to me . . .*

Just as Bloody Mary's voice swelled to a bewitched crescendo, coconut palms began popping up in the horizon. Goose bumps blossomed on my arms. We were driving, it seemed, into somebody else's fantasia.

When I saw the silhouettes of the casuarinas, Kenneth's motives became clear. The looming lighthouse only confirmed it: We were hurtling toward the Wees' old beach house.

Kenneth knew full well that I never wanted to see it again. Not the ruins, not the boulders where I sought shelter, and certainly not the ghosts. If I ever saw Taro among them, there's no telling the lengths to which I'd go to cause his ghost a moment's pain.

"Why've you taken me here?" I must have sounded enraged; in truth, I was much more unsettled than angry.

Kenneth shut off the radio. "I want to show you something."

"Turn back right now! You know I don't want to be here."

"Calm down. I want you to see what I've been working on—for *you*."

"I hate you."

"Ah, so you finally admit it."

We slowed down at the mouth of the old road, which had benefited from new construction. No longer private, it was now two lanes, each wide enough for a bus and very freshly paved. Ahead of us, a young Malay family of five traipsed along, the father carrying the youngest on his back. Kenneth gave them a friendly wave when they turned, momentarily stunned by our headlights. Grasping that we meant no harm, the father waved back, with a wide, easygoing smile. Slung over the wife's shoulder was a rattan bag with two long protrusions: badminton rackets.

"So?" Kenneth asked me. "Still want to turn back?"

I didn't answer. He drove on, a grin tickling the edge of his lips. We came upon other families walking by the side of the dark road and slowed down as we passed them. The luxurious beach houses had been flattened, as had most of the casuarinas that once lined the lane, leaving no trace of the gentlemen's retreat the coast had once been. To my relief, the Wee property, including its papaya trees, was completely gone.

Now it was a clear shot from the road to the surf.

The beachfront had been transformed into a kind of futuristic playground. Jutting out of the sand like gargantuan mushrooms were concrete barbeque pits. A dozen light posts stood, tall as telegraph poles, with bulbs so bright that the beach appeared to be made of snow, not sand. Between the posts, youths had stretched out nets and were playing badminton. Others kicked balls. Everyone looked happy; the light was so intense that it gave them all halos. I couldn't help but find the scene eerie and jarring, especially coming upon it after miles of unlit road.

"I convinced the Ministry to let me turn this place into a workers' paradise. The official opening's not till next week, but I was told people have already been finding their way here. You know me—I had to see it for myself." Kenneth turned off the engine and we sat in the shadows, surveying the beach. He was beaming. "This is only the prototype. If my plan goes through, we'll have one of these in Woodlands, Kampung Klang, Taman Seletar, and then someday, maybe even in place of that awful slum next to Wonder World. People are tired of the dark."

"I'm happy for you, Ken, really I am. But I don't see how this has to do with me."

He unbuckled his seat belt and leaned close, staring into my eyes. "You don't say."

"Stop being so bloody obscure."

"You don't see them, do you?"

"What?"

"Ghosts. I don't see them in your eyes."

I stepped out of the car and scanned the shoreline for the eternal martyrs, those rebels I once resented for ignoring my cries of help. I expected to find them frozen shoulder-deep in the high tide, oblivious to the changes that have come to the beach. But the beach appeared to be pristine.

I strained my eyes some more, bracing for the sight of Taro—Taro, my shame and sorrow—whose soul, I was sure, would never have surrendered quietly to the night. But under the glare of the blazing lights, as waves frothed in and out across the sand, the most I saw were hazy, powdery shadows.

"Well?" said Kenneth, grinning with great mirth. "Very *clean*, isn't it?"

"Yes." I couldn't bear to crush his joy with the more nuanced truth—that they weren't actually gone, only nicely hidden.

"Now do you realize how silly it is for you to question our bond? We are bound, Cassandra. You and I. Darkness and light."

"How did you do this?"

"Experimental bulbs, from Japan. Nobody there's even given them a go yet. They burn much brighter than traditional bulbs and last much longer. We got the first shipment to leave Hiroshima. The chap who developed it said he was inspired by the blast." He chuckled bleakly. "The extreme brightness, you see, alters the landscape, thereby wiping out all the old associations people might have with a certain place—erasing its memory, in other words. With nothing for us to remember them by and nothing for them to remember us by, the dead cease to exist. Or that was my theory, in any case—a theory now proven positive, thanks to you."

"And the Japanese invented this?"

"Don't be small-minded. They, too, want to move on with their lives. They've become experts at reinvention. In the end, it's good business for everyone."

I squinted at the blazing white beach. I saw more shadows amongst the fun-seekers. Faint and vague, probably harmless, yet undeniably still there. Loitering.

"Do these bulbs create a kind of visual"—I searched for the word—"sieve?"

"No, no. It's just light, pure light." He sighed, contented. "You and I, we've never just sat around, passively accepting the hand fate has dealt us. You and I, we've always fought for our own destinies. It's the same principle here. Strip away the darkness, the negativity, and even the worst places will forget their wounds. They'll begin to heal. The Isle shouldn't have to stay dirty. Ghosts don't have to live forever."

We watched the badminton players for a while. Could he not see that the lights turned them into paler, grayer—ghostlier—versions of themselves?

"Feeling sentimental?" He reached over and fondled my chin.

"Not at all."

"See?" he said, leaning in for a kiss. "I told you fresh air would do you good."

One of the many things I learned about Kenneth over the years was that he was at his most treacherous when he seemed at his happiest.

In retrospect, I must say I'm glad I learned about his impending nuptials by reading it in the papers. This allowed me to digest the news alone at home. If he'd told me in person at a restaurant, say, I would have had to rein in my shock and fury, offer congratulations, et cetera. He would've had the pleasure of watching me flail as my act wore thin—and I would have had to plunge my steak knife into him.

The cruelest stroke, alas, was that the winner of his hand should be a particularly horrible ghost from the past, one I hadn't seen returning: Violet Wee. Was she the "old friend" he'd run into, from "prehistoric times"? Probably.

I remembered how violently Kenneth once recoiled at the very mention of her name—and the frisson of delight I'd felt at having found someone who felt about her the way I did. How we had laughed together at the plump sourpuss and her demonic dog; our mutual dislike for Violet was the *first* thing that had united us.

The half-page announcement Kenneth had bought in the pages of the establishment *Tribune* was every bit as gaudy as the advert for facial blotters that ran beneath it, its cursive font mimicking the twirls of a villain's mustache. It answered a few of my questions about Violet, though not all. After the war, she'd apparently fled to family friends in Belgravia, London, and had stayed there all this time. It appeared likely that this London connection might have sealed the deal for our Anglophile Mr. Kee.

You and me, Cassandra. We're a team. I had been numbed by his peculiar brand of pillow talk into thinking we were two solitary people who saw eye to eye enough of the time to render us soul mates. I had to laugh at that notion now. More than rage at his betrayal, I felt shame at myself for having been so weak, so *blind*.

Of course, I hadn't been invited. I was glad for this, for it spared me the agony and the expense of a wedding present. But that didn't mean I couldn't attend.

How could I not? I had to see for myself how Violet looked in her wedding finery and whether Kenneth had acquired, just for one day, the sense to go easy on the pomade.

I went in the guise of a church mouse. I tucked myself into the stony folds of the St. Andrews graveyard, far from the parade of celebrants, dressed in a button-down cotton dress the same shade of gray as the headstones among which I stood. Lest anybody mistook me for part of the party, I brought along white chrysanthemums, the pompons of grief. I looked every bit the part of a woman mourning a death, which in a way I supposed I was. I was a widow many times over.

There appeared to be two very different sets of guests: doddering Peranakan towkays in batik shirts with their long-faced wives, emanating prestige and entitlement, likely the old associates of the late Mr. Wee, and a more modest group united by familial traits—birdlike in build and touchingly unaccustomed to having car doors opened for them. I lumped this latter lot with the groom and tried to guess which of the elderly women was his mother. Surely the monthly recipient of his cash-stuffed envelopes, the silent witness to her son's mounting successes, had to exude an unmistakable leonine pride? But men and women, young and old, Kenneth's people all seemed cowed, overwhelmed, even grateful to be included in the occasion. I found their humility unexpectedly moving.

The last sedan delivered two familiar faces—Cricket and Issa, looking self-conscious and stiff in their white, tailored suits. Issa's movements had an added awkwardness because he was lame and had to be helped out of the backseat by Cricket. His impatient scowls told me that this disability shamed him. Also in this car were two women, both Indian, who I assumed from their pale purple dresses were Violet's bridesmaids. It was only on closer observation that I realized they were Cricket's wife and teenage daughter.

Finally, a black Rolls-Royce drew up, the only such mastodon on the Isle. The Balmoral loaned it out at famously extortionate rates, and I was curious if Kenneth had managed to talk them down or if he paid full rate. Or did Violet foot the bill? From it the bride- and groom-to-be finally emerged. There were no flower girls, no fawning legions, and as much as I wanted to mock them for it, no hubristic fanfare.

Despite their chariot, it was a quiet, unfussy entrance that they made. Kenneth in a tasteful, if plain, white suit and Violet, almost unrecognizably slim, in the most chic wedding dress I'd ever seen. It was something Audrey Hepburn would have gladly worn: a white shoulderless, figure-hugging bustier ending in a loose, flowing silk skirt. Her arms, once so rubbery, were sheathed in elbow-length silk gloves. In mien, this strange woman was essentially still Violet, but in physique she had become elegantly frail in the way only the rich knew how.

They appeared cheerful, yet not overly so. I hated them for having such a surplus of joy that they could afford to rein it in on this most immoderate of days.

They paused for a few photos by the Rolls-Royce and then for a few more at the church door. That was it. They disappeared inside. The only glaringly false note to this theater of reticence, the only tell-tale smudge of immodesty, was the adornment on Kenneth's left wrist. Even from where I stood, I could see his outsize gold watch—as loose and ungainly as the heirloom he'd once so cherished and in all probability the one and the same.

The transfiguration of Kenneth Kee was now complete.

Standing in the St. Andrews churchyard, I was more than mildly tempted to call forth the denizens of its small collection of graves. But I did no such thing. I had too much respect for the dead to send them on the petty errands of a spurned woman.

Beating my own unfussy retreat, I left the bouquet of white chrysanthemums on the step of the church, just as the old pipe organ began to moan.

When I glanced back at the graveyard, I realized I hadn't been alone. The dog-man had been leaning on a tomb a few feet behind me. And there he lingered. Unlike me, he seemed not to understand it was time to go.

— 16 —

Legacies

Was he still my friend? Was he *ever* my friend? We never had time for labels. We had been content to be lovers, if never in word; we were phantom companions.

My flesh, on the other hand, was all too real.

The week after Kenneth's wedding, I felt subtle changes in my body—the curvature of the belly, the rounding of the hips—as if *I* were the one who'd gone through the matrimonial rite. Dread trickled in when I missed that first monthly cycle, then another, but it was the doctor's words, so routine for him, that took my breath away. Not that he'd been judgmental. I'd paid him very well to offer no opinion except the medical.

I took to my bed for three days, furious at my body for its betrayal, unwilling to accept the invader growing larger inside me; then I wept for a few more days, but by this time, the tears had turned into those of joy. At forty, I realized this would probably be my last chance for a child.

There was, however, the tricky matter of the father. The baby was half his.

I resolved to raise the child alone, whether Kenneth wanted anything to do with it or not. This was less a brave decision than a self-protective one. In my heart of hearts, I knew I needn't bother to ask. He had no interest in being a father. I'd seen him cower away from children on his walkabouts. "They're so *unreasonable*," he had said.

In practical terms, being an unwed mother would cause me no problems. I had no relatives I could shame, no rigid social expectations to live up to. I was a woman of independent means who stayed out of the spotlight, and if worse came to worst, the Isle's most powerful men would protect me—they needed my services.

But I knew I had to tell Kenneth. Unlike him, I wanted our relationship to be as uncomplicated as possible. It was in this spirit that I had him over for dinner when my next client list was due. Personal feelings aside, and I took pains pushing them aside, we were still an enterprise—business partners, at the very least.

You and I, we're a team. Mutually beneficial, symbiotic, and now biological.

When he turned up at my door, having rung the doorbell like any stranger, my stomach fluttered: He'd never looked so polished, so dapper. The shirt was Pierre Cardin. From his body language—shoulders pulled back, chin up—I knew there'd be nothing to discuss on the topic of his marriage. I almost lost my nerve.

His smile retracted. "What is it?"

"I'm having a baby."

"Is it mine?"

I was stunned that he'd imagined any other possibility. "Yes, of course...But I don't want you to feel you have to be responsible for anything. I'm perfectly capable—"

He reached over suddenly and enclosed me in a wordless embrace, sinking his head into my shoulder. I heard jagged little intakes of breath, shudders, and felt a river of dampness down my neck. Kenneth was weeping. However, I couldn't yet tell if these were happy or unhappy tears. He lowered his hands to my waist, rubbing his fingers along my midriff with a kind of neurotic nostalgia. I held my breath.

"I can't believe it," he whispered. "We're going to have a child together."

When we pulled apart, I saw his shimmering eyes.

"And you thought I wouldn't want to share this...development with you. What kind of a monster do you take me for?"

"A married man."

He laughed a deep-belly laugh, devoid of sarcasm or irony, and released another torrent down his dimpled cheeks.

"After all this time, after all these years...Cassandra?" He spoke my name as if it were a thing of wonder. "We've lived with bigger secrets than this. Bigger, unhappier secrets. I will make sure you and...our child...are well taken care of. No matter what happens, I promise to be involved in your lives."

I was speechless.

Again he embraced me tightly, caressing my spine, my waist, my thighs, pulling our growing child into himself until we three became one. Bound like this, I had a strange thought: The child was really more his than mine. If the fetus had any choice, it would surely leap from my belly to his, cleaving to the parent who loved it better, the parent who greeted the news of its existence with joy.

"I feel closer than ever to you," said Kenneth. "I feel like I've been suffering a disease and that I've been cured. This is the happiest moment of my life."

I could have wept. But experience warned me not to let my heart trust my ears until I had time to parse his words.

He lowered himself into a chair and pulled me toward him. There he lifted my blouse to nuzzle my belly.

"We'll have to make plans," he said. Swift as lightning, he lifted his face and I saw his eyes. Puckish delight. "We'll have to prepare."

"Ken, I don't want to . . . I'm perfectly capable of having this child on my own."

He didn't seem to register my words—or want to. "I was wondering how, if at all, your condition is affecting your acuity."

"My acuity?" I quickly took his meaning. "I don't think it's made a difference. Apart from the morning sickness and the fact that I'll have to get used to running around with a little person inside me."

"Well, so long as your eyes are as effective."

"They are. This won't compromise my work, if that's what you're worried about."

He reached into his pocket, and I had every expectation he'd whisk out a new set of clients' names and utter his usual line. Instead, his hand stopped short and he shook his head, smiling, almost bashful.

"What am I doing? Let's not sully this special night with business. I'll bring you the list tomorrow."

We sat silent for a while. I glimpsed us in the mirror on the wall, each of us staring in a different direction, our faces revealing our true state: slack, exhausted, confused. No doubt our minds were still digesting the news, but we looked like a couple who'd just had a row.

I wanted nothing more than for Kenneth to be out of my apartment. I didn't want to witness the changing of his mind, the expressions of regret, the formation of excuses, and especially not the nervous drinking; I wouldn't have been able to bear that. He knew it, too.

"She was a war hero, you know," he murmured at the door. "Three years at Wonder World."

What was I to make of this information? That he'd married Violet out of guilt? Pity? Admiration?

When I said nothing, he tried again. "Will you manage all right?"

I nodded, and he left.

Early the next morning, I found a brown envelope slipped under my door. I knew it was the new list, dropped off by Kenneth the same way he dispatched money to his mother every month. Just looking at the envelope— no doubt the same kind he used in those deliveries—made me queasy. Would I, too, become a recipient of his cold, scheduled largesse?

The name atop the list was Hiram Desker, meaning he was most important. I'd never before heard the name, but that wasn't unusual—he may have been as secretive as me. We were to meet at the old opium warehouse on the Black River, known best to me as the former HQ of one very vicious Rat Brigade.

Kenneth had no cause for concern. My eyes were perfectly fine.

The taxi dropped me off on Edinburgh Bridge at noon, and I walked across the river. With the sun directly overhead, neither the living nor the dead there created shadows and so were at first glance indistinguishable. But I could always tell the ghost boatmen, vegetable haulers, and fat-bellied merchants from their living kin. The dead exuded nostalgia; it burned in their eyes as they watched their old colleagues. They longed to sweat again, to join in the clamor, the exertion, the grunting camaraderie. The action was all they knew, and only in death did they realize it was all they loved.

Did I feel strange walking through this valley of death while carrying a child within me? Yes, but not in any way I could have predicted. I became more aware than ever of the new power in my possession, a power that was growing by the day: life. It was the ultimate rebuke to death and perhaps still the closest thing we know to a cure.

At the tail end of the river, the old opium warehouse stood, faded and worn. Its painted letters were barely readable: U—T-D Co-pany of M—chants of E-gl-nd. A panel of its slanted tin roof had collapsed inward and was drooping like the broken wing of some monstrous metallic bird. The word *AWAS*—Malay for "DANGER"—had been spray-painted across the rusty gate in black. You might think that this desolation would make it the perfect home for ghosts, yet none roosted here. They wanted no part of its gruesome legacy.

As I approached the gate, I began shaking. Uncontrollably.

When I accepted this assignment, I hadn't realized how powerful a hold the warehouse still had over me. My successes had left me overconfident. Here was a site unlike any other.

"Daniel," I whispered, in case he was here, lingering by the river. Of course he wasn't.

What did Hiram Desker hope to build here on this soiled spot? Was he a magnate of shopping arcades? A housing developer? The possibilities might have seemed endless to an ambitious industrialist, but my own narrow mind registered only misery.

I already had my diagnosis for this client. The only proper use of this plot was to burn everything to the ground, salt the earth, fence it off, and entomb it under concrete. The moment he arrived, this was what I'd tell him.

The sun blazed down on me as I waited for him at the high metal gate. The noonday heat would have been hard on anybody, but being pregnant, I felt almost baked alive. I stood there for fifteen minutes, and still nobody. My impulse was to flee the accursed place, but I couldn't, not until I saw Desker. His perch atop the list meant he was enormously influential, and I didn't want to make a powerful enemy.

After another five minutes, my patience was gone. I kicked the rusted gate, which swung open with a low, mournful yawn. The interior yard lay in shadow. The instant I stepped through that threshold, I knew: I was no longer alone.

I was being watched—by many pairs of eyes.

The rusted gate shut itself behind me with a clang.

From within, the old warehouse loomed far darker than it had from the road, blackened with dirt, mold, and soot. One enormous panel of the wall had been sliced off, revealing the building's gaping black innards. I felt life pulsing within it, although I couldn't be sure it was human. It drew me deeper nevertheless.

"Mr. Desker?" I called, my words reverberating in the hollow darkness. "Hiram Desker! Are you here?"

I made my way into the hangar. It was even more cavernous than I remembered. Inside, there was no sound, just the air's poised stillness, as if a great being were holding its breath. Thankfully, none of the formaldehyde reek of the Rat Brigade remained. I smelled only the coppery dampness of rust, rain, and animal waste, odors I'd grown used to in my ghost-hunting.

The place was bare, but it felt oddly full, with its undulating shadows, floating motes, and the golden square on the ground formed by the sun pouring through the skylight. In a religious painting of yore, some prophet might have stood in such a corridor of light—pate glistening, palms turned up. With nobody there, the picture looked incomplete.

I eased myself into that tunnel of light, letting the sunbeams gild my skin.

As I moved, footsteps sounded, mimicking mine. But they weren't mine. They came from the deep murkiness, impenetrable to my sun-dazzled eyes.

"Hello?" I cried.

I stared into the darkness. The hangar seemed infinite. But nothing could intimidate me now. I was safe in my box of light, my invigorating womb. I must have glowed not just with the promise of one life, but two.

Again, footsteps.

"Mr. Desker!" I waved at the darkness, while a voice within me warned, *Taro*.

And a ghost did appear as I focused my eyes—vague, then brighter, whiter, until it assumed a radiant silhouette, becoming someone whose beauty left me breathless.

Daniel—as young as before.

Fair skin, thick brows, a look of gentle inquiry. So it was *he* who Hiram Desker wanted me to evict. It seemed cruelly poetic that my work should reunite us.

"Have you been here all this time?" My voice cracked.

He nodded. A weird worm of a smile formed across his lips, buckling into a twitching, ungainly rictus. Was he struggling to speak? Or was he sneering?

"Oh, Dan, speak to me!" I cried. "I've missed you."

I was moving toward him when a series of unnatural whines sounded overhead, the tragic yowls of rusty things parting ways. I peered up at the sun through the roof. The ball of fire winked at me—winked, because something solid dangled between us, flapping with the lightness of a paper kite.

But of course it weighed more, much more. And with the full force of gravity, this traitorous piece of old roof plunged down upon me.

When I awoke, the pain had burrowed into my belly. I say it was my belly but it actually felt deeper and more intimate than that. The pain was in a place that didn't have a name but that felt absolutely vital. I wanted to reach into that spot and squeeze the pain until it seared to a halt, but I didn't know where to order my hands—the place had no name and no memory.

And it had no face.

My child had no face.

"Morphine!" a voice yelled.

And then I was gone again, dreaming of clouds, green lobes, clouds within clouds, lobes within lobes. Years could have passed in this way, with these images suspended in their own unchanging reality. I clung to them, desperate to stay in their realm, but of course, even death had to end.

When I returned to the world, I refused to see anyone. Their prayers could do nothing to lessen my loss. My first words to the nurse were a plea for silence:

"I know."

My body fared no better than my soul. My hands wore mittens of bandages. I couldn't scratch itches or wipe away tears. It hurt to move my head, but I had to survey the rest of the wreckage. My left knee was imprisoned in a plaster cast. God only knew what ugly treasures lay beneath. Thankfully, my right leg was intact. Seeing these wounds, I remembered how I'd tried to free myself from a titanic weight. Then darkness.

How many times can one woman die?

Three times Kenneth tried to visit me. Three times I turned him away. I didn't want to see his reaction to the news that I'd seen Daniel, that it was Daniel who might have done this to me. Nor did I wish to witness the relief on his face at being let off the paternity hook.

As for Hiram Desker: Had that tardy wretch saved me, pulled me out from under the roof? Had he driven me to the hospital? Did he even exist? I had my doubts. But it no longer mattered. All my medical expenses had been quietly covered, and I was left an outsize packet to buy off my wrath. Nine months' wages.

I lay in the hospital, mending. When I was finally ready to leave, a trainee nurse—chubby, wobbly, and green—saw me into a waiting cab. She must have thought she was doing me a kindness when she bade me her fare-thee-well:

"It was a boy."

I was young.

And then I was old. Just like that.

When I returned to my apartment and finally saw myself in the mirror, it appeared that twenty years, not two months, had passed. Never mind the cuts and bruises—my hair was completely white.

In a matter of weeks, I'd had both past and future ripped from me. My youthful black hair and my baby—both gone. Luckily I was still numb, all negation, all morphine. I combed my unruly hair into a matronly bun and powdered over my discolored cheeks. Once I had this mask, I painted my lips red and drew black arches over my brows.

If I could no longer possess my own face, I would borrow my mother's.

It was eerie how much I resembled her. I'd inherited everything I loathed about her face, including the dreaded tadpole eyes, the stunted lashes, the amoebic freckles. But I'd also hijacked everything that had supposedly made her pretty—prominent cheekbones, cushiony lips, a passable set of teeth. I'd fled across the oceans, but blood would never let me go.

It was in this maternal armor that I returned to the Black River. During my long days in the hospital, I'd had plenty of time to think. I burned to get to the bottom of what had happened that afternoon. I had to know.

Surely Daniel would tell.

But I wasn't the only thing that had changed in those two months. I had told the taxi driver to take me to the old warehouse, but when we arrived, there was nothing. Not even the admonishing gate. The plot had become flat, anonymous ground, the handiwork of wrecking balls, bulldozers, and the good old-fashioned broom. It was entirely *clean*.

I decided to put Hiram Desker's blood money to good use: I would take Li out of Woodbridge and place him in a new private institution. There, he would spend his days and nights in his own air-conditioned room, instead of being feasted upon by thirsty mosquitoes. I could even guarantee the new place was clean. The developer, H. M., had been one of my best clients.

Walking through Woodbridge, for what I imagined would be the last time, I was filled with nostalgia—the pear-shaped Indian and Eurasian nurses, the ubiquitous blue pajamas, the clusters of dazed walk-ins awaiting evaluation. Even the smell of disinfectant had its homey pull, not unlike the musty scent of an old maiden aunt.

And then I smelled another perfume, an even stranger one, made of Fab detergent, Florida water, and prickly heat talcum powder. An elderly woman in a jade-green cheongsam, bedecked with pearls and with meticulously coifed hair, walked past me toward the entrance—in fuzzy white bedroom slippers. Living or dead, I couldn't at first tell. I nodded to her, but she ignored me; her eyes were glazed.

"Don't let her scare you," one of the young nurses told me. "She's a medical mystery. Completely catatonic until the last Sunday of every month. Then she suddenly jumps up, hops in the bath, puts on her green dress and funny perfume, and takes a taxi to the Metropole hotel for high tea. Like a Swiss clock. Our *cuckoo* clock, we call her. Then after tea, she comes straight home and turns back into a pumpkin."

The Metropole? Could she be—of course, she was: Mrs. Odell!

The nurse and I watched as Mrs. Odell walked out the door, whereupon a waiting taxi pulled up for her. She struggled to get the cab door open. Instinctively, I started to run out and help her but the nurse stopped me.

"Let her. You'll only spoil her fantasy. She thinks she's still young. Anyway, each trip she takes now may be her last."

"How are her finances?" I asked.

"Her finances?" The nurse looked at me curiously. "She's been destitute for years. Luckily she's low maintenance. The Metropole's okay with her because she doesn't eat or drink anything. Imagine, they put her in a storeroom and she just *sits*."

"What's your name, Nurse?"

"My name?" she asked, even more surprised. "It's Cornelia. Why?"

"Well, Cornelia," I said, pulling out my checkbook and scribbling down a sum, "please see to it that Mrs. Odell has a comfortable life and a dignified death."

I walked quickly away before the poor girl could start asking questions.

Up two flights of stairs, another fantasist. Li greeted me at the door to his ward. "Back again so soon?"

I took one look at him and knew it would be hard to move him away. Now the longest-serving patient—next to Mrs. Odell, perhaps—he'd become Woodbridge royalty. He received me with a paper cup of iced water from the nurses' station. I drank it as if it were wine, sitting by his knee. As he leaned back into his rusty-legged, vinyl-backed throne, I surrendered: It would be wrong to force this king from his castle. He had to stay.

We were alone in the music room. His fellow patients had banished themselves, and the painted sunflowers on the wall were now his royal subjects. None, though, were as favored as me. He loosened my bun and ran his fingers through my head of white hair, as though I were still a thing of beauty.

"We were young," he whispered. "And now we're old."

He let his face grow slack, caught betwixt dreaming and waking, and began to tell me an old story from some secret place we both shared:

There once lived a family that tried very hard to be happy . . .

A year later, in early 1964, I returned to St. Andrews cathedral. This time, I was invited.

"Why lick your wounds when sweets abound?" Kenneth had whispered down the telephone. "Vi doesn't have to see you. But I want to. I *need* to. There'll be lots of people, so you'll be able to blend in. *Please*, come."

By this time, the newspapers had answered most of my questions regarding Violet's biography: She had moved to England after the war and earned a degree at the London School of Economics. From London, she'd managed her family's affairs—until, on a visit home, she bumped into her old friend Kenneth, waiting for a table at Mitzi's. The rest was history. They reclaimed the old Wee mansion in Tanglewood and made it into their Camelot.

What a difference a year made. This time, the grounds at St. Andrews were packed with limousines and hundreds of milling guests, dressed in the pastel shades of Easter. I looked absurdly out of place in my black blouse and skirt, but many of the guests were my former clients to whom my severity seemed perfectly natural. They each bade me respectful—even fearful—little nods as I passed them, none giving away our secret relationship with overt gestures of recognition.

My impulse was to flee and head to a bar, the seedier the better, to wipe out this nauseating show of renewal and fine millinery. But before I could make my move, Kenneth, ever vigilant, spotted me through the crowd. He shot me an almost imperceptible nod with eyes that conveyed honest gratitude, as if I were his only true friend in this sea of overly demonstrative huggers and cooers and kissers. He was wearing a pale blue linen suit that would have let him melt into this moneyed crowd, yet he wished me to behold his isolation, the loneliness of his own making.

During the service, I sat in the very back and pulled out my opera glasses. It might have looked gauche in a room where the only things being brought to one's eyes were handkerchiefs, but I had come for my eyeful, and an eyeful I was determined to claim.

Violet was in a pink sheath dress, sleeveless and chic, with her hair cropped short, all of it again in Audrey Hepburn style. Yet this time, the imitation only accentuated her grimness—she carried herself like a tragic flower of the past, more Camille than Holly Golightly. As she clutched the baby to her chest, Kenneth stood at her side, smiling yet eerily detached, as if he'd walked in on the wrong christening but was content to watch these strangers continue anyway.

The papoose itself—named Agnes Mary, after that dead mutt!—was just another baby. She neither laughed nor cried when the minister doused her wispy fluff of hair with water, losing a few drops on her white organza gown. In her unwillingness to appear either enthralled or horrified, the kid was pure Kenneth.

I couldn't help but think of *our* son and how he might have behaved in a similar setting. Surely my boy would have walloped a wail or squeezed out a resounding fart the second the minister touched his little head. He would have seduced the entire room.

Had he lived, my boy would have been almost six months old. I wouldn't be sitting in this church, of course; I'd be at home, tending to the sweet bundle's every whim. My nameless, faceless boy. Even now, the lad can bring tears to my eyes.

At that moment, I felt a sudden pressure building inside my brassiere. I was being pumped up with something: My nipples ached; my skin grew taut to the point of tearing. I placed a hand on my chest. Was this a heart attack?

The truth was less deadly but a fair bit weirder. My breasts had become swollen with milk.

I tried to make a quick exit once the ceremony ended, but the crowd made escape impossible. Somebody announced there would be more champagne and cake, and hearing those words, everyone stopped moving, clogging up the doorways.

A hand tapped me brusquely on the shoulder. Even before I turned around, I knew. I sensed the hostility.

Violet.

Her face was puffy with rage. No more Audrey Hepburn or tragic saint. She was now Bette Davis in fiery, bug-eyed mode. Without so much as a greeting, she yanked me by the sleeve and led me behind a Gothic pillar, her grip every bit as unyielding as when she was a sullen schoolgirl.

"I don't know what you think you're doing by coming here, but I know it's not the first time. I *saw* you at our wedding. Standing in the grave-yard." She began blinking as she fought back her tears. "It was my *wedding day*... yet you were there, watching me!" The tears gushed out now. "And those white chrysanthemums. I didn't tell Kenny but I knew it was you."

An amah walked over to ask Violet if she was all right, but she shushed her and sent her away.

"I know I've said horrible things to you but... that was the war. You have to understand, I lost everything!" Her face cracked open again. "Can't you just put it all behind us? The bitterness between us was strictly be-tween us. Don't drag my husband and my daughter into it. After what I went through, I never thought I'd *ever* be able to bear children. But I did, at my age. If you don't have a child, you can't possibly understand. I'm not going to let you take my happiness from me."

I walked away, not wanting her to see the tears welling in my eyes. She was right. Things had changed, and in her place, I would have fought for my family, too. But she remained aggressively blind to the fact that *she* was the spider who'd crept out of the woodwork and stolen *my* life.

Shouldn't I be the one crying, *Stop, thief*?

She pushed through the crowd after me and grabbed my shoulder once more.

"I was hoping I wouldn't have to beg but, Cassandra"—she took a deep breath—"*please*, will you stop haunting me?"

— 17 —

Lady Midnight

KENNETH TELEPHONED from his office several days later. He clearly had no clue about my confrontation with his wife.

"I saw you sitting at the back with your opera glasses," he said. "Did you notice her little hands?"

I admitted I did not.

"She was born without fingerprints!" He chuckled with a new father's pride. "It's the most wonderful anomaly. My darling girl has the smoothest little paws."

"That'll come in handy when she decides to steal the Hope Diamond."

"Or be a politician. I daresay this might portend a bright future in politics."

Kenneth, as usual, was speaking in riddles. You see, it was he who'd been enjoying the political spotlight.

With the backing of his Muslim comrade, Iskandar Ibrahim, and his Chinese immigrant comrade, Zhang Ming, he was campaigning for prime minister. The trio took wonderful photos together all over the Isle—at markets, in stadiums, on podiums with business leaders. Through it all, Kenneth continued to supply me with new clients, though the names were fewer and farther between. This was to be expected; the Isle was getting cleaner every day.

It never failed to impress me how he always knew when he stood a sliver of a chance and how best to expand this opening into a foothold. Nobody cares to remember this today, but Kenneth's opponent, the then-incumbent prime minister, was a Eurasian millionaire drunk put in place by the departing Brits.

In contrast, Kenneth promised Islanders what we all wanted: peace, prosperity, prominence, and, above all, a new beginning. When he gave speeches at grassroots rallies, his plummy locution vanished, replaced by a coffee-shop colloquialism; he took on the slurry, loose-jowled diction of cabbies and workingmen, yet the marvel was that he never ceased to sound lucid, forceful, and deeply passionate. When he spoke at gatherings of the powerful, his cool, Oxonian voice reemerged, and he peppered his sentences with terms like *Darwinian struggle* and *capricious fate*. The man may have had a split tongue, but he united all the groups with it.

Despite our troubled relationship, I followed his campaign every step of the way. He truly *was* the Isle's great hope. Nobody else came close.

Then during a crucial rally in working-class Woodlands, he made what sounded like an impolitic gaffe: "If I could drag our isle out of this lousy neighborhood and dock it up north, believe me, I would do it. We deserve better than this swamp!"

Hearing those words on the radio, I shivered. I remembered him sharing that sentiment with me on the rain-soaked steps of city hall, but to voice it on the radio . . . he had either committed the biggest blunder of his career or struck upon a vein of political genius. Of course, every hardworking Islander knew the frustration of being where we were, a tiny dot on the world's map surrounded by jungly, unambitious lands. But none of us dared to say it aloud for fear of insulting our neighbors.

Kenneth's sixth sense put mine to shame. The crowd loved it. His spontaneous-sounding complaint, with its perfectly calibrated blend of self-loathing and wishful thinking, would define him—and the Isle—for decades. It remains a key, perhaps *the* key, aspect of the Islander identity. For it expressed the right kind of dissatisfaction, the kind that inspires the relentless pursuit of prosperity.

I voted for him. Many, many others did the same.

In the general election of 1965, Kenneth won in a 66 percent landslide—according to the history books, anyway. In truth the figure was closer to 51. Still, I shouldn't begrudge my old comrade his victory. At forty-five, he became the nation's youngest leader, a vigorous boy wonder in a role previously filled by sweaty dinosaurs. And always by his side were his first mates, Issa and Cricket.

I smiled each time I thought about the countless hands he had to shake as prime minister, both in the hallways of power and on the street. He probably washed his hands ten times as fanatically as he used to, scrubbing at every groove until the lines began to fade. How apt, then, that his daughter should be born without fingerprints.

With Kenneth in power, slums and swamps began melting away. Low-cost, multistory coops took their place, each a bulwark against the encroaching jungle, each lit with the bravado of a shrine in the woods hoping to ward off the big unknown.

I knew it was only time before he'd call upon my services again. But he was patient. He waited four years.

It was three in the morning.

"Lady Midnight," he purred through the telephone. "From now on, I'm calling you Lady Midnight. It's safer this way."

Lady Midnight, or Zi Ye in Mandarin, was the pseudonym of a fourth-century courtesan who wrote poems lamenting the comings and goings of her lovers. If anything, I felt temperamentally closer to Li Ho, the outsider Tang poet who wrote about demons, graveyards, and weeping statues.

"If you're going to call in the middle of the night," I said, "you're not allowed to insult me. Lady Midnight—are you drunk?"

"No, no, just inspired..."

I could hear the rustling of pages being turned.

> "'She opens the window and sees the autumn moon,
> Snuffs the candle, slips from her silk skirt.
> With a smile she parts my bed curtains,
> Lifting up her body—an orchid scent blooms.'

"That's one of the verses Lady Midnight wrote from the male point of view, putting herself in the shoes of her lover. I always found her very understanding. So, far from insulting you—"

I sighed. But he went on.

"I think it's only fair that you have a code name since I have to have one. The Prime Minister and Lady Midnight." He chuckled phlegmatically.

"Actually, never mind, that sounds a bit like a Victorian bodice-ripper. One that ends very badly."

I sensed he *was* drunk. "Where are you, Kenneth?"

"Downstairs, in the kitchen, if you remember where that is in this house. I had a phone installed down here, next to the pantry. I told Vi it's so we can call the grocer the instant we discover we're out of milk. But this is the first time it's ever been used. Because when you're prime minister, you have people to make sure you *never* run out of milk." He laughed. "You should see this place. Vi's done a bang-up job. I told her to get rid of everything old and dark, basically everything the Wees had. That grotesque crucifix is gone, of course, and good riddance, too. We tore the whole place up. It's really quite nice now. All modern, clean. Two television sets—both in the bedroom so I can compare how two stations cover the same story and decide which one to sue the next day. You should pop over for tea sometime. Actually, on second thought," he snickered, "don't. I'm sure there are guests in my house I never want to know about."

"Where's the wife?"

"Upstairs. Asleep."

"And your daughter?"

"Upstairs, asleep as well."

"You need something. That's why you're calling me at this unholy hour."

"Yes, you're right. I have needs. Immense, unholy needs. I miss having you under me, writhing and squealing. Oh, the moaning. You were so good at it, too—you knew how to submit. I still think about it all the time, by myself, in the bath. Nostalgia's an incorrigible *snake*."

"What do you really want, Kenneth Kee?"

He paused, sobering up. "I know you have a waiting list. But I'm hoping to pull some strings. I've got someone you may want to put at the top."

"Some mighty big shot?"

"Not that you'd think so."

"So who is it?"

"Me." He laughed again, more carefully this time. "Heard of a li'l place called Redhill?"

Redhill was the slum where Li and Father lived during the war, only it'd since been given a name by the government—red hill, like a bump or a sore, an irritant. Over the years, it had grown into by far the Island's largest slum. Thousands lived there in nineteenth-century squalor. But the reason Redhill would attract Kenneth's attention, of course, had less to do with its poverty or its sensational stabbings and acid disfigurations or even its residents—they never registered to vote. It was its location. The slum sat on fifty acres of prime land.

"Well?" he asked when I said nothing.

"Trouble getting those people to leave?"

He chortled. "Oh, you know it, then. I need say no more."

"I'm not getting involved in this one. People actually *live* there."

"Yes, that's the problem: people. It'd be so much easier if they were just ghosts. We gave them two months and offered some incentive—enough to get them started elsewhere. No takers. It's like some kind of a cult over there. I wouldn't be surprised to hear there's a sacrificial pit in the middle of that thing. Vestal virgins, for all you know. A real bloody nuisance."

"Have you gone to Issa?"

"You know how he stands on these things. He gets very...sonorous." Pause. "So what do you say, Lady Midnight? Lord knows I'm not asking you to do anything *bad*. Couldn't you just give the place a quick look-see and offer a tip or two? I mean, if I do the wrong thing, it'll be a PR disaster. Not to mention it'd be *wrong*. What about a few words of sage advice, eh?"

"What do you want with the land?"

"Schools, hospitals, offices. Things we can actually use. But mainly roads. We can't do anything or get anywhere without roads, and Redhill's smack in the center of everything. We've got new flats up the road ready to house these people, all mod cons, fairly decent schools. I know these grub-eaters hate change, but once they're moved, trust me, they'll be so much happier. I'll pay you just to take a look."

I mulled it over. If I didn't help, he was likely to strong-arm the tenants, and the clash could be ugly.

"A look?"

"Just one look." He paused. "Does five thousand sound about fair?"

"Ten sounds fairer."

"Ten it is, then. I'll have a boy bring you the envelope in the morning."

Despite its prime location, it wasn't easy to get to Redhill. Kenneth's minions had shut down its closest tram stop; buses no longer stopped within a mile of its walls. That was the plan: to isolate the slum, to make life there so inconvenient that sterile pigeon holes in high rises would seem like a godsend.

What Kenneth hadn't reckoned with was that these people were hardy adapters. When their electricity was cut, they stole power from nearby poles—the slum still glowed by night. Water was not a problem either; it was collected from the sky, just as in olden times.

I got off the tram at Wonder World, now a deserted government-owned lot, and walked a half mile past more government-owned land before the wind brought along the first unmistakable odors of slum life—kerosene smoke, overused cooking oil, putrefying garbage, and human waste. It was another half mile before I saw the corrugated tin panels encasing the slum itself. My goodness, it had grown since Li and Father lived there. The slum was no longer a makeshift *kampung* but a patchwork city of grays, reds, and browns, and jammed with clotheslines. It announced, *We're here to stay.*

And so were its dead.

Hundreds stood at its perimeters, perhaps mistaking Redhill for a way station between purgatory and hell.

Instead of one entrance, the slum now had ten. I looked for the one I'd used all those years before to visit Li: It was still there, nearly hidden by a rusty metal door.

But there was something new. The passage was guarded by parang-wielding toughs, unshaven boys in dirty singlets—werewolf versions of what Li had been. They promenaded listlessly along the outer edges of the village, each with a Doberman on a leash. The dogs began snarling as soon as they smelled me, showing me their yellow, jagged teeth. Their animosity tugged their chains tight.

The boys stopped walking. All eyes were on me, full of suspicion. I was everything they were not—old, female, civilized.

"Are you from guvment?" a ruffian shouted in Hokkien. "My dog don't like smelly guvment pussy."

I offered him a serene smile. "I'm here to see my father."

"Who the hell's he?"

"Oh, you won't know him. He's from before your time. May I enter?"

"What d'you mean before my time? How would you know about my time?"

"He died many years ago. But his ghost still lives here."

The boys seemed to find this uproarious. They cackled and swapped lewd, misogynistic phrases, colorful ones that worked only in Hokkien.

"If you're trying to scare us, you're wasting your breath." He raised his rusted parang, eager that I register—and fear—its blood-spattered blade. "We live, eat, and sleep with ghosts."

I pointed to the blade. "In my day, I carried one of those, too."

Again, my young friends broke into high-pitched laughter.

"You're a wonderful comedian, old woman!" someone said.

"Doesn't this place feel like hell? Just an observation, not a judgment. Why live here when there are brand-new flats waiting for you?"

"Because we're one big family here," the first boy said. "We look after one another. If we move into flats, do you think they'll let us all stay together? 'Course not! They'll split us up, make us live next to Indians, Malays, Arabs, and who knows what! A big family don't like to be split up. That's how others take advantage of us."

"What about crime?"

He hacked out a gob of phlegm. "That's outsiders! Outsiders come in, do bad things, then blame everything on us. That's why we got these." He yanked on his dog's chain and made it yelp. "And these." Again he brandished the parang.

"I swear I've no interest in stealing anyone's wallet. I just want to pay my respects to my father. May I?" I nodded at the entrance.

"No." The boy stated this soberly. His face suddenly grew solemn, adding years to my initial estimate of his age; he could have been thirty. He walked toward me with his sleek black beast, which paced ahead of him, growling, impatient to sink its fangs into my flesh. The boy's arm flexed as the tightened leash started to jerk.

In a second, the Doberman was barely a foot from me, so close that I felt the wet waves of heat from its mouth.

"There is something not right with you. You're dirty. Our dogs can tell.

They don't like you. So I suggest you leave now, before anything bad happens." He issued this warning coldly, hoping to send me scampering, but I caught a trace of fear in his eyes. He snapped the dog back. "There are worse things in this world than ghosts. You, for one."

I would never be allowed inside; this much had been made clear. But I'd gotten my answer. The people of Redhill weren't afraid of being haunted.

"Thank you," I said to the boy, and nodded my farewell. "If you happen to see my father, tell him I tried."

As I walked away, his friends sent me their best, over the gnashing teeth of their canine wards.

"You're old!"

"You're ugly!"

"Your cunt stinks like squid!"

Kenneth called me that night, again far too late. But this time I was waiting.

"Well?" he asked.

"You're not going to like what I have to say. The place is packed with ghosts."

"And?"

"The people who live there are used to them. So even if you got me to give them a good scare—and I won't—it's not going to work."

"Bloody parasites. They're all Chinese, aren't they?"

"Mainly. It was that way even during wartime."

"Knew it! Low-class Chinks are the worst. Tenacious rat bastards. They probably get all their ideas from Red China. Just for that, I'm going to make English our official language. It'll be my gift to that lost constituency. No more of that everybody-speaks-his-own. How can we afford such freedoms when we're still made up of cretins fresh from the bog?" He paused to catch his breath, calm himself. "What do you propose I do?"

"Give them time to get used to the idea of moving. They'll buckle. They'll see how much easier their lives could be and they'll go. It's the only way. On your part, make them *trust* you. They think you're going to break their village up and cut off their ties."

"'Course, I'm going to cut off their ties!" he shot back. "How else will I prevent them from conspiring against me? They sow unhappiness, these

410

squatters. They feed on each other's discontent—and they fester. I can't afford to give them time. My bulldozers are waiting."

I was dismayed that he was taking their rejection so personally. Yet I was not surprised.

"Well, Prime Minister, you asked for my diagnosis and I gave it to you. I would caution against the use of force—they're very much on the defensive. They have dogs and machetes."

"Dogs and machetes—you joking? Any decent army's got to at least have guns."

"They might have those, too. Just give them time, Ken. Give them time."

"Why are you on their side?" he snapped, and the phone went very, very quiet.

I woke two days later, in a sweat, rays of sunlight cutting past the window shades and striking my eyes. They were especially bright, especially intense, and they knifed in at a weird angle. In my nightshirt, I walked to the living room and clicked on the radio news, as I did every morning.

"Rescuers are still unable to determine the cause or the extent of the damage. What is certain is that the accident took place in the early hours of the morning and that many homes have been lost. The fire captain puts the dead at three hundred, though he warns that this number is likely to rise . . ."

Fire captain? I switched to the Cantonese station, where the female news announcer was much more agitated and emotional.

"The police is urging everyone to please, please, keep away from the area so the rescuers can do their work. We know you may have relatives there—everyone seems to know somebody who lives in Redhill—but please, keep the area clear. All right, I'm getting news now that the latest death toll has risen to four hundred and thirteen . . ."

Redhill. Four hundred and thirteen dead. For the first time, I wished I had a television set so I could see what was actually unfolding.

411

"The most important thing you can do now, as a community and as a nation, is stay away. The fire is continuing to grow . . ."

I got dressed and dashed out to hail a taxi.

"Wah!" the cabdriver exclaimed as soon as we drove up to Wonder World.

A giant gray cumulus was rising beyond the park's crimson walls. The car couldn't move any farther. The streets were crammed with people—refugees, looters, gawkers like me—neither coming nor going but standing agape, blocking the traffic. It was hard to know which was louder, the police sirens or car horns, or if the smoke we were inhaling came from the fire or the stalling vehicles.

I hopped out of the taxi, pushing my way through the throng—some living, some dead—until I came face-to-face with a grim Sikh policeman.

"No" was all he had to say.

Behind him lay an obstacle course of fire engines and snaking hoses, all flaccid. Firemen in black helmets and khaki shorts dragged their feet. They'd already written the project off as a lost cause—too many hours of too much fire and too little water. Soaked in sweat and dejection, some of them threw off their helmets and mopped their wet heads.

Beyond this barricade, the black-tipped flames leapt hungrily, very much alive. As walls melted away, structures toppled like dominoes. Each time one came crashing down, voices inside screamed.

Survivors squeezed out through holes the firemen had sawed in the slum's walls. In their arms were whatever they could carry—chairs, table frames, mattresses, funerary urns. An old woman in pajamas clutched a mountain of photo albums; another pulled along a clothesline of air-cured ducks, dragging the whole lot in the mud. There was surprisingly little panic. The refugees looked unnervingly calm, not even stopping to argue. The act of escaping had pushed them into placidity. Or perhaps deep in their hearts, they were relieved to have been forced to flee this miserable ark.

The dead were the ones who wailed. I tried to avoid them, but they were all around me. Mothers shrieking for their sons; sons shrieking for their mothers. As during the war, the newly dead were too consumed by shock to notice their surroundings. I would be better off returning in a few days to console them.

The moment I got home, I rang Kenneth's office. Though I had no actual proof—Kenneth being Kenneth would have made absolutely certain there would be no proof—I had no doubt the fire was his doing. Like Taro, he was much too clever to get his own hands dirty. He would have bribed a few anonymous thugs, hungry, amoral kids seeking an excuse to play with fire. Our city abounded with candidates.

"I'm afraid Prime Minister is not available, madam," came his secretary's matronly voice. "Whom should I say is calling?"

Always a tricky question for someone who was supposed to be invisible.

"Lady Midnight." As soon as I said it, I realized how ridiculous it sounded.

"Oh, yes, in fact, Prime Minister did tell me to expect a call from you. He's on a diplomatic mission to Java, but due to the incident at Redhill, he's cutting short his trip and will return this evening."

Of course. Being out of the country was the perfect alibi. *The incident at Redhill.* Her bureaucratic coldness made my blood boil.

"What about Iskandar Ibrahim or Zhang Ming? Can I speak to either of them?"

"I'm afraid both Iskandar and Zhang are no longer here. They tendered their resignations two days ago. Personal reasons."

Issa and Cricket, both? "Can you tell Ken I expect a call from him, at my home. A house call, preferably."

The secretary went silent, stunned by my directness, my lack of respect. She recovered soon enough. "Certainly," she said, then added, in a mocking lilt, "Lady Midnight."

Kenneth never called. Nor did he show up in person. Of course I realized he was run ragged during that national catastrophe, rushing to the scene to pose for pictures as he consoled the ones who'd lost everything, racing to the podium to declare, teary-eyed, a Day of National Mourning, promising the victims wonderful new flats, then hurrying yet again to the secret conference of his planners where he gave the okay to his waiting bulldozers.

Reelection time was nearing and this was business as usual.

The *Tribune* was packed with his photos during those weeks—sleepless eyes, gray ash in hair. The boy prime minister was no more. He looked at least sixty. With my own head of white hair, I knew a bit about paying the price.

I typed out my terse letter of resignation and hand-delivered it to the guard stationed outside Parliament House.

Lady Midnight was no more. I burned the black clothes, the file folders with all the lists and invoices. Everything related to my ghost-hunting career was gone. Exorcised.

By ignoring my advice, Kenneth had sent me a clear signal: He could and would do whatever he wanted. Cricket's and Issa's sudden resignations only confirmed this; at least, I told myself, I wasn't the only one who felt cast aside.

After dropping off my letter, I went to see Issa at his Arab Street apartment and tried to persuade him to have tea at the Kandahar coffee shop. He agreed only when I told him that I, too, had severed my ties with our old friend.

"Better late than never, I suppose," he said. "But I know how *flexible* your vows are, Cassandra. Remember when you swore you'd never get involved with spirits again? Then before I knew it, there you were, *profiting* from your gift. I never said anything because it's none of my business, but I was disappointed. You'll never know how much I regret teaching you. Because in the end, you're just like the rest of them."

The accusation stung. I was nothing like Kenneth. "Quelling them is *not* the same as calling them up. I was working to clean the Isle up. I did it for all of us."

"Lie to yourself all you like."

I looked him in the eye, wondering if I still had a friend in him—and wondering, too, if I'd been lying to myself.

"What really happened at Redhill?"

He smiled and folded his hands. "No comment."

Cricket was even less forthcoming, though I'd never have guessed it from his effusive new manner. I met him at the tea room of the Metropole hotel, where decades ago I'd gone looking for Odell and found instead his widow.

Each time I brought up Kenneth or Redhill, he steered the conversation to property values or my health, and offered me more Earl Grey, more scones—anything to get me off the subject. He talked about his family and the rigors of splitting time between two households: His first wife, whom I'd seen at Kenneth's wedding, was Indian, from a Hindu background, and he had married his second, a "very bossy little" Roman Catholic Peranakan, just before the government outlawed polygamy.

Two families! As with Issa, I was moved by how we had drifted apart over the years, how I hadn't made any effort to keep abreast of his life, his thoughts. The darkest effect of my time with Kenneth suddenly became clear—the casualty wasn't my heart but my *world*. During those years, with secrecy guiding both my work and my life, I had turned isolationist, voluntarily becoming my own island. Two families. Too late to close this chasm now.

"When I was younger, I used to worry about being lonely, and now look at me!" Cricket chuckled, and lit up a cigar. "I just don't have the patience for politics anymore. My wives and my children, they take up all my time and energy." He poured me more tea. "I'm glad you've expanded your wardrobe—black was not a happy color. Now that you've come back to life, you should think about settling down, too. It's not too late, you know. It'll do wonders for erasing bad memories, believe me."

Over the next years, I followed Cricket's exploits in the news. He went into the soft-drink business and did quite well for himself, eventually owning the largest bottling plant on the Isle. Each time I drank a bottle of Fanta Grape, I thought of him smiling at me.

Issa, on the other hand, disappeared. I'd called at his apartment again but the landlord told me he'd moved out in a hurry, leaving no forwarding address. Nobody in his neighborhood, not even the owner of the Kandahar coffee shop, had any idea where or why he had gone. Even odder, I thought, none of them appeared to care in the slightest. Issa, a pillar of the tight-knit community and former right hand of the prime minister, had upped and vanished and nobody cared. It could only mean one of two things. Either they hated him or were harboring him from outsiders like me.

"People come and go here all the time," said an old Arab at the Kandahar, the *teh halia* bubbling with gingery heat in his glass. "Didn't you hear? PM says our island's the crossroads; we're the *blahdy* center of the *blahdy* world."

Without his former comrades, the prime minister embarked on a building spree, like all the best dictators. To be fair, he built no monuments in his own honor or stadiums in which to deliver his sermons. It was his vanity that he should always appear humble, pragmatic, never vulgar. And so he erected apartments, schools, hospitals, and factories from north to south, making the entire island a testament to his caring.

His new idea was to turn the Isle into a base for foreign businesses—British and American petroleum refineries, Swiss banks, Japanese electronics firms. In return, Kenneth made these companies employ a high quota of Islanders, even in management, righting the exclusionary wrongs of old British rule. If he couldn't sail the Isle to the developed world, he would bring the developed world to it.

I found most of Kenneth's plans admirable; they brought prosperity and stability to our country. What I objected to was the disinterment of graves in cemeteries for nothing nobler than golf courses and shopping centers, playgrounds to subdue a restless, gentrifying middle class—and worse, the Medusa's head of motorways he was planting near the city center, over where Redhill had been. With each such project, I called his office with new warnings. He was playing with fire. Never once did he call me back.

I had to do something. One afternoon, I made my way to the construction zone that was the Redhill Memorial Highway—oh, the false piety of the name! There, looking at the progression of concrete Xs each five stories high, I was hailed by two ghosts who'd perished in the blaze, a schoolboy and an old man.

As gray dust from the excavating cranes and dozers fell over our heads like snow, an echo of the fire that had brought us all here, they spoke to me:

"I was a light sleeper so I heard them," said the boy in Teochew, his emotions still raw. "They came in the night, like shadows. At first I thought they were thieves, you know, the ones going round, but then they threw a burning match into our room. I tried to wake my mother and my two small sisters. But the fire... It's not fair! I didn't get to run or say good-bye. My mother and sisters were killed in their sleep. That must be a happier way to die because I haven't seen them here, and I've been waiting. I don't leave in case they come back, but to be honest, every day, my memory grows weaker."

What the older ghost had to say was grimmer still: "Two live babies were buried at the base of these pillars last month. I tell you, I saw them put those crying twin babes in the ground. A Taoist geomancer came in and blessed them; then they threw the soil over them. I know of this superstition from my old home village. In Swatow, we believed in such things because we were uneducated brutes, but I didn't think people would believe in the same rubbish here. Now, I'm an old man and I'm not bitter about dying, but I want everyone still alive to know that wrong has been done here. People must know! Those poor babies may have been orphans, but their lives were robbed! It's a horrible, meaningless sacrifice."

I knew the testimonies of dead men would mean nothing to Kenneth, who was too occupied with the big picture to truly be a great man. But they weren't worthless to me.

I got down on my knees. I said a prayer for the dead twins and for my two confidantes, who, surprised that anyone cared, began to fade before my eyes.

— 18 —

The Prime Minister and Lady Midnight

EVEN TO THOSE WHO KNEW HIM WELL, Kenneth Kee became increasingly hard to grasp. While ideas of free love and personal liberation were flourishing in the West, he fed himself on the works of Han Fei, the ancient Chinese philosopher known for his cunning statecraft. Kenneth called it pragmatism; I called it paranoia.

For here's how Han Fei spelled out the qualities of the ideal leader:

He is so still that he seems to dwell nowhere, so empty that no one can seek him. He reposes with non-action above and his ministers tremble with fear below.

Han Fei also said one should hire only minions whose loyalty could be bought and exile those who exceeded their duties; their facility, after all, meant they could switch sides. I often found myself wishing Kenneth's head had been filled with Machiavelli instead. It would have kept him much nicer.

So it came as a great surprise to me when, early in the year 1972, he called me out of the blue.

"I have your sisters."

"What do you mean?"

"My people seem to have located them. Or at least, their last known address."

I was speechless. I'd mentioned them to him just once—decades ago— and he had remembered.

"I know it's taken years, but I feel I owe it to you. I can't guarantee they'll still be there, but it's the best my sources have been able to drum up."

I flew to Shanghai the following week, with Kenneth's office arranging a secret visa to get me into Mao's China. That was the first and only time I took advantage of my proximity to his power. I'd never accepted so much as a chocolate Yule log from the prime minister's office at Christmas, when even the night watchman took home two.

China in 1972 was nearly unrecognizable from the country I left in 1929. The joie de vivre and glamour of prewar Shanghai had vanished, replaced by a whole population in identical blue workers' coats; the only ones who didn't wear them were small children and the dead. Instead of the reassuring mandarin peel and mothball smells of my childhood, the city air was heavy with the stinks of the new China—cigarettes, mentholated ointments, and moonshine—all three sometimes emanating from a single person, in this case my assigned driver, Old Chen.

Most of my beloved buildings in the French Concession had vanished, as had the old rickshaws. Now everyone pedaled around on chunky, creaking bicycles, flooding the streets from dawn until the city shut down hours earlier than before. There was no more neon, no more billboards advertising British gin. I felt a complete stranger, a foreigner. Did Kenneth really send me here for my sisters or to show me what a *true* totalitarian state looked like?

"Do you remember when Shanghai was glorious?" I asked Old Chen, who I guessed to be around seventy and old enough to remember.

"No, madam," he replied. "I lived in a sampan on the river. It was never glorious to me—not 'til now."

The Chinese had reclaimed the city, but I realized these were not *my* Chinese. The streets had been renamed and renumbered by forceful nationalists to suit the forceful, nationalist mood. Our street, Rue Bourgeat, had become ChangLe Lu, or the Street of Long Happiness, and it was on ChangLe Lu that my sisters supposedly still lived.

As Old Chen's car wove its way along the street, avoiding bicyclists, I realized we were approaching our old address. The white colonial-era town houses had fallen into disrepair, divided and subdivided into dreary little units. It sickened me to imagine my twins clad in those dreary blue coats, cooking broken rice in some windowless room, their noses blackened with soot.

I had Old Chen drop me off at the old *Paradis* children's park, now called People's Space 45 and completely shorn of trees. The patch was barely the size of a primary school playground. Perhaps its edges had been chewed away by road expansion, or perhaps the park had always been this small.

Three codgers in blue coats trudged through the grassless lot, their breath curling from their mouths in white floral tufts. I scanned the grounds for the gated rose garden. It was gone. The old hedge maze survived but had been sawed down to knee height, probably to guard against private acts that might sully this public space. Gone, too, was the potting shed against which Li had handled his first cat. With these old markers eradicated, the park was clean. Not a single ghost. The Red Guards had done a thorough job: The place was now inhospitable to the living as well as the dead.

A few trees remained, denuded of leaves. I made my way to the largest, which I remembered as a great flowering mulberry bush. Deep inside its skeletal frame, too bristly to reach into, I spied tiny, rolled-up scrolls in scarlet, turquoise, and indigo, the hues still rich. These were the old sweet wrappers, of course. I hadn't seen such colors since arriving in Shanghai, where aside from the workers' blue, everything came in washed-out shades of gray. They gave me hope, these bright shards. Perhaps my sisters could be just as untouched by history. After all, I'd always thought of them as magical girls. Why wouldn't they be magical women?

Something caught the corner of my eye.

I turned to see a moving patch of black. A white-haired man in a long black cape walked briskly toward the far edge of the park. He carried a cane—in cinnabar red.

Could this really be?

I raced across the park, curbing the temptation to shout, and trailed him onto the road. But the old rascal kept disappearing—behind a bank of toilets, behind a street cobbler's stand, around the corner of an abandoned stable—only to surface again, ever more distant, ever more fleeting. After five minutes, I lost all sight of him, if it *was* him.

I made my way by memory to our family's old town house. Just as I'd guessed, it bore the new address Kenneth had given me. My sisters had stayed constant through all these years! But everything else had changed. Not only was there no gate between our house and the street, but also the outside world seemed to have flooded into the property like a tidal wave, sucking out all barriers in its undertow. The front door was missing. As for the windows, the glass had been haphazardly replaced with boards and blankets. The walls, once so strikingly white, were now mold black and guano gray. I hadn't lived here in decades, yet I felt defiled. I wanted to find somebody—anybody—so I could scream at them. How could they let this happen to my family's house?

Nobody could possibly live here. This was not a home. This was a photo essay torn from the pages of *Life* magazine: the Ravages of Communism. But I had come all this way, and I wasn't about to leave without going inside.

As I stepped over the threshold, a small boy scurried through the dark on all fours. He pushed past me and sprinted out into the sunlight, trailing behind him a ragged woolen flag, probably a blanket. I felt like running after him, to smack him for daring to steal from my sisters. But had he? In truth, he could have come from any of the subdivided coops. Where our cozy sitting room once stood there was now an entire apartment with its own locked door. The same was true of the kitchen and the servants' quarters beside it.

I looked up the old stairs. I had a feeling that my sisters, if they'd truly chosen to remain, would have fought to be assigned the place of their youth—the narrow hallway once clogged with their cot.

Climbing the freezing steps, I found two apartments. My parents' old room made up one, its door locked. The twins' space formed the other, its door wide open.

And there I saw them.

Xiaowen and Bao-Bao stood in this grimy, unlit hallway, one braiding the other's hair. I'd been right about them being oases of color. Both wore short-sleeved cotton dresses, one peony pink, the other sky blue—the colors of springtime.

My eyes welled up the instant I saw them. They were so terribly young—teenagers still—their cheeks flushed, their hair long and black and lustrous. I just stared at them for several minutes, soaking in their radiance.

I wanted to believe I could tell them apart. But I couldn't. Rather than hurt their feelings with an error, I whispered both names—"Xiaowen! Bao-Bao!"—and moved in to embrace them together. It didn't matter that my arms went right through them. They felt my love—they had to have.

"Oh my God, how I've missed you two."

They stared back at me impassively, amused by my emotional display but also baffled: why them?

"Don't you remember me?"

Again, two pairs of doe eyes stared, blank.

I yearned to hear them talk, to match their teenage voices with the baby ones I knew. I wanted them to call me, *Jie jie*, if only to humor me, and to tell me what had happened to them. But they seemed unwilling or unable, and returned, fully absorbed, to their activity. When the one finished braiding her twin's hair, she undid the plait, combed the hair straight with her fingers, and began braiding it all over again, ever patient, ever loving, as if trying to perfect the art. I could imagine her repeating this to infinity and, entranced by their presence, could have stood here watching them forever, had it not been for the bitter cold.

"Xiaowen, Bao-Bao," I tried again. "Say something!"

They smiled a response, but both sets of eyes closed me off. It was nobody's fault. These two had learned to sieve out the living, as I'd often done with the dead, and I could find no way to break through. We stood on opposite sides of the greatest divide.

Taped to the wall behind them was an old illustrated poster. Chairman Mao's round, beaming face loomed like the sun over an idealized family. Dressed in the coveralls and red scarves of the worker class were a suntanned father, a powdery-pale mother, a girl and a boy, both around seven years old, and a pair of identical toddler girls. A cocker spaniel romped in the foreground, clenching a spanner in its teeth.

I knew instantly that the image had been lifted from one of our studio portraits, the ones Father left behind—us at our finest hour, reimagined for the coarsest of times.

"That's us!" I pointed to the image. "That's our family!"

But my sisters chose not to hear me.

Like Father had once done, I stared at the twin girls in the picture, unable to tell who was who.

I wanted to take the poster with me—it was all that was left of my family. But alas, it would only remind me of what I'd never have again. The only place I could ever hope to keep us all together, out of space, time, and history, was in my mind.

And so, at age fifty, with half a century and my ghost work behind me, I devised a quiet life for myself.

422

Since working invisibly was what I did best, I settled into another profession in the shadows. I became a librarian.

It was during this time, while watching over the reference reading room at the National Library of the Black Isle, that I encountered that pair of Belgian anthropologists, Lucas Van Kets and Marijke Jodogne. Both gaunt and so blond as to be nearly white-haired, with skin burnished ochre by the sun, they struck me as castaways from another continent's wreck.

But it wasn't just their odd complexion that got my attention. They staggered into my reading room with the hollow eyes of academics reeling from having their theories blown to pieces by life—in their case, by the grueling reality of six months on the ground in Zaire, the former Belgian colony where even running water remained a luxury.

For two weeks, they treated the cool, quiet, rational atmosphere of my reading room as both ashram and womb. One day at lunchtime, I slipped them ham sandwiches from a nearby coffee stall and directed them to the back stacks, where they devoured them ravenously. From the books they requested, I followed the drift of their research—they had a preoccupation with Borneo headhunters and cannibal cults—and soon grasped that they were vastly misinformed about our region, readily misled by juicy conjecture, and were headed into murkier waters still. Although it wasn't my business, I felt obliged to right their course. I took them to tea at the Metropole. We struck up a pleasant rapport over scones and I told them a few anecdotes—inadvertently giving them the "interview" that would appear in their book *After the Ghost*, which at the time, given their bumbling approach, I believed had no chance whatsoever of seeing print.

Their photo of me in the cemetery, the one that labeled me "Native Girl," was snapped by Lucas when I took them to Forbidden Hill to look at its variegated graves. The "bones" they claimed I was digging up were in fact bits of some litterbug's fried chicken lunch that, as one with strong civic pride, I felt compelled to pick up. Their cheap attempt to make me seem like a practicing witch doctor came as a betrayal. I regretted the tea and sympathy.

Yet, the intrepidly energetic Belgians *did* lead me down an interesting rabbit hole. In the course of their poking around, interviewing headhunters on one of the nearby Spice Islands, they'd stumbled across a former resident of the Black Isle who had impressed them with his strange charisma. *"Diabolique."* Marijke grinned. They'd met him on a clove plantation where he was preaching anarchy, and described him as a bald, nameless Malay with a bad leg. When they mentioned the scars across his chest—from being tortured, the man claimed, by bigoted government spies on the Black Isle—I felt my heart take a little skip. So *that's* what happened to Issa.

He was leading a small army of former commandoes into the Isle's upcountry jungles where, the Belgians told me, he planned to launch attacks on the city itself.

"But why would he tell this to you?" I asked Marijke.

"I think he wants to get the rumor out, to frighten people."

"Or to warn them," Lucas added darkly.

Knowing the Belgians' credulity, I didn't trust their story. No doubt Issa felt betrayed by Kenneth's maneuvers—as had I—but it was ludicrous to think of him, now a frail old man, plotting against his own beloved city. It sounded absurd that he'd call his fellow Islanders "colonizers, slave owners, and infidels." I assumed the Belgians had embellished the tale with horrors they'd witnessed in Africa.

Two months later, a homemade time bomb exploded in the Chinatown bus depot. It was a busy Monday morning—eleven people died, and fifty were seriously injured. That same afternoon, another blast claimed the lobby of the Hong Kong and Shanghai bank building on High Street, killing three customers, two of them schoolgirls who had been opening their first savings accounts.

I called Kenneth's office. His secretary put me through immediately.

"It's Issa," I said.

"I know," he said.

"Then why didn't you stop him?"

He paused and coughed out a guffaw, concealing his fury.

"He's made it impossible to find him. He won't talk to me. I have men on the ground—Malay men, Muslim men, because that's what this is *apparently* about—trying to infiltrate his group. But, as you know, he's got the jungle on his side. He's been spouting all kinds of rot about wanting the Isle returned to its 'original owners,' as if they'd done such a fantastic job in the first place, and he's using Islam as a ruse to rally those types around him. But it's not about Islam, is it? We both know he's always been more of a self-styled pantheist or at least a pagan. The frustrating thing is that there are dolts on this island who'll succumb to his rubbish."

"He's got commandoes with him. Former navy men, people like that."

"We're well aware of that." I could hear him grinding his teeth. "Don't you think we've been working twenty-four hours a day for the past two years looking for them?"

"But the Isle's not that big!"

"And you're a bloody *librarian*!" He held himself back from saying worse. "Look, I'm already having the worst day imaginable. I have to get back to work."

Rather than fight him, I said something I never imagined I'd say to him again:

"Let me help."

It took a few days, but through the mysterious, invisible veins of the underground circuit, my request for a meeting was ferried to Issa's ear. To my surprise, he agreed. I suggested we meet at midnight at his father's grave in the cemetery on Forbidden Hill, where he would feel protected by spirits he could corral at a moment's notice.

Of course, I'd picked this spot also because if I was endangered, I, too, could call up an army of my own. But I felt confident that neither of us would break our sacred treaty and disturb the dead.

At the stroke of midnight, in the silent heart of the cemetery, a voice boomed out of the darkness, "Your hair's gone white."

I turned. "Iskandar."

He smiled. "I forgot about that. I thought you'd sent an old woman in your place."

He was dressed in a white long-sleeved shirt and khaki slacks, more or less what he'd worn on our first meeting on this mount. But I was startled by how he'd aged. His hair was gone and he limped along with the help of a cane. Other than his smile—still the image of potent ambiguity—he looked like the average Malay grandfather, not an idealistic freedom fighter or some unstoppable satanic mastermind.

My first impulse was to embrace him. But as he hobbled toward me from behind the moss-covered gravestone, I could tell he didn't wish to be touched. His eyes brimmed with mistrust.

"Why?" I asked.

"Because he hates us. He hates all of us. The man is built on hate. But you knew that from the beginning. You made that bargain yourself when you became close to him."

"If it's a bargain, as you say, then you made one with him, too, for far longer than I did."

"True, but I had to do it, for my cause. The same way he went with the British when it suited him, went against them when it stopped suiting him. Isn't that politics? And now he's going after us."

"Us?"

He smiled. "Oh, Cassandra. Of course I don't mean you. I'm referring to all of us who don't fit into his master plan—the ones who make his Isle *dirty*, the ones he wants to make disappear. The underdogs, the original people, the dark ones, the ghosts. I had to do something before he began purging us." His voice rose. "The Isle belonged to *us* first! Before the Dutch came and the Portuguese and the British came, before *you people* came, we were doing perfectly well for ourselves. We had our land and our water and our spices—God was on our side. This was *our* paradise—ours!—and then you people with your greed and your ambition came and snatched away our souls."

I winced at the cruel readiness with which he flung "you people" at me.

"I know you think I quit his government because of the fire. But I didn't give a damn about Redhill—that place was full of your kind. No, I quit because of what he said a long time ago to win the election. Surely you remember. He said he wanted to move the Isle away from these waters because this part of the world wasn't good enough for him. I knew that this was how he'd always felt but to proudly say it out loud, to stir up the kind of feelings that a comment like that would stir up, that's *wicked*. You people stole our land and yet you feel the right to condescend?

"I was filled with so much rage and shame. Every night when I went home from work, my neighbors would stare at me as if I'd sold my soul to the devil. I wanted to quit right then but I couldn't. I knew I had to resist, to learn his ways, to use him against himself. And the moment I left, I felt reborn."

"Do you feel better off now, killing innocent people?"

"Innocent?" he scoffed. "There are no innocent people on this island."

"What do you want?"

"You, of all people, should understand, Cassandra. I no longer want to be in the shadows. I no longer want my people to be in the shadows."

"And through violence, you'll get the attention you deserve?"

He laughed at me, like I was a naïve little girl.

"No, you misunderstand me. I don't want attention. All I want is respect and dignity for my people, for us to be returned what is *rightfully* ours, what is *owed* to us." These words seemed to soften him, and he grew quiet, almost ruminative. "As soon as he got elected, he dropped me like a stone. Do you know how difficult it is to talk to him? He surrounds himself with soldiers and gunmen, as if he's some emperor everyone's out to kill. It's been like this for years. I could never get a minute alone with him. He always had somebody around guarding him, as if he trusted that stranger more than he trusted *me*—me who saved his life more than once. Wouldn't you find that insulting?"

"Yes," I said. And I understood. But I was here to stop Issa's attacks, to forge a truce. "If there's something I can tell him for you, what would it be?"

"I want to meet him, face-to-face, and talk to him alone, like old times, the way you and I are talking now. I'd like to believe he's still got that much humanity—and humility—left in him."

I nodded, and to my surprise, he embraced me.

We stood there in that cemetery on the hill, two worn-down soldiers looking down through the night at the city we'd fought to create. The Black River lay beneath us, uncoiled like an onyx snake. On its banks were warehouses and godowns now silent, black and asleep. The only light came from the Edinburgh Bridge, the serpent's metallic waistline. It shone like a white cummerbund. And such a clean bridge it was, too. No pedestrians passed over it—the bombs had kept people at home—and no ghosts either—the lights had taken care of that.

Issa pointed. "Let's meet there, tomorrow midnight."

I went to see Kenneth that same night. It was my first time visiting the prime minister's office, and I was stunned at how his personal style had colonized the Victorian grandeur of Parliament House: bare white walls, uncarpeted wood floors, and the pervasive smell of 4711 cologne. The cologne, he explained, was to ward off the old British smells that still clung to the cracks.

"Cheesy feet, gammon breath, and goaty underarms."

Not having seen him in the flesh for years, I felt weak-legged with longing. For my youth perhaps, and an earlier Kenneth. It wasn't that he looked any different from his newspaper photos or televised appearances—he was even wearing his campaign uniform of gray-blue shirt and pants. No, it was his presence—the smell of him, the darting eyes, the quick, slippery smiles, the quintessence of Kenneth that nobody but me grasped.

We stepped into his chamber. His desk was flanked by two framed pictures. Both were color panoramas: one showed a Jakarta slum, the other downtown Geneva.

"This is so every time I decide on policy, I see the two possible scenarios and I'm reminded of why I do what I do," he said. "Order . . . or chaos."

"And you walk the middle path—tyranny."

He stared at me, mystified, it seemed. "What crude and appalling labels you use, Cassandra. Didn't you learn anything by going to China? The root of my success, *our* success, is that *we*, as in *all* Islanders, share a secret. You're not exempt. We all understand it, we all abide by it, and the secret is this: We came here with nothing but we sure as hell aren't going to leave with nothing. And so long as we keep this secret that others like to call greed or ambition, so long as we hold on to it like a *family*, we won't end up poor and depraved like our neighbors."

An assistant brought us a midnight snack—warmed-up chicken rice from Mitzi's, served on the gilded, embossed china of the prime minister's office.

"I know, the takeaway version just doesn't have the same snap." He shrugged. "The chicken seems . . . wan. But beggars can't be choosers. I can't just waltz into any old coffee shop like you. I've lost that luxury." He popped a piece of thigh meat onto his tongue. "So what did our former comrade want?"

I gave him Issa's list of conditions: no police, no weapons, no recording devices; in short, no nonsense. Naturally, I neglected to share with him some of Issa's more outlandish views.

I wanted to believe that Kenneth's drained, haunted look was sincere. I'd seen that same expression at his baby's christening—bewilderment that his outer self had run ahead and done things without first consulting his inner self. But what did it mean?

"I wish I'd kept him closer. Him and Zhang—even *you*." He laughed dryly. "You may not believe me, but there's a big part of me that just wants to ditch everything here and run off into the jungle with him. Just *vanish*. There's such a purity to how he views the world. It's almost"—he searched for the right word—"comforting."

"Comforting for him or for you?"

He didn't answer. But I wondered if, like me, he had grown weary of his world and wanted something simpler—not the jungle perhaps, but something else.

As I was leaving, he took my arm.

"I know we have history between us, but I think you understand." He looked me in the eye. "I've always done everything for the Isle. You do know this, don't you?"

"I'd *like* to believe it."

"Well"—he gave me a tired smile—"that's a start."

I went home to catch a few hours' sleep. The prime minister remained in his office, surrounded by a phalanx of bodyguards.

When I returned to Parliament House the next morning, the air was thick, monsoonal. It was exhaustingly muggy, even by Island standards, and this made everyone tense. Or almost everyone. Kenneth sat behind his desk with the distant, meditative aura of a monk, fondling the rosary of his gold Rolex. Was he actually thinking of ditching everything? After all, it would make a frightening sort of poetic sense. But I kept those thoughts to myself; his lieutenants seemed jittery enough.

I went over the plan again, Kenneth nodding neutrally after each point. At midnight, he would stand alone on the Edinburgh Bridge's north end. The streets within a one-mile radius would be closed off to traffic. I would lead Issa from the Forbidden Hill cemetery down to the bridge's south end, then disappear into the night, my work done. Each man, carrying his own black umbrella, would walk toward the center of the bridge. The meeting would be almost romantic.

"Are you nervous?" I asked. I certainly was. So much could go wrong: Issa saying something to Kenneth to enrage him, or vice versa. Above all, there was the haunting possibility that Kenneth might abdicate and turn civilian again.

He gave me the frozen smile of a politician forced to squander his Sunday at a supermarket opening.

"It's going to be all right." He patted my arm. "Disregard what I said last night. That was just the tension talking. No matter what happens tonight, I'd like you to know I appreciate you. I couldn't have done all this without you."

I turned back one last time. "Don't run away."

Kenneth stared at me with deadened eyes, his decision already locked in place. Nothing I said could change his mind.

"Don't you be late," he replied.

The rainwater gushed downhill, a fast-moving river crashing into the backs of our heels. I guided Issa down Forbidden Hill, clutching his arm so he wouldn't slip and fall. Water sloshed inside our shoes; we might as well have gone barefoot. The storm was bearing down sideways and ricocheting off the hard ground. The umbrella we shared was no match for this deluge.

His cane useless, Issa almost lost his footing several times. He clucked his tongue, his annoyance so vast it was almost as if he wanted to call the whole thing off—the threats, the men hiding in the forest, and especially this troublesome reunion.

I, too, wished that he could wash away the colossal past with a sad laugh—it was all a stupid joke gone wrong—and surrender himself.

But it was a fantasy that the Isle's fate could be decided by the messiness of one persistent rainstorm.

"How do you feel?" I asked.

"Optimistic."

It wasn't the answer I'd been expecting. As the white lights of the bridge came into view, the arrogance melted from his face. He tightened his grip on my arm as we stepped across another puddle. I felt the time was right for an overdue confession.

"Iskandar." Just saying his full, majestic name brought an ache to my heart. "Years ago, I did something very stupid. I tried calling forth the spirits, in the back of the Wees' house."

"Did you succeed?"

"No."

"Then you should have nothing to worry about."

"But I think I released something. The badi."

"Why do you think this?"

"Because it crawled out of the grave in the form of a dog-headed man. That was how they buried Mr. Wee, you know—they sewed Agnes's head onto him."

Issa's silence agonized me more than anything he could have said.

"Say something, Iskandar."

"You should have put it back in the ground."

"But I didn't know how."

"Well, I suppose, the damage has been done."

I froze. "What does that mean?"

"It means, my friend, that if the badi wants nothing more from you, you'll never hear from it again. But if it feels it still has unfinished business, you can be absolutely sure you'll meet again." His eyes darkened. "A bit like Kenneth Kee."

We reached the south end of the Edinburgh Bridge. So this was it. Issa seemed to sense it, too. He looked at me with a bit of the old tenderness. "I'm glad you're with me."

But was I?

Through the rain, I glimpsed the black silhouette of a man on the other end of the bridge. Black raincoat, black umbrella. I waved to him and he waved back, watch glinting. There was nobody else about, no other sound but the unrelenting claps of rain.

Issa clutched my arm. "I'm sorry."

I didn't know what to say in return, so I gave his arm a squeeze. I refused to look him in the face, refused to acknowledge that this murderer had also been my friend.

I let go of him and gave him the umbrella. It was the cue. He began to cross the bridge, slowly. At the other end, Kenneth began walking also, just as cautiously. I held my breath like a nervous mother, impatient for my children to settle their playground spat. Let both boys be softened by this heartless rain. If there had to be brutality, let it come from above.

Pulling my hood over my wet head, I waited. As both men neared their meeting point, the thin black line where the lips of this cantilevered beast kissed, I turned to leave.

I couldn't bear to watch, or even hear them argue, not that I could have heard a word through the storm.

But I did hear something. A loud *clap*, as if the thunder god had intervened to end their quarrel. It was followed by a second bang, sharper, louder.

When Issa dropped his umbrella, I knew this to be no act of God. He collapsed quickly, uttering something I couldn't catch.

I ran along the bridge until I came to his body, doubled over on the ground. The umbrella was bobbing, shuddering on the wet road. I kicked it aside.

Blood poured out of him. The rain spread it so I couldn't tell where he'd been hit. He was bleeding, it seemed, from every pore. His eyes were open, blinking, in shock. He'd been anticipating a duel, but not like this—silenced even before the match began.

Seeing this scared old man, my long lost friend, I sank to my knees and held his shoulders. I found the hole above his left ear, the blood nearly black, the brain matter throbbing. The other shot had pierced his chest. It was over. I lowered him gently back onto the ground and stared at Kenneth, who stood like a statue a few feet from us.

"You snake! Am I next?"

He dropped his umbrella and raised both palms, to show me he wasn't armed, that it wasn't he who'd fired the shots—as if this made his hands any cleaner. He lifted his face to the sky, drenching his hair, soaking his cheeks. Enacting a self-baptism—but for whose benefit? He already had the face of the damned.

Behind him, two figures in black raincoats slithered away in the dark. Elite army snipers, no doubt.

"We do not negotiate with terrorists," said the prime minister. "We *cannot.*"

He walked toward me. My eyes followed the glinting gold Rolex on his left wrist—a maddening sight amidst all this blood. When he got close enough, I lunged for it, trying to wrest it from him and hurl it into the rushing waters below.

My hands slipped. Blood, even in the rain, remains slick. He kicked me in the chest like a cur. I fell back into a puddle thickened with Issa's blood.

In that moment, the rain seemed to lift at the prime minister's command. At the north end of the bridge, where he had been standing earlier, I saw a ghost. Not Issa.

A dog-headed man, his face slick and black.

Then in a flash—nothing.

The prime minister kept winning, election after election. The people loved him. And why not? He kept the Isle clean, safe, well lit. He uprooted the jungles, vanquished the terrorists, and sucked dry the swamps. He gave everybody what all reasonable people wanted—honest work, affordable food, a roof over their heads, and the freedom to buy whatever they desired when they weren't working, eating, or sleeping. Eventually, even his opponents came to accept that material comfort wasn't necessarily a bad thing.

When the Isle became too limited to fulfill his ambitions, the prime minister didn't tow it away to better climes, as he'd once blithely promised. He'd learned to love the strategic importance of being where all the world's trade passed and instead sculpted the Island to his own will. By filling in the sea with sand and concrete, our Prospero widened his canvas, rounding out its southern coast until our diamond-shaped Isle became a fat-bottomed teardrop anchored in the waters of the Pacific.

As surveyors scrambled to chart the Island's expanding boundaries, the prime minister laughed and went on building. He scorned all clichés. Instead of erecting shrines to himself like so many of his peers in the postcolonial world, he continued to deploy sleight of hand—humility, in adherence to his own vaunted "Confucian values"—and let prosperity itself become his monument.

By the early 1980s, Geneva was finally within sight. In spite of his cruelty to me and all those he'd felled along the way, I was proud of his accomplishments. He had reinvented the Isle.

I was a beneficiary of the new order, after all. I liberated Li from Woodbridge and brought him home to live with me. This move was possible only because of the generous pension accorded me by my years at the National Library and, above all, my earnings from my days as the government's ghosthunter. On the Black Isle, to this day, it pays to retire as a good civil servant.

Li and I spent our days like a quaint old couple. On the rare occasions my young neighbors glimpsed us shuffling off together to the nearby 7-Eleven, they took him for my husband. I never bothered to correct them. Though we were barely sixty, the new generation treated us with the veneration reserved for those in their seventies or eighties, the result, no doubt, of my white hair and the moral education classes the prime minister instituted in all the schools. Nobody stared at Li for being soft in the head—they took his sloppy grin as the expression of a sage.

At home, Li watched television for much of the day, thank heavens. I admit I was a terrible companion and abandoned him in front of the set whenever I could. I had long since grown tired of his stories about our sisters and Shanghai. He could sit in front of the telly forever, giggling at cartoons and cowering from the casual violence of a show like *Dallas*. But the programs on Japanese war criminals, which I could never stop myself from watching, always left him shrieking and sobbing. Early in his stay, it occurred to me that his wit might be magically restored with a sip of my blood; he refused. But other than these outbursts, Li was as passive and easy to care for as a cat. If I placed a glass of milk before him, he drank it; if I led him to the bath, he removed his clothes. Whenever he was troubled by some fugitive thought in the middle of the night, morphine did the trick—for him and for me.

I spent my days like any other retiree spared the time-draining commitment of grandchildren: grocery shopping, tending to the upkeep of my apartment, reading voraciously, and enjoying French chocolate and cognac of a startlingly high quality, thanks to Kenneth's lenient import laws and low taxes. Best of all, early every morning before the humidity became intolerable, I took long walks in the Isle's famed Botanic Gardens, always stopping by the lake with breadcrumbs to feed the black swans.

More years passed, and the Isle continued to thrive.

Unlike my fellow citizens, I did not think the prime minister a deity. I'd had the disadvantage of having known him when he was merely a man. And unlike them, I chose not to close my eyes to his tactics. In the pursuit of a wholesome, family-first culture, he barred anything he associated with "the flesh trade"—everything from Tunisian belly dancers, once a popular attraction at hotel lobby bars, to any Hollywood movie that showed women taking off their tops. To stem the influx of "antisocial, hippie values," he banned not only long hair on men, but also the music of male musicians sporting haircuts longer than a pageboy, the likes of Mozart and Beethoven excepted.

"We do not negotiate with hippies," I could almost hear him saying in his stern campaign warble, followed by the humbler addendum: "We *cannot* negotiate with hippies." Like most Islanders, I had internalized his sermons. I could conjure up his voice and put imaginary words into his mouth:

"As a society in transition, we will not take our survival for granted. We *cannot*. We must constantly be vigilant of the tiger behind the door."

Or:

"We do not tolerate free speech here because we *cannot* afford it. Look at America, the so-called freest nation in the world. Look at the murderers, drug dealers, and rapists prowling her streets. Is it really freedom if you can't even walk home at night without fearing for your life?"

The Islanders seemed not to mind the way he shredded their cultural life. After all, he made them, and a multitude of foreign corporations, rich. The teardrop island, once so tattered, need weep no more. Unless, of course, one was given to littering, spitting, or jaywalking, in which case there were plenty of reasons to wail, including public humiliation, imprisonment, and multiple whacks on the derriere by the government's official cane.

The prime minister's frenzy for neatness culminated in the installation of urine detectors in all public elevators. This was how they worked: The doors locked in the offending party, and come the next morning, the guilty person's mug would be splashed across the *Tribune*. Front page, no less. Naturally, this unique punishment received mocking editorials in foreign newspapers, but the detectors quickly won me over—for there are few things as revolting as being trapped in a moving box sloshing with a drunkard's midnight piss.

Peace and prosperity left most people content—even the old rebels. I never heard a peep of complaint from Cricket, who had leapt from being the Isle's soft-drink king to an emperor of real estate. He'd apparently made his fortune the old-fashioned way—buying low, selling high. He was honest and above-board, for all I knew, with his two wives, multiple houses, and an infinity of children. I saw him in the papers time and again, a Mandarin dumpling with cigar, pipe, and sometimes both.

As for the prime minister, he and I proceeded on parallel tracks, never speaking, never meeting. But I knew we were both after the same thing—to free ourselves of ghosts, even if we meant it very differently.

For my part, I was all for ensuring that my dear brother met with a peaceful death—insomuch as the end could ever be kind. I wanted him to feel no need to return to his old places ever again. I'd seen how our sisters were trapped in their private diorama, forgotten yet not protesting, as meek as two dormice in the bear's claw of fate. I didn't want that same class of eternity for Li. He'd already lived much of his life as a lost soul, squiring the same old thoughts round and round his head. It'd be only too cruel if he had to spend his afterlife as one, too.

I watched his flesh sag and his joints grow weak—a mirror of myself, I'm loath to say. Through love and neglect, especially neglect, I tutored him to let go of the world and its cares, of old Shanghai, and especially of me.

The last thing I wanted was to find him in my home after he was gone.

— 19 —

The End

Li DIED on July 31, 1990, a few days shy of our sixty-eighth birthday.

Our parting was peaceful. One afternoon, he simply fell asleep and failed to wake up. People always seem surprised to learn it's possible to die of pneumonia in the tropics, but it is. Pneumonia's not picky.

A strange thing, to outlive your twin. It's as if you've either been given a reprieve, and for that you warily give thanks, or that you've taken more than your fair share from the communal storehouse, and for this you bear great guilt. Then there's the troublesome thought you must try to disguise: You are relieved to have him gone.

On our birthday, a surprisingly cool Tuesday, I took his ashes in a plastic bag and embarked on what I decided would be my last walk around the Black Isle. I was now ready to leave everything behind, for there's nothing lonelier than standing in the land you once loved only to find no trace of what you'd first loved about it. It's easier to live some other place, in a featureless void even, where you may reassemble all your cherished memories, free of the intrusive taint of the now.

I had to leave.

But before that, I took my final stroll along the grand avenue spanning from Tanglewood to the city. Kenneth's handiwork was everywhere—he'd dug up its huge, spreading rain trees and replaced them with canals. So instead of shushing leaves, birds, and cicadas, all I could hear now was nonstop pounding from the city as construction hurtled ahead on his underground transit project.

Still I toured my Isle with a proprietor's right, scattering parts of me, in the dusty form of my lost twin. It's animal instinct, I think, this compulsion to mark the places you've been, even if you never intend to return.

Walking through the city, I gazed upon shopping plazas and gleaming office blocks where once had been mass graves. Even the worst plots had become desirable. Where the Rat Brigade warehouse once stood, the discotheque Opium now flourished. Old clients had stopped heeding my warnings. Perhaps I should have been firmer—less laissez-faire, more Kenneth Kee.

Where others saw a glittering skyline, a Manhattan of the East, I saw nameless tombs writ large: Redhill, Wonder World, the Metropole, even the eccentric Troika restaurant—all casualties, RIP. Chinatown was China-town in commercialized nostalgia only. Our row of tenements in Bullock Cart Water had been "restored" by engineers in an apparent tribute to calamine lotion and the neighborhood repeopled by youngsters who considered themselves bohemian, by which they meant they drove to their jobs at city hall in Alfa Romeos rather than Honda Accords. As for the World's Busiest Airport, inaugurated with fighter jets trailing pink smoke, I saw what lay beneath its concrete runways: the beach where martyrs, murderers, and a love-mad octopus once roamed.

Everywhere, there were cameras monitoring what I did, at street junctions, outside public loos, at the registers of every shop and cafe. I had to hold back my urge to wink at them, a private greeting to the man I knew to be the ultimate owner of all these eyes—my long-lost friend, Mr. Prime Minister.

Of course, not everything was new. The spirits had returned to the city and grown defiant, roaming the squares where even the brightest lights blazed. Displaced from their places of rest, they spent their days gliding through shopping arcades and riding in taxicabs, just like everybody else. I could tell them apart only by watching closely—the dead's distinguishing trait being envy. They were, after all, second class.

Their quiet resentment told me this peace between the worlds would not last. But it was no longer my job to intercede, and I didn't want to be present to witness the clash.

When I returned from my walk, I booked a one-way ticket to Tokyo, to depart in a few months' time. It was a move I'd contemplated for years. If I let myself die here, I was condemning myself to become a ghost. This I already knew: I'd never be able to let it go. So why Tokyo? A city that large could swallow me up. I would look invisible, be invisible, and no one, not even *he*, could find me there. Living amidst my wartime foes, I would never engage with anyone; I'd never care. It was the best way I knew to die alone.

Best of all, Tokyo would not be the Black Isle. In exile, I would be free to let my memories shine, blossom like those old sweet wrappers tucked forever in the mulberry bush: the Isle of forty, fifty, sixty years past, a fragrant city drenched for eternity in sweat, smoke, and slouchy, off-tempo cha-cha.

As it happened, my getaway was trickier than I'd hoped. Perhaps the ghosts had glimpsed my itinerary.

It began with rumors. Seven soldiers, healthy boys aged eighteen and nineteen, supposedly vanished during routine training in one of the few remaining jungles, only to be found days later—gruesomely disemboweled and strung up on trees. "Pontianaks!" screamed the tabloids. Naturally, the government crushed such talk. Still, the night the scandal broke, my phone rang—as expected—and my answering machine recorded a message from the prime minister's office, urging Lady Midnight to call back ASAP.

Lady Midnight did not. Her work was done.

As public panic over the soldiers' deaths mounted, the city saw another calamity. A brand-new tourist hotel on South Bridge Road, the unfortunately named Hotel New Babylon, collapsed, taking a hundred foreigners. It was a site I'd advised the developer O.W.K. not to build on many years ago, because the spirits from the graves beneath were too many. Sadly, the promise of lucre proved stronger than my words. Again, my phone rang— four separate times, with Kenneth making the fourth call himself. Again, I did not respond.

I was a retired librarian and soon not even an Islander anymore.

On October 31, 1990, my bags were packed. I'd given away most of my things to the survivors of Hotel New Babylon. All that I wanted to keep, including a small ziplock bag of Li's remains, I stuffed into two medium-sized suitcases that would go on the plane with me. I would buy whatever else I needed in Tokyo.

On my final night, I went to bed on a bare mattress, staring at bare walls. Or at least, I tried very hard to fall asleep. My heart, that sad old thing, was pounding like a child's on Christmas Eve.

When the telephone rang, it came almost as a relief. I hadn't announced my plans to anyone, yet I knew that certain people had it within their power to follow my every move. I was determined to frustrate him, to ignore the rings and let him miss his chance to wish me good-bye.

In the end, though, curiosity got the better of me. It was 12:37 a.m. when I picked up the phone.

The caller was Violet.

"I have to speak to you, in person," she whispered, her voice distorted by a thickness in her throat—from crying, it sounded like. "Please, Cassandra. You're the only person I can turn to. Ken . . . he's not well."

"How does that concern me? I'm not his wife. That privilege is yours."

"I'm begging you." Desperation made her shrill. "I'll send a car to your place in five minutes."

"I'm not going to you." Not only did I not want to see her, but I also didn't want to see what they'd done to the house. I had my own memory of the Wee manse sealed away.

"All right, then. We'll speak in the car. Please, Cassandra. Just a few minutes of your time. I promise you . . . I will make this worth your while."

Seven minutes later, a black Jaguar came to a halt outside my apartment building. As the tinted window lowered, revealing Violet in the backseat, I stepped out of the shadows and showed myself.

The driver, a silent Malay, waited for me to buckle up and began driving slowly toward the city. Anyone who saw us through the blackened glass might have thought they were witnessing the setup of some eerie film noir: two grim old biddies journeying into the night.

Violet's face was puffy from hours, perhaps even days, of distress. She had regained all her old weight plus the accumulated sagging of age. But her directness was the same as ever.

"I *know* about you and him." To my surprise, her voice held no rancor. "At this point, none of it matters. All that matters is that you're the one person who can save him. He's locked himself in his study since this morning, drunk on champagne, refusing to come out. I fear this is it. He's *given up*."

She broke into a heaving sob. I couldn't tell what her words meant— was Kenneth threatening to quit or to kill himself? Either scenario seemed unlikely, for this was a man who had survived far worse.

"He's never known what it's like to fail," she continued, "to have his judgments questioned. Now, with these crises. And with you leaving..."

"Don't try to pin the blame on me." I stared out the window. The tinted glass made everything look artificially dark. Was this how Kenneth saw the world?

"I'm not blaming you for anything. There's no time for blame. We both care about him—that's why I've asked you here. Something else horrible has been happening, something the press has yet to uncover. But it's only a matter of time." She took a deep breath. "It's those underground tunnels, for the new trains. You know we've been using a lot of workers from Thailand. Good, hardworking boys from the north. Well, since last week, they've been dropping like flies."

"How many?"

"About thirty so far."

"Thirty?" The poor things, perishing in foreign earth, far from home.

"But there's nothing wrong with our safety or engineering," she added quickly. "The boys just collapsed and went into a kind of coma; those who couldn't be woken up died within the hour. The three who've come forth—the ones who did wake—all talked about winged female demons appearing to them in their sleep. Apsara, you know, those flying things from Eastern mythology."

I knew them well but said, "Have you ruled out gas leaks?"

"If only. Of course, that's the first thing the contractors checked, but it's nothing like that. No, no. It's nothing that can be explained, not conventionally. Ken thinks it's supernatural." She laughed uncomfortably. "But if he says so in public, can you imagine how the world's going to view him? Honestly, he couldn't care less what his own wife thinks of him, but the world? That's his greatest fear, to be taken as a fool.

"As a Catholic, I'm reluctant to believe in any of this myself, but I also know that on the Isle, the rules have always been different. There are too many things here I cannot begin to understand, things that somebody like *you* might know more about."

"Me?"

"Yes, Lady Midnight."

The car stopped at the foot of Forbidden Hill, now partially bald and the site of massive construction. Colorful banners on the pedestrian walkway

announced, ANOTHER PROJECT BY THE MASS TRANSIT AUTHORITY. INCON-
VENIENCE NOW FOR AN ACCELERATED FUTURE! Behind it were towering
plywood scaffolds.

It looked neat and civilized on the outside, but I'd seen how construction was carried out on the Isle—poor foreign workers fed on inadequate
food descending into holes wearing inadequate gear. But unlike the dozens
of sites around the city that chugged along twenty-four hours a day for the
advent of the underground train, here no machinery was rumbling. Work
had apparently come to a halt. I tried to see if there was anybody who
might give me a hint about what was happening but didn't see a soul.

"This is where the men perished," said Violet. "All in one location. We
sent the others back to their little villages, paid them enough to be quiet."

Up at the old cemetery on the side of the Hill, part of which peered
from above the pretty scaffolds, the shrubbery was gone, and the tombs had
been reduced to rubble. Oh, Kenneth Kee, how cheap your promises...

"Just look at what he's done," I said. "Even if *you* don't believe in—"

Violet cut me off. "The shortest route between Chinatown and city hall
was straight through this hill. We had no choice."

"There's always a choice. You could have dug around it. No passenger
would have noticed the difference of one minute in their journey."

"Be that as it may," she went on, suddenly firm, "the tunneling is complete."

"Then it's too late. Isn't it?"

"Maybe not. If it's true the spirits of the dead have been causing these
disruptions, you could find out what they want. Tell us how we can stop
more incidents from happening."

I glanced at my watch: 1:15. I should have been in bed ages ago.

"Cassandra." She clutched my hands. "I'll give you a million dollars. Out
of my own pocket. That's all I ask of you—please. You'll have the money
tonight, I promise. Tell me what they want. Or our Ken's *lost*."

She mentioned the sum as if it were immaterial, as if I were one of those
workers she had so casually paid off.

"Ahmad will take me home," she said, throwing a nod at the inexpressive
driver. "Then he'll come back here and wait for you. Please. If not for Ken,
then for our beleaguered island. It's *yours*, too, you know."

The truth was I *did* know.

I slipped through a crack in the plywood scaffold—one of the few advantages of being skinny as a twig. At sixty-eight, I was far from spry but could always stretch myself out if ever I had to outsmart a barrier. I was never any good at respecting boundaries.

Lying before me, glazed pale blue by the moonlight, was an enormous crater at least two stories deep—the site of the future underground station. Pylons, cinder blocks, and metal webbing peered curiously out of the mud, alongside an extended family of digging equipment, their yellow scooping arms frozen in midthrust. At the hill's base, I spotted the entrance to a tunnel—*the* tunnel—its dirt ceiling and sides propped up by wood trusses in the manner of a mine shaft. Light flickered from within, the only hint of movement in this vast nocturnal still life.

I looked up the denuded hillside and jumped back in fear. I was being watched—not by dead workers but by thirty people in garb from decades and centuries past, the permanent residents of Forbidden Hill. They stood motionless, like a macabre display at a wax museum. Their eyes shone with hatred.

A breeze ruffled my hair and I felt myself go as rigid as the bulldozers in the crater. I'd never had ghosts direct such furious looks at me, their friend and advocate. If they decided to attack, I was finished. What a sad, misunderstood end it would be, too—dying, it seemed, while on patriotic service to the prime minister.

How could I have taken Violet's bait? The ghost world was no longer my domain. I was old, out of practice, outnumbered. I was a *librarian*, for God's sake. Instead of standing here, fighting the unknown on behalf of a man who was no longer my lover or even my friend, I should have been savoring one final night in my apartment, luxuriating in old memories or nursing a giant mug of Ovaltine. Not this.

I cursed Violet's tears and my own vanity, although guilt, too, surely had a hand.

No matter—it was too late to slink away.

A dark silhouette appeared at the mouth of the tunnel. It was a small boy, not menacing like the others. He gave me a friendly wave. I knew the ghosts had chosen such an emissary to put me at ease, to disarm me.

I waved back and suddenly felt as if he and I were about to resume a conversation we'd begun not long ago. On a topic I knew well.

The boy beckoned for me to follow him into the tunnel. For a second I hesitated. Then I walked to the edge of the crater, glancing at the static sprawl of machinery below and the watchful wax gallery above. The whole universe had apparently stopped to enable this moment—my communion, after a long hiatus, with the dead. The ghost world was requesting my return.

For better or worse, I entered its womb.

Crunch, crunch. The loose gravel underfoot advertised my arrival.

The boy vanished. Before me lay a path lit with bulbs from a bygone era, their carbon filaments glowing and hissing as I neared, fading away as I passed, like bewitched tapers. These fixtures were soldered to the walls, their wiring so antiquated I wondered if I was imagining the whole thing. Who would possibly use such lighting at the end of the twentieth century?

I got my answer soon enough. The glaring figures on the hill had been only a preview. The tunnel widened into a grotto, and there, gathered in the dank, stood my real audience—hundreds of men and women, like some secret society of the dead, reeking of the upturned grave. The boy guide was among them, standing at the fore, and I finally caught a glimpse of his face—or what was left of it. The flesh had been eaten away by maggots, and in place of his nose was a hollow oozing slime. He had no eyes.

My knees went soft.

The others were just like him—bony, ravaged, decomposed, what all human beings look like after their time on earth was done. I'd never seen so many gathered in one place, with all their attention focused on one thing: me.

What did they want from me? Pity? Revenge? I wasn't about to stay long enough to find out.

I turned to leave, but more of the dead materialized, their movements stiff and jagged, closing me off from the way I had come. I suddenly thought of the Minotaur in his maze and wished I'd brought my own ball of string. I wasn't ready to die yet, not here, not when my escape from the Isle had been so close. So damn close.

"Forgive me," I whispered. "Forgive us."

My words reverberated through the cave as if I'd shouted. Every step I took produced an inordinately loud crunch.

Faces emerged, distinct, in the flickering light only to melt back into the darkness once more. Malays, Chinese, Parsees, South Indians, Eurasians, Anglo-Saxons, Jews... every one devastated by the elements, devoured by time. Every one missing eyes.

One face in the middle of the crowd burned into the light—and stayed. It was a Chinese woman, her gray skull exposed through a scrim of long, white hair. I recognized her jade-green cheongsam; she wore no pearls, however—the undertakers doubtless stole them because she had no children to complain.

"Mrs. Odell!" I cried, my voice quavering.

She stepped aside. Standing behind her was a skeleton in a gray suit. His head hung limply on his shoulder—Mr. Odell, of course. Although their appearance frightened me, I knew they would do me no harm. I'd paid for her burial; I'd ensured their reunion.

But without eyes, could they even recognize me?

"Help me, please!"

The stench of rotting flesh flooded my nose and mouth as if liquid, and I forced back the urge to gag—it would only reveal my fear, my revulsion, my mortality. The Odells didn't come forward. There was no choice; I had to wade through the others to reach them.

I kept my eyes low. The light, thankfully, was dim and erratic. Pushing through this gathering of corpses, the ground crunching beneath my feet, I told myself to think of the place as an abandoned butchery. The slabs were extruding the juices of putrefaction, yes, but like flesh and bone, decay was the stuff of life and nothing to be afraid of.

Nevertheless, the hairs on my arms prickled. My knees grew weaker with each step. I felt as if everyone in the cave was holding their breath—if they had any breath left to hold—waiting for me to be completely enclosed in their midst so they might crush me and claim me as their own.

The end would be painful; this much I knew. They had cause. I would be punished. I would be made to suffer. But my dying would be nothing compared to my death. I'd be condemned to walk the earth *as one of them*.

The ghost-hunter becoming a ghost. The archness of the irony.

"Mr. Odell," I pleaded as I staggered on, eyes still on the ground.

As the light shifted, I discovered that the dreadful crunching underfoot came not from loose gravel. I was stepping on fragments of bone, rosaries, coffin shards, black clumps of human hair. A shiver rushed up my leg as I lifted my left foot and saw a set of teeth. Beneath my right foot was a large chip from someone's headstone, its dedication in Farsi. Every step I took was another desecration. The entire tunnel was filled with lost memories, all of them mixed and mashed. Soon, trains would rumble through here, turning this final resting ground into a crossroads, a spot of perpetual transit.

If the ghosts took me, I, too, would be absorbed into this anonymous jumble. It would be as if I'd never lived...

Calm down, I warned myself. Panic only ensured I *would* become a ghost. Calm down. Go to the Odells.

But there was no happy reunion when I reached Odell and his wife. The two pushed their cold, hard bodies toward me. They didn't stop at an embrace. No, they wanted more. They began squeezing me, Odell from the front, his wife from behind. Perhaps to be born into death, both parents were required, as in life.

I shut my eyes and took a deep breath. The reek by now had ceased to register as mere smell. The air had grown so heavy it was becoming impossible to inhale.

Yet I had to try pleading once more. "I can do more for you alive than dead."

Even as I spoke those words, my desire to live was slipping away. I was exhausted, nauseated, my lungs empty. Terror was being overtaken by the dull ache of resignation. Why fight? Wasn't I already old and wrecked?

I stopped struggling, but my death parents went on squeezing me tighter and tighter. I felt the cracking of bones, though I couldn't tell if they were theirs or mine. The three of us were now so enjoined, so complete. It took me by surprise, my readiness to submit—to sleep, to suffocation. I no longer cared if the world forgot me. I was in my parents' arms. This family of death was more than enough for me. Their misery was all-consuming, deeper and more relentless than any I'd known—because it never had to end.

It was a greedy grief. All I had to do was yield. Completely.

But somewhere in the muddy labyrinth of my mind, I thought of the pontianak, the war, the girls on Blood Hill... I'd survived worse monsters. Why surrender now?

And in that moment, an annoying buzz began nipping at my ear. It wasn't quite a voice, but the shadow of a voice, like the shushing I'd heard at the cemetery years ago. Only now I could understand it. A language whose meaning suddenly washed clear.

Look around, Odell beseeched. *Look what you've done.*

Not me, I wanted to protest. But I had no voice to speak with.

Other whispers began, in a myriad of tongues so soft and tangled they sounded like wind blowing through the undergrowth.

You promised us this would never happen. You promised us we could rest.

Then two words exploded through the grotto, in the coldest crackle: *Kenneth Kee.*

With that, my death parents released me back into the living. Air rushed into my lungs and I dropped to the ground, wheezing and gagging.

They had believed what I'd told them. I would be more useful alive than dead.

Violet's driver took me home for a change of clothes and then on to the prime minister's home. When he dropped me at their door, he whispered, "Good luck."

Even in the night, the old Wee house glowed. Kenneth had maintained Mr. Wee's all-white palette, except the prime minister's paint shimmered, a brighter, whiter white.

Violet had been watching from the window. She opened the front door before I could even ring the bell. The foyer was a startling sight—done up, to match the exterior, in antiseptic white. The servants had been dismissed, which was just as well. I was in no mood for tea or even cognac.

A large childhood portrait of Violet in a short blue dress hung along the staircase, the only thing adorning the bare walls. I hadn't remembered it from the old days, though the prepubescent scowl was certainly true to life.

"My daughter," Violet said quickly, nodding at the painting. "She's all grown up now. But this is how we prefer to remember her." She clutched my arm to secure my fullest attention. "So, what did you find out?"

"Let me speak to Kenneth."

Violet glared at me with her old stubborn hostility.

"Believe me, Vi, seeing him is the last thing I want to do, but the spirits have given me no choice."

"Tell me what they want, and I'll relay it to him."

"This is something I have to tell him in person. It involves what he and I did before you came into the picture."

Her stony mien crumbled. "Years ago, I asked you, I *begged* you, to stop hounding us—"

"Vi, *you* asked me here tonight."

Gripping the side of the staircase for support, she unleashed a banshee wail. If Kenneth had cared a whit about her, he would have come running. But from the barren halls of the house came not a sound.

"Why can't you ... Why don't you just make them *go away*?"

"Because I didn't summon them. He did."

For his study, Kenneth had chosen the old library, where I'd stumbled into him while seeking refuge from my own engagement party. We were so young then. At that first meeting, the possibility of anything between us was absurd. What we shared then, aside from a mutual distaste for Violet, was a mutual mistrust. Now, all these years later, we had come full circle.

Violet knocked on the door.

"Ken!"

The door unlocked with a sharp click but remained shut.

"Ju*sh*t Cas*sh*andra," said Kenneth, his voice ravaged.

"Ken!" Violet repeated, trying to force the door open with her shoulder. But Kenneth had placed his weight against it. It refused to budge.

"No!" he howled, angrily this time. "I *said, jusht* her."

The second I stepped into the room, he slammed the door in Violet's face and locked it.

I heard her muffled whimper, followed by some indistinct curse hurled at him or me, most likely both of us.

The air conditioner wheezed and rumbled, even though, at three in the morning, it was quite cool outside. For a man who once claimed to hate air-conditioning, he'd clearly succumbed to its appeal as a buffer, sealing himself off in his own climate.

"Plea*sh*e," he said, gesturing for me to sit.

Before I could properly situate myself, Kenneth retreated to the swivel chair behind his rosewood desk, no doubt worried I'd say something cruel about the stink of alcohol that surrounded him like a mist—or about how his lisp had returned. The stark white walls didn't do his complexion any favors, nor did his drab gray shirt and pants. He was startlingly gaunt, with purplish bags under his eyes, but I knew his pallor didn't just come from the lack of sun and sleep. It took more substantial blows for a man of such hubris to look this bad. This wasn't the vigorous leader from news photos or TV. This was an old man.

I examined the room. His desk faced outward, bank manager style, ready to receive clients in a pair of leather armchairs that looked like they'd never been sat in—until now. Mr. Wee's mahogany bookcases had been ripped out, no surprise. They were replaced by an industrial trolley, the kind used to ferry books around libraries, and on it sat atlases, dictionaries, and the *CIA World Factbook*, all in their latest editions.

"Lady Midnight." He waved for my attention. His nails were slate gray and chewed to the quick. "Well, *ish* he here, *li*s*h*ening?"

"Who?"

"Daniel, of course."

I shook my head, appalled. But my answer seemed to relax him. His eyes grew keener.

"So, tell me," he began again, his lisp miraculously cured. "How did I get myself into this fix?"

He waited a second, gauging my reaction, then reached behind his desk, theatrically pulling up two fresh champagne flutes from a hidden drawer. His hands were steady; despite his act, and what his wife believed, he was completely sober. Ignoring my objections, he raised a sweating, quarter-full bottle of Dom Pérignon from an unseen ice bucket and filled our glasses to the brim. The final few sips in the bottle he poured straight down his throat.

"I am drinking, yes, but I am not drunk." He smiled. "You'll have to pardon my histrionics. It was the only way I could get Vi to go and get you."

I felt a shiver of rage. "And you knew Vi was the only person who could get me to come. Because the situation had to be damn serious for her to go begging her old foe."

"Clever girl."

Clinking his glass to mine, he spilled a few drops of champagne on his polished tabletop. He mopped it up with his sleeve. I pushed my flute away, rejecting both his drink and his theater.

"But you did come," he said, impressed with himself. "Funny how it always takes a catastrophe to bring us together. First the war, then the emergency, now this."

I glared at him, hoping to make him abandon his glass.

"Oh, don't worry. I get these bottles by the bateau. The French ambassador says I'm very easy to please—and I am, but only with the right vintage." He gargled his drink, then gulped it. "You are not amused. Well, I suppose there's nothing really amusing about me anymore, is there? I'm no longer the omniscient Papa, what with the chaos, forces out there, beyond my control."

"You don't get to absolve yourself so easily. It *was* in your control, all of it. Those are people's graves you're destroying."

"Tough love." He smirked. "Always with the tough love. Glad I never tried to tame you or I might be missing a hand or foot by now. Or God forbid, worse..."

"We promised them, Ken."

"No, no, no. *You* promised them. I said I'd *try*. My loyalties lie with the *living* citizens of the Black Isle. Always have. Don't you understand? I don't *see* them. It's not that they're not real to me, only that they're...abstract."

He gulped down the rest of his drink.

"When you're lucky enough to be prime minister, you have a cabinet of capable men and women who take care of problems for you. Under my guidance, they make their careful calculations, weighing the pros and cons of every move, and then we enact an agreed-upon plan—problem solved, like magic. You see, that's *my* kind of sorcery. I have people so I don't have to deal with people, keeping my citizens abstract to me and me abstract to them—thus the illusion of mastery. The trouble is," he chuckled, "when the problem *begins* as an abstraction, I don't have anyone who knows how to handle that. Once upon a time, I did, of course, and she was fairly good at her job. Sadly, like all the best minds, she was impossible to keep. You wouldn't happen to know a replacement, would you?"

"I'm leaving the Isle tomorrow. Nothing you can say or do will change my mind. I'm done with ghosts, I'm done with the bloody Island, and I'm done with you." I said all of this matter-of-factly so he wouldn't think I was trying to outdo his melodrama. "This is my final piece of advice. The ghosts want you to see Forbidden Hill for yourself. They want you to understand what you've done to them."

"They want me, do they?"

"Yes."

"Ah, everyone seems to want me—but you."

"Self-pity was never your best mode, Prime Minister."

He grew quiet, withdrawing into himself, as he always did when working through a problem. My defenses went up. He may have been old and beaten down, but this was still Kenneth Kee.

"And after I go and *visit* them, do you think they'll leave us alone, let the Isle go back to the way it was?"

"I honestly don't know. But it would be a start."

He nodded again, in private contemplation.

I stood up. I'd made my case, seen the house, met the man, felt the panic. My assignment was complete.

"Wait. Please." His voice was soft. "You and I really should . . . We have to talk about the past. I mean, we should have done that, before tonight. In a less antic atmosphere. We should have gone about things differently— very differently."

He rose sharply from his chair and walked toward me, eyes darting as if he couldn't bear to look at my face.

"You and I should have been together," he whispered. "We should have damned the cliché and done the whole thing—got married, had kids, lost our looks side by side. Instead of this. It's madness that we did this to ourselves."

"I don't want to hear it."

"Nobody understands my jokes here." He laughed bitterly. "And I mean, *nobody*! I find myself talking to you—this is where I commune with you, just so you know—because talking to your ghost is better than talking to my wife, my servants, my ministers, all of them combined. And sometimes these conversations get to be so intense, so real, it's almost as if you were *actually* here with me. I finally understood how it is that you manage to live with the dead around you all the time. I reckon it's very much the same thing. A spiritual connection with someone that nobody else can see or understand, someone who just refuses to let you go. A ghost is like a very persistent *secret*, isn't it?"

I turned away. I didn't want him to catch the agreement in my eyes, especially if this parade of feeling was just another of his stratagems.

"I've done you wrong, Cassandra. And I've done myself wrong because I acted against my own happiness."

"We wouldn't have been happy together." Not with our battling beliefs, not with the cycle of recriminations that was bound to have come following my loss of our child. I knew by now to mistrust such fantasies. "Regret's a chimera, Ken."

"*Of course* we would have been happy." He looked at me, his face gleaming with conviction. "Of course we would! But I ruined it, didn't I? I've begged your ghost for forgiveness a hundred, a thousand times. Your ghost, not the real you, of course... So let me confess to you now, Cassandra, *in the flesh*. I speak with all the certainty in the world when I tell you we *would* have been happy if *I* hadn't done certain things."

He clutched my elbow.

"It was I who lured you to that warehouse. It was I who made the roof fall. *I* killed our future together."

At this, I felt a pang, a swelling, of old, buried rage. Though I could never prove he'd been responsible, deep in my heart I *knew*. How long had I waited for him to say these words, to lay claim to his crime. Yet now that he'd done it, I could only stare at him suspiciously. Was this a penitent's confession or the plea of a confidence man at the end of his rope?

Before my heart could do anything foolish, I heard my voice say, "It doesn't matter. None of it matters."

Gently, I pushed his hand away and walked to the door. Those long-ago things happened not to me but to my lost doppelganger, a headstrong young woman named Cassandra whose sad history I would soon be leaving behind.

"And there's Issa. What I did to him haunts me all the time. It'll haunt me till the day I die, and even after that... Don't let me be a ghost, Cassandra."

I *had* to flee—now—before Kenneth could spin his terrible web and ensnare me once more. I couldn't amend his past for him.

"Tell me you forgive me," he whispered, sobs causing his thin shoulders to shake. "I was so afraid of what you had. I was jealous, insecure."

He made a grab for me again with his damp, clammy hands. I shook them off more roughly than I'd meant to—they were so shockingly cold.

"Tell me, Cassandra. Just tell me, I'm begging you ... I don't want to be a ghost."

"It's a bit late for that, don't you think?" If I could play that scene over again, I would have made my voice kinder than it was then. "What you can still do is go to Forbidden Hill. See it for yourself."

"But I'm frightened." He looked at me with plaintive, watery eyes, the eyes I'd once seen on a kitten whose neck was about to be snapped.

"If you *don't* go, your life's work will be meaningless. They'll destroy the Isle."

He lowered his head. "Yes ... there is that."

When I closed his study door behind me, Violet was waiting. Her face was hard, as if she'd been bracing herself for this final encounter. She saw me to the foyer.

"I've spoken to your bank. The full sum is in your account. You can withdraw or transfer any or all of it. There are no strings. It's clean."

I nodded. Thanks would have been inappropriate.

"Let's keep this strictly between you and me."

Again, I nodded.

As I walked out of the house, I saw Mr. Wee standing in the porte cochere like a guard, free of the dog's head. It appeared that the man's impulse to stay had trumped the badi's instinct to roam, though he was probably one of those genteel house spirits who stayed behind out of duty and decorum rather than any personal feeling. Having learned the hard lessons of involvement during his lifetime, this Mr. Wee didn't acknowledge me; now cold and unencumbered, he was one ghost who'd endure for centuries.

I went to a bank machine that same night. It was all there.

One had to give Violet credit where credit was due—the woman never told a lie.

At the airport, something was amiss. From the stewardesses at check-in to the Sikh policeman standing by passport control, the staff was languidly, indulgently glum. I was about to lodge a complaint—I was still a demanding Islander—when I saw that the lady behind the courtesy desk was weeping as if her beloved had just forsaken her.

The gate opened late. Until I hobbled through the aerobridge and found my window seat in business class, I worried that every little delay was conspiring to make me miss my flight—perhaps a final treat from Kenneth Kee.

"Good afternoon," I said to the tense-looking woman in the seat next to me, thankful she wasn't the talkative type.

She nodded and, as the plane began taxiing, picked up the late edition of the *Tribune* she'd carried onboard, dampened and smeared, it seemed, with somebody's tears. My farewells all said, I hadn't bothered to look at the papers that morning, not even out of last-minute nostalgia. But the headline now cried out to me, bold and black:

PRIME MINISTER KEE DEAD
ENTIRE NATION MOURNS

A land mine went off in my heart. Oh, Kenneth, I thought. Poor Kenneth.

Yet even as I was shaking from the shock, I can't honestly say I was surprised. I'd known this outcome was possible from the moment I entered his study. I'd played out the scenarios in my head. But that his end had *actually* come, that he had failed for the first time to outwit the Fates...I tried to fight back emotions too complex and explosive for me to detail what they were. My tears flowed all the same.

"I know," said my seatmate. "I'm frightened without him, too."

She offered me a tissue. I demurred and took her *Tribune* instead. The front-page story was terse, composed in great haste by a nameless hack. The facts were few. The prime minister, they wrote, had been on a late-night surprise "inspection" of the tunnel under Forbidden Hill, so concerned was he for the safety and well-being of his workers. For the tireless prime minister, the writer stressed, this type of impromptu visit was not uncommon. But this time, while he was in the tunnel, a scaffold collapsed. The esteemed leader "could not be saved." He was killed by his own boundless compassion, the article stated—not as metaphor but as fact.

I read it twice, trying to tease out hints of the truth between the lines. Had Kenneth sacrificed himself or did the spirits take him by force? But as always, the *Tribune* was hermetically sealed within its own propaganda.

I had no doubt he was terrified as he walked into the tunnel. I had no doubt he regretted taking my advice. But I wondered if he'd also been moved by the desecrated graves, if he was at all remorseful.

Did the ghosts show themselves to him? Did he, for the first and last time in his life, see what I always saw? Did the dead smother him as they had almost done me? Was it quick and painless or long and agonizing? Had he saved the Isle?

And if, by some crazy chance I had been in his final thoughts, was it love or was it hate? Would he now become a ghost, as hungry for my blood as the ghosts had been for his?

As we lifted off the earth, I took a deep gulp of air. I could feel the plane battling me, as if I were the cargo pulling it down, tethered soulwise to a tenacious platoon of ghosts. They wouldn't let me go; not Father, not Daniel, not Mr. Wee, and certainly not Kenneth, whose wrath was fresh-born. As for Taro? The Isle had robbed me of my showdown with him.

The jet engine roared, the walls rumbled, the vents spewed white vapors. I gripped the armrests and did my part, lifting my weight off the seat, making myself as light as gravity allowed.

When the clouds appeared, racing by my window like excited lambs, my tears finally abated.

The plane swooped back over the Island, this time high enough to escape its pull. The city lay below us like an architect's scale model with all its landmarks faithfully reproduced. Balmoral Hotel in white, city hall in gray, green rectangle for the Padang, pastel patchwork for the warehouse district riding the black eel that was the river. To the north, there was no more "up-country," only one concrete heartland after another, all centrally planned in Soviet clusters and painted in condescending, calming hues. Each township was a monument to Kenneth's terrible taste. Salmon pink was a recurrent scheme, as was kelp green, the color of his old MG roadster. These estates were even more hideous from the air than on the ground, and the destruction of the jungle far more advanced than I'd supposed. Except for the verdant patch of the Botanic Gardens and the two nature reserves, every green smudge appeared to be an afterthought; I knew for a fact that most of these were private golf clubs, open only to the very rich.

The plane glided on, higher.

How small this teardrop island really was, even after its multiple expansions. To its south lay the broccoli heads of another land, lusher, larger, fed on darker soil. It seemed to be edging across the strait as I watched, a mother waiting to reclaim her child. And in the waters to the north and east, yet other isles, younger, smaller, and manifold, each a wellspring of viral fecundity, all creepers and thorns, ready to infect the Black Isle should its coast draw any closer.

Alas, poor Kenneth, your Isle has drunk its fill!

Without you, the Isle has lost its greatest distinction—the gifted mendacity, the calculated overreaching so necessary for a tiny port to become a beacon of success. From my God's-eye view, I could tell its shine was already fading. The somnambulists would carry on, of course, cheap carbon copies with none of your vision or verve, and certainly none of the history that gave rise to your vision and verve.

I gave the place twenty-five years, fifty at most, before it vanished back into the swamp.

"Good-bye, my dirty Island," I said. "Please help me to forget you."

THE PROFESSOR IS WITH ME. She's heard the rest of my testimony—sitting through the final chapter in a state of hand-wringing tension.

This morning, we're all caught up. On the same page, as it were. Her eyes are bloodshot, either sleep-deprived or moved, quite likely both.

"How do you stand it," she asks, "living in Tokyo?"

"The language barrier helps. I'm not bothered or excited by what they twitter on about here. It's all noise to me."

A glint enters her eyes. "You're talking about ghost chatter, aren't you?"

"I'm talking about the living *and* the dead. That's how the mind works, you know. Don't understand something? Out it goes. At a certain point in one's life, curiosity goes away. Sociability fades. I'm an old woman, Miss Maddin—I mean, *Professor*. I ask for only two things in this life: peace and regularity."

She smiles. "I believe there's a third."

"And what is that?"

"Posterity."

"Overrated, I now think."

"All right. Then you won't mind me doing this." She collects my microtapes and plops them into her blazer's ample pockets.

"Only if you give me what's promised." I stand up.

"Of course." She smiles. From another unseen pocket—the woman's full of secret slits—she withdraws a flat silver box, the type that held cigarettes when people still smoked. "For your spells."

I take the curious thing from her. Peace offering? I open the lid carefully. Instantly, a plume of fine powder flies into my face. The rest remains static, crumbs and clumps in varying shades of gray.

I know this material too well: bone ash.

"I never really knew my father," she says. "But it did occur to me that his ashes might bring him to you."

Suddenly, I understand everything.

His ashes, hence his ghost.

I shut the box, blow the dust from my trembling hands, and look at her properly, with new eyes.

Here before me is a *living* ghost. Kenneth's narrow, close-set eyes, Violet's pale complexion and bushy brows. The calculation of the one, the indignation of the other. Anybody could have seen it, felt it. Why hadn't I?

"Do you hear me, Cassandra?"

I have to squeeze both my elbows to keep from twitching. Kenneth's spirit, his ashes, his child—all three have entered my fortress. His triad of posterity.

"Were you too entranced by the significance of your own story to *see*?" Agnes Mary Kee shakes her head, now impatient. "Of course, a ton's been written about my father. But all of it's either hagiography or abuse. He's always a deity or the Devil, nothing in between, never just a man.

"About a year ago, I was appointed head of the Black Isle's Board of National Memory, meaning I'm now the custodian of the Isle's history. The official history, that is. I think Papa would have been tickled. But how do I safeguard the national memory when I still have huge gaps in my own?

"When I was little, your name was whispered around our house like a curse. But my parents refused to tell me who you were, which only made you more mysterious. The phone my father used, next to the pantry—that was an extension. I listened in upstairs. I never forgot your voice, your name, and your adorable repartee...Lady Midnight." She laughs. "Am I embarrassing you?"

"Too late for that now."

"As soon as I had the power, I tracked you down. Because of your age, I had to act fast. Memory, after all, isn't eternal. I dropped hints—mutilated your sacred book, phone calls in the middle of the night—signs to get you in the mood for confession."

"And you sent your father's ghost."

"That was a bonus. I'm glad it worked."

"So what do you really want from me, Agnes Mary?"

Hearing her name, her voice grows quiet, conciliatory. "You could have stopped him, you know. Saved him. Yet you did nothing."

"Your father would have perished whether I'd shown up or not."

She avoids my gaze, gathering her nerve. When she feels sufficiently prepared, she squares her shoulders, draws a deep breath, and gestures for me to sit back in the sofa. It seems she, too, has a story, one rehearsed and refined over years.

"I was sent away to boarding school in England when I was ten. The painting you saw of me at the house—that was done a week before I was put on the plane, kicking and screaming. Mummy couldn't wait to be rid of me.

"Papa didn't like children. You were right about that. You were also right that he was afraid of them; he felt they could see through him. He did like me, but that was vanity. I worshipped him. He always said I was more his than Mummy's, and she *hated* that. But that's neither here nor there. I was sent away to school and eventually I landed in Balliol, his old college at Oxford. I don't know what kind of strings Papa had to pull, because I was never a very good student. I always had this gnawing doubt about whether I'd got in on my own merit or because I happened to be the daughter of Kenneth Kee. But I went along with it because I knew how much it meant to him: If he had gotten me in, it meant he'd had to make some odious pact with *somebody*, and I wasn't going to humiliate him by rejecting the spot."

"You think like your father," I say.

She nods vaguely, taking it as neither compliment nor swipe.

"I always felt in the way. Even when I went home to the Black Isle for the long holidays, nobody quite knew what to do with me. Papa was always busy. Mummy . . . well, Mummy was a sad case. She was so madly, I wouldn't say in love, rather in *awe* of him that she let him speak to her as if she were a half-wit. It was painful to watch, and eventually, even I had nothing but contempt for her. So once I was done with university, having claimed the degree Papa never got for himself, I decided to find a job in Europe and remain there, sparing myself being caught in the family . . . dysfunction.

"I moved to London. I had a normal life, which I cherished more than anything. That ended on October thirty-first, 1990. You see, it was still All

459

Hallows' Eve over there when my mother called. I was throwing a costume party, dressed up as a ghost and horrifyingly drunk. A ghost—what an irony! I was flown home, of course, for the state funeral. Closed casket, fawning speeches by his enemies. Just horrendous. Mummy looked like a corpse herself. A mummy. Most of the reporters didn't even recognize her at first because she'd been kept in the shadows for so long.

"After the service, I was trapped alone at the house with her. Without Papa filling all the rooms, it was suddenly just the two of us, and the emptiness shocked us both. He *really* was gone. She was in tears the whole time, but fierce, angry tears this time. I'd never seen her as forceful or furious as on the night of the funeral. She began raving endlessly about this diabolical, larger-than-life force who'd tried for years to bring our family down, this enchantress who killed Papa. That mysterious name from my childhood came up again. Lady Midnight.

"My mother, you may know, never drank. But that night, she popped open all the remaining bottles of Papa's champagne. We sat at the dining table drinking, just the two of us, virtually strangers, surrounded by maybe forty or fifty bottles of Dom Pérignon and a house that seemed to grow darker by the minute. As we got drunker and drunker, she gave me the history lesson of my life. She told me how you'd connived to marry into our family by seducing her naïve brother, and how during the war, while her father was doing all he could to protect the family, you led the Japanese straight to the house. She held you responsible for her father's and her brother's deaths and said that if it hadn't been for you, she wouldn't have had to endure those three years...

"After the war, she found solace in her church. But even then, you wouldn't leave her in peace. You'd show up uninvited at family celebrations like an evil fairy godmother. And, of course, there was your special friendship with Papa.

"You see, *you* were our family curse. Papa's death only convinced her you were even more dangerous than she feared. Because you'd even murder the *prime minister*. She believed she and I were next. 'Don't let her win,' she whispered in my ear that night, clutching me with her ice-cold hands. 'Don't give in to that demoness.'

"After she'd completely exhausted herself, she begged me to sleep with her, on Papa's side of the bed. She was terrified of being alone in their room. She said the house was haunted, that she saw shadows everywhere. She said she needed to be held and caressed. By this time, her voice was hoarse and mascara was running down her cheeks. I was terrified. I thought she'd gone insane. Of course, I refused her. Then she begged to sleep in my bed with me, and I refused her again.

"I told her to turn on all her bedroom lights and take a sleeping pill. I knew she had a huge collection of those things—all politicians' wives do. Later that night, while I was sleeping in my old room, I felt a cold shudder rip through the house. I don't know how else to describe it. A wave of air came up and brushed against me, making my skin prickle. That was my first, and still my only, supernatural episode. Instantly, I had a sick feeling. I ran to Mummy's room, which was lit up bright as day, with every light switched on. And there I found her—hanging from the chandelier."

I gasp. I didn't know. I hadn't even guessed. Vi, poor, raging Vi.

"No doubt you never heard. The whole thing was covered up, of course. The *Tribune* didn't report her death till days later, and even then they said she'd died of heartache from missing her great husband. That 'fact,' as everyone knows it, has become part of our national lore. The national lore I'm now supposed to protect.

"I arrived back in England an orphan. It turned out that my father had been horribly in debt. He'd sunk his own money into some of the Isle's bigger projects, thinking he'd eventually reap profits. But he was a politician, not a businessman. He'd expected I would inherit my mother's money, but, well, you already know the end of that story: She'd given whatever was left of it to *you*."

She pauses to let that thought sit with me—and it does, painfully. I lean forward to touch her arm but she pulls away.

"Our house was absorbed by the state. Nobody asked about the prime minister's daughter because he'd never discussed me. Maybe if I'd been a son, things might have been different. As it was, I didn't really exist. Those people you saw at my christening, none remembered me. People have a very short memory on the Isle.

"I worked very hard to make things right. And as you can well imagine, I developed a very keen taste for history. Everything I told you about myself and my work is true. I became a specialist in the history of the Black Isle. I bided my time. And when the Board of National Memory was formed,

I felt it was the perfect time to reclaim my place in the sun. I thought I would finally be able to find this Lady Midnight and solve the mystery surrounding Papa's death. Naturally, the Board was only too thrilled to have me, the daughter of the late, great Kenneth Kee. As always, I wondered whether I'd won the position on my own merit, but this time, I was determined not to be troubled by doubts. Nobody was as qualified as I was on the subject of the Black Isle.

"My husband, a good Canadian named Ernest Maddin, left me after five years of marriage. No children, luckily. He said I'd become possessed, haunted by imaginary demons. But I'd heard your voice on the phone. I knew you were real. And honestly, my mother didn't have much of an imagination—she couldn't have made you up.

"And now we're finally united. Shadow and shadow. If you worry I'm here to seek a nation's revenge for the murder of its leader, put your mind at rest. I'm here for entirely selfish reasons."

Again I ache to rebuff her talk of "murder," but as I'd learned with other dark souls, I have to let her finish.

"I even remember you at my christening. Not that I saw you, but I *felt* you—I felt the discomfort you created in my mother. She was never quite the same after that. All through my childhood, she was jittery and paranoid, always looking over her shoulder. Whenever we left the house, she held on to me for dear life, convinced that somebody would try to whisk me away. Only much later did I realize it was you she feared. Lady Midnight again. You had a hold over my father that she knew she could never equal, and because of that, you were *always* there. Lady Midnight, Lady Midnight, Lady Midnight."

She grabs a couple of tissues from her pocket, fluffs them into a bouquet, and buries her face in it.

"I'm grateful to learn your side of the story, Cassandra. But I hope you'll understand how . . . impossible it is for me to forgive you."

I wait for her tears to slow. "I'm sorry, child."

She chooses not to hear me. After wiping her face clean of tissue bits, she checks her wristwatch. When she speaks again, her tone is different—flat, frightening, like a civil servant of the Black Isle. "You may want to pack an overnight bag."

"What for?"

"I'm taking you for a change of scenery."

"What if I refuse?"

"Then you refuse. I'm not going to force you. But when I told you I had what you've been searching for, when I said this would be a fair exchange, I didn't mean the ashes."

"Then what did you mean?"

"Bring a coat. It's going to be cold down there."

We take a taxi to Tokyo Station, a redbrick neo-Palladian curiosity smack in the glass and steel Marunouchi district. It brings to mind some of the colonial buildings we have on the Black Isle, except being Japanese, it looks as if it were put up just yesterday by a dollhouse manufacturer.

I've never been here. I've never felt the need to leave this city.

Agnes Mary Kee navigates us through its crowded, serpentine pathways to a platform for the Shinkansen bullet train, one of those duck-billed marvels that's taken the epic journey on the Tokaido Road, made famous by those Hiroshige woodblocks, and reduced it to a mere three hours. I worry for an irrelevant second that she intends to throw me in front of it, but no, we hop on. The train leaves exactly on time.

We are headed south by southwest, on the nonstop express.

The seats are hard but the toilets are clean. Classic Japan. I don't complain. I stare like a cat at the mad tangle of telephone wires and the residential blocks that define every suburb for a hundred miles beyond Tokyo. I can't tear my eyes away, waiting for the scenery to start. Hiroshige-san has promised me Mount Fuji. Mount Fuji before death.

"You left very few clues, Cassandra. Then one day, I contacted the War Crimes library in Tokyo and discovered that you're a regular, which only makes sense, I suppose. You could never let things go."

"That makes two of us, then."

She looks out her window with a smile.

Distant and gauzy, beyond low-slung villages that will never matter, Mount Fuji juts into view like Mother Earth's ancient pudendum, the white hairs combed neatly flat. She stays with us a good while, and I feel a chill just seeing all that snow. When we leave the mount behind, the real countryside begins, with alpine hillsides blanketed thick and white. A blizzard whips by in a hurry, making the entire carriage rattle.

By the time we arrive in Kyoto, the air is clear again. But still frigid. The cold has tinted Agnes's cheeks pink, like a child in an old Chinese lithograph. There really is a lot of Daniel in her look—more so than Violet, really—and I feel a sort of tender kinship toward her. She's almost family, after all. We both represent the end of our respective bloodlines. We're each the last woman standing.

Outside the station, she hails a taxi and hands the driver an address. He nods and off we go. To the end of my hunting—or so she claimed.

Kyoto is old and calm, not just an anagram but a mirror image of Tokyo. The city itself is split through the middle by the Kamo River, its banks lined with ancient wood houses and shops with slanting tile roofs. Each resembles a little temple, and many of them are precisely that, shrines to handmade crafts: roasted rice crackers, sandalwood incense, powdered green tea. I've long assumed that Tokyo's lifeblood was its countless octogenarians, but Kyoto truly is the city of the old. The toothless and the bent claim every pedestrian crossing, independent and lively as they go about their day on wooden clogs. No self-pity. And maybe related to it, the ghost population is almost nil.

We get out at a sedate temple district on the edge of the city, aglow with lantern light. The sky has turned brooding, overcast. Agnes leads me along a walled street and through tall red-orange doors. And lo, we're in an enormous compound, with long, tile-roof buildings and a dry rock garden. Perfectly manicured pine trees shoot out of perfectly measured spots in the gravel.

I glance around. There are English words on a sign: SANJUSANGENDO TEMPLE.

"Has this been a kind of pilgrimage?" I ask. "I haven't been religious, not for a long while now."

"Nobody's making you pray, Cassandra. Quite the contrary."

It is closing time—four o'clock, with the setting sun, not that I could see it for the clouds. Tourists and pilgrims brush by us as they leave in one continuous trickle, nodding and smiling. The entire complex is suddenly deserted. A handful of lonesome figures in samurai garb wander the property, but I don't count them—they will likely remain here long after the doors are locked.

Steady chanting emerges from some unseen sanctum, keeping rhythm with a wood percussion bell. Monks.

I envy the monks their tranquillity.

A robed groundskeeper monk has emerged from one of the shorter wooden buildings. He doesn't so much as glance up at us, becoming instantly absorbed in the serious business of floor sweeping. Beyond this building sits a crowd of gravestones.

"Are we going there?" I point, following my instincts.

"If you like."

We walk over, slowly because gravel is hard on my feet, and finally reach the temple's miniature cemetery. The stones are arrayed in flawless blocks, some with long wooden tablets covered in well-wishes. I search among them for the name I know, the name I expect, but the kanji letters are engraved too tightly for my eyes.

"Which one is he?" I ask.

"What you're looking for isn't here," says Agnes. "These graves are much too old, much too valuable. This temple was built in 1164 for a retired *emperor*." She indicates the longest building, which stretches over a hundred yards. "I mean, in that hall, there are a thousand and one gold statues of Kannon, the goddess of mercy. They're really magnificent. Shame we got here too late to see them."

"But I've seen them," I assert. "On TV not long ago. You can also buy charms in their shop to ward off headaches, knickknacks that guarantee high marks on exams. The gods here are bribable, apparently."

She clears her throat. "In any case, I haven't brought you here to sightsee."

"I hoped not."

As we walk by the short wooden building, my eyes are drawn back to the lone groundskeeper in his saffron robe and thick white slipper stockings. He looks like a relic from a different millennium—if not the one before, then the one yet to come. It's become clear that his job is not to chase the stragglers off the lot. He's frightfully old, little more than a bald skeleton, living out the kind of fate I used to fear: manual labor unto death. Yet he looks blissful. Is this nirvana—or Japanese perversity?

His hands are brown and twiglike but they have a young man's firm grip on the rake. The strokes are sturdy as he sweeps bits of errant gravel off the pathway and back into the rocky pool. This doesn't look like a man whose back ever troubled him. He's almost not a man but some walking essence of sagacious calm, ready to be distilled, bottled, and sold in the temple's gift shop.

"See anything you want?" Agnes says.

I walk closer to the man. He still doesn't notice us, though we couldn't have been more than twenty yards away. His mind is fully engaged in the chanting of his colleagues: The body we see out in the yard is a mere vessel. Bit by bit, I click together the jigsaw of his features—the high, chiseled cheekbones, the straight Peking nose, the slant and hood of once-arrogant eyes, the hunch hinting at a taller, more vigorous youth.

Hands that once struck me, held me, caressed me, and struck me again.

Taro. My God, it really *is* him.

A surge of nausea rises up my chest. She really did find him! Yet why am I so surprised? She found *me*.

Agnes smiles. "Lieutenant Colonel Rukumoto. He's why you went to the archive week after week, isn't he? Looking for revenge."

"I had a feeling. But only a feeling," I gasp. "He's so very, very old."

My heart is racing.

It's true I've sought him, all this time. I may have seen the beach house go up in flames, but I never met his ghost. And one of the surest things in this world is that a man like Taro would have a ghost, and an angry one, too. Searching for him, with its attendant promise of vengeance or news of his death, with its promise of relief, has sustained me, given structure to my later days. It became its own ritual, long after my rage had grown dim. Yet I never dreamed I'd actually find him, least of all with someone like Agnes.

But was this really a peace offering?

"You don't forget and you don't forgive, do you, Lady Midnight?"

Agnes is different now. Her eyes have a crystalline, automatic hardness. The contempt has returned to her voice, and I know she hasn't had to dig deep to find it. She's inherited her father's talent for conjuring up slights and turning them into weapons.

It's all right. I accept the wrath of this poor, fatherless girl. Because here we are, bound in this cold wind, under the heaving gray sky, staring at the very man whose long-ago actions turned us both into the monsters we are now. If this didn't seal our weird kinship, then I don't know what could have.

"Learning about my father has been my personal project. You've helped me. In return, I present to you *your* personal project."

She reaches into her blazer and draws out an antique keris, ceremonial but sharp, perhaps stolen from a museum. She pushes its hilt into my palm.

"Go on. You *want* him, don't you?" She turns my shoulders until I'm facing the oblivious monk. "This is a settlement between the damned. Trust me, nobody's going to miss either of you."

I cup the keris in my freezing hand, and an electric current runs through my arm. This is what temptation feels like—cold, tingling, stiff.

Taro is here for my taking, at one hundred years old. He looks so placid I wonder if he'd resist at all. Would he even recognize me, a miserable crone aged eighty-eight, coming at him for crimes committed seventy years ago? Our geriatric pas de deux would be the stuff of legend—or comedy.

Watching him sweep, vulnerable, in soft garments, I can almost believe he's put himself here to await precisely this fate. Japanese perversity.

"Go on," Agnes whispers behind me.

Telling Agnes my story has revived my rage, lured my bloodthirst back from the dead. Has she been auditioning me for this very moment?

One quick, delicious slash to his throat, and I will right the wrongs of seventy years. I will do it for Daniel, taken away from me before his time. Father, Mr. Wee, even Violet, too. There will be no witness but she who put me up to the task.

Look at that villain, Cassandra. Think of the dead. Here's your chance.

I take a few steps toward him, Buddhist gravel crunching under my shoes.

Puffs of condensation flee my mouth as I exhale; they want no part of this. My fingers wrap themselves around the keris, trying their best to make the cold thing snug.

The monk goes on sweeping, his rhythm unchanged. He keeps his eyes fixed on the ground, either open to the entire universe or closed off from it—I can't tell which.

All of a sudden, he stops sweeping and turns. My heart jolts. Has he seen me? But no, his head tilts up.

There is a shiver above us. The gray clouds shrug off specks of silver, and the air becomes gauzy. Snow is drifting down.

The old monk's face comes alive with a boy's delight. His eyes crease—

there's a sparkle to them I'd never seen before—and he unfurls his pink tongue, stretching it as far as it will go. He catches a few flakes and closes his mouth, greedily savoring them. I can almost feel what he's thinking. He's not saying hello; he's saying good-bye.

I turn to Agnes. "That's not him."

Snow is beginning to pour down now, but the flakes only swirl around Agnes, not actually touching any part of her. The heat rising from her body seems to have created its own weather system, refusing solace, repelling peace. The tears stay liquid in her eyes. She has willed them not to fall.

I press the keris back into her soft hands. "Not anymore."

At Kyoto Station, we part ways. But first we shake hands like foes at the inception of a duel. Before I let her go, I examine her fingers. Her fingertips are impossibly smooth, line-free.

"My father always said it was a gift," she says. "But I always saw it as more of a curse. One of the few things we didn't see eye to eye on."

"Your father," I say. "Thank you for bringing him to me one last time."

Her face thaws. Curiosity, and something approximating hope—no, hunger—enlivens her eyes. In her desperation, I see the neglected girl who would do terrible things to win back her father's heart—even after his death.

"By the way," she says, feigning casualness, "did he say anything?"

"Yes." And because this lost girl has brought me the peace I now feel in my soul, I lie: "He told me you were the only thing he ever loved."

She bites her lip and smiles. "Thank you. But he would never use that word."

I try to draw out our farewell, make her realize we're nearly kin. She could have been my daughter; I was almost her aunt. "Will we meet again?"

"You and I?" She shakes her head. "I hope not."

"Agnes, I do wish you'll find a way to forgive me. To let go of all this history."

My words are met with silence.

She puts me on the Shinkansen to Tokyo and remains on the platform, watching me as my train departs. I see her lips mouth "Good night" and her face is cold once more, but I knew her father too well to mistake this for a lack of feeling. What I can't tell is if she's going to stay on in this city of temples, or if she has tapes to burn, ashes to bury, as soon as I disappear from view.

It's night on the train. I can see nothing out the window but blackness and my own reflection, greenish and pale beneath the pitiless lights. My eyes are tired now. I'm even cheated of Mount Fuji.

Night has come early, and along with it, the sobering truth.

Taro was now spent, penitent. Killing this changed man would only condemn me to an eternity of self-hatred and regret. Kenneth's threat would be fulfilled: I would have become a ghost—as he has, for his own unforgivable acts.

Agnes is a clever girl, with her father's sixth sense about deeds and consequences. Was this ultimate punishment what she intended for me all along? I'll never have the answer. But my refusal to comply denied her story its rightful conclusion. She will have to dream up a happier ending.

I look around the compartment. What were her words again? *Trust me, nobody's going to miss either of you.* Drunk salarymen snoring, old ladies nibbling on rice balls, a young man with a pair of Rollerblades on his lap, apparently dozing. I agree. None of these people will miss me.

So be it. My end will come. However it does, whenever it does, I vow to go peaceably. I have told my story. I will not be a ghost.

When I reach home tonight, I will celebrate like a grateful woman—with cognac, chocolate, and a good book. I'll savor every sip, every bite, every word. And then at long last, I will close my eyes.

At Tokyo Station, I weave through the pulsating throng. It's rush hour and I'm engulfed in one endless pinstriped horror, the combined detritus of the district's office blocks, snaking toward the underground. I can't walk fast enough. Finally, past the turnstiles, at the top of the down escalator, I stop moving altogether and let the hurrying bodies jostle, overtake, curse me for being old, slow, stupidly in their way, for I am what they all fear—sudden, aberrant stillness.

But by God, do I feel alive in my stalling!

I take a deep breath and let the escalator carry me down.

References

Here are some books I consulted for information and inspiration.

On the very real and dark research conducted by the Japanese Army during WWII:

Unit 731 Testimony by Hal Gold (Yenbooks, Tokyo, 1996) and *A Plague Upon Humanity: The Secret Genocide of Axis Japan's Germ Warfare Operation* by Daniel Barenblatt (HarperCollins, NY, 2004)

On the War in the Pacific, from a British colonial perspective:

Forgotten Armies: The Fall of British Asia 1941–1945 by Christopher Bayly and Tim Harper (Belknap Press, Harvard, Cambridge, MA, 2005)

I first encountered the Japanese myth of Kiyohime in this book featuring the haunting and horrifying woodblock prints of Taiso Yoshitoshi (1839–1892):

Yoshitoshi's Strange Tales by John Stevenson (Hotei, Amsterdam, 2005)

And last but not least, this encyclopedic anthropological gem:

Malay Magic: Being an Introduction to the Folklore and Popular Religion of the Malay Peninsula by Walter William Skeat (Dover, NY, 1967)

Acknowledgments

John Powers, loving husband, bolster, booster, and buoy.

Mitch Hoffman, brilliant, steadfast editor.

Barbara Braun, my agent, and John F. Baker—miracle workers.

Mark E. Doten, the boy wonder who fished me out of the bog.

Jessica Levin, my first "civilian" cheerleader.

Patricia Williams, Kathleen Clark, and FuzzCo, all of whom tried to make me presentable.

Anne Twomey, who designed such a fine-looking book jacket, Kim Hoffman, Lindsey Rose, Siri Silleck, Carrie Andrews, and everybody at Grand Central/Hachette who worked so hard to bring this monster out.

The constant Nico, and the cats who came a-visiting along the way: Pheebs, Snugs, Spike, Zero, Minnie, Momo (Mokes), Katara, Lill, Taco, and the late, great Bandit.

The wonderful friends who collaborated on my book trailer: Marijke van Kets, Lucas Jodogne, Carla Dunareanu, Jeremy Haik, and Hannah Mir Jayanti. Thank you!

Those who offered wisdom and kindness, from ancient times:

Philip Cheah, Pierre Rissient (the Whistling Snake), Melissa Franklin, Gretchen and Barry Mazur, Steve Erickson, Richard Peña, Laurie Ochoa, Rey Buono (high school drama teacher with whom I fought and fought)...and all the characters in the newsroom at *The Straits Times*'s "Life!" under Richard Lim and T. Sasitharan when I was there as a rookie covering movies—I have never forgotten you.

You are all my favorite ghosts.